IMMORTALIS

Also by R. A. Salvatore

THE ICEWIND DALE TRILOGY
The Crystal Shard
Streams of Silver
The Halfling's Gem

THE DARK ELF TRILOGY
Homeland
Exile
Sojourn

THE DARK ELF BOOKS
The Legacy
Starless Night
Siege of Darkness
Passage to Dawn
The Silent Blade
The Spine of the World

THE CLERIC QUINTET
Canticle
In Sylvan Shadows
Night Masks
The Fallen Fortress
The Chaos Curse

THE SPEARWIELDER'S TALES
The Woods Out Back
The Dragon's Dagger
Dragonslayer's Return

THE CRIMSON SHADOW
The Sword of Bedwyr
Luthien's Gamble
The Dragon King

*Tarzan: The Epic Adventures**

*The Demon Awakens**
*The Demon Spirit**
*The Demon Apostle**

*Echoes of the Fourth Magic**
*The Witch's Daughter**
*Bastion of Darkness**

Published by Ballantine Books

IMMORTALIS

BALLANTINE BOOKS • NEW YORK

A Del Rey® Book
Published by The Random House Ballantine Publishing Group

Copyright © 2003 by R. A. Salvatore

ISBN 0-345-44122-2

Map by Laura Maestro

Manufactured in the United States of America

IMMORTALIS

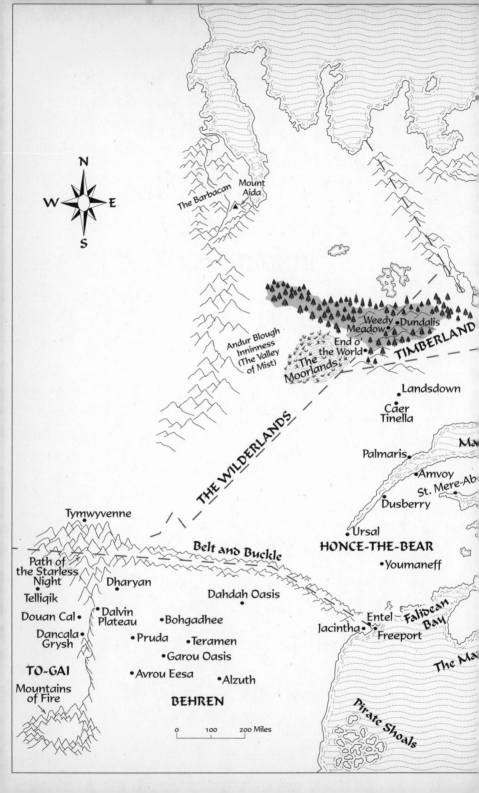

DOR

THE
JULIANTHES

(The Weathered Isles)

Pireth
Vanguard

MIRIANIC
OCEAN

aval
Gulf of Corona

Saints   Pireth
              Dancard

Pireth Tulme
Tinson
Macomber

St. Gwendolyn
by the Sea

The Broken Coast

THE LANDS OF
CORONA

PROLOGUE

"You let her go!" Marcalo De'Unnero screamed, every muscle in the strong man's body standing taut. He was past fifty, but appeared much younger, with the suppleness of youth still showing about his hardened muscles and with his black hair still thick upon his head. The excommunicated Abellican monk had been a fighter for all of his life and carried the scars of a hundred battles. But they were only superficial scars, visual reminders, for within the skin of Marcalo De'Unnero resided a body in perfect health.

For that was one aspect of the magic of the enchanted gemstone—a tiger's paw—that, through the power of the demon dactyl, had merged with the essence of the man.

At his side, Sadye put her hand on his arm, trying to calm him, for his outburst had raised more than a few eyebrows around the throne room of the new king, Aydrian Wyndon, who called himself Aydrian Boudabras. Many of the dukes of Honce-the-Bear were in attendance this morning, including Kalas, who led the elite Allheart Brigade, and Bretherford, who commanded the great fleet of warships. And none of them were used to any man, particularly not one of the Abellican Church, speaking to the king of Honce-the-Bear in such a manner.

Seated comfortably on the throne across from De'Unnero, Aydrian seemed hardly bothered, though. He wore a wry grin, which made him look even younger than his nineteen years, especially given his unkempt locks of curly blond hair and his large blue eyes. That too-innocent look had been stamped upon Aydrian's face since the events of a few days previous, when he had wrestled the tormented spirit of Constance Pemblebury from the nether realm and had used the distraction to murder King Danube Brock Ursal.

"You fear Jilseponie?" the young king replied, his voice steady and calm.

De'Unnero paused and tilted his head, scrutinizing Aydrian, who seemed to understand the puzzlement and smiled all the wider. Until very recently, Aydrian had been De'Unnero's pawn, and willingly so. As the son of Jilseponie, who had been Danube's queen, Aydrian held some tenuous claim to the throne. Using him, De'Unnero and Abbot Olin had pushed their agenda to the highest levels of the kingdom, to the throne itself. Now the pair intended to use that secular victory to bring them to prominence in the Church they believed had abandoned them. In their eyes, Aydrian had been no more than a means to a personal end. More recently, though, since the joust when Aydrian had defeated all challengers, including the great Duke Kalas, things had begun to shift in the relationship between De'Unnero and Aydrian. Slowly but surely, Aydrian had begun to assert more and more control.

De'Unnero saw that, and now, for the first time since he had met the young son of Elbryan and Jilseponie in the wild lands to the west, he was beginning to fear it. At first, after the young man's ascension to the throne, De'Unnero had watched him and had marveled, thinking him a most beautiful and cunning creature. But now, given the realization that Aydrian had truly allowed Jilseponie to walk out of Ursal, De'Unnero was growing ever more angry.

"Do you not understand the danger that Queen Jilseponie poses to us? To you?" the Abellican monk explained.

"Perhaps we should discuss this in private with Aydrian," Sadye said quietly to the monk, and she pulled him tighter. But De'Unnero didn't even look at her, so fixed was his glare upon Aydrian.

"My mother is nothing," Aydrian declared, and he looked all around, widening his response to include all in attendance so that he could answer every question raised by his surprising decision to allow Jilseponie simply to ride out of Ursal. "I saw her heart on that day," he explained. "When she learned the truth of me, that the son she had abandoned to die was alive and well, it was the end for her. Jilseponie Wyndon is no threat. She is an empty shell. I could have been merciful and simply killed her that day. But after her abandonment of me, after she left me for dead, I chose not to be so merciful."

As he said this, he paused and looked about, and so did De'Unnero, to see a couple of the noblemen nodding and smiling—even proud Duke Kalas, who had once been King Danube's best friend. Indeed, Jilseponie had made more than a few enemies in the court during her tenure in Castle Ursal, and that enmity had allowed the conspirators to drive a wedge through the accepted line of ascension.

"Let her sit and rot, tormented by the errors of her past," Aydrian went on. "Death is sometimes merciful, and I wish to show no mercy to wretched Jilseponie!"

De'Unnero thought to respond, but the murmurs about him told him clearly that he had few allies in this room against Aydrian's decision. He still believed that Aydrian had made a tremendous error. He knew Jilseponie well, had battled against her for most of his adult life, and understood that she was a formidable foe, perhaps as formidable as Aydrian could know in all the world. "We will see her again," he did say, and ominously. "On the battlefield."

"And when we do, she will watch her friends and allies die, then she will die," Aydrian calmly assured him.

"You do not understand the power of—"

"I understand it better than do you," Aydrian interrupted. "I took her measure, fully so, while she stood on that trial stage on the day of my ascent. I saw into her, saw through her, and I know the power of Jilseponie! And I know that power is diminished, and greatly so, by my reappearance in her life. Oh yes, my friend—my friends!—I know my enemy, and I do not fear her in the least. And neither should you. The execution of Jilseponie in a quiet and hidden place within Castle Ursal would have done us no good as we strive to reunite the kingdom. Indeed, if word had gone out of such an act, it might have martyred the witch. No, let our would-be enemies see her impotence in this, and lose all heart to resist us. Or let them witness her devastating demise if she chooses to come against me. They will lose all heart for continuing the fight. Jilseponie's role in all of this might not be over, but if she has any impact left in the coming events, then it will be one to benefit us."

The young man's words, and the calm and assured way in which he had spoken them, had De'Unnero back on his heels. Who was this young king he had helped to gain the throne? Who was this young man, once his eager student and now acting as if he was the teacher?

De'Unnero didn't know, and started to question, but Sadye tightened her grip on his arm, and when he looked at her, her expression begged him to let the subject drop from public discussion.

She was right, the monk knew. If he persisted here, he might actually be undermining Aydrian with the other noblemen, allies desperately needed if the new kingdom was to hold, if the legitimacy of Aydrian Boudabras was to spread out from Ursal to the north.

"Perhaps I am too reminded of who Jilseponie once was," the monk quietly admitted.

"She is not that woman any longer," Aydrian replied. "She is old and she is worn. Her road has been long and difficult, and her decisions have risen from the dead to haunt her every thought. She is nothing to concern us."

"She was once mighty with the gemstones and with the sword," interjected Duke Kalas, a warrior much like De'Unnero in spirit—which was probably why the two hated each other. He was a large and dashing man, powerfully built yet graceful in stride, the epitome of the nobleman warrior.

"Her skills with the sword have diminished with age and lack of practice, no doubt," Aydrian replied. "But even if she was at her peak of strength, and even if Elbryan was alive and fighting beside her, I would easily defeat them. As for the gemstones . . ." He paused and held up the pouch of stones, a magnificent and varied collection that had once belonged to Jilseponie.

"Well, she has none, and if she acquires some, I will have to defeat her in that realm. It is not a battle that gives me the slightest pause, I assure you."

Not a person in that room doubted his confidence. And none who knew him, who truly understood the power that was Aydrian, doubted his claim.

"And what of Torrence?" asked Monmouth Treshay, the Duke of Yorkey, referring to the one living son of Constance Pemblebury and King Danube, a bastard child who had been placed third in the line of ascension, behind Danube's brother Prince Midalis, and his own older brother, Merwick. Aydrian had slain Merwick in a duel after the death of Danube. As he had with Jilseponie, Aydrian had allowed Torrence to ride out of Ursal.

Well, not quite like Jilseponie, De'Unnero knew.

Aydrian turned a curious smile on the man, sizing him up, as did De'Unnero. Aydrian's hold over some of the dukes was tenuous. Kalas, the most powerful of the noblemen, had settled firmly in Aydrian's court, and that brought legitimacy to the new king that few of these southern dukes would dare question. For Kalas controlled the Allheart Knights, and they, in turn, controlled the general army of Ursal, a force that could sweep aside any resistance in the southland. Monmouth Treshay, though, had seemed less enthusiastic from the outset. The older duke was obviously torn. Yorkey County served as the retreat where most of the Ursal nobles spent their leisure time. Constance Pemblebury had lived there for most of the last years of her life, as had her children. The arrival of Constance's ghost exonerating Jilseponie might have brought Aydrian some measure of legitimacy with Duke Monmouth, but the ensuing fight, where Aydrian had defeated and killed Prince Merwick, had obviously not sat well with the man.

"How many would-be kings or queens will you allow to roam freely about your kingdom?" Duke Monmouth pressed.

In response, Aydrian grinned and looked over to Duke Kalas, who nodded grimly, his expression telling them all that he wasn't approaching the problem of Torrence with as much enjoyment as was Aydrian.

The intrigue of the moment was not lost on Marcalo De'Unnero, nor was he pleased to realize that Aydrian had decided to use Kalas in his secret plans for Torrence Pemblebury. Though such plans were prudent, no doubt, the monk did not like it one bit that Aydrian was stepping out from him, was taking control here and without any apparent consideration to him!

Gnashing his teeth with boiling anger, De'Unnero turned to Sadye for support, for surely she would see the same problem here as he.

He stopped short when he regarded the small and beautiful woman, the woman who had stolen his heart with her enchanting music and her wisdom, with her wheat-colored hair, grown to her shoulders now, and those shining gray eyes.

For though Sadye continued to hold De'Unnero's arm, her gaze was not fixed upon him, but upon another. She stood there, transfixed, a bemused expression on her face as she watched the every movement of . . . Aydrian Boudabras.

"We will journey to Vanguard and my uncle, the prince," Torrence Pemblebury told the man sitting next to him, one of the five soldiers who had chosen to leave Ursal with the deposed would-be king.

"Perhaps we would be wise to resettle in Vanguard," said the man, Prynnius by name, and the only Allheart Knight to abandon the court of the new King Aydrian. Prynnius had been one of the primary instructors of Torrence's older brother Merwick in the early stages of his Allheart training. Though a friend of Duke Kalas, Prynnius could not abide the killing of Merwick and could not bring himself to swear allegiance to Honce-the-Bear's new king. "Far from Ursal and the court of Aydrian. Far from the Allhearts and Duke Kalas, and far from the turmoil that is obviously about to befall the Abellican Church."

"You say that in the hopes that Aydrian's arms will not be so long."

"He will not penetrate Vanguard short of an all-out war," Prynnius said with conviction. "I know Prince Midalis well. He'll not welcome Aydrian—surely not!—for he is the greatest threat to Aydrian's legitimacy. All the kingdom knows that Midalis should have succeeded Danube."

"And with Merwick next in line, and myself behind him," said Torrence. "And yet this new king allows me free passage out of Ursal."

"His personal mercenary army is well paid, and now he has added the bulk of the army of Danube's Honce-the-Bear, the very same army that you would need to call your own to do battle with him," said Prynnius. "Perhaps he sees you now as no threat, and perhaps you—we—would be wise to keep him thinking that way."

"The greater our advantage of surprise when we strike back?" Torrence said eagerly.

"The longer we may both stay alive," Prynnius corrected. "Surrender your claim to the throne, in your heart at least, for the time being, young Prince Torrence. You have not the strength to do battle with King Aydrian."

Torrence sat back, crossed his arms over his chest, and assumed a petulant expression. "You think he's won," the young man stated bluntly.

"He has won," Prynnius agreed, and Torrence shot him an angry glare. "He has Ursal and he has the Allhearts. He has all the land to Entel and the sea, and he has Duke Bretherford and the fleet. Honce-the-Bear is his, I fear, and I see no way . . ." He paused as the coach lurched to a stop. Up in front, they heard the driver yelling at someone to clear the road.

Prynnius leaned forward and poked his head out the coach's window.

"Ye get outa the way!" the driver yelled. "Don't ye know who I'm carrying, ye fool highwaymen?"

"Highwaymen?" Torrence asked, coming forward in his seat. He slowed though, when he noted the grim expression on Prynnius' face, when he noted the man shaking his head slowly, his eyes telling Torrence clearly that he recognized some of the supposed highwaymen who had intercepted their coach.

"It would seem that our new King Aydrian is not secure in his victory as we presumed," Prynnius remarked, and he looked at Torrence and shrugged, then pushed open the coach door and drew out his sword as he exited the carriage.

Torrence sat there numbly, trying to register what this was all about even as the sounds of fighting erupted about him. He heard the hum of bow-strings, and heard one man call Prynnius a traitor to the Allhearts. A moment later, the coach shook as someone fell against it, then Prynnius opened the door and slumped in. He looked up at Torrence, his face a mask of resignation and defeat.

And then he lurched, and Torrence looked past his wincing face to see a man standing behind him, a man dressed as a common thief but wielding a fabulous weapon that no commoner could possibly afford. Prynnius jumped again a bit as the man twisted that sword within him.

With a growl of rage, Torrence grabbed up his own sword and dove forward, but the killer nimbly moved back out of reach.

Torrence sprawled across the dying Prynnius, half out of the coach. He started to scramble forward to pursue Prynnius' killer, but then he got hit from the side, and hard, and then got hit again. Dazed, he was only partly aware that his weapon had slipped from his hand. He hardly understood that he was being dragged from the coach, he hardly felt the boots and gauntlets smashing against him, pounding him down into darkness.

"Does it so bother you that your protégé has stepped forward from your shadow?" Sadye asked quietly, the blunt question and her innocent tone throwing a bucket of water onto the fires that burned within Marcalo De'Unnero. "Is that not what you would want from him?"

"What do you mean?" the monk asked, shaking his head in disbelief. They were back in their room in one of the buildings near to Castle Ursal reserved for visiting lords—which De'Unnero had pretended to be during the usurping of King Danube's throne.

"Did you and Abbot Olin truly expect Aydrian to remain dependent upon you for his every move?" Sadye asked. "Did you truly wish that? How, my love, are you to get about the business of converting the Abellican Church to your vision if you are needed for King Aydrian's every move? How do you and Abbot Olin expect to truly defeat Father Abbot Fio Bou-raiy and men like Abbot Braumin Herde if you are busy concerning yourself with affairs of the state?"

"Aydrian may err, and such an error could cost us everything," De'Unnero replied, not convincingly.

"Only yesterday, you were singing his praises and admiring the beauty that is Aydrian," Sadye pointed out.

"I was giddy with victory, perhaps."

Sadye scoffed and gave a doubting little chuckle. "Aydrian took control of the situation here in Ursal sometime ago," she reminded. "It was he who facilitated the trial of Jilseponie Wyndon, discrediting both her and King Danube. It was he who tore Constance Pemblebury from the realm of death itself, that she might act on his behalf in ending the reign of Danube. It was he who pulled Duke Kalas back from that same dark realm and thus manipulated the man into subservience. Do not underestimate him! Take great heart and hope that your pupil has risen to become your—"

"My better?" There was no hiding the bitterness in De'Unnero's tone as he spat those two words.

"Your peer," Sadye corrected. "And you will need him as such if you are to have any hopes of dominating the Abellican Church. Yes, with Aydrian's armies behind you, you might sweep away Bou-raiy and his followers, but to gain the heart of the Church, you need to do more than that. Be pleased, my love, that young Aydrian has stepped forward to worthily fill the throne."

Marcalo De'Unnero slumped back on his bed as those words settled within his thoughts. Sadye was speaking wisely here, he knew, and it was surprising for him to recognize that he and Sadye had almost completely swapped their viewpoints in a period of a few days.

Aydrian's road to win the entirety of the kingdom would be a difficult one indeed, but De'Unnero's quest to remake the Abellican Church into what it once had been, into something even greater than it had once been, would be no less so.

For a long time, De'Unnero sat there, considering the events of the last few tumultuous weeks, considering the actions of Aydrian. The turning point, he knew, had come that day on the jousting field, when Aydrian had defeated, and seemingly killed, Duke Kalas, only to reach into his enchanted soul stone and tear Duke Kalas back from the netherworld.

So much of this amazingly quick rise to the throne had been facilitated by Aydrian, without consulting either De'Unnero or Olin. And now it was continuing.

It did not sit well with Marcalo De'Unnero that Aydrian was acting so much on his own here, and yet Sadye's reasoning made good sense. The first part in the plan De'Unnero and Olin had concocted called for getting Aydrian on the throne, and now that had come to pass.

The second part of that plan, the takeover of the Abellican Church, had just begun here, in St. Honce, and would carry them all the way to St.-Mere-Abelle, so they hoped. If the kingdom was to be Aydrian's and the Church the province of Olin and De'Unnero, then, yes indeed, it would bode well for the monks if Aydrian proved capable of handling his end.

But still . . .

Marcalo De'Unnero glanced over at Sadye, to see her standing there, looking off into the distance, a wistful smile on her face.

He could guess whom she was thinking about.

*   *   *

When Torrence awoke, he was back in his coach seat, and the coach was rolling through the streets of Ursal in the dead of night. He was gagged and lightly bound, but he didn't even think of pulling free of his bonds, for three others were in the coach with him: burly men, all armed, and all staring at him intently.

The coach went through the side gates of the castle, and up to a little-used door, where a pair of men waited, chains in hand.

Torrence was roughly grabbed and pulled from the seat, his arms yanked behind him and chained at the wrists. They ushered him through the servant areas of the castle, through the kitchen and the scrub rooms, then through a door and down a long flight of stairs to the dungeons.

Panic welled up inside the deposed prince as his entourage silently dragged him along the cellars, to another flight of wooden stairs that took him even deeper beneath the great castle. Down this second flight, they stopped and pulled the gag from Torrence's mouth, roughly turning him about to look back under the stairs.

There a hole had been dug, one about the right size for a body.

Torrence instinctively recoiled from the open grave, but firm hands held him in place.

"That will not be necessary," came a voice the young prince surely knew, one that offered him a glimmer of hope. He turned to see the approach of Duke Targon Bree Kalas, the nobleman who had been his mother's dearest friend for so many years.

"Leave us," Kalas instructed the others, and the guards moved off without question, back up the stairs.

"Glory to St. Abelle that you found me," Torrence said, as Kalas walked beside him and unlocked the shackles that bound his wrists. "I know not what those ruffians would have done to me. Why, it seems as if they even prepared a grave . . ."

Torrence paused as he considered the moment, as he realized that Duke Kalas was in possession of the keys to his shackles. He stared down at the open grave, then slowly began to turn about.

"Forgive me," Duke Kalas whispered, and Torrence spun about wildly to face him.

Kalas's sword plunged into his chest, tearing his heart in half. Stunned and shaking in the last moments of his life, Torrence grasped the bloody blade.

"Forgive me," Duke Kalas whispered, and he held his hand up to silence Torrence's breathless questions. "Forgive me, Constance."

Kalas yanked his blade free and Torrence tumbled back, into the open grave.

"Damn you, King Aydrian, as you have damned me," Duke Kalas muttered under his breath as he stood there and considered his handiwork.

He could hardly believe that he had just killed Torrence, who had been as his nephew, the son of his dearest friend.

But Duke Targon Bree Kalas, above all others, had witnessed the true power of Aydrian Boudabras, a power that transcended death itself. In the face of that terrible strength, it was simply not within the man to refuse the young king.

"Sleep well, poor Prince," Kalas said quietly, and sincerely. "This is not your time. This is not the time of any who hold to the old ways. Be with your mother and father, young sweet Prince. And with your brother. There is no place here left for you."

With a sigh of profound regret, Duke Kalas dropped the sword to the dirt and slowly walked up the stairs, passing the men who would go down and finish that dark work in that dark place.

PART ONE

AND NOW
I AM KING

And now I am king, like so many before and so many yet to come. To most people, this accomplishment would be the end of their goal, the achievement they believed would place them in the lists of the immortals. But notoriety in one's time, great fame spread to the far corners of the world, is little security against the passage of years. King Danube Brock Ursal may be remembered for a while, since he ruled during a time of great crisis, both with the DemonWar and the plague. But few even now remember his grandfather, and fewer his great-grandfather. His name, too, will fade with the passage of time.

As will my father's. As will my mother's.

And now I am king, and this is just a platform, the first rung on a ladder that will climb to include Vanguard, Behren, To-gai, Alpinador, and even the Wilderlands to the west.

Do you hear that, Lady Dasslerond?

I will command the known world and beyond. I will own the Abellican Church, which will become greater under my rule, and which will suffer no rivals. My image will be engraved from southern To-gai to northern Alpinador; my boot print will forever stain the ground of Andur'Blough Inninness and my name will survive the centuries, beyond the memories of the oldest elves.

Those who brought me to this point, particularly Marcalo De'Unnero, do not yet understand the truth of Aydrian Boudabras. They do not understand that I see two shadows at Oracle, one who would speak to their weaknesses, and one who knows the truth of immortality—one who reveals to me that conscience is the halter the gods have placed upon mortal man.

De'Unnero and his cohorts do not understand that with this recognition, I am beyond all of them. The monk fears my mother, and is incensed at me for allowing her to walk freely out of Castle Ursal. I doubt that she will come against me again; I doubt that she has the heart now that guilt shows so clearly in her pretty eyes. She wears the halter of the gods, and it is a burden upon her that will allow me to destroy her with a thought, if necessary.

Better for me to allow her to witness it all, for her to watch the rise of her discarded son. She was once the hero of the people of Honce-the-Bear, who saved them from the demon dactyl, who led them to salvation from the plague. With her as my witness, my fame will spread even more quickly. It will gall Jilseponie as she comes truly to understand that she is my legitimacy, that her renown allows me to further my own. Her reputation is my ally even as she may become my enemy.

In that event, too, there is nothing but gain. A warrior is judged most of all by the enemies he defeats. Fio Bou-raiy, Prince Midalis, Lady Dasslerond, and perhaps Jilseponie Wyndon Ursal.

It is an impressive list.

I only hope that I may find more formidable and worthy adversaries.

I have heard of a dragon flying about the wastelands south of the Belt-and-Buckle.

The pleasure will be mine; the judgment will be kind.

And now I am king.

—AYDRIAN BOUDABRAS

❖ 1 ❖

The Shadow
in the Mirror

The shadow in the mirror drew him in, and Aydrian could not get the thought of Jilseponie out of his mind. Unlike the unrelenting hatred he felt for the woman, a rush of warmth came over him, as if this shadow was communicating to him that Jilseponie was his answer here. Not for glory. Not for power.

For what, then?

Salvation?

Aydrian leaned back against the wall in the small darkened room he had set up for Oracle, this mystical connection to the shadows in the mirror. The elves had taught him Oracle, and had taught him that in looking into the mirror, he was seeing those who had gone before. Aydrian wasn't sure of that. Perhaps Oracle was more a way for him to look within his own essence and heart. Perhaps these shadowy creatures he saw in the mirror—and he saw two, whereas others usually saw only one—were messengers of the gods, or his own attunement to godlike wisdom.

It was here, at Oracle, that Aydrian had learned to comprehend the power of the gemstones. It was here, at Oracle, that Aydrian had first come to understand the manner in which he might reach his coveted immortality—*immortalis* in the ancient tongue of man and elf.

So now he watched, basking in the continuing rush of warmth and softness that accompanied the thoughts of Jilseponie—imparted, he understood, by this one shadow. But then the second shadow appeared across the way, and Aydrian was immediately reminded of the truth of Jilseponie, that she had abandoned him to die, that she had, in effect, forced him into slavery at the hands of cruel Lady Dasslerond!

Moments later, all warmth and thoughts of some mystical salvation flew away from Aydrian, replaced by his hatred for the witch Jilseponie, the pretend queen. He watched as the two shadows came together, not to blend into something larger and greater, but in an apparent attempt by each to overshadow the other.

Aydrian couldn't help but grin at this continuing battle. Other people who knew the secret of Oracle saw one shadow, but he had two, and it was precisely that, these two warring viewpoints on every issue, that led Aydrian to realize that he was truly blessed. Unlike the lockstep fools who followed Oracle without question, Aydrian forced from Oracle the power of reasoned resolution. Each step was worked through logically and in his heart.

He laughed aloud, recognizing then that the first shadow was his own conscience, was the shackle the gods had placed about the neck of mortal men.

In that revelation, the issue of Jilseponie was settled once more. The witch would watch his rise to greatness beyond anything the world had ever known. She would die—of her guilt and with his smiling face watching her go—while he would live on forever.

Now very different images filtered through Aydrian's thoughts. He visualized a map of Honce-the-Bear—the southern reaches, from Ursal to Entel, shaded red; the rest, uncolored. Like crawling fingers, the red began to spread. It moved north from Ursal to engulf Palmaris, and as soon as the city fell under his control, all of the Masur Delaval, the great river that cut through the kingdom, bloodied. In the east along the coast, the red moved north from Entel, sweeping along the Mantis Arm toward St.-Mere-Abelle.

Yes, Aydrian understood that the conquest of St.-Mere-Abelle would be the final victory to secure all of Honce-the-Bear south of the Gulf of Corona. The thought of that monastery, the seat of power for Father Abbot Fio Bou-raiy and the Abellican Church, made him consider another problem: what to do with Marcalo De'Unnero and Abbot Olin, both of whom desired to rule that Church?

Aydrian asked the shadow in the mirror. *What of Abbot Olin?*

He envisioned the map again, and now the red fingers crawled south of Entel, around the edge of the Belt-and-Buckle, to Jacintha, the seat of Behren's power.

A knock on the door brought Aydrian from his contemplations, shattering the moment of Oracle. He looked up, his expression angry. But only for a moment, for as he considered what he had just seen, he realized that he had his answer.

The coach rolled through the southern gate of Palmaris, much like any other. The city was open, for despite the rumors filtering up from Ursal, this was a time of peace in Honce-the-Bear. Thus no guards approached the coach or inspected its contents or passengers. If they had looked in through the curtained window, they might well have recognized the woman sitting there, though she seemed barely a shell of her former self.

Jilseponie was hardly aware that her driver had crossed into Palmaris. She sat quietly, her arms crossed before her, her face still showing the lines of the tears that had marked the first days out of Ursal. She wasn't crying any longer, though.

She was just numb.

She could hardly comprehend the truth of Aydrian, could hardly believe that her child was not dead, but had been stolen from her by the elves and raised all these years apart from her. How could he have become the tyrant that she had seen in Ursal? How could a child born of her and Elbryan have become the monster that was Aydrian?

And he was a monster. Jilseponie knew that profoundly. He had torn Constance from the grave and, Jilseponie believed, had used her to murder Danube. He had stolen the throne of Ursal. And all of that under the guidance of Marcalo De'Unnero!

Marcalo De'Unnero!

To Jilseponie, there was no purer incarnation of evil than he, unless it was the demon dactyl Bestesbulzibar itself! How could Aydrian have taken up with the man who had murdered his own father?

It made no sense to Jilseponie, and in truth, the woman had not the strength to try to sort out the confusing morass.

Aydrian was alive.

Nothing else mattered, truly. No other questions could find their way to a reasoned conclusion within Jilseponie in light of that terrible and wonderful truth.

Aydrian was alive.

And he was the king, the unlawful king. And he was in league with De'Unnero and of like heart with the hated man.

That was all that mattered.

The coach lurched to a stop, and only then did Jilseponie realize that the road beneath them had turned from dirt to cobblestone, and that the fields beside them had changed to crowded streets, farmhouses to shops and taverns. The door opened and her driver, an older man with sympathetic eyes, offered her his hand.

"We're here, milady Jilseponie," he said tenderly.

Palmaris. A city Jilseponie had known as her home for much of her life. Here she had found refuge after the catastrophe that had destroyed Dundalis to the north. Here she had found her second family, the Chilichunks. Here she had married, though it had ended abruptly and disastrously. Here she had ruled as baroness. Here her friends presided over St. Precious. And here, Elbryan had been killed, as he and she had defeated the demon within Father Abbot Markwart. Moving as if in a dream, Jilseponie drifted out of the coach and onto the street. She was dressed modestly—not in any of the raiments suitable for the queen of Honce-the-Bear, surely—and so her appearance caused no stir among the folk moving about the crowded city avenue.

Jilseponie slowly looked around, absorbing the sights of the city she knew so well. Across the wide square stood St. Precious, the largest structure in the city, a soaring cathedral that could hold thousands within its stone walls, and that housed the hundred brothers under the leadership of Bishop Braumin Herde.

The thought of her friend had Jilseponie walking toward that cathedral, slowly at first, but then breaking into a run to the front door.

"Seems a one needin' her soul mended, eh?" a passerby remarked to the old driver, who stood by the coach, watching her disappear into the abbey.

"More than you'd ever understand," the driver replied absently, and with a sigh, he climbed back to his seat and turned his coach about, for the south road and Ursal. He had been explicitly instructed not to approach Bishop Braumin or any of the other leaders of the city, and while the old driver thought it strange that no formal emissary had come north from Ursal to this important second city, he knew enough of the history here to gather the motivation behind the silence.

King Aydrian, and more specifically, Marcalo De'Unnero, wanted to make the announcement personally.

"Few if any will oppose you openly," Aydrian said to Duke Kalas, as the pair, along with Marcalo De'Unnero, Abbot Olin, and some other commanders, stood about the large table in what Aydrian had turned into the planning room. A large map of Honce-the-Bear was spread before them, with the areas currently under Aydrian's secure control, notably the southern stretch from Ursal to Entel, shaded in red—just as he had seen at Oracle.

"None will stand before my Allhearts," Duke Kalas said.

Marcalo De'Unnero smirked at him, quietly mocking his proud posture. "Not openly, perhaps," the monk corrected. "The key to our victory will be to look honestly into the hearts of those you leave in your wake. Will they accept King Aydrian? And if not, how great is their hatred? Enough for them to take up arms against him?"

"Most will do as they are told," Abbot Olin insisted. "We have seen this before, during our march from Entel. The people care little who is leading them as king, as long as that king is gentle and fair toward them." He looked to Aydrian. "I suggest that Duke Kalas' journey be more a parade of celebration than the conquering march of an army. You are not invading the kingdom of Honce-the-Bear, after all, but rather spreading the word that the kingdom is rightfully yours."

"Many might not see it that way," Duke Kalas reminded. "Certainly, Prince Midalis and his followers . . ."

"Who are mostly in the distant land of Vanguard," Abbot Olin went on. "You will find few along the road to Palmaris who readily embrace Prince Midalis, if they even know of the man. We must simply tell them the truth of the situation: that Aydrian is king, and accepted as such by the Ursal nobles. Almost to a man, the common folk will go along without argument."

"For how could they begin to argue?" Marcalo De'Unnero added with a snicker, one that was shared about the table.

But not by Aydrian. "Let us not forget that he who leads Palmaris is a great friend to Jilseponie, and certainly no friend to Marcalo De'Unnero," the young king pointedly reminded. "Bishop Braumin Herde will oppose us, no doubt."

"Do you believe him foolish enough to denounce your authority?" Duke Kalas asked. "Do you believe that he will force the army of Ursal to crush the folk of Palmaris?"

"I know not, but certainly St. Precious will not open wide her doors to Marcalo De'Unnero and Abbot Olin," Aydrian remarked.

De'Unnero looked to Olin, and then to Kalas. For that moment, at least, it seemed as if the fiery monk and the warrior duke were in complete agreement. Kalas even nodded as De'Unnero replied, "Then we will open the door for them."

"St. Precious will be a fine prize," Abbot Olin said. "I greatly anticipate seeing her halls."

"But you will not," Aydrian said bluntly, and the declaration brought looks of surprise from all about the table, particularly from Abbot Olin himself—and the old abbot's expression fast shifted from startled to suspicious.

"Abbot Olin will have better and more pleasing duties to attend," Aydrian explained to the curious stares. "We have all heard the reports of the tumult in Behren, of the revolt of the To-gai-ru and the downfall of the Chezru Chieftain. Behren is a country drifting aimlessly now, with no leader, spiritual or secular. Perhaps it is time for Honce-the-Bear to come to the aid of our southern brothers."

"What are you saying?" De'Unnero asked incredulously.

"You believe that I should go to Jacintha?" Abbot Olin asked, almost as doubtfully. "To lend support and friendship?"

"To assume the mantle of leadership," Aydrian declared, and the doubting expressions only magnified, and a few murmurs of disbelief followed. "We cannot allow this open door to close to us," the king explained, and he began to walk about the table, settling his gaze on each leader in turn. "Not now. Behren is in desperate straits. The people have just learned that their Chezru religion was founded on a complete falsehood, and was in fact one based on the same gemstones that the Yatols use as proof that the Abellicans are demonic. The people of Behren are desperate, I say, for both a friend and a leader. Abbot Olin will be that man."

"To what end?" De'Unnero demanded, and his tone drew a dangerous look from Aydrian.

"Behren will be mine, perhaps before the fall of Vanguard," the young king explained to them all, and there was no room for debate within his tone.

"How thin will we stretch our armies?" De'Unnero asked.

"It will take fewer than you believe," Aydrian shot right back. "We have the wealth to bribe enough of Jacintha's garrison and the confused Yatols to our side. If this is done properly, and I hold all faith in Abbot Olin, our conquest of Jacintha will be nearly bloodless. And once Jacintha is ours, once we have given the people a new religion and a new hope to grab on to, once we have shown them that we are their friends and brothers, my kingdom will spread from Jacintha to engulf every Behrenese town."

De'Unnero started to argue further, but Aydrian cut him off.

"I have seen this vision and I know it to be true," Aydrian proclaimed. "Go to Entel, Abbot Olin. Speak with the pirate fleet we used to secure Entel from Danube. Duke Bretherford will support you with several warships. Gather enough of an army together, not to crush Behren, but to convince those scrambling for power there that you are the necessary alternative to the chaos that now grips their land. Our coffers are deep with gemstones."

Before De'Unnero could argue further, which he obviously meant to do, Abbot Olin voiced his intrigue. "Could this be possible?" he asked, his eyes verily glowing.

Aydrian and everyone else spent a few moments studying the man. It was no secret in Honce-the-Bear that Abbot Olin of St. Bondabruce in Entel favored Behren, perhaps even over Honce-the-Bear. The reason this senior Abellican abbot had been defeated by Fio Bou-raiy in the last election for Father Abbot of the Church was his close association with Chezru Chieftain Yakim Douan and the Behrenese people. To the Abellicans, Olin had always been a bit too comfortable with the southern kingdom.

And now here was Aydrian, hinting that the southern kingdom might be his.

"More than possible, it is likely," Aydrian assured the eager man. "Understand, Abbot Olin, that you will come to Jacintha as a friend, and more than that, as a savior. The Yatol priests will follow you because you will bring them the security they have lost with the downfall of the Chezru Chieftain and the chaos it has created among the flock. And because you will pay them—they are a greedy lot!"

"Not all will abandon the way of Chezru," Abbot Olin warned.

"But enough will to marginalize the others, and you will have enough power at your disposal to ... well, to dispose of those who prove most troublesome. I expect that Jacintha will be yours, my friend Abbot Olin, and very quickly. And from there, I have no doubt that you will spread your influence and spiritual kingdom, and my secular kingdom, in rapid manner."

Aydrian looked away from Olin, to the others. De'Unnero was staring at him blankly, trying to absorb it all, obviously, while Duke Kalas was just shaking his head, his expression still doubtful.

"Fear not, Duke Kalas, for Abbot Olin's press to the south will take little of your resources from the duties of securing the main prize, the kingdom of Honce-the-Bear," Aydrian remarked. "He will use part of the mercenary armies that brought us to Ursal, and not the professional armies of the kingdom." He looked back to Olin. "You go there offering friendship and support above all else."

"And it will be an honest offer," Abbot Olin replied.

"Indeed," said Aydrian, "as long as they ultimately agree to the rule of King Aydrian Boudabras."

Olin's face darkened for just a moment, but then he grinned, and replied, "Of course."

He hugged her and he held on for a long, long time. For Bishop Braumin Herde there was usually no more welcome sight than Jilseponie Wyndon, his dear and trusted friend, the woman who had led him through the fires of Bestesbulzibar and the hellish swirl of the rosy plague.

This day, though, the sight of Jilseponie tore at the man's heart more than it elevated him. In all his years beside her, even during the plague, Braumin had only once seen Jilseponie this downtrodden, and that after the death of her beloved Elbryan. And aside from his fear for his wounded friend, the mere fact that she was here, and not sitting as queen of Honce-the-Bear, set off alarms in his head that many of the rumors creeping up the river might well be true.

"We have word of the death of King Danube," remarked Brother Marlboro Viscenti, standing across the room from the hugging pair. "Truly I am sorry."

Jilseponie, her face streaked with tears once again, moved back from Braumin. "It was Aydrian," she tried to explain, though their looks told her plainly that these two had no idea of who Aydrian truly might be.

"Aydrian Boudabras," said Braumin. "Yes, the proclamation has come up the Masur Delaval that this young man is now king of Honce-the-Bear, though what that means for us all we do not yet know. I have never heard him mentioned in the royal line."

"There are other rumors," Viscenti started to add, but Braumin waved his hand to silence the man.

Jilseponie, though, steadied herself and looked back at the thin and always nervous Viscenti. "Rumors of a change in St. Honce, one that shall spread throughout your church," she said.

Viscenti nodded slowly.

"Our new king was aided in his ascent by your own Abbot Olin," Jilseponie confirmed. Then she paused and took a deep breath. "And by Marcalo De'Unnero."

"Curse the name!" Bishop Braumin cried, and Master Viscenti stood there trembling, wincing repeatedly with his nervous tic.

"How has this happened?" asked Braumin, and he moved away from Jilseponie, stalking across the room. "How did this come about without warning? A young man, unheard of, suddenly proclaimed king? There is no sense in this! What claim might Aydrian Boudabras hold to the throne of Honce-the-Bear?"

"He is my son," Jilseponie said quietly, though if she had shouted it, if she had brought in a thousand people to shout it, it would not have struck Bishop Braumin and Master Viscenti any more profoundly.

"Your son?" Viscenti echoed incredulously.

"He is but a child?" Abbot Braumin asked. "You bore King Danube a babe? Why did we not—"

"He is a young man," Jilseponie corrected. "The son of Jilseponie and Elbryan."

Both monks stood dumbfounded, Viscenti shaking his head and Braumin just staring at Jilseponie, trying to find some reason in this unbelievable turn.

"How is that possible?" the bishop of Palmaris finally managed to ask.

"The child I thought lost on the field outside of this very city was not lost," Jilseponie explained. "He was taken away and raised in secret by . . ." She paused and shook her head.

"And now corrupted by De'Unnero and Olin, to the doom of us all," reasoned Viscenti.

"So it may prove," Bishop Braumin answered, when it was apparent that Jilseponie would not. "And Duke Kalas and the armies have thrown in with this phony king? It seems impossible! What of Prince Midalis? Surely he will not stand idly by while this pretender to the throne dismantles his brother's kingdom, and the Abellican Church, as well!"

"Prince Midalis may go against him, but he will not win," Jilseponie said, her voice becoming little more than a whisper.

"Many will rally to him!" Viscenti declared, and he shook his fist in the air. "The throne of Honce-the-Bear is not one simply to be stolen, nor is the Abellican Church a willing victim of such treachery! Abbot Olin will be thrown out in disgrace! And Marcalo De'Unnero—we should have burned that fool at the stake years ago. I can hardly believe that he is even still alive! Like the demon dactyl, he is! Unending evil!"

"Surely Aydrian's claim to the throne is tenuous, at best," Bishop Braumin reasoned, all the while patting the master's hands to try to calm the volatile Viscenti, who had not been well of late and had been warned by the healers to try to remain calm—something that was surely against the man's instincts!

"His claim is enough so that the general populace will accept him," said Jilseponie. "It is enough so that the nobles who were not in Danube's favor at the end have the excuse to embrace him. Aydrian came to Ursal with an army at the ready, and once the throne was taken, he only added to that army with Danube's own soldiers." She looked at Bishop Braumin with sincere sympathy, and slowly shook her head. "He has Ursal, and will sweep through Palmaris, long before Prince Midalis can organize and offer any aid to you, should you choose to oppose Aydrian. Of that much I am sure. And allies will not be easily found, especially here in the southwestern reaches of Honce-the-Bear, so dominated by Ursal and the corrupt dukes. The common folk will welcome Aydrian because to do otherwise would mean doing battle against him, and that, they have not the power to do."

"The Church will not succumb to the threats of a usurper and his treacherous cronies!" Bishop Braumin declared. "Palmaris will offer resistance to this King Aydrian, and St. Precious will never open her doors to him, or for Marcalo De'Unnero and the traitor, Abbot Olin."

"You would pit your city against the legions of Ursal?" Jilseponie quietly asked, and her words stole more than a little of Braumin's bluster. Palmaris was no minor city, and its garrison was strong and deep and well seasoned. But they would be no match for the Allheart Knights and the thousands of soldiers of Ursal.

"For the city, I . . . I do not know," Braumin admitted, but the helpless shake of his head didn't last for long and the fires quickly returned to his dark eyes. "But on my life, I vow that neither Aydrian nor the cursed De'Unnero will enter this abbey, unless they are dragged through the gates in chains!"

"Do not make such a vow!" Jilseponie scolded. "You do not understand the power that will come against you!"

"You would have me welcome them?"

"I would beg you to flee!" said Jilseponie. "To St.-Mere-Abelle, and from there to Vanguard, if that is necessary. If you stay . . ." Her voice failed her then, and she began to pant, trying to catch her breath. She would have fallen to the ground had not Braumin rushed forward and caught her in his grasp, holding her tightly once more.

Aydrian waved them all away and continued to stand at the map table as the noblemen filed out, talking amongst themselves. De'Unnero grabbed that open door and stepped beside it, as if he meant to close it behind the others while he remained in the room.

"Go to St. Honce with Abbot Olin," Aydrian said to him. "Help him to prepare the formal documents declaring the change in the Abellican Church."

"And what is that change to be?" De'Unnero asked, and he looked back to the hall to make sure that Olin was far away by then. "Are we to proclaim Olin as Father Abbot?"

"For now, our friend Olin will serve as the official Abellican emissary to Behren," Aydrian replied. "That is all we need to tell your brothers. Soon, Olin will be named Father Abbot of the Abellican Church *in Behren*."

Not surprised, De'Unnero nonetheless chuckled. "You make it sound so easy."

"That part will be easier than placing Marcalo De'Unnero as Father Abbot of the Abellican Church in Honce-the-Bear," came Aydrian's response, one that had De'Unnero's dark eyes glowing. "While most of the country south of the Gulf of Corona will fall to me without bloodshed, we both understand that your Abellican brothers will not so easily accept you as their leader."

"They are not my brothers, so killing them will bring me little pause," De'Unnero replied.

"Then go and begin the process of your ascent," Aydrian told him. "Invite all who would come to join you in the march of King Aydrian, as the kingdom is solidified, as the church is renewed. Do not overtly threaten any who refuse, but—"

De'Unnero stopped him with an upraised hand. "I understand how I must proceed, now that it is clear that Abbot Olin and I are to walk diverging roads."

"The more you convince with promises, the easier it will be to destroy those who refuse," Aydrian said.

De'Unnero smiled wryly and left the room, closing the door behind him.

Aydrian turned back to the table, to the large map of the world. He ran his hand from Ursal to Palmaris, then from Entel across the Mantis Arm, following the coast all the way to St.-Mere-Abelle, the most coveted prize of all, and the one he knew would prove the most difficult to attain.

"You see?" he asked.

Across the way, a drapery moved, and Sadye walked out into the open.

"Tell me," Aydrian asked her, "what did you perceive of Duke Monmouth of Yorkey?"

"He fears you," the woman replied, walking to stand beside Aydrian at the table. "And he hates you. Though neither emotion is as strong in him as in Duke Kalas."

"And yet the fear within Kalas is so profound that it dooms him as my ally," Aydrian remarked. "What of Bretherford?"

Sadye looked up at him, her gaze lingering on his young and strong and undeniably handsome features for a long while. "I do not know."

"The southland must be secured before I do battle with Prince Midalis," Aydrian explained to her. "That will be a process more of measuring the loyalty of the noblemen who service each region than of conquering the commoners."

"King Danube was loved by the common folk, as was your mother."

"The common folk care not at all who is their king," Aydrian told her, and he looked away from the map, locking stares with her, and smiled. "If they are eating well, they love their king. If they are starving, they despise him. It is not so difficult a thing to understand."

"And you will feed them well," Sadye said.

Aydrian looked back at the map, running his hand from those areas already shaded red to those areas, all the rest of the world, he intended to overtake. "I will win with kindness and I will win with cruelty," he said calmly, matter-of-factly.

The fact that they were standing almost directly above the dungeon staircase, beneath which rotted the body of Torrence Pemblebury, only strengthened that statement.

"Long live King Aydrian," Sadye said quietly, and she gently touched his arm.

Aydrian didn't look at her, knowing that his indifference at that moment only strengthened his growing hold over her, only heightened her growing hunger for him.

*   *   *

"What are you going to do?"

The question was simple and straightforward enough, but it echoed confusingly around the thoughts of Bishop Braumin Herde.

What are you going to do?

About the abbey? About the city? He was the appointed bishop, which meant that both were under his guidance. He knew in his heart that he could not welcome any change to the Abellican Church that included Marcalo De'Unnero. The man was a murderer. The man had brought nothing but chaos and misery with him whenever he had come through Palmaris. He had once been bishop here, and had executed one merchant horribly and publicly. As henchman to Father Abbot Markwart, he had imprisoned Elbryan and Jilseponie, Visccenti and Braumin, among others.

Braumin understood that he now had to keep these two tumultuous, shattering events in Ursal separate. On the secular level, Aydrian was now king of Honce-the-Bear, and whether that was a legitimate claim or not, the fact that he apparently had the armies of Ursal to back him up made it a claim that none could oppose without dire risk. On the spiritual level, the mere thought that Abbot Olin was in league with De'Unnero discredited the man wholly within the Abellican Church, the Church that had been moving steadily toward the vision of dear Avelyn Desbris, De'Unnero's avowed enemy.

Slowly, Bishop Braumin turned to face the questioner, Brother Viscenti, his dear friend who had been through so much beside him, all the way back across the decades to their mutual discovery of the truth of Avelyn under the tutelage of dead Master Jojonah in the catacombs of St.-Mere-Abelle.

"St. Precious will not open her doors for them," the bishop declared. "Never that. Let De'Unnero and his newfound henchmen knock those doors down, if they will. Have them burn me at the stake, if they will. But I'll not surrender my principles to that man. I'll not encourage his misguided view of the world."

"Almost every brother here will stand firm with you," Viscenti replied.

Braumin Herde wasn't sure if that was welcome support or not, because he understood clearly what that might mean to his beloved companions. He almost said something to deny Viscenti's words, but he bit the retort back, reminding himself that he, as a younger man, had been more than ready to die for his beliefs. He had stood beside Elbryan and Avelyn when that surely put him in line for the gallows. Could he ask those beneath him now to surrender their own principles and beliefs for the sake of their corporeal bodies?

"St. Precious will lock them out and keep them out!" Viscenti boldly declared.

"And if they overrun us, then our deaths will not be futile," Braumin assured him. "The Abellican Church must make a principled stand against De'Unnero, whatever the cost, because to do otherwise would be to abandon everything we hold dear."

"But what of the city?" Viscenti asked. "Can we demand as much from the common man? Should we bar the gate and man the walls and allow the folk of Palmaris to be slaughtered by this new king?"

That was the rub. How Braumin Herde wished at that moment that King Danube had never appointed him bishop of Palmaris!

"I think you should deny him entrance, or at least, deny his army entrance," the surprising Viscenti remarked. "If this man who claims to be king wishes to parley, then allow him that, but in such a meeting, make it perfectly clear that Marcalo De'Unnero, curse his name, is not welcome here. Perhaps we can drive a wedge between them. Perhaps we can persuade Aydrian to speak more openly with his mother."

"You ask me to take quite a risk," said Braumin. "And if King Aydrian refuses to parley? If he demands the opening of the gate? Do we face war with Ursal, brother?"

Brother Viscenti leaned back and pondered the possibilities for a long while. "I would expect that the people of Palmaris, given the truth of their choices, would fight Aydrian to a man and a woman," he replied. "These are the folk who witnessed the Miracle of Avelyn. These are the Behrenese welcomed as part of Palmaris when no one else would have them—forget not, for they certainly have not forgotten, that De'Unnero and his Brothers Repentant persecuted them most horribly in the days of the plague! These are the folk who saw the folly of Markwart, and De'Unnero, who saw the beauty of Elbryan and Jilseponie, and of Bishop Braumin Herde. If you would so readily die for your principles, my friend, should not they be given the same opportunity?"

Bishop Braumin chuckled at the strange irony of that implication, that it was his duty to allow his flock to be slaughtered.

He strode across the room and hugged his dear friend, patting him hard on the back. Yes, Braumin Herde was quite grateful to Brother Viscenti at that moment, for the man had indeed helped him sort through the swirl that was in his mind.

"Jilseponie has gone to Roger," Viscenti remarked. "Watch the fire of Roger Lockless when he learns of the events in Ursal. He will rally Palmaris, if you will not!"

Braumin pushed Viscenti back to arm's length. "Or both of us, or the three of us, will rally all the region as never before!" he said with a determined smile.

Just beneath that determined smile, that shared pat on the back, though, lay the realization that the coming darkness might be the greatest threat ever to face the city of Palmaris. For always before, when the hordes of the demon dactyl threatened or the foul stench of Father Abbot Markwart pervaded the air, Palmaris had had an ally in the greater city of Ursal.

This time, though . . .

❖ 2 ❖

Warnings on the Winds

T he feel of the breeze on their faces came as welcome relief to the two elves who had spent weeks wandering the dark ways of the Path of Starless Night. This journey had taken much longer than their original trek under the mountains, when they had been heading to the south, for Belli'mar Juraviel and Cazzira of Tymwyvenne were determined properly to mark those paths leading through the Belt-and-Buckle, leading from Tymwyvenne to To-gai, the land they hoped now to be securely the province of Brynn Dharielle. For while Juraviel had left the ranger in the southland, he had not done so with a light heart, and he was determined to keep track of her progress in freeing the To-gai-ru from the conquering Behrenese.

Despite that burning curiosity and his deep feelings for Brynn, Belli'mar Juraviel hadn't regretted his decision to turn back to the north. His responsibility was, first and foremost, to his people, the Touel'alfar, and to his home, Andur'Blough Inninness. Lady Dasslerond had sent Brynn to the south to free To-gai because she had thought the To-gai-ru more sympathetic to her people than the Behrenese, and because she feared that the stain of the demon dactyl, the rot that had begun to infect precious Andur'Blough Inninness, might force the Touel'alfar on that southern road in the near future.

That need seemed much lessened to Belli'mar Juraviel now that he had come to know Cazzira so intimately, however. Not because the stain of the demon dactyl was any less dangerous to his precious homeland, but because he had found the race of the Doc'alfar, the lost cousins of the Touel'alfar. And as his relationship with Cazzira had grown, Juraviel had come to understand and believe that the elves of Corona would indeed reunite into one community.

The two races were different, physically. Though both were about four feet in height, and lithe of build, the Touel'alfar were possessed of translucent wings. And while the Doc'alfar had dark hair and very light skin, the result of living in their dark and foggy homeland bogs, the Touel'alfar had colors more reflective of the daylight, bright hair and light eyes and skin glowing with the warmth of the golden sun.

But now, over the months, Belli'mar Juraviel had come to look deeper into Cazzira, beyond their physical differences, and had come to see a soul that was very much akin to any of the Touel'alfar. They were one people, of one heart, and with mostly superficial physical differences that would fade over time as their communities rejoined.

That was Belli'mar Juraviel's hope, at least, and his plan. And so he had come back through the mountains, to the northern slopes near to the Doc'alfar land of Tymwyvenne, with Cazzira by his side, and with a third elf, not yet born, growing within Cazzira's womb.

"This is not the same tunnel that we entered with Brynn those years ago," Juraviel remarked, squinting as he surveyed the region, his eyes unaccustomed to the light—even though it was late afternoon and the sun was already beginning to set.

"But we are near," Cazzira assured him, and she pointed to the northwest, to a distinctive mountain peak that looked somewhat like the wrinkled face of an old man. "Close enough, perhaps, so that the scouts of Tymwyvenne are looking upon us, their deadly weapons readied to strike at you should you make any untoward movement against me," she added, flashing Juraviel that mischievous grin of hers.

"Let them attack, then!" Juraviel cried dramatically, and he flung himself against Cazzira, crushing her in his loving hug, the both of them laughing. He pushed his lover back to arm's length, his golden eyes locking with hers, which were no less distinctive and startling, the lightest shade of blue that contrasted so starkly with her raven locks. How deeply did Belli'mar Juraviel love this Doc'alfar! And in looking at her, every time he looked at her, he knew that Lady Dasslerond would come to see the beauty of it all, and the benefit of rejoining their long-lost cousins.

Sometime later, with the moon Sheila shining brightly overhead, the two elves moved along the lower slopes of the foothills, Cazzira leading in a generally westerly direction. They would not make Tymwyvenne that night, she had explained to Juraviel, but she was fairly certain that they would see the magnificent woodwork of the elven city's great gates early on their second day of travel.

They set camp in a clearing up above the bogland and skeletal trees that marked the region of Tymwyvenne, taking little care to conceal their campfire. For they were in the realm of the Doc'alfar now, secure from any intruders save Cazzira's own people.

The night was quiet about them, with only a gentle breeze blowing. A bit of a chill carried in on that breeze, but it was nothing their generous fire couldn't defeat.

"You will press King Eltiraaz to send us off immediately to your people?" Cazzira asked as the two lay side by side, staring up at the moon and the stars.

"Better that you and I make the first journey to Caer'alfar," Juraviel explained. "Lady Dasslerond will be no more trusting of your people than your King Eltiraaz was of me when first I ventured onto your lands. It is my Lady's duty to move with caution concerning the welfare of her people, and I would expect no less of her." He rolled to his side so that he was facing Cazzira directly, looking into her light blue eyes, which had so captured his heart. "But you will melt her caution," he said quietly. "Together you and I will forge the bond anew between our peoples, to the gain of Touel'alfar and Doc'alfar alike.

"To the gain of Tylwyn Doc and Tylwyn Tou alike, you mean," Cazzira teased, using the Doc'alfar names of the respective races, and pointedly and playfully putting her own people first. She moved her hand onto Juraviel's shoulder as she spoke, and he suddenly grabbed her wrist and pulled her arm back, pinning it.

"Touel'alfar and Doc'alfar!" he demanded.

"And if I refuse?" Cazzira countered.

"Then I shall have my way with you!" Juraviel replied. "Unless of course, the wondrous sentries of the Doc'alfar are about, ready to spring to your defense!"

Cazzira laughed. "The same wondrous sentries who managed to capture Belli'mar Juraviel on his first pass through their land, and with ease!"

"Aha!" Juraviel said dramatically, pointing one finger into the air. "But how do you know that was not my plan all along? To get captured so that I could steal from your people."

"Steal?"

"Your heart, at least."

"My heart?" Cazzira echoed incredulously. "Could you be so foolish as to believe that I have any romantic feelings toward you, Belli'mar Juraviel?"

With great dramatic flourish, Juraviel rolled away from Cazzira, clutching his heart as he went. "Ah, but you have shot an arrow into *my* heart!" he cried. "Mortally wounding—"

"I had thought to do the same," came a third voice, startling both from their play. Juraviel increased his roll and twisted about, coming swiftly to his feet, while Cazzira propped herself up on her elbows.

Both relaxed when they saw a familiar figure enter the firelight, that of Lozan Duk, who had accompanied Cazzira on the initial capture of Juraviel and Brynn Dharielle. He looked much like Cazzira, except that he was a bit broader in the shoulders and his eyes were dark, not light. The Doc'alfar scout spent a long moment studying the pair, his expression curious and obviously amused.

"Your journey to the southland was successful, I presume," he said. "Has the ranger Brynn unified the To-gai-ru tribes as securely as Juraviel and Cazzira have unified themselves, I wonder?"

Cazzira scrambled to her feet and rushed across the clearing to wrap her dear old friend in a great hug. Juraviel followed her over, taking Lozan Duk's offered hand in warm embrace.

"You have been gone too long," Lozan Duk said to Cazzira. "Our land has seemed empty without you. We have found so much less fun in hunting intruders." As he finished, he turned his smile and his gaze over Juraviel.

"Too long, indeed," Cazzira agreed. "I cannot wait to look upon Tymwyvenne again!"

"But you mean to stay only a short while," Lozan Duk prompted, glancing from Cazzira to Juraviel and back again.

"And how long were you spying upon us?" Cazzira asked.

Lozan Duk laughed aloud. "When first I came upon you, and recognized that Cazzira and Juraviel had returned, I wanted to rush right in and welcome you, both of you," he explained. "But then it seemed as if I was intruding on a personal time, and so I started away, prepared to return in the morning."

"And then you heard my mention of returning home, with Cazzira," reasoned Juraviel.

Lozan Duk looked at him earnestly and nodded. "You speak of momentous things, Belli'mar Juraviel of the Tylwyn Tou."

"I hope for momentous gain, for my people and for yours," Juraviel replied.

Lozan Duk really didn't have a response for that, so he just paused for a bit to consider his dearest of friends, returned to his side. For many years, he and Cazzira had been hunting partners, and partners in just about everything else. There had never been anything romantic between them, so there was no jealousy in his eyes as he considered her now, just gratitude that she had returned.

That expression of gratitude fast shifted to a look of curiosity, though. "There is something . . ." the elf started to say.

Cazzira's smile gradually widened, until the whole of her delicate and beautiful face was beaming in the moonlight.

Lozan Duk's jaw dropped open and his eyes followed Cazzira's gaze down to her slightly swollen belly. "You are . . . ?"

"I am," Cazzira replied. "It will be the first child born in Tymwyvenne in a quarter of a century, unless other births occurred during my absence."

"No others."

"And it will be the first child born of Tylwyn Doc and Tylwyn Tou parentage in . . ." She paused and looked over at Juraviel.

"In more than the longest memory of the eldest elves," he answered.

"But what does it mean?" Lozan Duk asked, a simple question that held so many layers of intrigue for all of them. Was this child to signify a union of the peoples, a reunification of sorts? Or was it to become a bastard child of both races, accepted by neither?

"It will mean what we make it to mean," Cazzira said determinedly. "The child is a product of love, true and honest love between Tylwyn Doc and Tylwyn Tou. Let there be no doubt of that."

Lozan Duk shook his head slowly as he considered his surprising friend, and gradually his gaze shifted over to Belli'mar Juraviel, this surprising visitor to his land.

"What says Lozan Duk concerning the child?" Juraviel asked bluntly, not sure how to read that expression.

The other elf took a long moment to consider the question, to digest all of this startling news. "If you make Cazzira happy, then you make Lozan Duk happy, Belli'mar Juraviel," he said at length. "She is my friend—as true a friend as I have ever known—and I stand beside her in all of her choices. She has chosen Belli'mar Juraviel as her companion in love, and has chosen Belli'mar Juraviel as the father of her child. That is all that I need to know about the truth of Belli'mar Juraviel's heart." He looked down at Cazzira's belly and smiled warmly. "Any child of Cazzira will be a beautiful creature."

"As will any child of Belli'mar Juraviel," Cazzira added.

"Then the child is doubly blessed," said Lozan Duk, and he held out his arms, and Cazzira fell into a welcome hug.

From the side, Belli'mar Juraviel nodded hopefully.

Lozan Duk led the pair away soon after, moving quickly along the trails leading toward Tymwyvenne. They met other Doc'alfar along the way, and all greeted Cazzira and Juraviel with open arms.

As did King Eltiraaz when at last the companions came before his gleaming wooden throne in the great hall of Tymwyvenne. He rushed down from his royal seat to embrace Cazzira, and welcomed Juraviel back with a warm handshake.

"So much we have to share," he said, returning to his throne. "I wish to hear every step of your journey to the south, and hope that all went well, and is well, with Brynn Dharielle, this extraordinary human that has made the Tylwyn Doc reconsider our actions against human intruders within our borders. You will be pleased to learn, Belli'mar Juraviel, that not another human has been given to the bog since you and your companion passed through."

Juraviel was indeed thrilled to hear that news. When first he and Brynn had encountered the Doc'alfar, it was behind an army of zombies they had created from human intruders, giving the people to the bog in a ritual that put them into an undead state.

"The humans are not without merit," Juraviel replied.

King Eltiraaz nodded, his thorny crown bobbing. "But they are a volatile race," he said. "They lack the stability of the Tylwyn folk. Even now, my scouts are out to the east, where momentous changes have come over the kingdom of the humans." He gave a great sigh. "I do not pretend to understand them and their frenzy, but perhaps we will learn.

"But enough of that," King Eltiraaz went on. "Your tale will be a long one, I trust, since you've walked a road for years. Begin at the beginning, if you will!"

Cazzira was smiling, and even started to speak, but when she turned to regard Juraviel, and when King Eltiraaz likewise looked at the Touel'alfar, they saw he wore a troubled expression.

"What is it?" the Doc'alfar king prompted.

"What changes in the east?" Juraviel asked.

King Eltiraaz and all the Doc'alfar looked at him curiously, as if they did not understand why that could possibly matter. "The human kingdom shifts often," Eltiraaz said. "I doubt—"

"Please, tell me what you have learned," Juraviel pressed, for a nagging feeling of dread filled him, and a sudden great fear for his friend Jilseponie. "Is not Danube Brock Ursal the king of Honce-the-Bear?"

"He is dead, from what we have learned, though you must understand that even my scouts most knowledgeable of the ways of the humans do not understand the subtleties of their language."

Juraviel held the elf king's stare and fought hard to keep his breathing steady. Something within was telling him that those friends he had left behind were somehow involved, and probably not for the good.

"King Danube is dead," Eltiraaz went on, "and his wife, Queen Jilseponie—"

"Jilseponie? Queen?" Juraviel blurted. It made sense to him, of course, for before he had left Andur'Blough Inninness with Brynn, the Touel'alfar had heard rumors that Danube had been courting Jilseponie every summer.

"Yes, her name was Jilseponie," King Eltiraaz explained.

"Was? Is she not still the queen?" The panic was evident in Juraviel's tone.

"Upon Danube's death, she left the great human city," King Eltiraaz told him. "From what we have learned, she is not in the favor of the new king."

"Who is this king?"

"Aydrian," Eltiraaz replied, and Juraviel sucked in his breath.

"Yes, and apparently he is a new addition to the royal line," King Eltiraaz explained. "He is not of the blood of Ursal, but of that of Wyndon."

Belli'mar Juraviel felt as if the whole world was sliding away from him at that awful moment, felt as if he was receding into some surreal dimension. Aydrian was king? He knew in his heart that Dasslerond had never planned such a thing, and that if this really was the Aydrian he had known in Andur'Blough Inninness, the child of Elbryan and Jilseponie, then something had gone terribly wrong.

"You know of him?" Cazzira stated as much as asked.

Juraviel hardly heard her. "I beg of you, King Eltiraaz, learn more of these events, for they hold great consequence, I fear, for my people."

"How so?"

"If this Aydrian is who I believe, then my people are either more intimately tied to the humans than ever before, or they are in more danger from the humans than ever before," Juraviel honestly replied. "I must learn more of this new human king, and quickly."

Cazzira put her hand on his arm, and when he glanced at her, he realized that the desperation must have sounded clearly in his voice. He looked at her helplessly for a moment, then turned back to the Doc'alfar king. "And I fear that my time here is short," he went on. "I must be away, as soon as is possible, to my people." He looked back at Cazzira, who nodded. "I pray you allow Cazzira to accompany me, and perhaps others of your court."

King Eltiraaz wore a curious expression. "I thought that we had long ago agreed on a decidedly more gentle approach to heal the ancient breach between our peoples. Such a meeting cannot be forced, we agreed."

"If Aydrian is king of the humans, then I fear for my people," Juraviel admitted. "And I ask King Eltiraaz to aid us in this, what may be our time of need."

"And so doing, endanger his own people?" the Doc'alfar king asked without hesitation, his tone growing more grave.

Juraviel conceded the point with a nod. "I must go," he said. "And I pray you do not hinder me."

"Then you must tell me more of this Aydrian," King Eltiraaz insisted.

Juraviel considered the question for just a moment; he could not deny that it was a reasonable request.

"I will tell you all that I know, of Aydrian and his parents," he agreed.

"And of your fears," the Doc'alfar king added, and Juraviel nodded.

"And we will tell you of our travels to the south, through the Path of Starless Night, through the lair of the dragon, Agradeleous, and across the wild grasslands south of the mountains," Cazzira put in. She looked at Juraviel, whose expression showed less patience with that prospect. But then Cazzira added, "And we will tell you of other developments that may sway your decision concerning Belli'mar Juraviel's journey home, and what role I, and others of our people, might play in that journey."

Juraviel understood her reasoning then, and he knew it was sound. Cazzira was going to leverage their love and their coming child, to try to force her king's hand in opening up the dialogue between Touel'alfar and Doc'alfar.

"Yes," Juraviel agreed. "We have much to share with you. And I beg of you to send your scouts out wider while we speak, to learn all that they can learn of King Aydrian and the affairs of the humans."

"Which humans, Belli'mar Juraviel?" King Eltiraaz asked. "Those to the east, or those to the south?"

Juraviel, who had considered himself out of the tales of Brynn Dharielle, took a long moment to ponder that question, for he realized that if the Aydrian he knew was indeed the new king of Honce-the-Bear, the implications might prove far-reaching indeed. "Perhaps both," he replied. "But for now, let us learn of the dramatic changes within the kingdom to the east."

❖ 3 ❖

Amidst the Fires

He never made it back to the Mountains of Fire and the Walk of Clouds, his beloved home, the monastery of the mystical Jhesta Tu. Pagonel, weary and battered and feeling every bit the four decades of life he had known, had left the northern city of Dharyan-Dharielle in the spring, intending to return to the monastery in the distant southland. He had much to report, after all, given the momentous events that had literally reshaped the region of Behren and To-gai. The Jhesta Tu had a friend now in Brynn, who led the To-gai-ru, and with the often antagonistic Behrenese in disarray, the Walk of Clouds seemed poised to prosper and grow in peace.

But it was precisely that disarray in Behren that quickly turned Pagonel's path. In the reclaimed Behrenese city of Pruda, before he had even reached the halfway point of his journey home, Pagonel had heard rumors of war. All the southern coast of Behren had erupted in battle, with Yatols Peridan and De Hamman resuming their old feud now that the overseeing power of the Chezru Chieftain was no more. That news alone was troubling enough to Pagonel, though certainly not unexpected. But the second rumors of mounting conflict sounded even more ominous.

Apparently, the Yatol of Avrou Eesa, a most unpleasant imperialist named Tohen Bardoh, was gathering strength. At the truce between To-gai and Behren—between Brynn and Yatol Mado Wadon, who spoke for the great Behrenese city of Jacintha—Yatol Bardoh had led the prime opposition. Bardoh had left the field outside of Dharyan-Dharielle a bitter man, and one whom all the parties involved in the truce agreed might prove to be troublesome.

Rumors now seemed to support that very speculation. If Bardoh was indeed gathering a great army, then likely they would soon be fighting for the city of Jacintha, for the heart of Behren itself, and the fate of the Jhesta Tu and of Brynn and her To-gai-ru kinsmen was surely involved. Yatol Mado Wadon, the logical successor to the dead Chezru Chieftain as Yatol of Jacintha, might soon be challenged, forcefully so, by Yatol Tohen Bardoh.

Bardoh hated the Jhesta Tu, and more than anything in the entire world, Yatol Bardoh hated Brynn Dharielle, known as the Dragon of To-gai. In her journey to free To-gai, she had conquered his city of Avrou Eesa, and had made the man look like a fool in the process, not once, but twice. Pagonel had no doubt that if Bardoh won the struggle and seized control of Jacintha, his friend in Dharyan-Dharielle would soon find herself once more at war— and this time with an enemy far more determined to see her end.

Pagonel owed it to Brynn to learn more about these troubling reports, and to determine if she and her legions should join in the fighting before the issue of Jacintha was decided. She had made something of a pact with Yatol Mado Wadon, after all, forcing him to agree to her keeping Dharyan as her own by using the threat of Bardoh against him. If she had not held the city, then Bardoh would surely have taken it, thereby strengthening his already considerable position among the remaining Behrenese leadership. Better for Yatol Wadon that she kept the city, she had reasoned effectively to the man, and when she had symbolically named the conquered and held city Dharyan-Dharielle, adding her To-gai-ru name to its previous Behrenese name, she had done so with the intent that this city would serve as a bridge between the two peoples.

If in control of Behren, Yatol Bardoh would only cross that bridge with a conquering army at his back.

The Jhesta Tu mystic, wearing his traditional red-and-orange robes, drew quite a few stares as he crossed through the Dahdah Oasis to the west of Jacintha. In the centuries of the reign of the Yatols, few Jhesta Tu walked the lands of Behren, but now Pagonel wore his robes openly so that he could gauge the reaction and thus, the significance of the recent changes.

There were no soldiers in the oasis this day, which surprised the mystic, given that much of the army was in the process of returning from the battle-scarred areas to the west. He had wondered if he would encounter the majority of the Jacintha garrison here, a logical stopping place on the road back to the east.

All that he found were merchants, though, their caravans clustered in various sections about the watering pond.

"A fair day to you," Pagonel greeted one man, a farrier, as he worked on the infected foot of a hobbled horse.

The man looked up at him, his jaw dropping open despite his obvious attempts to remain calm and controlled.

"Ah, be you de man who made de peace?" the farrier answered in his heavily accented voice, a dialect that Pagonel knew to be from the Cosinnida region of southeastern Behren.

"I am a man dedicated to peace, yes," Pagonel answered, dipping a slight bow.

"Den you be in de bad place now!" the farrier replied with a toothy grin and a burst of laughter.

Pagonel looked around at the many caravans, at the quiet, slightly rippling pond. "I see no armies drawing their lines of battle."

"Not yet, but soon," the farrier explained. "That Yatol Bardoh, he be very very angry. We see many soldiers returning to Jacintha, but many more do not. Or when they do, it will be in line with Yatol Bardoh, we hear, to take de place from Yatol Mado Wadon. It be very very bad, I tell you."

Pagonel was more than a bit surprised that the man was being so forthcoming with him. Obviously, Behren was in flux here, an uncertain time where information gained and given would be crucial to the well-being of all. As he stood there with the farrier, others drew closer, listening with more than a passing interest.

"We be going to this new city," the farrier said, and Pagonel noticed a few other merchants nodding.

"Dharyan-Dharielle," the mystic said.

"You know de place, yes?"

"I do, and can promise you all that the woman sitting as governess there will welcome you with open arms," Pagonel told them with complete confidence. "It is the desire of Brynn Dharielle that her city serve as a bridge between the Behrenese and the To-gai-ru, and that it remain an open city, exchanging goods and exchanging ideas. You will find your journey well worth your time, I assure you."

That brought a lot of hopeful nods from the men and women, all of whom were so obviously on edge from the mounting tension within Behren.

"You break de bread with me this night," the farrier said.

"And with me!" a merchant chimed in.

"And me!" said another, and so on down the line.

Pagonel readily agreed, knowing that the insights he gathered from these nomadic merchants would likely provide a greater understanding of the true goings-on within Behren than anything the leading Yatols might tell him.

"The events in Behren are of great importance to the new king of Honce-the-Bear," Master Mackaront of St. Bondabruce, the longtime emissary of Abbot Olin to the Chezru Chieftain, told the new leader of the Yatols within Jacintha.

"I would think that your new King Aydrian has problems of his own," Yatol Mado Wadon replied with obvious skepticism.

Mackaront spent a long while studying the man, his posture, and his movements. Mado Wadon was an old man, older than Mackaront's fifty years, and the very foundation of Wadon's world, the religion and spirituality that had guided his entire life, had just been stripped out from under him. He was frightened, obviously, and likely doubting the decision that had led him to dispose of Chezru Chieftain Yakim Douan. The pressure was growing on him, clearly, as more and more reports of the gathering strength of Yatol Tohen Bardoh filtered into Chom Deiru, the Yatol palace in Jacintha. Mackaront understood his fears to be justified, given the many territorial disputes that had erupted throughout the fracturing kingdom, particularly those just to the south, where Yatol Peridan seemed to be taking advantage of the fact that many of his neighbor's soldiers had been pressed into service during the war in the west against the To-gai-ru and had not yet returned.

"You must understand that our new King Aydrian was guided on his ascent by none other than my master, Abbot Olin," Mackaront said, a statement that he had offered several times already during this important meeting.

"Olin, who befriended Chezru Douan," Mado Wadon remarked.

"Abbot Olin, who loves Behren," Mackaront was quick to correct. "My master befriended Chezru Douan because Chezru Douan spoke for Behren. He holds no anger over the events that led to his friend's downfall, though he is certainly saddened by news of Douan's death."

"A most pragmatic man." There was no mistaking the sarcasm in Yatol Wadon's voice.

"As he was saddened in learning that the Yatols chose not to look more deeply into this joining of beliefs, Abellican and Chezru, that seemed exemplified by the actions of Yakim Douan," Mackaront said, and Mado Wadon's eyes popped open wide.

"Douan was a fraud, and a murderer!" the Yatol cried. "He used the evil gemstone to steal the bodies from unborn children, claiming them as his own in his pursuit of physical immortality! Do not for one moment try to justify such a heinous act as that!"

"I do not," Mackaront said, shaking his head slowly throughout Wadon's tirade. "But do not deny that the discovery of Yakim Douan's actions have shaken your religion to its very foundations. Perhaps it is time to explore the possibilities of a middle ground here, between—"

"No."

The denial was not unexpected to Mackaront, and he realized that he might be pushing a bit too fast and too hard here. It was not really his place, at this time, to lay the groundwork for Abbot Olin's ascent to the leadership of Jacintha, but rather, to measure the level of desperation within Yatol Mado Wadon and use that desperation to pave the way for the first forays into Behren.

"Perhaps that is a discussion for you and my master on another day," Mackaront said.

"Doubtful," came the reply, the tone uncompromising.

Master Mackaront, no novice to the inevitably narrowed viewpoint of long-term clergy, accepted the response with a nod.

"Aside from that, my master is well aware that you are in dire need here," Mackaront said. "He is a friend of Jacintha, first and foremost, and as such, a friend and ally to Yatol Mado Wadon."

The man held fast his skeptical expression, but Mackaront could see the cracks growing in that façade—cracks wrought of desperation, he knew.

"Abbot Olin is not without resources at this time."

"I would think that King Aydrian would need all of those resources and more, usurping a kingdom as mighty as Honce-the-Bear," said the suspicious Yatol Wadon.

"A nearly bloodless ascent, and one that has only added to Aydrian's considerable strength, I assure you," Mackaront explained. "Entel is secure—more secure than you can imagine—and Abbot Olin's position in the Abellican Church has never shone more brightly. We have resources to spare, and we offer them to you in this, your time of need."

"In exchange for?"

"As a gesture of friendship. The troubles of the Chezru religion are a great source of concern for Abbot Olin, who has always understood that the Abellican and Chezru churches were not as opposed as many believe. Abbot Olin, who loves Jacintha as he loves Entel, desires stability in Behren, for only in the calm of order might the greater questions concerning the dramatic events within Chezru be properly explored."

"And your master believes that he should have a voice in such discussions?"

"He would be grateful if you and your fellow Yatols included him, of course," said Mackaront. "Abbot Olin is a man of philosophy and education. He is no ideologue locked into a particular focus so strongly that he believes there is nothing left to learn. Inquisition and exploration lead to the truth, though it is a road that may continue for centuries to come."

"Fine words," Yatol Wadon said, with a hint of sarcasm holding in his tone. "But words for another day. Tell me what you offer."

"Yatols Peridan and De Hamman will continue to play out their fighting—there is little we can do to stop that," Mackaront explained, and Yatol Wadon predictably scowled at the words. It was important to him, after all, to calm the side battles so that Yatols like the two warlords to the south of Jacintha could aid him in his more important cause.

"What we will do is keep the fighting balanced, allowing neither to gain a major advantage," Mackaront went on. "Trust me in this. Events have already been put into motion to secure that end."

"You presume much," Yatol Wadon replied, an edge of unmistakable anger creeping into his voice.

"We understand much," Mackaront corrected, not backing down. "The best scenario for you and for Jacintha is to keep all of the other regions away from your expected personal struggle with Yatol Bardoh."

Wadon's expression showed that he had been thinking in exactly the opposite direction.

"You alone defeat Bardoh and secure Jacintha, and your position will not be questioned by any of the others," Mackaront explained. "And you will defeat Yatol Bardoh, and soundly, because my master is your friend."

He ended with a grinning expression, locking stares with Yatol Wadon. He could see that Wadon wanted to deny his claim, desperately so.

But he could not.

Mackaront recognized clearly that Mado Wadon was not pleased by his announced plans for Peridan and De Hamman, and that the Jacintha leader understood exactly what was going on here. Abbot Olin was forcing his hand and his allegiance. And yet, whatever he thought of that, there was nothing that he could do about it.

That last line, *because my master is your friend,* was not so veiled a threat. If Mackaront's master was not Wadon's friend, the implication seemed clear enough that Abbot Olin would quickly become Yatol Bardoh's friend.

Master Mackaront excused himself then, ending with a polite and respectful bow. He didn't want to press his advantage too strongly, after all.

The ten thousand Bearmen soldiers crossing the eastern stretches of the Belt-and-Buckle, the tremendous fleet of pirate ships leveling the conflict between Peridan and De Hamman, and the fleet of Honce-the-Bear warships even then assembling in Entel harbor, preparing to deliver soldiers of Aydrian's army to Jacintha, would do that all on their own.

And then Abbot Olin would arrive, the friend of victorious and indebted Yatol Mado Wadon.

CHAPTER

❖ 4 ❖

The End of the World
As They Knew It

"*S* *audi Jacintha,* the ship of Captain Al'u'met, sailed out of Palmaris," Duke Bretherford informed his guests on *River Palace,* the royal ship of the Honce-the-Bear fleet. "We have reason to believe that one of the masters of St. Precious, likely Marlboro Viscenti, was aboard."

"Heading for St.-Mere-Abelle," Duke Kalas reasoned, looking to Aydrian.

The young king nodded and grinned. "My mother reached them. She set them all in a frenzy, I would guess."

"We can assume that word has reached Fio Bou-raiy, then," Marcalo De'Unnero put in. "St.-Mere-Abelle will lock down her gates."

"Good," Aydrian replied. "Put them in their hole. They will be easier to catch that way."

"Spoken like one who has not witnessed the power that is St.-Mere-Abelle," the former monk sharply warned, and all about the table, eyebrows arched at De'Unnero's surprisingly blunt rebuttal of the king.

But Aydrian merely grinned all the wider. "Still you doubt and fear," he said to the fiery De'Unnero. "When will you come to trust me?"

There were far too many tangential implications reaching out from that question for De'Unnero to begin to answer.

Across the table, Duke Bretherford cleared his throat.

Aydrian turned a wry grin the smallish man's way. "Speak freely here," the young king instructed, though he knew that Bretherford would do no such thing—knew that if Bretherford revealed his honest feelings about all of this, then Aydrian would probably be forced to kill him on the spot. Duke Bretherford had been a dear friend of King Danube's, and of the whole Ursal line. It was he who had first taken Prince Midalis to Vanguard, those decades before, when Midalis and Danube's father was the king of Honce-the-Bear.

Duke Bretherford glanced over at Kalas briefly, and Aydrian did well to hide his amusement at the exchange between the two. He held Kalas firmly, he knew, and Kalas had convinced many of the other dukes to swear fealty to this new king. As far as Kalas was concerned, Aydrian was the best choice for Honce-the-Bear, particularly in restoring the kingdom to what it had been before all the trouble with the demon dactyl. His nostalgic view of a blissful kingdom those decades ago had been generally well received by some of the dukes.

Others, like Bretherford—arguably the second most powerful duke in the kingdom, for he most controlled the great Ursal fleet—had come to Aydrian's court with considerably less enthusiasm.

"You do seem willing to allow your enemies to gather their strength," Bretherford remarked. "You say that this is because you are confident of victory, but is such a strategy not inevitably to cost more men their lives and to make this conflict, if a war it must be, even more bloody?"

Aydrian was acutely aware of the others in the room sucking in their collective breath at that remark—certainly an inappropriate remark for any nobleman to make of his king. This was a test, Aydrian knew, to take his measure not only to Duke Bretherford, but to some of the other noblemen as well. He took his time, pondering the question and his answer as the seconds slipped by—and that was not anything that the impulsive and cocky Aydrian Boudabras was known to do!

"My mother will prove to be more a hindrance to our enemies than a useful ally," he began, and he looked all around as he spoke, even at De'Unnero. "As for the Abellican monks . . . well, better that they know of the events in Ursal. No doubt they have heard a skewed version of the truth, but better that to measure their loyalty to the throne. Let them stand on one side or the other now, and be done with it." The young king didn't miss the slight grin that escaped De'Unnero at his words, nor the satisfaction splayed on the face of Duke Kalas, who hated the Church above all else and who would surely welcome an assault against St.-Mere-Abelle, whatever its reputation.

"A skewed version?" Duke Bretherford dared to ask, and De'Unnero started to argue, and Kalas started to berate the man.

But Aydrian called for calm. "This is all yet unfolding," he told them. "We have much to learn of these folk before we label them as friend or enemy. For now, let us continue our glorious march to Palmaris. The disposition of that city will go far in telling us what we might expect as the word of my ascension spreads throughout the kingdom."

He dismissed them all, then, explaining that he was tired, and he went to his private quarters and lay down on his bed. And there, his physical form rested, but his mind wandered.

Aided by the powerful soul stone, Aydrian slipped out of his corporeal form and glided unseen across the deck of *River Palace*, to the taffrail, where Kalas and Bretherford were conversing.

"Are you so quick to dismiss Prince Midalis?" the smaller Bretherford asked. "To forsake the line of Ursal, that has served Honce-the-Bear for so many years?"

"I have seen the truth of our young king," Kalas calmly replied. "With all of my heart, I believe that he is the proper ruler of Honce-the-Bear."

"Despite your feelings about his parents?"

Duke Kalas shrugged. "Jilseponie has her strengths, and great weaknesses. The strengths are what she passed along to Aydrian. And were you not ever more a friend to Jilseponie than I?"

"I pitied the woman," Bretherford replied. "My loyalties were ever with King Danube, as I thought were yours."

Aydrian watched with great interest as Duke Kalas straightened and squared his shoulders.

"I blame Jilseponie for the downfall of King Danube," he said.

"And you embrace her son?"

"There is irony in that," Kalas admitted. "But no inconsistency. The blood of Jilseponie gives Aydrian claim to the throne, but—"

"Above Prince Midalis?" Duke Bretherford interrupted.

Kalas stared at him hard. "You should take care your words, my friend. Aydrian is king of Honce-the-Bear, and he holds the power of Ursal behind him. I pray that Prince Midalis comes to understand and accept this."

"And Prince Torrence, as well?" Bretherford asked, and it was obvious that the man wasn't really buying deeply into any of this.

Aydrian caught Kalas' slight wince at the mention of Torrence Pemblebury, but he was certain that Duke Bretherford did not notice.

"We will see," Kalas replied. "Aydrian is king. He has the Allhearts and the garrison of Ursal behind him, as well as the army that followed him and understood the truth of his ascension before he even rose to the position. He will secure the kingdom, through negotiation or through war, and he will reshape the Abellican Church—"

"That hope is what binds you to him, I'd guess," Bretherford interrupted. He turned out over the taffrail and spat into the water. "Are you hoping for a war to bring about a change in the Church to fit the visions of the crazy Marcalo De'Unnero?" he asked incredulously. "Or is it just the thought of a war within the Abellican Church that has you thrilled? Is that it, my old friend? Maybe King Aydrian will weaken the monks and push their Church to the fringes of the kingdom. Is that what you're wanting?"

Kalas leaned on the rail and did not bother to respond.

Aydrian was smiling when he returned to his waiting body.

The one-armed Father Abbot of the Abellican Church sat perfectly straight in his chair. His gray hair, as always, was neatly trimmed and perfectly styled; not a strand seemed out of place on him—physically. But none around Fio Bou-raiy, not the visiting Abbot Glendenhook of St. Gwendolyn, not Machuso or any of the other masters at St.-Mere-Abelle, and not Viscenti, who had brought the news from St. Precious, had ever seen the man so obviously shaken.

They were in the newly remodeled audience hall of the great abbey, on the eastern edge of the complex, overlooking the All Saints Bay. This large room, a hundred feet square, had been three separate halls, one on top of the other. But Father Abbot Bou-raiy, with visions of expanding the Church during the time when one of its sovereign sisters had sat the secular throne as queen, had desired something grander for the abbey, a place where he could entertain noblemen and perhaps even King Danube himself. So the ceilings and floors had been removed, leaving one huge hall that soared to nearly sixty feet, with a balcony running the length of the wall opposite Bou-raiy's grand throne, and all the way down the left-hand wall as well. The floor, a black-and-white patchwork of large marble tiles, was actually below ground level and was accessed by a single anteroom, the great double doors opening from the west, to the left of Bou-raiy's throne, and directly across from the most imposing design in the entire place: a huge and circular stained-glass window, set in the eastern wall above the wide staircase that ascended the thirty feet to the balcony. Filled with glass of rose and purple, blue and amber, the design on the window depicted the mummified arm of Avelyn Desbris, rising from the flattened top of ruined Mount Aida. A one-armed priest—obviously Bou-raiy—his brown robe tied off at one shoulder, knelt before the sacred place, bending low to kiss the bloody hand.

When he had first entered the room, Viscenti's eyes had widened indeed at the spectacle of the great window. A mixture of awe and revulsion had crept through him, for it was well-known throughout the Order that Bou-raiy had argued vehemently with the then–Father Abbot Agronguerre *against* traveling to Mount Aida and partaking of the Covenant of Avelyn.

Viscenti shrugged away his negativity, reminding himself that he had no time for such inconsequential worries at present. It was good, he realized, that Father Abbot Bou-raiy had now so obviously embraced the deeds of the hopefully soon-to-be Saint Avelyn. The Abellican Church would need such a boost, given the news from Ursal!

Father Abbot Bou-raiy had listened, without the slightest interruption, to the words of Master Viscenti, the tidings of the great upheaval of secular Honce-the-Bear, but also of the impending upheaval, perhaps even greater, that was sure to befall the Abellican Church.

A long silence held the audience room in this, the greatest of cathedrals.

"There can be no doubt of the identity of the coconspirators?" Fio Bou-raiy finally asked. "It was Abbot Olin and truly Marcalo De'Unnero, the same monk who served under Father Abbot Markwart, the same monk who was consumed by the tiger's paw gemstone and driven out of Palmaris by Jilseponie, the same monk who led the errant Brothers Repentant in the time of the plague? It was De'Unnero?"

"By the words of Jilseponie, who knew this man better than anyone, it was the same Marcalo De'Unnero," Viscenti confirmed, and he twitched repeatedly, any control he held over his nervous tic washed away by merely speaking the cursed name aloud.

"What does this mean?" asked burly Abbot Glendenhook, standing in what had long been his customary position, both figuratively and literally, at Fio Bou-raiy's side. With news of the grim tidings sweeping the land, Abbot Glendenhook had rushed back to the mother abbey to confer with his trusted friend, the Father Abbot.

"It means the end of the world as we know it," another master glumly remarked.

Fio Bou-raiy snapped his ever-imposing stare over the man, denying the claim visually before he had ever spoken a word. "It means that our time of peace and growth has ended, temporarily," he corrected, his voice stern and steady once more. "It means that we of the true Abellican Order may find ourselves besieged with informants and perhaps traitors, and possibly even by an army from the throne that we always before considered our ally. Surely none among the leadership of St.-Mere-Abelle are unused to adversity, Master Donegal. We have been weaned on the DemonWar, on a time of great upheaval within our order, and on a plague. Are you so quick to surrender?"

"My pardon, Father Abbot," Master Jorgen Donegal said, offering a submissive bow. "If Abbot Olin is in league with the new king of Honce-the-Bear, I doubt that he will be friendly toward the current leadership at St.-Mere-Abelle."

"Abbot Olin is Abellican first," Fio Bou-raiy declared. "He understands his position and his responsibility to this church."

"With Marcalo De'Unnero at his side?" Marlboro Viscenti found himself asking before he could find the wisdom to bite back the words, for that simple question deflated any momentum that Father Abbot Bou-raiy might have been gaining here. Bou-raiy hated De'Unnero profoundly, a feeling that was surely mutual. If Abbot Olin was indeed in league with the infamous former monk, then he was surely no friend to St.-Mere-Abelle, nor to the current incarnation of the Abellican Church!

"Ursal will demand change within the Church," Abbot Glendenhook observed.

"They already have, according to Jilseponie," said Master Viscenti. "By her account, Abbot Ohwan was reinstated at St. Honce, but only as a plank for Marcalo De'Unnero to walk to the post of abbot."

"The crown has no power to determine abbots!" said Glendenhook.

"Then it has begun already," Fio Bou-raiy put in, and the same despair that had been evident in Master Donegal's voice was showing around the edges here, too. "If this is all true, then we must assume that Abbot Olin and his henchmen are restructuring the Abellican Church to fit their needs."

"Bishop Braumin Herde believes that Ursal will demand that Olin assume the position of Father Abbot," Master Viscenti said bluntly, and though everyone in the room fully expected that, given the line of reasoning, hearing it aloud brought more than a few gasps of astonishment and despair.

Fio Bou-raiy held steady, though, and looked at Master Viscenti hard. "And where does Bishop Braumin stand on this issue?" he demanded.

Marlboro Viscenti stood up very straight, his slight frame seeming to grow very tall and formidable. "Bishop Braumin supported the election of Father Abbot Bou-raiy," the master from St. Precious reminded. "But even if he had not, Bishop Braumin is a true Abellican, and he would not support any usurpers trying to steal away our Church."

Only after speaking the words aloud did Viscenti realize the irony of them, for hadn't Braumin and all the others come to power through those very means? When Markwart had gone astray, Braumin and Viscenti had led the charge beside Jilseponie and Elbryan to take the Abellican Church from them.

"The Church is not astray," Viscenti quickly added. "We have learned so very much over the last two decades, culminating in the Miracle of Aida. We follow the way of St. Abelle, and soon-to-be Saint Avelyn. We follow the orders of St.-Mere-Abelle and Father Abbot Fio Bou-raiy with all confidence that those orders are in accordance with the precepts upon which we build our faith. Bishop Braumin will not forsake St.-Mere-Abelle nor Father Abbot Bou-raiy in this, at the price of his own life! If Marcalo De'Unnero desires to enter St. Precious, it will either be as conqueror or in chains. There is no negotiating that point!"

The stirring words seemed to bolster Fio Bou-raiy and all the others in the room.

"You say that De'Unnero and Duke Kalas are marching north from Ursal toward Palmaris," the Father Abbot prompted.

"The last report I heard, before Captain Al'u'met sailed me out of the Masur Delaval, was that they had advanced halfway up the river to Palmaris," Viscenti explained. "They are absorbing all the countryside as they proclaim the new King Aydrian. There have been some skirmishes, but nothing of any note, for the people have no rallying call denouncing this treacherous usurper. It is likely that Prince Midalis in Vanguard has not even learned yet of the death of his brother and his nephew Merwick, nor that his other nephew, the only other person in the royal line, is missing. Captain Al'u'met sails even now for Vanguard, but it will be weeks, months perhaps, before Midalis can muster any reasonable response. Until then, King Aydrian, with the legions of Ursal and Entel behind him, stands unopposed among the unwitting populace."

Fio Bou-raiy folded his fingers before him in a pensive pose and spent a long time digesting the words. "Then we must inform the people," he decided. "Then we must hold out against this treachery and rally the resistance against phony King Aydrian until Prince Midalis arrives."

"Thousands will die," Master Donegal remarked.

It wasn't really Viscenti's place to speak, for the remark had been directed to Fio Bou-raiy, but he among all the others held the weight of his previous actions and not just his convictions to answer, "Some things are worth dying for, brother."

Father Abbot Fio Bou-raiy sat up straighter and gave an appreciative nod to Viscenti. "You must return with all speed to St. Precious," he instructed the nervous master. "Tell Bishop Braumin that he must lock down Palmaris against this army. If Aydrian declares himself as king, then the army he commands is not the army of Honce-the-Bear, is not the army of the Ursal line, and must not be given admittance to a city loyal to that line."

Strong words, Master Viscenti knew, especially coming from the man who had the most to lose, and who was secure in what was arguably the most fortified bastion in all the world. But Viscenti didn't disagree with the reasoning. Some things were indeed worth dying for, and worth asking others to die for.

"Dispatch official emissaries to every abbey outside of Ursal, even to St. Rontlemore," Fio Bou-raiy instructed Master Donegal, referring to the second abbey of Olin's hometown of Entel, a place that had long been under the shadow of the more prestigious St. Bondabruce and powerful Abbot Olin. "Let none forget the truth of Marcalo De'Unnero, and let none misinterpret the actions of Abbot Olin here as anything other than treachery and blasphemy."

"Do we know for certain that Abbot Olin will not approach us civilly and with explanation?" Abbot Glendenhook dared to ask.

"He has overstepped his boundaries here, and there is little he could say to convince me not to excommunicate him," Fio Bou-raiy declared flatly, and that brought more astonished and nervous gasps, and more than a few concurring grunts.

Master Viscenti was among those concurring, and he dipped a low bow and begged his leave.

"Our wagons are at your disposal to return you to the Masur Delaval," Fio Bou-raiy told him, and Viscenti left at once, determined to stand beside Bishop Braumin when the darkness fell, a darkness that he couldn't help but believe would be the end of the world as he knew it.

Duke Bretherford sat on the edge of his cot in his private room on *River Palace*, leaning forward and rubbing his hands repeatedly over his grizzled face. He heard the stirring on the deck outside of his room and saw the light around the edges of his dark curtains and supposed that it must be morning.

Another night had passed him by with only fitful short periods of sleep. It had been that way since he had returned to Ursal, rushing in upon hearing the news of Danube's untimely death.

His whole world had changed, so quickly, and Bretherford couldn't sort through it. He spent hours tossing and turning, trying to find a place of acceptance, as had Kalas and so many of the other Ursal noblemen, but he had found no answers. He wished that he had been there on that fateful day, to witness the events. Perhaps then he might be more willing to embrace this young king and the promises the other nobles were whispering. Perhaps then he might be able to place Prince Midalis in a different light. Perhaps then . . .

Bretherford looked over at the small table set beside his bed, at the nearly empty bottle and the glass beside it.

He brought that glass in close, swirling it around, getting lost in the golden tan liquid.

Then he swallowed the whiskey in one gulp and moved to pour another, but a knock on his door stopped him short.

"What'd'ye want?" the tired man called.

How he changed his tone and his demeanor when the door pushed open and King Aydrian walked in!

"My King," Bretherford blurted before he could even consider the words. He scrambled about and ran a hand through his thin hair. "I am not ready to receive—"

"Be at ease, my good duke," said Aydrian, and he stepped in and closed the door behind him. "I desire no protocol here. I have come to ask a favor."

Bretherford stared at him dumbfounded. The king of Honce-the-Bear *asking* a favor?

"This has all come so quickly," Aydrian remarked, and he saw himself to a chair across from Bretherford's bed, and waved for Bretherford to remain seated when the man finally composed himself enough to try to stand and salute.

"You know that Abbot Olin has departed for Entel?" Aydrian asked.

"I suspect that he is well on his way, yes."

"Do you know where he will go from there?"

"Jacintha," said Bretherford, and Aydrian nodded.

"This is a dangerous mission," said the young king. "The Behrenese are not to be taken lightly. They present potentially formidable opposition, though I know that Honce-the-Bear will never again see as clear an opportunity as we have right now to strengthen our ties to our southern neighbor."

To conquer her, you mean, Bretherford thought, but he kept his face expressionless.

"Abbot Olin has a great fleet at his command, but he must coordinate its movements with the movements of a land army, as well," Aydrian explained. "It will be a daunting task, I fear, and with my attention now so obviously needed along the Masur Delaval, Abbot Olin will find little support from Ursal."

Duke Bretherford couldn't help but narrow his eyes with suspicion.

"Of course, the fleet at Abbot Olin's command is not—how shall I say this delicately?—conventional."

"Pirates and vagabonds," Bretherford dared to say. "The same dogs I have chased along the southern stretches of our coastline for years."

"Better to harness the dogs, eh?" Aydrian asked.

Bretherford was hardly convinced of that, and so he didn't reply.

"Better if I could spare the Ursal fleet, I agree," Aydrian remarked. "But Palmaris may not be so welcoming, and then there is the not-so-little matter of St.-Mere-Abelle, and Pireth Tulme, Pireth Dancard, and Pireth Vanguard after that."

"It is ambitious," Bretherford remarked, hoping that the sarcasm in his voice would not be so evident as to have Aydrian execute him.

"It is necessary," Aydrian corrected. "As is our pursuit of the heart of Behren, at this time. And it is attainable—all of it! But I fear that I may have distributed the able leaders at my command errantly here—of course, I had little knowledge of the dukes and commanders before decisions had to be made."

"You wish me to sail to Entel?" Bretherford asked skeptically.

"I cannot spare the ships it would require for you to safely make such a journey," Aydrian explained. "I wish you to *ride* to Entel."

"To what end?" Bretherford asked, and he rose from the bed, holding his arms out wide. "If the fleet remains on the Masur Delaval, then what am I to do . . ."

"Abbot Olin has warships of his own," Aydrian explained. "I need you there, my good duke. I need you to go and join with Abbot Olin, to take command of his seagoing operations. The delicacy of this situation cannot be overstated, and as such, I need the most experienced commanders I can find supporting Abbot Olin."

Duke Bretherford could hardly spit out a response. King Aydrian was saying it so cleverly, but what he was really doing here was placing Bretherford out of the main picture and off to the side.

"My King," the duke finally replied, "you speak of Abbot Olin's fleet, but in truth they are but a ragtag group of opportunists."

"And so your work in controlling them to Abbot Olin's needs will be no easy task," Aydrian was quick to reply. "But I have all faith in you, Duke Bretherford. Duke Kalas assures me that there is no more able man in all the kingdom at handling the movements of a fleet. The lives of ten thousand of Honce-the-Bear's soldiers will rest squarely on your shoulders, to say nothing of the overall designs concerning Behren. If Abbot Olin's mission proves unsuccessful, then we can expect those Behrenese pirates to use the turmoil within Honce-the-Bear to strike the coast from Entel all the way up the Mantis Arm."

It made perfect sense, of course, and that was the beauty of the plan, Bretherford knew. Bretherford realized that this was not about Olin, for if Aydrian was truly afraid of the potential consequences concerning Jacintha and Behren, he would have merely held the greedy abbot in check and waited until Honce-the-Bear was fully secured before turning his sights to the south. No, this was about getting Bretherford out of the way and far from Prince Midalis, the duke knew. Aydrian had Kalas securely in his court, and that meant the Allhearts, and they meant the Ursal garrison and the majority of the Kingsmen, and perhaps even the Coastpoint Guards of the southern mainland. But the fleet, like the waters they sailed, were more fluid in all of this, and Aydrian understood that the duke of the Mirianic could bring a powerful allying force to Prince Midalis as easily as Duke Kalas had brought the ground forces to Aydrian!

And so however Aydrian might parse his reasoning, the truth of it was that Bretherford was being shuffled out of the way, and away from the main body of Honce-the-Bear's great navy.

The duke was somewhat surprised as the truth unfolded in his thoughts. Why hadn't Aydrian just dismissed him, perhaps even had him murdered? Why this pretense of more important duties?

As he came to understand, Bretherford's estimate of young Aydrian as a tactician heightened considerably. The duke was on the fence concerning the disposition of the kingdom, and Aydrian saw that clearly. And so the young king was putting him into a position where his skills would serve Aydrian well. Aydrian feared him, Bretherford knew—feared that he would take the fleet and hand it over to Midalis. But no such fears would accompany the duke of the Mirianic to Entel, especially when the great bulk of his command would be left behind.

"Your estimate of my understanding of the Behrenese might be exaggerated," Bretherford started to say, trying to wriggle out of this.

"You are the man who will escort Abbot Olin by sea to Jacintha," Aydrian said firmly. "You will coordinate the movements of his naval assets along the Behrenese coast and provide him with the plans for transporting soldiers from Entel to Jacintha, or to whatever other coastal city Abbot Olin chooses."

"You propose to place a duke under the command of an abbot?"

"I have just done so," Aydrian corrected, his tone firm. He had come in pretending to ask a favor, but now he was obviously issuing an order. "You serve the throne, do you not?"

His pause and expression told Bretherford that Aydrian was not going to let that seemingly rhetorical question pass by without a direct answer.

"I have served Honce-the-Bear for all of my life."

Aydrian grinned. "And you continue to serve the throne of Honce-the-Bear?"

Bretherford didn't blink as he stared at the young king.

"The throne now claimed by Aydrian Boudabras?" Aydrian clarified, so that there could be no irony, no double meaning, in the demanded answer.

"I serve the throne of Ursal," said Bretherford.

"The voice of that throne in Jacintha will soon be Abbot Olin," Aydrian told him. "Abbot Olin travels to Behren at my request and as my emissary. The fact that he is an Abellican abbot is of no consequence. He serves me at this time, and you will answer to him."

Bretherford wanted to respond to that, wanted to remark something

along the lines that Duke Kalas might not be so thrilled to hear of these unexpected developments, but Aydrian's expression told him clearly that
there was no room for debate here. The young king hadn't come in to *ask*
anything. He had come in to push Bretherford out of the way.

The duke supposed that he should be grateful that Aydrian had seen this
way out, and had not merely ordered him thrown into a dungeon, or quietly
beheaded.

But still . . .

CHAPTER

❖ 5 ❖

Adrift

I t wasn't often that a Jhesta Tu mystic would be well received in Chom
Deiru, for the Yatols of Behren had spent centuries condemning the
Jhesta Tu as heretics and demon worshipers. The mystics were particularly disliked by the Chezhou-lei, the Behrenese corps of elite warriors,
who considered them as rivals.

When Pagonel arrived at the gates of the Chezru palace, dressed in his
telltale robes, the initial reaction to him was consistent with those notions.
The two warriors standing guard outside the great doors of the building
stared at him wide-eyed and mouths agape, and after recovering from the
initial shock, both dropped their spear tips level with the mystic's chest.

"Peace," Pagonel said to them, holding his empty palms up in a non-
threatening manner. "I am Pagonel, who is well-known to Yatol Mado
Wadon. I am he who traveled to Dharyan on behalf of your Yatols upon the
death of Yakim Douan. I am he who represented the wishes of the Yatols to
the Dragon of To-gai, thus ending the war."

As he spoke, the spears gradually eased to the side and down, and when
he finished, one of the guards nodded to the other, who fast disappeared
into the palace.

A few moments later, Pagonel was ushered through the doors, and though
more guards surrounded him and a few shot threatening glances his way,
the mystic understood that he had done well in coming here, that he would
indeed get his desired audience with Yatol Mado Wadon.

They escorted him into a small waiting room and left him there, and he
heard the door lock behind them as they departed.

Pagonel put his back up against the wall opposite the door, sank down
into a low and comfortable crouch, and waited. The minutes turned to an
hour, and still he waited, digesting all that he had seen on his journey from
the west, replaying all of the events and conversations in an attempt to
understand better the depth of the situation in this tumultuous land.

Finally, the door opened, and Pagonel was surprised to see that it was

Mado Wadon himself who entered. The man was quite old, with hair thinning to wisps of nothingness and heavy drooping lids half-hiding his dull eyes. He moved his withered little frame into the room just a step, then turned and motioned for Pagonel to follow. The Yatol said nothing as he walked with Pagonel in tow through the arching corridors of Chom Deiru, past the great artworks of the Chezru religion, the tile mosaics along the wall depicting the great struggles within the Behrenese church and culture.

How meaningless many of those murals now appeared to Pagonel, given the revelations of the previous Chezru Chieftain! The actions of Yakim Douan, using the soul stone to steal the bodies from unborn babies so that he could live on in a new corporal mantle, mocked the murals depicting the Abellicans of the north as heretics for using those same stones. The great deception of Yakim Douan laid waste to the many Chezru images of glorious Transcendence, the process that the Chezru had considered as a passage of knowledge, the incarnation of a new God-Voice to be found among the children of Behren. Only in walking these halls now, in looking at the murals that formed the core of Chezru beliefs, did Pagonel truly appreciate how profound an effect the deceptions of Yakim Douan would have on this land. The very core of Chezru had been shattered.

What emptiness must now follow?

They went into a small private room, with two chairs set before a glowing hearth and food and drink already put out on a table between them.

"You have come with word from Brynn Dharielle," Yatol Mado Wadon remarked before Pagonel had even sat down. His voice sounded as old as the wrinkled man looked, and as weary, cracking slightly on nearly every syllable.

"I have come hoping to receive word from you that I might relay to her," the mystic replied. "My road to the south showed me growing problems within your kingdom, Yatol."

"Yatol Bardoh has not been among those sending their well-wishes," Yatol Wadon said dryly. "He left the field of Dharyan—"

"Dharyan-Dharielle," Pagonel corrected.

"Dharyan-Dharielle," Yatol Wadon agreed. "He left the field with a great host of soldiers at his disposal, and with all of them knowing only that great tumult had come to Jacintha. They are uncertain, and in such a state, they are likely open to the suggestions of Yatol Tohen Bardoh."

"Suggestions that you suspect will not be in favor of the present situation in Jacintha, nor the present leadership," the mystic reasoned.

"Tohen Bardoh has ever been an ambitious man."

"As we have discussed before, to a degree," Pagonel remarked. "Your agreement of a joint, open city under the command of Brynn Dharielle was based primarily on these very fears, was it not?"

"And now I pray that your friend the Dragon does not disappoint me. It is in the interest of Brynn Dharielle and of To-gai that the present leadership in Jacintha overcome any threat by Tohen Bardoh. If Behren is united under him, he will not tolerate the addition of Dharielle to the name of the city Dharyan. He opposed the end of the siege of the city, vehemently so. You know this as well as I."

"Do you believe that he is strong enough to go against the Jacintha warriors?"

"Many of those warriors have still not returned from the field outside of Dharyan-Dharielle," Yatol Wadon explained.

"They stood down readily enough when word came to them from Jacintha."

"True, but I assure you that at that time few in Behren wished to continue battle against the Dragon of To-gai. This is a different matter. All across the kingdom there is war now, as old disputes renew without the control of the Chezru Chieftain to mute them."

Pagonel sat back and considered the startling admission. To have a Behrenese leader revealing such a weakness within his country to a member of the Jhesta Tu was incredible enough, but when that Jhesta Tu was well known to be in league with the To-gai-ru, the admission became even more unbelievable.

Pagonel sat back and folded his hands before him. That Yatol Mado Wadon was able to speak so bluntly and openly to him here confirmed the level of desperation that was obviously growing within the man. That Yatol Mado Wadon would even receive Pagonel in anything more than a polite manner in a general audience chamber was a clear indication that the man was deathly afraid of Bardoh. Apparently, the rumors of the Yatol of Avrou Eesa building a tremendous army were not understated.

"Brynn Dharielle has fewer resources at her disposal at this time than you may believe," the mystic honestly replied, for he understood that such information would not imperil Brynn in any manner. Certainly Yatol Wadon was in no position to even think of striking against her.

"Her dragon alone—"

"Fewer than you may believe," Pagonel interrupted. "And there is no formal agreement between Dharyan-Dharielle and Jacintha."

Yatol Wadon's dull eyes widened and he gripped the arms of his chair, seeming ready to spring up and assault the mystic.

"Her course seems clear, though," Pagonel remarked, and that settled him back just a bit. "What do you ask of her?"

The simple question seemed to catch Yatol Wadon off-balance for a moment, for what indeed might Brynn be able to do? She wouldn't march her army from Dharyan-Dharielle to Jacintha to protect the ruling Yatol from another Yatol, after all!

"I have come to understand that she is no friend of Yatol Bardoh," Yatol Wadon said hesitantly.

Pagonel merely smiled in response to that monumental understatement. Yatol Bardoh was the man who had ordered Brynn's own parents murdered. He was the Behrenese leader who had conquered To-gai so brutally a decade before, a man who had never expressed anything but contempt for the To-gai-ru and their traditions. Bardoh had left the field outside of Dharyan-Dharielle, but he had not done so with a light heart. More than anything else, he had wanted to retake the city and be rid of the Dragon of To-gai.

"To fully engage Jacintha, should it come to that, Yatol Bardoh will need the north road," Yatol Wadon explained. "He will need Dahdah Oasis, else the promises he feeds to his soldiers will die in the desert sands."

"You would like Yatol Bardoh to be looking over his shoulder at another enemy as he marches toward Jacintha," Pagonel remarked.

"Or looking over his shoulder at another enemy as he marches on Dharyan-Dharielle," Yatol Wadon was quick to reply. "He covets Jacintha, agreed, but he covets Brynn's city for even more personal reasons, and he may come to believe that retaking Dharyan for Behren will elevate him among the people and make his march toward Jacintha all the more plausible."

That disturbing thought had carried Pagonel every step of the way to Jacintha.

"It is time to open a dialogue between our two cities," Yatol Wadon said.

The mystic nodded. "Your words are wise, Yatol. I will carry them to Brynn Dharielle. You must prepare your emissaries to accompany me quickly, for the road will grow more difficult with time, I fear."

"They are already prepared," Yatol Wadon told him. "They would have left this very day had not you unexpectedly arrived in Jacintha. Upon hearing of your arrival, I had hoped that you would present yourself as a formal emissary from Dharyan-Dharielle, and I would be lying if I told you that I am not disappointed to learn that this is not the truth. Your friend is not so seasoned in her role as leader, I suspect, and so her ignorance of the present mounting danger is forgivable."

Again Pagonel nodded, though he hardly agreed with the assessment. Certainly this issue with Bardoh was more Mado Wadon's fight than Brynn's, though the consequences to Brynn and to To-gai could be dire, should Bardoh prove victorious. Still, it was not a point worth arguing with Yatol Mado Wadon over at this time.

There would be plenty of other more important arguments to make, Pagonel was sure.

CHAPTER

❖ 6 ❖

When Conscience Knocks

A ydrian awoke in a cold sweat. He was lying on his back, staring up at the darkness, but the blackness stirred and images of dead Constance Pemblebury assaulted him, her pale arms reaching out for him in his mind.

Hovering behind her was a huge face, elongated and twisted in agony, and despite its contortions, Aydrian certainly recognized it, for he keenly remembered the horrified look on King Danube's face as the cold hand of death had closed over his heart that fateful day up on the trial stage in Ursal.

Had these two ghosts come to haunt him?

The young king shook himself further awake and the images dissipated, leaving him alone in the dark. "Only a dream," he told himself.

Slowly, the young man composed himself enough to roll onto his side. He had killed. He had killed Danube, and Merwick, and Torrence, as well as the unfortunate driver and the other escorts. All had been murdered on his orders.

For the most part, Aydrian never considered such things, keeping his vision along the greater road that lay before him, his ascent to immortality, his elevation of himself above all others. He believed in that road, desperately so.

But the price . . .

Aydrian winced as he considered the dead already left in his wake. Many had been deserving of their fate—like the pirates who had tried to double-cross him on the return from Pimaninicuit—but others perhaps not so deserving. And worse, Aydrian understood that the dead thus far would be but a minuscule fraction of those who would fall in the war that would inevitably engulf Honce-the-Bear, or in the conquest of Behren, or of Alpinador.

Aydrian rolled out of bed, propelled by the guilt and the sudden doubts. He rushed out of the house he had procured in this small village north of Ursal and ran over to the grouping of wagons, which included his personal coach. He waved away the confused and concerned guards and climbed into the coach, closing the door behind him.

The moon was up. The lighting was just right.

Across from his seat, Aydrian pulled aside a small curtain, revealing the mirror he used for Oracle.

He sat back and stared, letting his thoughts flow freely within him. He felt the pangs of guilt and did not push them aside, though he did offer internal debate against them.

Conscience must be the guide of any true leader.

The thought came out of nowhere, and it startled Aydrian. He digested the notion, panic rising within him as he considered the implications.

And then he looked at the mirror, at the shadowy form that had taken its blurry shape in the lower left-hand corner.

Waves of guilt assaulted him; a silent plea arose within him beckoning him to abandon this road of certain war.

In that moment, it all made sense to him, and he grimaced, tormented, as he considered the cold body of Torrence Pemblebury lying beneath the dungeon stairs of Castle Ursal. In that moment, Aydrian felt adrift.

In that fleeting moment.

King Danube played in the arena of glory.

The second shadow appeared, taking greater shape in the mirror.

That last thought rang out again within the young king. Danube, too, had been king of Honce-the-Bear. Danube, too, had made decisions of life and death, and had gone to war. This was the game of humanity, the quest for glory, the quest for immortality—though few humans understood the truth of it, Aydrian knew.

And they were all going to die, after all, every one. Was Aydrian to assume responsibility for those who died in his ascent to the throne and to immortality? Was he to bask in guilt because he, above all others, had come to understand the truth and futility of the human condition, and had figured out a way to circumvent that seeming inevitability?

The young king's breathing came faster, and he closed his eyes tight against the onslaught of terrible images as he absorbed it all, as he considered those who had died and those many more who surely would be slain along his road. He was robbing from them.

Days? Weeks? Months? Even years? the shadow in his mind asked him. How much was he truly taking from the pitiful mortals? And would they, to a man and woman, not take the same from him if ever they came to understand the truth of eternity and immortality, as did he?

Aydrian opened his eyes and looked at the mirror, to see that only one shadow remained there, in the lower right-hand corner.

King Danube played in the arena of glory, he heard again in his thoughts. *He desired the same as you, but was not as strong as you.* The reasoning seemed sound to Aydrian. What hubris Danube possessed to claim himself king of Honce-the-Bear! And if he did not have the strength to survive a challenge, then his overblown pride was certainly misplaced. Aydrian was possessed of more pride, perhaps, but he knew in his heart that he had the strength to back it.

Sometime later, the shaken young man stepped out of his coach and headed back to the procured house. He felt somewhat better; the demons of guilt had been put aside for a while.

He was surprised, when he opened the door to his sleeping chamber, to find Sadye sitting within. A single candle burned on the small table before her, illuminating her with its soft glow, the light seeming to flow right into her yellow-brown locks. She wore a simple nightshirt that only reached down to the midpoint of her shapely thighs, and her hair was unkempt.

Somehow that only made her more alluring.

"Where did you go?" she asked immediately, true concern evident in her voice.

Aydrian put one hand to his chest, his expression skeptical. "Me?"

"You are the only one here, Aydrian."

"I went out into the night air," he explained, walking past her to take a seat on the edge of his bed. "To be alone. To think."

"To think?"

Aydrian shrugged.

"Planning the strategy sessions?"

"No," he answered simply, staring off to the side, and when he looked back at Sadye a moment later, he saw true concern on her face, and true curiosity.

Again, he merely shrugged.

"We will enter the village of Pomfreth tomorrow," Sadye said to him, politely changing what was obviously an uncomfortable subject. "By all reports, the townsfolk are preparing a celebration in honor of their new king."

Aydrian managed a little smile at the news, and it was one of honest relief. "I am glad that they accept what has happened without opposing me," he explained. "It would not do my heart good to lay waste to a simple village."

"Marcalo believes that we must have one sizable fight at least before we reach Palmaris," Sadye said. "To show the rest of the common folk of the kingdom the futility of opposing the rule of Aydrian."

"Sometimes I believe that Marcalo De'Unnero just likes to fight," Aydrian replied. He took a good long look at Sadye to measure her reaction to that statement, then he just gave a helpless chuckle, and asked, "Why are you here?"

"I learned that you had wandered out. I was concerned," said the woman.

Aydrian started to ask about Marcalo, but then the former monk appeared suddenly at the open door, hardly dressed and looking none-too-pleased. He stared at Aydrian, then even harder at Sadye, studying her intently.

Obviously uncomfortable, Sadye got up and straightened and lengthened her nightshirt modestly. "Aydrian left the building," she explained to the monk. "You should instruct him that such unexpected and unannounced forays into the night could bode evil for us all. He is the king, yet I fear that he has not yet come to understand what that means, or what he means, to the kingdom he rules."

Marcalo looked from Sadye to Aydrian as she gave her little speech, and he nodded and grunted a bit in agreement. But he wasn't being deflected that easily, Aydrian recognized. His concern at that time had less to do with Aydrian leaving to go outside than with Sadye leaving his bed to come to Aydrian's private room.

The fierce monk said nothing, though, just placed his arm behind Sadye as she walked out, ushering her all the more quickly.

Aydrian leaned over and blew out the candle, then sat alone in the darkness. He considered De'Unnero and Sadye for only a moment, and was far more amused than concerned.

Then he thought of the village they would enter in the morning, and he was indeed relieved at Sadye's words that the scouts believed that this one, too, would succumb to the rule of the new king without confrontation.

Yes, Duke Kalas and his minions could roll over any feeble force that the quiet villages north of Ursal might offer. But better for them all if the people continued to follow the lead of their nobles, strengthening Aydrian's hold even more upon the kingdom.

And better, Aydrian understood—though he did not openly admit it, even to himself—for his own peace of mind and his own contented slumber.

Duke Kalas and his Allheart Knights, all resplendent in the shining, meticulously crafted and fitted silvery armor, led the march into Pomfreth, as they had led the way into every village since the march from Ursal had begun. Not far to the east, the Ursal fleet, *River Palace* among them, cruised the Masur Delaval. And behind the ranks of the Allheart Brigade clustered ten thousand soldiers, all formed in tight ranks, showing the discipline of a trained army. In their center, atop a magnificent black stallion, sat King Aydrian, and his armor outshone that of the Allhearts. Specially made and fitted by a legendary smith, and enhanced by Aydrian with several magical gemstones, it offered better defenses for its wearer than any other suit of metal in all the world. The Allheart armor was comprised of overlapping silvery plates, but Aydrian's was trimmed not only in silver, but with gold. Dark lodestones were set in a circular pattern about a gray hematite that was placed directly over Aydrian's heart. His helm was bowl-shaped, less ornamented than Duke Kalas' plumed helm, perhaps, but designed to give the great young warrior complete visibility. Lined in gold, it tapered down the back of Aydrian's head and neck, but in the front, it only covered halfway, to the bridge of his nose, with thin golden strips outlining his blue eyes as if they were the wide-cut strips of a bandit's mask.

To Aydrian's right sat Marcalo De'Unnero, dressed in the simple brown

robes of an Abellican brother, his face locked in its seemingly perpetual scowl.
He had brought quite a number of the younger brothers from St. Honce
along with him on the march, mostly to serve as replacements in the chapels
where village priests didn't appreciate or embrace the change that he was
bringing to the Church.

To Aydrian's left sat Sadye, her three-stringed lute slung across her back,
the wind blowing her brown hair, which was growing quite long again,
across her face.

In the distance to the north, they heard the cheering.

Sadye looked up at Aydrian, whose face showed a clear sign of relief. Apparently the reports were true and he would be welcomed as an accepted
king, not as an enemy conqueror.

They sat and waited a bit longer, until Duke Kalas and his entourage
came galloping back out from the cluster of houses.

"Form up to march through," Aydrian told the commanders sitting astride
their mounts in a line behind him. "You will camp north of Pomfreth this
night. We march tomorrow at dawn."

The commanders broke ranks immediately and with practiced discipline.
With every town they encountered, there were two routes, march through
or overrun, and thus far, the latter had not proven necessary. Still, Aydrian
and all the others understood that the farther north they marched, the more
likely they were to encounter resistance. And, of course, Palmaris lay at the
end of this northern road, where Bishop Braumin would not likely prove so
accommodating.

The seventy-five Allhearts galloped into formation beside and behind
their king, and Aydrian nodded to De'Unnero and to Sadye, thus beginning
the triumphant parade into Pomfreth.

All the peasants lined the main road through the small village, cheering
wildly for "King Aydrian!" and waving towels at the young man as he paced
his mount, the legendary Symphony—the horse his father had ridden to the
Barbacan to defeat the demon dactyl—slowly through the town. He nodded to the people every so often, but mostly he watched the road before
him, aloof and above them all. That was what they would expect of their
king, De'Unnero and Kalas had explained to him. That was what the frightened rabble truly needed from their king. Aydrian was the foundation of
their identity. He was not one of them, and was not anything that any of
them thought they could become, but was, rather, their deity in the flesh. As
king, he was the symbol of their nationality, and the man upon whom they
relied to protect them, to provide for their basic needs, and to guide them
to a better place, secularly and spiritually.

And so Aydrian kept his eyes mostly straight ahead, offering occasional
glances and nods, and trying to appear as regal and dominating as possible.

"The parson?" he heard Sadye whisper at his side, talking behind him to
Marcalo De'Unnero.

Following their gazes, the young king noted a man in the distance, behind the lines of waving peasants. He stood leaning on the white wooden door of the town's small Abellican chapel. He was not cheering. He was not smiling.

Aydrian glanced at De'Unnero. "He may need convincing," he quietly remarked.

"He may need burying," De'Unnero replied, and he veered his horse away from the royal entourage. He motioned for the crowd to part, then trotted his mount across the open ground to the chapel and the lone man.

Aydrian paid the scene no heed, confident that Marcalo De'Unnero would handle the situation as he saw fit. Aydrian had long ago decided that De'Unnero would set the tone concerning the conversion of the Abellican Church to his own conservative vision. However De'Unnero conducted the conquered Church was irrelevant to the young king, so long as that Church remained a loyal ally to him in his pursuit of the wider conquests. Secretly, Aydrian hoped that De'Unnero would take the Abellican Church mercilessly and would bring it to a posture that evoked fear in the common man. Let the Church do the dirty work in keeping the common folk in line, leaving the way open for him to become a truly beloved king. Let De'Unnero become the tyrant that Aydrian clearly recognized was lurking in his heart; Aydrian would only shine all the brighter beside him.

His entourage remained behind as Aydrian paced Symphony to the center of the town square. Magnificent upon the magnificent stallion, the young king surveyed this newest group of his flock for some time, letting them bask in the sight of him while he took some measure of their enthusiasm. What he sensed most of all, as in all the other towns, was fear. The common folk of Honce-the-Bear were afraid of change. Common folk took comfort in routines. How well Aydrian had learned this when first he had run away from the wicked elves, settling in with villagers in a nondescript and wretched little place named Festertool in Westerhonce. In their routine, ultimately boring, lives, those folk had taken solace in the emptiness. That was the way of commoners, Aydrian understood keenly, and all that he had to do to win their love was offer them security within their little corners of the kingdom—and to look resplendent upon his great horse.

"Good people of Pomfreth," he began, speaking loudly, his voice resonant. He kept his line of vision just above the heads of the gathering, as he had learned, and he swept one arm out in a grand gesture. "You have heard of the passing of good King Danube, and no doubt the news has saddened you as it has saddened all of the court of Ursal."

"The king is dead!" cried one man from the back of the gathering, a man that Duke Kalas had planted in the town ahead of the army's approach, as he had done in every town.

"Long live the king!" came the appropriate responding cry in many voices, repeated over and over in a mounting cheer for King Aydrian.

Aydrian sat quiet and let the momentum gather, then play out to renewed silence.

"I march now, with the army of Ursal behind me, to comfort you and assure you all that there is no struggle within the kingdom," he explained. "King Danube is dead, and I, as the son of Jilseponie, have rightfully and legally, by the late king's own words, assumed the throne of Honce-the-Bear. You see with me Duke Kalas and the Allhearts, and many of the nobles of the court of Ursal.

"Let the word spread throughout the land that a new and just king has ascended. Let the word spread from this town throughout the land that this King Aydrian is a friend to the folk of Honce-the-Bear, and that I will serve you as your king with the same love and affection of my worthy predecessor, King Danube!"

It was all he had to say. The folk erupted into great cheering, calling out the name of King Aydrian. All signs of nervousness and fear were flown now, in light of his assurances. He had told them exactly what they had desperately hoped to hear.

And now he could move on, confident that he had secured his kingdom just a little bit more.

The town's grandest house—which wasn't much of anything, really—was gladly turned over to Aydrian soon after, and he entered with Sadye by his side, both glancing toward the small chapel, into which Marcalo De'Unnero had disappeared with the parson.

"With each town taken, your relief grows more evident on your face," Sadye remarked, as soon as they were alone.

"Each town is farther removed from Ursal, and so more likely to offer resistance to the change."

"Resistance?" the woman asked doubtfully. "Against the army you carry in tow? Duke Kalas would burn Pomfreth to the ground so quickly that your march through would hardly be slowed. Aye, more quickly than the little speech you are required to give at every stop."

Aydrian's fast-souring expression stopped her abruptly. Sadye put a hand on one hip and leaned a bit, studying the young king.

"Or is that it?" she asked. "You fear having to kill people."

"Fear?" Aydrian echoed with the same tone of doubt Sadye had just used. "No, I do not fear anything or anyone. Nor will I hesitate to trample anyone who gets in the way of this march I intend to make from one end of the world to the other. But I do wish to keep the slaughter at a minimum, you see. I take no pleasure in killing—that joy is reserved for those like your lover."

Sadye stiffened a bit at that remark, though neither she nor Aydrian were quite certain of which part of the comment had stung her—the statement that De'Unnero took pleasure in killing or the mere observation from Aydrian that De'Unnero was her lover.

"I do what I must do," Aydrian explained. "I walk a road of greater purpose and design than these peasants could understand—greater even than any of the nobles and generals can understand."

"Greater than Marcalo can understand?" Sadye asked.

"His purpose is narrower," Aydrian replied. "His purpose is determined by the weight he carries from his bitterness toward the Abellican Church. It takes less to satisfy him. The prize of St.-Mere-Abelle, of executing those who moved away from the vision he embraced for the Church, will suffice. So yes, greater than Marcalo can understand."

"Greater than Sadye can understand?" the woman asked, without missing a beat.

Aydrian's blue eyes, so much like those of his mother, bored into her, and a wry smile grew on his handsome and strong face.

Sadye shrugged, prompting an answer.

"No," Aydrian said with a shake of his head. "Sadye understands. She wants no less for herself. That is what drew you to Marcalo's arms, is it not? The search for something greater, something more exciting and more gratifying?"

Unsure of the young man's direction, Sadye put on a frown and assumed a more defensive posture, turning one shoulder toward Aydrian.

"What will Sadye do when Marcalo's vision pulls him to St.-Mere-Abelle, I wonder?" Aydrian teased. "Sovereign Sister Sadye?" He laughed as he finished, but Sadye did not find the preposterous title so very amusing at that moment.

"Where will Sadye look, I wonder?" Aydrian went on undaunted, and he walked around her, reaching out one hand to play with her hair as he moved behind her.

He pulled away quickly at the sound of someone approaching, and he was glad that he did when the door opened and Marcalo De'Unnero strode in.

"The town fell under our embrace easily," said the monk. "Though I do not trust the parson. He claimed allegiance, but if our enemies find their way to him . . ,"

He stopped and looked hard at Aydrian, then at Sadye. "What is it?" he asked.

Sadye blew out a big sigh and managed a laugh. "Our young Aydrian became quite defensive when I observed that he was relieved to learn that there would be no fighting this day," she explained, and she hopped over to De'Unnero's side and wrapped her arm playfully about his waist.

De'Unnero gave a snort. "As we all should be relieved," he said seriously, "with every town that gladly throws its allegiance to Aydrian. We will find battle soon enough—probably at the gates of Palmaris, if not before. The more of the kingdom that comes over willingly, the greater our claim of legitimacy against Prince Midalis."

"And against Fio Bou-raiy," Aydrian put in, eliciting a wicked smile from De'Unnero.

"I do believe that our friend Sadye is bored," Aydrian remarked offhandedly. "She spoils for a fight. Take care, Sadye," he warned. "Boredom is the impetus to greater heights, 'tis true, but it can prove the enemy to those who do not truly understand the heights to which they aspire."

The irony of that statement in light of their private conversation, especially with De'Unnero nodding his agreement at her side, was not lost on Sadye. But she wouldn't give Aydrian the satisfaction of seeing it on her face, and so she just laughed absently and moved off, towing De'Unnero with her.

Aydrian watched her go, every step.

Ever was he the ambitious lad. Ever was he ready to conquer every challenge.

A Soft Wall of Resistance

"I want you to go with me," Jilseponie said to Roger Lockless, a diminutive man, stunted by a childhood illness that had nearly taken his life. But while Roger was short in stature, he was long on character. In the war with the demon's minions, Roger had stood firm as a beacon of hope, a lone hero to forlorn people. And he had stood strong beside Jilseponie and Elbryan through the ordeal of Markwart. Roger had grown under Elbryan's tutelage and proven to be the best friend Jilseponie— Pony—could ever know.

"Go?" Roger asked hesitantly, and he glanced to the side of the table, where his wife Dainsey was looking on silently. Like Roger, the woman appeared somewhat frail, with spindly limbs. She had nearly succumbed to the rosy plague, was on her last breaths when Jilseponie had brought her to the mummified arm of Avelyn Desbris. Dainsey had been the first to taste of the Miracle of Aida, but though she had beaten the plague, she had never fully recovered her previous robust health. Now her hair was gray and thin, and her eyes were sunken back in her skeletal head.

"To Dundalis first," Jilseponie explained. "I must find Bradwarden. And then to Andur'Blough Inninness—though that journey I expect to make alone."

"You will go and question the elves?" Roger asked skeptically.

"How can I not?"

"How can you?" Roger countered. "Do you believe them to be your friends?" He shook his head and insisted, "They are not your friends. Surely this development proves that beyond all—"

"Dasslerond must answer for this!" Jilseponie demanded, and the flash of power and anger in her blue eyes set Roger back a bit. Again, though, the diminutive man looked over at Dainsey, who was nodding at him approvingly, and gathered his strength.

"Lady Dasslerond is not your friend, Pony," Roger said quietly.

Jilseponie started to answer, but was given pause by his suddenly somber tone, by the obvious implication that he knew something here that she did not.

"When you were in Ursal, sitting as queen, Dasslerond's people came to me," Roger quietly explained.

"You knew of Aydrian?" The flash of anger was there again, suddenly and explosively, and Jilseponie even leaped up from her seat.

"No, of course not," Roger replied, and he placed his hands on her shoulders in a calming motion. "Lady Dasslerond's people came to me in Ursal, asking that I watch you carefully. Dasslerond fears you, and always has, for you possess something that you should not—in her eyes, at least."

Jilseponie eased back into her chair. *"Bi'nelle dasada,"* she reasoned, her voice calm once more. "Lady Dasslerond fears—has ever feared—that I will teach the elven sword dance to the soldiers of Honce-the-Bear."

"Her people are not numerous," Roger remarked. "They fear for their very existence."

"And that gives her the right to steal a child from the womb?" Jilseponie cried, her voice rising in indignation once more.

"'Course it doesn't, and no one's saying such a thing," Dainsey interjected.

"I know how you feel—" Roger started to say.

"No you do not," Jilseponie insisted.

Roger conceded the point with a slight nod. "We have an enemy rising right here in our midst," he said. "Why will you go to the elves to begin another war, when one has come to you?"

"There are questions—"

"For another day," Roger interrupted.

"For now!" Jilseponie shot back. "This battle within the kingdom is not my war. I have no more wars in me. De'Unnero be damned—and he shall, I am confident—but he and Aydrian are a problem for the folk of Honce-the-Bear."

"Not of Jilseponie?" Roger asked, and the woman stared at him hard. "You will abandon these people? You have served them all your life."

"And given all that I have to give."

"That loss is yours more than theirs," Roger replied.

Those words stung Jilseponie profoundly, but they did little to change her mind or her course at that moment. "I leave for Dundalis in the morning. I intend to ride hard all the way. I welcome your company, Roger, and yours, Dainsey, but I will go alone if not beside you."

With that, the woman rose and walked out of Chasewind Manor, the greatest mansion in all Palmaris, formerly the house of the ruling Bildeborough family. Jilseponie had lived here when she had ruled this city as baroness and then as bishop, and she had passed the house on to Roger and Dainsey as her stewards when she had gone south to marry King Danube.

She had barely exited the place, though, and had not even reached the gates across the courtyard, when she was assaulted by the sound of galloping horses and the shouts of a roused populace. She stood there on the front walk of Chasewind Manor, dumbfounded by the rising energy within the city—and it was a general tumult across the city, she could tell, even from where she stood on the elevated western edges.

She stood quiet and she listened, picking out the calls of the heralds.

A moment later, Roger and Dainsey were out beside her.

"Braumin has roused them," Roger observed. "He has decided to fight."

"And the folk're welcoming the choice," Dainsey added.

Jilseponie looked at them both and started to reply, but then the shouts rang out very near to Chasewind Manor's gate, as a rider galloped by, crying, "Long live Prince Midalis!" followed by the stinging, "Death to Aydrian!"

Jilseponie swung about, her face a mask of horror and anger, her breathing suddenly shallow.

"It won't come to that," Roger assured her, moving right beside her and wrapping one arm about her waist. "They are frightened, that is all. The bluster of criers is to rouse the people to a cause. They cannot—"

Jilseponie held her hand up to stop him. She understood quite well the need for such strong words when the folk would soon be asked to stand firm against an army.

But that didn't lessen the sting.

"So you have decided to fight," Jilseponie remarked when she caught up to Bishop Braumin and Master Viscenti a bit later on, in Braumin's office on the main floor of St. Precious.

"The choice was never ours to make," Braumin said to her. "I held audience on the square outside of St. Precious."

"Without sending word to me or to Roger in Chasewind Manor?"

"I had not planned it to be so definitive a speech," Braumin told her, and she knew the man to be sincere. "I planned to tell the gathering simply to measure their feelings on this."

"You understand what you ask of them?"

"I know what they demanded of me," Braumin replied.

"As soon as he told them the truth of our self-proclaimed king, and the truth of his companion, the folk needed no convincing," the recently arrived Master Viscenti put in. "They will not tolerate the return of Marcalo De'Unnero unless that return is with chains about him!"

"They are loyal to the line of Ursal, and the crown has been stolen," Braumin added.

Jilseponie stared at him hard, recognizing clearly the conflict that remained within the man. Yes, he was somewhat relieved that the people had grabbed on to his simple statements of fact and taken control of the momentum from that point forward, but there remained within Braumin a good deal of guilt and trepidation about all of this.

"You will lock the gates and not allow Aydrian entrance?"

The bishop of Palmaris squared his shoulders. "I will."

"And what will you do when Aydrian knocks those gates down?"

"Are we to surrender to him?" Braumin asked, suddenly animated, waving his arms and storming about. "Can the strongest simply take the throne with impunity? Are we not a land of tradition and law?"

Now it was Jilseponie's turn to stand quiet and hold fast to her stance.

"If you fight beside us, we have a chance," said Braumin.

Jilseponie was shaking her head before he ever finished the sentence. "I have business that will take me far from this place, likely never to return."

"You will forsake us in this dark time?" Viscenti put in.

"The day is dark, I do not doubt," Braumin added. "But who are we if we allow our mortal fears to defeat our principles? Who are we if we choose the comfort of the flesh over the serenity of the soul? We know what has happened here. We see the injustice clearly."

"And you resist that injustice," Jilseponie remarked.

"As should you. Are you not the same Jilseponie who stood fast beside Elbryan against the direst of odds? Are you not the same Jilseponie who would have given her life before denouncing her principles in the face of the demon-possessed Markwart?"

Jilseponie gave Bishop Braumin a pleading look, as desperate an expression as the man had ever seen, as she answered, "He is my son."

"Then we cannot win!" Viscenti lamented, and he turned away, throwing up his hands in despair.

"You cannot win in any case," Jilseponie said to him. "Not here, not now. You have seen my strength with the gemstones, and believe that such power would bolster enough to resist. But I have seen Aydrian's strength, and it is greater still! He will knock down the gates of Palmaris if they are closed before him."

"Then all hail King Aydrian!" Master Viscenti dramatically cried, swinging about to face the woman. "And all hail Father Abbot De'Unnero! Damn the traditions of Church and State alike! Damn the—"

"There is a third course open to you," Jilseponie said to Braumin.

The bishop glanced at Viscenti, who quieted at once, and both turned to Jilseponie, eager for her counsel.

"Defy Aydrian with a soft wall of resistance," Jilseponie explained. "Make a stand here if you must, but do not include all of your resources in that stand. Allow your line to bend, all the way to Vanguard."

Bishop Braumin looked even more intrigued.

"Only the unified opposition of the folk of Honce-the-Bear holds any hope of defeating Aydrian now," Jilseponie went on. "He holds the Kingsmen army of Ursal at his disposal, the Allheart Knights among them, and many thousands more in reserve, gathered from the lands about Entel. The people do not know enough to deny his claim as their king, particularly

when that claim is made at the end of an Allheart lance. Such a common denial of Aydrian, if it is to grow, cannot begin until Prince Midalis publicly
makes his claim to the throne."

It all made sense, of course, except . . .

"You ask me to surrender the city," Braumin remarked.

"I ask you to save the garrison for Prince Midalis," Jilseponie corrected.
"For he will need every ally he can find before this is ended."

"You will go to him?"

Jilseponie stepped back and offered no reply, for in truth, she hadn't
thought that far ahead. A moment later, she just shook her head. "I'm going
home," she said softly. "At this time, I need to go home."

Master Viscenti started to argue that course, but the perceptive Braumin
understood clearly that nothing more could be said here, and so he held up
his hand to silence Viscenti. He reached out and took Jilseponie by the
shoulders, looking her right in the eye.

"Forgive my . . . forgive *our* callousness," he said softly. "You have been
through so very much. You owe the people of Honce-the-Bear nothing, my
friend. Go home and heal, Jilseponie."

"Bishop!" Viscenti started to say, but again Braumin stopped him with
an upraised hand. He walked away from Jilseponie then, moving quickly to
his desk, and from the top drawer, he produced a small pouch.

"Take these with you," he offered, handing the bag of gemstones to Jilseponie. She motioned as if to resist taking them, but Braumin only pushed
them toward her more forcefully. "Use them as you see fit, or use them not
at all. But you must have them." He looked deeply into her eyes, the caring
look of a dear friend, and nodded. "Just in case."

Jilseponie took the pouch, and the two monks moved for the door.

"A soft wall of resistance?" Bishop Braumin asked.

Jilseponie merely shrugged and walked out of the room and the abbey,
the two monks in tow.

"It is my fervent hope that you will find your heart and your strength and
join us in this battle," Bishop Braumin said to her. "We have fought so hard
to win the Abellican Church to Avelyn's vision, to bring the common man
more fully into our protective fold. Marcalo De'Unnero would destroy all
that we have accomplished in short order, I am sure."

"Avelyn's vision?" Jilseponie echoed softly and skeptically, for she wasn't
even sure of what "Avelyn's vision" might truly be. She thought of the
"mad friar" then, the drunken brawler she had met in a tavern not far from
Pireth Tulme when she had been serving in the Coastpoint Guards. This
man who had defeated Bestesbulzibar in the bowels of Mount Aida at the
cost of his own life. This man who had taught her the gemstone use. What
might Avelyn think of all of this? Would he, perhaps, be as weary of it all as
was she?

A wagon pulled up then, unexpectedly, and all three turned to regard the
driver, a diminutive man.

"Come along," Roger said to his friend. "We've a long road ahead and I intend to make a good start this day."

Despite her glum mood and true despair, Jilseponie Wyndon Ursal could not deny her smile at the sight of Roger and Dainsey sitting in a wagon laden for the road.

The long road that would take her home.

CHAPTER

❖ 8 ❖

The Lesser of Two Evils

"They wear the colors of a Jacintha legion," the tall and lean
Paroud informed Pagonel, his accent, like his name, telling
the mystic that he was from the southwestern corner of Behren, the Cosinnida region. Pagonel had been surprised, when Yatol Wadon's
assistant had introduced him to the three Jacintha ambassadors, to find a
Cosinnida man among them. Cosinnida was the province of Yatol Peridan,
after all, who was causing dire troubles for Jacintha by pressing the war
against Yatol De Hamman. It merely illustrated to the mystic how tumultuous the situation in Behren truly was at that time, with no real battle lines
delineated.

The two men, along with the other two emissaries from Yatol Wadon,
stood on a rocky bluff to the north of Dahdah Oasis, looking down at the
sanctuary. They had marched out of Jacintha a few days before, bound for
Dharyan-Dharielle to strengthen the alliance between the great cities. Tipped
off on the road by some merchants, the foursome had veered to the north
and the higher ground.

Sure enough, a legion had entered Dahdah, nearly three hundred soldiers, and wearing the colors of one of the Jacintha garrisons.

"Perhaps they are merely tardy on their return, and have at last found
their way home," remarked Pechter Dan Turk, the oldest of the ambassadors. He was a short man with thick gray hair hanging to his shoulders
and a great gray moustache. His skin was ruddy and, like those of so many
of the open desert people, his eyes seemed locked in a perpetual squint.

"They have wandered for months?" the third of the Jacintha contingent,
a strong-jawed and heavily muscled man named Moripicus, asked doubtfully. "Even the stupidest of soldiers understands that the sun rises in the
east, yes? And since Jacintha lies on the eastern coast, finding their way
home should not have presented much of a challenge, yes?"

"They are not returning to Jacintha," Pagonel observed, and the other
three looked at him curiously.

"Not directly, at least," the mystic clarified. "They are loading their wagons with supplies—more than an entire army would need for the march from here to Jacintha, especially if that walk was to be along the open and easy road."

That was true enough, all of them realized as they looked more closely. The group had come in to Dahdah to resupply for an extended march, it seemed, and likely a march into the barren desert.

"Bardoh?" Moripicus asked.

"That is what we must discern," said Pagonel.

Pechter Dan Turk laughed aloud. "If they are allied with Yatol Bardoh, then they will be less than welcoming to the emissaries of Yatol Mado Wadon!"

"And even less welcoming to a Jhesta Tu mystic, one might suppose," added Paroud.

Pagonel nodded but didn't respond. A moment later, he started walking toward the oasis.

"Where are you going?" Moripicus demanded.

"To get some answers," replied Pagonel. "You three can go in if you choose, but move to the road back in the east a bit, and enter openly along it. We have no affiliation, and no knowledge of each other. I will rejoin you to the west of the oasis this same night."

"What are we to do now, then?" Paroud asked, as soon as Pagonel moved out of sight.

"We might just move around the oasis from the north and await the mystic on the western road," Pechter Dan Turk offered.

"With our skins empty of water?" Moripicus asked.

"With our skins still on our bodies!" Pechter Dan Turk replied.

"Information is our ally here," Moripicus scolded him. "We go to grovel at the feet of the smelly To-gai-ru and we do not even know for certain that Yatol Bardoh is assembling any force against Yatol Mado Wadon. There lie our answers."

"We can walk right in," Paroud agreed. "Greetings, possible traitors! We are ambassadors from Yatol Wadon, whom you wish to kill!"

Moripicus narrowed his eyes as he stared at the sarcastic man from Cosinnida.

"We are no such thing," Pechter Dan Turk put in. "We are . . . merchants. Yes, merchants! Traveling the road about Jacintha."

"Without wares?" Moripicus said dryly.

"In search of wares!" Pechter Dan Turk insisted.

"Without money?" said Paroud, before Moripicus could point out that obvious shortcoming in the disguise.

"We . . . we," Pechter Dan Turk stammered over a few possibilities, then just shook his head and blurted, "We buried our money in the desert nearby! One cannot be too careful about thieves, after all!"

"Yes, and when we tell that to hungry renegade warriors, they will take us into the desert at spearpoint, and when we cannot give them any money, they will run us through and leave us for the vultures to pick clean!"

"But . . ." Pechter Dan Turk started to argue, but he was cut short by Moripicus.

"We are scholars."

The other two looked at him doubtfully.

"Is not the Library of Pruda now reassembled in Dharyan-Dharielle?" Moripicus asked. "So we will become scholars, walking the road to the Library of Pruda, and if any of the soldiers down there take exception to that library now being in the city of the Dragon of To-gai, we will simply agree. Tell them that we despise the thought of our great scholarly works being in the hands of dirty Ru dogs."

"Yes, we are going merely to ensure that the precious works survive," Paroud added, catching on to the possibilities.

"Scholars, scholars from Pruda, and without political aspirations or affiliations, except that we all hate the To-gai-ru," said Moripicus.

"An easy enough mask to carry," agreed Paroud, who did indeed hate the To-gai-ru.

"Then why go to Dharyan-Dharielle?" asked the oblivious Pechter Dan Turk. "The place is crawling with Ru!"

The other two just looked at each other and rolled their eyes, then started back to the southeast, to strike the road far out of sight of Dahdah.

Several merchant caravans were in the oasis, as usual, but the place was dominated by the presence of the soldiers. They were everywhere, at the water's edge and mingling about every caravan with impunity. They inspected wares, and simply took what they wanted.

Pagonel felt the eyes upon him as soon as he walked into the oasis area. He was not wearing his Jhesta Tu robes for this dangerous return trip, but he certainly did not seem to fit in among the dirty rabble and loud merchants. He took care not to make eye contact with any of the warriors, so as not to begin any confrontation. He was here to gather information, not start a war.

He moved quietly across the shade of a line of date trees nearer to a merchant wagon, whose owner was apparently confronting a soldier.

"You cannot just take what you wish to take!" the merchant cried, and he reached for a silken swatch the soldier held.

The soldier pulled his hand back and blocked the advancing merchant with his free hand. "I have a sword," he warned, flashing a toothy smile.

The merchant backed off a step and waved his fist in the air. "I have a sword, too!" he insisted.

"Ah yes, but I have three hundred swords," the soldier retorted, and he nodded. Three other men descended on the poor merchant, herding him back toward his wagon, slapping and kicking him repeatedly, and laughing all the while.

"The authorities in Jacintha will hear of this!" the man cried. "I have friends in Chom Deiru!"

That was all the soldiers needed to hear, but not to any effect the merchant had hoped. He was still waving his fist in the air when the nearest soldier drew out a dagger and plunged it into his side. He wailed and fell away—or tried to, for the other two similarly drew out knives.

The three fell over him, stabbing him repeatedly even as he slumped down to the ground.

Pagonel had to fight every instinct within him not to intervene, reminding himself repeatedly that to do so might hold greater consequences than the unfortunate murder of this one man.

"Are you a friend of this man?" the soldier with the clean hands and silk swatch demanded when he turned to see Pagonel standing there watching.

"I am a simple traveler," the Jhesta Tu mystic replied.

"To where? To Jacintha?"

"I have come from Jacintha," Pagonel answered. "My road is west."

"He's got Ru blood in him," said one of the men who had finished with the dead merchant.

"Yeah, he's got the stink of Ru all about him," agreed a second, and all three moved to join their companion, who was holding the stolen silk. Two even fanned out a bit, somewhat hemming the mystic.

"You know what we do to Ru in Behren, eh?" remarked one of the bloody knife-wielders, and he brandished his blade threateningly.

Pagonel kept a proper amount of attention on the blustering man, but he noticed the arrival of his three companions, then, wandering into the oasis area down the eastern road. They nodded and bowed to every soldier they passed, trying to be diplomatic, even submissive, but in truth doing nothing more than drawing attention to themselves.

They made their way quickly past the various groups of soldiers, walking swiftly, but then Paroud noticed Pagonel, the soldiers moving in closer, and he stopped short, all three gawking in the mystic's direction.

"I desire no trouble, friends," Pagonel said quietly. "I have come from the southland, following rumors of turmoil. My masters wish to help, if they may, in healing Behren's wounds."

"Wounds?" asked the soldier with the silk. He looked to his friends and they all laughed. "All that is wounded are the coffers of the imposter Chezru! They have been torn asunder, their gems and jewels spilling out."

"Spilling out to our waiting hands!" another added.

"You march to Jacintha?" Pagonel asked.

"You ask too many questions," one of the men retorted. "Who is your master?"

"Yes, tell us where we must send your headless body," another added.

The two men who had fanned out to each side moved in closer then, brandishing their knives dangerously close to the seemingly unarmed mystic.

Pagonel glanced to the side, to see another group of soldiers closing fast on his three traveling companions. Those three noticed it as well.

Paroud broke left, screaming as he ran back toward the east. He would have been captured almost immediately, and likely gutted, but then Moripicus pointed at Pagonel, and shouted, "Jhesta Tu!"

Every soldier in the area froze in place, and all eyes turned toward Pagonel.

The mystic felt the soldiers at his sides move in a bit closer, felt them tense up, as if preparing to strike.

He moved first, snapping his hands up suddenly, smashing the back of his fists into their faces. The man directly before him struck out hard with his knife, a slash aimed for Pagonel's face.

But the mystic was far below the strike as the blade cut past, having dropped into a sudden low crouch.

Pagonel punched across with his right hand, smashing the inside of the soldier's right knee and buckling his leg out. A quick reversal had Pagonel's elbow smashing the inside of the man's left knee, similarly widening his stance, and then the mystic brought his hand back to center and turned his arm to the vertical and delivered the coup de grace by punching straight up between the stunned man's widespread legs.

He lifted the soldier right off the ground with the weight of the blow, and given its location, all fight went out of the soldier. The man sucked in his breath, clutched at his groin, and slowly tumbled down to the side.

Pagonel wasn't watching, though. As soon as he delivered the crippling blow, the mystic brought his hand back in close and leaped a sideways somersault to the right, landing lightly on his feet in perfect balance and coming up suddenly and ferociously before the knife-wielding soldier. He led with his forearm as he rose, pushing aside the man's feeble attempt to stab at him, then driving his arm across the man's face, knocking him backward.

As Pagonel retracted, the soldier was still stumbling, his head still up from the blow, offering a fine opening at his throat.

Pagonel's stiffened left hand took that opening, though the mystic held back enough so that he did not actually kill the man.

The soldier gasped and fell away and Pagonel swung back the other way to meet the charge of the third.

More to dodge it than to meet it, actually, for the mystic fell suddenly again, spinning as he dropped and swinging one foot out wide to trip up the advancing soldier.

Up came Pagonel as the man flailed and stumbled in a turning descent. The mystic's fists hit him, left, right, left, on the chest as he went down, and Pagonel leaped away.

It had all happened in the blink of an eye, it seemed, and so the soldier holding the stolen silk swatch was still not even ready with any kind of defense. He flailed his arms wildly before him to fend off the mystic, but Pagonel wasn't really engaging him anyway, but rather, was using him as a springboard to the top of the merchant's wagon. A great leap brought the mystic up high and he planted his foot on the flailing man's shoulder and leaped away from there, easily gaining the wagon roof and rushing across to the other side.

Paroud heard Moripicus' cry, and though he felt sorry that his friend had betrayed Pagonel, he was certainly glad for the personal reprieve! For those soldiers who had begun to take up the chase on him stopped suddenly and swung back the other way.

The frightened man mingled into a group of merchants, scrambling through their ranks and out the back side of their wagons, making his way to the lower ground by the water's edge. Then he ran along that edge, using the distraction to get all the way out of the oasis. He ran flat out down the eastern road, back the way he had come, back toward the safety of Jacintha.

Across the way, Pechter Dan Turk similarly used the distraction to move away, but he, unlike his companion, headed for the west.

Moripicus hesitated at his spot for a short while, watching Pagonel's furious escape attempt, and even whispered, "Forgive me, mystic," then turned to follow Pechter Dan Turk.

He turned right into the blocking chest of a soldier, though, and one who had obviously heard his soft plea for forgiveness.

· Pagonel hit the ground softly, his legs buckling under him as he fell sidelong to the sand. He reversed his momentum completely and rolled back under the wagon, coming to his belly directly beneath it. He pushed up hard with his hands, lifting himself right from the ground to slam up against the undercarriage of the wagon. Out snapped his hands and feet, pressing out against the frame and locking the mystic in place.

Soldiers swept by the wagon, scrambling all about to catch up to him. A couple were even cunning enough to fall and glance under the wagon, but none moved under enough and turned his eyes up to see the splayed mystic in his perch.

Gradually, the tide of soldiers swept away, but Pagonel had to hold his position much longer, he knew.

He heard a commotion over by the area where he had engaged the three men, heard a familiar voice pleading for mercy.

"I warned you!" Moripicus begged. "I told you he was Jhesta Tu, yes?"

"And how did you know?" an angry soldier demanded.

Pagonel took a deep breath. He could tell from the soldier's tone that this was not going to go well for Moripicus. The mystic dropped to the sand, landing on hands and knees and looking out toward the voices.

Just in time to see Moripicus forced down to his knees, his head pulled forward forcefully by a soldier tugging his hair, while two others held his arms back.

Pagonel was about to shout out, and to roll out from under the wagon, but it was too late, and all he could do was avert his eyes as another soldier brought his great khopesh swinging down to behead the man.

Tellingly, the executioner invoked the name of "Chezru Tohen Bardoh" as he carried out the death sentence.

Pagonel gave a quick scan of the area, trying to sort out the other two Jacintha emissaries, but neither was to be found. With great regret, the mystic went back up tight under the wagon and waited for the cover of darkness.

Pechter Dan Turk crouched behind a dune, shivering in the cold night air and terrified that pursuit would come out from that now-distant oasis. He knew Moripicus was dead, though he had already been out and running to the west before the execution, and knew, too, that he would also be killed if the soldiers caught up to him.

What to do?

He thought that he should return to Jacintha to report this tragedy to Yatol Wadon, though he didn't like the prospects of trying to slip past the legion.

What then? Was he to go on to Dharyan-Dharielle? The man had been uneasy with the prospects of dealing with the foreign To-gai-ru all along, but now the thought of going in there alone positively terrified him. At that time, though, huddled in the cold desert sand, the sounds of the night about him, the fires of the legion glowing in the black sky to the east, Pechter Dan Turk would have been relieved indeed to see the gates of the city of the Dragon of To-gai.

A noise to the side startled him, and he snapped his gaze that way, his eyes wide. He trembled and huddled, trying to stay lower in the sand.

A pair of pale eyes stared back at him for a moment, and then the creature, a small, doglike lupina, wandered away, skittering fast and looking back at him. A single lupina didn't seem much of a threat, but Pechter Dan Turk knew enough about the open desert to realize that where there was one lupina, there were usually a dozen more.

He knew that he had to move, had to find some defensible ground where a host of lupinas couldn't come at him all at once. He wanted to go, he consciously willed his arms and legs to unfold and to start away, but he simply couldn't begin.

And then a hand tapped him on the shoulder.

Pechter Dan Turk locked in place, a silent scream reverberating throughout his tense body. His leg felt warm from his own release.

"One of your companions is dead," Pagonel said softly. "The soldiers killed Moripicus in the name of Chezru Bardoh."

So relieved was Pechter Dan Turk to hear the familiar voice of the mystic that he hardly registered the significance of the words Pagonel spoke. He managed to turn his head to regard the man in the dim starlight. He smiled widely and nodded stupidly, and managed to begin breathing again, in short gasps.

Pagonel took him under the arm and helped him up. "We must be on the move throughout the night," the mystic explained. "Where is Paroud?"

"He ran back to the east," Pechter Dan Turk replied unsteadily. "He was gone, poof, at the first sign of trouble."

"That is good," the mystic said. "Let us hope that he got safely away. Yatol Mado Wadon must be informed that his suspicions are sadly proven true. Yatol Bardoh is gathering his strength and taking considerable strength from Jacintha in that process."

Pechter Dan Turk looked at him as if he did not understand.

"Your companion was executed in the name of *Chezru* Bardoh," Pagonel said again, emphasizing the stolen title.

Pechter Dan Turk shuddered so tightly that it seemed as if he was about to explode. "This is very bad," he said. "Very bad. Yatol Bardoh is not a kind man!"

"I know him all too well," Pagonel replied. "Fortunately for any hopes Jacintha has of forming an alliance with the To-gai-ru, Brynn Dharielle knows him well, too."

Pechter Dan Turk nodded nervously, and Pagonel led him off at a swift pace across the darkened sands.

❖ 9 ❖

The Second Prize

"Twenty thousand?" Marlboro Viscenti asked Bishop Braumin. The two of them stood at Palmaris' southern wall, looking out over the farmlands and the many campfires that had sprung up this night, the fires of King Aydrian's army.

"Perhaps," Braumin replied, as if it did not matter. Indeed, the numbers seemed hardly to matter, for the bishop had taken Jilseponie's advice and had built a soft wall of resistance. Most of Palmaris' garrison was gone now, along with a large percentage of St. Precious' hundred brothers, slipping out to the north in the hopes of catching up to Prince Midalis as he executed his inevitable march out of Vanguard.

What a difficult decision that had been for Braumin! To surrender Palmaris, with hardly a fight.

He looked around inside the city walls, to see the bustle of preparations. He had given the remaining residents the option of joining in the resistance to the new king and his march, or of simply hiding in their homes, with no repercussion and no recriminations. He was surprised at how many had chosen the way of resistance.

Surprised, and a bit saddened, for he knew that the armies of Ursal would run them over.

Led in spirit and resolve by the five thousand Behrenese of Palmaris—most of whom had come to the city only recently, in the years since the plague—the remaining citizens had decided to lock the gates and offer no hospitality to this usurper named Aydrian. The depth of their commitment to stand beside the line of Ursal and the Abellican Church of Bishop Braumin made Braumin wonder if he had chosen correctly in sending nearly a thousand warriors away.

Or perhaps he should have sent all the soldiers away, and all the citizens who would join them, as well. Leave Palmaris deserted before the advance of the usurper and the wretched De'Unnero!

The bishop chuckled at the impracticality of it all. The fall would soon enough come on in full, and winter arrived early in those areas north of Pal-

maris, the only escape route from the advance of Aydrian. If Braumin had
led the folk of Palmaris into self-imposed exile, he would have been sen-
tencing a good number of them—the majority, even—to certain starvation
and death from exposure on the harsh road. And those who did get to
Prince Midalis would hardly have bolstered the prince's cause, but would
have dragged him down beneath their dependent weight.

So a partial withdrawal and a partial defense.

For Braumin, there would be no withdrawal. He meant to fight Aydrian—
or more pointedly, fight De'Unnero—to the bitter end. Before sunset, word
had come that the Ursal fleet was shadowing the army up the Masur Delaval,
and would likely seal off the river before the morning.

"You need to leave once more," Braumin said to Viscenti.

The skinny man turned sharply toward him. "I stand with you!" he
insisted.

"You stand as witness," Braumin corrected. "From across the river. You
will bear witness of the fate of Palmaris and St. Precious to our brethren in
St.-Mere-Abelle."

Viscenti seemed to be trembling more than usual. "That is the duty of
Bishop Braumin. You, and not lowly Master Viscenti, can go to St.-Mere-
Abelle and force Father Abbot Bou-raiy to strong action against De'Unnero."

"Father Abbot Bou-raiy will need little prodding in that direction,"
Braumin assured his friend. "My duty is here, to the people of Palmaris."

"Palmaris will not stand long against King Aydrian."

"But Bishop Braumin will hold true to the end," Braumin explained. "I
will serve as a symbol of hope and defiance for the common folk of Palmaris, and for my brethren as they prepare for the long struggle against
Marcalo De'Unnero. As Master Jojonah led the way for us, so I shall take
up that beacon and help to guide our people through the long night of
Aydrian."

Viscenti shook his head through every word of the dark and prophetic
speech. Jojonah was a martyr, having been burned at the stake by Father
Abbot Markwart. The image of Jojonah had indeed led the way for many of
the younger brothers of the Abellican Church: the way to Avelyn, the way
to the Miracle of Aida.

But that didn't change the fact that Jojonah was dead.

"You go and I will stay," Viscenti insisted.

Braumin turned his gaze over the man, the bishop looking every bit of his
fifty years. "I am not just the abbot of St. Precious," he quietly and calmly
explained. "I am the bishop of Palmaris. As such, I have sworn my loyalty
to Father Abbot Bou-raiy and to King Danube and Queen Jilseponie. And
mostly, to the common folk of Palmaris, Abellican, and Chezru. I am staying, Master Viscenti, and I am ordering you across the river, this night,
before the fleet can close the way. You will bear witness to the fall of Palmaris, the fall of St. Precious, and the fall of Bishop Braumin. You will go to
St.-Mere-Abelle and tell them, and you will hold strong the course against

Marcalo De'Unnero above all else. There are few I would trust with this most important mission, my friend, my ally. Only because I know that you will carry on do I have the strength within me to do as I know I must do."

Viscenti started to argue but Braumin draped his hands over the man's shoulders and held him firm.

"Go," he bade the diminutive master.

Tears welled in Master Marlboro Viscenti's eyes as he crept out the back door of St. Precious soon after, rushing with his escorts to the Palmaris long dock, where a group of Behrenese fishermen were waiting to ferry them across the great river.

As dawn broke across the eastern horizon, the spectacle of the force that had come against Palmaris was revealed to the townsfolk in all its splendid glory. A line of soldiers stretched the length of Palmaris' southern wall and more! Their banners waved in the morning breeze, showing their various legions, or, for the Allhearts, their noble family crests, and one design flew above all others: the bear and tiger rampant, facing each other above a triangular evergreen. How significant that banner seemed to Bishop Braumin, a perversion of Danube's own and the Abellicans' own! Danube had ridden under the bear rampant. The Abellican evergreen flew above the guard towers of St.-Mere-Abelle. Aydrian had taken both as his mantle, and had added the tiger—the tiger for De'Unnero, Braumin understood.

The Allheart Knights centered that line of Kingsmen, in their gleaming magnificent armor, the best in all the world, and astride their solid and unshakable To-gai pinto ponies. And in their center sat the grandest spectacle of all: young King Aydrian in his shining gold-lined armor, sitting astride the legendary Symphony, the horse of Elbryan the Nightbird. That stallion, draped in armor plating and a red-trimmed black blanket, seemed on edge, stomping the ground repeatedly.

Trumpets announced the dawn and the arrival of the young king of Honce-the-Bear.

To Braumin Herde, standing on the parapets near to the city's southern gate, those trumpets heralded naught but doom.

A trio of riders came out from the line, trotting their muscular ponies toward Herde and the southern gate. When they stopped before the gate, the rider in the center took off his great plumed helm and shook out his curly black hair.

"I am Targon Bree Kalas, Duke of Westerhonce, former Baron of Palmaris," he announced.

"You are well known to me and to the people of Palmaris," came Braumin's reply, and only then did Kalas seem to take note of the bishop. "Under King Danube, we were allies, Church and State joined in harmony for the good of the folk of Honce-the-Bear."

"Bishop Herde! I bring you greetings and great tidings!" Kalas said with sudden enthusiasm.

"That King Danube is dead," said Braumin.

"Rest his soul, and long live the king!" Duke Kalas responded, and he swept his arm out to the side and behind him, back toward Aydrian.

"Why do you come to the gates of my city with such an army, Duke Kalas?" Braumin Herde asked, his tone suddenly a bit more demanding.

"We are the escort of the new king, the rightful king by Danube's own proclamation on that day when he wed Jilseponie," the duke explained. "Behold Aydrian, the son of Elbryan, the son of Jilseponie! Behold Aydrian, the king of Honce-the-Bear!"

Braumin Herde glanced up and down the line at the puzzled expressions worn by the defenders of Palmaris. This was a bit much to ask of them, the bishop felt at that moment. Kalas was speaking truthfully, and yet Braumin was asking the folk of Palmaris to deny this heir of their two greatest heroes. And that, on top of asking these folk, these brave folk, to stand strong against a trained and outfitted army without the bulk of their own garrison to support them.

And yet, here they were, shoulder to shoulder, manning every spot on the wall.

"Tell me, Duke Kalas," Bishop Braumin began slowly and deliberately, "what words from Prince Midalis on the ascension of this new king? From obscurity has he risen, a name that few north of Ursal had ever heard mentioned, I would guess. He is the child of Jilseponie and Elbryan, and yet, Jilseponie had no idea that he existed before the fall of King Danube."

"Then we should be glad that God has given us this gift that is Aydrian," Duke Kalas replied. "To lead us through the dark times."

"And upon whose wisdom does this young king rely?" asked the bishop.

"On yours, of course, and rightly so. And pray tell us, who else? Who is it that sits astride his horse right behind the young king?"

Even from this distance, Braumin Herde could see Duke Kalas' face grow very tight.

"Might it be Marcalo De'Unnero, Duke Kalas?" Braumin Herde pressed, slamming home the critical point to the assembled Palmaris folk, and indeed, he heard De'Unnero's cursed name being whispered up and down the wall. "The same De'Unnero who once ruled Palmaris? The same tyrant who terrorized the folk of Palmaris in the name of Father Abbot Markwart?"

Those questions brought murmurs and shouts of discontent all along the city wall.

"King Aydrian's ascent was the doing of King Danube, who in his wisdom—" Duke Kalas began.

"Who in his ignorance that Jilseponie had ever given birth, errantly referred to a child of his own loins with his new queen, should that event ever come to pass!" Bishop Braumin interrupted. There, he had said it: an outright denial of Aydrian's claim; an obvious, intended resistance to this march of the young would-be king.

Bolstered by his own recognition that now it was out there openly, Braumin

Herde plowed ahead. "We of Palmaris will accept the sovereignty of King Aydrian when and only when Prince Midalis of Vanguard offers his blessing. We bid you return to Ursal now, with no threat from us, until such time as Prince Midalis, the brother of King Danube who had long been named as rightful heir, can come south from Pireth Vanguard to place his claim to the throne or to condone the ascent of Aydrian. Only then will we of Palmaris swear fealty to the crown."

"I, we, did not ride here to secure an alliance, Bishop Braumin Herde!" Duke Kalas roared back. "You . . ." He swept his arm out dramatically to encompass all of those listening. "You all have sworn fealty to the crown of Honce-the-Bear. We have ridden north in a time of great celebration, in announcement that the crown has passed, in accordance with King Danube Brock Ursal's own wishes and words, to King Aydrian Boudabras. Open wide your gates, Bishop Braumin, and cease your treasonous proclamations. Your king has come to visit!"

"Go home, Duke Kalas," Braumin Herde replied without the slightest hesitation. "We have heard your words, and Aydrian's claim to the throne, and we are not moved. Especially so when we consider the theft of the Abellican Church that is even now commencing."

"Open wide your gates and greet your new king with proper respect," Duke Kalas warned.

"When Prince Midalis arrives, he will be greeted accordingly," Braumin replied.

Duke Kalas stared hard at the man for a long while, then scanned the length of the wall, his eyes narrow and threatening. "Is this the decision of Palmaris, then?" he asked, and his reply came forth as a volley of jeers, telling him to go away.

"So be it," Duke Kalas said to Bishop Braumin. "Do tell your gravediggers to stock up on extra shovels." He replaced his great plumed helm on his head, then brought his horse about suddenly and galloped back to the Ursal line, the other two Allheart Knights in tow.

"Ye did well," the man standing next to the bishop of Palmaris remarked, and he patted Braumin on the shoulder.

Braumin offered a grateful nod in reply. He wondered, though, if that man would feel the same way when Palmaris' walls came tumbling down.

"Jilseponie is behind this treason," Duke Kalas spat when he returned to his place beside King Aydrian. "You underestimated the power of the witch, and now before us, the gates are closed!"

"Perhaps we should thank her, then," Marcalo De'Unnero remarked, and the duke and the others stared at him curiously.

"If all the kingdom willingly joins with King Aydrian before Prince Midalis can move south out of Vanguard, the war will be over before it ever begins," the duke reasoned. "Better for us all if—"

"Do you so fear a fight?" De'Unnero interrupted, cutting short the man's argument. "Perhaps Palmaris will prove a valuable lesson for the rest of the kingdom. Perhaps it is time that we show the people of the land the price of denying the truth of Aydrian Boudabras."

That brought a few nods from those close enough to hear, and Kalas let go of his argument and turned to Aydrian for his orders.

Aydrian's blue eyes bored into the man, reminding him of his encounter with death, reminding him of his journey to the dark realm, when Aydrian had literally pulled him back to life. Those eyes told Kalas profoundly that this man, and not the pitiful Abellican Church, held the secret to life after death, held the secret to immortality itself.

"March to the wall, Duke Kalas," Aydrian commanded. "If they do not open the gates, we will tear the gates down."

The duke nodded his obedience, then spurred his pinto away, gathering up his commanders, organizing the first charge.

To the side, remaining quiet, but watching intently, Sadye took a good measure of Aydrian. She could see the strength of the young king. She could see the vision of the man. He was so beyond those around him, De'Unnero included, so enwrapped in a journey of greater glory that he feared nothing at all. Truly, he was king, of Honce-the-Bear and beyond. Truly, all the world should bow before him, for he was . . . above them.

Sadye caught herself with a deep breath, hardly believing the thoughts that had flooded through her. She studied Aydrian carefully, his intense blue eyes peeking out from the golden rims of his helm, his blond hair showing all about the edges. She looked at his armor, the most magnificent suit in all the world, and she knew even beyond that, that the man beneath those metal plates was more magnificent still.

She did step back from her own fluttering heart to note something else about young and strong Aydrian though, something that she could not miss in his eyes. A twinge of regret, perhaps?

Then the trumpets began to blare, and the thousands of Kingsmen infantry took up their determined march toward the city.

Sadye took up her lute and began to play, a song of battle.

Bishop Braumin watched the approach with a heavy heart. There was no turning back now, no more speeches to give. He had told the people of Palmaris the truth as he had honestly measured it, and they had made their decision to resist this young king. And now the resistance was put right before them.

The soldiers advanced methodically; behind the line, the Allheart Knights, nearly a hundred strong, assembled their ponies in the center of a larger line of cavalry.

A few arrows went out from Palmaris' wall, falling far short of the still-distant force. Bishop Braumin began to call for a halt to the ineffective fire, but changed his mind. They were nervous, he knew.

A few balls of burning pitch soared out from Palmaris' tower catapults, to more effect, but still falling far short of the needed defense to deter such an army as approached.

Braumin turned left and right, scanning the wall. The brothers of St. Precious who had remained behind had been given specific gemstones and specific tasks in aiding the defense. Braumin had strategically placed them for maximum effect.

To kill as many attackers as possible.

That realization brought with it tremendous guilt and regret, and old Braumin, no stranger to war and conflict, had to work hard to keep the waves of despair away.

The march progressed in orderly fashion, but then the soldiers entered the area close enough for effective fire. Lines of arrows reached out from Palmaris' wall, slashing into the long ranks. The first blood stained the field outside the city that morning, and the first cries of agony rent the air, and tore at Bishop Braumin's heart.

The march broke into a full charge, the Kingsmen roaring out their battle cries and coming on hard. But for all their pomp and presence, for all their glory and military strength, the group that had come to Palmaris was not really prepared to assault a walled city. They had no ladders with them, no ropes with grapnels, no siege towers or battering rams. They came on, shouting and cheering, and with their armor protecting them, the ranks were hardly thinned when they at last reached the city walls.

But then what?

Many spears went up over the walls, and volleys of arrows went at the city's defenders, and many did fall.

But with the support of the magic-wielding monks, the return fire was far more effective, archers leaning over the walls to shoot down into the milling throng.

Kingsmen herded about the strong and fortified city gates, trying to press them open, to no avail!

The Allheart charge came on then, and was nothing short of spectacular, the thunder of hooves shaking the ground.

And Braumin's gemstone-wielding monks replied with a barrage of lightning and fire, concentrating on the area about the gates, jolting the soldiers about.

One monk leaped out from the wall, calling the name of Avelyn, and as he landed amidst the throng, he released the power of his gemstone, a ruby, and blasted a fireball in the midst of the attackers, consuming himself and them.

Flaming men ran out of that conflagration, waving their arms and screaming pitifully.

Bishop Braumin turned away and blinked hard against his tears.

*   *   *

From across the field, Aydrian watched the events with growing trepidation. His conscience assailed him, demanding of him that he stop this battle, this march, this war—demanding of him that he find a way of peace.

They are the cattle! Screamed a voice in his head, so suddenly, the same voice that had guided him across the Mirianic to Pimaninicuit to retrieve the gemstones, the same voice that had led his way across Yorkey County to Ursal, the same voice that had shown him the way to destroy King Danube. It was the voice from the mirror, the voice of Oracle, the voice that had shown him the lie of Dasslerond and the promise of his inner strength. *They stand before you because they fear you,* it told him. *They deny the truth of you because they fear the lie that is their ridiculous faith!*

Aydrian unwittingly argued with that voice, feeling as if he was a second shadow in the same mirror, like one of the two blurry forms that he used to see at Oracle, which were always at odds. One had told him to listen to Dasslerond, to accept the wisdom of the elves as a gift, while the other had denied that course.

That latter voice, the voice that was now talking to him, had brought him so far from Andur'Blough Inninness, and at all but these crucial and painful moments, it seemed to hold Aydrian heart and soul.

But in light of the scene before him, against the assault of gruesome and horrific images, against the cries of pain, Aydrian's other voice could not help but question his course and his desires.

That confusion held him in place for many seconds, and showed no sign of resolution. And then a third voice, a physical voice, entered the conversation suddenly and with surprising clarity and certainty.

"You outshine them," Sadye said to Aydrian, moving her mount right up beside Symphony and putting her hand on his arm. "You are the path to glory and greatness! Let not the cries of the flock deter your course!"

Aydrian looked at her, surprised.

"The people, of Palmaris and of your own army, are already dead!" the woman insisted. "They have been dead for most of their lives, though they simply haven't realized it!"

She held Aydrian's gaze a few moments longer, then nodded toward the city walls and the continuing battle.

Aydrian spurred Symphony to leap ahead. He took up his sword, Tempest, with its set gemstones.

A blue-white glow surrounded rider and horse, and then it, and they, were lost in the sudden, explosive burst of fire. That fiery ball dissipated almost immediately, but the flames did not, and on charged Aydrian and Symphony, rider and horse aflame!

Bishop Braumin, along with everyone else, defender and attacker alike, could not ignore the spectacle of the charging Aydrian Boudabras. Braumin wanted to call out for a general focus of the defense against Aydrian, wanted all of his archers and all of the brothers to concentrate their attacks on that single target. If Aydrian fell, would not all of this become moot, after all?

Before the bishop could begin that call, and with many arrows already reaching out toward Aydrian, he felt something, a buzzing in his head, something he could only describe as a white noise.

Confused, the bishop took up his graphite, holding it forth and reaching for its powers to loose a lightning blast at Aydrian.

But he couldn't quite get there, couldn't quite find his focus in the stone, against that buzzing white noise.

Braumin opened his eyes to see Aydrian, no longer aflame, astride Symphony behind the main tumult at the gates. The young pretender king held Tempest aloft and seemed deep in concentration.

Braumin understood. In Tempest's hilt was set a sunstone, the stone of antimagic, and Aydrian was using it now to send out the white noise, the antimagic. Braumin had seen such things before, but what stunned him was the realization that Aydrian's antimagic wave had not been targeted at him, but rather, at the length of Palmaris' wall! The young man was denying all magic use by the defenders and was stealing the strongest advantage that he and his brethren held against the armored soldiers of the crown.

"It cannot be," Braumin muttered. He glanced down the line, to note the confusion on the faces of his brethren as they stared at their gemstones as if they had been deceived.

Without the supporting magic, the tide soon turned against the defenders. The Kingsmen abandoned their tactics of trying to break through the gates, and turned into defensive squares, protecting their archers with their armored bodied and great shields, while those archers increased the barrage against the walls.

The more skilled soldiers, with their stronger bows, began to turn the tide.

And still the antimagic wave held strong. Another brother, apparently misunderstanding, leaped over the wall, ruby in hand, apparently with plans similar to his charred brother. He hit the ground hard, but no fireball erupted from his hand.

He was still working at the gemstone, still trying to bring forth its magic, when the soldiers fell over him and hacked him down.

"It is not possible," Braumin muttered, and he looked from his gemstones to Aydrian, to the son of Jilseponie. The woman's warning about his strength echoed in Braumin's ears at that desperate moment. Jilseponie had told him that Aydrian's power was beyond him, was beyond them all.

As if recognizing the amazement mounting within Braumin, Aydrian opened his eyes and looked up at the bishop, and even flashed a slight smile.

Then, suddenly, Aydrian started into motion, dropping Tempest in line with the city gates. The white noise disappeared from Braumin's thoughts, but before he could even register that fact, a tremendous blast of lightning exploded from the gleaming shaft of the magnificent elven-forged sword that Aydrian held so deftly, bursting out in a sudden flash to smash against the Palmaris gates.

Metal melted under that searing heat, and supporting stone pillars split apart, and in the flash of an instant, the great city gates were gone, replaced by a pile of smoking rubble.

Braumin's eyes widened in horror.

The Allhearts led the charge into the city.

The defense broke apart, the folk and brothers running for cover.

And in denial of any possible countering strike, the white noise returned.

Bishop Braumin stood in the front gatehouse of St. Precious Abbey, looking out over the main square of the city, now occupied by the army of Ursal. The fighting had gone on, in pockets of resistance, throughout the day and long into the night. But now, the morning after Aydrian's assault, the city was quiet once more.

Braumin could only imagine how many had died out there in the fighting. He had heard that the Ursal soldiers were offering little quarter to the dark-skinned Behrenese. He felt profound guilt for retreating to his abbey, along with many of the remaining brothers. He should have been out there among the folk, fighting to his last.

No, he shouldn't have, he reminded himself. When the gate had fallen, when the soldiers had charged into the city, the general battle was ended, the outcome a foregone conclusion. If all the folk of the city had taken up arms and charged back at the Allhearts and the Kingsmen, they would have been slaughtered to a man, woman, and child. And so Braumin had called for, and had followed to the letter, the predetermined plan. The defense of the city was never considered plausible for any length of time, and so the bishop had never called for that. If the wall was taken, so went the order, the people were to flee back to their homes.

The fight had come quickly to St. Precious, as Braumin had known it would. He had hoped that his resistance would be stubborn and very costly to the invaders. He had hoped that he would strike a profound and devastating blow to the ambitions of the young usurper Aydrian.

But now that the soldiers had finally closed about the abbey, now that they were at last within range of Braumin's fury, the white noise had accompanied them, denying the magical response.

And they had come prepared, Braumin saw. They had taken the artillery from Palmaris' wall, dragged it to the corners of the square, and reassembled it over the course of the night.

The bishop winced as the first bombs smashed against St. Precious' wall. He looked across the square to Aydrian, who stood resolute with Tempest upraised. He looked to Aydrian's side, to Marcalo De'Unnero, who stood calm, staring back at him.

*   *   *

"Braumin has ever been a stubborn one," De'Unnero explained to Aydrian and Kalas, as the bombardment of St. Precious continued around them. "He will not surrender, and will willingly die for his cause. He was like that when he stood beside Elbryan, your father, against Father Abbot Markwart."

"Is such strength of character not to be commended?" Aydrian asked.

De'Unnero nodded. "Braumin is a fool, and misguided," the monk explained. "He followed Jojonah and Avelyn and helped to create this ridiculous imposter of a Church."

"Nearly as ridiculous as its imposter predecessor Church," Duke Kalas remarked.

De'Unnero shot him a glower. "The people here believe in Braumin, and deeply," he went on, speaking to Aydrian and trying to keep his gaze away from Kalas. "If we tear down St. Precious and kill him in the process, they will remember, and it will not reflect favorably on the man who would be their king."

"You just said that we could not turn him," Duke Kalas remarked.

De'Unnero had no answer.

But between them, Aydrian merely smiled.

Bishop Braumin felt a sense of relief as he finally managed to loose a bolt of lightning at the attackers sometime later, as the white noise finally diminished somewhat. Apparently, there was a limit to Aydrian's strength and stamina, though that limit seemed far beyond anything any other mortal man or woman had ever achieved!

So now the monks could use their magic again. But apparently the attackers had anticipated such a turn, for the square was all but abandoned, and the bombardment continued only from afar, with catapults launching their bombs from behind the cover of adjacent buildings.

Braumin knew that the end was fast approaching. St. Precious was in shambles, with fires burning in several places, and the integrity of the walls and the strong gates seemed in question. And Braumin understood that Aydrian, if he so chose, could smash down those gates as easily as he had breached the city itself.

But he had not, as yet.

Braumin had no answers. Only twenty brothers remained inside the abbey with him, and they had abandoned all futile efforts to bolster the failing defenses or even to put out the fires. They were assembled in the main chapel, praying, and, like Braumin, waiting for the end.

The bishop moved past them, offering reassurances that God was with them, and then continued out of the room to the back side of the abbey.

At the back wall of the abbey, Bishop Braumin looked out over the rolling waters of the Masur Delaval, and across the towering masts of the Palmaris warships that had closed on the docks as Aydrian had taken the wall. His dear friend Viscenti was out there, he knew, looking back at him.

Braumin clutched his soul stone closer and fell into it. He sent his spirit out, rushing across the waters. St. Precious was lost, he knew. Palmaris had fallen. But there was a lesson here that had to get to St.-Mere-Abelle. There was a measure of Aydrian that would prove invaluable to the brothers who would defend that great abbey, that greatest fortress in all the world, when Aydrian Boudabras at last came against them.

Braumin's spirit did find the weeping master. He went to the man, knowing that he could be no more than a warm feeling to the confused Viscenti. Markwart had once used the gemstones for actual communication across the miles; Jilseponie could do so, to a degree, as well—but not Braumin. He had never been very powerful with the stones, and so all he could do now was approach Viscenti and concentrate with all his heart and soul on that which he had witnessed, hoping to impart some sense to the master of the power of this enemy Aydrian.

Viscenti reacted to the presence of Braumin by standing up suddenly, his eyes going wide.

Braumin called out to him and focused on those images of Aydrian's exploits.

He held the connection for as long as he could, though he had no idea of how much added information he had offered to Viscenti in the one-way exchange.

A voice broke his concentration.

Braumin turned suddenly, and then nearly fell over, for there before him stood Marcalo De'Unnero, wearing a wry smile, and wearing, as one arm, the limb of a tiger, its end bloody.

"And so we meet yet again, Brother Braumin," De'Unnero said.

"Ever enduring is evil," the bishop replied.

"Ever enduring is your folly," De'Unnero replied with a laugh. "Need I tell you that the king of Honce-the-Bear has seen fit to relieve you of your duties as bishop of Palmaris?"

Braumin started to answer, but truly had no reply, and so he just stood there, shaking his head.

"You know who he is, of course," De'Unnero continued. "You know that Duke Kalas announced him honestly. Jilseponie came through here and told you."

"Told me the truth of this monster, Aydrian," Braumin replied.

"The truth?" De'Unnero mused, and he moved inside the doorway and stepped to the side. "That is a curious term. So many truths are bantered about, are they not? The truth of Markwart. The truth of Avelyn. The truth of Father Abbot Fio Bou-raiy. Abbot Olin might not agree with that last one."

"It is not his place to disagree with the College of Abbots."

"An infallible body indeed," said De'Unnero. "Here is your truth, Brother Braumin. Aydrian, the son of Jilseponie, the son of Elbryan, is king of Honce-the-Bear. The noblemen support him. The army supports him. The Church supports him."

Braumin stared at him doubtfully.

"Oh, not the imposter church of Father Abbot Bou-raiy and misguided Braumin Herde. The real Abellican Church, rising once more from the disaster that was Avelyn. Aydrian is king of Honce-the-Bear. That, Brother Braumin, is the truth."

Braumin steeled his gaze at the hated De'Unnero.

"It is a pity that you cannot see that," De'Unnero went on. "We are enemies only by your choosing."

Braumin nearly choked at that remark.

"I do not hate you, brother, though I know you are misguided," said De'Unnero. "I offer you now a chance to reassess your actions, to see the light of the former and greater Abellican Church."

"Spare me your lies!" Braumin interrupted strongly, and when De'Unnero laughed again, he added, "And your mercy!"

Braumin started forward then to attack the monk, though he knew that De'Unnero would surely and easily dispatch him. He stopped short, though, as another figure entered the room.

"Meet your new king," remarked De'Unnero, who had not even flinched at the charge.

"Greetings, Brother Braumin," said Aydrian. "I have heard so much about you."

"Save your soft words for those who do not understand the truth of Aydrian," Braumin countered as strongly as he could manage, though he was surely shaken by the spectacle of the young king in his shining silver-and-gold armor, at the gemstones glittering across his metal breastplate, at the familiar sword strapped at his hip. "How dare you come here in conquest?"

"How dare you deny me entrance?" Aydrian calmly asked.

"If you are the rightful king, then you have nothing to fear from us, for when Prince Midalis accepts you as such, the people of Palmaris—"

Braumin stopped, unable to breathe, as an invisible hand clamped upon his throat. He could hardly believe the strength of that magical grasp, denying him breath, even lifting him up to his tiptoes.

Braumin surely thought his life would end then and there, but Aydrian's magical hand let him go. He nearly fell over, his hands going to his throat.

"Brother Braumin," Aydrian began, slowly and deliberately, "the people of Palmaris, the people of all Honce-the-Bear, will accept me as their king, or they will be put out. It is that simple."

"Murdered, you mean," Braumin managed to gasp in response.

"A king defends his kingdom," said De'Unnero.

"But you can help to prevent that tragedy," Aydrian said to him. "It need not lead to violence and death."

Braumin looked up at him, the now-former bishop's eyes narrowing. "You wish to manipulate me into approval, in the hopes of securing Palmaris against the doubts that will grow when the rightful king marches south from Vanguard," he reasoned, spitting every word with utter contempt. "I will say nothing to aid the usurper Aydrian!"

Aydrian smiled and looked at De'Unnero, then back at Braumin. His smile only widening, the young king held up a gray stone, the same color as the stone that Braumin held in his hands.

"Or perhaps Bishop Braumin will say whatever Aydrian wants him to say," the sinister De'Unnero replied.

PART TWO

DARK FINGERS NORTH AND SOUTH

That voice was with me on the battlefield, guiding my hand—the same voice that I found in the mirror at Oracle.

I still do not know what it is!

The Touel'alfar taught me that humans are not immortal. I am doomed to die, in flesh and in consciousness. I and all akin to me are doomed to nothingness. And yet, at the same time, the Touel'alfar taught me Oracle, that state of meditation where I could find my way in the darkness. At Oracle, I am supposedly guided by my forebears, by Elbryan the Nightbird, my father. But if Elbryan is no more, if his consciousness is gone, rotted with his body, then how do I subsequently contact him? Or do I? Is Oracle, perhaps, merely a place where I can more deeply see that which is in my own mind? This is what I initially believed it to be. Were my instincts correct from the very beginning?

There's the confusion, for I know from personal experience that Elbryan's consciousness lives on. When I went to the grave of Elbryan and claimed Tempest and Hawkwing as my own, I reached that spirit and pulled it forth! I nearly pulled it completely from the realm of death, and believe that I could have done so, had I chosen to pursue that course!

Is it that the spirit lives on, but is trapped in emptiness unless brought forth by a living person, such as at Oracle or on the cold field that day by Elbryan's grave? Do we become in death huddled and trapped blurs, shadows of what we once were, and wholly dependent upon another conscious, free-acting being to summon the power to temporarily break us out of death's bondage?

It is an intriguing thought, for if that is the case, then is there, within the gemstones, a way for me truly to cheat death? To live on beyond the span of Lady Dasslerond's years? To live on forever? Is there, within the gemstones, a way in which I might offer eternal life to those around me?

This is what Duke Kalas believes, and it is the only reason he follows me so devoutly. On one level, Kalas knows me as a usurper, as the one who stole the throne from the bloodline of his beloved friend and king. Kalas hates my mother and was no friend to my father—and the duke steadfastly believes—or rather, believed—that the throne of Honce-the-Bear must be reserved for the select few who are properly bred to be king. And yet, he is one whose loyalty I do not doubt, not for one instant. I hold Duke Kalas solidly in my court because he was dead, by my hand, and I gave him back his life! Duke Kalas, who long ago lost faith in the Abellican Church, who long ago lost all of his faith, now sees in me the promise, or at least the hope, of immortality.

He will never go against me.

Can I offer that which he so desires? Am I the way to eternity? I honestly do not know. Twice now I have waged battle with death, and in neither instance was I impressed by the netherworld's grasp on the departed spirit. And there may be something more, something tangible and physical—a joining of mind and body and spirit in a union untouched by pain and age. The shadow in the mirror has hinted of this, has told me quietly that I can achieve such a union through the powers of the hematite and that in that state, I will be beyond the reach of spears and disease and death itself. Perhaps I will find my answers, to my own immortality and to that of those around me. Perhaps I will find my answers, will find all the answers, within the swirl of a soul stone.

It is all too confusing, I fear, and all too distracting. Of one thing I am certain: only the great are remembered. Those people who stand above the populace, those people who stand above the kings, they are the ones spoken of as the years become decades and the decades become centuries.

It is my destiny to rule. I know that. The voice on the field, be it that of Elbryan or one merely expressing that which is in my own thoughts and heart, speaks truly. I prefer that my march be a peaceful one. I do not enjoy the killing. But I know I lead the world to a better place. I know that when Aydrian is king of all mankind, the world will come to realize greater peace and prosperity than ever before. And so the end result is worth the bloodstains of the ignorant. And so those who die in the name of King Aydrian are dying to create a better world.

It is in this knowledge and confidence that I am able to deny the screams of the dying. It is in this sense of destiny that I find my way along the road of life.

There was another voice on the field outside of Palmaris that day. When I hesitated, there was one beside me, reminding me.

Sadye has come to understand my march. Sadye, wise Sadye, knows the profound difference between mortality and immortality, between living and surviving, between invigorating excitement and deathly routine. She fears nothing. She shrinks from no challenge. She engaged Marcalo De'Unnero **because** he was the weretiger, not in spite of that fact. She exists on the very edge of disaster because she knows that only *there can a person be truly alive. She is keeping me there, as well, herding my march along a straight and determined line. She is holding me on a precipice, and the stronger the wind that blows behind us, threatening to blow us over that cliff face, the wider is her smile.*

Sadye knows.

—King Aydrian Boudabras

His Widening Sphere of Influence

For as long as anyone could remember, the piping of the Forest Ghost had haunted the forests of the Timberlands about the towns of Dundalis, Weedy Meadow, and End o' the World. And so it was this night, the delicate melody drifting through the trees, seeming so much a part of the night that many of the folk of Dundalis did not even notice until a friend pointed it out.

The three visitors to the town surely marked the piping of the Forest Ghost as soon as it had drifted in on the evening breeze, though, for they had come here in the hopes of finding that very piper.

"Bradwarden," Roger Lockless said with great reverence. "It is good to hear his music once again."

"I'm thinking that Pony's agreein' with ye," Dainsey remarked with a smirk. She stared at Pony, drawing Roger's gaze there, as well.

There sat Pony, on the front porch of Fellowship Way, the town's single tavern, her eyes closed and rocking gently in rhythm with the music.

Roger and Dainsey looked to each other and smiled wistfully, glad to see that a measure of calm had come to tortured Pony's beautiful face. They let her sit there for a long, long while, basking in the moonlight and the melody, before Roger finally remarked, "Bradwarden is not far."

Pony opened her eyes sleepily and looked over at the couple.

"Shall we go?" Roger asked her.

Pony hesitated for a moment, then shook her head. "Not we," she said. "I wish to speak with Bradwarden alone, at first."

Roger hid the wounded look before it could blossom on his face.

"'Course ye do!" Dainsey said. "But ye best be goin', then. Bradwarden's not one to stay about for long, from all that I heard o' him."

"You heard right," Pony agreed, and she pulled herself from the wooden chair and straightened her breeches and tunic, pointedly adjusting the pouch of gemstones hanging on her belt at her right hip. With a nod to her friends, she started away, skipping down the few steps to the main road of Dundalis village. With a look around at the quiet routines of the Dundalis night, she headed straight out to the north.

The forest night swallowed her in its profound blackness, but Pony was not the slightest bit afraid. These were the haunts of her childhood, where she and Elbryan had run the same trails that she moved along now. Far out of town, the music floating in the air all about her, she seemed no closer to finding Bradwarden than when she had been sitting on the porch. That was part of the centaur's magic. His song was simply part of the night and never seemed to emanate from anywhere specifically. It was just a general tune, filtering fully about the trees. Standing there, turning slowly, Pony could not begin to guess the direction of the piper.

With a determined nod, a reminder to herself of what Dasslerond had done to her, the woman reached into her gemstone pouch and brought forth a hematite, a soul stone. She moved it in close to her breast and closed her eyes, focusing her thoughts on the smooth feel of the gray stone. There was a depth to this one above all the other enchanted gemstones, an inviting richness, and into that gray swirl went Pony's thoughts, and into that gray swirl went Pony.

She escaped her mortal coil and moved out, looking back at herself as she stood motionless, clutching the stone that had become the link between her body and her spirit.

Free of her mortal bonds, Pony soared out on the same night breezes that carried the centaur's melody. She floated up high, above the canopy, and willed herself along at great speed, covering the distance more quickly than even mighty Symphony ever could.

When she found Bradwarden, she found, too, a warmth in her heart as profound as that she had felt when she had first seen Braumin and Roger again. There he was, eight hundred pounds of muscle. From a distance, an ignorant onlooker might have thought him a large rider on a small bay mount, but up close it became evident that the rider and mount were one and the same, for Bradwarden's muscular human torso, waist up, rose where the neck of his horse body should have begun.

Intent on his music, the centaur's eyes were closed as he held the bagpipes tucked under his powerful arm, while his hands worked the many openings along its neck. His hair was still black and wild, with a full beard and great curly locks, and though he was older now, no slackness had come into his corded muscles. The centaur looked as if he could crush stone under that powerful arm as easily as he was squeezing the air out of his musical pipes.

Pony's spirit slipped down near to him and hovered about for a few moments, until the centaur, apparently sensing the presence, popped open wide his intense eyes. His song ended with a discordant shriek.

The centaur glanced all around, seeming on his guard and confused.

Pony didn't move her spirit any closer. One of the great risks of spirit-walking was the ever-present instinct of the spirit to dive into a corporeal body. Spirit-walking was a prelude to possession, and possession, Pony knew, was nothing to be taken lightly. Still, the woman dared to reach out to Bradwarden, to impart to him a rush of warmth and friendship.

"Bah, but it can'no be," he muttered, and then he blinked and looked about curiously, for the sensation was gone.

With Bradwarden located, Pony wasted no time in setting out as soon as her spirit rushed back through the soul stone and into her corporeal body. She had marked the way well and knew enough of the area to measure accurately the distance and the time it would take her to reach the piping centaur. When she heard the song renewed, she gained confidence, and a bit of a smile, that she had reassured Bradwarden enough to keep him in place.

A short while later, the piping stopped again, but this time it wasn't because Bradwarden had felt the presence of a ghost, but rather, that he had recognized the presence of a dear old friend.

"Ah, so many're the times I've wondered if I might be seein' ye again, Pony o' Dundalis!" he said as she walked out of the shadows of the trees before him.

Pony's lips began to move, but she couldn't begin to get a word out at that moment, and so she just rushed across the small clearing and leaped up against the centaur, wrapping him in a tight hug.

"The queen is out without an army at her side?" Bradwarden asked, finally managing to push her back to arm's length. "But yer husband'd not be happy by that . . ."

He stopped and looked at her curiously.

"My husband is no more," Pony admitted. "King Danube has passed from this world."

"Then ye're on yer way to find Prince Midalis," the centaur reasoned, but his tone was quite telling to Pony, revealing to her that he held more trepidation at her announcement than perhaps he should have.

"When Prince Midalis comes through here, it will be at the head of his army," Pony replied. "And that army had better be a formidable one if he is to hold any hopes of taking the throne that is rightfully his."

Bradwarden looked at her knowingly and slowly nodded.

"You knew of him," Pony stated.

"Midalis?"

Pony shook her head and stepped back, out of the centaur's reach. "Do not play coy with me, Bradwarden. For too long, we have been friends. How many enemies have we stood against, side by side? Was it not Bradwarden himself who saved me and Elbryan at the Barbacan after we did battle with the demon dactyl?"

"Oh, but don't ye go reminding me o' that!" the centaur wailed dramatically, his tone going lighter. "Ye got no way o' knowin' how much a mountain hurts when it falls on ye, woman! Ye got—"

He stopped short, for Pony stared at him hard, not letting him change the subject and wriggle away so easily.

"You knew of him," Pony said again, sternly. "And I speak not of Prince Midalis. I speak of Aydrian, my son, and you knew of him!"

Bradwarden's lips tightened and seemed to disappear beneath his thick beard and mustache.

"You did!" Pony accused. "And you did not tell me! Were you in league with Lady Dasslerond all along, then? Do you find it so easy to deceive someone you name as friend?"

"No!" the centaur shot back. "And no." His voice softened, as did his expression. "I met yer boy two years ago, when winter began its turn to spring. He had Tempest and Hawkwing, and had brought Symphony to his side."

"So I have learned," Pony said bitterly.

"Ah, but it's a sad day for all the creatures o' the world when Symphony's at the side o' that one," the centaur lamented. "And no, woman, I was no party to Lady Dasslerond on this, and though I've e'er seen the wisdom o' the Touel'alfar, never before has such a mistake been made."

"You've known for years, and yet you did not come to me and tell me," said Pony in the voice of a friend betrayed, a voice thick with sadness and disappointment.

"And how might I be doing that?" the centaur said. "Ye're thinking I might be galloping into Ursal to talk to the queen?"

Pony looked at him and gave a sigh and a helpless shrug.

"Ah, but ye're right," the centaur admitted. "I should o' done more, though I wasn't knowing what I might be doing! But ye got to believe me on this, me Pony, me friend. Yer son's got not the blessing o' Bradwarden."

Pony shrugged again, then came forward and wrapped Bradwarden in a hug, and though that embrace was supposed to show the centaur that all was forgiven, was in effect supposed to comfort Bradwarden, as the centaur wrapped his muscular arms about Pony and held her even closer, it was she who was most comforted. The tears began to flow, and she let them come forth. Her shoulders bobbed with sobs, but Bradwarden held her steady and tight.

Sometime later, Pony moved back from the centaur and gave a little self-deprecating laugh as she reached up to wipe her tears away.

"What a silly old woman I've become," she said.

"Ye're neither," the centaur replied without hesitation. "If ye're feeling a bit old now, then ye've the right, I'm guessing. Not many who've seen such pain as Pony."

"And it is only beginning, I fear."

"Bah, it's one more thing for ye—for us—to go out and beat, don't ye know?" Bradwarden said.

Pony looked at him skeptically. "You want me to fight against my own son?"

Bradwarden didn't even bother to answer.

And Pony understood, and she gave another sigh of resignation.

"Prince Midalis will be riding hard to put things aright, and he's to be needing Pony at his side," the centaur said.

"And Pony's to be needing Bradwarden at her side, to hold her on her feet," the woman said.

The centaur flashed that typical grin of ultimate confidence and promised with a wink, "I'll keep the mountain off o' ye."

"Do not underestimate the Palmaris garrison," Duke Kalas warned. "They have been hardened by many trials over the years. Their leaders are veterans of battles."

"We can hunt them down and kill them, and quickly," argued Marcalo De'Unnero. "Before they cross through Caer Tinella, if we are fast."

Seated across the table from the two men, Aydrian leaned back in his chair. They were certain that Bishop Braumin had pulled a trick here in Palmaris, slipping a large portion of his trained militia out of Palmaris' northern gate before Aydrian's forces had arrived. Very shortly before, from what the young king and his men had learned in interrogating citizens of the conquered city. Now, a few days after the fall of St. Precious, they could assume that the escaped garrison was well on the way to Caer Tinella and Landsdown, the two largest towns north of Palmaris, halfway between the great city and the Timberlands region, where Aydrian's parents had lived.

"We must move quickly," De'Unnero implored Aydrian. "We have tarried too long already."

"The securing of Palmaris is all-important," remarked Duke Kalas. "Winter will fast descend upon this region and we must have complete control of the city, and have it in full operation."

Aydrian nodded. They had already discussed this at length. The first priority for this stage in strengthening his hold on the kingdom was to secure Palmaris in good order. The people would tighten their ties to Aydrian only if he did not too greatly disturb their lives. Thus, after the conquest, when his soldiers had charged through the streets, he had held them in great restraint. Palmaris had been taken with minimum casualties, and with even fewer repercussions to the conquered folk. One by one, the prisoners taken in the conquest had been interrogated, and almost all had been released. Aydrian's soldiers had told them to go home, to tend to their families, and to understand that the new and rightful king of Honce-the-Bear was a just and decent man who harbored no vengeance against those misinformed souls who had dared oppose him.

"You would allow an opposing army to run about the edges of the conquered land?" De'Unnero asked Kalas. "These garrison soldiers have family remaining within the city. Do you not believe that they will try to come back and reclaim their homes?"

Kalas laughed, as if that hardly mattered.

De'Unnero conceded the point. They had ten thousand Kingsmen in the Palmaris area, including the Allheart Knights. The Palmaris garrison might have put up a strong defensive stance against Aydrian's force if they were huddled behind the city's strong walls, but now, operating as the invader, the Palmaris garrison would be sorely outmanned.

"They will not turn back," Duke Kalas said to Aydrian. "They ran north because they are confused. They seek Prince Midalis to guide them, but they'll not reach Vanguard before the winter begins to blow. Let them go! Give Prince Midalis more mouths to feed through the difficult months of winter. It will be a ragtag and homesick bunch he marches back to Palmaris, do not doubt."

Aydrian nodded at the seemingly sound reasoning. The best estimate was that a few hundred men had fled to the north. He wasn't overly concerned. He had Palmaris, and that was the immediate goal. Now he could secure the immediate region about the city, perhaps as far north as Caer Tinella and Landsdown.

But the real prize, the one Aydrian coveted above all else, the one Aydrian wanted even more desperately than De'Unnero wanted St.-Mere-Abelle, lay not to the north, but to the west.

Of course, he hadn't told his commanders of that little side trip just yet.

"Prince Midalis remains a threat only if he can find his way to weak spots in our ever-lengthening line," Aydrian remarked. "He will try to strike behind us, or strike wherever our main force is not. He will not be able to do so before winter, nor will he be able to find any way around us if we force him to march all the way from Vanguard.

"Let us secure our hold from Entel to Ursal, from Ursal to Palmaris," the young king reasoned. "Let us show the people of these most populous parts of Honce-the-Bear that the Kingdom of Aydrian will bring them peace and prosperity, for that is all they want, after all. They care little for the name of their king. They care for the food on their tables."

"Midalis' claim is no small thing," said De'Unnero. "He will inspire many against us."

"The longer we keep him away, the less inspiration he will provide," Duke Kalas put in. He looked to Aydrian and gave a knowing smirk. "It is of great importance that we determine the prince's route, and that we make his trail as long and difficult as possible. The farther from Ursal that we do battle with Prince Midalis, if it must come to that, the less support he will find."

"Soon enough," Aydrian replied, and he looked to De'Unnero.

The discussions of the secular kingdom sat heavily on De'Unnero's strong shoulders, and he sat there, tapping the tips of his fingers together before him.

"Patience, my friend," Aydrian said to him. "We will turn our eyes to St.-Mere-Abelle soon enough."

"Not soon enough for me," De'Unnero admitted.

"We are not yet ready," Duke Kalas put in. "Trust me when I say that I wish to see the fall of St.-Mere-Abelle as much as do you! But we must control the sea, and that we cannot do with winter approaching. And we must isolate Prince Midalis."

"We will take the sea, and the Mantis Arm," Aydrian assured them both. "When we approach St.-Mere-Abelle, it will be from the east and the west, with every other abbey of Honce-the-Bear already secured, save St. Belfour of Vanguard. Fio Bou-raiy will find no support from without."

Marcalo De'Unnero nodded, and worked hard to keep the simmering anger from his expression. He knew the plan, of course, for it had been an intricate part of his and Olin's design long before Aydrian had ever ascended the throne. But Aydrian had altered that plan without consult by dangling a carrot before Abbot Olin that the old fool could not resist. How might Aydrian facilitate the sweep along the eastern coast of Honce-the-Bear with his entire mercenary army diverted to the south, to Jacintha?

"Time is our ally, not our enemy," Aydrian said to the monk, as if reading his thoughts exactly. "A church must be maintained from without, not within, and as we bring more and more abbeys around to our way of thinking, the present Father Abbot's influence will shrink and shrink to nothingness. We will speak to the people while Bou-raiy and his companions fester in the dark corridors of St.-Mere-Abelle."

He stopped and nodded, leaned back and smiled, as if everything was going along right on schedule.

Aydrian dismissed the courier with a wave of his hand, and when the man started to argue, the young king put on a great scowl.

The courier left without further delay.

"Abbot Olin must have dispatched him to the north to find us before he had gone halfway through Yorkey County," De'Unnero remarked.

Aydrian looked at the monk, who seemed more amused than anything else. The courier had come into Palmaris with an urgent request from Abbot Olin, begging that more soldiers be released to him for his efforts in Jacintha.

"Olin cannot even know the disposition of the enemy allayed before him," Aydrian remarked.

"Likely he has come to know that some of the mercenaries we hired on our march to Ursal have returned to their homes," reasoned De'Unnero, and he noted that Aydrian excluded the use of Olin's title—not a minor oversight.

"That was not unexpected."

"Abbot Olin desires Jacintha more than you can understand," De'Unnero went on.

"He has ten thousand hired mercenaries, a fleet of bloodthirsty pirates, several Ursal warships with well-trained crews, and the garrison of Entel, two thousand strong and second in Honce-the-Bear in experience and equipment only to the Allhearts. Having that force, if he cannot assume control of a nation torn asunder, he is hardly deserving of our respect."

Again, the level of disrespect toward Olin coming from the young king surprised De'Unnero. "Do not take Jacintha lightly," he warned.

"The Behrenese are killing each other, by all accounts."

"True enough, but that may change quickly when a foreign army walks into the great coastal city. Abbot Olin is being cautious. We still do not know the disposition of the Coastpoint Guards manning the eastern coast. If they do not come over to King Aydrian, Abbot Olin will be forced to hold his garrison in place to ward any possible incursions."

"The Coastpoint Guards will not go against Entel!" Aydrian insisted. "They are but a few hundred in number, if all joined in the effort, and Entel is a great city. And the Abellican brothers in Entel serve Olin."

"The brothers of St. Bondabruce," De'Unnero reminded. "There is a second abbey, St. Rontlemore, whose abbot and brothers have never been friends of Abbot Olin."

"A minor abbey compared to St. Bondabruce," Aydrian argued.

De'Unnero conceded the point with a nod. Indeed, it seemed to him as if Abbot Olin should have more than enough strength to accomplish his mission, if there was indeed opportunity for Honce-the-Bear now to insinuate itself into the affairs of Behren. Olin had all the assets that Aydrian had claimed, and more, for the largest cache of nonmagical gemstones taken from Pimaninicuit remained in St. Bondabruce, and with that wealth, Olin should be able to swell his ranks two- or threefold if necessary.

Still, the level of agitation within Aydrian at that time struck the monk as curious.

"Abbot Olin will not fail us," he said to the young king.

"I fear that I may have to travel there," Aydrian replied.

"It is warmer, particularly with winter coming on in full. We will find no trouble from Midalis until the late spring, at least, and probably not until midsummer or beyond. If you are needed for the efforts in Jacintha . . ."

"No!" Aydrian said flatly, his tone surprising the monk. "I have business here."

De'Unnero looked at him closely and curiously. "What is it?"

Aydrian moved as if to answer, but stopped suddenly and waved his hand. "It will all sort out, and soon enough," he said. "If Abbot Olin requires me, then I will go to him, and swiftly."

"Even on that horse of yours, it will take you a month and more to reach Entel."

"There are ways to make a horse run faster," Aydrian assured the monk. "There are methods with the gemstones to leech the strength from others and give it to the horse, and Symphony will prove most receptive."

"Two weeks, then," De'Unnero conceded.

"If I am needed, and I hope that it will not come to that."

"If you go, you go with the understanding that we are in complete control of Westerhonce," said the monk. "The two cities to the north will fall to

Kalas in short order, and he will sweep out to the west, securing all the land."

Aydrian nodded, and with that, De'Unnero turned to go. He still had much to do in sorting out the captured brothers of St. Precious. Some had shown signs of possible conversion, though most, predictably, had remained stubborn.

"If I go to Jacintha, you cannot join me," Aydrian remarked before De'Unnero had gotten out of the door.

De'Unnero turned about and considered the young king, considered his tone most of all.

"I'll not leave Duke Kalas alone here with such a force," Aydrian explained, a perfectly logical though ultimately unconvincing addition.

"I have no desire to travel anywhere but to the east," De'Unnero assured him. "To the gates of St.-Mere-Abelle, where I reclaim my Order and church in the name of St. Abelle."

Aydrian agreed, offering yet another nod, but then as De'Unnero turned once more to go, he surprised the monk once again by adding, "But I would wish Sadye to travel with me."

The blunt remark froze De'Unnero in place. In the quiet moments that followed, he replayed all the looks he had seen Sadye giving to Aydrian over the last few days—nay, over the last few weeks! Sadye was so much closer to Aydrian's age! And De'Unnero understood that which most drew the attention and elicited the excitement from the bard. She loved power and she loved danger. She had welcomed De'Unnero into her arms because of the thrill of dealing with so dangerous a creature as the weretiger. With that serving as the basis for her lust, how could one such as Sadye not be drawn to Aydrian Boudabras? He was young and handsome and as great a warrior as any in the world, De'Unnero included. He was king, and his domain would soon enough encompass all the known world! And he was dangerous. Oh yes, De'Unnero saw that clearly. Aydrian was a dangerous young man, one who was growing more confident and more powerful by the day.

The monk turned slowly to regard his ally, who had been once, but certainly no more, his student.

"You wish Sadye to leave my side to accompany you?"

"Of course." It was said so simply, so matter-of-factly.

De'Unnero didn't want to have this fight at this time. "I cannot be without the both of you," he said. "There is the little matter of the weretiger."

"I can give you complete control of the beast," Aydrian promised.

De'Unnero's eyes narrowed.

"I can," Aydrian said to that doubting expression. "I can put the beast back inside of you because I know where to find your humanity. I can show you that, and teach you to use the gemstone to reach the desired level of calm."

De'Unnero didn't reply.

"I offer you freedom," Aydrian said after a long pause, with no response forthcoming from the stunned monk. "I offer you independence from me."

De'Unnero didn't reply.

"It must come to that, must it not?" Aydrian asked. "I cannot remain in St.-Mere-Abelle with you, after all, once that place is taken. I presume that you will rule the Abellican Church of Honce-the-Bear from that great mother abbey, while Abbot Olin rules the Abellican Church of Behren from either Entel or Jacintha. If that victory is to come to pass, you must learn to hold control over the beast by yourself."

"And in exchange, I am to give over to you the woman I love?" came the skeptical reply.

Aydrian shrugged, and De'Unnero saw that he, too, was not ready to have this fight at this time. He was probing.

"Her road will be hers to choose, in the end," Aydrian admitted.

"Her road was already chosen." With that, the monk turned again to leave.

"And what life will you offer to her in St.-Mere-Abelle?" Aydrian questioned, a parting shot that surely stung De'Unnero. For indeed, what life would Sadye find in the dark corridors of that male-dominated abbey?

The monk had no answers. He walked out of the room, but Aydrian's voice followed him.

"I offer her the world," the brash young king said. "The *whole* world!"

❖ 11 ❖

Posturing

A cold wind blew strong in Belli'mar Juraviel's face as the trail wound about to the northern slope of the mountain. The ground fell away before him, descending to a blanket of thick gray mist, covering a wide vale.

How well Juraviel knew these trails about his homeland. How well he knew the valley before him, Andur'Blough Inninness, with its tree city of Caer'alfar, the home of the Touel'alfar. He had been gone for nearly five years, and had been on the road often before that over the last two decades.

Now it was good to be home, though the specter of Aydrian, King Aydrian, held his smile in check.

He looked back along the trail, to see his companions, Doc'alfar all, moving along.

"What have you done?" came a sharp voice among the trees to Juraviel's left, long before the elf's companions had caught up to him.

Despite the uncharacteristically harsh tone, Juraviel recognized the voice of To'el Dallia. He turned and scoured the trees, and sorted his kinswoman out from amid the tangle of branches.

"Long-lost cousins, too far removed," Juraviel replied solemnly.

To'el Dallia moved to the end of one branch, near to Juraviel, and studied him closely. She wanted to say that it was good to see him—he could see the warm familiarity clear upon her sparkling features. But there, too, resided a dark cloud, a deeper expression of true concern.

"It is no time to bring strangers to Andur'Blough Inninness," To'el Dallia scolded. "Go to them and turn them away, and be fast about it!"

Juraviel nearly laughed at the absurd remark, and would have had he not caught the hints of deep and sincere distress resonating within his friend. For there was never a proper time to bring strangers to Andur'Blough Inninness! Few outside the Touel'alfar were ever permitted to look upon the beauty of the elven valley, and those were only the rangers-in-training, or other unexpected guests given shelter in times of great distress, as Lady Dasslerond had done with Juraviel's human traveling companions, refugees all, when the demon dactyl had come upon them on the open road so many years before. That last unexpected and uninvited incursion had also brought the demon Bestesbulzibar himself to the elven valley, and the profound stain that the creature had left behind, the growing rot upon the beautiful ground, had led to . . .

All of this, Juraviel understood, and only then did the implications of Dasslerond's uncharacteristically generous act that day on the open road ring true to him. Because of the presence of the dactyl in the elven valley, because of the stain and the growing rot, Lady Dasslerond had sent Brynn south to free To-gai, thus securing a potential escape route for the Touel'alfar should they ever be forced out of their valley. Because of that stain, Juraviel had gone south with Brynn, whereas rangers would normally have departed alone. It was his presence that had saved the girl from the normally unmerciful—to humans at least—Doc'alfar.

And because of that stain, Dasslerond had taken Jilseponie's baby, and had raised him to be her weapon against the demon sickness.

All of it resulting from that one incident on the road.

With a helpless shrug, Juraviel realized that if what he had heard about the rise of Aydrian in the east was true, the implications had only begun to play out.

He looked over at To'el Dallia then, still visible though she had retreated somewhat, and he noted the curious, even stunned, expression on her face. As if sensing his stare at her, the female turned to regard him once more, and asked again, "What have you done?"

"I have brought our cousins home," Juraviel answered. He swept his arm out to the south, to the approaching band. "I give you Cazzira, my wife, and among those beside her is King Eltiraaz himself, who leads the Doc'alfar of Tymwyvenne."

The names meant nothing to To'el Dallia of course, except for one. "Doc'alfar?" she echoed, hardly able to get the name out of her breathless throat, and so stunned was she that she apparently hadn't even registered the fact that Juraviel had just announced one of them as his wife.

Curious stares, some showing great alarm, and a cold wind followed Captain Al'u'met's every step.

The sailor from Behren was no less curious in looking back at the scenes around him, the deerskin tents and the blond-haired people. Giants they seemed! Though Al'u'met was not a short man, he surely felt like one in the southern reaches of Alpinador. At last the good captain understood so much more vividly the mighty reputation of the warrior Alpinadoran barbarians. Not a man in this small village had an arm thinner than the Al'u'met's leg, discounting the Bearmen who had accompanied him, an entourage which included Prince Midalis and Abbot Haney of St. Belfour.

It was more than a little intimidating to the captain, but Prince Midalis seemed to know his way about the settlement and was obviously recognized by most of the barbarians. Midalis held himself with regal bearing. He was in his forties, but still had the physique and energy of a man fifteen years his junior. He looked much like his brother, King Danube, though he had ever been of a leaner build than the somewhat portly king. Both had the thick black hair of the Ursal line and the penetrating blue eyes, orbs that could shrivel most men under their intense stare. Midalis wore a beard, trimmed short and low on his strong jawline.

Beside him, Abbot Haney seemed a frail figure. Thin and well-groomed, the man walked with a much stiffer gait than did Midalis, the result of spending many, many hours seated at a desk, working with quill and ink rather than with heavy tools or weapons. He had gone bald on top, which made his forehead seem ridiculously high, and he had developed a laziness in one eye that made it droop a bit. Still, though the recent years had not been kind, the abbot carried himself with dignity and poise.

It struck the tall and dark-skinned Al'u'met how odd-looking a trio they truly were.

A large man, even by Alpinadoran standards, emerged from a tent near the back of the settlement. His hair was long and thick, with feathers woven in on one side. He wore a sleeveless deerskin tunic and had a leather strap tied about his right upper arm, which only emphasized his enormous muscles.

His features were strong and stern, severe even, but he did smile when he saw the visitors.

"Bruinhelde!" Prince Midalis called to him. "It has been too long, my brother!"

The large man stepped forward to greet the prince. They clasped hands, but the barbarian pulled Midalis closer, wrapping him in a great hug. He glanced over at Al'u'met often, though, apparently almost as surprised by the appearance of a Behrenese man in Alpinador as were the other villagers.

"You found us too easily, eh?" the large man said in somewhat broken Bearman language. "We should do better to cover our tracks when we travel, if a simple southerner can follow them."

"Only because this southerner was trained by Andacanavar of the north," Prince Midalis was quick to reply, and that brought an even wider smile to the barbarian's face. "Where is our friend these days?"

"He travels about the northland," Bruinhelde started to answer, but he stopped suddenly. "Forgive me," he begged and he half turned and swept his hand invitingly toward his tent. "Join me. We will have much food and strong mead."

Prince Midalis nodded and motioned for his friends to follow him into the tent, and each ducked in turn beneath the doeskin flap. Though Bruinhelde was the leader of all the southern tribes of Alpinador, there was little in the way of luxury or ornamentation in here. The place was well stocked in comfortable furs, though, and soon enough, Bruinhelde's attendants made good on his promise, bringing heaping plates of food and skins full of strong Alpinadoran mead.

"You know Abbot Haney," Prince Midalis started, and the barbarian leader nodded and offered a warm look to the man. "And I give you Captain Al'u'met of the good *Saudi Jacintha*, a merchant ship sailing out of the great city of Palmaris."

"The comforts of my tribe to you," the barbarian said graciously. "You are a long way from the water. Though I do remember you, from the wedding of King Danube and Jilseponie."

Al'u'met bowed slightly, impressed.

"Captain Al'u'met came to me with confirmation of disturbing news, my friend," Prince Midalis explained. "News of the death of my brother."

"It wounds my heart," the barbarian replied genuinely, after giving Midalis a solemn look and nod. "I named King Danube as my friend."

"There is more," Prince Midalis began, and he glanced over at the captain, who had sailed into Vanguard with the tales of Aydrian Boudabras and Marcalo De'Unnero. "And this, too, will wound your heart, I fear. We come to you because it is important that your people know what is happening in the kingdom to the south. We come to you because we doubt that the new imposter king of Honce-the-Bear will honor the border between our countries if his army marches this far to the north."

"Imposter king?" Bruinhelde echoed, surprise and anger equally evident in his tone. "What of Jilseponie, then? What of Midalis?"

The prince turned to Al'u'met and motioned for him to begin. And so the captain recounted the tales of the events in the southland again, in great detail.

Bruinhelde listened, riveted, for more than two hours, and when Al'u'met finished, the Alpinadoran leader sat there for a long while, digesting all the information. "What do you ask of our friendship?" he asked Midalis.

The prince glanced around at his two companions, then back at Bruinhelde, his expression alone conveying his sincere gratitude that this great warrior leader had even deigned to ask such a question.

The problem was, in that time of confusion, Prince Midalis didn't really have an answer.

It was with great reluctance that Master Viscenti finally turned his back on the Masur Delaval and Palmaris truly to begin his second journey of the month to St.-Mere-Abelle. The monk had tarried long about the eastern banks of the great lazy river, grabbing every tidbit of news that had filtered across the waters. But finally, with Palmaris secured by the forces of Aydrian, the fleet had turned to the east, securing those cities along the riverbanks, and even off-loading legions of Kingsmen, who struck out on expeditionary missions about the region.

Marlboro Viscenti found himself in a long line of refugees fleeing for St.-Mere-Abelle, and when he had at last arrived at the great and ancient monastery, he found a city of tents on the fields before the gates, with nearly as many people as had congregated there during the time of the great rosy plague! They were afraid, Viscenti understood. Afraid and confused, and thus looking to the one solid foundation upon which they could throw their trust.

He wondered if Fio Bou-raiy, who had been no friend to the plague victims, would be more generous with this current crowd.

Inside, Viscenti found the great abbey all astir, and he was stopped with practically every step, hordes of brothers congregating about him, begging for information. He told them all as little as possible that would allow him an escape, for he had been met at the abbey gates by emissaries of the Father Abbot, bidding him to come straightaway for an audience. Finally, with help from some of the Father Abbot's closest masters, the visitor managed to get to the private audience chamber.

Fio Bou-raiy was obviously not in good spirits this day. He met Viscenti with a scowl and a simple question, "What happened?"

"Aydrian happened," the monk from St. Precious replied. And then he recounted all that he knew of the fall of Palmaris.

Even as he had finished telling the story of the battle proper, Fio Bou-raiy interrupted. "We have heard that Bishop Braumin has spoken in favor of this new king. And in favor of Abbot Olin and Marcalo De'Unnero." There was no mistaking the anger behind those words, a sign that the ever-suspicious Bou-raiy was believing the stories of Braumin's· capitulation completely.

Master Viscenti lowered his eyes, for he had heard the same tales from many of the folk fleeing the great city. With their own ears they had heard Bishop Braumin's endorsement of King Aydrian, so the informants from the conquered Palmaris had said.

"I have heard the same," the nervous master admitted. "And it has troubled me all these days since the fall of Palmaris."

"A fall, or a surrender?" Father Abbot Bou-raiy asked sternly.

"A fall!" Master Viscenti insisted. "I witnessed that with my own eyes. The folk of Palmaris fought valiantly, but they were overwhelmed! The brothers of St. Precious held on stubbornly, until flames licked the walls of the abbey and the forces of Aydrian forced their way in!"

"You saw all of this, and yet you escaped?"

"I watched much from across the river, and that which I believed I saw was confirmed by the first folk fleeing the city," Viscenti answered.

"The same folk who claim that Bishop Braumin endorsed the new king and new Father Abbot?"

Viscenti started to give a helpless sigh, but then answered, "No," with some conviction. "No," he reasoned, and things started to sort themselves out a bit more clearly in his mind. "Those last reports of Bishop Braumin's endorsements came later. Likely it is a disinformation campaign by the imposter king. Perhaps these people reporting the tragedy were placed—"

"Spies?" Fio Bou-raiy interrupted, and he shook his head in dismissal. "No, Master Viscenti. You have seen some of the same people as I, no doubt.

They have come here of sincere intention and sincere confusion. And many tell the same tale."

Then Viscenti did give that sigh.

"And what answer have you for this?" Fio Bou-raiy asked. "Has Bishop Braumin lost his faith? Is this the same man who stood against Father Abbot Markwart when all seemed lost?"

"It is!" Master Viscenti insisted.

"Then what answer have you?" the Father Abbot demanded.

Master Viscenti lowered his gaze, for though he did not doubt the reports from so many, he did not have any idea of what might have happened, or of how this might have happened.

Of course, neither Viscenti nor Fio Bou-raiy nor anyone else in the room had any idea that Aydrian Boudabras was powerful enough with the soul stone to possess the body of one as learned and formidable as Braumin Herde, and force that mouth to say whatever he wanted it to say.

"Then you will need us more than we need you," King Eltiraaz remarked after Lady Dasslerond had revealed to them and to Juraviel the truth of the new king of Honce-the-Bear.

Juraviel, now fluent in the languages of Doc'alfar and Touel'alfar—languages that were not far apart—translated Eltiraaz's words, taking great care that every inflection was properly represented. For Eltiraaz wasn't being in any way condescending, nor was he bargaining for anything from a position of power. He was making a statement, and in generous tones that made it quite clear that he intended for his people to aid the Touel'alfar in this possibly dangerous time.

Juraviel had been stressing that to Dasslerond throughout that entire first week after his return to Andur'Blough Inninness. At first, the Lady had been incensed to learn that he had stepped so boldly as to bring anyone to the secret valley, even though the news of who Juraviel had brought in had surely stunned her, as it had stunned all of the Touel'alfar. Few among Juraviel's people even suspected that the Doc'alfar still survived.

Gradually through that week, though, Dasslerond had come to agree with Juraviel's decision to bring Cazzira and the Doc'alfar king, and that understanding alone had told Juraviel just how dire the protective Lady considered the situation with Aydrian to be.

"If Aydrian is all that I suspect, then you will find our need to be a mutual thing," Lady Dasslerond countered anyway.

Juraviel caught the grimace of Cazzira, who understood his native language as well as he understood hers. He nodded her way, a reassurance that his Lady's response was not meant to incite any hard feelings, then correctly translated to King Eltiraaz, adding his own comment that it was good that they had come together at this time.

King Eltiraaz studied the Lady of Caer'alfar for a long while. "How do we proceed?" he asked. "If this young Aydrian is as powerful and vengeful as you believe, and he commands the tens of thousands of human warriors, then what are we to do?"

Lady Dasslerond had no direct answer, but she reasoned, "We must stay as far from Aydrian as possible. And we must learn all that we can about him and his intentions. We may have allies in our fight, his mother among them."

"And what of Brynn?" Juraviel asked. "She should be informed."

Lady Dasslerond considered the prospect for some time, wondering if the rise of Brynn Dharielle would offer some hope, a retreat for all the elves, perhaps, or an ally in the potential war against Aydrian.

"Are the Doc'alfar familiar with the *brista'qu'veni*?" she asked Juraviel, referring to the Touel'alfar magical way of throwing their voices to the evening breeze, a whisper on the wind that could carry across great expanses of ground to others of their kind who knew how to interpret the message.

Juraviel started to translate the question, but Eltiraaz stopped him with an upraised hand, obviously understanding, and nodded.

"There is a way to strengthen such an idea," the King of Tymwyvenne added, and he reached into his pouch and brought forth a shining purple sapphire, a gemstone as spectacular as that which Lady Dasslerond kept. The Doc'alfar lifted the stone toward Dasslerond. *"A'bu'kin Dinoniel,"* Eltiraaz intoned. "The gem of the air and the mists."

"Tel'ne'kin Dinoniel," Lady Dasslerond responded, and she brought forth her shining emerald and moved it up beside the sapphire. "The gem of the precious land."

"Sundered on the day of tou and doc," Eltiraaz went on, turning to those surprised onlookers about him. "The emerald a gift to the Tou, that they could hold their valley precious and safe. The sapphire a gift to the Doc, that veiling mists would follow their retreat. There is a familiarity within these sister stones that once joined their owners, the Lord and Lady of Andur'Blough Inninness, in harmony."

"Then let us find again that bond, cousin King," Dasslerond suggested. "And let us organize a line, north to south, from Andur'Blough Inninness to Tymwyvenne."

"And farther south, through the mountains and the lair of Agradeleous to the steppes of To-gai and the ears of Brynn Dharielle," King Eltiraaz added.

"The dragon will allow it?" Dasslerond asked.

"He is a friendly beast, though he might require a fine tale or twelve to allow passage," Juraviel explained. "And of course, none should disturb Agradeleous' treasure. He would not look kindly upon such an act, though if he holds anything of value to our cause, he might be persuaded to share."

"A dragon who shares with alfar," Dasslerond mused. "It seems such an improbable thing."

Across the way, Eltiraaz understood and chuckled. "Tylwyn Doc and Tylwyn Tou reunited in a common cause," he replied, and he echoed Dasslerond's phrase perfectly. "It seems such an improbable thing."

Lady Dasslerond accepted that with a generous shrug.

All of the Touel'alfar gathered in a circle on the wide field outside of Caer'alfar, the same field where Brynn had been named as ranger, and Elbryan before her. In the center of the circle, which also included Cazzira and the other visiting Doc'alfar commoners, face-to-face, stood Lady Dasslerond and King Eltiraaz. All gathered sang a common song, one known to Touel'alfar and Doc'alfar alike, of a time far, far removed, when the race of Tou were one.

"As we were sundered, so let us be joined," Lady Dasslerond intoned.

"Not two peoples, but one," replied Eltiraaz.

"Of differing bodies but like hearts," said Dasslerond.

"Of common purpose and common goal."

Lady Dasslerond began lifting her hand first, palm up, the emerald showing clearly. Eltiraaz did likewise, until their hands were above them, side by side. In the dark night, the gemstones began to shine—an inner glow, Juraviel realized, and not a reflection of the rising moon.

Lady Dasslerond brought the emerald straight over her head, and said, *"A'bu'kin Dinoniel!"* That was the name of Eltiraaz's gem, of course, but when the wielder of the sister gem spoke the words, the emerald pulsed suddenly, sending a ring of green light out from its sides. The light drifted down, encircling Lady Dasslerond until it settled on the ground about her feet.

"Tel'ne'kin Dinoniel!" Eltiraaz cried, lifting the sapphire above his head, and a purple ring pulsed out from the gemstone, similarly drifting down to the Doc'alfar king's feet.

Both began to repeat the phrases over and over, and more rings came forth, cascading down across their blurring forms. And then the two leaders began to turn circles, stepping out as they did so that the pattern of the ring elongated and crossed through each other now and again.

King Eltiraaz reached out to Lady Dasslerond, and she took his hand and allowed him to pull her in close, both still spinning and reciting the name of the other's enchanted gemstone, and rings of purple and green cascaded down about both of them.

"A'bu'eh'tel'kin Dinoniel," both said together, which referred to both at once as the gem of earth and air and mist, and the rings shifted, blending together, and instead of just falling to the ground, they seemed to come alive with the dance, rolling up and down the spinning pair.

Despite all the danger in the world, Belli'mar Juraviel could not feel anything but joy at that triumphant moment.

At his side, his pregnant Doc'alfar wife squeezed his hand.

CHAPTER

❖ 12 ❖

Surrounded by Allies?

Brynn ran her hand along the deep trio of scratches torn into the wall. She had asked Agradeleous to clearly mark the way back to his lair using a series of codes she and the dragon had devised, and so he had, with great claw marks showing at every fork and intersection. Some showed the correct path, others revealed the incorrect path, and Brynn knew the subtle differences in the dragon-claw signposts.

When she and the dragon had worked out the coding, it had been with hopes that she would never have to use them. The mere thought of Agradeleous elicited mixed feelings in the woman. On the one hand, the dragon had undeniably aided her in freeing To-gai; without him, she never would have been able to so frustrate the Behrenese in their own lands. In addition to his obvious battle prowess, Agradeleous had actually provided Brynn with a method of quickly moving her warriors up and down the cliff divide that separated To-gai from Behren. Also, the dragon's great speed and tremendous strength had allowed Brynn to keep her force supplied while they were out in the hostile open desert.

Without Agradeleous, Brynn could never have won against the Behrenese, could never have forced a truce that brought freedom back to the To-gai-ru tribes and transformed the city of Dharyan into Dharyan-Dharielle, a place where the cultures could exchange goods and understanding. This city, Brynn believed, would serve as the bridge between the peoples and would shine as the hope that Behren and To-gai would live in peace as separate and complementary lands.

But the gains of the dragon had come with a price—a terrible price for Brynn Dharielle. To defeat the Behrenese, she had been forced to turn loose the power of the dragon, and that awful, indiscriminate might had shaken her to the fabric of her conscience. She had watched Agradeleous level settlements and turn avenues into walls of flame. She had heard the screams of the dying—she heard them still, echoing in her dreams. Brynn's greatest fear was not that the Behrenese would conquer her people once more; it was that she would be forced to use Agradeleous again, to loose that terrible weapon once more.

All the way back here in the northern stretches of To-gai, with Pagonel by her side, Brynn had told herself and the mystic that she would rouse Agradeleous for scouting purposes, and perhaps to hold as a threat to keep Yatol Tohen Bardoh in check.

She truly wanted to believe that.

Every claw mark in the long tunnel had reminded her of the sheer strength of the dragon. Every claw mark had brought a shudder.

But she persevered, forcing away her own guilt and pointedly telling herself of that gain Agradeleous had brought. Her people were free; they were not only finding again the old ways of the To-gai-ru, but because of Dharyan-Dharielle, they were reaching further, examining the more modern world and allowing it to slip quietly into their rich culture. To-gai-ru children in Dharyan-Dharielle were even learning to read in the great new library Brynn had assembled from the remains of the formerly glorious Library of Pruda.

Coming to retrieve Agradeleous, however, brought her always back to the notion that those gains had not been realized without cost.

"You cannot raise an army sufficient to keep Yatol Bardoh from conquering Jacintha, should he move against that city," Pagonel reminded her, as if sensing her doubts. "You would have to rouse all of To-gai. Would they heed such a call to go to the defense of Behren? And should you ask that of them?"

Brynn looked at him, standing quietly in the flickering torchlight. They had gone over this before, of course, when Pagonel and Pechter Dan Turk had arrived in Dharyan-Dharielle with the news of Bardoh's mounting power. Setting the defenses of Dharyan-Dharielle in place, Brynn and the mystic had quickly raced off to the west and north, to the entrance of the Path of Starless Nights. She had left Tanalk Grenk, her trusted advisor, to see to the defense of the city and the rousing of the To-gai-ru riders, though she wasn't sure yet what she might do with that army.

"I am confident that we can hold our city against Bardoh," she replied, though that wasn't really answering the mystic's question, because she really had no answer to the mystic's question.

"Your people have found freedom again, and nothing short of a complete and united Behrenese invasion will truly threaten that," Pagonel agreed. "And I do not think that Yatol Bardoh will go against Dharyan-Dharielle at this time. And should he make that error, yes, all of To-gai will rise against him. He knows that. He has too much to lose, since his real prize lies in the east, along the coast.

"If you wish to go to the aid of Yatol Mado Wadon, as we implied in the truce, and as would obviously be to the longer-term benefit of your own people, you will need Agradeleous," the mystic finished bluntly.

"Longer-term benefit?"

"You cannot deny that if Tohen Bardoh wins in Jacintha, he will soon enough turn his sights upon Dharyan-Dharielle."

Brynn started to respond, to argue, but she bit back the retort. Pagonel was right. Of course he was right, and as much as she hated to admit it, the suffering that Agradeleous might soon bring to the land would pale beside the tragedy of allowing the wicked Tohen Bardoh to take control of Behren and unite the kingdom under his imperialistic designs.

The woman pressed on, telling herself determinedly that time was running short. For all she knew, the fight for Jacintha might already be on in full.

Later that same day, the pair heard the rhythmic rumbling sound of a sleeping dragon.

Soon after, they came out of the narrowing tunnel into a wider chamber stacked with coins and assorted items that glittered in the torchlight. It wasn't the main chamber of the dragon, Brynn knew, for that one, where she had first encountered Agradeleous beside Juraviel and Cazzira, was much larger and much more treasure-filled. This area was barely large enough to admit the dragon. No other exits were apparent, though the chamber's sheer walls climbed high and straight, and there seemed to be a ledge far overhead.

Brynn looked to her companion, to see him studying the piles of glittering objects intently. Following his lead, she quickly figured out what had so caught his interest. There was little of real value here—even the coins were of silver or copper, mostly.

"Aha!" came a sudden roar above them, and then a sliding sound from the tunnel they had just exited, a portcullis or stone block, perhaps, told them that they had walked into a trap.

Instinctively, Brynn spun back toward the tunnel, to see that it was indeed blocked by a solid piece of stone. She swung back and drew out Flame-dancer, her elven sword, setting its blade afire with but a thought to the ruby embedded in its hilt. Her eyes darted about, taking note that Pagonel was gone from sight, and then she looked up, taking note of the attacker.

"Agradeleous!" she called, even as the dragon's great head came over the ledge, the long serpentine neck sweeping down at her.

The dragon stopped, his reptilian eyes going wide. He gave a snort, smoke rushing out the nostrils set on either side of his long snout. "Ah, little one!" he said, his tone suddenly changed. "For the second time, I mistook you for a thief!"

The dragon gave her the once-over, and Brynn, given the source of most of the armor she wore and the sword she carried, could only shrug.

"Yes, but that first time, you were a thief, weren't you, little one?" Agradeleous said, and he gave a chuckling snort, which sent a burst of flame and smoke out his nostrils.

"I borrowed the items," Brynn corrected, sliding the sword away. "For a lifetime—my lifetime!—and that is not so long a time to one such as Agradeleous."

"Not so long indeed!" the dragon agreed. "And consider the items yours, gifts from Agradeleous to one who has given him so many fine tales and memories! Greetings again, little one! It does me good to see you here, but I am surprised that you chose to come alone."

Brynn glanced all about.

"Not so alone, great wurm," Pagonel said from the side, and the mystic stepped out of the shadows, and truly it seemed as if he was materializing out of nothingness. To Brynn and the dragon, who had come to understand the Jhesta Tu well, it was not so surprising.

"Ah, mystic, welcome!" Agradeleous boomed. "Do you like my trap? A dragon cannot be too careful, you understand, now that his lair is well-known. You humans number a fair portion of thieves among your lot."

"And since all of your gains were honestly earned . . ." Pagonel dryly remarked.

"Code of dragons, mystic," Agradeleous explained in a similar tone. "Eat the owner and keep everything on him that sparkles."

Pagonel looked around. "You have been well nourished."

"This?" the dragon asked skeptically. "This is but a trifling!" He lowered his head nearly to the ground. "Climb atop my head that I can take you to my true chambers, my friends."

As soon as they were up in the larger chamber above the ledge, the dragon stepped back and began to reshape its form, bones cracking and breaking apart, shifting until Agradeleous wasn't too much larger than the two humans, though he still projected a much larger and heavier aura.

"Come along and see the splendor of my gains," the dragon said.

For Pagonel's benefit, Brynn allowed Agradeleous to give them the grand tour through the several chambers stocked with the treasure of the ages, roomfuls of glittering gold coins and gems and jewels. Each room glittered with pieces of crafted armor and shining weapons, everything from the delicate and curving Chezhou-lei swords of wrapped metal to the heavier broadswords favored in Honce-the-Bear. Every so often, the dragon would stop near to one piece and recount the great battle in which he had won the trinket. And grand stories they were, of the world from a time long before Brynn and Pagonel had been born, before their parents' parents' parents and beyond had been born.

"You have come with a new tale, I hope," the dragon said when at last the tour was ended.

Brynn looked to Pagonel. "A new tale, indeed," she said, "and perhaps a new adventure."

That widened the dragon's eyes again, and as the surprise wore away, Agradeleous looked at Brynn curiously. "So soon, little one?" the dragon asked. "What trouble have you started this time?"

Though she had seen that same expression so many times over the last couple of years, Brynn could not help but smile when she noted the look on Pechter Dan Turk's face when she introduced him to her new friend.

Pechter Dan Turk, of course, knew of the wurm—Brynn had been named "the Dragon of To-gai" for a reason, after all—but to come face-to-face with the great wurm just outside of Dharyan-Dharielle was something altogether different than seeing him from afar, or simply hearing tales about him.

"I have adjusted the saddle to carry three," Brynn explained to the man.

Pechter Dan Turk's eyes nearly fell out of their sockets, and he reflexively backed away, waving his hands in horror before him.

"You wished for help to save Jacintha," Brynn scolded. "Here is your help."

"We are to ride . . . that?"

"We came all the way from the northwestern corner of To-gai to Dharyan-Dharielle in a single day," Pagonel put in. "The speed of Agradeleous alone will allow us to better determine our next moves, and will give us the power to communicate quickly with Yatol Wadon to coordinate our efforts against Yatol Bardoh."

Whether the shaken man was even registering that claim was impossible to say, for Pechter Dan Turk stood there shaking his head and waving his arms, and saying "Agradeleous," under his breath.

"Agradeleous?" he asked more firmly a moment later. "You mean that . . . that beast, has a name?"

Agradeleous narrowed his reptilian eyes and issued a low growl that reverberated like a small avalanche.

"In To-gai, we have many sayings that echo the wisdom of not insulting a dragon," Brynn commented.

"I would guess that to be a common sentiment through all the lands of men," Pagonel agreed. "And a common sentiment among all the races of creatures who are not yet gone from the world."

"Can I eat him?" Agradeleous asked, and the poor emissary from Jacintha seemed as if he would melt where he stood.

"Enough of this," Brynn demanded a moment later. She strode forward, past the lowered head of Agradeleous to the dragon's shoulders, where she grabbed a leather strap. With a fluid movement, she pulled herself up into her riding position atop the beast's great shoulders. "Come along," she bade the other two. "The day is yet young. Let us go and see how far Tohen Bardoh has progressed."

After practically pulling the reluctant and terrified Pechter Dan Turk into place in the third seat of the saddle, they set off at a great pace, Agradeleous sweeping past Dharyan-Dharielle, where half the people who noticed the wurm cowered and the other half cheered. Straight as an arrow's flight, the dragon moved down the eastern road.

The very next day, the foursome came upon Dahdah Oasis, and to their surprise, there remained absolutely no sign of Yatol Bardoh's forces, not even the renegade Jacintha legions that Pagonel and Pechter Dan Turk had encountered when they had first come out from Yatol Wadon's city. Fearing the worst, Brynn prodded the dragon in close to the great Behrenese city that same night, settling him down under cover of darkness on the lower foothills to the north of Jacintha.

Pagonel and Pechter Dan Turk left immediately, but Brynn did not go, explaining that she and the dragon would continue to scout the region, and would rejoin them at the appointed place.

The mystic gave Brynn a knowing look and an approving smile before he departed. He understood indeed. Brynn would not accompany them and had taken that option away without discussion, because doing so would mean that she would have to let Agradeleous roam free while they were busy in Jacintha.

There were too many innocent people in the region for Brynn to allow that.

"The city is still in the hands of Yatol Mado Wadon," Pagonel reported upon his return to Brynn and Agradeleous. The mystic had not returned alone, and had even added a second representative, Paroud, to accompany him and Pechter Dan Turk. While Pagonel came in to explain to Brynn, Pechter Dan Turk stood on the edge of the small clearing, coaxing his obviously nervous companion to come forward, telling him that it was all right, that the dragon, the great Agradeleous, was a friend and no enemy.

Finally, the justifiably frightened Paroud moved forward, extending a series of low and ridiculously polite bows to Brynn and the dragon.

"The turmoil within Behren has settled then," Brynn reasoned. "And we can send Agradeleous home."

The dragon rumbled, seeming none too happy with that notion.

"The situation has only worsened," Paroud blurted, finding his voice in a sudden and explosive burst. "Yatol Bardoh has joined ranks with Yatol Peridan of the Cosinnida region, my homeland, far to the south. He . . . they, threaten Yatol De Hamman, and once they have overrun him, there is nothing to stop their march to Jacintha!"

"That Yatol Peridan has willingly joined with Yatol Bardoh does not bode well for Yatol Wadon and Jacintha," Pagonel agreed. "Their combined forces will prove considerable, I fear."

Brynn stared hard at the mystic, silently asking him for guidance here. What was she to do? Could she go to Dharyan-Dharielle and round up a force to throw in with Mado Wadon and his struggles? How could she ask that of her people after the oppression the Behrenese had laid upon To-gai for more than a decade?

"We must not move prematurely," Pagonel said to the two nervous emissaries, though in truth, he was quietly answering Brynn's obvious concerns. "Go to your Yatol Wadon and ask of him what Brynn might do."

"He has already told us of the aid he requires!" protested Paroud. "He needs soldiers, as many legions as To-gai can muster, and quickly!"

"You presume much," Brynn said curtly, somewhat deflating the man.

Something about Paroud wasn't sitting well with her. The Behrenese had long been a tribal people, loyal first and foremost to their particular region within the greater kingdom. Paroud was from Cosinnida, obviously, yet here he was vehemently demanding help in defeating his ruling Yatol. Perhaps there was an undercurrent of ambition here, Brynn mused. Perhaps Paroud believed that Yatol Mado Wadon would move quickly in replacing Yatol Peridan with a more trusted man from Cosinnida.

It all meant little to Brynn, of course, but as she considered the machinations underlying the tumultuous state in Behren, she was reminded once again to proceed with great caution.

"The situation will prove very fluid," Pagonel put in, seeming to share the woman's thoughts. "Let us learn all that we may. Perhaps a visit from Brynn and Agradeleous will dampen the designs of Yatol Bardoh and the willingness of Yatol Peridan to choose such an ill-advised ally."

"Perhaps," was all that Brynn would say, and her gaze never left the emissary, Paroud. Her tolerance for presumptuous Behrenese was not great, and while she wanted Behren under the control of someone like Mado Wadon, who had seen the wisdom of making peace with the To-gai-ru, there was, after all, a limit to their friendship.

On a warship not far from Jacintha harbor, and flying the flag of the kingdom to the north, Abbot Olin and Duke Bretherford listened carefully as Master Mackaront recounted a similar tale of the changing situation south of the great Behrenese city.

"Mado Wadon is terrified," Mackaront remarked. "He understands well that the march of Bardoh will be relentless once Yatol De Hamman's forces have been destroyed. Mado Wadon now openly asks for whatever assistance we can offer, and rumor flies throughout Jacintha that he is looking west for help as well, to the Dragon of To-gai and her fierce warriors."

"And have the To-gai-ru answered that call?" Abbot Olin demanded, his smug expression wiped away by the mere thought of Jacintha finding her needed aid elsewhere. He had a fleet of warships laden with warriors ready to land south of any attacking army, and ten thousand more warriors ready to sweep down from the mountains in the north, catching the attackers in a deadly vise.

"No," Mackaront replied. "There are no reports of any army moving along the northern road from Dharyan-Dharielle. It is doubtful that Brynn of the To-gai-ru will be able to gather any substantial force together in time to halt the charge of Yatol Bardoh." The man offered a confident chuckle. "It is doubtful that Brynn Dharielle will be able to rouse her warriors to any cause that involves aiding Behren. The hatred between the two peoples runs deep, I assure you, despite the forced treaty."

Abbot Olin smiled wickedly at that welcome news.

"And thus, Mado Wadon bids you to join with him as soon as possible," Mackaront began, but Abbot Olin cut him short.

Olin glanced over at Duke Bretherford. "You have spoken with Maisha Darou?"

The duke nodded. "As you expected, Yatol Peridan approached him and bade him to redouble his efforts very soon after the alliance was sealed with Yatol Bardoh."

"And he understands his continuing and expanding role?"

"A few bags of gems always clear the mind of a pirate," Duke Bretherford replied sourly.

Abbot Olin gave a laugh and looked back to Mackaront. "There you have it."

"Then I can assure Yatol Wadon . . ."

"Of nothing," Abbot Olin quickly corrected. "Yatol Wadon will wait until I deem the time proper. The desperation of Jacintha is our ally." He looked around at the two men. "Yatol Wadon will welcome us with open arms. I will be the savior of Jacintha, and that will give us the foothold we need."

"To convert the Behrenese to the Abellican religion?" asked an obviously skeptical Duke Bretherford, who had been in a sour mood ever since he had arrived in Entel, and all during the journey here to Jacintha, even though Abbot Olin had given him *Rontlemore's Dream* as his flagship and it was truly as grand as anything in the Ursal fleet, *River Palace* included.

"To find common ground between our religions," Abbot Olin corrected without any hesitation.

"To bring them into your flock," the duke responded.

"However you interpret it," Abbot Olin allowed. "Your King Aydrian desires Behren, and so we shall deliver Behren to him. It is that simple."

Duke Bretherford nodded and lifted a mug in obedient salute. He understood well that this was more about Olin than Aydrian. Yes, the young king was ambitious, but this move into Behren—and before the monumental issues within Honce-the-Bear had even been properly settled—was more about the craving of Abbot Olin.

Duke Bretherford had been around the court of Ursal long enough to understand that Aydrian had decided to put Olin out of the way here, as he had put Bretherford out of the way. And what better prize to show to Olin than the city of Jacintha and all the land about it? Bretherford couldn't deny the effectiveness of the move, for he did not doubt that the forces secretly arrayed by Honce-the-Bear to defend Jacintha would prove more than sufficient and would indeed allow Olin to begin a power grab. Despite that, though, a nagging doubt did hold fast in the thoughts of the duke of the Mirianic, one that had grabbed at him since the change of power in Honce-the-Bear.

One that included the name of Prince Midalis.

Under Cover of Darkness

"This is crazy," Roger whispered. "You're certain to get us both killed!"

Bradwarden didn't answer, for the centaur was too busy staring at the remarkable and unexpected scene before them.

The mighty Allheart Brigade, along with legions of Ursal Kingsmen, swarmed over the towns of Caer Tinella and Landsdown. There had been no resistance, for the invading soldiers marching north out of conquered Palmaris had found the two towns substantially thinned of their populace.

"Ye gived them a warning, did ye?" Bradwarden asked.

"We did not go in," Roger replied. "Pony wanted to get to Dundalis as quickly as possible, so we bypassed the cites altogether on our ride north."

"Well, someone came through," the centaur remarked.

"The Palmaris garrison," Roger reasoned. "Many of them left the city right behind us. They would have stopped here, and would have warned the people to flee."

"Or to accept the new king," said Bradwarden. "And it seems as if a fair number done just that. But I wonder where them that ran might've gone to. Not to Dundalis, or we'd've seen 'em on the road."

"Vanguard," said Roger. "They went to the east with the Palmaris garrison to join up with Prince Midalis."

"They're goin' to be finding a long and cold road, then. Winter's to come on early this year, and earlier still in the forest lands north o' the gulf." The centaur looked all around, his gaze finally settling on Roger. "Ye go in there tonight, playing the part of a simple townsman."

"In there?" Roger asked incredulously. "Do you know who might be in there? Marcalo De'Unnero is likely about, and if not him, then surely Duke Kalas. He knows me. If I go into Caer Tinella or Landsdown, I don't think I'll soon be coming out."

"We got no choice in the matter."

"We?"

"Well, yerself at least. We're to need more information if we're to get all the way to Palmaris and get anything done," the centaur explained.

"Then we'll sneak about the perimeter and learn what we might," Roger offered. "Sentries have big mouths and lack basic discretion. I'll go down and find a place to hide near a group, and we'll know all that we need to know."

As he finished, he snapped his fingers and flashed a smile, and started off toward the town.

"Ye go right in," Bradwarden ordered. "Ye go to the common room in Caer Tinella and ye'll hear more in a drink than ye'll get all the night near the half-frozen and miserable sentries."

Roger glanced back, but Bradwarden's expression brooked no debate.

With a sigh, the small man headed off.

He kept the cowl of his cloak up high, but not so high as to make it look as if he were trying to avoid being recognized. Roger had always been a resourceful fellow. In the time of the DemonWar, he had used his skills at hiding and thievery, as well as his persuasive manner, to keep a band of refugees from these very towns well fed and well hidden. Until Elbryan and Pony had arrived to lead the hapless band of villagers into a greater union against the minions of the demon dactyl, Roger Lockless had provided for them and kept them safe, mostly by outwitting the powries.

But those were just powries—ferocious and tough dwarves, yes, but . . .

But this was Marcalo De'Unnero.

The mere thought of the man sent shivers coursing along Roger's back. If De'Unnero was here, and happened to recognize Roger, then nothing in all the world—not Bradwarden, not Pony—could save him.

As he moved along the streets of Caer Tinella, with more soldiers about than townsfolk, Roger began to become more at ease. This was his home, after all, the town where he had been raised into adulthood.

He neared the common room, as Bradwarden had bade him, but upon reaching the door, found that the place was nearly deserted. On an impulse, Roger turned aside and moved swiftly along a side street, coming to the home of an old friend.

He knocked gently, and when there was no answer, he glanced around to make sure that no one was watching, then quietly picked the lock on the door and moved inside. The place did not show signs of any hasty packing, and when he saw pieces of the man's battle armor and a fine sword leaning against the side of a stone hearth, Roger was fairly certain that his friend hadn't deserted the town.

That made sense, Roger knew, for the owner of this house, Captain Shamus Kilronney, was not one to shy from a fight.

Roger moved into the sitting room, plopped into a chair right before the dark hearth, and waited.

A couple of hours slipped by, and Roger became nervous and agitated.

Might something have happened to Shamus? he wondered. Had the man protested the new king too loudly and been thrown into a jail cell?

Roger had just made up his mind to go and find out, and was even up from his seat and heading toward the door, when it opened suddenly and a very weary-looking Shamus Kilronney walked in. He tossed his hat on the table near to the door and moved a chair back as if to sit in it, and then, in a movement most uncharacteristic for the normally calm and composed man, he flung the chair across the room to crash against the wall.

"It has not gone well, I take it?" Roger asked, moving out of the shadows.

Shamus jumped at the sound and the sight of him, moving right into a defensive posture. But he relaxed visibly when he recognized that it was Roger.

"What are you doing here?" asked the former soldier, once a leader of a Kingsman contingent that served in Palmaris.

"A pleasure to see you again, too," Roger answered dryly.

Shamus seemed suddenly off-balance and totally flustered. "Of course," he stammered, and he moved forward, extending his hand to his old friend. "Roger!" he said, and instead of shaking Roger's hand, he wrapped the man in a great hug.

All of this was so out of character for Shamus Kilronney, and that fact told Roger more than a little about the present occupation of Caer Tinella.

"How quickly the world changes," Shamus said, taking a seat and motioning for Roger to sit across from him. "Tell me, where is Jilseponie? Is she safe after the unexpected death of King Danube? Is she . . ."

Roger patted his hands in the air to calm the man. "Safe? Yes," he answered. "In body at least, though to be sure, the truth of Aydrian revealed has been more than a bit of a shock to her."

"Is it true, then?" asked Shamus, leaning forward eagerly. "Is the new king truly her son?"

"As they say," Roger conceded. "But though he has the blood of Elbryan and Jilseponie flowing through him, he is not akin to either by any action he has shown."

"I know not where this will lead," said Shamus. "But to evil, no doubt. Prince Midalis is not to allow this without a fight. All the kingdom will be torn apart!"

"Has Aydrian come to Caer Tinella?"

"He remains in Palmaris."

"And what of Marcalo De'Unnero?" Roger pressed, leaning forward in his seat. "Has he come here?"

"De'Unnero?" Shamus echoed, and he seemed both confused and as if he was about to fall over. "What has Marcalo De'Unnero got to do with any of this?"

"Who represents King Aydrian here?"

"Duke Kalas, who leads the Allhearts."

"And the good duke has not seen fit to tell you of Aydrian's principle advisor?"

"De'Unnero?" Shamus asked, again with complete incredulity. "Does he even live on?"

"De'Unnero precipitated the rise of Aydrian in Ursal," Roger explained.

"It cannot be!"

"Jilseponie herself told me of this," Roger explained. "There can be no doubt. If he is not here, then likely he remains in Palmaris with Aydrian. That is the hope, at least," he added, and he couldn't help but glance all about nervously. "Better that than to have him stalking about the region, half man and half beast."

Shamus Kilronney ran his hand through his thinning and graying hair repeatedly, as if trying to get a handle on all of the startling news that had overwhelmed him these last days. "It all makes no sense," he remarked. "Duke Kalas is not an evil man, and yet it appears as if he has forsaken the line of Ursal. And why would he ever go in league with Marcalo De'Unnero?"

"Is he truly?"

Shamus Kilronney seemed intrigued by that prospect, but only for a moment, then he nodded. "He took the towns in the name of King Aydrian, and those soldiers of Palmaris who came through here a couple of weeks ago insisted that the new king's march to Palmaris was led every stride by Duke Kalas."

Roger could only shrug.

"I am to meet with Duke Kalas this very night—he may be on his way here at this very moment," Shamus explained. "Sit with us and perhaps we can together begin to unravel this mystery."

"Hardly," Roger said with a chuckle. "Kalas has never been overly fond of me, and hates Jilseponie above all."

"We can reason with him—"

"He will throw me in chains and drag me back to Palmaris, if I am fortunate," Roger said. "No, I have no desire to face the likes of Duke Kalas." As he finished, he rose from his seat and moved to the curtained window beside the door. He drew back the curtain just an inch, and peered out, and noticed a group of soldiers heading his way.

"Kalas?" asked the perceptive Shamus.

Roger nodded. "I beg you not to betray me," he said. "I do not know how all of this will fall out, my old friend, but I doubt that I will ever find myself in league with the likes of Duke Targon Bree Kalas!"

"Begone, and be quick, then," Shamus agreed, and Roger moved swiftly out of the room even as there came a loud knock on the door.

Shamus hesitated a few moments to give Roger a head start, then walked over and pulled wide the door. A group of soldiers entered, nodding deferentially to Shamus, but pushing past him and into the house. At once, they began moving about, searching every cubby and closet, overturning blankets and falling to the floor to peer under anything high enough off the floor for a man to squeeze beneath.

Shamus started to protest, but changed his mind and held his words. He had spent most of his life in the Kingsmen, serving Baron Bildeborough of Palmaris and other dignitaries, and he understood that these men were only acting as they had been trained to do, securing the house before the arrival of their lord.

Not waiting for any all clear, the ever-confident Duke Kalas strode in.

"Duke Kalas," Shamus said with a low bow. "Too long has it been." He heard banging in the other room then and stifled a grimace, hoping that Roger had not been found.

"I am surprised to find you here, Captain Kilronney," the duke admitted, taking a seat at the table and motioning for Shamus to do likewise.

"This is my home," Shamus answered. "Where else would I be?"

"On the open road with Jilseponie, and others of like mind," Duke Kalas bluntly replied. "It would not be the first time you have taken up with her against the crown."

The insult was not unexpected, of course. In the dark days, Shamus had indeed stood strong beside Elbryan and Jilseponie, and had even been with Elbryan at the Barbacan when Duke Kalas and Marcalo De'Unnero had led an army there to capture the ranger.

The other soldiers came into the room, then, and to Shamus' relief, they weren't dragging Roger Lockless.

"I will concede that I stood with her, and with Elbryan," Shamus replied, not backing down. "But never did Jilseponie truly stand against the crown. You know that now, Duke Kalas. In her efforts against Father Abbot Markwart, she was correct, and—"

"Spare me the recital of the virtues of Jilseponie," Duke Kalas said dryly. "I have heard too much from her and about her these last years. I can only hope that she ran off into the forest and was eaten by a bear."

"Or a tiger?"

The obvious reference to De'Unnero made Kalas sit a bit straighter suddenly, and narrow his eyes.

"Yes, I have heard of Marcalo De'Unnero's unexpected return," Shamus confirmed. "Though I admit that I am more than a little surprised to find that he and Duke Kalas are on the same side once again."

"This is not about Marcalo De'Unnero," Duke Kalas snapped back, and the harshness in his tone betrayed how strongly he felt about the fallen monk. "This is about putting the kingdom of Honce-the-Bear back as it was, about restoring . . ."

"The name of Ursal?"

"Captain Kilronney," Duke Kalas said quietly, evenly, as clear a threat as Shamus had ever heard.

Shamus held up his hands, showing that he would let the issue drop.

"I am as surprised by the turn of events as are you, I assure you," Duke Kalas went on. "But I am also certain that our land will prosper as never before under the command of Aydrian."

"How can you know?"

Duke Kalas fumbled over a few words, then just shrugged. "There is more to him than to any man I have ever known," he said quietly, and Shamus looked at him intently, never having seen the proud and headstrong Duke Kalas seem so humbled. "If ever there was a man born to be a king, then it is surely Aydrian."

"His breeding is impressive," said Shamus, and Kalas scowled.

"He rises above the many shortcomings of both mother and father," the duke insisted. "And pray, do tell me of his mother. Has Jilseponie passed this way?"

"She has not, and until your arrival and news that she was on the road, I had feared that she remained in Ursal, imprisoned."

"You are telling me that the Palmaris garrison did not march through here?" Duke Kalas said suspiciously.

"They did indeed, but had little to offer," Shamus replied. "Nor did I question them intently, as they were merely rushing through, along the road to the north and east. To Vanguard, I presume."

"And many of the townsfolk went with them." It was a statement and not a question.

"Many indeed. Prince Midalis and King Danube fostered great loyalty in this region, to be sure, but no more so than did Jilseponie Wyndon."

Again Kalas scowled at him.

"Tread carefully, good Duke," Shamus warned. "The name of Jilseponie is not discredited up here north of Palmaris, whatever her reputation in the city and on the roads south. The people of Caer Tinella and Landsdown, and all along the road to the north, remember well all that she and Elbryan did for them."

"Which is why I would expect that the reports we have of her heading north out of Palmaris are likely true," Duke Kalas replied. "Yet you say that she did not come through here."

"She did not, and if she had, then surely I would have seen her and spoken with her, and I assure you that I have not."

Duke Kalas stared at Shamus hard for a few moments, then, seeming satisfied, gave a nod.

"Just because she did not come through here does not mean that she didn't pass this way," Shamus offered. "Never has she called Caer Tinella her home."

"It may be that she is farther north," Duke Kalas agreed. "Back in Dundalis."

"And you will march that way?"

"No," Kalas said without hesitation. "That is not my mission. The Timberlands are not important at this time."

"Even if Jilseponie is there?"

"I have not come out in search of Jilseponie," Kalas explained. "And if I never see the witch again, I will die a happy man. My assignment was to take these towns for King Aydrian, and so I have, and now I will swing west with my legions and the Allhearts to secure all the lands in a ring about Pal-

maris, which now embraces Aydrian in good spirit. Even Bishop Braumin
has spoken for the new king."

Shamus nodded, though the significance of that was not lost on him, nor
was the curiosity of it. Hadn't Braumin been one of Jilseponie's staunchest
supporters for all these years?

"I came here for more than idle chatter," Duke Kalas said suddenly, and
he sat up straighter in his chair. "It is obvious that the folk of the towns
have taken you as their leader."

"I would hardly say that."

"But I have said it, and I am not surprised," said Duke Kalas. "King
Danube took it as a great loss when you left the Kingsmen and your service
to the crown. For many years, many of us considered that your future
would be bright within the hierarchy of the kingdom, even after your decision to side with Elbryan and Jilseponie."

Shamus wanted to point out again that he had been proven right on that
point, but he held the words to himself. He knew how stubborn Duke
Kalas could be, and knew that to this day Kalas had never embraced the
myth of the heroes of the north.

"I wish you to return to service," Duke Kalas went on when no protest
was forthcoming. "I tell you with all my heart that King Aydrian will lead
Honce-the-Bear to greatness beyond our comprehension. But as magnificent as he is, he will need competent leaders in his ranks."

Shamus was only partly aware of the fact that a slight breeze could have
blown him over at that moment. To hear Duke Kalas, of all people, so ex-
horting the virtues of another! It was so uncharacteristic of the proud man
as to be unthinkable!

"I have long retired," Shamus did manage to stutter. "I have little desire
to pace the open road again, my Duke."

"I have shown you no road," Duke Kalas replied. "I seek only stability
in these towns, and I believe that you can deliver that stability, for King
Aydrian."

"And against Prince Midalis?"

"A fair enough question," said Kalas. "And I pray that it never comes to
that, for if Midalis goes against Aydrian, he will be destroyed. But we will let
them play out that drama, should it come to war. For now, I seek only to assure the folk of Caer Tinella and Landsdown that all is as it was. I hope to
coax back those who have fled because of their unfounded fear. Aydrian is
no conquering king, but one who loves this land above all."

The words rang hollow on many levels, but Shamus could not deny that
he was glad to hear them. Whether his loyalties lay with Jilseponie or with
the nobles of Ursal was not the point—and was nothing that he could investigate at this time, in any case, having seen neither the former queen nor her
son. What truly mattered to Shamus Kilronney at that moment was exactly
what Duke Kalas had just said to him: the stability of Caer Tinella and
Landsdown.

"We have seen too much war," Shamus said.

"Then remain out of any that might march your way," offered Duke Kalas. "Keep these towns safe and secure. Assure the folk that King Aydrian is no enemy, but an ally who will not forsake his people at any cost."

"Then why have you come in with an army, Duke Kalas?" Shamus dared to ask. "If what you say is true, then why not send a courier with the news, bidding support for the new king?"

"Because there will likely be war, and we know not when we might find it," the duke explained. "A sizable portion of the garrison of Palmaris, guided by errant loyalties, have marched out of the city. We know not when we will encounter them."

"And you wish to ensure that they are not welcomed in Caer Tinella and Landsdown through the winter months," Shamus reasoned.

"I doubt they are anywhere near here," said Kalas. "But yes, there is that small fact. I will be gone from this place soon, but I am leaving a force behind to secure the towns and to help them through the difficulties of the winter months. I would have you aid them in their cause."

Shamus Kilronney spent a long time staring at the man. He really had little choice in the matter, he knew. His loyalties, first and foremost, were to these towns he now called home, and leading them against the legions of Ursal would be nothing short of suicide and complete disaster.

A few moments slipped by, with Shamus not answering.

"Yet, you were a friend to Jilseponie, not De'Unnero," Duke Kalas did remark.

"No more a friend to De'Unnero than are you," Shamus countered effectively.

"True enough," said Kalas. "Then I can inform King Aydrian that Captain Kilronney will hold the towns of Caer Tinella and Landsdown in his name?"

Shamus thought on it for a moment, and said, "We will not become enemies to those who do not come to us as enemies."

It was enough of an assurance for Duke Kalas obviously, for the man stood up and motioned for his soldiers to lead the way out. "The force I leave with you will not be substantial," he explained. "Your duty will not be to engage Prince Midalis, if this way he rides—and surely he will!—but to send riders far and wide that we might offer the proper defense in Palmaris to the south."

"We want no fight here," Shamus assured him. "But tell me again, on your word, that you do not hunt for Jilseponie."

"Old loyalties die hard?" Duke Kalas replied with a chuckle, then he added, "Marcalo De'Unnero was not pleased at Aydrian's decision to leave her to the Timberlands, if that is where she has fled. He wanted nothing more than to press on after her. Personally, I hope she simply fades away, never to be seen again."

Shamus grimaced and held a hard stare, but allowed him that.

It had gone better than expected, but the captain was glad indeed when he shut the door behind the departing duke and made his way back to the sitting room.

A soot-covered Roger Lockless was just crawling out of the chimney as he entered.

"You heard?"

"Every word," Roger answered. "My body wears the aches of middle age, but my hearing is acute, I assure you. Especially when the subject is one so dear to my heart." Roger dusted himself off and gave a little laugh. "I'm amazed that Duke Kalas was so quick to trust you. He has to know that these two towns might prove pivotal in any march of Prince Midalis— and these are no longer the minor villages they were in the days of the demon dactyl. Five thousand call this region home now, and more than half, including many hardy warriors, are on the road to join Midalis!"

"Duke Kalas trusts me not at all, though he understands that I am honor-bound as a soldier," Shamus explained. "Likely he will leave many in his force to watch over me specifically, and I hold no doubt that at the first indication I offer in swaying at all toward Prince Midalis, should it come to that, they will have me chained and dragged all the way to Ursal."

Roger looked at him hard, all hint of a smile long gone.

"Take care where you stand in this, Roger Lockless," Shamus honestly warned him. "And pray keep Jilseponie safe. This is not a war that will easily be won, I fear, and the enemies are not clearly defined this time, as they were with the minions of the demon dactyl. Choose wisely, for all our sakes!"

"You can't believe there is legitimacy in Aydrian."

Shamus gave a shrug, as if it did not really matter. "We are a long way from Ursal," he explained. "If King Danube had died years ago, our lives here would not likely have been any different than they are now. Unless this Aydrian proves to be a tyrant, levying crushing taxes and impressing the folk of the land into service to his kingdom, then what real difference does it make?"

"These are not the words of the Shamus I knew!" Roger insisted.

"Perhaps not. But they are the words of a man who has known too much battle."

"Have you no loyalty to King Danube?"

"I did."

"And what of his brother, then? The rightful successor?"

Again Shamus shrugged. "We know nothing of Prince Midalis' designs at this time. Would you have me lead a revolt against the Allheart Knights and legions of Kingsmen? Would you have me lead my people into slaughter, or back out into the wilds of the forest, to run and hide from an enemy we cannot hope to defeat?

"Besides, how do we know that young Aydrian will not prove to be the true offspring, in spirit as well as blood, of Elbryan and Jilseponie?" the man went on. "And if that is the case, Honce-the-Bear may yet know its best days."

Roger could see the logic in that, and in not resisting the overwhelming forces of Duke Kalas at this time. But he countered, and with great effectiveness, by reminding the former Kingsman of Aydrian's sidekick, saying merely, "Marcalo De'Unnero."

Shamus gave a resigned nod and smirk that fast turned to a scowl.

He would cling to his hopes, Roger understood, and so would many in the kingdom, but those hopes were placed upon the shoulders of a man who had risen to power under the tutelage of a monster whose past exploits could not be ignored.

Roger went back out into the forest before the dawn, and found Bradwarden waiting for him at the appointed spot. He recounted the events to the centaur, who listened carefully, nodding all the way through and giving little indication of whether he approved or not.

Expecting a more vociferous response from the volatile creature, Roger said emphatically, "They refuse to draw the battle lines!"

"Wisely so," said the centaur. "Shamus Kilronney's not to be leading his people to slaughter, and if ye're thinkin' they've got a chance in the world o' fighting the army that's marched out o' Palmaris, then ye're thinking wrong."

"We have to do something," Roger argued.

"And we'll see if it comes to pass," said the centaur. "Prince Midalis'll be heard from afore this is ended, don't ye doubt, but right now, it's seeming to me to be his fight to start, then ours to choose sides."

Roger paused and considered that for a moment, with Shamus' warning that he should choose sides carefully echoing in his ears. "And we do nothing?" he asked.

"Oh, we got plenty to do," Bradwarden replied. "We got a friend in the north who's needing us, and a friend in the south who's in more trouble still. I'm standing by me friends, whate'er the cost, and so is yerself, if ye're the Roger Lockless I'm knowing."

Roger looked at him curiously, not quite understanding. He caught the reference to Pony, obviously, but who might the friend in the south be? Braumin Herde? Did the centaur think that he and Roger and anyone else they might find had any chance at all of getting to the man, if the man was even still alive?

"Climb on me back," the centaur instructed. "We got a long run to Palmaris ahead of us, and I'm thinking to make it quick!"

Roger, still perplexed, did as instructed, and the centaur leaped away, his large hooves tearing up the turf.

"I'm thinkin' it's good that we got so many soldiers behind us," Bradwarden called back to him. "That'll mean less to fight once we get to the city."

Roger just held on.

❖ 14 ❖

The Weight of Responsibility

B rynn reviewed the assembled To-gai-ru riders arrayed behind Tanalk Grenk: several hundred in number. He had brought them out of Dharyan-Dharielle and along the road to support their beloved leader, the Dragon of To-gai.

The woman gave a doubtful look over at Pagonel and Agradeleous, the dragon in his bipedal lizardman form. They were back in the west now, closer to Dharyan-Dharielle than to Jacintha, after a swift flight that had added the emissary Paroud to the group of riders.

"They number not nearly as many as I would have hoped," Paroud said curtly. "But they are Ru . . . To-gai-ru warriors, after all, and renowned for their ferocity."

"Many more are moving toward Dharyan-Dharielle as we speak," Tanalk Grenk answered him. "Doubt you the might of To-gai after the defeat of your own kingdom?"

Paroud started to answer, but Brynn cut him off with a simple, "Enough!"

She looked again to Pagonel, silently pleading for his help. What was she to do? Send this army charging to the aid of Jacintha and reinforce the Behrenese secured there with more and more To-gai-ru as they rode out of To-gai to her call? The exchange she had just witnessed between Grenk and Paroud was a telling reminder of the enmity between the peoples, a basic distrust that went back many hundreds of years. Given that, was it right for Brynn to ask her fellow To-gai-ru to die for the cause of Behren, for the security of a Yatol priest who had gladly served the previous, imperialistic Chezru Chieftain? Had Yatol Mado Wadon even questioned the decision by Chezru Douan to invade To-gai and conquer Brynn's people?

And yet, she could not deny that the other player in the drama that was now Behren was a man she hated even more profoundly. Yatol Bardoh had been the executor of the invasion, a brutal and unmerciful man who had murdered To-gai-ru without the slightest hesitation.

Including Brynn's own parents.

She closed her eyes and tried to calm herself. Personally, she wanted revenge on Bardoh, but would that justify throwing To-gai into the middle of the Behrenese civil war?

She opened her eyes when she felt a light touch on her arm. Pagonel motioned her to follow him to the side, where they could privately discuss the matter.

"To engage Yatol Bardoh's forces within the city of Jacintha, should they breach the wall, would be foolhardy," the mystic cautioned. "Your warriors are better suited to the open desert and roads. Use them to nibble at the perimeters of Yatol Bardoh's force." He paused there and spent a long moment studying Brynn's doubting—scowling, even—look. "If you choose to use them at all," he added.

"Can I?"

"They look to you as their leader," Pagonel replied. "If you instruct them to go to war, they will go to war."

"And can I, in good conscience and with the benefit of To-gai in mind, ask that of them?" Brynn clarified.

"Would To-gai see a benefit if Yatol Bardoh assumes the leadership of Behren?" Pagonel answered. "He has made no secret of his continuing designs on your homeland."

It was true enough, and there lay Brynn's dilemma. If she let this civil war continue and Tohen Bardoh proved victorious, then To-gai would likely know war soon enough. And certainly, Bardoh's first move would be to try to reclaim Dharyan-Dharielle for Behren.

Of course, Brynn understood her limitations quite clearly. She looked back at the small force of riders. Would throwing her warriors and herself into the middle of the conflict even make a difference in the outcome?

There was the rub, and the weight that tipped the scales within Brynn's thoughts. She looked at Pagonel and nodded appreciatively, then moved back to the others on the road. For the last two weeks, she had tried to avoid this moment of decision. All along the way to Agradeleous' cave and back again, Brynn had hoped that Mado Wadon would crush Tohen Bardoh and be done with it before she ever had to declare openly whether or not she would engage To-gai in the fight.

Now she had run out of time.

"Go back to Dharyan-Dharielle and organize all of those coming in," she instructed Tanalk Grenk.

"You must be quick, then!" Paroud advised. "If you are to assemble a larger force, then do so at once, or it may prove too late for Yatol Wadon!"

Brynn shot him a brief look, but turned back to her trusted commander. "Organize the defense of Dharyan-Dharielle, and of all the paths leading into To-gai," she ordered. "If Yatol Bardoh proves victorious, he will turn against us, I do not doubt. And we will be ready for him."

"We will," Tanalk Grenk promised.

"What foolishness is this?" Paroud demanded, the weight of it all sinking in. "You will forsake us in our hour of need?"

"Forsake you?" Brynn asked incredulously.

"You feign friendship with Yatol Wadon to get that which you desire, but when that friendship is tested—"

"Friendship?" Brynn interrupted. "I have never feigned friendship, nor claimed friendship, with Yatol Wadon."

Paroud stammered and nearly fell over himself, gesturing protests wildly. "When Yatol Bardoh was at your gates . . . when you were in need . . . was it not Yatol Mado Wadon . . ."

"Who recalled the Jacintha garrison and stood down the army because he dared not risk another costly fight?" Brynn finished for him. "Understand me in this. I am no enemy of your Yatol Wadon. But I understand, as do you, that his decision to forgo the battle at Dharyan-Dharielle was for his benefit and the benefit of Behren."

"He let you keep the city!" Paroud screamed at her. "A Behrenese city!"

"Because his choice was either me or Yatol Bardoh, who he knew would soon enough attack him," Brynn replied. "No, my decision is made, and it is for the good of To-gai." She looked to Tanalk Grenk and nodded for him to go, and he gave a deferential nod of his chin and swung his pinto pony about, organizing the warriors for the ride home.

Paroud started to protest again, but Brynn walked right up to him, eyeing him coldly.

"I will not ask the To-gai-ru to shed blood for the sake of the Behrenese," she said with complete calm. "Not when the memories of Behrenese cruelty remain so keen in their minds. If Yatol Wadon desires a true alliance between our peoples, even a friendship, perhaps, then it is his responsibility to foster that friendship."

Paroud stood very still for a long while, digesting her blunt retort. "It will be a difficult course for Yatol Wadon to take if he is dead."

"That would be most unfortunate," Brynn replied. "And I will try to help prevent that where I might."

Paroud's look went to one of confusion. "You just said . . ."

"That I would not ask my kinfolk to bleed for Behren," the woman explained. "For me, this feud with Yatol Bardoh runs much deeper."

"One woman?" Pechter Dan Turk dared to say with obvious skepticism. "A warrior, to be sure, but hardly an army."

"One woman and one Jhesta Tu," Brynn replied, looking to Pagonel, who nodded grimly.

Off to the side, Agradeleous gave a roar.

"And let us not forget," Pagonel added.

It started as a trickle of fleeing refugees, desperate and desolate, wandering up the road from the south. Soon it built to a flood, filtering about the ramshackle buildings of the slum outside of Jacintha proper and marching to the wall. These were the people of Avrou Das and Paerith, the main cities of Yatol De Hamman's domain. Before the questioning of those on the leading edge of the refugee line had even begun, Yatol Mado Wadon understood the implications.

De Hamman's province had been overrun by the combined forces of Bardoh and Peridan. Now there remained nothing between that joined army and the walls of Jacintha.

The refugees poured in all through the day and night, in a line that showed no signs of ending. Finally, Yatol Wadon ordered the gates closed. But still they came, wandering to Jacintha because they had nowhere else in all the world to go. Thousands milled about the brown fields beyond the city and the shanties beyond Jacintha's strong walls. They were desperate people with little to eat and drink, and with no hope left in their dull eyes.

On the second night after the grim procession began, scouts returned to the city with word that there was a distinctive and bright glow in the sky to the south, and Mado Wadon understood that Avrou Das was burning.

Soon after, one of the refugees was brought to see the Yatol of Jacintha, and so battered and dirty was the man that Yatol Mado Wadon at first did not recognize him—not until he spoke.

"I expected the loyalty of Jacintha," he said, his voice heavy with grief and pain and simple weariness.

"Yatol De Hamman," Mado Wadon said, and he moved near to the man and reached up and placed his hand on De Hamman's dirty cheek. "We did not know."

"You knew that Tohen Bardoh had assembled a great force, and knew that he had turned south," De Hamman argued.

"But to what purpose?"

"Is that not obvious?" De Hamman countered. "My land is in ruin, my cities burning. So many of my warriors were already weary from their long struggle with Peridan, and so many more were siphoned off from Avrou Das to aid in Chezru Douan's foolish war in the west."

"But I had no way of knowing Tohen Bardoh's plans," Yatol Wadon protested. "He could have just as easily thrown in with De Hamman as with Peridan." If not an outright lie, the Yatol's reasoning was certainly porous and suspect—and obviously so to everyone in the room. Yatol Bardoh had made his designs on Jacintha quite public from the beginning of the insurrection, and given that, turning his forces southward would have obviously prompted an alliance with Peridan, who was fighting Jacintha-backed De Hamman.

Still, for whatever reason, the desperate Yatol De Hamman did not press the point any further.

"We could not resist them," the defeated man remarked. "They arrived unexpectedly on the field south of Paerith, and with the reinforcements of Yatol Bardoh, Yatol Peridan's line was five times that of my warriors. Many broke ranks and fled, and those who remained were slaughtered to a man. Paerith was in flames that same day. I tried to organize some defense of Avrou Das, but . . ." He just shook his head helplessly, then closed his eyes and cried, his shoulders bobbing.

"We will stop them," Yatol Wadon promised. "We will turn them back and pay them back for this atrocity committed against you and your flock. And I will help you to rebuild your cities, my old friend. On my word!"

That seemed to comfort Yatol De Hamman somewhat. He sniffled away the tears, looked at Mado Wadon, and offered a hopeful nod.

The Yatol of Jacintha motioned to his attendants then, to take Yatol De Hamman to a private room where he might clean up and find some rest. Then Wadon himself went to his bedroom, followed by images of battle and Jacintha burning.

He slept not at all.

And the next morning, when the scouts returned with a better assessment of the disaster just south of the city, Yatol Wadon realized that he might not be sleeping well for a long, long time.

"Avrou Eesa, Pruda, Alzuth, Teramen," Rabia Awou recited, the list of towns—nearly all of the major cities of western Behren—that had thrown in with Yatol Bardoh in his march against Jacintha.

Yatol Wadon closed his eyes as the recital continued, including the southeastern stretches of the kingdom, Yatol Peridan's domain of Cosinnida. Given the source of this information, Rabia Awou, Wadon couldn't dismiss it at all. Rabia Awou was the best scout of Jacintha, a man of disguise and intelligence, who could transform not only his appearance, but his demeanor, as well, and infiltrate the most secretive of societies. Once long ago, Chezru Douan had used him to infiltrate a ring of thieves working the docks of Jacintha, and the small, slender, brown-skinned man's work had been nothing short of brilliant, and his information nothing short of perfect.

"Pruda?" he did ask doubtfully, for Pruda, the former center of learning in Behren, had always remained neutral in the ways of war.

"The folk of Pruda resent the fact that you allowed Brynn Dharielle to keep the contents of the library she stole from their beloved city," Rabia explained.

Yatol Wadon looked at him incredulously. "How was I to get them back?" he asked. "Would the good people of Pruda like to lead the march into Dharyan-Dharielle against the Dragon of To-gai?"

Rabia Awou just shrugged, as if it did not matter to him. And of course, it did not. "They seek one to blame for their great loss," he explained. "They blame you."

"Yatol De Hamman said that the combined army that took the field against him was five times his number—"

"Then that was less than half of Bardoh's army," Rabia Awou said grimly, and the weight of that statement nearly knocked Yatol Wadon over.

He knew at once that Jacintha was surely doomed.

Hardly thinking, the man turned to the side, to the room's eastern window, and gazed out across the bay at the tiny specks on the horizon.

In the early-evening twilight, Brynn and her companions could see clearly where the line of refugees ended and the wave of pursuing warriors began. Agradeleous put the woman and her three companions down on a high dune overlooking the north–south coastal road. The flames of Avrou Das were clearly visible in the south, and even more poignant than that tragedy were the screams of terror rolling over the flat sands.

"Take your beast and go to them!" Paroud insisted to Brynn. "Are you to stand here and watch while people die? Have you no conscience or concern?"

From behind the man, Agradeleous gave a low, rumbling growl, and Paroud slowly turned about to regard the dragon.

"If you call me a beast again, I will eat you," the dragon promised, and the ambassador from Jacintha seemed as if he would faint dead away.

"Tohen Bardoh knows how to fight Agradeleous," Brynn replied, and she was speaking as much to clarify her own thoughts as to explain her actions to the others. "I dare not reveal the dragon before his forces are fully engaged."

"I will eat them all," Agradeleous declared, and when Paroud pointed to the dragon and looked back at Brynn, as if to acknowledge the dragon's agreement with his logic, the dragon added, "Starting with Paroud."

Again, the man seemed as if he might just fall over.

"We will go to the south," Brynn decided. "If I know Tohen Bardoh, that is where he will be found, hiding behind his lines until victory is assured." She looked to Pagonel as she finished, and the mystic nodded his approval.

When darkness fell the dragon was off again, swinging back to the west, then banking south, only gradually making his way back to the east to complete the circuit behind the rear position of Bardoh's lines.

From on high, Brynn marked the campfires well.

"You would make me come out here personally?" Yatol Wadon said, trembling with anger. For not only had he been forced to climb into a small boat and travel all the way out to *Rontlemore's Dream* to meet the abbot of St. Bondabruce, the man would not give him a private audience. Duke Bretherford and Master Mackaront were on hand, sitting at either side of Abbot Olin, while Wadon had only been allowed to enter the cabin alone.

"Consider yourself fortunate that there is a 'here' to come out to," replied Abbot Olin, wearing a superior grin as he glanced left and right at his two underlings.

A frustrated and frightened Wadon turned his eye on Mackaront. "You told me that the provisions were already being made! You told me that Abbot Olin was already aiding Jacintha. Where are the soldiers, Master Mackaront? Where is the help we need when Yatol Bardoh's army is within a day's march of Jacintha's southern gate?"

Mackaront, wearing a grin to match Olin's, turned deferentially to his abbot.

"Our reach is greater than you understand, my friend," Olin explained. "But why would I place Honce-the-Bear soldiers into battle on behalf of Jacintha, without even knowing if Jacintha truly desired our help? I do not so willingly send my countrymen to die, nor am I thrilled at the prospect of telling good King Aydrian of his losses after the war—the war to which we have not yet been invited."

All energy seemed to flow out of Yatol Mado Wadon at that moment, his shoulders slumping in defeat. "Would you have me beg?" he asked somberly.

Abbot Olin scoffed at him. "Your begging is of no practical use to me."

"Then what, Abbot Olin?" Yatol Wadon asked. "What am I to offer in exchange for your aid. Surely you understand that your position will be stronger if I rule in Jacintha than if Yatol Bardoh conquers the place."

"Truthfully, Yatol, I know of no such thing," Olin replied. "I have known Yatol Bardoh for years, and ever have we held a fondness for each other. He was much more tolerant of Chezru Douan's arrangement with Entel than many in Douan's own palace of Chom Deiru."

Yatol Wadon couldn't help but wince at that last remark, for the reference was true enough concerning him specifically.

"But still you are here, and I have Master Mackaront's words as a guide," the desperate Yatol reasoned. "You are prepared to step in against Yatol Bardoh—you have said as much. So please spare me the cryptic games, Abbot, and speak that which you desire."

Abbot Olin came forward suddenly. "I will fend Bardoh's forces and save Jacintha for you," he said bluntly. "And as a reward, I will be seated in Chom Deiru beside you."

"There is always a spare room . . ."

"Not as your guest, Yatol," Abbot Olin clarified. "But as your equal!"

Yatol Mado Wadon blanched and blinked repeatedly.

"Together we will forge a relationship between Abellican and Chezru," Abbot Olin explained. "You and I will seek the common ground of our respective religions and we will use that ground to build a new religion."

"You wish to bring the Abellican Church to Behren!" Yatol Wadon accused, seeing the coy words for what they were.

Abbot Olin slipped back in his seat into a comfortable position and looked again to his two commanders. "I offer you a place beside me," he said. "One of luxury and comfort."

"A place for a stooge to give you credibility, you mean!"

"And if I do mean exactly that?" Abbot Olin retorted. "Your religion is in shambles, and you know it. All the pretense of Chezru died with the revelations of Yakim Douan's deceptions. You scorn the sacred gemstones of the Abellican Church openly, and yet your leader, your God-Voice, used those very stones to seek immortality. Do you really believe that the religion of Chezru will survive this?

"And so I offer you an alternative," Abbot Olin went on. "Together we might rebuild the trust of the Behrenese people. Consider your options before you so readily dismiss my offer, Yatol. If I defeat Bardoh for you, Jacintha will survive. If I remain out here . . . well, I wonder how high the flames will leap over Jacintha."

Yatol Wadon glanced all around, seeming like a cornered animal. But again, he suddenly seemed to deflate, as if all the fight had been taken from him. "Stop him," he begged Olin, his voice no more than a whisper.

Abbot Olin's smile widened nearly to take in his ears. "I am fighting for a seat in Chom Deiru," he explained to the Yatol. "I fight well when the rewards are so great."

Abbot Olin turned to Bretherford and nodded, and the duke rose and left the room. He paused at the door and glanced back at the abbot, his expression ambiguous, as it had been since the rise of Aydrian, and all along this wild and unexpected journey.

"Go back to your . . . to our, city, Yatol Wadon, and instruct your archers to hold their shots as the warriors of Honce-the-Bear cross along your western wall," Abbot Olin explained. "Muster your own forces along the city's south wall alone."

"The south wall and the docks," Yatol Wadon replied. "We have information that Yatol Peridan has assembled a great fleet."

Abbot Olin and Master Mackaront both began to laugh. "Along the south wall alone, Yatol," he reiterated. "Your docks will not see battle."

Yatol Wadon stared at the man hard, not understanding.

But Abbot Olin merely laughed again, not explaining.

Screams erupted among the ramshackle buildings just outside Jacintha's southern wall, and flames quickly followed.

Yatol Mado Wadon and his assistants watched the beginning slaughter from the bell tower of Chom Deiru. The legions of Bardoh and Peridan—many of them wearing the colors of the Jacintha garrison!—marched among the buildings, wantonly slaughtering the dirty peasants as they tried to scramble out of the way.

A huge host of frightened commoners, peasant and refugee alike, swarmed the city proper's southern wall, beating their hands against the soft stone and pressing hard against the gate, so hard that several fell dead, crushed by the weight of the terrified, frenzied crowd.

"Tell them to fight back!" Yatol Mado Wadon yelled at those around him. "Prod them on! Pour burning oil on them from the walls if you must to turn them back into the fight against Bardoh's dogs!"

"Yatol, they have no weapons to use against the soldiers," one of the attendants tried to explain, but old and angry Wadon slapped him across the face to silence him, then said through gritted teeth, "Tell them to fight back."

The screams grew louder, as did the press on the wall, which was exactly what the enemies of Jacintha desired, Yatol Wadon knew. Bardoh the merciless was using the peasants as fodder, forcing the Jacintha soldiers to waste arrows on their worthless hides, or to pour oil on them. Using their fear, Bardoh had turned the hundreds into a human battering ram.

Yatol Wadon turned to gaze out to sea, where a fleet of warships was gliding into clear view. These were not the low-running sleek pirate boats that Peridan had reportedly used, but the greater warships of Honce-the-Bear. From his high vantage point, Wadon could see signalmen on the prows of those approaching craft, waving large red flags.

The Yatol glanced back to the north, to the mountains. "Hurry up, Abbot Olin," he muttered under his breath.

South of the city proper, the screams began to diminish, and Yatol Wadon heard the call of his parapet battle commanders. In seconds, the fight was on in full, with the city defenders firing their bows over the wall and artillerymen launching their catapults, sending huge balls of burning pitch soaring out to the south. But Bardoh and Peridan had not come unprepared, and the returning fire, including a barrage from a high dune far away that almost took down large sections of the wall in a single volley, was no less devastating.

Yatol Wadon cupped his hand across his brow to shield the glare and peered out to the southwest, to that high dune, to a line of catapults that had been dragged into position.

The second volley was soon airborne, a combination of boulders and flaming brands, and in seconds, several structures about Jacintha's southern wall went up in flames.

"The advance begins in full!" proclaimed Abu Das Abu, the undercommander for Yatol Peridan's waterborne legions. The obese man sat on a huge padded chair specially constructed to hold his girth. Once a great warrior, considered a match for even a Chezhou-lei, Abu Das Abu had been sorely wounded in a tragic wagon accident many years before and had lost all strength and feeling in his lower torso. Normally in the harsh Behrenese society, such a debilitating injury would have meant a death sentence, but so valuable was Abu Das Abu's battle cunning that Yatol Peridan had kept him on all these years. It was Abu Das Abu who had led Peridan to the pirate leader Maisha Darou in the early days of his conflict with Yatol De Hamman, and that alliance had given Peridan a decided edge over the Yatol to the north.

And now, with the greater promise of Jacintha itself, and indeed, all of Behren, that alliance had seemingly paid dividends once again, for Maisha Darou had responded to Peridan's plea with a tremendous fleet of ships.

Abu Das Abu had more than five thousand warriors on those ships, sailing fast to the north, paralleling the charge of the infantry as it neared Jacintha's southern district and wall.

"We will let the fighting begin in earnest, then sweep into the docks," Abu Das Abu directed Maisha Darou. "Yatols Peridan and Bardoh will pressure the city's defenses. Jacintha will need every warrior to hold the wall, and so the docks will be ours!"

Maisha Darou reflected the obese man's wicked smile. "We will find a favorable tide coming in from the north," he explained. "We must tack deeper out to sea so that we are not seen by the watchers on the docks. They will expect an attack from the sea, but from the south and not the north."

Abu Das Abu looked at the man suspiciously for some time, weighing every word. Darou's course change was not in the original plan, and while Abu Das Abu wanted the infantry to reach the city first, the fleet could not lag too far behind.

"I know these waters," the pirate said, clapping the big man on the shoulder. "Once we get out past the southern coastal current, our speed will amaze you. And there is a swirl out there and a back tide that will rush us in to Jacintha's docks faster than a To-gai pony."

"Back tide?" Abu Das Abu asked doubtfully. "I have never heard of such a thing."

But all that Maisha Darou would reply was, "You will see," and the pirate walked away, motioning to his pilot to tack hard right, turning the ships out to the deeper waters of the great Mirianic.

Just as Duke Bretherford had instructed.

"You see, Yatol Peridan, it is all in the execution," Yatol Bardoh said smugly, watching the pounding at the southern wall of Jacintha from a position on the high ridge, beside his formidable battery of catapults and great, spear-throwing ballistae. "Now, as soon as your Abu Das Abu takes his force onto the docks, all pretense of Jacintha's defense will shatter, and we will have the city."

Peridan started to respond, but reflexively ducked as another great volley went out from the artillery beside them. He shook his head in absolute amazement at the effectiveness of those batteries. These were Yatol Bardoh's trump card, as Abu Das Abu's force was Peridan's. Bardoh had spent weeks with his forces doing nothing but building these great war engines. Their power would bring down Jacintha in short order, he had promised Peridan, and—and this was the real prize in Bardoh's eyes, Peridan knew—would evict the troublesome Dragon of To-gai from the Behrenese city of Dharyan.

And it all seemed to be going extremely well. Even from this great distance, Peridan could see that the city's defenders were sorely pressed. Sections of wall were down, and large fires had begun to rage. And all the ground before the wall was strewn with the dead peasants and the pitiful refugees who had swarmed north from De Hamman's towns before the charge of Peridan and Bardoh. Now, if only Abu Das Abu would reach the docks . . .

And he should be there, Peridan knew, but there were no indications of any action along the city's eastern side, though in truth, he couldn't see it well enough from his vantage point to gauge properly.

His relief was palpable when an aide came riding hard toward the ridge-line, crying out that there were ships in the harbor.

"Abu Das Abu," Peridan announced to Bardoh, and the Yatol of Avrou Eesa grinned wickedly and nodded his approval.

"Ships in the harbor!" the messenger cried again, his horse struggling up the ridge. "Great warships! Flying the pennant of the bear and tiger!"

In the blink of an eye, the smiles disappeared from the faces of the two Yatols.

"Honce-the-Bear?" Yatol Bardoh said to the man, who dismounted and began scrambling toward the great leader.

"Yes, Yatol," the messenger replied. "They are Bearmen, no doubt. There are whispers that Abbot Olin is among them!"

"Where is our fleet?" Yatol Bardoh demanded of the messenger, and he turned as he spoke, throwing the question at Yatol Peridan, as well.

"I do not know!" the messenger shrieked.

In his rage, Yatol Bardoh turned and motioned to Ung Lik Dy, his personal Chezhou-Lei bodyguard, and the muscular man stepped forward immediately and with a sudden movement, whipped the delicately curving sword from its sheath across his back and in a single fluid motion, took the head from the messenger's body—so quickly that the man didn't even have the time to cry out.

The head rolled across the dirt and wound up staring back at the head-less body, which was only then beginning to sway and topple, and the messenger's eyes and mouth widened in unison, as if in that moment of his death, he had suddenly realized what had just happened.

"You told me that Abu Das Abu was reliable, Yatol," Bardoh growled at Peridan.

"He is likely circling the Honce-the-Bear warships even now, preparing to sink them in the harbor," Peridan stammered, and all the while he was speaking, his gaze alternated between Ung Lik Dy and the head of the messenger.

"What are they doing here?" Yatol Bardoh demanded, and before Yatol Peridan could answer or Bardoh could press on, there came the winding of horns, so many horns!

The two men spun about, as did everyone else on the ridge, and even from this distance, the charge of the Bearmen was purely stunning.

They swept along the western wall of Jacintha in tight formations, squares of infantry leading the way, their shields interlocked and spear tips gleaming in the morning sunlight. Flanking them came a line of cavalry, a thousand at least, all armored, rider and horse.

"How is this possible?" Yatol Peridan said, his voice barely more than a whisper.

"He has allied with Honce-the-Bear!" Tohen Bardoh screamed. "The fool is just like his predecessor, a friend to the Abellican gemstone wizards more than to his own people, and more than to his own religion. But he will not survive this, despite his alliance!"

He glared at Peridan. "Order a full retreat to this ridge. We cannot stand in open combat against the Bearmen with their heavy-plated armor, but they cannot hope to pursue us for long. Let the hot sun steal their strength! By the time they arrive at this ridge, they will be falling from exhaustion, and then we will come back at them!" Bardoh turned to his artillerymen. "Fill the area about the Bearmen with burning pitch, and be prepared to wheel the cata-pults away at a moment's notice. We have no idea what other sundry alliances the dog Wadon has made!"

As he finished, all of the artillerymen who were looking his way suddenly blanched, their eyes widening, their jaws drooping open. Following that lead, Tohen Bardoh saw indeed what other alliance Yatol Wadon had forged, in the form of a great dragon swooping in at their ranks!

The Behrenese cried out and broke ranks, fleeing every which way as the dragon dove for the line of catapults. Peridan fled down the ridge, and Bar-doh moved to follow, but his Chezhou-Lei warrior grabbed him by the arm and tugged him back toward the rushing dragon, correctly guessing that the wurm would not be able to compensate for their move and would swoop right above them.

"Bardoh!" Brynn cried recognizing the hated man. She knew at once that Agradeleous could not possibly react in time, though, and so she flipped her leg over the dragon's neck and dropped into a roll in the sand.

Agradeleous kept his path true and the first two catapults went up in flames beneath the power of his fiery breath. The third war engine fell, too, toppled by the dragon's mighty claws.

Brynn rolled over and over and over, absorbing the shock of the impact. She came up in perfect balance and swung about, glancing back over her shoulder in time to see the dragon's destructive run, and to see a second form, Pagonel, similarly drop to the sand.

Brynn charged on after Bardoh. All about her, Behrenese soldiers scram-bled and shrieked, and not one would turn to face the formidable woman.

Not one, except for Ung Lik Dy.

Bardoh continued to flee behind him, but the Chezhou-Lei warrior stood resolute, parting his feet about shoulders' width and rocking back and forth a bit to get complete balance in the soft sand.

"We are not enemies," Brynn said to him, coming up before him with Flamedancer, her slender and strong elven sword, held out to the side. "Or we need not be. How many Chezhou-Lei must die in these times? Was not the disaster in the Mountains of Fire enough for you?"

She knew, despite her claim that they were not enemies, that her refer-ence to the Mountains of Fire would spur the man to action, for in that place, not so long ago, she, the Jhesta Tu mystics, a pair of elves, and Agra-deleous had decimated the Chezhou-Lei order.

Ung Lik Dy leaped forward, his magnificent sword cutting a circle at Brynn's eye level, once and then again. Before the ducking Brynn could even think about stabbing forward under that slashing blade, Ung Lik Dy altered the momentum so that his sword was cutting diagonal slashes be-tween the two combatants, forcing Brynn to retreat instead.

And she did, and with perfect balance, for she was schooled in *bi'nelle dasada*, the elven sword dance.

Once out of range, she set herself, feet perpendicular, right foot in front with her toes pointing the way to Ung Lik Dy and the bulk of her weight centered over that back, balancing foot. She brought her left hand up in the air behind her further to solidify her balance, and let Flamedancer weave delicately before her, like the teasing sway of a serpent.

The Chezhou-Lei came forward in a sudden rush, sword spinning in those diagonals. He changed hands repeatedly, altering the cut, and when Brynn tried to parry, he turned the blade into the diagonal, nearly getting past her outstretched sword.

Brynn made a mental note to dodge, not parry!

The tireless Ung Lik Dy pressed on, his shining sword humming as it cut through the air. He only seemed to be gaining momentum and speed, and Brynn was retreating as fast as she could, while still maintaining the balance needed to fend off the dynamic warrior.

She thought of calling to Flamedancer then, to ignite the blade and thus startle the warrior. She held back, though, wanting to get a better measure of her opponent before playing so desperate a deception. Under different conditions, Brynn might have held the fires of the sword altogether, for the sake of honor, but at that time, her goal was not to win a test with a Chezhou-Lei warrior, but to get to the dog, Bardoh!

She continued to dodge and to back away, allowing Ung Lik Dy to play out his momentum. Soon enough, she planned to turn back on him.

Or so she thought.

For out of the corner of her eye, she noted two of the other Behrenese warriors, apparently gaining heart with the sight of the deadly Chezhou-Lei warrior, coming in hard at her. She had to turn to fend, she knew, but she could not without getting decapitated by the warrior!

In the pair came, spears lowered, and Brynn had no practical defense. She reversed her movement and went ahead instead, and suddenly, stab-bing her sword up high to ring against the Chezhou-Lei blade to tap it just enough to break the man's rhythm.

And then she tucked in her hip and spun, knowing that she had no chance to avoid getting skewered.

But then a form came rushing between Brynn and the two spearmen, turning as it went, and turning their spears aside.

Pagonel lifted his elbows in that turn, expertly slamming the first and then the second warrior in the face, in rapid succession. One went down, while the other staggered a few steps to the side, stumbling some ten feet from the Jhesta Tu mystic.

Pagonel stopped his rush, planted his feet immediately, and leaped back the other way, up high and turning to the horizontal.

The stunned warrior tried to lift his spear, but he was too late, and the mystic came in over it, double-kicking the man in the face and laying him low on the sand.

Too engaged with the Chezhou-Lei, Brynn didn't watch the spectacle, but despite their desperate dance, she realized that her opponent couldn't help but be distracted by the sight of a hated Jhesta Tu.

At that moment Brynn did call to her sword, and the blade flamed to life. She snapped it up high, and bade the sword to extinguish, then snapped it back down low.

But the Chezhou-Lei, his eyes tricked by the burst of fire up high, didn't follow that sudden downward movement, and so his defenses went up high, as well.

And Brynn's thrust came in hard below his sword, catching him in the throat.

Sputtering and gasping, the warrior fell away.

Brynn didn't hesitate, sprinting past him as he fell, in full pursuit of the running Bardoh, though in the up-and-down terrain of the immediate area, she was not sure where he had gone.

But then Agradeleous was there, flying beside her, and she called out to him to guide her to Bardoh.

"He is right there," the dragon answered, looking ahead and to the left, just over another windblown dune. "A tasty morsel!"

"No!" Brynn screamed at him, and the wurm pulled up.

Brynn didn't bother to offer an explanation, just sprinted ahead and leaped over the ridge, nearly landing on the terrified Bardoh. He threw up his hands in a gesture of surrender, but the pose didn't even register to the outraged woman.

Yes, Brynn remembered this man, oh so well. He was the invader of To-gai, who had enslaved and tortured her people. He was the man who had ordered mass executions of To-gai-ru, simply to teach the hated Ru some discipline. He was the man who had murdered her parents when she was but a child.

That last thought was sweeping through Brynn's mind even as her elven sword was sweeping through Tohen Bardoh's neck, lopping his head from his shoulders.

Caught by Her Own Gemstone

"**B**ut aren't ye looking like a great feeder o' the pigs this fine morning!" Dainsey Lockless cried out in a spirited tone when she and Pony moved to the back, private rooms of Fellowship Way, the Dundalis tavern named after the place in Palmaris where Pony had grown into womanhood. A scented candle was burning nearby, giving the room a soft and smoky aroma, and a shade was drawn over the room's lone window, keeping out the brilliant sunlight. All in all, the place gave Pony the impression of a room where someone might go to die. Dainsey's words had been obviously exaggerated, for the man at whom she had aimed that phrase so energetically seemed far from worthy of the mood. Old and weary, Belster O'Comely was propped upon several pillows, making his great girth seem even larger. He had always been a man of many chins, as the saying in Dundalis went. Now it looked as if he had found many more.

His shirt was less than fresh; his hair, what little was left of it, unkempt; and he was sorely in need of a shave.

"And here I am thinking that the only thing I'll ever feed to the pigs again might well be my own flesh," he replied in a phlegm-filled voice with as much energy as he could muster—and the exertion had him coughing violently a moment later.

Pony went to his side and instinctively brought the soul stone out of her pouch. "Tell me where you're hurting, Belster."

The portly tavernkeeper, larger now by far than Pony remembered him, looked up at her warmly and smiled. "Ye got a cure for age, do ye?" he asked. "Where ain't I hurting? There's the better question!"

It struck Pony how much Belster's enunciation had taken on the accent of the Timberlands region. She didn't dwell on it, though, for she couldn't resist that wry grin, and she moved forward and wrapped her dear old friend in a great hug.

"Ah, but there's the best healin' any man could ever want," Belster remarked.

Pony pulled back. "You've a tavern full of patrons, old man," she teased. "Why are you in bed?"

Belster's expression became very serious. "Bah!" he snorted. "It's been this way ever since I hurt the leg, ye know. Kept me in bed—and in bed, things've only gotten worse."

"Because ye've gotten fat, ye old fool," Dainsey scolded, and Belster laughed at her.

"Does your leg still trouble you?" Pony asked, reaching down to feel the man's knee, and as soon as she touched it, Belster gave a little hiss and a jump, showing her just how tender it still was. She remembered her wedding day to King Danube those years ago, when she had first learned of Belster's bad leg, and now she scolded herself privately for not rushing right up here to aid the man!

"Some days are better than others," Belster admitted. "I can tell you when a rain's coming, to be sure!"

Pony was glad to share his smile again. Belster had been such a great friend and protector to her in Palmaris in the days of Markwart; she hadn't realized how much she had missed the man until this moment, sitting beside him in his small tavern in the heart of the Timberlands. How strange it seemed to her! And yet, how much at home she felt. It was as if she hadn't seen Belster in decades, and as if she had been beside him only yesterday, all at once.

"I can help to heal that knee," she said, showing him the soul stone. "But your belly is your own to fix, and you'll not do that by lying here on your pillows!"

Belster just smiled in reply. Pony started to move toward his leg, but he grabbed her tightly by the arm and made her turn back to face him. "So good, 'tis, to see ye again," he said softly, and he reached up to run his hand over Pony's golden hair. "Ah, the fine times we had! We gave that demon Markwart all that he could handle! And now look at yerself: the queen of Honce-the-Bear!"

He stopped suddenly and looked at her curiously, and Pony knew that a revealing cloud had surely crossed over her face.

"No more the queen," she told him. "King Danube is dead and the throne has been claimed by another."

"Was her own boy, Aydr—" Dainsey started to say, but Pony stopped her with a sudden fierce expression.

Pony turned back to Belster immediately, softening her look. "It's just me, Pony, again," she said. "And that is the way I desire it to be."

But Belster, who had seen so much in his years, who had made his living all his adult life as a tavernkeeper—and as such, as a man who listened to secrets—wasn't so easily deflected. "Whose own boy?" he asked.

"It is nothing to concern yourself with," Pony answered. "Honce-the-

Bear will be whatever it will be, and Ursal is of no concern out here, surely. I have come home, Belster. I have left the court of Ursal far behind, and that is my choice. I care nothing for the events in the far south, and very little for the routines of Palmaris, except in how they affect our friend, Braumin Herde. I have come home, seeking the peace of Dundalis. This is not the time for Queen Jilseponie, but just for Pony."

She looked back to his leg, elevated on still more pillows. "Your friend Pony, who plans to get you up and about in short order," she finished, feeling again the tender spots on that knee.

She could tell that Belster was looking past her, to Dainsey, and so she glanced the woman's way, to see her chewing on her lips.

Belster, in his typical manner, was pressing the point even before Pony turned back to regard him. "Whose son?" he asked. "Aydr?"

"Aydrian," Dainsey explained. "Aydrian Wyndon, who calls Pony and Elbryan his parents."

Pony spun and flashed her an alarmed look, but Dainsey stood resolute, shaking her head.

And she was right, Pony knew in her heart. Who were they to keep such a secret from Belster O'Comely, the man who had never been anything but the very best of a friend to them both?

Pony closed her eyes for a moment before turning back to Belster, trying to figure out how she could begin to explain Aydrian. She was surprised to learn that she'd have less to tell than she anticipated.

"Oh, by the demon dactyl itself," Belster was muttering. "Lady Dasslerond, what'd ye do?"

Pony's eyes popped open wide and she stared hard at the man. "How could you know?"

"Who'd the elves take ye to when they dragged ye off that field after yer fight with Markwart?" Belster replied, his voice stronger than it had been to this point, and stronger than Pony expected it could possibly be, given the man's condition. "Ye went out with a child in yer belly and came back without one, and I never was believing the elves' tale of what had happened!"

With great effort, the man pulled himself to a sitting position. He motioned for Dainsey to go and pull back the room's curtain, then looked Pony in the eye. "Now ye tell me," he said. "And ye tell me all of it. Don't ye go protecting Belster for Belster's sake, ye hear me?"

Pony stared at him for a moment, caught off her guard. But only until she remembered who this man truly was, and remembered that he had been there, in times good and in times bad, standing with her, defending her, hiding her, and nursing her. He had demanded the truth from her, and how could she begin to think that he deserved anything less than that?

And so she told him everything, of the rise of Aydrian and the fall of Danube. And of the return of Marcalo De'Unnero, which seemed to pain Belster most of all.

When she had finished, the three sat in silence for a long time until Belster finally gave Pony a curious look. "He hates ye?" the man asked.

"Aydrian believes that I abandoned him to the elves, and they were less than kind, from what I can gather," Pony admitted. "He hates me profoundly—I am surprised he suffered me to live."

"Poisoned by the tongue of Marcalo De'Unnero, no doubt," Belster reasoned. "Ever was he the serpent. So much better we'd all be if ye had killed the man in Palmaris those years ago."

"But I did not," Pony replied, and she managed a smile as she added, "Though to be sure, I tried!" The smile was short-lived, though, lost in the realization of the darkening world. "And now De'Unnero is with Aydrian, and that is the reality."

"And ye've fled," said Belster. "But why here? Shouldn't ye be in Vanguard, standing beside Prince Midalis?"

"You would have me fight Aydrian?" Pony replied, her tone so downtrodden and defeated as to dismiss any arguments that might be forthcoming. "Nay, I've no anger for him—how could I?"

"Ye're full of anger! It's in yer eyes!"

"Oh, yes," Pony agreed.

"For the elves," Belster said suddenly. "Oh, but ye hate them, don't ye?"

Pony stared at him for a long, long while, her expression as firm an answer as anyone would ever need. "Let me get your leg mended," she said. "And then you get yourself out of that bed. And then you clean up and find your spirit! Belster O'Comely's not ready for the grave just yet!"

Pony left him a short while later, satisfied that she had done much to help him reverse the downward spiral his injury had caused. Dainsey was with him still, and more than ready to prod him out of his bed and over to the well for a much-needed cleaning!

As she moved back to the tavern of Fellowship Way, Pony did not replace the soul stone in her pouch, though. She hadn't used the gemstones much in the last few years, but the connection had come easily to her once more. Now she looked at the stone, into its enticing gray depths, and considered its other possible uses.

She had meant to stay in the tavern for a bit, just to watch the ordinary routines of this place she had once called home, but she found herself walking out almost immediately, moving across the small village to a house the good-hearted and generous folk of the town had offered to her and Dainsey and Roger when they had first arrived.

Inside, she drew curtains over the home's single window, then moved to a quiet corner, rolling the stone about her fingers all the way.

And then she fell into it again, and used it to loose her spirit. Freed of her mortal bonds, she flew out of Dundalis, off to the west, toward the distant mountains she knew housed Andur'Blough Inninness and Lady Dasslerond.

For a long while, Pony's spirit roamed those mountains, seeking the elven valley. But to her dismay, she did not locate it that afternoon. She had made progress, though, taking note of specific landmarks, including one or two that looked familiar to her. She had been to the elven valley on a couple of occasions, and had found it before with the soul stone. She knew that it was very well hidden, though, and suspected that Lady Dasslerond might be working hard with her own magic to ensure that it was even more secluded now.

When she returned to her waiting body, Pony was satisfied with her progress. Using the soul stone, she would soon have the mountains about Andur'Blough Inninness mapped out sufficiently for her to make the physical journey and confront the elven lady who had taken so much from her.

"What do you know?" Belli'mar Juraviel asked Lady Dasslerond when he found her standing on the edge of the forest, staring out at the mountains with a perplexed expression.

"She was here."

"She?"

"Jilseponie," Lady Dasslerond explained. "Her spirit came very close. She seeks us."

Juraviel looked at her curiously, his expression doubting. "How can you know?"

Lady Dasslerond held aloft her shining emerald, the stone of Caer'alfar, given to the elves by Terranen Dinoniel in the first coming of the demon dactyl. Among the most marvelous of the enchanted gemstones, the emerald was also among the rarest. And certainly there was no other stone in all the world quite like Lady Dasslerond's; the power of other emeralds collected at Pimaninicuit served no stronger magic than to speed someone's walking. But Dasslerond's was the stone of the earth itself, the stone that connected her to the ground beneath her feet. With it, she could distort distances, thus allowing her to travel across great expanses with a single step. With it, she could sense the grasses and the fields, and the animals that walked upon them.

And the spirits, perhaps, that hovered about them.

"She seeks us," Dasslerond said again. "She knows of Aydrian now, of course, and she is not pleased."

"We could not expect otherwise," said Juraviel, and sensitive to Dasslerond's dilemma and fears, he did well to keep hidden his relief at learning that Pony was alive.

"She is a human," Dasslerond said with her typical, thinly veiled contempt for those she considered the lesser race. "She could never begin to comprehend the greater implications of her son, and the greater promise."

"And the greater failure," Juraviel dared to add, drawing a sharp look from his Lady.

"Aydrian alone offered us the promise of saving Andur'Blough Inninness from the stain of the demon dactyl that will surely consume it," Dasslerond countered. "That decay was brought on by our selflessness in helping humans. We sacrificed for their sake."

"I do remember," Juraviel admitted, for it had been Lady Dasslerond's rescue of him and the band of refugees he was escorting that had brought the demon dactyl to the elven valley.

"And now we ask a sacrifice from one of them," Dasslerond went on. "Would not Elbryan, Aydrian's own father, give of himself to save Andur'Blough Inninness? His mother would not, surely, but Elbryan—"

"Jilseponie would," Juraviel strongly corrected. "Ever have you misjudged her, and underestimated her. She would have willingly sacrificed herself for the sake of the Touel'alfar, had that ever been asked of her. In quality of character, she is every bit the ranger as any we have ever trained."

Dasslerond's expression showed that she really didn't want to have this argument with Juraviel again. Not here and not now.

"She is not seeking us so that she can help us," came Dasslerond's dry reply.

"She just learned the truth of Aydrian," Juraviel replied. "I do not disagree."

"With me or with her?" Lady Dasslerond snapped, and her sudden, uncharacteristic anger told Juraviel just how on edge she was about all of this.

"I do not disagree with your assessment," Juraviel clarified, and he didn't bother to add that he wasn't really sure he disagreed with Pony's anger, as well. Surely he understood that anger; how could anyone be so deceived about her own child and not react with anger?

"She will search for us again," said Dasslerond. "And she will eventually find her way to Andur'Blough Inninness."

"In spirit," Juraviel remarked.

"And what is then to stop her from finding us in body, as well?" asked the Lady of Caer'alfar. "Perhaps of even allying with Aydrian to show him the way home?"

"She will not," Juraviel argued.

"It is not a chance that we can take."

"What do you mean to do, Lady?" Juraviel asked, alarms screaming at him in his mind. He knew how cold and merciless Dasslerond could be, especially toward the lesser races! And in most cases, Juraviel agreed with Lady Dasslerond, or at least understood her propensity to err on the side of caution. The Touel'alfar were not numerous, after all, and were not a prolific people. It would not take much to destroy them altogether.

But this was Jilseponie! This was Pony! This was the woman who had stood so strongly beside Elbryan! This was the woman who had faithfully carried the secrets of the elven sword dance, and of Andur'Blough Inninness, with her. This was the woman who had never been anything but a friend of the Touel'alfar, though Lady Dasslerond had never, ever treated her as such.

"There is, perhaps, a way in which I might facilitate the unavoidable meeting at a time and place of my choosing," Lady Dasslerond explained. "When Jilseponie returns in spirit, I will know of it, and I will find that spirit, and with this—" She held aloft the emerald. "—I can perhaps bring her out here in body, as well."

"Lady . . ." Juraviel said breathlessly.

"You will be there beside me," Lady Dasslerond continued.

Juraviel wanted to shout at her, to scream that she could not do this. This was Jilseponie, a friend to the Touel'alfar, a dear friend to Belli'mar Juraviel. He suspected that Dasslerond wanted him there to lure Jilseponie, perhaps to defuse her and help to get her off her guard. Or perhaps his Lady just wanted him to witness this so that she could assess his reactions to her stern judgment, and thus measure his loyalty to his people.

It was all too much for him in that horrible moment, and he truly wanted to scream out.

But he did not.

Pony knew that she was making fine progress toward finding the hidden valley when she went out spiritually from Dundalis again the next day. Many of the landmarks were familiar to her now; she remembered the images of certain, distinctive mountains clearly from her journey here beside Elbryan.

Pleased, she continued on for a bit longer, taking a wider search and trying to find the elusive trails that would take her to the mountain slopes overlooking the cloud-veiled valley. She hoped that perhaps she would see that gray shroud this very day. But then, wearying from the exertion of spirit-walking, she was forced to turn back for Dundalis and her corporeal form.

But a voice called out to her, both physically and telepathically.

Following that call back along a trail, Pony found the source, and if she had been in her corporeal body at that time, she surely would have had to be reminded to breathe.

For there stood Lady Dasslerond and Belli'mar Juraviel.

Belli'mar Juraviel! For all the hatred Jilseponie felt toward the Touel'alfar at that time, she could not deny the sudden burst of warmth she felt at the sight of her old companion and friend!

But even that could not balance her emotions at the sight of Dasslerond, the Lady of Caer'alfar, who had stolen her child from her, and who had created from that child of promise the creature Aydrian.

She flew back before them, and it took every ounce of willpower she could muster not to dive spiritually into Lady Dasslerond and do battle with her soul. She almost did just that, and actually started to, but when she did, she felt a very definite spiritual barrier there, and only then did she realize that Dasslerond was holding a gemstone of her own, a green-shining emerald.

"Fly back to your body," Lady Dasslerond said, speaking perfect Bearman. "I will go with you that we can have this . . . meeting, you so desire."

Pony hovered there, her emotions swirling wildly.

"I am one with my gemstone now," Dasslerond went on. "Go now, for I cannot maintain the connection to it and to you for very long! Go, or this meeting will be at its end!"

Pony knew that there was more to it than that; she understood implicitly that Dasslerond was trying to prevent her from finding the elven valley— perhaps out of fear that she would subsequently lead an army there to exact revenge. She had to make a decision, and quickly. Was her argument with the Touel'alfar in general or with Lady Dasslerond alone?

The sight of Belli'mar Juraviel standing beside the Lady of Caer'alfar, his expression clearly one of sympathy, helped her find her right course in the clash of emotions, and without offering a response to Dasslerond, the woman flew away with all speed across the miles, all the way back to her quiet and dark room in Dundalis and her waiting physical form. She dove back through the soul stone and into her body, expecting to find Dasslerond standing before her, and perhaps with a sword drawn!

And Dasslerond was there—sort of. For beside the image of the Lady of Caer'alfar remained the mountainous scene all those miles away, almost as if the two places had been suddenly linked, a distortion of distance itself!

There was Juraviel as well, and he lifted his hand to Pony, and without even thinking, she reached up and took it.

And then she was soaring again, but not spirit-walking! Somehow— through Dasslerond's magical gemstone, she realized!—she was physically moving across the miles.

In the blink of an eye, she was beside Dasslerond and Juraviel, standing on a windblown mountain pass outside Andur'Blough Inninness. Only then did Pony realize that she had been deceived.

Only then did Pony understand that Dasslerond had known her intent and had caught her first. She had no gemstones save the soul stone, and didn't even have her sword!

And she faced Dasslerond, the true power of the Touel'alfar.

CHAPTER

❖ 16 ❖

Three Ways to Win

R oger knew better than to close up under the cowl of his traveling
cloak as he walked the streets of Palmaris that windy late-autumn
night. The best disguise was often no disguise, he knew, and so he
walked about the gate area of Palmaris openly and seemingly completely
at ease.

He was certainly not at ease.

How could he be? He was in a city he had called home for many years, a
place where he had served among the ruling hierarchy, substituting for
Jilseponie herself when she had gone south to become Danube's queen. But
Palmaris was not his home any longer. Far from it. The city was in turmoil,
the citizens confused and upset. Aydrian was here, in command of the city
as the hated De'Unnero was in command of St. Precious. And all supposedly with the support of Bishop Braumin Herde, which was the most confusing factor of all. Roger Lockless understood that he would not be welcomed
here—which was why he had slipped in by hanging on to the undercarriage
of the wagon of an unsuspecting farmer.

He reminded himself constantly that he only had to get through this single night, and not even for much of the night, if Bradwarden's plan worked.

He made his way past the guardhouses and barracks that lined the wall,
all manned by Ursal soldiers now with the bulk of the Palmaris garrison
long fled to Vanguard. In a way, that was an advantage for Roger, since none
of these men recognized him, as the Palmaris soldiers surely would have.

Along this wall, too, were the city's long stables, huge barns with small
stalls with room for hundreds of horses. Roger knew the area well, and
knew where the garrison commanders had kept the finest of their stock.
Near that western end of the stabling area, Roger hoisted a bucket and
moved about with familiarity and ease, acting very much as if he was supposed to be there. He held his breath as he entered the barn area, though,
hoping against hope that Symphony was stabled nearby.

If not, then he knew where the horse would be: in the finer, and undoubtedly well-guarded, stables at Chasewind Manor. The mere thought of

going there unsettled him. The servants and groundskeepers would know him, after all, and no doubt the place was thick with Ursal men.

"It's about time ye got here!" an incredibly thin man with a shiny bald head and a dark and straggly beard assailed him as he entered with the bucket. "The damned mares've been screaming for their feed all the night!"

"I . . . I don't believe this is for them," Roger stammered, thinking fast on his feet. "I was told to deliver the meal to King Aydrian's own horse, and that one's not a mare, by all accounts."

"King Aydrian's horse?" the barn keeper replied, and his tone and incredulous expression confirmed Roger's worst fears.

"The big black," he said, hoping against hope.

"Ye got yerself a long way to carry the bucket!" The barn keeper snickered. "Or better yet, ye give me the bucket for the mares and get yerself another one at Chasewind Manor. They got plenty up there."

The man held out his hand for the bucket, and Roger readily turned it over.

"Ye best be running!" The barn keeper scolded. "I'd not be the one to keep King Aydrian's horse braying and kicking at the stall!"

Roger just nodded and walked out, devising a plan as he went, envisioning the layout of Chasewind Manor's grounds and stables—which of course were in the back of the house, in clear view of every sitting room! Worse still, that stable area was always well lit.

But Roger had to go there, and he had to hurry, for Bradwarden's song would soon fill the Palmaris night.

He had little trouble navigating the city to the more exclusive western region, and though there were more soldiers patrolling the streets in that area, there were more hedgerows for stealthy Roger to hide behind. Soon enough, the small man was standing along the wall of Chasewind Manor, not far from the main gate. He tried to act casual, surveying the area and sorting out the routines of the skilled soldiers guarding the grounds—Allheart Knights this time and not just ordinary Kingsmen.

Then, unexpectedly, Roger Lockless got his first view of Jilseponie's son. He knew that it was Aydrian riding in the open coach that rushed out of Chasewind Manor's gate. He only saw the man for an instant, but the young king looked at him directly and there could be no mistaking that resemblance. He possessed Pony's thick lips and thick hair, and Elbryan's eyes and jaw. In that moment of looking at him, Roger almost thought that he was looking upon his dead friend Elbryan once more!

To Roger's profound relief—after he had digested the truth of the encounter—the young king did not recognize him at all, and the coach wheeled away. Of even greater fortune, the guards seemed to relax almost immediately upon Aydrian's departure.

The shaken Roger grew even more unsettled a moment later, when a beautiful melody drifted across the Palmaris night. So unobtrusive was that song, so attuned to the night itself, that those around Roger didn't even seem to notice it.

But Roger surely did, and if Bradwarden was correct in his planning, then another in the city would not miss the significance of that song.

Spurred by a sudden realization of urgency, Roger moved swiftly along the wall, away from the gate. He knew the layout of the area well and, using strategic places of concealment, the small and nimble man made his way around the back of the compound. With a quick glance about, and a long and deep breath to steady his nerves, Roger slipped up and over the wall, dropping into the shadows of a widespread elm on the other side. Glad that there were few guards visible in the area, and hoping that no one was looking out from any of the many darkened sitting rooms at the back of Chasewind Manor, Roger hastily made his way toward the stables, where he could already hear a commotion brewing.

"Rouse King Aydrian!" he heard one man cry from inside the opulent barn. Every word was accompanied by an agitated whinny or the hard thump of a strong hoof smashing against wooden planks.

Without hesitation, fearful that Symphony might hurt himself in his anger, Roger sprinted right into the barn.

He found a trio of Allhearts standing before the great stallion's stall, one holding a whip and looking very much like he intended to charge into the stall and discipline the increasingly agitated stallion.

"He will kill you if you enter!" Roger cried reflexively, and he believed every word. Bradwarden was calling to the stallion with his haunting piping. Bradwarden, who had watched over Symphony and all the wild horses of the Timberlands for so many years, was musically bidding the great stallion to come home.

And there could be no doubt about the fact that Symphony wanted to go!

The three soldiers turned surprised expressions over at Roger. "Who are you?" one demanded.

"A man who knows this horse well, and who has known him since before the days when King Aydrian found him!" Roger answered. He rushed up to the stall and gently called to the magnificent stallion, and it was obvious, though Symphony retained his agitation, that there was some recognition there.

"We have to let him out, to run in the paddock," Roger explained, and if he had told the soldiers to fall dead upon their swords, they could not have worn more skeptical expressions. "It is the strength of Symphony," Roger tried to explained. "The stallion needs to run or he bursts with energy. Quickly! Help me to guide him out into the paddock. Let him run off the excess energy and he will rest more easily."

Not a soldier moved.

"He is a wild stallion, bred and grown in the open hills of the Timberlands," Roger desperately explained. "He can tolerate only short amounts of time in such an enclosure! Be quick, I beg you, or your king's horse will break a leg!"

"Who are you?" one of the soldiers demanded again.

"I was a stable hand in Caer Tinella when this magnificent creature carried King Aydrian's own father, Elbryan the Nightbird," Roger lied. He lowered his eyes perfectly, playing as if he was embarrassed to admit, "And I served Queen Jilseponie when she was baroness here in Palmaris, in the early days of her rule here soon after the plague. Few know of this, and I beg of you not to speak of it, but this same magnificent creature was also the favored mount of Jilseponie."

That brought a trio of stunned expressions, which was exactly what Roger was counting upon to give him enough credibility to dupe the fools.

"Please, I beg of you, if not for the sake of the horse, then to protect yourselves from the wrath of King Aydrian, help me to guide mighty Symphony out into the paddock," Roger pleaded.

"You cannot hope to control the beast!" one of the soldiers argued. "If we open the door, he will run you down!"

"No he won't," said Roger, and he looked up at the horse. "You'll not harm me, will you, Symphony?" he asked softly and the great stallion stopped its whinnying and kicking for a moment to consider Roger, as if he had understood every word. Roger didn't wait for an answer, but used the opportunity offered by the moment of calm to move to the door and quickly unbolt and open it. Before the guard could react, Symphony moved right up to Roger and nuzzled him, seeming to calm down immediately.

Roger looked to one of the soldiers, who tossed him a halter. He started to put it on the horse, but paused to stroke the horse's face—and to strategically allow Symphony to edge a bit farther out of the stall.

Roger moved as if to put the halter on again, and leaned in to whisper soothingly into the horse's ear. He didn't ask the horse for calm, though, but rather, urged Symphony to run!

And then Roger fell away, crying out as if he had been injured, and Symphony bolted past him and past the three startled soldiers. Head down, the stallion galloped out of the barn, and snorting and bucking, charged about the compound.

"Catch him! Oh, catch him!" Roger wailed, knowing full well that none of them would get near the great horse. His ploy worked to keep the soldiers off of him, though, and they ran out after the horse, calling out for help.

"Run on, Symphony," Roger whispered. "Follow the centaur's call, back to one who deserves you." He paused a moment, listening intently and taking some hope as the commotion moved away from the stables, toward the front gate.

And then the small man wisely made his own escape, heading out the stable's side door and into the shadows of another great tree. Or at least, that's where he had hoped to go.

"Master Lockless?" came a call right behind him, and though he didn't immediately recognize the voice, Roger knew that it was a question of surprise alone and not of identity. He stiffened and stopped and slowly turned about, to find a stunned old Illthin Dingle, one of Chasewind Manor's gardeners, looking back at him.

"Master Lockless!" the old man said again, more emphatically. "But I thought ye'd gone out to the north with Jilseponie."

Roger moved a finger to pursed lips, hoping to quiet the man somewhat, and he glanced all about nervously. "So I did, good Master Dingle, and now I am back to see this king who is her son."

Illthin cocked his gray-stubbled, grizzled face. He wore his hair long and tied in a gray ponytail, giving the old man a carefree appearance that fairly well matched his often unpredictable personality. "Ye got to do better than that, Master Lockless," Illthin said with a knowing grin.

Roger looked all around, then settled himself into place. "True enough," he admitted. "I returned for Symphony, and Symphony alone."

"Ye didn't now!"

"I did. Symphony is not the horse of this new king, worthy though he may be . . ."

"Ye're not for believing a word of that!" Illthin said with a phlegm-filled laugh.

"Symphony is not the horse for this new king," Roger reiterated deliberately.

"Oh that ye believe suren enough," said Illthin. "It's the other, *worthy,* part . . ."

Roger straightened and didn't flinch or blink.

"Many're feelin' the same way," old Illthin said. "Despite the words from Bishop Braumin. Curious, that. I'd not've expected Braumin to turn in favor of that one! Not after he had men die holding back King Aydrian at the southern wall."

"What did Bishop Braumin say?"

"He spoke for the king—the rightful and lawful king, he called him," Illthin explained. "And for Abbot De'Unnero of St. Precious—now there's a turn o' the moss for ye!"

Roger Lockless listened to it all silently. He didn't doubt the veracity of what Illthin was saying, and it wasn't hard for Roger, no stranger to the ways of gemstone magic, to figure out how Aydrian might have so manipulated Braumin into saying things so preposterous as that.

"Perhaps all is not what it seems to be, good Illthin," he replied, and old Illthin laughed again.

"I pray you say nothing," Roger bade the man. "For Symphony's sake, if not my own."

Illthin eyed him suspiciously.

"For Jilseponie's sake, if not my own," Roger added, and that seemed to melt the man's doubting façade.

Before Illthin could respond, the commotion moved about the side of the great house, with many men in pursuit of the agitated Symphony.

"I must be away," Roger said, and he and Illthin shared one last agreeing look before Roger Lockless melted into the shadows, expertly picking his way back to and over the wall.

By the time Roger had worked his way back around the compound, many soldiers, some astride To-gai ponies, were charging out the main gate and down the street in pursuit of Symphony. Roger did not know that it was Illthin who, feigning terror and running from the charging horse, had conveniently opened the gate to make his own escape, and thus allowed Symphony to break free of the compound.

The chase went on through the streets of Palmaris, but it was really no chase at all, for no horse could match the stride of Symphony, especially no horse carrying a rider. And none of the Allheart ponies were behaving with their usual discipline in any case, all lured by the same centaur piping that was leading Symphony home.

Palmaris' northern gate was open, as always, and no one there had a chance to close it in time when they realized the identity of the stallion charging their way. One soldier bravely and stupidly stepped out to block the horse, but Symphony just ran him down, knocking him to the ground.

And then the stallion was running free across the rolling farmlands north of the city, following the promise of Bradwarden's melody.

The promise of freedom, the promise of home.

For Aydrian, meetings such as this one were among the most useless and boring aspects of his running adventure. During all the planning with Abbot Olin and De'Unnero to design his ascent, Aydrian had been forced to sit through similar sessions, where the principals gathered to go over and over and over their upcoming actions. What amazed and dismayed Aydrian most of all was his absolute understanding that the gatherings, as they grew repetitive, did nothing productive. These were meetings to calm the nerves of the various leaders, to comfort them and reassure them that they were acting properly.

Aydrian needed no such reassurances anymore. He had his guidance from the shadow at Oracle. Day by day, he was growing more confident in his abilities and more aware of his limitations, few that they were. To Aydrian, these bureaucratic exercises were merely delays along the course to the inevitable.

He had to admit that this one was more important than most of those previous, though. This one was not for the benefit of Marcalo De'Unnero, who was busy putting the house of St. Precious in order, or Duke Kalas, who was off in the northland securing Caer Tinella and Landsdown, nor for any of the other war leaders who had traveled with Aydrian from Ursal. This meeting concerned the leaders of Palmaris—other than Bishop Braumin, obviously, who remained locked in a room in De'Unnero's St. Precious.

Aydrian looked around the huge table in the great hall at them, reminding himself of their importance to his cause. Palmaris would be the pivotal city if Midalis ever came south, and having the support of these many lords, the great landowners and influential citizens, would go far in making certain that Palmaris was not welcoming to the dispossessed prince.

But still, it was tedious, at best, and whenever Duke Monmouth Treshay of Yorkey, the formal host at the event—though they had gathered at the home of a prominent Palmaris landowner—addressed an issue to the Palmaris lords, then referred to Aydrian, the young king had to sit up straighter and remind himself to care.

"So, as you can well see, my lords," he heard Monmouth saying, "the transition of power in Ursal was nearly bloodless, and would have been completely so if all in attendance had simply accepted the declarations of King Danube himself."

"King Danube was your friend, Duke Monmouth," said one man, a wealthy merchant who often visited Ursal.

"Indeed he was, and I was proud to call him so!"

"Prince Midalis was your friend, as well, was he not?" the merchant asked, and that got Aydrian's attention! "When he ventured south with the Alpinadoran barbarians to attend the wedding of Danube and Jilseponie, was not Duke Monmouth pleased to see him? Did you not ride with him the very next morning?"

"True enough, Lord Breyerton," admitted Monmouth. "And I shall still call Prince Midalis friend if, when he learns of the transition of power, he accepts the desires of his dead brother who was king. And I expect he will."

That brought more than a few doubting stares from around the huge table, Aydrian noticed. Given Monmouth's doubting expressions back in Ursal, Aydrian understood those doubts. Indeed, the young king had many times wondered if he might have to "replace" Monmouth, perhaps brutally so. Thus, soon before beginning the march out of Ursal, Aydrian had visited Monmouth Treshay, not in body, but in spirit, and he had shown the man the glories he might know in Aydrian's shadow.

And he had shown the man the horror he might realize out of that protective shadow.

Lord Breyerton looked directly at Aydrian in what could only be interpreted as a challenge, which caused more than a few of the others to widen their eyes in alarm. "And if he does not?" the bold lord asked. "If Prince Midalis claims the throne as his own?"

"He has no legal claim," the all-too-convinced Duke Monmouth replied strongly. "He—"

"He has no throne to claim," said Aydrian, the first words he had spoken since the opening of the meeting more than an hour before. "The throne of Honce-the-Bear is occupied. That is the simple truth of it. If any others are to make a claim on this throne, given to me by my stepfather in his wisdom, then they are traitors to crown and country and will be accordingly dealt with by the soldiers who serve crown and country."

"Many people support Prince Midalis," the defiant Lord Breyerton dared to remark. Eyes about the table opened even wider, and more than one man gasped.

"Is Honce-the-Bear now a product of the will of the people, Lord Breyerton?" Aydrian asked. "If the people had decided that King Danube was not a good king, could they have simply found a replacement and set him upon the throne? What sort of anarchy do you profess?"

"Indeed, what idiocy is this?" asked another of the gathered lords.

"It is an honest question!" Lord Breyerton declared. "If there is to be war—"

"Then you should choose wisely your alliances," Aydrian interrupted. "If in his disappointment, Prince Midalis cannot accept the vision of King Danube and acts foolishly and traitorously, then he will face the wrath of the crown. You have seen but a fraction of my army and my power, I assure you, and yet Palmaris wisely relented their folly before the city was laid to waste. Even Bishop Braumin, so dear a friend to my mother, came to understand the inevitability and the correctness of my rule. This is no longer about who will sit on the throne of Honce-the-Bear, Lord Breyerton, for that issue is long decided.

"And as your king, I have come to understand that I must reach out to the great cities and the great men who lead them," Aydrian went on. "King Danube ruled long and ruled well, mostly because he understood that his eyes and ears alone would never suffice for a kingdom as large and powerful as Honce-the-Bear. His wisdom lay in his ability to recognize the attributes of others and to allow those other great leaders the freedom to serve the kingdom within their own judgment."

That last line had nearly every head bobbing, had several of the lords staring with hopeful and sparkling eyes. Olin and De'Unnero had schooled Aydrian well here. A king who offered the ambitious and greedy merchants free reign over their own little kingdoms within Honce-the-Bear would be a beloved king indeed—at least by those people who mattered. Even Lord Breyerton seemed a bit off-balance, as if suddenly torn between the carrot Aydrian had just subtly dangled and his loyalties to Prince Midalis.

Aydrian recognized clearly the conflict within Breyerton, and he determined then and there to sway that conflict in his direction.

The lords continued to argue amongst themselves for a bit, until a page rushed in, running over to stand beside Lord Breyerton. The young page bent low, whispering excitedly into Breyerton's ear, and the lord's eyes widened immediately.

"What is it?" Aydrian asked of him.

Lord Breyerton rose from his seat. "A minor disturbance, my King," he said, and it was clear that the man was quite unnerved. With a quick bow, Breyerton turned and started away.

"Lord Breyerton!" Aydrian said suddenly, stopping the man in his tracks. Breyerton turned about to look at the king.

"What have you learned?" Aydrian coolly asked.

"There is a disturbance by the north wall, my King," Breyerton admitted. "A group of Palmaris soldiers have taken control of the smithy. Some of your Kingsmen were wounded, I am afraid."

Aydrian rose and moved beside the man. "Lead on," he instructed.

"My King, the area will be dangerous," Breyerton protested, and several of the others, especially the escorting Allheart Knights, seconded the notion. "You have not even your armor to wear."

In response, Aydrian gave a wry grin and put a hand to the hilt of Tempest, belted at his hip. "Lead on, Lord Breyerton. I wish to speak with these . . . confused men."

"My King—" Breyerton started to argue, but Aydrian cut him short.

"Lead on," he insisted, and he practically shoved the man out of the door.

The Allhearts and Duke Monmouth were close behind, followed by the other lords. This particular house wasn't far from the northern wall and the area of the disturbance. As soon as they exited the building, they could hear the sounds of battle.

Needing no guidance, Aydrian moved ahead of Breyerton, striding confidently toward the sounds. He found many of his Kingsmen encircling a small barn set against the northern wall of the city. Nervous horses nickered and skittered about a small corral to the side of the structure. A few men lay dead about the place, most wearing the armor of the Palmaris garrison, but a couple showing the insignia of Kingsmen. All about the area, hundreds of Palmaris citizens looked on at the spectacle, mostly from distant balconies or from behind the protection of stone walls or water troughs.

Their focus quickly shifted, though, from the fighting to the unexpected arrival of the new king of Honce-the-Bear.

As always, Aydrian found that he liked the feeling of so many people looking at him, of so many people looking on in awe of him. He shook away the distraction, though, and continued ahead, reaching into the pouch on his hip to sort through the gemstones.

The front of the smithy was open, an orange-glowing hearth showing within, but bales of hay had been piled there. Every so often, a man would pop up and loose an arrow out at the encircling force, only to have it answered by a barrage of return fire.

Aydrian drew out Tempest and put a soul stone into his left hand and continued to stride right past the ring of his own soldiers, heading for the smithy. When one of the commanders took the cue and started to call to his men to follow their king into battle, Aydrian turned and hushed him and waved him away. Similarly, when Aydrian's Allheart escorts rushed up beside him, one grabbing at him to pull him back to safety, the young king shoved them away and ordered them to stop.

"You cannot approach, my King!" a frantic Allheart Knight cried.

"Find cover and watch," Aydrian commanded. "These men do not understand the truth of their new king, so I am going show them."

"I am sworn to protect you!" the Allheart insisted. "With my life, and I willingly give it, my King!"

"King Aydrian, be reasonable!" cried Lord Breyerton. "Allow the soldiers to put down the traitors! That is their duty."

"Come not another step beside me," Aydrian said, and the young king kept walking.

"You have not even your armor!" Breyerton protested, but Aydrian merely grinned, knowing from the receding voice that the man had not only stopped, but had rushed back behind some cover.

Aydrian strode out from the encircling ring of barricades and cover, into the open area before the confiscated smithy. He was in plain sight of all of them now, of the rebels, of his own soldiers, and of the many Palmaris onlookers.

He saw an archer pop up from behind a hay bale at the side of the door and he fought hard not to flinch, not to slow his stride at all. The greater shadow in the mirror of Oracle had told him he could do this, that he could find a place between spirit and body where he could not be harmed.

Aydrian clutched the hematite more tightly and fell into its swirl. He kept enough of his physical consciousness to witness the archer let fly his arrow—and Aydrian had to fight hard to resist the reflexive urge to snap Tempest across to attempt a deflection.

The arrow dove into his side and he felt a burning explosion of pain.

But only for a second, and the young king didn't swerve a step. He kept his breathing steady and focused his thoughts on the wound, visualizing the damage and sending waves of soul stone healing power to the region.

Still keeping stride, the young king reached down and pulled forth the arrow, casually tossing it aside. He lost some blood, but not much, for the waves of healing magic had the wound closing almost immediately behind the withdrawing arrow.

Another archer popped up, straight in front of Aydrian.

But Aydrian didn't want to feel that pain again and so he raised Tempest's tip even as the man leveled his bow. And he reached into the graphite set into Tempest and sent forth a bolt of lightning even as the man loosed his arrow. The line of cracking energy blasted the arrow into harmless splinters, then slammed the archer, launching him into a short flight back into the smithy.

Aydrian changed the sword's angle and loosed another stunning bolt, this one hitting the ground right before the hay bales with a thunderous report, shaking every building on that side of the town and blasting away the makeshift barricade, and a couple of hidden defenders, as well.

"You defy me?" Aydrian shouted as he calmly and confidently strode into the smithy.

A man came at him hard from the right, spear stabbing, but Aydrian casually reached Tempest out that way, rolled it about the man's spear, over and inside, and shoved the thrusting weapon out wide. A quick retraction and sudden stab, and then again, and then again, had the spearman falling backward, a stunned expression on his face, his hands clutching at his chest in desperation.

But Aydrian hadn't finished any of the three stabs, putting only superficial wounds into the rebellious Palmaris soldier. Enough to stop him, certainly, but not to kill him. Aydrian didn't want to do any more of that than was necessary.

Another desperate man charged out from the shadows, and then another beside him, both brandishing swords. They came in hard and fast—too much so!—and Aydrian knew that they were terrified.

And Aydrian knew that they were right to be terrified.

Tempest slashed across hard to the left and down, taking the thrusting tip of one sword with it, then came back up and across in the blink of an eye, deflecting the second blade only an inch from Aydrian's face, moving the sword up and out.

Falling into the stance of *bi'nelle dasada*, the young king moved back suddenly, out of range, and the pair of hastily retracted and then rethrust blades fell short of the mark. And both attackers were suddenly off-balance from the unexpected and clean miss, with not even a parrying blade to counterbalance their desperate thrusts.

Now Tempest snapped right and left, tapping one blade and then the second just enough to open a lane between them. Before the two soldiers could even put their weapons back in any kind of defensive line, the perfectly balanced Aydrian rushed ahead and stabbed the man on the right in the thigh, sending him howling to the floor. Aydrian retracted Tempest way back, then turned the tip over to the left and shot the blade that way, cutting under the second swordsman's weapon as he tried to swing it Aydrian's way.

Up went Tempest, lifting the swordsman's blade and arm as it went, and Aydrian stepped in behind, moving right near the man, and hit him with a short and chopping left hand to the chin.

He went down hard.

Instinctively, Aydrian spun about, slashing his blade across, and picking off an arrow as he did!

The archer was in the loft, along with at least one other man.

Aydrian picked out a path to the ladder, but before he even started away, he heard a feral roar behind him.

De'Unnero, he knew before he even turned, and sure enough, the former monk, half in human form and half in the form of a great tiger, bounded past him and easily leaped the ten feet to the loft, bowling over the archer as the man frantically tried to fit another arrow to his bowstring.

Aydrian gnashed his teeth as he heard the monk's devastating work up above, as blood began to run freely through the spaced planks of the loft.

One man came to the edge and moved as if to leap out, screaming wildly, but he barely got off the ledge before a great paw hooked his shoulder and brutally tore him back to the loft. His screams continued, even intensified, and Aydrian could see one arm flailing wildly.

And then it suddenly stopped.

Commotion from behind stole Aydrian's focus and he turned about to see the Allheart and Kingsmen soldiers rushing into the smithy. With a sigh of frustration, Aydrian sheathed Tempest.

Before he put his soul stone away, the young king went back to work one last time on the wound from the arrow, just to make sure he had properly repaired it. A few moments later, satisfied that he had, he slipped back out of the trance of the stone. He heard Marcalo De'Unnero, who had come down from the loft and was standing over by the door, shouting at Duke Monmouth, scolding him for allowing Aydrian to walk into such danger.

Aydrian smiled, considering that Monmouth had been given no choice in the matter. Or maybe he was just smiling because he liked hearing De'Unnero so utterly outraged.

One of the rebels from the loft came forward then and pitched over, falling hard to the floor at Aydrian's feet and splattering the young king with blood.

De'Unnero was there in an instant, lifting an arm that was still a tiger's paw as if to finish off the man.

But Aydrian held him back, then reached down and grabbed the wounded Palmaris soldier with his right hand. He fell back into the soul stone and sent a burst of healing energy into the man, but the poor fool was too far gone, fast falling into the realm of death.

Aydrian snarled and fell into a kneel beside him, and then, as he had done on the field with Duke Kalas so long ago, the young king's spirit leaped through the portal of the soul stone and chased the spirit of the dying man into the dark realm.

A few moments later, Aydrian opened his eyes and fell back, and on the floor before him, the seemingly mortally wounded man coughed and sputtered and looked up, completely overwhelmed.

But very much alive.

Aydrian grinned and looked around at the many obviously impressed, obviously awed, onlookers.

Only Marcalo De'Unnero didn't seem very pleased. He came forward to crouch before Aydrian and roughly pulled the young king to his feet.

"What folly is this?" the monk cried, then quickly lowered his voice.

"Less carnage and more manipulation, if you please," Aydrian calmly replied, and De'Unnero could only stare at him in a stupor.

"You think this a game?" the monk asked.

"I think it an opportunity," Aydrian answered, and he pushed De'Unnero aside—pleased to see Sadye standing there directly in his line of sight, watching closely.

Aydrian went to the man he had just saved and roughly pulled him up. "Do you not understand who I am?" he asked the man, who was trembling and obviously completely overwhelmed. "Do you not understand that I was born to be your king?" As he finished, Aydrian looked up, as if addressing them all.

"Ye . . . yes," the healed man said, blinking, crying, trembling, and melting down to the floor.

"Clean this place, bury the dead, and bring the prisoners and wounded to Chasewind Manor," Aydrian commanded his soldiers. "But do not mistreat them! We will learn much from them," the young king declared. "And they will learn the truth of King Aydrian of Ursal. They will learn that we are not their enemies."

The others began to filter off, giving Aydrian and De'Unnero a moment alone together.

"What are you . . ." De'Unnero started to ask, but then he just stopped and shook his head, clearly at a loss, clearly caught completely off his balance here—almost as much so as had been the man Aydrian had pulled from the realm of death.

Aydrian certainly understood that nearly blank expression. It was not easy for De'Unnero to see his former student step so far ahead of him!

With a snort and another helpless shake of his head, Marcalo De'Unnero walked away.

Sadye went up to Aydrian then, though she was looking back at her departing companion.

"He is only beginning to understand who I am," Aydrian said to her, drawing her eyes to his own. "He is beginning to recognize that I am beyond him now."

Sadye looked at him curiously, and a bit suspiciously.

"He fears that his own position will be compromised," Aydrian went on. "He fears that I do not need him, perhaps that I will even begin to see him and his well-earned reputation as a detriment to my progress."

"What are you talking about?"

"The truth," Aydrian replied, and his blue eyes sparkled with intensity, boring into her. "And you know it. But Marcalo De'Unnero does not."

"He has done so much for you," Sadye reminded. "He found you in the Wilderlands and showed you the way—all the way, from the Timberlands, back south to Ursal and all the way to Entel. The gemstones of Pimaninicuit were his doing, and those riches more than anything else have funded your ascension. Are you so quick to forget?"

"I have forgotten nothing," Aydrian replied. "If I had, then I would have left De'Unnero in Ursal, for his true usefulness to me ended on the day King Danube died. Do you not believe that I would have found more acceptance here in Palmaris if I had not arrived beside the hated former bishop?

"But I'll not forsake him," Aydrian went on. "And I will grant him his Abellican Church, as he so desires."

"You act as if everything from this point forward will be your doing alone."

That wry grin returned, and it was a quite convincing and clear answer.

"I taught these rebels the truth of Aydrian this day—those who were not slaughtered to satisfy the blood thirst of Marcalo De'Unnero. That man who was so close to death will welcome Aydrian as king, and will tell others of rebellious disposition to lay down their arms and embrace the savior that is Aydrian." He paused and tilted his head back, just a bit, so that he was looking down at Sadye more completely, and more suggestively. "When will Sadye come to accept that same truth, I wonder?"

Sadye brought a hand up to brush a strand of hair from in front of her gray eyes, a gesture that told Aydrian just how much he had rattled the normally unshakable woman. She held his stare for a short while longer, but then had to relent, and she turned and started away.

Aydrian touched her shoulder lightly and she stopped as surely as if the strong young man had grabbed her and tugged her back, and when she glanced back at him, he moved his hand from her shoulder to the side of her face, lightly running the back of his fingers down across her pretty cheek.

Sadye closed her eyes and her breathing deepened for just a moment, then she blinked her eyes open and walked away.

Aydrian knew that he had gotten into her soul in that moment. She was walking away from him, stubbornly defiant to the bitter end, but he knew beyond any doubt that she wanted to turn about and leap into his arms. He knew something else, too, and the knowledge rang sweetly in his thoughts: in many ways, Sadye almost hoped that he would kill De'Unnero and be done with it, alleviating any guilt or fears that she might harbor.

Oh yes, he had touched her soul.

Pony pulled the blanket tight about her, never blinking as she stared at the elven Lady. She had no idea how Dasslerond had accomplished this feat, taking her from Dundalis so completely that she was still wrapped in the blanket she had thrown across her shoulders when she had sat on the floor of her room to meditate.

"Aydrian is my son," she said.

"He is," Lady Dasslerond answered, her tone flat and showing no emotion at all.

"You stole him from me, on the field outside of Palmaris."

"I did."

Pony felt her legs go weak for just an instant, and then felt a sudden surge of strength course through her body, imploring her to leap ahead and throttle the diminutive elf.

"And if I had not, then both mother and child would have died on that field, the victims of the demon dactyl," Lady Dasslerond went on, stealing a bit of that urge. "The victims of the same demon dactyl who had defeated Jilseponie and was chased away by the rescue of the Touel'alfar."

"That does not afford you the right—"

"The same demon dactyl that once found its way to Andur'Blough Inninness, after I had rescued yet another group of humans from its clutches.
Once there, the beast placed its stain upon the ground, upon the lifeblood
of our valley. Only the child taken from Jilseponie on the field, where she
and he surely would have died, offered the promise of defeating that growing demon rot."

Pony stammered and sputtered, recognizing the logic but denying the
conclusion. "That does not give to you the right to steal my child!" the
completely frustrated woman yelled at last.

Dasslerond's reply came as an emotionless and distant stare, as if Pony's
words had meant nothing at all to the Lady of Caer'alfar.

Which of course, was true.

"How can you stand there and look at me like that?" Pony asked. "Do
you care not at all what you have done to me? To Aydrian?"

"I saved your life, and his."

"You stole a child!" Pony yelled at her, but her strength was going even
as she finished the sentence, and she continued with a voice that was clearly
wavering. "Could you not have come back for me? Could you not have
brought me to him? Have told me at least that he was alive and well?"

Dasslerond did flinch, just a tiny bit, but it was stopped by a strong re-
sumption of her icy visage. "Your life was saved at a price."

"Never one that I agreed upon!"

"It does not matter," the Lady of Caer'alfar said. "I acted as my people
needed me to act, for the good of the Touel'alfar—indeed, for the very sur-
vival of the Touel'alfar. That was my concern, and not the broken heart of a
human woman. You are no enemy of the Touel'alfar, Jilseponie. Do remember that our intervention back in Dundalis those decades ago when the
goblins overran the town allowed you to live. Do remember that our sacrifices were considerable in the war against the demon dactyl, and for the
good of man as much as for the good of the Touel'alfar. You know *bi'nelle
dasada*, and many other secrets of my people, and yet we have taken pity on
you and allowed you to live. This is no small matter, Jilseponie. Release your
anger toward us, here and now. Our days together are at their end."

"We have never had any days together," Pony spat back at her.

Dasslerond conceded the point. "My duty is to my people, as yours is to
your own, first and foremost," she said. "And your duty now demands that
you do battle against the forces that have darkened your lands."

"You ask me to wage war against my own son?"

"Do you believe that any of us have a choice?" asked Dasslerond. "You
do not understand who he is. He is mightier with the gemstones than any
who have come before, and greater with the blade, perhaps, than was Elbryan himself! He has Oracle—we thought that the gift would inspire him
to follow his true path. But alas, he has found naught but ill counsel there!"

"And ill counsel from those humans closest about him," Belli'mar Juraviel
added, and neither Pony nor Dasslerond was about to disagree with that.

"Fear him," Dasslerond warned the woman. "You cannot understand the truth of him until it is too late for you."

"For you, you mean," Pony accused.

Dasslerond didn't flinch at all, didn't even blink. "Return to your people," she said, and she moved her hand holding the emerald up before her. "Defeat your son, for the good of the humans if not for the good of the Touel'alfar. Forget that we exist, Jilseponie, for your own sake . . ."

The elf's voice began to waver and fade, and Jilseponie felt herself receding, back to Dundalis, she knew. But she lifted her own stone, too angry to let it go at that, with too much hatred for the superior-minded Lady of Caer'alfar. She dove into the hematite, releasing her spirit, and charged at Dasslerond.

She nearly overwhelmed the elven lady in that initial assault, nearly got through the iron willpower of Lady Dasslerond that had kept together the Touel'alfar and their enchanted valley for centuries.

But then there came a sudden distortion of distance, a spinning vision of landscapes, as Dasslerond, in her horror, abruptly retreated.

Pony felt as if she was falling from on high, as the spinning ground leaped up to swallow her.

And then it was over, suddenly, and she lay in a pool of cold water on a field of clay and soft mud. Her body aching from the hard landing, she pulled herself up to her knees and looked all about.

She was in the Moorlands, she realized. The desolate, goblin-infested wastelands far to the west of Dundalis. She glanced all around, though she knew that the elves were not with her. In that moment of confusion and attack, Dasslerond had retreated—likely back to Andur'Blough Inninness.

And Pony was left alone in a desolate and hostile region, without food and without a weapon.

She fell back and put her wet and muddy hands over her face, defeated.

❖ 17 ❖

The Dragon Revealed

I t took the thump of Agradeleous landing beside her to break Brynn from her trance. Seeing the headless body of Yatol Bardoh lying in the sand before her was almost too much for her. The image, the reality of having finally avenged her parents, made her think back to her childhood days on the steppes of To-gai. The circumstances around her childhood had not been happy: the Behrenese conquerors were a brutal lot; and her parents, both resisting the occupation, had been almost constantly on the run. Still, Brynn's mother and father had nurtured her and loved her, taught her the old ways. They had taught Brynn that there was something bigger than she, something bigger than all of them, and that they were a part of it, living in harmony with the soil, the plants, and the animals. They had given so much to her in the few years they had known her.

And then they were gone, taken by the wickedness of this man, Tohen Bardoh—now a headless corpse bleeding into the dirt before her.

"The battle continues," came a voice, and Brynn looked around to see Pagonel coming over the dune behind her.

Brynn moved to join him, and saw the Chezhou-lei warrior sitting in the sand, rubbing his throat. She shook her head, confused, certain that her strike should have proven fatal. But then she figured it out and looked over at her companion.

"You healed him."

"He will not fight us again," said the mystic. "Was I to allow him to die?"

"He tried to kill us."

"He protected his master, as his code of honor demanded." The mystic glanced back at Bardoh's corpse, drawing Brynn's gaze with his own. "His master needs protecting no longer."

Brynn considered the words and the logic. Ever was Pagonel tempering her fighting spirit, ever was he edging her toward mercy.

Ever was Pagonel making Brynn a better person and a better leader.

"The battle continues," Pagonel remarked, and they both looked back toward Jacintha, where the sounds of metal ringing against metal and the screams of the wounded and victor alike echoed in the air.

"Where are the emissaries?"

"Hiding," the mystic explained. "Come. Perhaps the sight of Brynn and Agradeleous will convince these warriors that nothing more is to be gained here."

Brynn turned with him and started for the dragon, but she stopped and ran to the side instead, scooping up something from the sand. Pagonel was already astride the dragon when she got there, offering her his arm to pull her up behind him.

A short run and but two flaps of Agradeleous' great leathery wings had them up into the air, flying to the east and banking to the north. Spying ships out in the harbor, Pagonel bade the dragon to stay along the coast, in full view of whoever was out there, be it friend or foe.

The sounds of battle diminished almost as soon as the great shadow of Agradeleous rolled across the battlefield. Behrenese traitor, loyalist, and Bearman alike rushed out from before the terrible splendor of Agradeleous, forgetting their own battles in the face of this much more significant danger.

And there sat Brynn astride the beast, clutching with one hand as the dragon swerved left and right and with her other hand aloft and in clear view, holding the head of Yatol Bardoh.

The Jacintha loyalists cheered.

The Behrenese followers of Peridan and Bardoh cowered and begged for mercy.

The soldiers of Honce-the-Bear filtered back, tightening ranks defensively. Unsure of this new presence, stunned by the sight of a dragon, the men of the northern kingdom continued their well-disciplined retreat right through the southern slum of Jacintha and back to the city wall.

Out in the harbor, Abbot Olin, Master Mackaront, and Duke Bretherford found themselves drawn to the rail, along with the other crewmen, to view the spectacle of the great beast. They had heard of dragons, of course— mostly in old legends—but none of them had ever actually seen one.

"The Dragon of To-gai," mumbled Mackaront. "Then she is more than a legend, more than the imaginings of frightened Jacintha soldiers."

"Our soldiers are in retreat," Abbot Olin realized. "What does this portend?"

"Wisdom?" Bretherford asked dryly.

"The cheering along the wall names the dragon as an ally," answered Master Mackaront, who was well aware of the previous agreements between Brynn of To-gai and Yatol Wadon, and who better understood the significance of this unexpected arrival. "It is Brynn Dharielle, come to the aid of Yatol Wadon."

Abbot Olin started to turn to face the man, but couldn't take his eyes from the spectacle of the beast as it swooped about the battlefield south of the city. "Send couriers to the docks," he instructed Mackaront. "Nay, go yourself! Find out what this means."

"You fear the arrival of the beast will bring trouble for you with your new friend Yatol Wadon?" Duke Bretherford asked when Mackaront walked away.

"Not so," said Abbot Olin. "It is Brynn, once a friend of Aydrian from what De'Unnero and Sadye have told me. It is possible that our new young king has just found a great ally."

If Abbot Olin could have pried his eyes from the dragon at that moment, he would have noticed that Duke Bretherford didn't seem altogether pleased by that prospect.

Agradeleous didn't join Brynn and Pagonel as they entered Jacintha later that day. There was no need to send the populace running in fear, after all, as would have undoubtedly occurred even if the dragon had gone in using his lizardman form.

The pair were greeted warmly by the soldiers at the southern gate and taken through the streets of Jacintha to the palace of Chom Deiru. Neither missed the significance of the many soldiers in the streets that night, particularly the many soldiers of Honce-the-Bear.

"It would seem that Yatol Wadon found another ally when he learned that To-gai would not aid him," Brynn remarked.

"Long before that," Pagonel corrected. "Such an army as this could not have been pieced together so quickly. It would seem that your friend who now leads the northern kingdom had determined weeks ago that he would support Yatol Wadon."

His reference to Aydrian drew a look from Brynn. She had hardly been thinking of the young ranger these last weeks, too engrossed was she in setting up her own kingdom and, of late, in rousing Agradeleous and plotting her moves in favor of Wadon.

"Or perhaps it was Abbot Olin of Entel," Pagonel went on. "He has had a long relationship with Jacintha, by all accounts."

Brynn had no idea of the situation, for she had little knowledge of Honce-the-Bear. She had heard that Aydrian was king soon after she had forged a truce with Behren and settled into Dharyan-Dharielle, but it had been a single courier with only vague information. Was it possible that Aydrian was here in Chom Deiru waiting for her?

She got her answer—that he was not—a few moments later, when she and Pagonel were escorted into a grand dining hall where a huge feast had been set out. Paroud was there, along with Pechter Dan Turk, who ran forward to greet Brynn warmly.

Pechter Dan Turk then led the pair about the long table, which bent in a semicircle about the tables piled with food. So much food! More than Brynn had ever seen! Enough to feed a To-gai-ru tribe for half the winter.

And yet, there were only about twoscore people assembled, stuffing their faces, spilling their drinks, tossing half-eaten racks of pork and lamb to the floor without regard.

Pechter Dan Turk showed Brynn and Pagonel to Yatol Wadon first, and the old Behrenese priest nearly leaped across the table to embrace Brynn.

"You have brought the head of Bardoh, yes?" asked the man beside him, Yatol De Hamman, as he looked down at the sack Brynn carried.

She lifted it and nodded. "It is given as a show of support to Yatol Wadon," she said. "Though I wished to leave it outside of this place where you are feasting."

"Your escorts insisted that we bring it in," Pagonel added.

"Of course they did!" cried the exuberant De Hamman, and indeed, it was obvious that he was thrilled to see his enemies vanquished. He motioned to a guard, who rushed over to take the satchel, and then, to Brynn's disgust, the soldier pulled forth Bardoh's head and placed it upon the table of food, in a predetermined spot, raised and central, at the end of a headless pig body.

Immediately, all of the feasting Behrenese rose up and lifted their glasses of wine in toast to the death of the traitor Bardoh, and then in another to the arrival of the Dragon of To-gai.

Brynn hid her disgust well.

At a nod from Yatol Wadon, Pechter Dan Turk led Brynn along the table, introducing the various Behrenese lords and Yatols and the Jacintha garrison commander. Then he took her to the three foreigners in attendance, Bearmen all.

"I give you Abbot Olin of Entel," Pechter Dan Turk said, and the old monk rose and extended a hand covered in bejeweled rings toward Brynn.

Not understanding that she was supposed to kiss the back of that hand, Brynn gave it a rather lame shake.

Abbot Olin only smiled at her, then turned to the two men standing on his right. "This is Master Mackaront, my emissary to Jacintha," he said, indicating another monk. "And beside him is Duke Bretherford of the Mirianic, a lord in high standing with King Aydrian Boudabras."

Brynn couldn't help but reveal her interest in that name as it was unexpectedly spoken, her light brown eyes flashing as she looked from Bretherford back to Abbot Olin.

"Do you know of my king?" Abbot Olin asked her.

"It is possible," Brynn replied. "But it was many years ago, good Abbot. I knew an Aydrian once."

"Trained by the Touel'alfar in the Wilderlands beyond Honce-the-Bear," the abbot agreed, and Brynn could only stare at the man. "The son of Elbryan the Nightbird and Jilseponie Wyndon Ursal, who was queen of Honce-the-Bear before him. Yes, I suspect that it is the same Aydrian you once knew, good lady. Could there be two such extraordinary young men with the same name?"

Abbot Olin looked past Brynn, as if only then noticing Pagonel standing beside her. "You have walked a strange and unexpected road, good lady," he said, a bit too politely. "And find yourself in strange and unexpected company."

Pagonel didn't flinch at the obvious insult, both in words and in the smirking way that Abbot Olin was regarding him, but Brynn surely took up the defense of her friend. "Could any less be said of Aydrian?" she remarked.

Abbot Olin merely bowed and lifted his glass of wine in a salute.

Sensing the sudden tension, Pechter Dan Turk ushered the pair along to the far end of the table and their two assigned seats.

The food was wonderful and plentiful, the drink potent and brilliant, and a constant stream of entertainment—singers, musicians, and amazing dancers and acrobats—came through the dining hall, but neither Brynn nor Pagonel ever really settled in comfortably. Around them, the talk centered mostly on the appropriate punishment for Yatol Peridan and his traitors, and for those Jacintha warriors, many killed, some captured, and others fleeing across the desert, who had joined with Yatol Bardoh.

It struck Brynn as curious that Abbot Olin was participating so greatly in the discussion, and in what seemed to be more than just an advisory role.

Pagonel caught it, too. "It would seem that your friend Aydrian has forged a strong alliance here, one that goes beyond lending aid to Yatol Wadon in his time of desperation."

Brynn didn't like the tone of Pagonel's voice, one full of concern, but she wasn't really a part of the general discussion about the table, nor did she seem welcome to be. At one point, she did inquire of the man seated on her other side, a lesser Yatol, of the arrival of Abbot Olin, but he only replied cryptically that the Jacintha garrison was stronger than ever before, and that all of Behren would soon enough be put back in order.

When at last the feasting subsided, and the music went quiet, Brynn and Pagonel rose to leave. The mystic motioned Pechter Dan Turk to them, and the emissary, one of the few men in the room who had not passed out on the floor beneath the table, escorted them away.

First they went over to say their farewells to Yatol Wadon, who was standing off to the side, conversing with the trio from Honce-the-Bear.

It was Abbot Olin, though, and not Wadon, who stepped forward to greet Brynn and the Jhesta Tu, and it was obvious that the old man had indulged himself quite heavily that night. "Your action this day was that of a friend, and it will not be forgotten," the abbot said to her, his voice slurred.

Brynn accepted his handshake, but looked past him to Wadon, who was smiling, surely, but in a manner that seemed somehow strained to her.

"I wish to meet with you again, good lady of To-gai," Abbot Olin said with great enthusiasm. "I wish to learn more of your people, and of that curious mount of yours! Such a wonderful beast would be of great help to us as we secure the kingdom, no doubt."

"No doubt," Brynn replied, and she gave a polite bow and went with Pagonel out of the room, passing through the two sentries—two Honce-the-Bear sentries—posted at the door.

"Great help to *us*?" Brynn whispered to the mystic. "As *we* secure the kingdom?"

"So Aydrian looks south," Pagonel quietly replied. "With more than a passing interest. We might do well to learn more of him."

Sometime later, as Brynn slept soundly by a fire on the darkened plain west of the city, Pagonel took Agradeleous on a ride back to the east. The pair flew past Jacintha, hugging the north to keep the dragon's telltale silhouette hidden behind the line of dark mountains. They stayed near to the mountain range to its very end, settling at last upon a rocky embankment overlooking the Mirianic. Not far from the shore, a grouping of Honce-the-Bear warships was moored, and a line of smaller boats stretched out from them, gliding between them one at a time.

Every so often, a scream echoed over the dark waters of the Mirianic.

"The water about the boats is thrashing," Agradeleous remarked.

Pagonel squinted, but his eyesight was no match for that of the dragon. He could barely distinguish the silhouettes of the great ships, let alone the water about them.

"It churns white," the dragon explained. His sentence was punctuated by another shriek from the distant ships.

Pagonel sat on the stone and crossed his legs tightly before him. The mystic placed his hands on his thighs, palms upraised, and fell back into himself. He became aware of his mind-body connection, and consciously severed it.

His spirit stepped forth, a separation of mind and body much as the Abellicans could do with the soul stone, though to a much lesser extent. It was enough to get Pagonel's consciousness over to those distant vessels, though, just briefly.

But long enough for him to sort it out.

The Honce-the-Bear ships had captured the force of Behrenese traitors who had not landed at the docks of Jacintha. Now the Bearmen were sorting their prisoners, likely interrogating them to find which had truly turned traitor to Yatol Wadon and Jacintha.

Many of them, their hands lashed behind their backs, were being thrown into the water between the boats.

There, the sharks feasted.

❖ 18 ❖

A Desperate Call
on a Cold Wind

Pony pulled the blanket more tightly about her to ward the cold wind. It was wet, though, and the wind was damp, gathering moisture from the many pools and bogs that marked the Moorlands. Mud caked Pony's shoulder-length blond hair, and it seemed as if it would never dry in the perpetual gloom of the area. Tired from her exertion against Dasslerond and from the emotional battering just seeing the treacherous elven lady had given to her, the woman could barely find the strength to move along. A big part of her simply wanted to slip down into the soft clay and die.

Dasslerond had told her to fight Aydrian, for the sake of them all, and Pony couldn't rightly disagree with that assessment. But how could she bring herself to do something like that against her own son? And how could she—or anyone else for that matter—find a way around the power that was Aydrian? Pony had felt that power, all too clearly. Her son could bend the will of Symphony. Her son could reach into the realm of death itself and pull Constance Pemblebury back from the grave.

It all seemed moot to her anyway, that gloomy day wandering the Moorlands. She knew enough about the region to understand the depth of her peril there. Most of the water about her was fetid, and there was little food to be found. Winter was fast coming on in the more civilized lands to the east; on the moors, the damp wind already had the bite of that cold season. She needed shelter and a fire, but there was little to be found and no wood about to burn. And this forsaken place was the domain of goblin tribes and of darker things.

Pony still held her hematite gemstone, but it would do little, she knew, to warm her or put food in her growling belly, or turn the spear of a goblin warrior.

She wandered along, stubbornly putting one foot in front of the other, hoping against hope that Dasslerond's gemstone throw had put her near the eastern edge of the Moorland wilderness.

When day turned to night, the woman huddled against the side of a clay overhang, shivering, as the Moorlands came alive about her.

The cry of a wolf was answered again and again, some of the howls uncomfortably close. Pony pulled her blanket up tighter about her, right over her head at one point in a futile effort to block it all out.

Eventually, she did fall into the inviting swirl of the hematite, at first thinking only to spirit-walk the area about her to see if any danger was closing in. But soon after, her spirit flying free of her body, she rushed back toward the east, seeking vicarious comfort in the warm fires burning in the countryside farmhouses.

And there, somewhere north of Palmaris, perhaps in the Caer Tinella region, the woman felt a sudden and familiar connection. It was a fleeting thing, just a feeling, and nothing that she had the strength to locate specifically.

Her spirit cried out for help in that flash of recognition. She imparted images of her surroundings, trying to be as specific as possible, trying to remember exactly that last real landmark she had wandered past.

But then the woman knew she had to fly back to her body, and quickly! She popped open her eyes and pulled aside the blanket.

And heard the goblins, snuffling in the dark, not so far away.

Frantically, Pony pulled herself from her hollow, gaining her feet and stumbling along the other way. She thought to discard the blanket, but immediately changed her mind, not wanting to leave a trail. Besides, that blanket was the only potential shield she possessed.

She came around the clay mound to find a pool blocking her way, the dark and still waters as murky as the sky above.

Pony glanced back, knowing that the creatures had caught her scent. But where to run? By all the old tales, some Moorland bogs were bottomless things; others served as home for creatures ancient and terrible.

With a steadying breath, the woman stepped ahead into the chilly water, moving slowly and smoothly to keep from splashing, and also so that she could test the ground before putting her foot down. Expecting to be swallowed up with every step, but knowing that certain danger was close behind, she pressed on.

She knew that she was making more noise then, splashing with every stride through the thigh-deep water, but she didn't slow. For the goblins were there, on the bank behind her, their lamplight eyes scanning the darkness.

She heard a splash close behind her and glanced back to see a spear bobbing in the darkness. Now hoots and shrill calls echoed out at her, and from the continuing sound, she could tell that her enemies were fanning out, left and right, about the pool.

Pony ducked low and lifted her gemstone, falling into it once more, using the portal to break her spirit free. She flew across the night air to the southern bank of the pool, where a trio of goblins was running. Right for the middle beast she went, charging headlong, with all of her willpower, into its corporeal form.

And there she struggled, both against the spirit of the goblin and against her own revulsion at this horrible act. Of all the powers of the gemstones, none was darker than this.

She had caught the goblin by surprise, obviously, for the creature knew nothing of gemstone magic, knew nothing of disembodied spirits, and knew nothing of such spiritual battles. Still, sheer instinct had the wretched thing fighting back against Pony's intrusion, immediately and desperately, struggling for its very life.

But Pony was still strong with the gemstones, and with the soul stone in particular. In her last weeks in Ursal, she had spent many hours tending the sick and the poor, using this same type of stone.

The goblin's spirit was expelled.

It would be a temporary thing, Pony knew, as she came to see the world through the creature's eyes. She stumbled and nearly toppled, for the balance of the body was very different from that of a human. Goblins were smaller and more wiry, and ran with a loping, low to the ground gait, often using their long arms to tap the ground for balance.

Still, despite that and despite the goblin's spirit trying to fight its way back in, Pony managed to lift the creature's crude spear and jab ahead, drawing a shriek from the goblin in front of her. When that creature pulled up, Pony jabbed it again, harder, right in the back. The goblin turned about, howling and lifting its own crude weapon.

Pony stabbed it again, and then again before it could settle into any kind of defensive posture. The creature spun desperately as it went down to the sand and Pony retracted to stab it yet again.

And then she felt a dull thud and then a burst of pain against her back and she was stumbling forward into the muck.

She managed to half turn as she fell, to see the third of the group bearing down on her, its cudgel lifted to smash her again.

At that moment, Pony relinquished her hold on the goblin's body, her spirit flying free and the goblin's disembodied spirit rushing back to reclaim its corporeal form.

It got there and blinked through its own physical eyes again, just in time to see the descending cudgel, just in time to feel the explosion as the crude club crushed in its forehead.

Pony didn't see it, her spirit flying back fast across the lake, past her body and to the far bank, where another pair of creatures was moving swiftly.

She went at the trailing one, thinking to possess it similarly. She got the upper hand almost immediately, as she had with the first creature, and managed to wrestle some control of the beast.

But possession was the most difficult and taxing of the gemstone magics, and in her already weakened state, Pony could not maintain the hold. She did wrest control enough to launch the goblin at its leading partner, diving onto its ankles and tripping it down to the clay. As it turned to respond, and with the spirit of the possessed goblin frantically assailing her in an effort to regain its body, Pony managed to punch out with the possessed fist, smacking the confused creature before her right in the face.

It responded with a snarl, its arms flailing, its face coming forward to bite at her—at the goblin, rather, for Pony let go as that horrid sight approached, her spirit bursting free and rushing back to her waiting body with all the urgency of a surfacing man who has been under the water for too long.

The woman charged the rest of the way across the bog, abandoning all attempts at carefully feeling her way. She pitched forward onto the muddy bank and tumbled down to the clay. She scrambled to her feet, balling her blanket about one arm and digging her free hand into the clay to scoop up a ball.

Two of the goblins from the south were almost upon her; the third, the one she had possessed, lay screaming in agony along that southern bank.

The two came in side by side, one leading with its crude spear, the other with its cudgel raised to strike at her. Pony threw that soaked and muddy blanket across the tip of that leading spear, then easily sidestepped and launched the ball of clay right into the face of the second creature. The stunned goblin continued its charge, but it instinctively straightened back onto its heels. Pony dove to the ground at its ankles, launching it over her into the mud.

The woman scrambled frantically, turning about to defend as she rose. But she was out of practice, her reflexes dulled by age and by the emotional turmoil that had commanded the last years of her life. She saw the first goblin stubbornly coming in at her, its spear unwrapped from the entangling blanket and leading the way. She knew that she had to turn about to get past and inside that leading tip.

But she could not.

Pony hunched away as the spear caught her in the side and began to slide into her. She grabbed the shaft with her left hand, slowing the progress, then grimaced and accepted the pain as she rotated forward a half step and lashed out with her right hand, smacking the ugly little creature right in the face. It fell back from the impact, and Pony took the spear in both hands and helped the retreating goblin along, pulling the weapon back out of her side. She didn't let go then, though the waves of pain nearly stole the strength from her completely and weakened her legs beneath her. Knowing that if she allowed the goblin to get free it would surely finish her, the woman called upon all her years of training and discipline and ignored the burning wound. Instead of following her instincts and falling away, she charged forward, shouldering the creature down to the ground before her. She continued to press down, driving her shoulder into the goblin's face— and it promptly bit her!—while tugging relentlessly on the spear with both hands.

The goblin let go of the weapon and began battering her about the head and shoulders, biting all the while.

But then Pony put one hand beneath her and tightened all of her muscles, and in a movement that could only be achieved by one who had spent so many years of her life in martial training, the woman shoved up suddenly from the goblin. She turned a complete spin above the prone creature, reversing her grip on the spear as she went so that as she came around and fell back down atop the goblin, the spear led the way.

With all of her weight behind it, the crude but effective weapon drove into the goblin's chest. She felt the resistance as it clipped past the creature's backbone. Still she pressed down, the tip sinking into the soft clay beneath the creature.

The goblin went into a frenzy, a macabre dance of the last fleeting moments of its life, and Pony didn't even try to block the many blows raining about her. She turned and scrambled off, putting her knees and hands to the ground and grabbing up more clay, then rising fast in a spin to meet the resumed charge of the goblin holding the cudgel.

She hit the stupid thing in the face with a ball of clay again, but this time, instead of diving at its feet, she charged right into it, slamming her body against it and turning as she did. She cupped her hand over the goblin's and bent its wrist down suddenly and brutally, and as the wave of pain rolled up the creature's arm, its grip lessened enough so that Pony could pull the cudgel free.

She took up the weapon, spun, and swung, smacking the goblin hard across the head. And then she went into a frenzy, battering the creature down into the ground, hitting it repeatedly long after it had stopped moving.

In her frustration and pain, she might have continued to batter it for a long, long time, but she heard the approach of the two from the north, and rose to meet that charge. One held a short sword and the other, the one Pony had possessed, carried no weapon but came at her hard anyway with open hands, raking at her with its long and dirty nails.

But now she had a weapon, and now she was set. She danced back, and back some more, in perfect balance and moving always just out of reach of the outraged, and quickly overbalancing, goblins. She had no doubt that she could defeat them, and easily, except that blood—and she hoped that it was just blood!—was pouring freely from her side. She grasped at her wound with one hand, literally holding in her guts, while she worked the club about the leading sword of the goblin attacker, every so often swiping it the other way to fend the second creature.

Her opponents started working more in harmony, and Pony's legs began to go numb beneath her. The woman knew that she was in trouble. She stumbled, leaving an apparent opening, and when the too-eager sword-wielder stepped forward to fill that hole, the woman sprang forward, slapping not at the attacker, but at the weapon.

The goblin staggered out wide, leaving Pony a clear path to its unarmed companion. She went in straight, stabbing with the club instead of swinging it from out wide, and the heavy head of the weapon got through the goblin's sudden curl to slam it in the chest. Pony retracted immediately, sending the cudgel into a spin down under her armpit and then back up high, extending her arm as she went so that the next strike came from on high, smashing down atop the goblin's head, smashing its skull and dropping it to the ground like a stone.

Pony spun about desperately, and instinctively let fly the club at the charging sword-wielder. She didn't score a significant hit, but tied it up enough for her to follow that throw, charging past the extended blade and slamming hard into the goblin. The pair went into a death clutch immediately, Pony grabbing the goblin's forearm tenaciously to keep its sword out wide. She worked her feet for perfect balance and used her greater size to drive the goblin back toward the water. Then she tripped it up and fell over it into the cold and murky pool.

Pony pushed down on the creature's head hard with her shoulder, ignoring the pain as it thrashed about beneath her. She held the difficult angle stubbornly, pressing with all her weight as the goblin went into a frenzy, kicking and flailing. It let go of its sword and managed to get its hand in enough to tug at Pony's hair, but she accepted the pain and continued her press.

It seemed as if many minutes had slipped by, but finally the goblin stopped its thrashing.

Pony held it there for a while longer, ensuring that it was drowned, then she pulled herself off of it, crawling back to the pool's bank. She staggered aside, holding at her still-bleeding side, all strength flying from her. She reached for the healing soul stone, needing its magical energy, but to her horror, she found that she had lost it somewhere in the fighting! She glanced around, knowing that she had to find it.

But she hadn't the strength, and after a few staggering steps, the woman fell facedown in the clay and drifted off into a dark, dark place.

She wondered if Elbryan would be waiting for her.

PART THREE

WINTER

Palmaris is mine.

The great river is secured now by the fleet of Earl DePaunch, my chosen replacement for Duke Bretherford. He is a young and eager man, too concerned with his own ambitions to worry about any possible higher callings of morality and community.

He is the perfect undercommander.

As winter settles on the land, our hold on the great and important river will be strengthened and made unbreakable, and with that done, all will be in place for the next two thrusts: southeast to Entel, securing the heartlands of Honce-the-Bear; and the voyage of the armada north to Pireth Dancard and then Pireth Vanguard. I will have the whole of the kingdom by midsummer, and much of Behren as well.

The first reports coming back from Jacintha have been more than promising, and have silenced the critics among my advisors who feared that we had struck too far and too fast. Abbot Olin is in control of the Behrenese capital city now, and will have the entire southern kingdom soon enough, and it was none other than Brynn Dharielle who helped him achieve that initial victory. I cannot wait to see her again! Always have I cared for Brynn, and it will be through her eyes that I find my greatest satisfaction. Brynn will recognize me for what I have become and she will know that Lady Dasslerond was wrong about me. She will know that I am the epitome of the ranger, that I am more than the promise of my mother and my father, that I am more than the wretched Touel'alfar could ever have hoped to produce. Brynn will take pride in me; perhaps together we will rule the entire known world.

Perhaps not, but I will ensure that she is not forgotten in the maelstrom of Aydrian Boudabras.

Once I had thought that Brynn would ultimately become my bride, my queen. Two rangers, ruling the lands in a manner that the men of the world have never known. Now, though, I see another who must rise beside me. Every day that passes moves Sadye farther from the arms of Marcalo De'Unnero and closer to mine own. I will have her singing the songs of Aydrian alone soon enough, and now, I believe, De'Unnero has come to understand this. I hear it in the agitation of his voice whenever he speaks to me. I see it in the looks he tosses Sadye's way, in the fists too oft clenched at his sides. But he will step back, I am sure, because that which I offer to him—all the Abellican Church and the complete control of the weretiger within him—has ever been more important to Marcalo De'Unnero than any woman.

He will be happy for us. Or if not, he will remain silent.

Either way, I do not care.

Similarly, De'Unnero will not be alone in his criticism of my forthcoming decision, I understand. He suspects that I am seeking something in the area to the west—oftentimes has he questioned me about sending Duke Kalas and his forces on such a wide western sweep of the region surrounding Palmaris. When I tell them of my intentions, there will inevitably be doubters, even more so than when I sent Abbot Olin to invade Jacintha. This time, though, the prize is less apparent, for many of them do not even understand that the enclave of Touel'alfar exists. Aside from that, they will question my choice to go to war with an enemy that is irrelevant to the kingdom, and to any kingdom of man.

But nothing could be more relevant to me than the destruction of Andur'Blough Inninness and Lady Dasslerond!

And nothing in all the world will taste sweeter than the moment of my victory over the elves!

I will hear her surrender. I will hear her admission that she was wrong. I will hear her proclaim Aydrian as worthy of the title "ranger," as more worthy than any who came before him, including his legendary father!

And then I will stamp Andur'Blough Inninness flat.

It was not until very recently that I came to understand the depth of my hatred toward Dasslerond and her annoying little folk. I left Andur'Blough Inninness bitterly, to be sure, and after a struggle that would have cost me my very life had I lost. But still, for months and months, my feelings toward the Touel'alfar had been more along the lines of wanting to prove them wrong, of wanting to force from the lips of their pompous leader the honest admission that they did not appreciate me. The delicious irony of it all, of course, is that I have come to understand myself and my potential through Oracle, the elven gift to me, the discipline that Lady Dasslerond herself insisted that I master. At Oracle, I have come to see the selfishness of the Touel'alfar. At Oracle, I have come to see their unconcern for me, and for all humans. At Oracle, I have come to know their ultimate arrogance, their continual lies—not only to me, but to every human they have ever known. At Oracle, I have learned the darkness of Touel'alfar hearts, and the cruelty of Touel'alfar generosity. For they do nothing for the good of a human. They use that guise merely to gain full control, that they might manipulate their rangers to serve only the Touel'alfar.

But at Oracle, I learned to turn their duplicitous games back upon them. The large shadow in the mirror prompted me on, even as the smaller shadow told me how many wondrous things the elves might teach to me. And so I used them even as they tried to use me. I let them teach me the sword dance, the gemstones, and the way of the ranger.

How delicious will be the irony when I crush them!

I wonder if Brynn has come to see the truth of these wretched slavers. I wonder if, in her rise to the leadership of To-gai, she has been able to look past her personal gains to understand that she had merely been an instrument for Lady Dasslerond.

I wonder if she sees a shadow similar to my mentor in her darkened mirror at Oracle.

If she does not, then I will become her shadow.

I hope to see her in the summer. I hope to tell her in great detail of the fall of Dasslerond and the wretched Touel'alfar. I hope that she will come to see the truth.

For it would truly please me if Brynn Dharielle, the Dragon of To-gai, walked this road beside me, willingly and with all of her heart.

But if not, then so be it. I will construct the road of immortality over the bodies of lesser men and lesser women. I will lead humanity to its pinnacle of glory and hope, but that can be achieved only through war.

Oracle has shown me this road clearly, and it is one I am prepared to walk. And Oracle has honestly shown me that this side journey I intend to make to Andur'Blough Inninness is not a necessary path to the conquest of the human kingdoms—as my doubting commanders will no doubt point out—but that it is a necessary journey for Aydrian the king nonetheless.

If for no better reason than to enjoy the sweetness of Lady Dasslerond's defeat.

—KING AYDRIAN BOUDABRAS

❖ 19 ❖

Stretching His Fingers

The work along the Palmaris docks was nothing short of furious. A line of wagons stretched the length of the city's long wharf as one Ursal warship after another slid into line. The Kingsmen drilled along the docks, learning techniques for getting ashore quickly and efficiently and establishing defensive positions. Several ships were brought into dry dock for repair, recaulking hulls, and even replacing severely weathered planks. Second and third anchors were added to the larger ships, to hold them steady against potential winter gales.

Not the Palmaris gales, though. Anyone observing the preparations who understood the region and seamanship would quickly come to the conclusion that many of these warships were soon to be departing, and to the north, into the open Gulf of Corona.

And they would be taking extra crew—soldiers—along for the journey.

In a small stone house not far from the docks—which was actually the house that served as St. Precious Abbey's liaison house to the region, used by Marlboro Viscenti when he had sneaked out of the city just prior to Aydrian's arrival—seven monks had gathered to watch an extraordinary presentation by an extraordinary man.

King Aydrian sat between the brothers, a hematite in one hand and a graphite in the other.

"This stone," he explained, holding forth the hematite, "can serve you as a conduit to the other. Using the state of meditation offered through the soul stone, you will have easier access to the powers of the second stone." To finish his point, the young king lifted both stones before him, closed his eyes, and sent a jolt of electricity emanating out from him, stunning and surprising the brothers and knocking a couple right to the floor.

A few minor protests began, but Aydrian's laughter, which quickly became contagious, cut them short.

Aydrian started to explain, but then just jolted them all again, and then again, laughing all the while, as were most of the brothers. With De'Unnero's help, he had chosen only the most loyal and ambitious group of Abellican converts, and the promises of power he was now displaying for them simply overwhelmed any protests before they could gain strength.

"It is so very easy," the young king explained. It wasn't quite true, he knew, and certainly would not be as easy for these brothers to perform as it was for him, who had learned the deepest secrets of the gemstones from his shadow mentor at Oracle. If he had thought for a moment that these brothers would ever even approach his power and ease of use with the gemstones, this was one secret the young king would have certainly kept to himself!

Aydrian led the seven out the back door of the house, and into a narrow alleyway that he had ordered his soldiers to seal off to the public. And then he put the monks to work with the gemstones, one at a time, shooting bolts of lightning down the alleyway.

Most of the shots were truly pitiful, Aydrian had to admit, but he kept them at it, over and over, and what heartened him was that the seven showed little signs of tiring from the extended magic use, which proved, at least, that they were having a somewhat easier time of accessing the graphite using his soul stone technique.

At several points during the training, Aydrian fell into his own soul stone and stepped free of his mortal coil, moving to the training monk. He didn't go in to possess the chosen man, but affected a sort of spiritual joining, that he could guide the monk along his journey from soul stone to graphite.

A short while later, with the training on in full, the young king was drawn from his work by the sounds of an argument not too far away. Aydrian recognized the voices and was hardly surprised.

He left the young monks to their work and moved out of the alley and back into the stone house, where he found Marcalo De'Unnero and Earl DePaunch in heated discussion.

"It is folly!" De'Unnero declared. "The gulf is not to be challenged so late in the season when we have so much to lose and so little to gain."

"Perhaps you should ask our king about that before making such a statement," replied Earl DePaunch, a thin and severe-looking young man, whose tight little beard and thick black eyebrows only added to the intensity of his dark and too-eager eyes. DePaunch, an Allheart Knight, had been appointed by Aydrian to replace Duke Bretherford as acting duke of the Mirianic on the suggestion of Duke Kalas; and in listening to him now, his every word dripping in an almost obsessive intensity, it wasn't hard for Aydrian to understand the reasoning behind that recommendation.

As he finished, DePaunch drew De'Unnero's gaze over to the house's back door, where stood a rather amused-looking King Aydrian.

"All goes well, my friend," Aydrian said to De'Unnero. "Why are you so concerned?"

"The Gulf of Corona is an enemy we do not need," De'Unnero replied, and he glanced from Aydrian to DePaunch in a manner clearly asking the young king to dismiss the upstart young earl. "If the ships exit the Masur Delaval and find a gale blowing down from the Timberlands, we may lose a thousand men to an indifferent enemy."

"I have faith that our friend DePaunch here will properly sail the ships to Pireth Dancard and quickly secure the island," Aydrian answered.

"We will overwhelm them, my King," DePaunch snapped, coming to painfully straight attention. "I will have Pireth Dancard in my grasp within two weeks, and set the flag of King Aydrian waving from its high tower throughout the winter!"

"There, you see?" Aydrian calmly asked, drawing a sour look from the dangerous monk.

"You are sending but a third of our available ships," said De'Unnero, as if that alone showed that Aydrian was not as unconcerned as he appeared. "Why not send the entire fleet, after all, and truly overwhelm the small fortress?"

"The others will be needed to continue to patrol the river and to ferry our soldiers to the eastern banks."

"Prince Midalis has ships," De'Unnero reminded.

"Which is why I wish to take Pireth Dancard before we begin the next maneuvers to secure the southland," Aydrian explained. "With the island in our grasp, Midalis' ships, or any potential informant vessels he might have scouting about our coasts, will have no place to resupply. Taking Pireth Dancard will help to blind him to our movements." Aydrian paused and gave a wry little grin, then tossed a carrot out to the concerned monk. "And will seal off passage from St.-Mere-Abelle, for the brothers there have no ships capable of crossing the Gulf of Corona without stopping to resupply. We wouldn't want Fio Bou-raiy and his cronies to rush to Midalis' side, would we?"

"Midalis may be sailing south already," De'Unnero reasoned. "If he reaches Pireth Dancard before Earl DePaunch, the force you now send will not be sufficient to dislodge him."

"He is not," Aydrian said with great conviction, with absolute certainty, and he flashed his soul stone for De'Unnero to see, knowing that the monk was well aware of spirit-walking and Aydrian's power with the stones.

"I have not been idle here," Aydrian explained. "I do not send a third of my fleet into dangers without proper scouting. Prince Midalis' ships are moored in Vanguard harbor, just as we would expect for this season."

"Prince Midalis has many experienced sailors in his fleet, who know well the cold waters of the gulf," the monk retorted. "At anchor is a well-considered position for ships in this season."

Aydrian smiled at the unrelenting sarcasm. He was not growing tired of Marcalo De'Unnero questioning his every move. He understood the many frustrations, everything from Sadye to St.-Mere-Abelle, that were playing on the man's emotions, and he was glad of the questioning in any case. The ever-doubting De'Unnero was keeping Aydrian from getting careless, was forcing Aydrian to find a solution to every possible danger before committing so much of his resources. That was a good thing.

"It is not so far a journey," Earl DePaunch interjected, turning to face Aydrian, though he was answering De'Unnero. "I will get there. I will secure the island and put the fleet into tight mooring about its sheltered bays whenever a gale threatens. You will lose no ships, my King, and few men—and fewer when the brothers you so magnificently train perfect the methods you show them!"

Aydrian nodded his appreciation of the confidence, but he was watching De'Unnero more than DePaunch, and was quite amused by the monk's mocking expression aimed at the upstart and eager young earl. De Paunch caught the look, too, obviously, and he bristled with the pride so prevalent in the Allheart Knights.

"Brother De'Unnero fears any diversion from the goal he views as penultimate," Aydrian explained to the earl. "To his thinking, there remains one prize above all others. Is that not true, brother?"

De'Unnero returned the young king's stare, but did not otherwise respond.

"St.-Mere-Abelle looms as the crowning prize for our friend," Aydrian went on. "And indeed, when Marcalo De'Unnero is in control of the Abellican Church, our desire to return the kingdom to its former glory, and even to expand that glory, will be much closer to realization.

"Patience, my friend," Aydrian went on, turning to De'Unnero with a slightly condescending tone. "Let us secure the gulf and isolate Midalis, and then we might turn our attention to St.-Mere-Abelle. The foolish brothers will have no support from without, and likely will face great dissent from within. You will have your deserved prize. You will sit as Father Abbot of the Abellican Church of Honce-the-Bear while your friend Abbot Olin sits as Father Abbot of the Abellican Church of Behren. And be assured that I am well aware of the value you two bring to my rule."

They were simple words, of course, and ones that Aydrian had uttered to De'Unnero many times previous. But issuing the timely reminder now in front of Earl DePaunch, who was surely a man well on the rise within Aydrian's military hierarchy, created a calming effect on Marcalo De'Unnero. The monk looked at Aydrian long and hard, then merely nodded, his arguments defeated, and bowed and walked away.

Earl DePaunch flashed Aydrian a look that seemed to mock the departing monk, a grin that conveyed his amusement at how easily Aydrian had deflected the argument.

But Aydrian would have none of that. De'Unnero's reputation among the Allhearts and with Aydrian's court in general had been on the decline of late, as the monk's reputation had elicited nothing but scorn from the populace of the towns falling under their control, particularly here in Palmaris.

"That man is the greatest warrior in all the world," Aydrian said, and DePaunch's smile evaporated. "Besides myself, of course. He could defeat you or any of your Allheart brothers in single combat, one after another until the lot of you were dead."

DePaunch bristled again, his shoulders straightening, his expression tightening.

"Take that as no insult, my good Earl," Aydrian went on. "Even your Duke Kalas knows the truth of this. A man as proficient in the arts martial as Marcalo De'Unnero is a rare treasure indeed, the epitome of a generation of warriors. He is a man of honor and great fortitude against trials you cannot begin to understand or appreciate. Look upon him as a great ally, I beseech you, and know that when he sits in power of the Abellican Church, it will become again an institution allied with the throne in a manner beneficial to the nobility of Honce-the-Bear."

"Yes, my King," DePaunch said obediently.

"And do keep always in your mind, my good Earl, the certainty that if you mock Marcalo De'Unnero too greatly, he might just kill you."

So much for DePaunch's proud posturing.

"Enough of that," Aydrian was quick to add, not wanting to deflate his naval leader too greatly. "Turn your attention from the detractors of this all-important mission. That is an issue with which I must deal. Your duty now is clear before you. Prepare this fleet to sail, and these men to execute their tasks to perfection. I send you in all confidence—I listen not at all to those who doubt the wisdom of this expedition to Pireth Dancard because I hold absolute faith that you will secure the fortress in the name of King Aydrian. Once we have that island, the key to the Gulf of Corona is in our hands, and our enemies from the north will have far fewer options open to them concerning their route of attack.

"But beware and be vigilant, my good Earl, for it is possible that Prince Midalis will come against you before we are able to reinforce you. If the Vanguard warships come against Pireth Dancard, you must hold them off. You must make Midalis pay dearly."

"My King," Earl DePaunch said quietly, as if he could hardly get the words past the lump of pride swelling in his chest and in his throat, "I will not fail you. When you sail north after the winter, you will find Pireth Dancard flying the bear and tiger of King Aydrian, and you will find the men you now entrust with this most important mission standing ready to sail beside you in the conquest of Pireth Vanguard!"

Aydrian smiled, mentally patting himself on the back once again for the wisdom of his decision to take the main fleet from the aging and too-cautious Duke Bretherford.

"He is afraid, that's all," Sadye said to Aydrian later that day, the two of them alone in Chasewind Manor's luxurious rooms. "He holds confidence that we cannot be stopped, of course, but prefers a more methodical march across the world."

Aydrian gave her an amused look. "Since when has Sadye ever preferred a course of caution?"

That set the smallish woman back on her heels.

"Is this not the same Sadye who traveled the Wilderlands with a band of ruffians?" Aydrian asked. "The same Sadye who befriended Marcalo De'Unnero, indeed, who fell into his arms, because of the thrill of danger that he presented?"

Sadye's posture became one of petulance. "It was more than that."

"Was it?" Aydrian asked. "Oh yes, there was the promise of power, as well, perhaps the greatest aphrodisiac Sadye the bard has ever known."

She tried to hold her look, but Aydrian could see that his simple and honest reasoning was wearing at her edges. He moved very close to her—too close!—and she seemed to shrink back, just a bit.

"I understand you," Aydrian said, his voice barely above a whisper. "You and I both recognize the allure of power and of danger. You and I both understand that to live on the precipice of disaster is truly to be alive."

Sadye blinked repeatedly and her breathing became more urgent and intense. Aydrian could feel that breath on his face, full of the heat that was growing within her. He could see the sparkle in her dark eyes, an intensity wrought of simmering desire that threatened to explode into unbridled passion.

He leaned in a little closer, wanting her to be full of his scent and his breath, wanting her to feel the pull of his body.

Her chest rose and fell more quickly; she was drawn toward him beyond the warning of her common sense.

"I am expected at council," Aydrian said suddenly, and he stepped back, breaking the moment. He wanted Sadye badly. He had never known the love of a woman, but he understood the sweetness of it anyway, could see it in the sheer intensity of the woman's eyes, could feel it in the heat emanating from her body.

But not now. Not while they were still so far from the treasure De'Unnero coveted most greatly. He would trade De'Unnero the Abellican Church for Sadye, and the man would go along. Besides, Aydrian knew that he was making Sadye insane with lust for him, and he wanted to play that out, wanted to let the heat grow within her until she begged him to take her.

With a look that promised passion beyond anything the woman had ever known, Aydrian turned about and left the room, glancing back only one time.

Sadye was trembling.

Thoughts of her followed Aydrian out of Chasewind Manor and all the way across Palmaris to the meeting house near to the city's north gate. He found De'Unnero, Kalas, and all the other commanders who were not busy with DePaunch and the preparations at the docks assembled about a table on which was spread a map of Honce-the-Bear.

Aydrian moved to the table, stepping between De'Unnero and Kalas. He studied the map, noting the areas shaded red to indicate that they were considered well secured under his control. That included all of the kingdom south of Caer Tinella on the western side of the Masur Delaval, and all of the southland, across Yorkey County to Entel. Aydrian particularly noted the newest placement of the pointers they used to show the intended progress of a coming march. One moved out of the Masur Delaval to Pireth Dancard, indicating the course of DePaunch, while a second moved across the river from Palmaris and diagonally southeast, generally aiming for Entel or the coastal region just to the north.

"Proceed," Aydrian bade them, for he knew that all of the commanders had paused to allow him to digest the map in full.

Kalas looked to De'Unnero, motioning for him to continue his reasoning, and the monk promptly bent over the table and adjusted that southeastern-leaning arrow to a position more directly east, its tip climbing north from Entel in a direct line to St. Gwendolyn, the largest abbey along the Mantis Arm region of the kingdom.

After a moment's pause, Duke Kalas said, "You risk leaving pockets of resistance behind our lines. We have not secured every town south of this line and out to the Mirianic. Prince Midalis has loyalists there, I assure you."

"The longer we tarry, the more likely those pockets will fester into open rebellion," De'Unnero countered. "If we sweep north of them, those unsecured towns will be cut off and the people will understand the folly of resistance."

"Tarry?" came a question from a lord across the table. "Are you not the same man who cautioned patience and argued against launching Earl DePaunch to Pireth Dancard?"

"Brother De'Unnero wished to ensure that all precautions were properly explored," Aydrian interjected before the volatile monk could snap back. "And wisely so. There is a significant difference between a fast march and a late-season seaborne assault. The weather will not slow To-gai ponies, but a gale in the gulf could cost us dearly."

That brought more than a few confused looks from those around the table, from men who had supported Aydrian's determined decision to send DePaunch north.

"Brother De'Unnero wanted to make sure that all risks had been weighed—as Duke Kalas is apparently thinking now in aiming our march more conservatively toward Entel." Aydrian paused a moment and looked at Kalas, and then, with a supportive smile, to De'Unnero. "In this case, the dangers are even less considerable," he decided, and he placed his hand on the pointer, holding it firmly in line toward St. Gwendolyn. "If any rise behind us, we will quickly proceed south and destroy them. For our army that reaches St. Gwendolyn and the sea will likely be far less in number than the force that initially departs Palmaris. We will stretch our line across the kingdom, from the Masur Delaval to the Mirianic, and then turn up the coast and move inland from the river simultaneously." As he spoke, he put his hands at those two strategic points and slowly began to move them toward each other, timing them so that they would converge upon that single most coveted prize, St.-Mere-Abelle.

Aydrian was not surprised by the satisfied expression he found stamped upon the face of Marcalo De'Unnero. He turned his head about to regard Kalas, and found him nodding his agreement.

"It will be the most glorious march of the Allhearts and Kingsmen in centuries!" said the same enthusiastic commander who had berated De'Unnero.

"Ten thousand soldiers marching under the bear and tiger of King Aydrian," another agreed. "The very ground will tremble at our passing!"

"The army will be prepared for the challenge," Duke Kalas assured the king, and several seconded his sentiment.

"Duke Kalas can begin his march out of Palmaris at the earliest opportunity," Aydrian explained. "The season will be milder across the heartland than in Palmaris. For those Allhearts who will not go with Duke Kalas, but will remain in command of Palmaris, I bid you to gather exploratory forces and strengthen the flow of information all about us, from Caer Tinella in the north to Ursal in the south, and across all the stretches of the kingdom west of the river. Also, ready a fast-moving force to react to any open revolt anywhere south of Duke Kalas' proposed march. If a local lord begins resistance, you have my orders to crush him and at once replace him with someone loyal to me."

That brought enthusiastic nods from the warriors, to be sure, but also more than a few confused looks.

"You will be traveling back to Ursal then, my King?" Duke Kalas asked. "For you speak of my march as if you will not be involved."

"No, and yes," Aydrian replied, and when those answers sank in, a few more commanders affected confused expressions.

"Surely you are not considering sailing with Earl DePaunch to Pireth Dancard!" one man said with alarm, voicing the doubts shown on every face about the table—except of course, for Aydrian and one other notable exception: Marcalo De'Unnero.

Aydrian looked at the monk and could see on De'Unnero's face a complete understanding of his own intentions.

"Duke Kalas has secured the regions west of Palmaris," De'Unnero remarked, the perfect lead-in for Aydrian.

"The plans you lords have put in place to deal with the enemies of the crown that you recognize are laudable," Aydrian explained. "Yet there remains one more enemy, hidden in the west. This enemy will prove formidable only if we allow her to use her tactics of subterfuge and quiet destruction. If we face her on the field of honor, the threat will be fast extinguished."

He paused and considered the posture of those about the table, the looks of confusion and even suspicion. Aydrian understood those expressions, certainly. His ascension had thrust the kingdom into civil war, had forced these earls and dukes and Allheart Knights into standing against the man they always believed would become their king. And now Aydrian was introducing something completely new to them, yet another threat and yet another war.

"This will be my task throughout the winter," Aydrian explained, sliding up out of his chair to tower over the seated men. "While Earl DePaunch secures the gulf and Duke Kalas and you other fine lords strengthen our hold on the southland, and while Brother De'Unnero continues the erosion of the present-day Abellican Church and facilitates the revitalization of that wayward institution, I will march to the west, with four hundred warriors behind me."

"The Allhearts are ready to march, my King," said Duke Kalas. "I will personally pick the most able Kingsmen to supplement our ranks."

"Did you not hear me just explain that your duties to the crown will be in the southland?" Aydrian asked.

"But my King . . ."

Aydrian leaned over the table, hovering over Kalas, and—amazingly to the other lords and Allhearts, who had always viewed Duke Kalas as the strongest of their order—the man seemed to shrink and diminish beneath the mighty king.

"Do not ever presume to treat me as a delicate ornament," Aydrian reminded, his tone level. "I am the same man who defeated the uprising at the north wall, the same man who facilitated our conquest of this formidable city, the same man who won the tournament celebrating the fiftieth birthday of King Danube."

Aydrian wished that he could take back that last remark as soon as the words had left his mouth, for Duke Kalas winced—he had been the man Aydrian had defeated that day—and all the other lords bristled. Behind him, the young king heard Marcalo De'Unnero suck in his breath hard.

"If I am enough of a man even to ride in the same field as Duke Kalas," Aydrian improvised, "then surely I am warrior enough to defeat the dangerous enemy to our west."

Kalas's expression softened just a bit, but enough so for Aydrian to hope that he had salved the wound.

"Would you not all agree?" the young king asked, turning and standing straight, his waving arm throwing the question to all the assembly.

As the lords fumbled about their appropriate affirmative responses, Aydrian glanced down to his left, to see a tight-jawed De'Unnero resting back in his chair, his strong arms crossed defensively over his chest.

"Pray tell us the identity of this enemy, my King," Duke Kalas bade. "Do you fear the huntsmen of the Wilderlands?"

"I fear no one," Aydrian replied. "Not Prince Midalis, not St.-Mere-Abelle, and not the Touel'alfar."

Looks of astonishment came back at him; some of them had never even believed in the Touel'alfar, after all, and had known them only in the fireside tales told to them as children and in the wild rumors circulating through the streets of Ursal that Aydrian had been raised and trained by these mysterious elves.

"Oh yes, my lords, they are real, these elusive creatures of the Wilderlands," Aydrian assured them. "You have all heard the rumors of my origins, beyond my parental heritage, and those rumors are true. I know this enemy. I know where she lives. And I know how to destroy her, quickly and efficiently. I will go with four hundred—select the soldiers, Duke Kalas, and they need not be the finest of your warriors. Just give to me men able to withstand the elements of winter, men who possess the skills necessary to survive the harshness of winter in the Wilderlands, even in the lower mountains. Huntsmen and those raised on the northwesternmost borders of Westerhonce, perhaps."

"This is foolishness," came an unexpected reply from across the table, even as Duke Kalas was nodding his agreement. Aydrian and all the others looked over to regard the speaker, Duke Treschent of Falidean, the southernmost province of the Mantis Arm.

"You dare to question the king?" Kalas snapped, but Aydrian held up his hand, bidding Treschent to continue.

"I . . . I only . . ." Treschent glanced about nervously.

Aydrian began a slow walk about the table, his eyes never leaving the man, his stare, though it seemed neutral outwardly, melting the duke beneath it.

"You do not doubt my ability to destroy our enemy," Aydrian prompted.

"No, my King, of course not!" the squirming duke replied.

"No, you fear our hold over the kingdoms while I am away," Aydrian reasoned, and the other swallowed hard. "You question the depth of the acceptance of King Aydrian, and fear that the people will step into open revolt when I am away."

The duke swallowed hard again as Aydrian moved to stand right beside him, and several others about the table dared to whisper in private conversation.

"Is that not why I have men such as Brother De'Unnero and Duke Kalas supporting me?" Aydrian asked. He stayed there a moment, thoroughly diminishing the duke, then walked to the side, addressing the whole of the gathering.

"You are all afraid," he said bluntly. "And why should you not be? We have struck out boldly from Ursal, and thus far our road has been an easy one to walk. Only Palmaris has offered any real resistance, and even that . . ." He paused and chuckled easily.

"And now we face a dangerous sail to the north, and potential battle in the south," he went on. "And Midalis is always there, in waiting." He looked at De'Unnero. "And St.-Mere-Abelle is there, waiting. The greatest fortress in all the world, manned by more than seven hundred brothers trained in battle and mighty in gemstone magic. You are all wary, as well you should be.

"And now I tell you of a new foe, one which most of you never even knew existed. Your doubts are justified, except . . ."

He paused and looked around, to make sure that every set of eyes was looking his way, that every ear was tuned to his every word.

"Except that I am your king," Aydrian went on. "And I know this enemy, intimately so. And I know how to eradicate this enemy. And so I shall."

There were no whispers, and no responses, not even from Duke Kalas or Marcalo De'Unnero.

"You are dismissed," Aydrian said to them. "Go to your duties. Winter is fast approaching and we have much to accomplish before the turn of spring and the greater battles that season will bring."

With many glances to each other, and much nervous shuffling, the gathered nobles began to filter out.

All except one.

Marcalo De'Unnero remained in his seat with his back-leaning, almost amused posture, his arms still crossed over his muscular chest. Slowly, his eyes never blinking and never leaving Aydrian, he unfolded those arms and began to slowly clap his hands.

"You handled them as if they were children," he congratulated. "Yet most of them have been in positions of authority longer than you have been alive. So tell me, my onetime student, where have you come to know such politic?"

Aydrian gave a little shrug. "It is an extension of confidence, my friend."

"You are so certain that you are above them?"

"Beyond anything they could ever dream," Aydrian replied. "And you know that I am. If I treat them as children, it is because—beside me—that is all that they are."

De'Unnero's expression became somewhat incredulous. "You are simply amazing."

"More than you can imagine."

De'Unnero paused and looked away for a moment, then chuckled and turned back. "And you truly mean to march against Lady Dasslerond and her band?"

"It is a prize I covet as dearly as you covet St.-Mere-Abelle, and one far more easily attained."

De'Unnero's expression became very serious. "Do not underestimate the diminutive folk," he warned. "It was they who orchestrated the rise of your father. It was they who facilitated the downfall of Father Abbot Markwart and the previous Abellican Church. Those were no minor feats."

"If Lady Dasslerond is able to work from the shadows, she is formidable," Aydrian agreed. "But I intend to light those shadows with flames. She will not stand against me—this will not be our first encounter. Even then, when I was so much younger and inexperienced, Dasslerond was not the one who walked away victorious."

"I should go with you," De'Unnero said, and Aydrian was shaking his head before the predictable words ever came forth.

"Our hold on St. Precious is not so strong, and converting the brothers will prove far more valuable than merely eliminating them."

"Then wait until the spring, or until the next season, when the kingdom is secured."

"You believe that Dasslerond will not involve herself in our conquest? You do not understand her hatred of me, and her fear. She knows that I will come for her, as the monks of St.-Mere-Abelle know that the wrongs they perpetrated upon Marcalo De'Unnero will lead you back to them, at the head of an army mighty enough to topple them. If we wait for Dasslerond, she will become many times more dangerous to us."

"The winter in the Wilderlands will be difficult for so large a force."

"That is why I choose not to take twenty thousand," said Aydrian. "I have a full measure of Andur'Blough Inninness and Lady Dasslerond. Four hundred will suffice."

"I will return to you within three months' time," Aydrian went on when it seemed as if De'Unnero had run out of doubts to express. "And the threat to the west will be no more. If Duke Kalas is successful in his march across the southland, we will be well on our way. Then we might focus more fully on the march of Midalis, and when that inconvenience is eliminated, we will turn our attention to the greatest prize of all."

"While Abbot Olin continues his conquest of Behren," De'Unnero replied. "While our new commanders in Vanguard—the eager DePaunch, perhaps—draw up battle plans for the conquest of Alpinador. What then, my former student? Do we sail to the Weathered Isles and conquer the powries, as well?"

It was meant sarcastically, but Aydrian gave a look to show that the possibility did intrigue him.

"But let us not forget about Brynn Dharielle, this 'Dragon of To-gai' who sent Behren into such turmoil," De'Unnero went on undaunted.

"What is your point?" Aydrian asked, all signs of his previous amusement flown.

"Take care that we do not stretch too far, else more than you believe will slip through your widespread fingers," De'Unnero warned. "You have made many enemies out there, more formidable than you apparently believe."

"Or perhaps you merely underestimate Aydrian," the young king said.

"It always comes back to that."

Aydrian smiled.

"And if you are killed in the Wilderlands?" the monk asked. "What then for all of us?"

"There is no return for the noblemen and the Allhearts," Aydrian was quick to answer. "They have taken an open stand against Midalis, and so if they are to hold their coveted power, the prince cannot rise as king. There is no stepping back from this war. I will not be killed, but if that were to come to pass, then the gain to Marcalo De'Unnero would be even greater. You would win the war without me, of course, and then how much stronger would your Church become when the kingdom is truly leaderless? Duke Kalas will be appointed as Steward of the State, no doubt, but a steward is not a king."

De'Unnero was tapping his fingers before his face by then, his every movement showing that he was not about to disagree.

"So take heart, my friend, and hold faith in your"—he paused to flash a smile—"former student."

❖ 20 ❖

The Heart to Fight

The night was so dark that when she opened her eyes, she was not certain that she had. Or perhaps, if her eyes were indeed open once more, she had passed from the world she had known to a place of darkness, a place of shadows—to a place that did not know the light of life.

She closed her eyes once more and consciously tuned herself in to the sensations about her: the cold, wet clay beneath her face and bare arms; the numbness in her legs; the dull ache that permeated her side; the hot fire of pain burning brightly in her belly. She knew at once that she was very near to death, for a coldness crept up her legs, one so profound that it seemed as if her flesh was disappearing beneath its deathly touch.

She tried to lift her head, but could not. She wanted to turn to the side, to get the cold, gritty clay away from her mouth, but she could not.

She wondered then why she had stirred, why death had not simply taken her in her unconscious state.

She got jostled—again, she realized—by something hard pushing against her shoulder.

With tremendous effort, Pony slid her head along the clay enough to change her angle of view. At first she saw nothing except the darkness, but gradually, she made out a darker silhouette.

She got pushed again.

A horse's hoof.

"Symphony?" the woman mouthed, but silently, for she had not the strength to draw enough breath for audible words. She saw the silhouette rear up and kick its forelegs, and she felt the connection, intimate through the powers of the turquoise gemstone that Brother Avelyn had set into Symphony's breast.

"Symphony," she said again, this time whispering through the sand.

The horse nickered and pawed the ground anxiously, prompting her to movement.

But Pony had not the strength.

More insistent, Symphony pushed at her again, shifting her to the side. Waves of pain rolled up and down her side, but with them came the sensation of feeling, at least, a temporary reprieve from death. Pony wasn't sure that she wanted that reprieve, though. Wouldn't it be easier just to close her eyes and let the nether realm take her? To go to Elbryan? To escape the pain of goblin spears and the more profound agony that was Aydrian?

For there before her, hovering like a black wall against her willpower, against her very instinct to survive, was the specter of Aydrian, the mark of true despair. She had seen his power and the blackness within his heart. In looking into his blue eyes—so much akin to her own—Pony had understood the waste of what might have been and the terror of what he had become. She could not defeat him, nor could she bear to watch his rise.

And in the end, for her, there would be only death.

Symphony whinnied and stomped at the ground. The stallion pranced about Pony, snorted with every stride, kicking and bucking insistently. The sheer power of the old horse brought Pony forth from the dark contemplations, made her instead regard the resilience and determination that was Symphony.

In light of that, the broken woman was surely shamed.

In light of that, Pony suddenly felt foolish, lying there in the muddy clay awaiting death with a healing stone somewhere nearby!

She brought her hands up by the sides of her chest and tried to lift herself up. But it was too late, she was too far gone, and she fell back to the mud.

"Symphony," she whispered.

The horse moved very near to her and bent his head down, his lips nibbling at her ear and hair.

"Gemstone," Pony tried to say, but more important than the word that would hardly come, the woman projected her thoughts at the stallion, calling for the hematite, trying to make him understand.

But such communication was not possible without the soul stone, she knew.

Stubbornly, Pony considered Oracle, the gift Andacanavar had given to her so that she could reach out for Elbryan's spirit. She had not used the meditative process nearly enough over the last few years. Instead of finding a connection to Elbryan at those times when she sat in front of the darkened mirror, Pony had found only despair at the stinging pain of her loss. But now she went there, fell into that meditative state as surely as if she were sitting in a dimly lit room, staring into a mirror. She felt a presence about her, the shadow in the mirror.

Symphony sensed it, too, she knew, from the way in which the horse began snorting and pawing again, obviously agitated.

Pony sent her thoughts forth again, to the shadow that she knew was Elbryan. She replayed the goblin battle, from the time she had begun splashing across the lake, but she was watching it from a different perspective, as if she was looking on at her own actions from the side. She had been holding the soul stone at the pause in the middle of the pond, obviously, for there she had gone south and north, possessing the goblins and turning them against each other. And then she had come out on the bank, to face the charge from the south, and she had thrown her blanket at the goblin and had dived to the sand at the feet of a charging goblin . . .

A moment later, Symphony leaped about and rushed away. Exhausted, the shadow fast dissipating, Pony slumped back into the mud and closed her eyes. She heard some splashing, and then some more a bit later, and followed Symphony's snorts along the bank to the south.

But the cold and empty darkness invited her . . .

A rough push against her shoulder roused Pony once more a few moments later. She resisted the call, and got pushed again and then a third time by the insistent and indomitable stallion. Finally, she opened her eyes, to see a small piece of deeper blackness upon the ground right before her face. With a grunt and a sudden burst, Pony brought her hand up over that spot, over the soul stone.

She ran away from the inviting cold, and into the warm gray swirl of the hematite, freeing her spirit from the weariness and the pain. She felt something full of strength move up against her hand and hardly recognized it as Symphony's leg. But she pressed against it instinctively, the soul stone set firmly between her cold and half-numb hand and the great stallion's hoof.

Her spirit found the fugue area between those two corporeal forms, connecting with Symphony. She understood then what the stallion was offering, but her generous spirit instinctively recoiled.

Symphony pressed in closer and gave a great and insistent cry into the dark night.

Pony joined with his spirit, and pulled back strength from his spirit, infusing herself with the power of the horse. She instinctively recoiled, knowing that this was among the most profane types of possession, which in itself struck her as horrible. But Symphony wouldn't let her go. She recognized that the horse understood what she was doing and willingly lent her part of his own life force.

Energized, the woman reached down to her wound and put the healing powers of the gemstone to work.

Like warm water, the waves of healing magic cascaded down across the prone woman, filling her with warmth and relief from the pain. Soon after, those areas that had long ago gone numb from the wounds began to tingle with renewed life.

As all of this went along, another sort of healing found its way, quite unexpectedly, into a different part of Pony, into the most profoundly wounded element of the woman: her heart. She lay there in the muddy clay, keeping her energies rolling through the gemstone, transforming into magical healing, but focusing her thoughts on the unexpected events that had led her to this point. She remembered again the fight against the demon-possessed Markwart on the field outside of Palmaris. She had been beaten, and surely would have died without rescue by Dasslerond's elves.

That was when she had lost Aydrian to the Touel'alfar.

The woman managed to roll over then, to get her face out of the mud. She lay on her back, staring up at the stars, and then she saw . . .

The Halo.

Pony's heart leaped at the multicolored rings, as if her spirit were reaching for them. She remembered a day long ago, when she and Elbryan were but children, rushing out of Dundalis up the northern slope. They had glanced back to see this same magical sight. This was the source of the gemstones, and seemed to her so perfect a gift from God. She felt such a connection here, between memory and present thought, between her spirit and those of ones who had passed from this life before her. That ring told Pony that Elbryan was with her still, that the song of Nightbird lived on in more than just her own memories. It resonated in the trees and the birds, and in all that Elbryan had touched. It floated on the evening breeze as surely as Bradwarden's haunting melody.

A great sense of calm came over her, as profound a relief to her soul as the waves of healing magic had been to her body. She did not try to halt the tears spilling out of her eyes as she lay there viewing the corona, as she felt her spirit touching that of Elbryan.

He was there with her—she could feel it so keenly! He stood beside her; he had helped to guide Symphony to her!

And he was telling her something.

Pony thought back to the day of King Danube's death. She looked past the shock of the moment, past the horror of seeing the ghost of Constance Pemblebury, past the terror of watching her husband get pulled down to his death, past the sudden and brutal shock of the recognition of the son she did not know she had. In that moment in the mud, looking up at the corona, feeling the love of Elbryan all about her, Pony sought a different perspective. She forced away her rage at Lady Dasslerond and instead whispered a thanks to Dasslerond and the elves for saving her life and for saving Aydrian. She forced away the pain and resentment, pushed past her fear of the monster Dasslerond had created, and looked at Aydrian in a new context. He was her son. He was in great pain.

Great pain had brought him to this pinnacle of disaster. Great pain had fostered his resentment toward his mother. Great pain and Marcalo De'Unnero.

Pony let go of that name, as well, as soon as it had occurred to her. She had no room for rage at that moment.

And perhaps it was more than De'Unnero, the woman pondered, and a shiver ran up her spine. She considered again the circumstance under which she had lost Aydrian, in the midst of a spiritual battle with Father Abbot Markwart and with a creature quite beyond the scope of the frail old monk.

For the first time in so long, Pony felt that old spirit rising within her, the same fires that had carried her to Mount Aida to battle the dactyl demon, the same fires that had sustained her through her ordeal at the hands of

Markwart and the loss of so many she had loved, the same fires that had
bolstered her courage throughout the rosy plague and shown her the truth
of community and the way to the shrine of Avelyn.

She considered Aydrian again, and the errant monster he had become,
and she admitted to herself that she did not have the heart to fight against
her own son.

But Pony pushed past that, and confirmed within her heart that she did
indeed have the heart to battle Marcalo De'Unnero.

Without further ado, with the name of the false and discredited monk
filling her body with determination, the woman pulled herself from the
ground and moved beside the patient Symphony. She stroked the horse's
face lovingly, communicating her gratitude, then brought her face up against
the side of the great stallion's neck, feeling his warmth. With a whisper in
his ear for him to take her home, Pony climbed up on Symphony's back and
took hold of the thick black mane.

Off leaped the horse, running as no other animal in all the world
could run.

He carried her tirelessly across the Moorlands and into the forests where
the leaves had fallen thick upon the paths. He charged up every hillside and
gracefully and carefully descended the back slopes, moving ever eastward.

In short days, Symphony galloped through fields of caribou moss, like white
powder rising up the stallion's hooves and muffling the sound of Symphony's
thunderous passage, and when she recognized the rolling moss-strewn fields
about her, Pony knew that she was almost home.

She leaned forward over the horse and whispered a new instruction, and
Symphony knew her desire and certainly knew the way. One day about twilight, the horse pulled up near a diamond-shaped grove.

Pony slid down, only then realizing that the song of Bradwarden was
thick in the air about her, blending, as always, with the harmonies of nature.
Bolstered by the music, and by the presence she felt in this special place,
the woman moved into the copse of trees, to a place before two stone
cairns.

"I'll bring back your sword, Mather Wyndon," she promised. "And Hawkwing for you, my love. All that we worked to achieve will not be lost in the
wayward designs of our son."

"Yer words're music sweeter'n anything me pipes have ever blowed,"
came the voice of Bradwarden behind her.

Pony smiled and turned about.

"Ye seen the elf lady?" the centaur asked.

"Dasslerond and I did not part as friends," Pony admitted. "But we are
allies in this, of circumstance and not choice."

"Ye put yerself out to fix the errors o' the Touel'alfar?"

Pony gave a resigned little shrug. "Someone has to."

The centaur broke into a great bellylaugh then. "And once again, it falls to yerself. Ah, but what a life ye've known, Pony o' Dundalis! Pony who fought the demon in its hole, and fought it again in the body o' Markwart."

"And who might yet do battle with Bestesbulzibar," the woman said solemnly, and Bradwarden stopped his laughing and stared at her curiously.

"Prince Midalis will need me," the woman went on, not wanting to elaborate upon her fears at that time. "And now that Symphony has returned to me, I will find him."

"Ye can be thanking meself and Roger for springing that one from the stables o' yer greedy little son," the centaur remarked.

"There are no stables suitable for Symphony beyond the wide, unfenced fields of the world."

"True enough." Bradwarden let the conversation die for a moment, as Pony turned back to stare at the cairn of her beloved Elbryan. A profound sense of relief splayed across her beautiful face, as if her recent ordeal had shown her the truth of her life now, and of her duty.

And it seemed to the centaur, that it was a duty she was ready to meet.

"Ye're to ride out in the spring for Vanguard then?"

Pony turned back, shaking her head. "There can be no delay. I will ride into Dundalis this night and be on the road to Prince Midalis by midmorning."

"Ye'll be running against the winter," the centaur warned.

"As Symphony does every winter."

"True enough," the centaur admitted. "And it's not like I'm needing any warm bed, for I ain't found one yet that'll hold me!"

Pony's quizzical expression fast shifted to one of gratitude as she realized that Bradwarden meant to go with her every step of the way, and that nothing she could possibly say would dissuade her loyal friend from walking the road to war beside her.

"Ye don't be goin' in the morning, though," Bradwarden said to her. "Ye spend the day with yer friend Dainsey. She's frightfully worried about her Roger, and she's needin' ye now, I'm thinking."

"Roger?" Pony asked with sudden alarm.

"He went with meself to get Symphony from yer son," the centaur explained, and he didn't seem overly worried. "He come out o' the city, but turned back. Seems our friend Braumin's got himself caught by Aydrian and De'Unnero, and Roger's set on getting him free."

Pony spent a moment digesting that, and the feeling of dread returned to her tenfold. She trusted in Roger—he was resourceful and clever. But he was no match for Marcalo De'Unnero! And neither was Braumin Herde.

Pony almost shifted her thinking then, almost broke and declared that she would ride for Palmaris. But she knew that her duty was to a greater cause than her personal friendships. As with the ride to the Barbacan to battle the demon incarnate, her duty now was to Honce-the-Bear, was to the society of man. Her course led north and east, to Midalis, and so she would put any of her personal needs aside and trust in her friends and follow that road.

She found Dainsey in Fellowship Way, staying with Belster—who seemed much improved now after Pony's healing session. The bloom of life had returned to the large man's cheeks as the strength had returned to his legs. She found him behind the bar, tending to the many patrons, and he cried a river of tears when she appeared before him, and rushed about the bar to crush her in a hug as great as any father had ever wrapped about his daughter.

His mirth did diminish when she asked about Dainsey.

"She's in the back, worrying for her Roger."

Pony pulled back from Belster, who nodded as he let go of her, then she slipped behind the bar and down the small corridor to the door of Dainsey's room.

She knocked softly, and when she got no reply, she gently pushed the door open. Dainsey sat in a chair by the window, looking out into the dark night.

Pony crouched beside her, and it wasn't until she put a hand on Dainsey's shoulder that the woman even seemed to notice her. Dainsey turned and leaned into Pony's inviting hug.

"It's always a fight, ain't it?" Dainsey said. "Always one finding ye even if ye don't go lookin'."

"Roger does seem to find his battles," Pony agreed, but her tone was much more lighthearted than Dainsey's somber and fearful voice. "Not many have to come to him."

That remark seemed to cheer Dainsey up a bit.

"No friend of Roger ever needs ask for help," Pony went on. "Remember those days when you and he would come to visit me in Castle Ursal? Every look the snooty nobles offered my way was met by a look of challenge from Roger Lockless."

"Aye, and though they were knights all and trained in the ways of battle, and though their armor alone outweighed me Roger, if it'd come to blows . . ."

"The noblemen would have spent many hours on the ground," Pony finished for her, and now Dainsey did share her smile.

"He's after Braumin."

"So Bradwarden has told me," Pony answered.

"He's got the wretch De'Unnero between him and the bishop."

"Pity De'Unnero then," said Pony.

She stayed with Dainsey for several hours before retiring to her own room. She slept late—later than she had intended—but when she woke, she found Belster and Dainsey waiting for her, saddlebags full of supplies on the table before them.

"I spoke with Bradwarden last night," Belster explained. "We know yer road."

"We're all needin' ye now," Dainsey agreed.

An hour later, Symphony carried Pony out of Dundalis, with Bradwarden charging along beside them.

Vanguard was a long ride, and winter's bite was thick in the air.

But that was nothing compared to the enemy they would face soon enough, all three understood, and so they feared not the discomforts of the road.

For Pony, there were only the defeat of De'Unnero, the restoration of the crown, and the rescue of her son.

CHAPTER

❖ 21 ❖

The Price of Loyalty

"Season's end catch!" the old fish vendor cried in a cackling voice. "We gots yer river cod and white bass! Season's end!"

The figure bent low over the cart, pushing it with seemingly great effort along the cobblestoned street in Palmaris' northeastern section, not far from the great abbey of St. Precious.

"Season's end!" he called again, and he reached up and stroked his long gray beard—subtly shifting it back into proper place.

A pair of brothers wearing the brown Abellican robes moved up toward the cart.

"Season's end, you say, good fishman vendor?" one remarked.

"Aye."

The two monks moved right up beside the cart. "Master Lockless?" Brother Hoyet asked, his face a mask of curiosity.

Roger looked up, called out his fish once again, and gave the monks a wink.

"A grand disguise," said the other brother, Tarin Destou by name. "So many times did I serve as Bishop Braumin's second in the service at Chasewind Manor, and yet even standing here before you, it is hard for me to discern your true identity."

"That's the point, after all," Roger deadpanned. "Wouldn't be much of a disguise otherwise."

The monks looked at each other and grinned, then turned as one back to Roger.

"Ah, the white bass, ye say?" Roger said loudly as a couple of other Palmaris citizens wandered by. He reached into his cart and brought up a sad-looking specimen. "Fine choice, lads! Fine choice!"

Brother Hoyet took the smelly fish.

"What of Bishop Braumin, then?" Roger asked. "I had feared that De'Unnero, if not Aydrian, would have him killed as soon as Palmaris had fallen, but it is my understanding that he has made appearances since the conquest."

"He has spoken on behalf of King Aydrian several times since," Hoyet confirmed.

"To calm the city's populace and prevent wholesale slaughter, no doubt," said Roger.

"He has spoken on behalf of Marcalo De'Unnero, as well," Brother Destou added, and Roger couldn't help but wince. Never, under any threat or even for the good of the community he served, would Bishop Braumin Herde willingly stand beside Marcalo De'Unnero—unless they two were standing on a gallows and the noose was firmly about De'Unnero's neck!

"He has asked the city to embrace King Aydrian for the glory and good of Honce-the-Bear, and to dismiss their errant notions of Brother . . . of *Abbot* De'Unnero, to accept him as the rightful leader of St. Precious at this time, and as the likely Father Abbot of the Abellican Church in due and short order."

"Bishop Braumin would not say such a thing," Hoyet added.

"Not if they held a poisoned dagger to his back," Roger agreed. "Were you close to him when he spoke those words?"

"Three in line to the side," answered Hoyet. "It was no imposter, but Bishop Braumin."

"Or was it an imposter within Bishop Braumin?" asked Roger, who understood gemstone possession well enough to make the connection.

Both monks, who had obviously been thinking the same thing, nodded.

"De'Unnero?" Roger asked.

"It is rumored that the son of Jilseponie is mighty with the gemstones—greater even than his mother," Brother Destou explained.

"That he would do this marks him as no son of Jilseponie, whatever his physical heritage," Roger was quick to reply. "Know you where they keep Bishop Braumin? Is he well?"

"Beneath the abbey, perhaps," answered Hoyet. "Many new prisoners have been brought to the dungeons since the arrival of the new king. We are not allowed anywhere near to the entry rooms, of course. Only those brothers who arrived with our new abbot can get close to the dungeon stairwell."

"They hold him in chains—he is not well," Brother Destou added. "They drag him out and clean him when they need to use him for their purposes."

"Then you know where he is being held?" Roger asked Destou.

The monk shrugged. "I have seen the shackle marks about his wrist, and he is thinner by far. But I have not seen him taken from the dungeons of St. Precious."

Roger gripped the fish cart—he needed the support or he might have fallen over. He had suspected that all along, of course. As soon as he had learned that Braumin had not gotten out of the city, and had not been killed, but rather, was being used as a puppet for Aydrian and De'Unnero, he had suspected that his friend was probably not in a good and healthy situation, and likely in the dungeons of St. Precious or Chasewind Manor.

"Where has he spoken?" Roger asked.

"In the square, as is customary for an abbot of St. Precious," Destou answered.

"And has he traveled with the group of brothers from St. Precious to that customary spot?" Roger pressed. "Has he spoken after or during a rain? And if so, were his shoes wet before the entourage emerged from St. Precious?"

"They were," Brother Hoyet answered suddenly, his face lighting with the revelation. He looked at Destou, who merely shrugged again, apparently having not noticed.

"De'Unnero stays at St. Precious?" Roger asked.

Hoyet nodded.

"And Aydrian in Chasewind Manor?"

Another nod. "Though he is leaving any day now, marching west, by all reports," Brother Hoyet put in.

Roger's head similarly bobbed as he sorted it all out. He knew the dungeons of Chasewind Manor well. Many of his friends had been held there when Markwart had come to the city to battle the disciples of Avelyn, including Braumin Herde and Jilseponie. And of course, living in the manor over the last few years had given the ever-inquisitive Roger the opportunity to scout out the place top to bottom, all the catacombs, dungeons, and many of its secret passages.

"You will go to him?" Brother Destou asked.

"I would not be a friend if I did not," said Roger, and both monks bowed their heads, as if stung by the remark.

Roger appreciated their looks. The two had denounced Braumin to De'Unnero, he understood, else they, too, would have been thrown in chains. No doubt each was carrying substantial guilt upon his shoulders. A younger Roger would have scolded them for their cowardice, surely, but the man, who had learned so much under the tutelage of Elbryan and Jilseponie, appreciated their torment.

"You did not betray Bishop Braumin," the generous Roger said. "You have risked so much in meeting with me this day." He ended with a wink and began pushing the fish cart on past the pair. "Keep the white bass," he offered.

The two young brothers nodded, Hoyet lifting the fish in a bit of a salute, and then they hiked their robes more tightly about them against the cold wind and headed back toward St. Precious Abbey.

Had they been more perceptive, they might have seen the shadowy figure peering out at them with too much interest from a small window on the great structure's second floor.

Marcalo De'Unnero stood with a large gathering at the city's northern gate as Aydrian led the procession of four hundred Kingsmen out of Palmaris and off to the west. Bereft of his escaped stallion, the young king seemed little diminished. He rode a sturdy To-gai-ru pony, one of the many extras in the Palmaris stables since a group of Allhearts had sailed with Earl DePaunch into the Gulf of Corona.

Wagons rumbled out the gate behind Aydrian; the disciplined soldiers marched in perfect cadence, and half the city, it seemed, had gathered to watch the departure.

De'Unnero fast turned his attention from Aydrian to the clustered citizens, some of whom, he knew, were looking at him with great trepidation. Though a dozen years and more had passed, many in Palmaris remembered well the rule of Bishop Marcalo De'Unnero, short though it had been.

This time would be different, the monk told himself. He and Aydrian had set out a proper course for him within the city, one that would keep the people of Palmaris satisfied at least, if not enamored of their young king and his primary advisor. There would be no public executions. There would be no mass imprisonments, nor any edicts slashing the rights of the folk to go about their daily routines much as they had done through the last ten years.

Furthermore, there would be no formal declaration of De'Unnero as bishop, or even as abbot of St. Precious. As far as the folk of Palmaris were concerned, he was just an abbot from another abbey, serving as Aydrian's representative advisor to Bishop Braumin Herde.

Of course, Marcalo De'Unnero was much more than that. With Aydrian gone and Kalas involved in the control and complete subjugation of the southland, the monk was, in effect, the absolute ruler of Palmaris. Bishop Braumin was a name, and nothing more; with Aydrian gone, De'Unnero had no intention of even letting the bishop out of his dungeon cell. De'Unnero would use one of the converted masters of St. Precious to speak the edicts— proclamations said to have come from Bishop Braumin—but those speeches would be written by none other than Marcalo De'Unnero.

His charge was an easy one. He was to sit out the winter in peace and in control, to rest and be ready for the greater battles that would surely come in the spring.

Well, that was almost Marcalo De'Unnero's edict. He had forced one concession from Aydrian, something that he and Father Abbot Markwart had tried before, to results that proved rather disastrous to De'Unnero. His policy of reclaiming all magic gemstones had angered the Palmaris populace greatly against him, though Markwart and then Bishop Francis had used his fall from grace to further their cause of collection and to further the popularity of Francis. Many of the stones had been retrieved, and were still in Church coffers, but getting the rest of them was something that Marcalo De'Unnero believed to be the most important task he would ever undertake.

For the stones were the province of the Abellican Church, as far as De'Unnero was concerned, and the thought that so many were outside the Church, sold by the former abbots of St.-Mere-Abelle and often converted into easily used magical items by heretical craftsmen and alchemists, made him tremble with rage.

This time, De'Unnero meant to go about collecting the stones in a more diplomatic manner, though, much as Francis had used after De'Unnero's removal from Palmaris. Instead of threats, the monk would use payment to regain sacred and magical items. He had brought bags and bags of unenchanted, though valuable, gemstones with him for just that purpose.

Yes, De'Unnero meant to become a friend to the people of Palmaris, and of all the towns along the Masur Delaval all the way back to Ursal. Or at least, he would become the friend of the important and powerful people. Wealth could buy back many of the gemstones, or could buy information concerning which merchants and noblemen might be holding a stone or an enchanted item. Once he identified each criminal, De'Unnero would approach the man personally and offer payment.

If that was refused, De'Unnero would quietly return the same night and take the Church's rightful property.

The monk had consciously to remind himself to smile, standing there in the open at the northern gate. He knew that many eyes were upon him and so he fought his more instinctual urges to scowl and tried very hard to soften his visage.

It was not an easy thing for Marcalo De'Unnero to do.

Roger couldn't help but feel a few pangs of guilt as he nodded back to Brother Hoyet, the first in the line of nearly a dozen young monks set in place to escort Bishop Braumin through dark paths all across the city to the river, and then across the river to a waiting coach fast bound for St.-Mere-Abelle. It encouraged Roger to find that so many of the brothers of St. Precious would rally to help Bishop Braumin, knowing full well that, in doing so, they were putting their lives at a great risk. Marcalo De'Unnero was not a forgiving man!

But Roger had prompted them, had coerced them, had met secretly with Hoyet and Destou on many occasions, egging them on. He recounted to them Braumin's own humble beginnings as a revolutionary, along with Viscenti and Brother Castinagis and others who had secretly gathered with Master Jojonah those years ago, in the very bowels of St.-Mere-Abelle—then Father Abbot Markwart's stronghold—to keep alive the flame of hope that was Avelyn Desbris. Those brothers had faced similar penalties, but had followed their hearts and held true to their precepts. Some like Jojonah, who had been burned at the stake, had paid a heavy price. But all of them had accepted that potential cost for the sake of their conscience.

So it was now with Hoyet and Destou, and the nine others who had helped to organize this attempted escape, Roger knew. They were doing it out of love for Braumin and in trust of Roger.

"I'll not let them down," the man whispered quietly as he moved along the hedgerow that ringed Chasewind Manor. It was an easy enough scramble for him to get over the wall, touching down in the darkened yard behind the manor house.

He saw the silhouette of a man not so far away, as he had anticipated, as Brother Hoyet had arranged.

Elbryan would not have done it this way, Roger couldn't help but tell himself, as he considered yet another man in on the conspiracy. *Elbryan would have come in alone to rescue Braumin Herde, and would have left a trail of scattered enemies in his wake, if need be.* Roger knew it to be true, and knew that in asking for the help of these dozen men, he had put them in dire straights.

He saw no way around it. He was a decent fighter, but certainly no match for a trained soldier twenty years his junior! And certainly no match for an Allheart Knight!

And this place was crawling with both. Even from his perch back here in the shadows behind the house, Roger could hear the men inside, mostly soldiers. And he had seen the guards at the gate, and others marching in formation about the wall, despite the late hour.

"Here now, ye don't be coming in after the sun's gone down," came a cackling old voice, and the thin silhouette ambled toward Roger. "And ye don't come in at all over the wall. But through the gate, properly introduced."

The words were correct, as were the quiet tone and delivery. "Illthin?" Roger asked, and then he ducked low as the sound of marching soldiers echoed nearby.

"Come along then, ye lazy snoozer," the silhouette, who was indeed old Illthin, said to Roger, and he tossed a shovel at the man's feet. "I told Allheart Desenz that I'd have that tree upturned afore the dawn, and I'm not for getting a beating because a man half me age can't keep his eyes open long enough to dig a few roots!"

"Is there trouble here?" came a call, and the man leading the patrol moved over to Roger and Illthin, eyeing them suspiciously.

"Only because me worker here ain't worth the coins I'm payin' him!" Illthin grumbled. "Ye think ye might give him a few lashes for me, me good Kingsman?"

The soldier eyed Roger wickedly and reached for a club set on his belt.

"Wait! Wait!" Roger pleaded, holding up his hands defensively. "I wasn't napping. No, I . . . I had to . . ." He glanced about to the base of the wall and gave the front of his pants a tug to straighten them.

"All this trouble over a piss?" the soldier snapped at Illthin.

Illthin played his role perfectly, eyeing Roger with an edge of true suspicion. "Long piss, then," he muttered, and he waved the soldier away. "Get yer shovel, then, ye lazy dog, and if ye got any more in ye needing to come out, ye best do it in yer pants!"

Roger scooped the shovel and fell into a quick step right behind the muttering Illthin. "We'll never get it uprooted afore the dawn," the old man grumbled.

The soldier moved back to his patrol, and they took up their march, away from the pair as Illthin led Roger over to an aged tree by the large back porch of the manor house.

"You almost got me beaten," Roger grumbled.

"Better'n hanged, ye fool," the old man cackled back. Illthin looked to the ground about the old tree and motioned with his chin for Roger to get to work.

"We're really digging it up?"

"Until the change o' the guard, at least," Illthin explained. "And that'll be an hour." He motioned again, more insistently.

It struck Roger as humorous that even though he knew that Illthin was working for his own good, and for the sake of Bishop Braumin, the old man never seemed to be completely on his side. He drove his shovel into the ground, grunting as it clipped a thick root.

Within a few minutes, Roger was breathing heavily, and the strokes of his shovel came more and more slowly.

"Ha-ha," old Illthin laughed at him. "Are ye goin' to fall over dead then, Master Lockless?" he asked. "All yer pampered days taken the fight from ye, have they?"

Roger planted the shovel in the ground and leaned on it, staring at the old gardener. "This is no game," he said. "Though I'm glad that you've found a bit of mirth at my expense."

Illthin's cackling ended abruptly, and the man's thin grin disappeared into a suddenly serious expression. "Mirth?" he responded. "Now ye got sweat and mud on ye. Now ye're lookin' the part of a worker, and so now ye can go into the washrooms about the cook rooms."

Roger stared at him for a moment, digesting the logic, and he could only nod his agreement. The washrooms and the cook rooms—that was the area near to the stairwell to the dungeons.

"Bah, we'll have to wait for morning's light to get the damned tree down," Illthin said suddenly, and loudly, and it took Roger a moment to realize that he was speaking for the benefit not of Roger, but of the patrol marching around the corner of the building.

"Just go and get yerself cleaned and get some sleep," Illthin went on. "And ye meet me back here at the break o' dawn."

Roger nodded and leaned the shovel over to Illthin's waiting grasp; then, with a glance at the soldiers—none of whom seemed overly interested in him or in Illthin—he moved toward the house.

He got inside without incident and began making his way along corridors and through rooms all too familiar to him. The place was mostly quiet at this late hour, but he heard one group of men rolling bones, and another group arguing about the current politics in the kingdom—though none saying a word against King Aydrian, obviously.

Moving silently, using those skills that he had learned as a young boy in Caer Tinella and had then perfected during the powrie occupation in the days of the demon dactyl, Roger took a roundabout and inconspicuous course that brought him inevitably toward the servant quarters of the great house and the stairwell to the lower dungeon levels.

He came to a door, slightly ajar, with candlelight spilling out from within the room. He put his ear to the door, then dared to push it open just a bit and peek in.

Roger froze in place, for the room was not empty. A pair of large men, Kingsmen, were on guard within, one sitting and seeming asleep—or at least very near to sleep—and the other leaning against a cupboard at the far right of the room.

And there, on the left, was the door that led to the downward staircase.

Roger believed that he could get to it without being noticed by the groggy guards, but how then might he get back out, with Braumin in tow?

Roger glanced all around, looking for a solution. His hand went to his belt, where he had a small dagger sheathed, but the thought of attacking the guards was a fleeting one. Once Roger had been a decent fighter. Once . . .

The thief changed tactics then, inspecting the doorway and the crude lock. With a smile, Roger bent low, moved the door back to its original, nearly closed position, pulled forth a small pick, and worked that mechanism.

Then he peered in again, and quietly slipped into the room. He moved in a crouch, so low to the floor that none of the candlelight spilled over him. A movement to the side froze him in place, but when he finally mustered the courage to turn about, he saw that the source, the man standing at the cupboard, had merely shifted to get a bit more comfortable. Only then did Roger realize that the standing guard, too, was actually asleep, though why he hadn't pitched over, Roger couldn't begin to know.

At the cellar door a few moments later, Roger glanced back once to ensure that the guards were not in any way alerted. Then he reached up and gently tried the handle.

The door was locked.

Roger's pick went to work again, expertly and silently, and a few moments later, he went through the door onto the landing, pausing long enough to secure the door behind him.

He could hardly see the uneven and crude stairway stretching out below him, but there were fires burning below. Roger placed his hand on the wall to his right and started down slowly, grimacing every time a rickety old stair groaned beneath his weight. Soon enough, he was moving along an earthen-and-stone tunnel, speckled with puddles and echoing with the sound of rattling chains and of hammers beating on metal.

Apparently, King Aydrian and his cohorts had reinstated the old practice of having prisoners put to hard labor.

Roger heard the swish and crack of a whip, followed by a pitiful groan, and he knew that other practices had been reinstated, as well.

His stride increased in tempo as he considered that Braumin, his dear friend, might be among those tortured men, and around a few bends and down a couple of side passages, Roger looked upon the jailor and the prisoners. They were in a long earthen room, several standing, chained in a line along a stonework dais and standing before respective anvils. A great hearth blazed before them, and two other prisoners, wearing heavy gloves, moving the rods of metal to the hearth and, when they were heated to an appropriate glow, to the next freed-up anvil.

The jailor, a huge and heavily muscled man, paced up and down behind the dais, a whip in one hand, a short and thick sword in the other. He hurled an insult and then cracked his whip at one of the hammer-wielders, and the poor wretch cried out and fell forward to one knee.

"Bah, get up, ye traitorous dog!" the jailor roared at him, and the whip cracked again, laying the man even lower—which only infuriated the jailor even more.

"I telled ye to get up!" the jailor yelled again, and he lifted the whip to strike, but then swung about reflexively instead, sensing movement.

The burly man almost got his hand up in time to block the downward chop of one of the extra hammers. Almost, but he got hit squarely on the chest instead, and he staggered backward, tripping over the raised stonework and falling to his back.

Roger was over him in an instant, the hammer raised to keep him at bay. "Where is the key?" the small and dangerous man demanded.

The jailor held up one hand to fend any forthcoming blows, and shook his head with fright, his breath coming in short and raspy gasps.

"The key!" Roger demanded.

"There is no key!" one of the prisoners cried.

"Oh, ye've doomed us all!" said another, and the cries rose along the line—or started to, until one voice familiar to Roger rose above the others.

"Master Lockless?" Bishop Braumin Herde asked. "Roger?"

Roger looked up at his friend, but had to turn his attention back immediately to the jailor, who suddenly grabbed at his leg. Down came the hammer, but the jailor managed to deflect the blow, pushing it out wide and forcing Roger either to let go or tumble down.

Roger leaped back, pulling free of the man, who came up fast and charged at the intruder.

Or started to, for he got hit low across the ankles by the flying form of Bishop Braumin, and he fell headlong to the ground, landing hard right before Roger. He began to get up immediately, but Roger balled his hands together and fell down atop him, driving his hands onto the back of the jailor's neck.

The man fell flat, facedown.

Roger scrambled past him, up to the confused and frightened prisoners, falling into the waiting grasp of Bishop Braumin.

"Why are you here?" Braumin asked. "Roger, we cannot get away!"

Hardly listening, Roger fell to his knees before the bishop and went to work on the heavy shackle latched about Braumin's ankles. This was a more sophisticated mechanism than that on the door above, but there was no more proficient lockpick in all of Honce-the-Bear than Roger Lockless—a name well earned!

He had Braumin free in a few moments.

"What about us?" one of the other prisoners demanded.

Braumin looked pleadingly at Roger, who was shaking his head. "There are guards everywhere up above," Roger explained to the bishop. "It will be enough for me to get you out of here; there is no way that I can escort the lot of you!"

"These are not criminals, but men loyal to me and to our cause," Braumin countered. "You cannot ask me to leave them!"

That brought some grateful murmurs from the others.

"Then I do not ask," Roger replied. "I insist."

The murmurs sounded again, more as grumbles.

"And they will insist that I leave them, as well," Roger went on, "if they are truly loyal. This is not about your loyalty to them, or theirs to you, Bishop. This is about the need to get you out of here, and out of Palmaris."

Braumin, his face filthy, looked at him hard.

"While you remain in Palmaris, you are a voice against the people, from all that I have heard, and I know that it is not a voice that truly comes from Bishop Braumin Herde."

That statement seemed to hit the man profoundly, and Braumin slumped forward, his shoulders suddenly bobbing in sobs. Roger hugged him close and patted him across the back for a bit, until he composed himself enough to look up and look Roger in the eye.

"He possesses me," the Bishop whispered. "Aydrian, our king. I am not strong enough to begin to deny him. There is no resistance within me. He is strong, Roger, so terribly strong!"

"And that is why you must flee with me," Roger said, and he looked up so that his determined expression would encompass the whole of the group. "I must get him out of here, to offer a voice against King Aydrian and to stop his voice from speaking for King Aydrian! I ask the greatest sacrifice of you all—that you remain here as prisoners—for the sake of the true kingdom."

There was some bristling, and a bit of discussion, but Roger wasn't waiting for an answer anyway. He looked at Braumin, who seemed to agree, and then Lockless pulled the bishop away, suddenly, ignoring the protests and dismissing his own guilt.

Truly it bothered Roger Lockless to leave the men in that predicament, but he knew that there was simply no way he could get them out of Chase-wind Manor. He considered unshackling them, just for a moment, but he dismissed that, as well. What would he accomplish by doing so? No good for the men, certainly, though any distraction they provided in their futile flight for freedom might have helped him.

But no. He would not sacrifice them.

He got Braumin back to the stairway, and then up to the door. Roger bade him wait, then slipped into the room.

A moment later, he returned, pulling wide the door and bidding Braumin to follow.

The bishop froze in place, though, watching the writhing of the soldier on the floor, the man grasping futilely at his torn throat.

"Roger, what have you done?" Braumin asked, or tried to, before Roger hushed him, pointing at the second guard, who was sound asleep at the table.

"Do not make me kill another man," Roger whispered, great regret evident in his cracking voice. "I beg of you."

The two went through the room, and moved along the darkened corridors of Chasewind Manor, Braumin following Roger's every movement, often ducking behind drapery or into crannies to avoid the occasional soldiers.

They had almost gotten out of the house when a commotion erupted behind them, first the shout of the jailor, then the cries of, "Murder! Murder!"

"Run on!" Roger bade the bishop and he shoved the man ahead, driving him toward the back door, then out into the night, pursuit growing all about them.

They ran to the back wall. "Go! Go!" Roger told the man, pushing him up the wall as he grabbed its top.

Braumin, who had gained far too much weight over the years, struggled mightily to pull himself over, with Roger pressing behind him. "Brother Hoyet is in the shadows awaiting you," the man explained. "Run to him!" With a final heave, Roger got the bishop atop the wall.

Braumin hesitated, looking back at him and reaching down to offer his hand.

But Roger shook his head and moved away. "Go!" he bade the man. "Go and be quick!"

Roger turned and ran the other way, and before he had gone halfway across the yard, he heard the cries of the guards and knew he had been spotted.

So he kept running, putting as much ground between himself and Braumin as he possibly could. He rushed about the front corner of the great building, only to turn about and scoot the other way after nearly running into a group of guards.

He headed for the nearest wall, but had to turn again as another group appeared, angled to cut him off. He veered back to the other side, but those directly behind him were peeling wide that way, sealing him in.

"Wait!" Roger bade them, turning about and stopping fast, holding up his hands defensively. "Wait! I can explain!"

A soldier rushed in past the intruder's upraised arms, lifting his short sword as he came on, and Roger felt an explosion of agony across his skull.

And then he knew no more.

*   *   *

As soon as word of the escape reached him in St. Precious, Marcalo De'Unnero knew exactly where to turn. He had known something was brewing, for his spies had watched Destou and Hoyet, and had quickly identified the other brothers who were in with the potentially traitorous pair. But the brazenness of their move—breaking Bishop Braumin out of the most secure prison in the city!—surely surprised De'Unnero. He had thought that the monks had been planning their own escape from Palmaris.

De'Unnero was out of the abbey in moments, and given the movements of those watched monks over the previous days, he had a fairly good idea of where to look.

All the city was coming alive by then, with soldiers running about the streets and others riding hard to and fro, calling out.

De'Unnero ignored the clamor and moved into the shadows of an alleyway. He felt the beast rising within him, and he did not try to fight it.

A great cat came out of that alleyway, speeding for the riverbank area where Brothers Hoyet and Destou had been spotted two nights earlier. He knew that they would try to get Braumin out of the city as quickly as possible, across the river and on his way to St.-Mere-Abelle.

Along the bank, the tiger slipped into the shadows and noted the approach of a small craft. The part of him that was still a reasoning being resisted the urge to leap out into the water and overtake the small boat, slaughtering the boatmen. His caution was rewarded a few moments later when three forms came scrambling down the bank, two pulling the third along.

They splashed into the water and toward the boat, then cried out in terror as the great cat charged toward them, leaping for the haggard form in the middle of the trio.

Without the slightest hesitation, the other two, Hoyet and Destou, shifted to intercept, pushing Bishop Braumin away. The pair of younger monks lifted weapons to defend, but the weretiger crashed in hard, sending all into the river.

"Run on!" Hoyet cried.

Bishop Braumin eyed the approaching boat, but hesitated, looking back at the pair, who were struggling wildly to keep the tiger engaged.

"Make not my death irrelevant!" Destou cried, and his last word was jumbled as the cat reared before him and swatted him across the chest with its killing claws.

Braumin cried out and staggered ahead, crashing against the boat, which started away before he had even managed to scramble aboard, one man grabbing him to hold him fast against the hull, the other working the oars furiously to get the craft out into the faster current.

Bishop Braumin looked back to see one man, Hoyet, standing before the cat, a small sword flashing before him frantically.

And then he was down, the tiger leaping atop him and bearing him beneath the dark water. All was quiet for just a moment, then there came another splash as Brother Hoyet's lifeless body bobbed up suddenly, then settled, floating on the current.

The tiger leaped forth right after, hitting the river with a rush and swimming powerfully out toward the small boat. But they were in the currents now, being swept along more quickly than the cat could hope to swim.

Braumin was free.

But he felt trapped, surely, as he looked back at the river's western bank, as he imagined the waters running red with the blood of Hoyet and Destou, and he imagined the torn bodies of the two loyal men bobbing along. He thought of Roger, too, and knew the man had not escaped.

So many had died for him this night.

A large part of Bishop Braumin wanted just to let go of the boat and slide back into the water, letting the river take him.

But another part would not let him dishonor the heroic sacrifices of the brave men who had rescued him. They had freed him because they knew that as a prisoner of King Aydrian, he was unwittingly working against the cause of justice. A captured Braumin was a mouthpiece for a usurper king. A freed Braumin could speak against that imposter king and help rally men to the cause of Prince Midalis.

Braumin knew all of that logically, and he hoped that if faced with a similar situation, he would have found it within himself to act as bravely as Roger and Hoyet and Destou and all the others had this night.

But that didn't make their deaths hurt any less. Hanging on the side of the boat, no longer even trying to scramble in despite the numbness that was creeping into his body, the former bishop of Palmaris lowered his head and wept.

CHAPTER

❖ 22 ❖

Second-guessing

"Yatol Wadon! By great Chezru himself, we are most fortunate to have you in control of Jacintha at this most troublesome hour!" Yatol De Hamman cried, clapping his hands together and leaping and skipping across the great audience hall in Chom Deiru.

Across the way, a very dour-looking Yatol Mado Wadon sat in the throne normally reserved for the Chezru Chieftain of Behren. The old holy man was slumped forward, his wrinkled head in his hand, his eyes unblinking, and his stare more downward than at the bounding man heading his way.

Yatol De Hamman, so excited at the news that Yatol Peridan had surrendered, with his forces crushed, didn't even notice the confusing expression. "I have the most promising young apprentice ready to step into Peridan's place, after we execute the dog, of course," De Hamman explained, slowing as he approached the raised platform that held the throne of the Chezru Church, and thus the throne of Behren itself. Only then did he notice another figure, that of Abbot Olin of Entel, standing just off to the side. Flanked by Honce-the-Bear soldiers, the man seemed almost amused by De Hamman's approach, and that curious expression, combined with the look De Hamman then noticed upon the Jacintha Yatol, set off alarms within the excited man.

"You need not trouble yourself with replacements for Yatol Peridan," Abbot Olin explained in perfect Behrenese, with an accent befitting a man who had spent his life in Jacintha rather than in Entel. His hands folded before him, invisible within the wide sleeves of his brown robe, Abbot Olin moved forward to De Hamman's side.

"Surely we will not let him continue his rule," De Hamman replied, looking to Yatol Wadon. "He is not to be trusted."

"Yatol Peridan will be properly punished, fear not," said Abbot Olin. "And no, he will not be allowed to continue his rule in any manner. Should he be spared his life, he will then live out his days here, at Chom Deiru, under the watchful eye of Yatol Wadon and the palace guards."

Yatol De Hamman was more confused by the speaker than by the actual reasoning. Why was a priest of the Abellican Church relaying plans for a traitorous Yatol, especially with the serving leader of Behren seated right before them?

"We have already selected a replacement for Yatol Peridan," Abbot Olin went on. "A man of proper temperament and loyalties."

"We?" De Hamman asked, looking from Wadon to Olin and back again. "What business is this of an Abellican abbot?"

"Perhaps you did not notice that the soldiers who fought back the legions of Yatol Peridan and Yatol Bardoh wore the uniform of Honce-the-Bear," Abbot Olin answered. "Perhaps it missed your perceptive eye that the soldiers who moved to the south to expel Peridan from your lands wore that same uniform, and that they were accompanied by warships flying the flag not of Behren, but of your northern neighbor."

"And thus you have earned our friendship," De Hamman reasoned. "That does not equate to a voice—"

"Everything I relate to you, I say with the blessing of Yatol Wadon," Abbot Olin interrupted, and the two men stared at each other for a long, long while, with De Hamman trying to get a full measure of this foreigner.

"We cannot dismiss, nor should we, the friendship that Abbot Olin has shown to us, nor the aid that he has offered in our time of direst need," Yatol Wadon said, somewhat diffusing the tension—at least enough to turn De Hamman's focus back to him. "And it is strength we will continue to need, my friend, if we are to have any hope of restoring Behren to a singular and strong nation."

"A nation?" De Hamman dared to say, his voice barely more than a whisper. "Or a province of our northern neighbor?"

Abbot Olin burst into laughter. "We are your friends, Yatol De Hamman," he said. "Can you not see that? King Aydrian has taken a great risk in sending so many warriors to your aid at this desperate time, when his own kingdom is not yet secured. But he felt that a secure Behren was necessary for the safety not only of you and your fellow Yatols, but for Entel and all the Honce-the-Bear cities who regularly trade with Jacintha."

"And your assistance was appreciated," De Hamman said, somewhat dismissively, and he turned back to Yatol Wadon.

"And it came with a price," Abbot Olin assured him. At that De Hamman's eyes popped open wide and he slowly turned back to face the man.

"A price?"

"If I were to leave today, with all of my soldiers and my fleet, do you really believe that you and Yatol Wadon could hold Behren together?" Abbot Olin asked.

"Peridan is defeated, as is Bardoh."

"And Avrou Eesa has been secured? And Pruda? And Yatol Peridan's territory is in the hands of one loyal to Jacintha?"

Yatol De Hamman winced with each stinging question.

"The price of keeping the warriors of Honce-the-Bear is suffering the advice of an old Abellican priest," Abbot Olin explained. "Yatol Wadon understands our new arrangement, and accepts my counsel, and you would be wise to follow suit."

De Hamman bristled but offered no overt response.

"Who is to become the new Yatol of the province to my south?" De Hamman asked.

"Paroud, my trusted advisor," Yatol Wadon answered. "His loyalty cannot be questioned, and with him ruling below you, and answering to Jacintha, your province is more secure than it has ever been."

"Particularly true if you consider that Honce-the-Bear warships will continue to patrol your coast," Abbot Olin added. "As well as the pirate fleet, once loyal to Peridan, but now convinced that they would be a healthier lot if they served the Yatol of Jacintha."

Yatol De Hamman was not an inexperienced leader, and he knew a power play when he saw one. He knew, beyond any doubt, that Abbot Olin's price for the assistance of Honce-the-Bear was far greater than an advisory role to Yatol Wadon. But he knew, too, that there was nothing he could do about that. Wadon had all but lost the kingdom to Yatol Bardoh— and such an event would have precipitated a swift beheading of Yatol De Hamman, to be sure!—and only through the efforts of Abbot Olin had the present power structure within the tumultuous kingdom been somewhat secured. Yatol Wadon had accepted the price demanded by Abbot Olin of Entel because he had been given no practical alternative.

Could Yatol De Hamman say otherwise?

"You are surrounded," Abbot Olin said to the man, whose excitement had been dissipated by the unexpected turn of events. De Hamman straightened, wondering if he should meet the challenge in those words, when Olin added, "by friends."

De Hamman didn't know how to respond. Surely he was better off than he would have been had not Olin and his soldiers arrived to rescue the hierarchy in Jacintha. But the situation ground at his sensibilities. He understood the damage Chezru Douan had done to the order when he had been secretly using the magical gemstone, long considered the greatest of heresies by the Yatol priests of Chezru. Worse still was the design and manner of Douan's usage, to steal the bodies of babies in the womb to use as his own, becoming God-Voice over and over again through the last centuries. Douan's indiscretions had shattered the order and the faith of so many. The immediate problem was to hold the kingdom intact, and in that, Abbot Olin had surely helped.

But Yatol De Hamman understood, if Yatol Mado Wadon apparently did not, that the challenge immediately following the securing of the kingdom's body would be the securing of the kingdom's soul, and if that return to faith was to bear any resemblance to the ancient tenets of Chezru, then the presence of an Abellican priest might not prove such a beneficial thing.

The Yatol reminded himself that he had regained control of his province, that the threat of Peridan and Bardoh was no more.

Now they might move forward, wherever that road would lead.

With many pressing duties ahead of him, not the least of which was reorganizing his garrison from the scattered remnants, the man offered a gracious bow to Yatol Mado Wadon and a nod to Abbot Olin and took his leave.

From the side of the great audience hall, Pechter Dan Turk watched the proceedings with growing concern. At first glance, it had surprised the man that the often contentious Yatol De Hamman had so readily accepted the presence of the Abellican abbot, but as he considered the situation, he came to understand, as De Hamman had, that there was really very little that could be done to correct the situation at that time. Without Olin and the Honce-the-Bear soldiers, Yatol Mado Wadon's edicts held little bite.

Pechter Dan Turk moved a bit closer to the raised platform and perked up his ears as Yatol De Hamman made his way out of the great room. As an advisor, as with the soldiers in the room, he was considered a nonentity, and thus, Yatol Wadon and Abbot Olin could speak freely in his presence about the ramifications of the words with De Hamman.

"You were a bit abrupt with him," Yatol Wadon remarked.

"He annoys me," Abbot Olin admitted. "His life would have been forfeit had I not arrived. A bit of gratitude would not have been out of line."

"And a bit of respect from you would carry us a long way at present," said Yatol Wadon. "We will need Yatol De Hamman now. Tremendously so."

Abbot Olin gave a dismissive snort.

"Your warriors and ships dominate the coastal region, Abbot," Yatol Wadon reasoned. "In wars past with Honce-the-Bear, this has always been the case."

"We are not at war."

"And that is why your hopes of reaching farther, of encompassing the entire kingdom, have a possibility of fruition," Yatol Wadon explained.

Pechter Dan Turk's eyes widened and he had to fight hard not to gasp and reveal his interest.

"How will your armored warriors fare away from the cool coastal breezes, when the hot sun heats their armor so greatly that they can no longer even stand to wear it?" Yatol Wadon went on, and Pechter Dan Turk understood that the man was almost pleading here, as if he was trying to make Abbot Olin understand that the Behrenese were still needed to control Behren!

"The coast controls the commerce," Abbot Olin countered. "Commerce determines the health of the theocracy. If you have no trade with Honce-the-Bear, and indeed, no routes for merchant ships to connect your own greatest cities, and no roads from Jacintha outward upon which caravans might travel, then what have you left?"

"Yatol De Hamman understands how to wage war, and he alone might raise the forces necessary to strike westward to Avrou Eesa," said Yatol Wadon.

"Bardoh's city is virtually undefended," agreed the abbot. "It is ours for the taking."

"With Behrenese soldiers," insisted the old Yatol, and he did indeed appear very old and weary to Pechter Dan Turk at that moment. It was obvious that Abbot Olin was the one with the final say, and that observation sent a chill coursing along Pechter Dan Turk's spine. He had not missed the reference Olin had made. Abbot Olin had not said that Avrou Eesa was Yatol Wadon's for the taking, but had included himself in that victory!

The two leaders continued their private discussions for some time, turning the subject across many borders, from trade to the potential loyalty or lack thereof of Maisha Darou the pirate, to future trade policies between Entel and Jacintha and the proper assignment of soldiers, Behrenese or Bearmen, within Chom Deiru and the city as a whole.

In all of it, Pechter Dan Turk recognized clearly that Abbot Olin and not Yatol Wadon was in charge. On every issue, Olin made the statements and Wadon then countered with questions and concerns, some of which were answered by the Abellican abbot and others of which were summarily dismissed with a wave and a derisive snort. And how it hurt Pechter Dan Turk to see his beloved master so belittled by an Abellican heretic!

For the first time, Pechter Dan Turk wondered if he had done right in enlisting the aid of Brynn Dharielle to defeat Yatol Bardoh. For the first time, he wondered if the wrong side had perhaps prevailed. He had never been a supporter of Yatol Bardoh—though he had often considered Yatol Peridan a superior Chezru to the perpetually whining Yatol De Hamman—but Bardoh was Chezru, at least!

Only then did Pechter Dan Turk come out of his contemplations to realize that Abbot Olin and Yatol Wadon were both staring at him. For a moment, panic hit him, as he wondered if the two had somehow read his traitorous thoughts.

"Do we know how many of Yatol De Hamman's warriors survived the battle in the southern district of the city?" Yatol Wadon said, his tone making it clear that he was reiterating his unanswered question.

Pechter Dan Turk gave a sigh of relief, then stiffened and shook his head. "But I can quickly find the numbers."

"Do so," Abbot Olin ordered him. "At once!" He waved Pechter Dan Turk away and turned back to Yatol Wadon, and Pechter Dan Turk heard him remark, "We must set De Hamman on the road west immediately and force every province under our control."

The man's last words as Pechter Dan Turk moved out of hearing range struck the advisor particularly hard: "Perhaps we can entice the Dragon of To-gai to do war with any foolish enough to resist the changes that we know must befall Behren."

*   *   *

The guest quarter of Chom Deiru was quiet this night, in sharp contrast to the revelry of a gathering of the victorious Yatols and Chezhou-Lei warlords that was going on in the lower feasting halls. Pechter Dan Turk was supposed to be there among the revelers, and surely not here!

The man pressed on. He held his sandals in his hand, having taken them off so that he could more completely mask the sounds of his movements. Fortunately there were few guards about, and even more fortunately, Yatol Wadon kept a spare of all of the room keys hanging in an office—an office to which Pechter Dan Turk had full access.

The nervous man stopped before Abbot Olin's guest room and looked both ways along the quiet and dark corridor. He took a deep breath, praying that the Abellican wizard hadn't placed some gemstone-riddled wards about the portal, then he slowly turned the key and moved into the dark room. He fiddled in his pocket to produce a candle and flint and steel, then moved, shading the light with his free hand, toward the large desk opposite the door.

In but a few moments, he found an unsealed letter addressed to King Aydrian. Hands trembling, Pechter Dan Turk slowly flattened the parchment on the desk. He was versed in all the known languages, nevertheless Olin's scrawl was at first hard to decipher.

As the pieces and intent of the letter became apparent, Pechter Dan Turk began to tremble even more, his worst fears realized. Abbot Olin was not writing of aiding Yatol Wadon and Chezru, but was hinting that the Chezru were ready to receive the truth of the Abellican Order!

He was hinting that they were ready to be subverted to the precepts of that order!

Pechter Dan Turk brought his hand to his cheek, but he was shaking so badly that he wound up slapping himself repeatedly in the face. He read through the letter again, as well as he could decipher it, but found no comfort in any misunderstanding of his first passage through the foreign words.

Abbot Olin was here as an opportunist, not as a friend.

The trembling man considered his next move. He could bring this to Yatol Wadon and reveal the treachery . . .

That thought died before it ever gained any momentum.

Because in his heart, Pechter Dan Turk knew the truth.

Yatol Wadon would not be surprised. Yatol Wadon was a part of this conspiracy.

The man left the room in such a fit that he forgot his candle on the desk and even forgot to relock the door. He didn't go back to the feasting room, where he was expected, but rather, left Chom Deiru altogether, moving out along the streets of the city, where the revelry had become a general thing ever since the victory over Yatol Bardoh.

Victory? Pechter Dan Turk had to wonder. Could the intrusion of the Abellicans at the head of a Honce-the-Bear army rightly be called so?

The man left Jacintha altogether soon after, having procured a cart, horse, and supplies for his journey. He moved westward along the northern road, bound for Dahdah Oasis and beyond, to the city of Dharyan-Dharielle. What he might accomplish there, he did not know.

He only knew that he had to get away from the place that was no more his home.

CHAPTER

❖ 23 ❖

In Need of Glory

B rother Stimson of Chapel Aubeard had been handpicked by Marcalo De'Unnero to lead the contingent of monks accompanying the Ursal fleet because of his absolute loyalty to De'Unnero's cause and his strong proficiency with the gemstones. The young brother, barely into his forties, was one of the few of his generation who rejected the teachings of Brother Avelyn outright. Stimson's peers, after all, had come to their full power as Abellicans during the time of the rosy plague and the Miracle of Avelyn at Mount Aida. Brother Stimson, too, had partaken of that miracle, and he could not deny that God had touched the world through Avelyn to defeat the rosy plague. Still, to Stimson, the magical gemstones were the gift of God reserved for the chosen of God—the Abellican brothers. The notion of using these stones among the populace so readily, as was espoused by the followers of Avelyn, seemed absolutely abhorrent to the man.

And thus, Stimson was all in favor of the current revolt within the Abellican Church, where Brother De'Unnero and Abbot Olin were reshaping the chapels and abbeys in the image of the Order before the days of Avelyn. By extension, Stimson had become a loyal supporter of Aydrian Wyndon, as well. Without Aydrian, there could be no revolution within the Church, so went the thinking, and thus, though he had always been loyal to King Danube and though he had always understood the successor to Danube's throne to be Prince Midalis, Stimson would forgo the desire for that logical ascension.

The Abellican Church, after all, was paramount.

To Marcalo De'Unnero, brothers like Stimson were the most valuable of resources as he moved along with Aydrian to bring the kingdom into the proper fold. Thus, he had rewarded Stimson with this most important of missions. Seven brothers had sailed with the fifteen ships of Earl DePaunch out of the Masur Delaval and into the Gulf of Corona. They had shadowed the land for many days before turning straight north, taking a direct line to the target: the island fortress of Pireth Dancard. The weather had cooperated, with no early-winter storms blowing across the waters, but with a cold

228

westerly wind that the great ships had tacked into a fine, water-raising speed.
Right on schedule that cold sunny morning, the dark tower of Pireth Dancard
came into view.

Brother Stimson was among the first on the deck to spot it after the lookout's call came down. Standing at the front rail of *Assant Tigre*—the Behrenese words for *Attacking Tiger*, DePaunch's flagship named by Aydrian in
honor of Marcalo De'Unnero—Stimson gripped the rail tightly at the sight.
He heard the commotion behind him, many footsteps shuffling forward.

"We have the gemstones held ready," an excited Brother Meepause said
to Stimson, and he held forth his hand with the graphite and hematite
De'Unnero had given him. A couple of other brothers behind Meepause
did likewise, though Stimson hardly seemed interested at that moment. It
would be hours before any battle was joined, after all.

And Stimson secretly hoped that the gemstones, and all other firepower,
would be unnecessary. Pireth Dancard and the Coastpoint Guards who
manned it had not formally declared themselves for either Aydrian or
Prince Midalis, after all. It was quite likely that Earl DePaunch and the Allheart escorts would be welcomed by the soldiers. That would be for the
best, Stimson knew. The less battling that Aydrian had to do to stabilize the
kingdom would allow for more concentration in securing the contentious
Abellican Church.

"The bear rampant!" came the cry from the crow's nest, and Stimson
gritted his teeth as the man finished, "No tiger!"

Pireth Dancard was flying the pennant of the Ursals, not the new flag of
Honce-the-Bear, the bear and tiger rampant, facing off above the evergreen
of the Abellican Church. The island fortress should have known about the
change in flags by this time, though Stimson recognized that the Coastpoint
Guards stationed out here would have no appropriate pennant for King Aydrian available to them.

"There will be a fight!" one of the younger brothers behind Stimson remarked eagerly. "They ally with Prince Midalis!"

That seemed to be the feeling all about the ship and those ships nearby,
Stimson could tell in glancing around at the sudden commotion, at the eager faces and sparkling eyes. He held quiet his argument that perhaps the
soldiers out here were flying the only flag they possessed.

Signalmen flagged each other across the waters and the ships moved
from their fairly straight-triple line formation, with the vessels port and
starboard of *Assant Tigre* bowing out wide and tacking to slow, and those
behind sliding up into the vacated areas. In mere minutes, with the black
speck of Dancard on the horizon barely larger than it had been at first sighting, the ships had moved into an approach formation that created two rows,
seven up front and eight off center spaced right behind, instead of in three
columns of five in a front-to-back line. *Assant Tigre* centered that front line.
These were the "kill" ships, heavily armored and manned with regiments of
archers and the seven gemstone-wielding brothers. The eight smaller craft

behind, swifter and more maneuverable, each housed a pair of long-range catapults and soldiers trained in ship-to-ship combat.

"Each of you knows your duty," Brother Stimson said to his six fellow Abellican monks. "Since Earl DePaunch has chosen to concentrate us all on one vessel, we must be even more efficient and coordinated in our attacks. If resistance is discovered onshore, a catapult or a contingent of archers, then we must destroy that resistance quickly, before any real damage can be offered to this ship. Do you understand?"

Enthusiastic cries came back at him. Too eager, thought the older brother, who had seen a great riot in the days of the plague, a wild battle in the square of his small town northeast of Ursal. Stimson had heard men dying by the score, and despite his belief in De'Unnero and Olin and his acceptance that the Church and kingdom would not be secured without a fight, the man had little desire to hear those echoing screams ever again.

"Go and eat, if you have not, and make your peace with God before you find your positions," Stimson told the brothers. "Brothers, relax and understand that we still have hours at least before any battle will be joined."

With that, the commanding monk took his leave, moving to the center of the ship and the war room, to join in the discussion with Earl DePaunch and the other leaders.

He found DePaunch in nearly as agitated a state as had been the young brothers, and that he did not view as a good sign!

"I will move to within three hundred yards before I turn right and sail about the island," DePaunch explained.

"Three hundred is within the reach of some of their greater catapults, those set up high on the rocks, my lord," remarked one of the other commanders, Guilio Jannet, an Allheart Knight who had served for many years under Duke Bretherford.

DePaunch nodded. "But hardly could they prove accurate at such a range," he explained. "The back eight will be split, four escorting us and four swinging left about the island. No enemy ships will sail beyond our reach."

"I would suggest you allow four to continue to sail past Dancard," said Giulio. "In case some have already fled—or soon will now that we have likely been spotted."

Earl DePaunch thought on it a moment, then nodded his agreement.

"Pardon, good Earl, but are we not presuming much here?" Brother Stimson interjected. "We do not even know if these folk of Dancard are friends or enemies."

"They fly the flag of the Ursal line, not that of Aydrian," said one of the other commanders.

"Do they even possess the bear and tiger rampant?" the reasonable monk replied. "Do they even fully understand King Aydrian and the legions he commands? These are Coastpoint Guards, after all. Will they not be persuaded that ours is the proper cause when they see Allheart Knights among us?"

"Are we to sail into the shadows of their deadly catapults?" Earl De-Paunch retorted. "When four or five of these great ships King Aydrian has entrusted to me flounder in the waves, am I to then assume it would be proper to attack?"

"I only meant—"

"Their first response is the pennant they fly," Giulio added. "If a bear and tiger greeted us from above Pireth Dancard, then we would have sailed in as allies."

Brother Stimson recognized what was going on, and in truth, he had expected nothing different. Earl DePaunch was the most eager of young men, as was Giulio Jannet. Accepting Dancard as an ally to the throne would be a great gain for King Aydrian; defeating a hostile Dancard and forcing it under the flag of Aydrian would be a great gain for the careers of DePaunch and Giulio.

The ambitious earl was spoiling for a fight.

When Stimson moved back out on the deck, he found that the ship sailing beside *Assant Tigre* had brought down their colors and the crew were now running up the more traditional flag of Honce-the-Bear, the bear rampant that had served as Ursal's banner for more than a hundred years. The monk moved to the fore, beside his brethren, all of whom were watching the changing of the colors beside them.

"What does it mean, brother?" one asked Stimson.

The monk wanted to reply that it meant they would use that ship as a front in order to get close to the docks. He wanted to reply that it meant that they were going to get their fight, whether Pireth Dancard wanted it or not.

Instead, the monk just shrugged noncommittally. Marcalo De'Unnero had chosen him for a reason, he reminded himself. While he might not agree with the methods of Earl DePaunch, he surely agreed with the outcome of Aydrian's rule, especially as it pertained to the Abellican Church—the wayward Abellican Church, by Master Stimson's estimation.

The wind remained strong, filling the sails, and the fifteen ships remained under full sail, speeding for the island. Stimson and the others watched it grow and grow, until the tower set on the high rocks came into clear view, the pennant visible even without use of a spyglass. The island's southern docks were set right below it, down a rocky slope that housed a few buildings, including one long warehouse right on the water level. That hill was sparse of growth, with only a few patches of grasses and a couple of small trees, but it was well fortified, with crisscrossing walls of piled rocks leading up from the docks to the tower. Off to the right-hand side of the island, the eastern slopes, was a small settlement of stone houses, and there, as on the docks, a commotion was brewing, with many people staring out at the fast-approaching fleet.

Barely a thousand yards out, ten of the eleven ships dropped to half sail, battle sail, and as one, ten prows dipped lower in the water. The one remaining at full sail—the one to *Assant Tigre*'s right, flying the pennant of Ursal—sped on toward the long wharf.

"Be ready, Master Stimson," came Earl DePaunch's voice from behind. "When *Assant Tigre* makes her run, I expect you and your brothers to trace our glorious path."

Stimson looked at the man, and at Giulio Jannet beside him, both grinning and nodding, obviously eager.

Into his early fifties now, Warder Constantine Presso was among the oldest and most experienced leaders of the Coastpoint Guards. And among the most proper, with his neatly trimmed moustache and goatee and traditional blue, red-trimmed overcoat, complete with a black leather baldric running right shoulder to left hip. He was a tall man, and stood impeccably straight, shoulders wide and back, eyes never down. He had served at all of the major outposts of the rugged outfit, from Pireth Tulme to Dancard to Pireth Vanguard in the north. The man was well aware of the politics of Honce-the-Bear, and of the games that were often played by eager young commanders seeking a quick road to promotion.

Presso had been told immediately when the fleet had sailed into view, and had arrived at the tower's top in time to watch their precision and training in action as they moved from an open sailing line to battle formation.

And now he watched them in this latest ruse, or whatever it was.

"She flies the Ursal bear!" cried a man from somewhere below.

It was true enough, Constantine Presso could see; the lone approaching ship was not flying the strange pennant that seemed to verify the rumors of a change in power in Ursal, but rather the more customary flag of King Danube and his predecessors. But, the warder noted, the ship was even then running a second pennant up her mainmast, the white flag of truce.

Presso wandered about his tower top, studying the catapult emplacements set among the stones left and right and the great swiveling ballista upon the tower top itself. He moved back to the lip overlooking the docks soon enough and called for his men to "stand ready."

Then he again looked out at the fast-approaching ship, and the ten others gliding in behind it—and glanced west at the four others who had broken off from the back line and were moving at full speed about Pireth Dancard. Presso even offered a glance toward the north, where the two Dancard scout ships had long ago sailed, departing at the first sight of the approaching fleet as per their standing orders whenever a potentially hostile vessel approached the fortress. For Dancard was not built to hold out against a great foe, but rather to serve as sentinel to the mainland on the south and Vanguard on the north.

"What king do they serve?" came a confused cry from one of the Coastpoint Guards in position along the defending wall below the tower.

Warder Presso looked back at the leading ship, to see that both the pennant of Ursal and the white flag had been cut away from the fast-approaching warship. In their stead, the ship had run up the same flag the others were flying, along with a second fast-climbing the guide ropes: a white flag bordered in black and with a red X over the field.

In mariners' terms in Honce-the-Bear at that time, that flag was one demanding surrender.

Presso noted that the ship's catapult was set and ready to fire, pitch smoldering in its basket. He watched in disbelief as a great contingent of archers crowded the deck, all wearing the uniforms of Kingsmen. They dipped their arrows into unseen buckets below the rails and brought them up, tips aflame, and bent back their great bows.

Behind Presso, the ballista crew broke into action.

"Hold!" the warder ordered them.

Unfortunately for Presso and for Dancard, few on the island had been hardened by actual battle. Presso recognized the ship's movements as a goad and ploy—the full sail and continued course gave her away—but some of the younger and more frightened Coastpoint Guards did not.

A few arrows arced out at the ship; one Dancard catapult fired, then the second.

A ball of pitch hissed as it fell into the cold water at the ship's side, but the second found the mark, splashing across the unfurled sails and setting them ablaze. From that fiery deck came the response, fifty flaming arrows knifing across the docks of Dancard, followed by a returning ball of pitch that splattered across the lowest levels of the wall.

The wounded ship tacked and steered hard, bending low into a direct turn for the island's docks.

Up on the tower, Warder Presso closed his eyes and shook his head, understanding more fully the tactic. Momentum would carry the wounded ship to crash into the docks, where her crack crew would be fast ashore.

He looked past that vessel to the other ten, and to the ten fiery balls arcing gracefully into the sky.

Master Stimson, too, watched those responding catapults, taking note that of the ten shots, only six had been aimed at the dock areas. The four longer-ranged shots from the trailing vessels climbed out to the east to land among the stone buildings, ignited all flammable material within their splash zones.

Including people.

Stimson closed his eyes as he heard the screams again, just as in the riots of his youth. Not the roars of battle lust that turned to grunts of pain, as with combatants; these were the shrieks of surprise and terror that arose from the confusion of innocents caught up in a fight they could not comprehend. Even the pitch was different, for among the cries coming from the small village were intermingled the screams of women and children.

The Abellican master glanced back at Earl DePaunch and saw that the man was not alarmed by the apparently errant shots. Stimson understood;

DePaunch was goading Pireth Dancard on to a larger fight. He was leaving little room for common sense and a possible compromise here, little room for diplomacy. For now, suddenly, Dancard was fighting for her very existence. The soldiers were fighting not only to hold their docks, but to keep their families alive. Perhaps four hundred people lived on this island, but no more than a quarter of that number were soldiers, with the rest working as dockworkers and farmers and fishermen. And among those three-quarters of the folk were the family members, the wives and the children.

Stimson turned his attention back to the docks just in time to see the leading, wounded ship slide into the wooden pier. Great beams groaned in protest, on both ship and dock, and a section of the pier crumbled into the wash. Finally, the ship settled against the broken wood, burning and listing, but the crew didn't immediately debark. They lined the deck behind the blocking high rails and continued their barrage of arrows, great volleys sweeping across the docks.

Responding fire came at them from the rock walls, with a number of bowmen at least equal to the fifty archers on the wounded ship. The Coast-point Guardsmen were well drilled, obviously, sending in volleys continuously, a third of them firing, then the second group, then the last, and back around in perfect timing. Many of those arrows coming out carried flaming tips, only adding to the confusion and devastation on the wounded ship.

A thrumming from above turned Stimson's eyes to the tower top, to see a dark sliver flash out, a great ballista bolt diving down not at the wounded ship, but at one of the other approaching six. The shot was true, nearly, for the bolt skimmed the front of the boat to *Assant Tigre*'s far left, but glanced off the angled prow to splash harmlessly into the water.

Then came the second volley from the ships' light catapults, this time with all ten flaming balls splashing about the area just beyond the docks and lower rocks walls. The defenses were solid there, and the effect of the shot was minimal at best in terms of casualties. But the spreading bits of fire served the invaders well, for the defenders—slapping out smoldering pieces of splashing pitch or scrambling to find new positions away from the obscuring smoke—were clearly and necessarily distracted.

Some of the sailors on the wounded ship used the opportunity to continue their barrage, while others cut away the burning sails and worked to secure the craft more fully to the crushed dock area.

And the other six leading warships sailed in. The island catapults fired again, one scoring a hit high atop the mainsail of the ship immediately to *Assant Tigre*'s left. The fires hardly slowed the vessel, though, and the crew, intent on getting ashore, hardly paid the small flames high above any heed. Many rowboats hit the water all about the ships, soldiers scrambling down with practiced efficiency and taking up the stroke immediately to get ashore.

Only *Assant Tigre* kept its course, straight in to the docks, maneuvering directly opposite the wounded sister ship.

"Master Stimson!" came Earl DePaunch's prompt.

"Focus your energies, brethren," Stimson told his six Abellican companions. "The catapult left of the tower."

Warder Presso rubbed his face as he watched the continuing approach and battle below him. He had known from the start that holding the island against such a fleet, bearing so many warriors, would not be possible. He had hoped to thin the enemy ranks enough initially to slow down the progress until parley could be pursued, however, and fully expected that his well-trained men would do so.

Perhaps a catapult could put another two ships out of commission. Perhaps his archers would ward the docks for the remainder of the day—there was really only one safe approach to the island, and the long wharf would only accommodate two ships at a time. If he could win these first moments of battle, he would force his enemy to come ashore wholly by rowboat, a much more difficult and time-consuming proposition.

Despite the movements and the minimal effects of the second catapult volley, Warder Presso believed that he and his men were doing exactly that. The wounded ship would prove a difficult debarkation, given its angle against the broken dock, and the second ship moving in would have only a narrow channel upon which to gain access to the crushed wharf. A well-placed catapult shot would lock down the wharf altogether, he believed.

Warder Presso held his breath, knowing that his artillerymen would now attempt to do just that, using the second docking ship as a backstop for their bombs.

But then Presso's breath came out in a burst, and his eyes popped open wide in both shock and horror as seven distinct lightning bolts leaped forth from that ship, each reaching up to blast the area about the catapult below the tower on the right. The warder leaned over the wall to see a couple of artillerymen scrambling weirdly, limbs flailing, hair dancing, while several others lay about on the ground, some moving, some not. Wisps of smoke drifted up from the war engine itself at several locations, and as Presso watched in dismay, one of the support legs of the catapult buckled beneath it, toppling the engine to its side.

"Abellican monks!" cried the commander standing beside the devastated warder.

"Allheart Knights!" cried another man, drawing Presso's attention back to the wounded ship, to see warriors armored in the garb of the famed Allhearts moving across the planks to the dock.

A second volley of lightning bolts shot forth from the ship, wreaking similar destruction on the lone remaining catapult.

The only formidable magic-wielders in all the world, as far as Warder Presso knew, were the Abellicans who served the King of Honce-the-Bear. Pireth Dancard, an outpost of the same king, had little defense against such a magical assault.

Presso heard the ballista swiveling behind him, and he turned fiercely.

"Hold fire!" he cried. "And put up your bows!" he screamed over the edge of the tower, to the archers set about the defensive wall. He turned to his stunned commander and bade the man to run the white flag up at once.

"We must trust in the Allhearts and the Abellicans," he said to the group on that tower top. "They are the heart and soul of Honce-the-Bear; we must ask them for mercy."

"They serve the usurper king!" came the commander's reply, for indeed, the *Saudi Jacintha* had stopped through Pireth Dancard on her way to Vanguard weeks before with just such a report. "What of Prince Midalis?"

"We shall see," Warder Presso replied as he headed for the stairwell to take him down to the scene. "Without artillery, we cannot hold them off. We are outnumbered five to one, I would estimate."

"We have defensible positions!" the commander argued, and indeed, Pireth Dancard was networked with many winding tunnels set with numerous bottlenecks and traps.

"Defensible against our own people?" Presso retorted. "Defensible against gemstone-wielding Abellican monks? Those tunnels were built for last desperate use against powries, Commander, or against any other foe who would not give quarter. Are we to expect such treatment from our brothers of Honce-the-Bear?"

The commander tightened his lips, obviously biting back a sharp retort. But he held it to himself.

A thin voice from the tower top was not going to suffice in making the surrender general, and many more, attacker and defender alike, were killed or wounded on the docks and lower battlements. More volleys of flaming pitch came soaring in from the warships, striking the rocky hill higher and higher in succession until they reached right up to the gates of the sturdy tower. On came the Allheart Knights, covered by archery fire and more devastating volleys by the gemstone-wielding priests. By the time Warder Presso made it to the gates and flung them wide, the battle had nearly reached the fortress, with many more invaders coming ashore from the rowboats all about the dock area. Presso could hear cries from the east, as well, and he realized that the four trailing warships had sailed about the island, likely lobbing their catapult bombs intermittently.

Warder Presso took the white flag of surrender from the man beside him and waded out into the melee. Or at least, he tried to, for a sudden jolt of lightning, and then a second and third, perhaps even a fourth, jolted him and hurled him backward, where he lay helpless on the ground, his limbs twitching.

He took some relief when he noted another of his soldiers scoop up the flag and stubbornly run past, and then he knew no more.

"A glorious day," Earl DePaunch said to Master Stimson and Giulio Jannet. The three walked the lower reaches of Dancard's fortified southern expanse, the smell of burned pitch heavy in the air. About them, bodies were still being removed—twoscore of the defending Coastpoint Guardsmen had been killed, as well as more than sixty of DePaunch's men, many of them the brave souls on the sacrificial boat that was still jammed up against the damaged long wharf. Other noncombatants had been killed in the village area, but no count had yet been formulated.

"Warder Presso will survive," Master Stimson informed the earl. Stimson had worked on the man with hematite personally, and now the other six Abellicans were out among the islanders, helping to heal their wounds.

"Only to be hanged, likely," Earl DePaunch replied, and he gave a coarse chuckle, which Giulio Jannet quickly joined.

"Take care of such an act," Master Stimson warned. "Presso has served Dancard for many years and is much loved by his men and the townsfolk."

"You would have me ignore his act of treason?" Earl DePaunch asked with feigned incredulity, for they all knew that the actions of Warder Constantine Presso were hardly treasonous, and were, in effect, more self-defense than anything else. "Good brother, we cannot have renegade commanders opposing the rule of King Aydrian."

"Does the man even know our king's name?"

"He will," DePaunch assured Stimson, "right before the noose tightens about his neck."

That brought another laugh from Giulio Jannet, which DePaunch summarily joined.

Master Stimson looked away, considering his own duties. There was one Abellican priest out on Dancard, a Master Coiyusade. He was a fairly distinguished member of the Church, and had been heard at the last College of Abbots, in which Fio Bou-raiy had been elected Father Abbot. As his name indicated, Coiyusade was of Behrenese descent, though his family had lived in Entel for more than a century, and had intermarried with folk of Honce-the-Bear so frequently in the past that the master's skin was more the complexion of a man of Honce-the-Bear than that of a Behrenese. Despite his southern heritage, Coiyusade had voted for Fio Bou-raiy and not Abbot Olin at that College. The man had served most of his time in St. Rontlemore, the sister abbey and rival of Olin's St. Bondabruce in Entel.

He had wavered in his vote at that last college, though, Stimson remembered, and had nearly been persuaded over to Abbot Olin's side. Perhaps he could be moved toward the new reality of the Abellican Church.

A cry to the side turned the attention of all three toward a woman, running and screaming for her husband. She almost got to the flat rock off to the side of the wall where the dead were being piled before a pair of Kingsmen intercepted her, one shoving her hard to the ground and ordering her away.

Stimson realized that his task concerning Coiyusade would be much more difficult if such actions became common. He looked to Earl DePaunch, expecting a scolding of the soldier, who continued his harsh treatment of the woman, even kicking her a couple of times.

But Earl DePaunch just laughed again, and Giulio Jannet joined him.

❖ 24 ❖

Making a Man of Him

O n a cold and snowy winter's day, when folk this far out in the Wilderlands to the west were usually huddled before the hearth, families and friends close together to share body heat, all of the citizens of Festertool were outside, lining the main cart road through the small and remote village. They waved red kerchiefs and jumped up and down, cheering for their young king—this man, Aydrian, who had once lived in this town, and who had served all the region as Tai'Maqwilloq, the Ranger of Festertool.

Sadye hardly paid the jumping and shouting townsfolk any heed as she rode beside Aydrian, surrounded by the guarding cavalry of the few All-heart Knights who had accompanied them out from Palmaris. A score of Kingsmen had gone into the village before the main parade, ensuring Aydrian's safety. The rest of the troop, more than three hundred strong, marched behind Aydrian's group, with drumbeats cutting through the dull and snowy winter air.

And Aydrian was soaking it all in, beaming more proudly than Sadye had ever before seen him. They had come through several towns before this, of course, and with similar fanfare, but this one was different, Sadye recognized. This town had been Aydrian's first real experience with a human community after his escape from the Touel'alfar. In this town, he had learned how to speak the language of Honce-the-Bear, and had learned the other manners, subtle and not-so, of human interaction. In this town, Aydrian had risen from wayward boy to hero in a short period of time, and now he was returning, the ultimate conquering hero.

He seemed a beautiful person to Sadye in that moment, his face aglow with the cold and the pride, rosy cheeks and bright red lips accentuating those marvelous blue eyes of his. He wore no helm and had pushed the hood of his heavy cloak back off his head so that his golden hair, all tousled and unkempt, was shining above him with an almost supernatural glow. Everything about Aydrian seemed larger than life to Sadye at that moment.

Truly he was the king here, in every aspect of the word, and just being beside him sent a shiver coursing along her spine.

She was still staring at him when they reached the end of the lane, and Aydrian dismounted to stand before the town elders. He paused and glanced all around, surveying the group, and Sadye could tell by his movements and the sparkle in his eyes that he recognized more than a few.

"Hey, boy, are ye still needin' old Rumpar's sword?" one old man cried, and those around him laughed and tittered.

Until Aydrian fixed them with a warning glare.

Slowly, very slowly, Aydrian drew Tempest from its sheath on his hip, sliding the blade out into the air before him and lifting it high. That alone brought many gasps, and those only multiplied a moment later, when the brilliant blade erupted into leaping flames.

To his credit, Aydrian chose not to respond any more than that, and he promptly let go of the magical fires and slid the sword away.

"Good people of Festertool," he began, turning as he spoke to take them all in, "you knew me as your ranger, defending your boundaries from highwaymen and monsters alike. And now I have returned to you as your king."

A great cheer began somewhere to the side, and rolled along the line of townsfolk, growing with each passing second. No doubt, the Kingsmen standing among the crowd were urging them, Sadye knew, but in truth, it didn't seem to her as if many needed that prompt. Their cheers seemed genuine, the hopes of a nondescript and usually ignored little town who saw one of their own step forward to the highest glory in all the world. Sadye wondered if Jilseponie had received such a reception from the folk of Dundalis after becoming Danube's queen.

Aydrian caught her attention, then, looking over at her, his eyes sparkling with pride and also with something else, some intensity that caught Sadye off her guard at that moment.

Instinctively, she hugged her arms close in front of her, almost an attempt—a futile one—to deny the warmth that was suddenly flowing throughout her.

Their meal was served by a host of attendants, seeing to their every need, and while the food was rather plain, Sadye appreciated the great lengths to which Aydrian had gone to make this evening together something rather special.

She noted, too, the way he looked at her throughout the meal, and knew that the hunger in his blue eyes longed for something more than food.

This time, though, the woman was not caught off her guard as she had been earlier in the day. She did not recoil from Aydrian's stare, did not hug her arms defensively in front of her. Rather, she lifted her glass of wine—one of the few delicacies the army had taken out of Palmaris—and replied to Aydrian with a leading and teasing smile.

Aydrian dismissed the servants before he and Sadye had even finished their meal. And when she was done, he wasted no time in coming around the table toward her.

Sadye rose before he got there and moved to the window, pulling aside the curtain to look out on the quiet town of Festertool and the many camp-fires of the army gathered about it.

"The hero comes home," she said when Aydrian stalked up beside her, and her words slowed his deliberate approach somewhat. Still, he was right against her, looking not out the window, as was she, but at her. She could feel his stare boring into her, soaking in her delicate features.

Only after a moment did her words truly seem to sink in to him. "Home?" he asked. "This place?"

Sadye turned her gentle expression to him. "This is not your home?" she asked. "Where, then?"

The question seemed physically to push Aydrian back at step and he blinked repeatedly as if coming out of his intoxication with Sadye's obvious charms.

"Is it this place you name as Andur'Blough Inninness?" the woman pressed, and Aydrian was shaking his head before she ever finished.

"I do not wish to talk about this."

"These questions do not dig so deep, do they?"

"No, I don't wish to talk about this!" Aydrian said more emphatically, and he turned away. "Not here. Not now." He spun back on her almost immediately, moving close once again. "This is not the time," he said, his voice going softer but hardly diminishing—rather, it gained a husky quality and a sense of urgency.

Aydrian pressed up against her, his arm going about her so that she could not even begin to lean away. "Not now," he whispered, and he moved in to kiss her.

A deft twist and duck had Sadye sliding under that holding arm and moving back toward the center of the room.

Aydrian's eyes popped open and he spun to regard her, his expression caught somewhere between surprise and anger. "You refuse me?"

Sadye recognized the genuine confusion in his voice, and, as she had expected, the lack of true confidence behind his imperial façade. She didn't respond to him openly, not wanting to clear that confusion and those doubts, but merely smiled coyly.

Aydrian approached, but the graceful woman simply danced away.

"What game do you play?" the frustrated king asked.

"Game?"

Aydrian came at her suddenly with a move that would have served him well as a swordsman, closing the distance too quickly for Sadye to move aside.

And so she stopped him instead, with a simple change in expression, a sudden frosty stare.

Aydrian halted and shook his head.

"You just take what you will?" Sadye remarked. She nearly laughed aloud when Aydrian started to answer in the affirmative, and her fluid expression stopped him before he made that mistake.

"I am the king," he said instead.

"And so you have your kingdom."

"And so I have what I desire."

"No," came the woman's simple response.

"I could have any woman in the kingdom!"

"All but one, perhaps."

Aydrian clenched his fists at his sides and Sadye half expected him to stamp his foot in frustration. She resisted the urge to giggle at him. "My word is law," he argued, and then reiterated, "I will have whatever I desire."

He started forward, but Sadye's outstretched hand, backed by a look of intensity beyond anything Aydrian had ever seen from her before, stopped him as surely as any barricade ever could.

"No," she answered in denial of his last statement. "Because what you desire cannot be taken."

Those words seemed to calm Aydrian somewhat, and he settled back, looking at her curiously.

"You could take me, of course, by force," Sadye went on with a shrug. "I could not stop you, nor would any speak ill of the act, since you are king."

Aydrian's expression showed her that he was considering that option at that very moment, and Sadye realized that she had a lot of work to do on this flawed young man.

"There would be no gain," she explained. "You would find nothing but physical release, and if that is your goal, better that you seek out someone for whom you care nothing, or service yourself . . ."

"Enough!"

"But you would gain no mastery over me, Aydrian," the woman pressed on, narrowing her eyes. "Because I would detach myself wholly from the experience. You would not hurt me nor subjugate me because I would be there in body only."

"Perhaps that is enough!"

The woman chortled at him. "If you believe that, then you are a fool," she said, and she turned away, moving around the table. She needed time, and distance, because he needed to learn. Once she had achieved that distance, Sadye began to laugh aloud, not derisively, but to show him clearly that she knew something that he did not. "You broke Symphony to your will, yes?" she asked.

Aydrian wore a perplexed expression, and he just stared at her for a long time before slightly nodding.

"And yet, you never mastered the horse," she added.

"So says Sadye," came the dry reply.

"Did Symphony not throw you at the joust upon first opportunity? Did Symphony not run from you at the first opportunity in Palmaris?"

"The beast desired to be wild . . ."

"And yet every tale I have heard shows that Symphony went to Elbryan, and to Jilseponie, willingly. Has it occurred to you that those encounters were more than anything you ever knew of Symphony?"

Aydrian's face crinkled. "You speak of a horse?" he asked, shaking his head. "What has that got to do—"

"You can take whatever you want, King Aydrian Boudabras," Sadye said directly. "But some things cannot be taken, can only be given."

"It is De'Unnero, isn't it?" Aydrian shouted at her.

Sadye didn't dignify that with an answer. She turned from him and walked from the room, not even looking back. She heard his footsteps as he started to follow, but only smiled when those steps broke off suddenly. His emotions had dropped a solid wall before him, she knew, and it would not be one that Aydrian had any experience against, nor any weapons against. She had stopped him.

She had taught him the first lesson.

She went back to the house that had been set aside for her and spent hours preparing herself and her room, before finding an attendant and sending him across the lane to fetch young Aydrian. She wished that she could have waited a day or two at least before moving on to this next most-important lesson, but the army would march in the morning, and this was no lesson to be learned in a tent in the wilderness.

Aydrian locked a scowl on his face later that night as he walked across the small lane to the house Sadye was using. The young king could hardly believe that he was answering the call delivered by Sadye's appointed door guard. His first instinct was to send a stinging retort back to the woman who had so completely rebuffed him. But for some reason he did not understand, the young king of Honce-the-Bear was out and walking, his cloak pulled tight about him against the cold night wind.

He knocked on the door, but then just grunted and pushed through it, not waiting for any answer.

Immediately Aydrian's senses were touched, at every level. A fire blazed in the hearth to the left of the door, and many candles were set about the room, their lights sometimes crystal clear and other times dull glows behind the wafting layers of steam and scented smoke. Aydrian took a deep and intoxicating breath and a strange warmth washed over him.

He closed the door and moved deeper into the room, to a central collection of pillows and blankets set between hanging shades of delicate fabric. Only as he neared the pillows did Aydrian notice the music. Sadye's lute, he knew, the plucked notes hanging in the air until moving seamlessly into the next. The song was slow, but full of sharp and distinct sounds.

Then came a hissing sound, and Aydrian turned, to see Sadye drifting about the steam, pouring a pitcher of water on heated stones before going right back to her playing.

She was dressed in light layers of the same teasing gossamer-like material as the shades, which hardly covered her lithe body. She danced aside as she played, drifting in and out of the opaque steam, and behind the hanging shades, turning as she went. Water glistened on her delicate shoulders and on her hair, and a single droplet hung teasingly on her lip for a few moments.

"What is this?" Aydrian asked, his words lost in the continuing music of the lute. "What are you about?" As he spoke, he pulled the heavy cloak from his shoulders and tossed it aside, and Sadye flashed a mischievous grin and did likewise, pulling a veil from about her waist and leaving it in her wake.

Aydrian's eyes fixed on that beautiful bare belly, seeming soft and firm all at once, with a delicate curve at its bottom, where it disappeared behind the veil wrapped about the woman's hips.

Catching on, Aydrian grinned wickedly and threw off his shirt, stripping to the waist.

In a twirl, Sadye did likewise, but then she moved sidelong to him, with her arms blocking his view, just barely.

"Sadye, what are you about?" Aydrian asked.

She didn't answer, other than to fix him with one of the most intense gazes he had ever seen, her eyes alone nearly buckling the young man's knees beneath him. Almost panting now, barely able to draw breath, Aydrian stripped off the rest of his clothes and moved toward her.

But Sadye moved gracefully away from him, and when he rushed to catch up to her, she turned and froze him with another look, one suddenly cold and denying.

"Sadye?" he asked, he begged.

The woman brought a finger to her pursed lips, bidding him to silence. Only then did he realize that she had deftly removed the rest of her veils.

"What game is this, woman?" Aydrian said, his voice taking on lower and more insistent tones. Sadye moved around the other side of the circular pillow pile then, slipping behind another of the hanging screens, and Aydrian moved suddenly, and as purposefully as a charge in a sword fight, cutting her off so that there was only that thin sliver of fabric between them. He reached out and took her by the shoulder.

The music stopped and a frown crossed Sadye's beautiful face as she pulled immediately away from the man. "I told you before," she warned. "You will have me on my terms alone. Now retreat to the pillows."

Aydrian did let go, but he stood there staring at her for a long moment, shaking his head. "I am the king."

Sadye moved up to him, her body just brushing his, her lips moving delicately over his. A groan escaped him and he leaned forward, but Sadye was already retreating, moving in perfect synchronization with Aydrian so that his body was barely touching hers all the way back.

He stopped, finally, gasping, and Sadye came back at him, first waving a burning brand of some lavender-scented branch before her, then tossing it on the fire and coming in behind the alluring scent, this time to press more urgently against Aydrian, kissing him hard and passionately.

Aydrian crushed her in his arms, moving to align himself with her, wanting only to be one with her. Waves of passion flowed through him, dizzying him. He could hardly breathe; he needed release.

But Sadye pulled away, giggling, and took up her lute again, twirling behind another of the hanging screens.

Aydrian started to pursue, but stopped short, looking at her, his mouth moving as if he wanted to say something but couldn't find the words, his hands wringing at his sides, his entire body taut, as if he would simply explode.

"What is wrong, King Aydrian?" Sadye teased.

"What are you doing to me?" he asked. "What bewitching . . ."

"I am teaching you," the woman answered. "Be grateful for the lesson, else I'll end it now."

"I will take you!" Aydrian said through his gritted teeth.

"Then you will get so much less than I can truly offer," the woman said with another giggle. "Poor Aydrian. Always needing to be in control."

He shook his head and moved a step toward her, but she laughed and spun away.

"But do you not understand?" Sadye asked. "Everything you do, you do with complete command. Everyone around you, even Marcalo De'Unnero, has become your puppet. You, young King, hold all the strings."

"Not all, it would seem."

"Then be grateful to Sadye," the woman purred. "No, you do not control me, nor can you. With your great strength, you could ravish me, but that would bring you so much less of the sweetness I offer. With your mighty sword, you could execute me, and none would question, but even in dying, I would laugh at you, and you know it."

"Another once thought she controlled me," Aydrian warned, his tone suddenly ominous. "I am on my way even now to kill her for that."

"Ah, but Dasslerond controlled you for her purposes and her benefit," said Sadye, obviously not shaken at all. "I control you for the good of . . . you." She motioned again to the pillows, and this time, despite his obvious desire to resist, Aydrian lay down upon them.

Sadye continued her dance about him for some time, teasing him with different, almost complete views of her alluring body, and with the notes of her song and the scents wafting about the air, with the steam and the heat, and the moisture glistening upon her.

Gradually, so slowly, she went to him, and even then, lying beside him or kneeling over him, she took her time, teasing more than touching, bringing the poor young man to near insanity with desire.

Finally, she straddled him as he lay on his back and leaned forward to whisper in his ear, nibbling his lobe before she spoke. "You have earned me," she whispered. She moved her face back, looking down at him with an expression that was part smile and part serious.

And then she came down hard.

The room began to spin for Aydrian. He felt as if he was lifting into the air. He couldn't draw breath and he didn't want to. His legs went so taut that somewhere in the corner of his mind he feared the muscles would simply tear themselves apart.

Sometime later, Aydrian was still lying on his back, thoroughly spent, his mind whirling with the sweetest memories. Beside him, Sadye sat up against some piled pillows, her lute across her lap as she absently plucked at the strings.

"I never imagined," the young man said, his voice barely escaping his throat.

"Because you spend your every day in complete control—you even control the weretiger within Marcalo," Sadye explained.

"I am the king. I will rule all the world."

"Almost all," Sadye replied with a wicked grin and she pointedly crossed her legs. "You will never rule me. You will never control me. Understand that."

Aydrian's face went tight with anger.

"And that is why you will always appreciate me, and love me," Sadye finished. "You will always be a boy, Aydrian, if you are always in control of everything around you. I will teach you to be a man."

"What foolishness . . ."

"Because only in letting go of that iron-fisted control, only by letting your emotions step through your willpower, will you understand the other half of what it is to be human," Sadye explained in all seriousness. "Only when you embrace this other side of you, this passion, this freedom from control, this danger of the unknown, will you be complete, and only when you are a whole human being can you truly be a man."

Aydrian blinked repeatedly, but did not rebut.

"Marcalo was much like you," Sadye explained, and Aydrian winced through a shot of jealousy at the mention of her other lover. "So many powerful men . . . no, powerful boys, are."

"What of Sadye, then?" Aydrian asked.

The woman looked at him as if she did not understand.

"If you go back to him, I will—" Aydrian started deliberately.

"Kill me?" she interrupted. "Kill him? Kill everyone?"

"Do not play this game."

"You please me, Aydrian, in so many ways," the woman coyly replied. "Continue to do so and you have nothing to fear."

Aydrian leaned back and closed his eyes; all of it was too confusing to him at that moment, still basking in the loss of his virginity.

Sadye began to play again, then, and began to sing, softly, and her sweet voice was the perfect ending to a perfect night.

Aydrian drifted off to sleep.

Sadye sat there for a long while, looking at the beautiful young king, the beautiful young man. He was the most powerful man in all the world.

Except when he was with her.

❖ 25 ❖

Missionaries

B rynn stood on the eastern wall of Dharyan-Dharielle, replaying the events of the last couple of weeks over and over in her mind. She couldn't shake the image of Abbot Olin in Chom Deiru, nor the look upon his face—so smug, so self-assured.

So dangerous.

All of the reports that had followed Brynn home served to heighten that uneasy feeling. Bolstered by their great victory over their primary opponent, the Behrenese armies were on the march out of Jacintha. Several provinces and cities had already fallen back under the blanket of Yatol Mado Wadon and the principle city, which was what Brynn and her comrades had hoped from the beginning. But those armies were being accompanied by a large number of priests—not only Chezru, but Abellican! Many Honce-the-Bear soldiers were also filling the ranks of the "Jacintha" force, and at least one report from Dahdah Oasis claimed that it was the northmen, not the Behrenese, who were truly in command.

"You look as if you expect an attack from Jacintha at any moment," came a familiar voice, taking Brynn from her contemplations. She turned her head to regard Pagonel as he walked up beside her at the parapet.

"Abbot Olin seems to be an ambitious man," the woman remarked.

Pagonel nodded and stared out to the dark east.

"It is my fear that we fought not for Jacintha and Mado Wadon, but for Olin of Honce-the-Bear," Brynn explained.

"I have heard words to that effect," the mystic agreed.

Brynn turned on him. "What have we done?"

"We stopped Tohen Bardoh, and that bodes well for To-gai," Pagonel reasoned. "If your old nemesis had taken Jacintha, then we would have more than us two staring out to the east, and the expectation of attack would be a near certainty, I believe. And so do you."

"Bardoh would never have allowed the To-gai-ru to hold Dharyan-Dharielle," Brynn agreed.

"Then you have done well, yes?"

The fact that Pagonel had turned the statement into a question alerted Brynn to the fact that he was asking her to look deeper within herself here, to examine her feelings honestly and openly. That was why she valued Pagonel's company more than simple friendship. His calm demeanor went to the core of his rational being. His embracing of the Jhesta Tu code gave him a perfectly rational perspective on all issues, a clearheaded ability to weigh every situation in every context, large and small. When the Chezhou-Lei warriors had arrived at the Mountains of Fire, challenging the Jhesta Tu to battle, there had been little irrational emotion guiding the hand of the Jhesta Tu leaders, including Pagonel, just a simple estimate of the good and bad of it.

The Jhesta Tu were complete human beings, Brynn thought as she regarded the always-serene mystic. In Pagonel, she saw true contentment and harmony, and it was a state that she surely envied and aspired to.

"I fear that Abbot Olin has gained the upper hand over Yatol Mado Wadon," Brynn said after a bit more reflection. "The blanket of Jacintha takes on a decidedly Abellican point of view, by all that I am hearing from those cities that have capitulated to the marching army. Behren will soon be reunited, no doubt, north to south, east to west, but she will not be the same as before the fall of Chezru Chieftain Yakim Douan."

"How could she be?" Pagonel asked. "Douan's fall revealed a terrible betrayal, one that went to the heart of the Chezru religion and the leadership of Behren. The faith of the Yatols and of their flock was shaken, indeed, and perhaps shattered. Whatever form Chezru takes as it rises from the ashes of Yakim Douan's wreckage will, by necessity, be very different from the church as it was."

"But will it come to resemble the Abellican religion of Honce-the-Bear?" Brynn asked. "For that is what Abbot Olin seems to be about, and Yatol Wadon is apparently not disagreeing."

"Would that be a bad thing? The Abellicans have had their own trials in recent years—perhaps one day I will tell you of the fall of Father Abbot Markwart and the rise of the followers of Avelyn Desbris."

Brynn looked at him curiously. She had heard a bit of that tale, from the Touel'alfar and in her time as leader of To-gai, when she had learned that Aydrian, her old training companion, had assumed the throne of the northern kingdom.

"Aydrian's mantle as king would seem to speak of that very event, since his mother and father were among those who rode with Avelyn."

"And now Honce-the-Bear has come down to Behren to aid in their crisis," Pagonel said. "Perhaps Abbot Olin understands well this type of trouble and is sharing his expertise with a devastated Chezru leadership."

Brynn stared at him for a long while, knowing well that he was taking a position more to make her consider all the alternatives than to convince her of anything. "Or perhaps Abbot Olin has come in view of an opportunity here in the shattered and confused people of Behren," she answered.

Pagonel's expression showed her that he did not disagree.

"Is Abbot Olin expanding your friend Aydrian's domain?" he asked.

Brynn looked back to the east and shrugged.

"Would it not be a good thing for you and your people if that was the case?" Pagonel went on. "If Aydrian or his representatives come to hold sway over Behren, is not the threat to To-gai from the Behrenese reduced? He is your friend, is he not?"

"Perhaps it would be reduced."

"Then why do you trouble yourself over the aid we gave to Yatol Wadon, and perhaps to Abbot Olin by extension, in the battle of Jacintha?" the mystic asked. "You have pushed war farther from your border, it would seem, and is that not the responsibility of any leader?"

It made sense, of course, but the reasoning did not resonate within Brynn, because there was one other consideration. "And what of the Behrenese?" she asked.

"Would your friend Aydrian be an unworthy leader? A tyrant?"

"He is not Behrenese," Brynn answered. "And the Abellicans are not Chezru, nor do they completely understand the concept and faith of the Chezru people."

"A faith that has been shattered."

"But still, is conquest the answer to their suddenly unheeded prayers?" Brynn came back emphatically, and she could see by Pagonel's expression that he had led her to this place purposefully. "Have I helped to push the Behrenese under the rule of a foreign army and church, as my own people were subjugated by the Behrenese?"

"Will the Behrenese be better off because of that?" the mystic asked.

"No," Brynn answered without the slightest hesitation. "The same was said of the To-gai-ru, that the Behrenese were showing us a better way of living. They were teaching us to tame the land to our needs, rather than to live in accordance with the steppes."

"And you do not believe that truth?"

"No, because they were stealing from us our very identity," Brynn answered. "The old ways of the To-gai-ru were more than traditions, they were our very identity. To have that stolen away without choice . . ."

Pagonel's soft expression told her that he had been hoping for that very answer.

"No, I will not be comfortable if Honce-the-Bear entrenches itself in power over Behren," Brynn declared. "I will rue the part I played in such a course. Behren is for the Behrenese, and To-gai is for the To-gai-ru. If the people of Honce-the-Bear, even the Abellican priests, wish to aid Behren in this time of crisis, even if they wish to influence the wayward Chezru flock, that is acceptable. But using this crisis to conquer is not."

"Perhaps the time is fast approaching for you to meet with your old friend Aydrian."

"I have not dismissed Agradeleous," Brynn replied.

"Nor should you. We will need the dragon for mobility, if not for war."

"We?" Brynn loaded her voice with hope. She had thought that Pagonel would soon be on his way again to his southern home.

"The Walk of Clouds is an ancient place," the mystic replied. "It will be there for me a year from now, or two."

"Your place is at my side."

The mystic draped a comforting arm about Brynn's small but strong shoulders as the two of them stood there, staring out to the dark east.

"They wasted little time," Brynn said to her scout when he returned to inform her that the army headed by Yatol De Hamman and marching under the banner of Jacintha was even then assaulting Avrou Eesa to the southeast. Avrou Eesa had been the home of Yatol Tohen Bardoh and was one of the most important Behrenese cities, the largest and strongest of all within the western stretches of the kingdom now that Dharyan-Dharielle was under To-gai-ru control.

The woman looked to Pagonel, who was seated at her side. "I must go there," she said, and to her surprise, her advisor didn't immediately disagree, and didn't even look as if he wanted to. He sat there, staring ahead, holding a pensive pose and gently stroking his chin.

"I could get there and return in short order," he replied. "I could fly Agradeleous about the city and learn much."

"I wish to see for myself," said Brynn. "The manner in which Jacintha treats the citizenry of Tohen Bardoh's home city might tell us much about what to expect from the strange alliance that has formed in the east."

A slight agreeing nod was all the answer Pagonel offered.

Within the hour, Brynn and Pagonel rode out from Dharyan-Dharielle, accompanied by two hundred To-gai-ru riders. The dragon Agradeleous, back in his huge reptilian form, circled overhead, flying lookout with his keen eyesight and ready to heed Brynn's call.

She used the dragon a few times over the next couple of days as they made their way south along the base of the great plateau dividing To-gai and Behren. With Agradeleous' great speed and strength, Brynn flew up to the plateau top and brought in more of her warriors, many of whom had been assembled along this divide. Thus, by the time the troupe approached Avrou Eesa, less than a week after setting out from Dharyan-Dharielle, they numbered closer to five hundred.

After reconnaissance from the high perch atop Agradeleous showed them that the city had already fallen to De Hamman, Brynn brought her warriors within sight of the western walls, then broke free with Pagonel and a group of a dozen, riding in under a flag of truce.

The Dragon of To-gai, who had conquered this city in the war only months before, knew that she would not be warmly welcomed if any of the original Avrou Eesa guardsmen were still at their posts. But they weren't, for De

Hamman had swept the city, and the guards greeting the To-gai-ru from the watchtowers on the western gate were men of Jacintha.

And, Brynn and Pagonel both noted, a few light-complexioned warriors wearing the heavier armor of Honce-the-Bear.

The To-gai-ru group was admitted openly into the conquered city, and even cheered by some of the soldiers—and why not? Brynn thought. Hadn't she and her companions turned the tide in the battle for their home city? Had Bardoh prevailed, how many of these men would even still be alive?

"I will speak with Yatol De Hamman," Brynn said to the commander of the watch, and he motioned a pair of soldiers front and center and ordered them to take her at once to the Chezru temple Yatol De Hamman had set up as his temporary palace.

Before even entering that battle-worn but still impressive place, Brynn had many of her questions answered.

For laid out on the square before the temple were dozens of wounded soldiers, all wearing the red-stitched turbans associated with Yatol Bardoh. Obviously injured in the battle, or after the battle, these poor souls had little in the way of comforts. Many onlookers lined that scene of suffering, but none dared approach within the ring of Jacintha soldiers. Women pleaded for their husbands, and children cried, but the sentries seemed impassive to it all, casually marching the perimeter and enthusiastically beating back any who attempted to move in toward the lines of wounded.

Even more telling, Abellican monks and Chezru students walked among the wounded, bending low and speaking with them.

Brynn walked Runtly, her brown-and-white pinto pony, aside and dismounted, moving to join in one such discussion.

"The pain will end," a Chezru student was saying to one emaciated and grievously injured man. "We will bring your wife and daughter inside with us, and they will hold your hands as Master Mackaront here shows you the truth of St. Abelle and Chezru. You will learn the beauty of our joined hands, my friend."

The wounded man looked away in obvious disdain and the Chezru student straightened, spat upon him, and moved to the next in line.

Or started to, until Brynn stopped him. "How long have they been out here?"

The men turned to her; Mackaront flashed a toothy smile. "It is good to see you," he started to say, but Brynn stopped him with a severe look and an upraised hand.

"How long have they been out here?" she asked again.

"Three days," the Chezru student offered. "There were many more, of course, but some succumbed to their wounds." His face brightened. "But many more have come to see the truth, and are even now resting comfortably!"

Brynn turned her stern look over the Abellican master. "You hold their families and their very lives up before them with your offer of relief?" she asked incredulously. "Is this how Abellicans spread the word of their god?"

"They must accept the possibility that they have been deceived all these long years by a tyrant," Mackaront replied, and it seemed to Brynn that these were well-practiced words. "They must show some repentance, at least, to counter their years of blindness. We of St. Abelle are a generous and kind lot, but our God-given magic cannot be bestowed upon our enemies nor upon heretics."

Brynn tightened her jaw but resisted the urge to scream at him. She knew that she wasn't going to get anywhere, so she turned away, glancing back once to soak in the pitiful image of the wretch on the ground, then moved more forcefully to catch up and pass her companions, striding with grim determination for the palace.

She was the first to stand before Yatol De Hamman, and neither offered nor waited for any formal greetings. "How can you accept this?" she asked.

The man put on a confused look, one that Brynn didn't believe for a moment.

"You are forcing Behrenese to embrace the Abellican Church," Brynn explained. "You wear the robes of a Yatol of Chezru, yet you deny those robes and tenets before this holy place."

A commotion from behind turned Brynn, to see her companions standing calmly behind her, and to see litter-bearers taking in the same man she had seen lying before the feet of Master Mackaront outside the palace. A woman and a younger girl, the man's wife and daughter, obviously, flanked him, holding his hands and crying, while Mackaront moved beside him as well, clutching one hand to his chest, the other set upon the wounded man's injured side.

"Does your desecration know no bounds?" Brynn asked De Hamman.

"Desecration?" the Yatol replied skeptically. "Because we have come to understand the deception of Douan? Because we have embraced friends from the north?"

"Abellican friends," Brynn reminded. "Men who follow a different God, and men who have never been true friends of Behren." She did note a bit of a wince there, and suspected that maybe De Hamman's feelings didn't run quite as deep as his words seemed to indicate.

"Release the hatred from your soul, Brynn Dharielle," De Hamman bade her. "We live in enlightened times. Better times."

"You throw away everything that gave Behren its very soul!" Brynn argued, but then a hand on her shoulder calmed her, and she glanced over to see Pagonel standing beside her.

"As you embrace the heretic mystics of the Jhesta Tu?" De Hamman retorted.

Brynn let the comment go and forced herself to a place of calm. She understood the error of the analogy, of course—the Jhesta Tu weren't making any claims within To-gai, after all—and in that understanding, she allowed herself to dismiss the remark out of hand.

"Who leads Behren, Yatol De Hamman?" she asked. "Is it Yatol Mado Wadon? Or has Abbot Olin of Honce-the-Bear stepped forward behind this screen of 'enlightenment'?"

That, too, seemed to sting the man a bit, but then he shook it off visibly and regained his firm posture. "I would be dead now," he replied. "Without the aid that Abbot Olin brought to Jacintha in her hour of need, I would lie dead amid the bodies of so many good Chezru."

The simple statement did set Brynn back a bit.

"And dead to what heaven?" De Hamman went on. "The one promised by Chezru Douan? The same one that he was too afraid to face through all those centuries when he stole the souls of unborn children to perpetuate his own wretched existence?"

Brynn paused a long moment to digest that heavy remark, to consider the weight behind it. Yakim Douan's deception had been so horrible that it had torn Behren apart and shattered the foundations of the Chezru religion. De Hamman was not unique among the Chezru clergy, obviously, and the weight of war and suffering could do much to convert those less learned in their ancient traditions. With that thought in mind, Brynn glanced back at the curtain behind which Mackaront and the others had disappeared, and noted that no more agonized screams were coming forth.

"Is this friendship?" the woman asked De Hamman. "Or conquest?"

The man's response cut her to her heart, and warned her that great trouble might well be brewing in the kingdom to the east. "Does it matter?"

Information gathering

"We have at last a king who understands that the sacred gemstones, as the gifts of God, are the province of the priests who represent that God," Marcalo De'Unnero told an attentive gathering of monks one morning in St. Precious. "With King Aydrian's blessing, we might go about the task of returning the gemstones to the Abellican Church."

That announcement was received with many assenting nods and even a few cheers—although the brothers in attendance of course knew that De'Unnero and the monks he had brought out of St. Honce in Ursal had set about doing that very thing all along the march up the Masur Delaval.

However, one older brother, a master of St. Precious who had been in Palmaris for many years, seemed not so enthusiastic, and his expression was not lost on those around him nor on De'Unnero as he surveyed his brethren army.

"Master DeNauer?" he prompted.

The older man—older than De'Unnero, and appearing much older than the unnaturally aging weretiger—looked up with sleepy gray eyes. "Have you not tried this once before, Master De'Unnero?" DeNauer asked. "Was this not the mission of Bishop De'Unnero when he represented Father Abbot Markwart in Palmaris?"

Marcalo De'Unnero stared at the man, trying to place him, trying to remember him. Had this one been among the treacherous brothers surrounding Braumin Herde back in those days? A follower of Jojonah and Avelyn, perhaps? De'Unnero's scrutiny turned into a scowl and he felt the stirring of the beast within in simply thinking such things. He fought that feral urge away, temporarily at least, by reminding himself that he and Aydrian had screened the brothers of the conquered abbey cautiously, and that only those showing an open mind toward Aydrian and this new incarnation of the Abellican Church had been allowed to see the light of day since the conquest. And Aydrian's tactics in his interrogations, De'Unnero knew, went far beyond the insights of human perception. Aydrian had used gemstones to scour the thoughts of the surrendering brothers, to learn which among them were too far engrossed with the lies of Braumin Herde to be of use to De'Unnero's Church.

"And do you believe that Father Abbot Markwart was errant in everything he proposed?" De'Unnero asked, narrowing his dark eyes.

Master DeNauer rested back in his chair and didn't blink as he took in that threatening stare.

"Because you see, brother," De'Unnero went on when it was apparent that no answer would be forthcoming, "it is my understanding, and that of our new king, that the followers of Avelyn Desbris, in their elation over the end of the rosy plague and in their confidence since the fall of Father Abbot Markwart, have seized the opportunity to press too far in their understanding of the generosity of the Abellican Church. Perhaps we should open the coffers of every abbey, and hand out gemstones to every peasant who desires one. Perhaps we should even train such peasants to use the stones!" He moved about as he spoke, waving his arms with dramatic flourish. "Perhaps Brother Avelyn's belief that we of the Church are no different than those peasants whom we serve is the correct approach!"

"I have never heard such a thing attributed to Saint Avelyn," Master DeNauer dared to say, and the man's reference to Avelyn as a saint stung De'Unnero profoundly.

"Saint Avelyn?" De'Unnero echoed with great skepticism.

"All that remains is the formal declaration from St.-Mere-Abelle," Master DeNauer replied. "The canonization process has been successfully concluded, has it not?"

"No proclamation from St.-Mere-Abelle at this time holds any weight, dear brother," De'Unnero was quick to correct. "Not until, or unless, that body recognizes Aydrian as king."

"And by extension, Marcalo De'Unnero as Father Abbot?"

The question sent a surge of anger running through De'Unnero's body, one that awakened primal urges within him at every point. He needed Aydrian then, he realized. Or Sadye! Someone to tame the weretiger that was fast rising within him. He fought to reason with himself; if the beast came forth at this time and tore the bothersome DeNauer apart, then how would he ever hope to retain any semblance of control over the rest of the clergy? His credibility would be gone in the flash of a deadly tiger's paw!

He fought hard and fell into the discipline that Aydrian had shown him. He closed his eyes, found a point of meditation, and gradually resisted those urges. He tucked his right arm up under the wide sleeve of his robe, as well, and it was good that he had, for he knew that beneath the brown fabric was not the limb of a human, but the deadly tearing paw of a great cat.

But the mind controlling that paw, thanks to the teaching of Aydrian, was not the primal, instinctive brain of a great hunting cat.

De'Unnero opened his eyes and stared hard at the obstinate master. "When King Aydrian claimed Palmaris, an honest question of allegiance was asked of every brother," he reminded.

"Aydrian is king," DeNauer replied.

"And?"

"And the Abellican Church has veered from its course," the master admitted. "Abbot Olin should have been elected Father Abbot those years ago when Master Fio Bou-raiy was given the mantle."

"Even now, Abbot Olin shows us his worth as a great leader!" De'Unnero interrupted, seizing the moment. "He is expanding the Church beyond anything that has been done since the sixth century. His strides exceed everything that was attempted by all the Alpinadoran missionaries combined." He moved about as he spoke, basking in the glow of admiring eyes. "But," De'Unnero said, stopping suddenly and holding up his index finger to punctuate his words, "Abbot Olin's duties will keep him away for many months, for many years, perhaps. In his absence, King Aydrian has other intentions for the Abellican Church within Honce-the-Bear, and we ignore the wishes of our wise young king at our peril."

"Father Abbot De'Unnero!" one enthusiastic young brother cried out, and many others cheered their assent.

De'Unnero watched Master DeNauer as the applause grew, and noted that the man, though obviously less enthusiastic, was not openly disagreeing. Even his body posture hadn't gone tight and defensive.

"Master DeNauer," De'Unnero said when the cheering died away, "do you disagree with this premise."

"If I did, then I would not be here at this time, brother," the older monk replied, and De'Unnero did not miss the double entendre of his words. "But I am no fanatic for Avelyn Desbris," DeNauer went on, "though I believe him to have been a godly man, and perhaps worthy of sainthood. I question your decision concerning the magical gemstones not out of disrespect, but out of painful memories. How will Palmaris react this time when brothers arrive at the doors of merchants, demanding the precious stones? Stones purchased from the Abellican Church, no less, and for tidy sums?"

De'Unnero nodded as the man played out his reasoning. "We must first identify every stone," he explained. "And then we will contact the owners of such stones privately. We will not take the stones, as Father Abbot Markwart once desired, but rather, we will procure them with generous payment. King Aydrian understands the potential for anger in this action, and so he has provided us with the wealth we require to buy back the sacred stones that the Church should never have sold in the first place.

"We enter a new chapter in the history of our faith, brothers," De'Unnero went on, his voice excited and almost breathless. "No more will the Abellican Church operate outside the secular society of Honce-the-Bear. We now have a joining, of Church and State. King Aydrian is our ally." He turned a sudden sharp look over DeNauer, anticipating a retort. "And not as Jilseponie was supposedly our ally when she served as queen," he said before the man could offer an argument. "For King Aydrian understands the truth of our faith. His teacher was not Avelyn Desbris—yes, a godly man in many respects, but an errant one in many others! No, King Aydrian understands the truth of Brother Avelyn, and of Father Abbot Markwart. He knows where each was correct, and where each ultimately failed. We have the wealth, brothers. We have the strength of the throne behind us. Let us go now and reshape the Abellican Church in our wisdom."

That brought another cheer from the enthusiastic gathering, one that elicited a grin from Marcalo De'Unnero. He hated giving Brother Avelyn any credit, of course, but he understood the need to temper his orders with generosity. These younger brothers only knew Avelyn from the words of his admirers, men like Braumin Herde, and from those who had survived the rosy plague, they believed, because of Avelyn's "miracle." De'Unnero knew better than to openly compete with those beliefs. No, he would build upon them instead, nudging the brothers along the course he desired.

That same day, the brothers of St. Precious, armed with gemstones that could be used to detect magic and with lists compiled during the reigns of Bishop Francis and Bishop De'Unnero of merchants known to possess other enchanted stones, began their march across Palmaris. Watching them go out, Marcalo De'Unnero considered again the good fortune that had brought him to Aydrian. If this day's meeting had happened a few years ago, Master DeNauer would now be dead, torn apart by the weretiger. And all would have been for naught, with the brothers of St. Precious turning away from De'Unnero in horror.

But now . . .

Now there was hope. Aydrian had taught De'Unnero the control he needed to complete his rise within the Church.

From his window in St. Precious, the fierce master looked out across the great and lazy river to the east, imagining again the solid walls of St.-Mere-Abelle, the oldest and grandest abbey in all the world. He would rule from within those walls, he knew.

Or, with Aydrian's help, he would tear them down.

The watchman's cry of "Dragon!" had Brynn looking out to the south that late afternoon, several days after returning from her visit to Avrou Eesa. Soon after her arrival back in Dharyan-Dharielle, the warrior leader had sent Agradeleous out with her commanders to rouse the To-gai-ru warriors from their villages. She was afraid of the current events in Behren; the uneasy feeling that had engulfed her in Avrou Eesa had not diminished. Honce-the-Bear was on the march here, obviously, and her friend Aydrian seemed to be quite an imperialistic leader.

Brynn knew that part of her uneasiness was in fact coming from her recollections of Aydrian from their time together with the Touel'alfar. She had liked the young ranger, her only human companion for several years, but she had seen a distinct danger within Aydrian even then. Never, by all accounts, had any ranger given Lady Dasslerond such trouble! And it came from an inner fire, Brynn knew, that had exceeded even her own pressing need to see To-gai free of Behrenese rule. There was something about Aydrian—something too ambitious and eager.

Out of caution, and because the folk of the steppes were entering their slow hunting season anyway, Brynn had mustered the warriors all along the plateau divide and brought many into Dharyan-Dharielle as well, tripling the guard and launching scouting expeditions east along the mountains, south along the plateau divide, and into the desert areas in between. And of course she had this other huge advantage: the dragon Agradeleous. With his keen eyes and great speed, Brynn could watch the movements of any army across the desert sands.

So far, at least, De Hamman had not advanced beyond Avrou Eesa in any significant manner.

As the great dragon soared in closer, Brynn recognized that it bore a rider this day, and her heart leaped at the thought. There weren't many Agradeleous would allow such a perch, and given the dragon's direction, coming from the southeast, Brynn had a good idea of who it might be.

The dragon glided in to his customary perch in Dharyan-Dharielle, the flat roof of the central guard tower, and Brynn was thrilled indeed to see her suspicions confirmed, to see that it was Pagonel returned to her atop the dragon. She moved quickly to join the mystic, and met him coming out of that guard tower a few moments later.

"My heart is glad of your return," she said, and she wrapped Pagonel in a great and warm hug. The mystic had remained in Avrou Eesa after Brynn's abrupt departure, wishing to study further this curious comradeship that had apparently developed between the Chezru and Abellican religions. Though she had wanted her chief advisor standing beside her as she prepared To-gai for a potential advance from the east, Brynn had readily agreed with Pagonel's assessment that the situation needed further investigation.

"I had feared for you," Brynn admitted. "The Jhesta Tu have never been welcomed by either the Chezru or the Abellicans."

"But was I not the man who helped reveal the deception of Chezru Chieftain Douan?" Pagonel replied.

"Which made me fear that De Hamman and the others might bear some undercurrent of hatred for you. You unsettled their world, after all."

"I was treated with respect, if distantly," the mystic replied. "Though I suspect their politeness was born more out of my association with you than because of any of my actions in Jacintha against Chezru Douan."

"Distantly?" Brynn echoed. "You were given little access?"

"Little more than anyone else in the conquered city. Yatol De Hamman's official proclamations told me much, however. He cited the deception of Yakim Douan as the primary reason for the destructive and unnecessary rift between the two churches, Abellican and Chezru. It is obvious that the current leadership of Chezru has embraced the Abellicans as friends and allies on every level."

Brynn winced at that news, and shook her head.

"Yatol De Hamman even went so far as to claim that the two churches actually follow the same god, though with a different name, and the same hopes of eternal life in their common kingdom of heaven above."

"They have joined at the heart, and not just as allies," Brynn reasoned.

"Though in truth, I suspect that all churches could be similarly described," Pagonel went on.

Brynn smirked at the remark and looked at him slyly. "Even the Jhesta Tu?"

"Perhaps," the mystic answered. "But our knowledge of that possibility, and admission of that possibility makes us more tolerant of those who do not follow our specific guidelines."

"Will the spread of St. Abelle prove an enlightenment for the folk of Behren?" Brynn asked. "Or a shadow that will cover the desert kingdom?"

"That is the question," the mystic replied.

"I fear them. I fear Aydrian."

"There is little doubt that the move southward by the soldiers and priests of Honce-the-Bear was swift and deliberate," Pagonel agreed. "They came here with a purpose beyond bailing out the beleaguered remnants of the Chezru leadership in Jacintha."

"A purpose that has spread across the sands to our very feet."

"And what does that mean?"

The simple question had Brynn off-balance. "I know not," she admitted. "All preparations have been made against an attack, should one come, but I am not about to initiate a war on behalf of Behren against this insurgence of the northmen, especially when it seems that many in Behren accept and invite the Abellicans."

"There is another troubling consideration," Pagonel remarked. "Should a fight come back to To-gai, our enemies this time will be more potently armed—especially against our major asset."

"The dragon fears gemstone magic," Brynn agreed, and she looked up the tower as she spoke, to see Agradeleous' great reptilian tail swaying over the edge above her.

She looked back at Pagonel to see him nodding his agreement, his expression seeming to show that he not only agreed that the dragon did fear the gemstone magic, but that he also agreed that the dragon *should* fear the gemstone magic.

Roger grimaced as the guard loosened the ropes about his wrists, but he never took his eye off the man who had summoned him.

He was in one of the private rooms of St. Precious Abbey. The place was somewhat dim, having only one small window and that partially obscured by one of the many tapestries hanging from the walls. Roger knew this drawing room well, for he had spent many hours in it with Abbot Braumin and Master Viscenti during their tenure here in Palmaris. It had been one of his favorite rooms, tastefully decorated with interesting tapestries and a warm and inviting hearth fronted by a thick wool rug and three of the most comfortable chairs Roger had ever known.

Now, though, the place seemed cold and uninviting, though whether that was because of the present company or the lack of a fire in the hearth to counter the chill winter wind, Roger could not say.

"Begone," De'Unnero ordered the guards, and they obeyed immediately, leaving Rogers standing by the door and rubbing his sore wrists.

Of course, the battered man's wrists were hardly the worst of his wounds. That first hit De'Unnero had inflicted on the day of Abbot Braumin's escape had raked a line of gashes across Roger's chest and belly, and without treatment, without even clean water to wash the mud from his wounds, the gashes had not properly healed.

"I am very tired of this, Master Lockless," De'Unnero said, breaking the silence.

Roger lowered his eyes and happened to glance to the side, to the room's small desk and the wine-screw that Abbot Braumin kept there for his meetings with Roger and Viscenti. Roger looked back at De'Unnero, to see him moving toward the window, staring out and paying Roger no apparent heed whatsoever.

A slight step had the battered prisoner closer to the wine-screw.

"How long shall we continue our fight?" De'Unnero asked, looking over at Roger, who stiffened immediately. "How many decades?"

"I had thought our battle ended years ago," Roger answered. "When Markwart was thrown down."

De'Unnero gave a little laugh and looked back out the window.

"And then again when you led the Brothers Repentant to this city, disgracing yourself and damning yourself beyond salvation," Roger pressed on, and he moved to the side another step and slipped the wine-screw into his cupped hand. "You remember, don't you? When Jilseponie chased you out of Palmaris in disgrace?"

De'Unnero slowly turned to face him, all hint of mirth gone from his stern face.

"We thought you dead, De'Unnero," Roger said defiantly. "We hoped you were dead. All the misery you've brought . . ."

"Misery?" De'Unnero asked. "You and your pitiful friends have presided over the fall of the greatest institution in the history of mankind. And to this day, you do not even understand the damage that you have done, do you? You do not even understand that you have stolen from the people of Honce-the-Bear all sense of spirituality and ultimate justice?"

"You babble!"

"I speak the truth!" De'Unnero insisted. "You and your wretched friends, beginning with that fool Avelyn Desbris, have brought the descent of the Abellican Church from on high. Once we were seen by them"—he waved his hand out toward the window and the streets of Palmaris beyond—"as emissaries of God. The Father Abbot was more powerful than the king himself in holding the souls of the people. You took all that, for selfish reasons. First Avelyn, to cover his own crime of murder, then his lackeys. Jojonah. Elbryan. Jilseponie. And to a lesser extent, those fools who fell under the spell of those lackeys."

"I have little desire to argue the facts of the DemonWar with you, De'Unnero. Nor the ending of the rosy plague—I'm sure that you remember that small event, yes? If the faith of the people of Honce-the-Bear was shaken by the fall of Markwart—and well it should have been—then it was restored and heightened tenfold by those who made the pilgrimage to Mount Aida, where this man you name as a fool saved their mortal bodies!"

He thought his words would enrage De'Unnero, and expected the man to spring at him. In his shielded hand, he held the wine-screw ready, hoping for the chance to plunge it into Marcalo De'Unnero's chest.

"As you will, incorrigible fool," De'Unnero replied with a snort. "They are all dead now, you know? Avelyn. Jojonah—oh yes, I had the distinct pleasure of heaping the logs onto the pyre that burned that heretic. And Elbryan, by my own hand." He turned a wicked glare over Roger. "And Braumin Herde, you know, and by my own hand."

"You lie." Roger's voice lacked both strength and conviction.

"The river has taken him out into the gulf by now, of course," De'Unnero went on, seeming quite pleased with himself. "The fish have no doubt nibbled the flesh from his bones."

"You lie!" The denial came forth more strongly this time and Roger felt the rage welling up inside of him. He fought it back, understanding that De'Unnero was goading him here, much as he had just tried to goad the volatile monk. He saw that so clearly stamped upon the monk's face now, in the form of a superior smile.

"They are all dead," De'Unnero went on. "Remember Brother Castinagis? The poor lad died in a fire, yes? Up in Caer Tinella. I was up there at the time, taking young Aydrian to claim the sword and bow that are rightfully his. Oh yes, I saw that fire."

Roger felt his breath rush away and his knees nearly buckled beneath him. He stubbornly held his balance, though, not wanting to give De'Unnero the satisfaction.

"Only three remain," De'Unnero mused aloud. "And you are here, alive at my whim. The annoying little Viscenti has fled to St.-Mere-Abelle, of course, and so he will meet his deserved end soon enough. In truth, I care as little for him as I do for you. I could let him walk away without concern, as I could let you walk out of here a free man."

Roger spat.

"Because, of the three who remain, I care only for one, Roger Lockless. And you know where she is."

"You're a fool."

"You left with her and with your wife, fleeing like bilge rats before King Aydrian swept into Palmaris," De'Unnero remarked. "Do you think that all within the city are so loyal to you and to the witch Jilseponie that they would not tell me such things? Do you think that all of the brothers here at St. Precious, even, are so blinded by the lies of Braumin Herde that they would approve of the ridiculous changes that have swept through the Abellican Church?"

"Go ask your demon dactyl master for the information you so desperately desire!" Roger shouted at the man, and De'Unnero took a long stride toward him.

"Where is she?" the monk asked with deadly calm.

"I know not!"

"You do!" De'Unnero shouted, and he came forward—and Roger thrust out his hand, stabbing the wine-screw for Marcalo De'Unnero's heart.

The anticipation of feeling that instrument slide into the chest of his most-hated enemy turned suddenly into an explosion of fiery pain, as De'Unnero, with reflexes honed as finely as any man's alive, caught that stabbing arm at the wrist and jerked it out and over, turning Roger's elbow in and forcing the man to drop to one knee.

"Where is she?" De'Unnero demanded again, and he snapped his powerful arm out and down some more.

Roger heard the pop of his elbow a moment before the wave of agony crashed over him. He would have fallen to the floor, but De'Unnero grabbed him by the hair and jerked him upright. The poor man tried to grab at his broken elbow, but De'Unnero hit him a backhand across the face that sent him flying backward, crashing over the side of the small desk and crumpling against the base of the wall.

As his vision refocused, he saw De'Unnero towering over him. He tried to kick out, but the monk stamped upon his ankle and pinned it brutally to the floor.

"You went north with your wife," De'Unnero remarked. "Beyond Caer Tinella, so obviously to Dundalis. When I find your precious wife, perhaps I can persuade her to tell me of Jilseponie's whereabouts."

The mention of Dainsey brought a surge of power to Roger and he kicked out with his free foot, aiming for the knee of the leg pinning him.

But De'Unnero jumped straight up, then came down lightly on one leg behind the blow, and before Roger could retract his leg for another strike, the monk's other foot smashed into his face.

All the room was spinning.

"Make it easy on yourself and your wife, Roger Lockless," he heard De'Unnero saying, though it seemed as if the monk's voice was coming from far, far away. Roger felt himself being lifted into the air and set back on his feet. He forced his eyes to open and to focus.

Just in time to see De'Unnero's fist sweeping in at his jaw.

He felt the blow, and felt the wall crunch against the back of his head.

De'Unnero kept screaming at him, and kept hitting him.

Roger awoke sometime later, in the dirt of his cell that was turning to mud from Roger's own spilling blood. Aware of a presence behind him, the man turned his head about.

De'Unnero stood at his dungeon door, blocking the flickering firelight behind him, seeming even larger and more ominous in silhouette.

"We will speak again when you are well enough to feel the pain," the monk promised. "And well enough to understand the pain that will befall your dear Dainsey should you refuse." With that, the monk walked away.

Roger settled back into the mud. Hours had passed since the beating, he knew, and yet De'Unnero had stood there, waiting for him through all that time, just to make that one comment.

Even through the haze and pain of the beating, it was that last image of determined De'Unnero's imposing silhouette that stayed with Roger, that brought to him a sense of hopelessness beyond anything he had ever known.

When Aydrian
Came Home

The weather had cooperated wonderfully, and with his magical gemstones, Aydrian could light a fire on the wettest wood with ease. Those gemstones had made the trails so much easier, as well, for whenever they came upon a difficult obstacle along the road, Aydrian simply took out his malachite and used its levitational powers to take even the largest wagons across.

Thus the army out of Palmaris had made great progress out into the Wilderlands, crossing the frozen Moorlands without incident and moving up into the mountains. They all suspected that they were getting close to this strange enemy, the Touel'alfar—a fact confirmed that very night when whispering comments filtered throughout the encampment, melodic voices bidding them to "turn back," warning them to "go away, go home."

More than a few of the Kingsmen were unnerved by the ghostly whispers, but Aydrian wandered throughout the camp, full of enthusiasm, telling his men that the mere presence of the elven voices confirmed that they were drawing near to their goal.

"They try to scare us away," he explained, "because they know that they cannot beat us in the field. When we find Andur'Blough Inninness, as we soon will, the Touel'alfar will have to flee or die!"

Bolstered by his words and supreme confidence, the soldiers began shouting back threats and shaking their fists at those wind-carried whispers.

Convinced that the men were back in line, Aydrian went to his own tent, securing a pair of guards at the entrance and three others strategically placed around the sides. Inside, the young king lit no candle, but rather, sat in the darkness, clutching his soul stone. The elves were near!

His spirit walked out of his body a moment later, drifting through the encampment and tuning in to the whispers on the wind. Soon after, he found a group of Touel'alfar in a copse of trees in a shallow dell a few hundred yards to the north. They were in the branches, mostly, some alone, others sitting in pairs, and with all of them whispering.

Aydrian knew their tricks; the elves could magically throw their voices, could weave a net of sound or the absence of sound by the very timbre of their song.

He could be out here with a fraction of his army and send them all running, he knew, and he intended to do just that. But then, as his spirit was moving to depart, Aydrian noticed a familiar face among the elves, the only one who had truly befriended him those years ago when he was a ranger-in-training.

Belli'mar Juraviel.

The last time he had seen Juraviel, the elf was setting out on the road to the south with Brynn Dharielle. Apparently, after helping Brynn gain her throne in To-gai, Juraviel had returned.

Aydrian was sorry of that. Of all the Touel'alfar, he felt friendship with only this one, and he didn't want to be forced into destroying Juraviel with the rest of them.

But so be it.

His spirit soared back to his encampment and his waiting corporeal body, then a moment later, he burst outside. "I need our hundred best soldiers ready to march with me immediately," he told the guards at his tent flap. "Be quick to your Allheart leaders and see to it!"

The two men rushed off.

Aydrian looked to the dark north, a smile growing on his handsome and strong face. "First contact," he whispered. "First victory."

"They are well-schooled and disciplined," Juraviel said to Cazzira as they sat together on the low boughs of a tree. "I would have expected no less of a force led by Aydrian."

"Why is he coming?" Cazzira asked, and it was not the first time. "If these humans are as deserving as you have told my people from the beginning, then why has young Aydrian betrayed the trust of the Tylwyn Tou?"

Belli'mar Juraviel looked away, his expression grim. Dasslerond had told him of her last encounter with the young ranger, of Aydrian's magical assault that had nearly left her dead. She had known that he would return—which was why she had honestly bid Jilseponie to help her to fight the young king—and so this marching force had not been wholly unexpected.

Juraviel had led a sizable force of Touel'alfar out of Andur'Blough Inninness then, moving to shadow the approaching army, using the elven song to try to dissuade some soldiers.

It wasn't working.

"Blynnie Sennanil has them in sight," came the call of another elf from the base of the tree, and the pair looked down. "At your word, she and her archers will begin punctuating our warning with arrows."

For Juraviel, this order was about as difficult as any he had ever issued. On this point, though, Lady Dasslerond had been uncompromising; if the humans couldn't be persuaded to leave by magically enhanced whispers on the night breeze, then Juraviel was to strike terror into their ranks, stinging them in the dark, killing them as they slept.

He hesitated only long enough to remind himself of Dasslerond's expression when she had sent him out, one that left no doubts in his mind, as there were obviously none in hers, that Aydrian would indeed find his way to Andur'Blough Inninness, and that Aydrian meant to destroy it.

"At her discretion," Juraviel replied, and the elf below disappeared into the shadows.

"Perhaps someday you will find it in your heart to answer me," Cazzira remarked when Juraviel turned back to her.

Her tone and look stung Juraviel's heart. "Perhaps someday I will better understand why young Aydrian is so removed from the hearts of his father and his mother," he answered, putting a gentle hand on Cazzira's delicate fingers. "Nightbird was as great a human as I have ever known, and Jilseponie proved to be a worthy companion for him."

"You have never spoken of either with anything less than sincere admiration," Cazzira agreed. "But what of Aydrian? How is it that he, raised in the shadows of your valley, has turned so wrong?"

"It may be precisely that," Juraviel replied. "I do not believe that we were wise in bringing the baby Aydrian into our care that dark night on the field outside of the human city of Palmaris. Does a child not belong with its mother?"

"All ill has come from it," Cazzira agreed. "Jilseponie hates you, and Aydrian hates you.

Powerful enemies."

"Jilseponie is wounded and disappointed, but she is no enemy," Juraviel insisted.

"And Aydrian?"

"He is angry, and he is misguided—more so than I ever would have believed possible."

"They will not leave," Cazzira observed. "We will be forced to fight them."

That did not seem like a welcome option to Belli'mar Juraviel.

Cazzira shuddered then, suddenly, her dark eyes going wide as she glanced all about.

"What is it?" Juraviel asked, coming on his guard.

"A coldness," the Doc'alfar female replied. "I do not know. Something passed us, much like the sensation of the spirit departing the human bodies when we offer them to the bog."

Juraviel, too, glanced all around nervously, trusting Cazzira's senses, though he knew not what she meant. A moment later, they locked stares.

"I know not," Cazzira said again.

*   *   *

They marched in hard toward the copse, with Aydrian out front and leading the way, and with Sadye right beside him, playing a rousing song on her lute, the music lifting the spirits of the men all about their king.

"Touel'alfar!" Aydrian cried. "I will see your Lady Dasslerond!"

When no answer came forth, the young king lifted his hand toward the left side of the small and fairly contained grouping of trees and sent forth a burst of brilliant, stinging lightning. He shifted right immediately and fired again, singeing the trees and lighting several boughs.

He brought his free hand up behind him and waved left and right, and his disciplined force broke both ways, rushing to encircle the trees around both sides.

Aydrian strode forward powerfully. "Now, I demand!" he shouted. "Or I shall tear your precious valley down around you!"

A score of small arrows whistled out of the trees, every one slashing unerringly toward the young King. Aydrian didn't flinch, other than to grab Sadye and pull her defensively behind him. He knew the designs of the Touel'alfar and understood that all of those arrows would be tipped with silverel. He reached into the magical gemstones set in the chest plate of his magnificent armor and brought forth a wave of magnetic energy that turned the bolts as surely as any shield.

And then he reached out again with his graphite and loosed a series of devastating lightning strokes that cut searing lines through the trees. And then he shouted out for a charge, and his soldiers rushed the copse, waving swords and spears.

Arrows reached out at the charging soldiers, and several fell clutching devastating wounds.

In front of the trees, Aydrian watched closely, marking the source of an arrow and responding with a lightning blast that threw the poor elf out the other side, dropping her charred form to the ground.

"By god," Sadye whispered, her mouth agape. "Aydrian . . . this is . . ."

He wasn't even listening. He charged straight in behind that last blast of sizzling energy, bringing forth his magnetic lodestone shield and a second, bluish white glowing energy about his body.

He heard a cry, and recognized Juraviel's voice, the elf telling his kin to run away.

Under the trees went Aydrian, reaching into a third stone, the ruby set on the pommel of Tempest, his wondrous sword. The fireball engulfed the central area of the copse and had most of the elves running, and had a few others tumbling from the boughs, their bodies aflame.

Aydrian scrambled out to the right, to see an elf faced off against one of his soldiers. The poor lumbering Kingsman strode forward and took a roundhouse swing that never came close to hitting. The elf skittered back out of reach, then came forward with sudden and devastating efficiency, driving his slender sword in through a seam in the man's armor.

As the man fell away, clutching a brutal wound, a smiling Aydrian took his place.

"And so we meet, traitor," said the elf, whom Aydrian recognized as Tes'ten Duvii. "For years, I have desired my chance at laying low the errant son of Elbryan the Nightbird!" With that, the elf came forward, but in a measured way, the thrust of his sword more to measure Aydrian's response than any honest attempt to hit.

Aydrian didn't have time to play. He leveled Tempest at his enemy and sent a surge of energy through the graphite he had set in the pommel, and a bolt of lightning struck Tes'ten full force, lifting him from the ground and hurtling him backward to smash into a tree. Aydrian's lightning held the poor elf there for a long moment and charred the tree behind him.

"And so you had your chance," the young king taunted, though the elf was far beyond hearing him or hearing anything ever again. "Do you feel fulfilled?"

With a grin that was, in truth, more a grimace, Aydrian turned aside. "Juraviel!" he cried. "I know you are about! Come and face me here and now!"

But Juraviel did not come out, as far as Aydrian could see, and as abruptly as it had begun, the fighting was over.

"They're running off to the west!" one Kingsman cried.

"Do we pursue, my lord?" another man closer to Aydrian asked him.

Aydrian smiled and shook his head. "Let them run—all the way back to Andur'Blough Inninness. They have nowhere to truly hide."

Soon after, Aydrian's expeditionary force returned to the main group, bearing six dead and nearly a score of wounded, several seriously, and leaving behind the seven Touel'alfar who had fallen, all but one killed by Aydrian's magical blasts.

When they returned, Aydrian soon learned that his encampment had not been quiet in his absence, for groups of elves had begun striking at the soldiers helter-skelter almost as soon as he had departed. The men were doing well in responding, offering batteries of archers to launch devastating volleys in the general direction whenever a tiny arrow came in from the darkness, but as yet, they had located no enemy bodies.

"Kill them as they come into view," Aydrian said to his commanders. With Sadye beside him, the woman still obviously shaken from the fight at the copse, he went into his tent.

"They think that they can stand before me," Aydrian said. "They still do not understand the truth of Aydrian Boudabras!"

"How profoundly you hate them," Sadye remarked. "Back there, at the copse of trees . . ."

"I repaid the slavers," Aydrian interrupted, and he motioned for Sadye to sit beside him. Then he lifted the soul stone for her to see, offered a wink, and closed his eyes, falling into the hematite, spirit-walking once more.

Drifting into the trees, he soon enough found a pair of elven archers.

Aydrian didn't hesitate, sliding into the body of one of the elves, catching her off her guard and pushing her spirit from her body. He knew that he couldn't likely hold out for long—the Touel'alfar were strong of will, much more so than any human!—but he didn't need long. In control of the body for only that brief moment, Aydrian darted from the trees, waving his elven arms and crying out.

His spirit was pushed from that diminutive form, willingly so, in time for the returning elf to see the host of deadly arrows speeding her way. Any one of the ten that hit her would have slain her.

Back in the trees, the other elf was crying out for his foolhardy companion when Aydrian assaulted him as well.

But this one, more prepared perhaps because of witnessing the fall of his companion, fought back more forcefully, crying out "demon!" over and over again to warn his friends. He even managed to shout out, "Possession!"

The human archers homed in on those cries, though, and sent their arrows soaring into the trees. Ninety-nine of the hundred that came in missed the unseen mark.

But it only took one.

Weary from his great exertion, Aydrian nonetheless tried to continue, his spirit sweeping along the perimeter of his encampment.

But the Touel'alfar were never slow to react, and the young king found no others in the area.

Back in his corporeal form, Aydrian instructed his soldiers where to run out.

They returned shortly thereafter, bearing a grievously wounded elf, lying near death with an arrow through his side.

Aydrian found enough strength to use his hematite again to prevent the elf from dying.

"Keep him bound and under heavy watch," the weary king told his men. "This one will lead us true to Andur'Blough Inninness at first light!"

Belli'mar Juraviel and Lady Dasslerond stood on a high ridge along the mountains outside the mist-covered vale that housed Andur'Blough Inninness. The midday air was crisp and cold, a brilliant sun shining overhead. It all seemed so calm and peaceful, a moment frozen in time.

But both elves knew otherwise. Both knew that Aydrian and his army were fast approaching.

"He moves unerringly toward us," Dasslerond remarked.

Looking at her, her eyes closed in concentration, her green gemstone cupped in one hand, Juraviel knew that she spoke correctly. He knew it anyway, for the scouts had been coming in all morning, and every subsequent report showed that the distance between Aydrian's marching army and Andur'Blough Inninness was fast closing.

"I have ordered the skirmishers away from the humans," Juraviel informed his Lady.

Dasslerond looked at him out of the corner of her dazzling golden eyes. "The first line of defense of the Touel'alfar has always been to strike at any approaching enemy from the shadows," she remarked. "To wound our enemies in body and in heart in the hopes that they will turn from their folly."

"We cannot strike at Aydrian's flanks," Juraviel explained, though he knew that Dasslerond needed no explanation. "We have struck at him almost continually since the open fight at the trees. He finds our skirmishers and reveals them to his soldiers, or he attacks them with his own magics. A score of our people are missing, my Lady, and I fear that most are dead or captured."

Dasslerond closed her eyes at those burning words. The Touel'alfar were not a numerous folk in the human-dominated world, and twenty was no small number to their ranks.

"You would have us enter our valley and hide it within the mists of the emerald," Lady Dasslerond reasoned.

"At once, my Lady."

"Aydrian has a prisoner," Dasslerond informed him. "The emerald of our people has shown this to me. He scours her thoughts with his soul stone and she leads him, despite herself, to us."

"You can hide Andur'Blough Inninness even from her, then," Juraviel reasoned. "We must abandon her."

Again came that cold stare out the corner of Lady Dasslerond's eye. For a moment, she seemed as tall and terrible as Juraviel had ever seen her, but that instant passed, leaving Dasslerond appearing diminished and shaking Juraviel's faith in her before she ever admitted, "I cannot."

Juraviel's hopeful look turned to one of confusion.

"Our captive kin would demand no less of you!" Juraviel argued.

"I can leave her to her fate, though it troubles me," Lady Dasslerond clarified. "But even so, I cannot hide our valley from Aydrian."

Few words could have hit Juraviel as hard.

"Aydrian follows me into the magical realm," Lady Dasslerond explained. "His power is greater than mine. He unwinds all that I weave."

"Then we are lost," Juraviel remarked. "Or Andur'Blough Inninness is lost. We cannot hope to fight him."

"Hold out your hand," Lady Dasslerond instructed him, and after a confused moment, the male complied.

Lady Dasslerond's right hand went to her hip, drew forth her small dagger, then reached out and cut Juraviel across the palm. He flinched, but did not pull back from her.

The Lady of Caer'alfar reached out her left hand, opening it palm up and rolling the precious emerald to her fingers. Without flinching, without the slightest quiver, she reached over and cut her own palm, then rolled the emerald back into the palm, over her wound, and turned her hand over and placed it atop Juraviel's.

"Pestiil pe'infor testu," the Lady intoned.

Juraviel's eyes widened at the sound of the words, which meant, "So I give my knowledge." This was the beginning of the transfer of Touel'alfar power, a chant which, once begun, could not be halted.

Lady Dasslerond chanted on. Her words wound and disappeared to Juraviel's sensibilities, replaced by a sudden rush of insight as the secrets of the emerald began to unravel in his thoughts.

Juraviel closed his eyes and fell within himself. Time itself seemed to stop, or to flow at a different rate. His mind pictured places that he knew from his travels. He saw Mount Aida and Avelyn's arm—not a memory, but a present-time image of the place! He saw Dundalis and Tymwyvenne, home of Cazzira's people, far to the south. And he knew that he could go to these places through the power of the emerald. He could warp time and space itself within its tremendous powers.

All sensation suddenly stopped, leaving Juraviel in blackness. It took him a long while to open his eyes, and when he did, he realized that he and Dasslerond were no longer alone on that high ridge.

And he felt tired, so tired.

"Lady, what will you do?" he managed to whisper, when Dasslerond retracted her hand, leaving the emerald upon his. Truly Juraviel was glad when Cazzira moved next to him and put her arm about his waist, giving him needed support.

An honest smile warmed over Lady Dasslerond's face, and she seemed to Juraviel somehow changed, somehow freed of her burdens.

"Aydrian has come for a fight," she said, her voice serene, more so than Juraviel had ever heard. "I will show him the ultimate escape. Take all of our people out of Andur'Blough Inninness, Belli'mar Juraviel. Take them and your dear wife and our visiting Doc'alfar king and be long gone from this place. You have the gemstone now. You know how."

"Lady, you cannot!"

"Do not question me, Belli'mar Juraviel. I knew the dangers of Aydrian, and it was my own folly that brought those dangers down upon us. Now I must pay for my errors. Be quick, I insist, while the resonating powers of the emerald remain with my body and soul."

Juraviel reached up to wipe away the tears that were suddenly streaming down his face. "My Lady," he whispered.

Smiling with absolute contentment, Lady Dasslerond turned to Cazzira. "My life has been long and fulfilling. My regret, though, is that I cannot witness the true reunion of our peoples. Brave Cazzira, bear well the children of Belli'mar Juraviel, who will this day rule the Touel'alfar. And bid your King Eltiraaz to show mercy to his cousins, who need his benevolence this dark day."

"Of course, my Lady Dasslerond," Cazzira replied.

Lady Dasslerond lifted her bloody hand above her head and clenched her fist. She looked at Juraviel and Cazzira one last time out of the corner of her golden eyes.

Then she threw her head back, and she was gone.

Cazzira turned her questioning stare over Juraviel, who stood staring at the pulsing emerald, feeling its transmission of power to the Lady who had been one with it for many centuries. How keenly that energy flowed now! Juraviel could feel every pulse in his own cut palm, as if his life energy and Dasslerond's were joined in the hub that was the pulsating emerald.

Juraviel took a deep breath, steadying himself and steeling himself against the wave of regret and sadness. "We must be gone from this place, all of us, and quickly."

"What of Andur'Blough Inninness?"

Juraviel looked up at the mountains and slowly shook his head.

A great commotion erupted at the front of the marching army when the Lady of Caer'alfar appeared suddenly before them, literally out of thin air. Some men fell back, others charged.

But Dasslerond raised her bloody hand and reached back across the miles to the powers of the emerald. The ground heaved before her and rolled out like a wave, scattering the charging fools and throwing many of the others back against the trailing ranks of humans.

Some warriors lifted bows and let fly, but their feeble arrows never got anywhere near the gemstone-protected Lady.

But then one man strode forward, a wry smile on his face, and Dasslerond didn't even bother to try to throw her gemstone magic at him.

"Too long have I waited for this moment, Dasslerond," Aydrian casually remarked. "It was your grave error in training me. You made me too strong."

"My greatest error was in not allowing you to die on the field outside of Palmaris," Lady Dasslerond replied. "For I erred in my estimation of your parentage. I thought Elbryan to be your father, but in truth it was Bestesbulzibar!"

Aydrian laughed at her. "Because I reject you and your wretched kin? Because I have become too great to be controlled by the Touel'alfar? You fear me and taunt me because you know that you cannot defeat me!"

"I already have," Dasslerond calmly replied, and she lifted her hand and whipped it about, chanting as she moved and filling the air about her with the crimson mist of her flowing lifeblood.

Aydrian responded with a snarl and a burst of his own magic, lifting Tempest and surging his power through it, shooting a tremendous bolt of lightning at the slender figure of the elven Lady.

But that lightning dispersed about the wall of crimson mist, leaving Dasslerond untouched. Slowly she began to turn, keeping her hand up above her.

"So flows my blood, so flows my soul," she intoned. "So swirls my blood, so swirls my home."

"What foolishness?" Aydrian started to ask.

"In crimson mist and spirit wound, within my heart is valley bound."

Aydrian began to catch on, his eyes widening, his lips turning into a snarl. "No!" he cried, and he fired another lightning bolt, the greatest blast of all, and ordered his men to charge at the elf.

But Dasslerond continued to spin unabated before him, her upraised hand winding her in a globe of unbroken reddish hue.

Aydrian's soldiers charged, crying out for their king, but those in the front, whose weapons first touched Dasslerond's mist, were stopped cold, their weapons and then their bodies erupting in biting red flames. They fell away, screaming, and those behind skidded to a stop.

A snarling and growling Aydrian pushed through them to face his nemesis. "What witchery is this, Dasslerond?" he demanded.

"And none shall find this secret place," she went on, stopping her spin to face Aydrian directly. "Not a path and not a trace. And not a bird's call from within, and not the wind's unending hymn. Not friend nor foe shall know my home, unless the blood of my enemy mixes with my own."

She finished then, and seemed quite pleased with herself as she stood staring at the befuddled Aydrian.

"I am defeated, Aydrian," she admitted, and her voice seemed very thin at that moment, and her body itself seemed to be shrinking, as the red globe about her grew richer and larger. "But Andur'Blough Inninness is denied to you."

"I will find it!" Aydrian growled.

Dasslerond merely smiled, and then she melted away, leaving the glowing and pulsating crimson mist. Immediately it began to swirl, bringing forth a wind that had all of the humans except for Aydrian backing away in fear. Faster and faster Dasslerond's tornado spun, and then it swept up and away and flew off to the west.

"No," Aydrian growled and he freed his spirt from his corporeal body with a mere thought to the soul stone set in the chest plate of his armor.

He caught up to that mist and followed it, even rushing ahead as it neared Andur'Blough Inninness. For a brief moment, Aydrian's spirit was once again within the magical borders of the elven valley, the place where he had been raised from infancy.

But then he had to flee—and he was nearly trapped within and destroyed!—as Dasslerond's bloody mist came upon the valley, widening to encompass it all.

From a short distance away, Aydrian's spirit watched as all the valley of Andur'Blough Inninness fell within the swirl of that tornado, the enchanted fog that perpetually covered the place mingling with the crimson cloud, the very trees and ground warping within the swirl.

And then it was gone, as Dasslerond had gone, and Aydrian's spirit was thrown back into his body.

The weight of that return nearly knocked the young king from his feet, and would have had not Sadye moved to his side to support him. As he absorbed more completely the truth of what had transpired before him, the truth of Dasslerond's enchantment, he nearly fell over again.

"Damn you!" the frustrated Aydrian cried into the now-empty wind. "Damn you, Dasslerond!"

She was gone to the world now, having given herself to her enchantment. But his victory was a hollow one, Aydrian knew, for in going, she had taken from him any hope of conquering Andur'Blough Inninness.

And that place, he knew, meant more to Lady Dasslerond than her own life ever could.

PART FOUR

HEROES PAST AND HEROES PRESENT

The Bearmen have wasted no time in filling the void left by the revelations and downfall of Chezru Chieftain Yakim Douan. With Behren in turmoil, Abbot Olin has led the charge from Honce-the-Bear, and has done so accompanied by thousands of soldiers serving the new King Aydrian. A sizable portion of the northern kingdom's great fleet has joined in, as well.

I gather information of that northern kingdom as I find it, and with great interest, because this new king, this young Aydrian trained by the Touel'alfar, frightens me. He has seized control of the most powerful kingdom in all the world, somehow, and quickly and securely enough for him to look already outside his own borders to expand his domain. If he gains Behren, as it seems he surely will and possibly already has, then no force will be able to resist him.

I spoke with several Abellican monks in the city of Avrou Eesa and came to learn that their Church is in turmoil, with the reigning hierarchy holed up at the great abbey of St.-Mere-Abelle, not only opposing the legitimacy of Aydrian, but also the new order envisioned by Abbot Olin. And yet, despite this ongoing struggle within their own borders, this young king and the abbot of Entel have seen fit to insinuate themselves in the turmoil of Behren. Aydrian strikes with the design of an imperialist, and that, I fear, will mean danger for all the world.

Aydrian's confidence is stunning, especially from one so young—for he is several years younger than Brynn, even, and she is far below the age one would expect of someone sitting on the throne of a great nation. I see, therefore, in Aydrian, the first mark of a great man, for a great man is one who truly has come to understand that no one is better than he.

That confidence inspires ambition unbridled, and only with such a tool could someone truly rise to such heights. But only after those heights are attained can a true measure of the man be taken. For then the leader faces a challenge of empathy. With great success oft comes a sense of entitlement to that success. The wealthy merchant, the landowner, the feudal lord, the king, the abbot all risk the danger of dismissing good fortune as part of their rise, instead coming to view their fortune and power as something that separates them from the common folk. Even those whose position was gained through heredity instead of effort share this dilemma, oftentimes, illogically, more so.

Was heredity a factor in bringing young Aydrian to the throne?

Whether that is true or not, whether it was effort or heredity or a combination of the two, Aydrian's temperament might well prove to be the determining factor in the lives of hundreds of thousands of people *over the next few years. If he has internally elevated himself above the rabble, as his imperialistic exhibitions seem to indicate, then the world will know war on a grand scale, and for no better reason than to satisfy the ambitions of a few men.*

Brynn ascended to power through effort and determination and no small amount of luck. Had she not encountered Agradeleous on her journey through the Path of Starless Night, she would have lacked the tools truly to overcome the Behrenese. But with her rise to power, Brynn Dharielle never forgot the second truth of a great human. She has cried for every life destroyed in the To-gai uprising, To-gai-ru and Behrenese alike. She understands and appreciates the sacrifice and bravery of her own soldiers, the sacrifice of those To-gai-ru they left behind to tend the villages, and the pain brought to innocent Behrenese as well. Even the Behrenese soldiers, Brynn understands, are men swept up in a situation beyond their control.

Brynn cannot dismiss any of them, which is why she understands her position to be more of a burden than a pleasure, more of a necessary responsibility to her community than an avenue of self-gain. Her overriding desire is for peace and prosperity, for her own people and for her neighbors. She would be grateful if her rule over To-gai became an uneventful one, measured in the calmness of passing years rather than in the false glory of murderous conquest. If every kingdom in all the world were ruled by people of mind akin to Brynn Dharielle, then the brotherhood of man would know its greatest age.

And so I must come to understand this Aydrian and the motivations behind his insinuation in the southland. I must come to understand the motivations of those who have guided him on his ascent and who now serve as his advisors. Are they all akin to Abbot Olin, who so obviously has craved Behren and now seizes upon the southern kingdom's weakness to his own gain?

This danger cannot be underestimated, for young Aydrian is so obviously possessed of the first knowledge of what it is to be a great man. That knowledge, if not in league with the second tenet, is a truly dangerous thing.

A great man knows that no one is better than he.

But a truly great man appreciates, too, that he is no better than anyone else.

—Pagonel

❖ 28 ❖

When Aydrian
Comes Knocking

"They are efficient, if nothing else," Brynn said sarcastically. She stood next to Pagonel on the battlement of Dharyan-Dharielle, looking out over the southern sands where the great army of Jacintha had assembled under the dual banners of Chezru and, amazingly, the Abellican Church.

"Yatol De Hamman must have come straight from Avrou Eesa," Pagonel agreed. "I would have expected him to turn his attention to the south to solidify all of Behren under Yatol Wadon first." Still, the mystic gave a sigh of relief that they had not been caught unawares. In addition to the forces Brynn had ordered mustered at the plateau divide, the woman had sent out some of her own garrison commanders and the dragon Agradeleous to organize the line.

"You believe that he erred?" Brynn's hopeful look, the woman grasping at a possible weakness, reminded Pagonel of just how young and inexperienced she was.

"That, or we have underestimated the power of Jacintha with the addition of Abbot Olin's forces," the mystic answered, and he made it clear with his tone that he thought the latter the more likely scenario. "Few of Behren's western cities gave allegiance to Yatol Bardoh, and so with Avrou Eesa gone over to Jacintha, Yatol De Hamman might well believe—and might well be correct in believing—that Behren is once again under the great tent of Jacintha. Still, even if that is true, I would have expected Yatol De Hamman to move more cautiously before marching with such numbers to Dharyan-Dharielle."

"Abbot Olin wants all of traditional Behren back, it would seem," said Brynn, and Pagonel saw the hints of fires light behind her rich brown eyes, those same old simmering fires that had propelled the woman to victory over the Behrenese.

"It is not Abbot Olin who truly concerns me," the mystic said. "But rather, your friend who is now king."

"We do not know where Aydrian truly stands with all of this," came a defensive reply. "He may not even know of Olin's moves upon Jacintha."

"Abbot Olin came in with ten thousand Honce-the-Bear soldiers," Pagonel reminded.

"Most mercenaries."

"But all marching under the new flag of Aydrian's kingdom. And Abbot Olin was supported by the fleet of Honce-the-Bear. If Abbot Olin, who is not even the Father Abbot of the Abellican Church, can muster that strength on his own, then I would guess that your friend's kingdom is in true turmoil."

Brynn's expression told the mystic that he had won the point.

"Riders," Brynn remarked, motioning to the side, where a group of soldiers had broken away from De Hamman's gathered force and were running their mounts hard for Dharyan-Dharielle's southern gate. Brynn started off toward that gate, with Pagonel right behind, and they arrived at the battlement atop the eastern gatetower just as the group of riders pulled up outside. They carried three flags: that of Jacintha, that of the Abellican evergreen symbol, and that of truce. They walked their mounts right up before the closed gate.

"I bring great tidings!" cried the man centering the group, a burly Behrenese warrior, though not a Chezhou-Lei. He wore a great moustache that ran down from the sides of his lips and off his chin in tightly wound braids. His hair was black and bushy, sticking out all about his head from under the band of his turban.

"Deliver them, then!" Brynn cried back before the gatekeeper could answer.

The Behrenese soldier looked up at her, and recognition flashed on his swarthy features. "Dragon of To-gai!" he called. "My master, Yatol De Hamman, bids me inform you, with great joy, that Behren is united once again!"

Brynn turned a nervous glance over at Pagonel.

"We send our gratitude to you again, Dragon of To-gai, for your assistance in turning the battle against those who would have denied Yatol Mado Wadon of Jacintha the crown," the courier continued. "My master and his masters relay that they are indebted." As he finished, he dipped a polite bow, bending over the side of his roan horse's neck.

"Masters," Brynn said softly, so that only Pagonel could hear. "Not master."

"Abbot Olin has done well for himself," the mystic dryly replied.

"I speak for To-gai, and To-gai wishes Yatol Mado Wadon well as he seeks to lead Behren from the turmoil of war's aftermath," Brynn called down to the man. "But I am confused as to why your Yatol De Hamman sees fit to march upon Dharyan-Dharielle with his army."

"To march upon?" the man echoed doubtfully. "No, my good lady of To-gai. Yatol De Hamman wished to personally deliver to you the news of our great victory and of Behren's reunification. Thus we have marched north before turning east to our homes."

"Relay my congratulations to Yatol De Hamman, then," said Brynn. "And I bid you all speed and good fortune on your long march eastward."

The man assumed a pensive pose, then, as if she had caught him off his guard.

"Good lady," he called up a few moments later, "are not the gates of Dharyan-Dharielle open to Behrenese and To-gai-ru alike? By agreement and by word, is your city not an open city?"

"It is."

A wide smile erupted under that great moustache. "Then we bid you throw wide your gates and allow us admittance. We would rest and resupply, and commence the revelry of our great victory with our allies, the To-gai-ru!"

Brynn turned to Pagonel. "Well," she said, "there is a twist. The aggressor wishes the gates thrown wide."

"It would be far easier for Yatol De Hamman to send word to Jacintha that Behren's old border has been restored if he did not have to fight his way over your strengthened wall," Pagonel replied.

"Then you believe that De Hamman has paid us this visit for more than a courtesy call?"

Pagonel looked back over the southern sands to the great assembled force. "If Behren is truly secured and his intentions are as his courier has stated, then why would he come here with ten thousand warriors? Dharyan-Dharielle could not resupply them all in any short order, and Yatol De Hamman knows that. Nor is Dharyan-Dharielle a considerably easier march from Avrou Eesa than Jacintha itself. He has crossed a huge expanse of open desert to come to pay you a visit, my friend."

"Whereas his march back to Jacintha from Avrou Eesa would have been along a defined road, lined by oases," Brynn finished the reasoning.

"So will you open wide your gates?"

"As soon as I have finished opening the horse corral for the wolf pack," a determined Brynn replied, and she looked back out at the courier. "We have not the facilities for so large a force," she called. "Our stables alone would be overwhelmed. Nor do we have sufficient supplies on hand to carry such a force all the way to Jacintha. Twoscore at a time, you may enter and resupply."

The man hesitated. "My master, Yatol De Hamman wishes to be done here more quickly than that, I fear," he called. "He bids that you throw wide your gates, as per your agreement with Yatol Mado Wadon upon the treaty between our countries that ceded Dharyan into your province. We will not tarry long about your fair city, Dragon of To-gai. We have horses needing shoeing and waterskins for dipping."

"Indeed," Brynn replied. "And so you shall have your needs fulfilled— twoscore at a time."

"But my master—"

"Those are the terms, courier."

"There is a treaty here to be considered."

"And so I have," Brynn replied, her voice strong and firm. "Twoscore at a time."

The courier started to respond, but apparently thought the better of it. He motioned to his men and they wheeled their horses about and went galloping back to the Behrenese line.

Brynn looked to Pagonel and the mystic nodded his approval. Then she looked past him, to one of her guard commanders, and said quietly, "Muster all the warriors, but keep them below the wall top. Send the signalers to the towers."

"What word shall they send?"

"None as yet," Brynn explained. "Tanalk Grenk and his warriors are not far, nor is Agradeleous. If we need them, they will come with all speed."

The commander nodded and hustled away.

"Yatol De Hamman will waste no time," Pagonel remarked a few moments later, when the couriers were almost back to the distant Behrenese line.

"You believe he will dare to attack?"

"Or encircle," the mystic replied. "Yatol De Hamman would not take this initiative on his own—particularly not with soldiers of Honce-the-Bear among his ranks. He comes here under orders from Yatol Wadon."

"And Abbot Olin."

"Likely," the mystic agreed.

"But to what end? Does Abbot Olin act so boldly as to begin a war with To-gai before Behren is even properly secured? Were we not declared as allies only a few weeks ago in Yatol Mado Wadon's own palace?"

"We do not know if our fears are correct," Pagonel replied. "Perhaps this is, as the courier said, an honest visit."

Even as he spoke, though, the distant forces began to stir, moving left and right with practiced precision, widening the line as if preparing a charge.

"Perhaps the leaders of Jacintha now wish to test you for themselves. I hold no doubt that Abbot Olin's designs are imperialistic, and if that is the case, he surely desires this city returned to Behren."

"We held off the Behrenese once before," came a determined reply, but the woman's gritty resolve seemed less apparent when she turned to face the knowing Pagonel once more.

"The fall of Chezru Chieftain Yakim Douan precipitated the Behrenese retreat more than any victory won here," Pagonel said quietly. "How long would you have held off Yatol Tohen Bardoh if Jacintha had not recalled her forces?"

"True enough," Brynn admitted. "And now they are reinforced by gemstone-wielding Abellicans and the armored warriors of the northland." She paused a moment to reflect. "I trusted Yatol Wadon. Was that my error?"

"You could not have foreseen the insinuation of Abbot Olin's designs," Pagonel said to her.

From the center of the Behrenese line came forth another group of riders, this one centered by the familiar figure of Yatol De Hamman.

"Brynn Dharielle!" he called when he neared the gate. "What folly is this? Was our cause not one and the same when you ventured to Jacintha to aid in the struggle against Tohen Bardoh and the dog Peridan? Was it not your own fine sword that took the head of the hated Bardoh?"

"Indeed, Yatol, it was, and we were allied as you say," Brynn replied. "And so I am perplexed to see an army of Yatol Wadon's Jacintha assembled before the gates of my city."

She started to go on, but Pagonel nudged her. "Not publicly," he whispered.

Brynn looked back to De Hamman and motioned for him to wait, then she and Pagonel moved down the tower's staircase and out the small door set beside the city's great gate.

The mystic noted that De Hamman did not dismount as he and Brynn approached.

"You understand that we are friends, do you not?" De Hamman asked from his seat on high. "Despite our differences in Avrou Eesa, the name of Brynn Dharielle is not known as an enemy to Yatol Wadon's Behren."

"And how is it known to Abbot Olin's Behren?" Brynn replied, and Pagonel nudged her again.

"Your present kingdom is confusing to us, Yatol," Pagonel quickly added to quell the mounting antagonism. "You have struck so quickly and decisively that we are still trying to discern the source of such momentum."

"We wish Behren restored—is that any surprise to you, Jhesta Tu?" the Yatol replied, and he turned a rather angry look over Brynn. "Abbot Olin has aided us in that cause as an ally, as we believed that Brynn and To-gai were our allies."

"And so we were, and so we are, if your goal is to restore your kingdom to a peaceful state under the rule of Chezru," said Brynn.

"It is."

"Then the peace between our peoples holds fast."

"I shall instruct my commanders to bring in their weary soldiers," the Yatol replied with a forced grin.

"Twoscore at a time."

De Hamman's expression turned sour in an instant. "That was never in the agreement that secured Dharyan for Brynn," he reminded.

"That agreement was for open commerce and the admittance of scholars seeking the tomes of the library. I do not extend it to include an invitation for an army to enter the walls of my city."

"Even a friendly army?"

"No army that is not under the control of To-gai will enter."

"Dissolve the treaty at your peril, Dragon of To-gai," the Yatol warned. "We have come as friends—"

"Then dismiss the bulk of your forces," Brynn cut in. "Send them along the road to Jacintha and their homes, and you and your remaining commanders may enter, as friends. I am not dissolving the treaty, but neither am I willing to allow a foreign army entry. No more so than Yatol Mado Wadon would allow me to march ten thousand To-gai-ru riders into Jacintha, whatever pretense we placed upon our visit."

"A foreign army," Yatol De Hamman echoed. "There are many who would not consider a Behrenese army foreign to the city of Dharyan."

"And so it would not be," the warrior woman replied, hardly backing down. "But Dharyan-Dharielle is not Dharyan, nor is it Behrenese. This city is To-gai, by the agreement of Yatol Mado Wadon himself."

"An agreement forged under duress, perhaps?"

"One that he has no choice but to honor, whatever the circumstances of its inception."

"Choice," said De Hamman, and he turned about and looked along his great line of warriors. "A curious word." He swung back to stare hard at Brynn. "And our two kingdoms stand on a steep precipice, one whose outcome will be decided by the choices of their leaders. A precipice as sharp as the plateau divide that separates Behren and To-gai—and do note, Dragon of To-gai, upon which side of that dividing line Dharyan resides."

He sat up tall and crossed his hands over the horn of his saddle, assuming a posture of complete confidence as he finished, "Choose wisely."

"I already have."

Pagonel silently congratulated Brynn's decisions, and the way she had handled the obstinate De Hamman. The man had gone from a pitiful and whining victim only a few short weeks ago, when Yatol Peridan had chased him all the way to Jacintha, to an overconfident warlord, sweeping across the desert sands.

He was dangerous now, the mystic understood, because De Hamman surely recognized that this battle looming before him, should he choose the course of battle, would be the most difficult by far since the fall of Peridan and Tohen Bardoh. Had he already acquired enough hubris to actually make the attempt?

Or was he looking for an easier way to claim victory?

The mystic's reasoning had his eyes darting about, scrutinizing all of De Hamman's escorts, and so he was not surprised a moment later when De Hamman signaled for them to retreat back to their line and one man lifted the edge of a blanket set across the front of his saddle.

Purely on instinct, Pagonel snapped his right hand out against Brynn's shoulder, knocking the surprised woman sidelong to the sand. Along with her grunt of protest, the mystic heard the click of a crossbow—a distinctly Honce-the-Bear, Abellican weapon!—and then felt a sudden and nasty burn in his forearm.

Hardly pausing to consider the wound, Pagonel rushed forward and leaped up, his flashing leg knifing by the horse, which was rearing and protesting as the assailant tugged at its reins. The mystic's foot caught the would-be assassin in the gut, throwing him back and to the ground.

Yatol De Hamman kicked his horse into a swift retreat, shouting, "Attack! Attack! I am under attack!" Several of his entourage turned and charged away with him, but a trio of others came on at Pagonel and Brynn.

Brynn picked herself off the ground and drew out Flamedancer in one swift movement, lighting its fiery blade right in the face of a charging horse. The beast reared and Brynn rolled around to the side, using the horse as a shield against a second attacker.

With both hands tugging hard on the reins of the frightened horse, the rider initially offered no defense against Brynn as she came spinning around. He did manage to bring his sword out wide in an attempted parry, but Brynn slapped it away and stabbed him hard in the side. He lurched and screamed and his horse leaped away, clearing the path between Brynn and the second rider, who lifted his spear to throw.

Pagonel landed easily from his strike and leaped again, taking the vacated seat. He expertly pulled the horse around to meet the charge of one rider, a lowered spear coming in hard for him. A slight twist and lift had that spear going under Pagonel's arm as the rider thundered by, and the mystic dropped his arm over the weapon, locking it in place, and held on with the concentration only a Jhesta Tu could accomplish.

The rider improvised, bringing his second arm over, swinging a heavy morning star for Pagonel's head. But the Jhesta Tu ducked the awkward assault easily and countered with three short and heavy punches. Then Pagonel spun his horse the other way and tugged fiercely on the trapped spear, and the Behrenese rider slipped from his saddle as his horse ran off. He held on stubbornly for a moment, hanging in the air off the side of Pagonel's mount, until the mystic simply released the spear, dropping him to the sand.

To his credit, the Behrenese soldier deftly rolled with the fall, coming around and over to his feet. To his misfortune, Pagonel proved the quicker, sliding from his seat and halting and reversing his momentum as he landed, spinning a devastating circle kick just as the man tried to rise. Pagonel's foot caught him in the side of the head and spun him over in nearly a complete somersault. He hit the ground hard and did not try to rise.

Pagonel turned his attention to the initial assailant, but the crossbowman was up and running, apparently wanting no part of the Jhesta Tu in open combat.

The mystic spun back to Brynn, who had assumed a defensive stance before a spearman poised to skewer her!

But then both Pagonel and Brynn winced and averted their eyes as a barrage of arrows overwhelmed the rider, a sudden rainstorm of death from the Dharyan-Dharielle wall. He got hit a dozen times, and was knocked right off the back of his wounded and frightened horse.

"Grab the horses!" Brynn instructed, and she went straight for the wounded one, grabbing it by the bridle and tugging straight down to steady the beast, while whispering calming words in its ear to quiet it. Behind her, Yatol De Hamman's charge was on.

Before her, the horns of Dharyan-Dharielle began to blow, and the defenders lifted their great bows.

"A short-lived peace," Brynn remarked, as she and Pagonel rushed through the gate.

The mystic merely sighed.

On came the Behrenese charge, the line closing fast. Back up on the wall, Brynn held the bulk of her forces in concealment, bringing them up little by little to the wall top, and keeping them crouched behind the shielding crenelations.

She looked up to the tower and motioned to the signalmen, who lifted great mirrors and put them into the sunlight, directing rays to the west and the plateau divide.

"Let them come closer," she ordered her soldiers as she walked along the wall, steadying the nervous archers with her solid attitude. "Our first volley must prove devastating."

De Hamman's riders and infantry charged in headlong, moving practically to the base of the wall, launching spears and arrows.

And then the To-gai-ru warriors sprang up, a line so thick that it stood shoulder to shoulder the length of that wall, and the hailstorm of arrows drove hard into the Behrenese ranks, stopping cold the bold assault.

"He did not know so many of our warriors had come into the city," Pagonel remarked.

Even as he finished the statement, however, a surge of lightning bolts reached out from the back of De Hamman's line, smashing in hard against the defenders, splitting stone and sending men flying from the wall.

Dharyan-Dharielle's great ballistae and catapults responded, sending balls of fiery pitch and gigantic spears into the masses, many heading for the general direction of the Abellican gemstone users.

It went on for many minutes right there below the walls, and Brynn assembled a group of strong warriors beside her, and followed Pagonel as he ran about, shoring up defenses wherever they seemed about to fall.

A second volley of lightning bolts flashed in at the city, this time all concentrated on Dharyan-Dharielle's southern gate. Wood splintered and bolts crackled, and the gates buckled inward. And right behind the thunderous blasts came a surge by a group of armored Honce-the-Bear soldiers, driving their equally armored mounts hard against the weakened barrier.

"Hold that gate at all costs!" Brynn cried from the wall a short distance away. She looked at Pagonel for guidance, but he was already engaged in battling a pair of men who had scaled the wall.

"Run on!" the mystic shouted to her. He knew that he had to score a hit quickly here, and so he did, ducking the slash of one man's sword and sweeping his leg out wide to trip the man up. Not even finishing that kick, trusting that he had the man enough off-balance, the mystic sprang up cat-like at the second warrior, rushing in before the man could bring his sword to bear. Pagonel's stiffened fingers smashed hard against the man's wind-pipe, stealing his breath and his balance.

The mystic caught him before he fell to his death, though, wrapping him in a tight embrace and turning him about as a human shield against the first man who was trying to recover and come back in.

The attacker hesitated and Pagonel threw the limp man to the ground between them, and even as the standing attacker's eyes instinctively looked down at his falling comrade, the mystic leaped forward, turning his legs un-der him and kicking out, launching the attacker over the wall.

Pagonel turned to regard Brynn, but to his relief, she was already moving along.

Brynn leaped down to the courtyard, the rest of her entourage close be-hind. "Mount up!" she ordered, knowing that foot soldiers would likely be overwhelmed by the riders pressing at the gate.

Men screamed all about her, horrible sounds of battle that Brynn Dharielle had prayed she would never again be forced to endure. She could hardly believe the sudden turn of events, and it pained her greatly to con-sider that Aydrian, her companion for so many years, was in fact the source of this chaos!

With fierce determination, the leader of To-gai climbed up on Runtly and led her force to the courtyard directly before the collapsing gates.

"Fight well," she said.

"Die well," came the appropriate To-gai-ru response.

Out in the distance, horns began to blow, and many cries of "Tanalk Grenk!" came echoing down from the walls.

Brynn nodded grimly, knowing that her loyal and able commander would strike hard at De Hamman's flank and ease some of the pressure on the town.

More hopeful and excited shouts came from the wall, and Brynn fol-lowed them to see many men pausing for just a moment, and pointing to the southwestern sky.

"Meet my dragon, Yatol De Hamman," the woman said grimly. She wished she could go and watch that spectacle—she did indeed!—but then the gate creaked and cracked, and one of the great doors tumbled down into the courtyard. Charging over it even as it fell came the rush of Honce-the-Bear cavalry.

"Fight well!" Brynn called again.

"Die well!" came the eager battle cry.

Brynn was first in, her solid pony not shying in the least as she took it right against the flank of one larger horse, and tightly in between that and a second. Flamedancer flashed left and then right, defeating one attack and initiating a second. The Bearman rider managed to block and started to counter, but Brynn maneuvered Runtly expertly out of his reach, and then the pony leaped back in at him in perfect coordination with her second stab.

This time, her sword got past the man's defenses and banged hard against his fine armor, the elven blade driving a crease that had him lurching. Not wasting a second, Brynn spun Runtly around to face the other warrior, and urged the pony to buck, its hind legs coming up and kicking hard against the stunned man's dented armor, launching him from his seat.

Now one against one, Brynn worked her sword in a series of slashes, stabs, and defensive parries, twice ringing her blade off the back of the Bearman's helmet, and three times scratching his solid chest plate. He tried to counter repeatedly, but each of the lumbering blows of his far heavier sword were neatly picked off, or hit nothing but air as Brynn dodged and retreated.

All along that courtyard, the To-gai-ru riders, as skilled on horseback as any in all the world, matched the Bearmen cut for cut, using speed and agility to counter heavier weapons and armor. They gave no ground, but neither were they gaining any, and the press behind the Bearman was greater, slowly but surely widening the breach at the gate.

"Archers!" Brynn called, trying desperately to redirect more fire into that breach, but her warriors all along the wall were too engaged already to offer much help. She did see Pagonel right above the gate, directing the fire of the archers and keeping the wall clear all about them so that they could concentrate on the impending disaster below, but she feared it would not be enough.

Beyond the wall, more lightning flashed, some streaming up into the air, and the screams increased tenfold, along with a sudden roar of agony, a cry so feral and huge that it made many men stop their fighting and cover their ears, and made others simply turn away and flee.

Following the cry came the crash as the dragon fell from the sky, skidding hard into the wall right beside the opened gate. Stone crumbled at that impact, launching defenders and attackers alike from the wall top. Even some of those archers above the gate were thrown down.

But not Pagonel.

The mystic held his ground stubbornly and cried out to the dragon, pointing to the breached gate. "Here, Agradeleous!"

Dragon fire filled that breach suddenly, immolating those poor attackers behind the front ranks of riders.

Pagonel climbed over the wall and dropped the dozen feet to the ground amidst that burning carnage. All about him, all about the nearby dragon, Behrenese were fleeing in terror. "Come," Pagonel bade the dragon.

Another volley of lightning bolts, diminished from the originals, but stinging nonetheless, reached out to slam against the wounded dragon's side.

"I so hate monks and their nasty toys!" Agradeleous roared, swinging his
reptilian neck about to face the distant gemstone-wielders. One fleeing man
inadvertently stumbled too close to the angry dragon, and Agradeleous
wasted no time in grabbing him up in his great jaws. He lifted the flailing
man up high so that many could see, then snapped his great maw fully.
Pieces of the dead man fell all about.

Agradeleous growled and roared and forced himself up on his haunches,
brushing aside blocks of the wall that had tumbled atop him.

Men shrank away from the spectacle, for the dragon seemed unbeatable
and all-powerful.

But Pagonel recognized the way the beast was favoring one wing and
knew that Agradeleous was sorely wounded from the lightning. Agradeleous took a step out from the wall, as if he meant to go after the monks.

"No!" Pagonel called to him. "That is what they want!"

The dragon turned on him, smoke wafting from his nostrils, licks of
flame erupting from the sides of his mouth, and sheer hatred shining in his
reptilian eyes.

"They are ready for you," the mystic explained. "They have the weapons that were built specifically for your destruction. And they have the
gemstones."

The dragon growled again, long and low, and then roared as yet another
lightning bolt flashed in against his great scaled side.

Pagonel continued to coax and to warn him, bidding him into the city.

Almost as soon as the mystic and the dragon crossed through the felled
gate, the remaining Bearman warriors threw down their swords, and the
courtyard and wall were secured.

A few moments later, the city's western gate swung open and Tanalk
Grenk led his force into Dharyan-Dharielle. All about the walls, archers ran
toward that area to send volleys at the pursuing Behrenese.

In truth, though, the battle was over. With the gates secured by the imposing dragon, the Behrenese retreated.

As Tanalk Grenk rode toward her, Brynn nodded her appreciation and
deference, for she knew that he had played his role to perfection. He had
come down with his skilled riders from their positions just along the shadows of the plateau divide, just to the southwest of Dharyan-Dharielle. With
the typical and unmatched ferocity of the To-gai-ru, Grenk had struck hard
at the Behrenese western flank, then immediately turned his forces in a run
to the western gate, diverting many Behrenese and easing the pressure on
the southern wall.

"We have won no victory here today," Brynn told Grenk and all the others nearby. "But we have held our enemy at bay and have stung them hard."
She looked all around, the determination in her blazing brown eyes stilling

all doubts and all confusion in a moment of crystalline clarity. "Perhaps we
have stung them hard enough to make them turn back for their homes."

"If not, there is always tomorrow," said a determined Grenk.

His unabashed support touched Brynn at that desperate moment, for she
knew that more than a few of her people would be privately questioning her
leadership at that time. Had these attackers not come from the same man
Brynn had just helped seat on the throne of Behren, after all?

But she did not allow any of her doubts to cloud her eyes or her strong
features.

"Shore up the gate," she instructed her warriors, then she dismounted
and walked off with Runtly to shore up her own resolve, reminding herself
of the peculiar circumstances and telling herself repeatedly that she had
done right in fighting the wicked Tohen Bardoh, whatever treachery Yatol
Wadon and Abbot Olin now offered.

She had to believe that.

CHAPTER

❖ 29 ❖

The Hopeful Miscalculation

Abbot Glendenhook of St. Gwendolyn crumpled the parchment in his large and strong hands. His thick brow furrowed over deep-set eyes and he clenched his huge fist powerfully, the muscles on his massive arm tightening the fabric of his brown robes. More than any other master of the Abellican Order, Toussan Glendenhook had ridden Fio Bou-raiy's coattails to power. For many years, he had walked in Bou-raiy's shadow, and willingly so. Glendenhook had accomplished much on his own, especially in the arts martial, where he had risen as one of the finest warriors to come out of St.-Mere-Abelle—not on a par with legendary Marcalo De'Unnero, of course, but Glendenhook had been the best of his class.

Still, Glendenhook had always been very aware that he had no chance of ever rising in the hierarchy beyond the rank of master—until, that is, his friend Bou-raiy had ascended the dais as the Abellican Church's Father Abbot. Glendenhook had been there every step of the way with Fio Bou-raiy, supporting his friend. When Bou-raiy had made his successful bid for the position of Father Abbot, Glendenhook had lobbied long and hard for the votes. Subsequent to gaining the seat in St.-Mere-Abelle, Fio Bou-raiy had repaid his loyal friend with this appointment as abbot of St. Gwendolyn, a monastery traditionally run by a woman.

There had been little resistance to the appointment; the then–Master Glendenhook had rushed to the rescue of St. Gwendolyn when the rogue De'Unnero had come to dominate the place, organizing his infamous Brothers Repentant from the ranks of the plague-devastated abbey. Over the last couple of years since his appointment, Abbot Glendenhook had compiled a strong record at the abbey and among the people of the neighboring villages. His abbey was among the leaders in per capita attendance and donations, and though he was not really a great follower of Avelyn Desbris and the reform that had swept the Abellican Church, Abbot Glendenhook had not reined in his sisters, brothers, and masters when they had desired to go out among the people with the healing soul stones. Like his mentor, Fio Bou-raiy, Abbot Glendenhook had adapted to the change, if not embracing it, and had brought St. Gwendolyn back from the ashes.

And now this.

The burly man looked down at the crumpled parchment, trying to find every angle between the actual words. He was not surprised, of course, to learn that Duke Kalas was fast approaching St. Gwendolyn with his enormous army; Glendenhook and all the other citizens of central and southern Honce-the-Bear had watched Kalas' march from Palmaris throughout the winter, with every town falling into obedient line. Kalas had cut a line straight out to the coast south of St. Gwendolyn, and so it had been obvious for nearly two weeks that he would not stop there, but would turn north to finish his blanketing march.

But this decree, from Duke Kalas himself, had not been so predictable, especially coming in some thirty miles ahead of the front ranks of Kalas' force! The nobleman had formally announced his approach, and his demand that St. Gwendolyn be opened to him and to King Aydrian Boudabras, and that the brothers and sisters of the abbey formally declare Abbot Olin and Master De'Unnero as the rightful leaders of the Abellican Order.

"He knows that we, that I, will never accede to the demands of Marcalo De'Unnero," Glendenhook said to Master Belasarus, another transplant from St.-Mere-Abelle.

"Not in any form!" the master declared. "The man is a dangerous rogue! He is beyond the bounds of rationality itself. There is no place in the Abellican Church for Marcalo De'Unnero, curse his name!"

Abbot Glendenhook patted his large hands in the air to calm the frightened and angry master. "Of course there is no place for him. Father Abbot Bou-raiy has formally banished Marcalo De'Unnero—he did so almost immediately after De'Unnero's disgrace in Palmaris at the hands of Sister Jilseponie."

"And now Abbot Olin has embraced him?" Master Belasarus spat incredulously. "Has the man gone mad?"

"Beyond mad, it would seem," said Glendenhook. "It is no secret that Abbot Olin did not take his defeat by Father Abbot Bou-raiy well. But never could we have imagined this."

"They will march to the gates of St.-Mere-Abelle," Master Belasarus reasoned. "Father Abbot Bou-raiy will not open the abbey for them. Does King Aydrian mean to tear those great gates down?"

Abbot Glendenhook looked down at the parchment once again and offered only a shrug. That was an issue that would be settled later in the season, it seemed, likely before midsummer's day. For Glendenhook now, though, the issue was here before him in the form of this letter. Why had Kalas sent it?

Glendenhook and Kalas had met only briefly a couple of times in their lives. In many ways, they were men cut of the same mold. Both lurked in the background of the true power, Fio Bou-raiy and Father Abbot Agronguerre for Glendenhook, and King Danube and now, apparently, King Aydrian for Kalas. They were generals in their respective armies, Glendenhook for the Church and Kalas for the crown. There had been no animosity between them, at least none that Glendenhook had ever noticed. Was it possible that Duke Kalas had sent this letter so far ahead of the army to give Glendenhook the opportunity to gather up his staff and escape to St.-Mere-Abelle? By all accounts, the roads to the mother abbey were clear of any soldiers.

"What do you want of me, Duke Kalas?" the abbot said quietly.

"He knows that we cannot open our gates for a king demanding such change within the Abellican Church," Master Belasarus remarked.

Glendenhook looked up at him.

"Duke Kalas surely understands that we, none of us, will ever accept the rule of Marcalo De'Unnero," the master explained. "Nor of Abbot Olin, unless he wins the position he so covets by our rules at a College of Abbots."

"Where is Olin?" Glendenhook asked. "Is he still in Behren?"

"By all accounts."

A soft knock sounded on the door of Glendenhook's office. The abbot motioned to Belasarus, who answered, opening the door wide to admit Sovereign Sister Treisa, the highest-ranking woman at the abbey, and a likely successor to Glendenhook. Before the storm that was Aydrian had clouded the Honce-the-Bear sky, there had been rumors that Father Abbot Bou-raiy intended to move Glendenhook to another position, perhaps even as abbot of St. Honce in Ursal, to thus elevate Sovereign Sister Treisa and restore St. Gwendolyn to the control of a woman. Nearing forty, the comely Treisa seemed more than ready to assume the mantle. She had lived through many trials during her years at St. Gwendolyn, including the devastation of the rosy plague and the perversion of Marcalo De'Unnero. She had come through it all with grace and dignity, and had returned from her personal pilgrimage to Mount Aida to partake of the Miracle of Avelyn with such a profound sense of serenity that she calmed any room simply by entering. She had supported Glendenhook brilliantly over the last couple of years, since her return from a walking tour of the Mantis Arm, and the two had become as close as any brother and sister of the Abellican Order dared. There were even rumors that their friendship had gone beyond propriety.

But no one really cared to investigate the rumors, and many actually hoped they were true. For whatever reason and by everyone's estimation—even Glendenhook's—Sovereign Sister Treisa had made Glendenhook a better and more generous abbot.

Abbot Glendenhook rose when she entered, offering a warm smile despite his foul mood.

The sovereign sister didn't return that smile. "Duke Kalas will arrive in two days," she explained. "His army has been spotted to the south, moving hard and without resistance."

"They will have to cross through two villages, and securing them may slow them," Master Belasarus offered.

"I would not count on that," Treisa replied. "His army's ranks have swollen. By all reports, he left Palmaris with a few thousand."

"What is the estimate of his force in the field now?" Glendenhook asked.

"Twenty thousand, perhaps. Perhaps more."

The staggering number had Glendenhook sliding back into his seat.

"All towns are rallying to King Aydrian," Treisa explained. "Their menfolk are running to join in Duke Kalas' glorious march."

"One that will take him to the gates of St.-Mere-Abelle, no doubt," a dour Belasarus added.

"Twenty thousand," Glendenhook echoed quietly.

"Perhaps more," Treisa said again. "There are rumors of a second force moving north to the west of here."

"Encircling us," Belasarus reasoned.

"So many have joined him," Glendenhook said, shaking his head.

"How could they not?" asked Treisa. "Duke Kalas and his Allheart Knights in their shining armor have stormed into every village, praising King Aydrian. To contest them would be suicide."

"To follow them is to deny the true line of kings!" Belasarus protested.

"The common folk care little who is their king, master," Treisa replied. "They care only that their families have enough to eat, and that their children might live more comfortably than they. All this rattle of politics is background gossip for the folk, unless the rattle leads to the misery of war."

"Which it certainly shall when Prince Midalis arrives," insisted Belasarus.

"If he is not too late," said Glendenhook, and his pessimism seemed for a moment as if it would knock Belasarus from his feet.

"They join Duke Kalas because they have no one to lead them otherwise," Treisa reasoned. "Perhaps King Aydrian's army will fracture when and if Prince Midalis arrives. Perhaps not."

"And what is the role of the Abellican Church in all of this, then?" asked Belasarus. "Are we to cater to the demands of the usurping young king if doing so means demanding the abdication of Father Abbot Fio Bou-raiy for the likes of Abbot Olin and Marcalo De'Unnero?"

"Of course not!" Abbot Glendenhook said without the slightest hesitation. He held a stern stare upon Belasarus for a bit, then softened his strong features as he turned back to Treisa. "What counsel do you offer?"

The woman paused a bit, her brow furrowing pensively beneath her black hair and showing only the slightest wrinkles of age. She chewed a bit on her bottom lip, a common twitch when she was deep in thought that often brought a smile to Glendenhook; and she turned her hazel eyes to the floor. Finally, she looked back up.

"If King Aydrian had remained secular and had not involved the Church in his theft of the throne, then I would counsel inaction," she explained, "even though his ascent adversely affected another sovereign sister and forced Jilseponie from Ursal. But since it was Abbot Olin and worse, Marcalo De'Unnero, at Aydrian's side, we cannot step away from it. No distance that we put between Church and State will hold. It is clear now that Aydrian means to instate one of his cohorts into the structure of the Abellican Order at the very highest level. Twelve significant chapels have been rolled under Duke Kalas' present march, and only those brothers who pledged their allegiance to King Aydrian and to both Abbot Olin and De'Unnero remain in place serving their communities. All others were forced away, or worse."

"We have heard such rumors from the brothers seeking refuge here," Glendenhook agreed.

"And so we must stand, on one side or the other," Treisa went on. She looked at Belasarus, then at Glendenhook, forcing their undivided attention. "We cannot stand with Abbot Olin and the traitorous De'Unnero. We cannot sacrifice our mortal souls."

"Then fight or run?" Belasarus asked of Glendenhook.

The abbot looked to Treisa for guidance.

"Neither," the sovereign sister said, and she squared her shoulders. "Do not close our gate to Duke Kalas, for he will merely trample it down. Let us resist with inaction. Let us not run from them, nor march with them, but rather, merely sit where we are."

"Does that not signify our acceptance of Abbot Olin and Marcalo De'Unnero?" asked an obviously confused Belasarus.

Treisa shook her head. "We will not allow it to seem so. Not to Duke Kalas and not to the folk of the land. We will surrender without a fight, because we cannot win, but we will not serve King Aydrian or his kingdom as long as he embraces such treachery in the Abellican Church. Let our example perhaps begin the first fissure in Duke Kalas' army, a slender crack that will widen when the true king of Honce-the-Bear marches south from Vanguard."

"We must make this clear if our statement is to have any effect," reasoned Belasarus.

"And we must ensure that our surrender does not strengthen Duke Kalas," Glendenhook reasoned. "Organize an escape by some of the younger and hardiest brothers. Let them take our treasures, particularly our gemstones, along the coast to St.-Mere-Abelle."

"Duke Kalas will not appreciate that," said Treisa.

"And it will perfectly outrage Marcalo De'Unnero, which makes it all the sweeter," Glendenhook agreed.

"But we need something more telling," Master Belasarus reasoned. "Something to ensure that the people all around, especially those commoners who have joined with Duke Kalas, understand that we do not support King Aydrian."

Glendenhook considered what options he might have, then noticed that Sovereign Sister Treisa's face had suddenly brightened. He prompted her with a look.

"My sisters and I are nearly finished with the altar cloth intended for the final canonization of Avelyn Desbris," she explained. "The image of the up-raised arm of Avelyn placed against a solid red background—the same image that Father Abbot Bou-raiy commissioned for the new window in the great keep of St.-Mere-Abelle."

"What do you propose to do with it?" the intrigued Glendenhook asked.

"Let us fly it above St. Gwendolyn, proudly so!" said Treisa. "And right beside it, let us fly the bear rampant of the Ursal line. By all accounts, Duke Kalas marches under a different flag, that of the bear and the tiger rampant, the flag of Aydrian Boudabras."

Abbot Glendenhook nodded his agreement—such a show as that would spread ear-to-ear all along the eastern stretches of Honce-the-Bear.

"But doing so will ensure that Abbot Olin and Marcalo De'Unnero gain the altar cloth of Avelyn's upcoming canonization," reasoned Belasarus.

"It is worth the price," Treisa decided before Glendenhook could speak. "In our show, we will send a message to St.-Mere-Abelle, as well, offering our vote for Brother Avelyn's long-overdue ascent to sainthood, and we will remind all the kingdom of the miracle that precipitated his rise."

Abbot Glendenhook had never shared Treisa's enthusiasm for Avelyn Desbris. Nor had Father Abbot Bou-raiy. But Bou-raiy and Glendenhook had long ago discussed the matter, and had agreed that Avelyn's rise was an avalanche that would bury any who opposed it. After the Miracle of Aida, with a majority of Honce-the-Bear's population making the difficult pil-grimage to be cured of the rosy plague, or insulated against its deadly ef-fects, there could be no denying the rise of Saint Avelyn. The process should have been completed several years before, but the typically ponder-ous Abellican Church simply hadn't gotten around to it yet—mostly, Glen-denhook knew, because his friend the Father Abbot was holding the final canonization in reserve against any potential crisis in the Church. Only the Father Abbot could finalize the process, and that gave Fio Bou-raiy a large stick indeed to wave against any upstart young brothers, particularly Brau-min Herde and his fellows of St. Precious and in Vanguard.

"Any who stay will do so out of choice," the abbot decided. "All who wish to flee for St.-Mere-Abelle should go out this very afternoon. And I strongly suggest that most of your sisters make that flight, Sister Treisa. We have precious few women in the Abellican ranks as it is."

Glendenhook's expression went very serious. "I would ask of you that you, too, make the pilgrimage."

"Then you have little understanding of my faith, Abbot Glendenhook," came the stern reply. "In my God, in St. Abelle, in my Church, and in my abbot."

While on one level he wanted to yell at her and scold her, Abbot Glendenhook could not help but smile at the determined and strong woman.

"Master Belasarus," he said, without ever taking his eyes from Treisa, "I bid you to lead our delegation to St.-Mere-Abelle. Tell Father Abbot Bouraiy of our actions here, of the flags we proudly fly."

"But . . ." the man started to argue, but he stopped and sighed. "Yes, Abbot, it will be done."

All the horizon was filled with their spear tips, an army greater than anything ever seen by the three dozen remaining brothers at St. Gwendolyn or the two hundred people of neighboring villages that had come in for shelter. They were not as practiced as the Kingsmen or the Coastpoint Guards, and certainly not as spectacular as the Allheart Knights, but what the peasant warriors who had joined up in the glorious march of Duke Kalas lacked in shining armor and precision marching, they more than made up for with the sheer weight of numbers.

Grim-faced and dirty-faced, they stood shoulder to shoulder in a line stretching all around the three sides of the abbey that did not face the sea, and in ranks five deep. Allheart Knights rode all about, bolstering men with their cries of duty and glory for king and country.

Centering the line was Kalas' primary force, the Kingsmen who had marched with him out of Palmaris, and they alone would have had little trouble in overrunning St. Gwendolyn, Abbot Glendenhook realized.

From the front, western gate of the abbey, the abbot looked up at the two flags, flapping hard in the ocean breeze. At least he had made a statement.

Calls along the ranks advanced Kalas' force, thickening the ranks and tightening the line as they moved in closer. Over the hills behind them came great catapults, and carts beside them piled with heavy stones. Glendenhook could see the faces of the soldiers clearly now, could see their eyes. They were not afraid, not even the peasants, because they knew that few would die if battle was joined this day.

If Duke Kalas called for a charge, St. Gwendolyn would be overrun in a matter of minutes.

Horns blew along the ranks and the approach halted, the front lines barely two hundred feet from the abbey's high walls. From the center of the line came a contingent of Allheart Knights along with a rider bearing the flag of the new Honce-the-Bear. Duke Kalas centered them as they rode fearlessly up to St. Gwendolyn's gates, right in the open before the abbot and his brothers.

"Who leads this abbey?" Duke Kalas called up.

"One known to you, good Duke Kalas," Glendenhook replied, stepping forward to the edge of the wall so that the Allheart leader could get a good look at him. "Abbot Glendenhook."

The duke gave a deferential nod of his head. "I come bearing great tidings from Ursal, Abbot Glendenhook," said the duke. "Tidings sad and tidings glorious."

"That King Danube is dead and young Aydrian has assumed the throne," the abbot answered.

"I expected that word would precede my arrival."

"And so it has."

"And yet you fly the flag of old," the duke remarked. "We have brought a new one for you."

"It is not one that we desire."

Duke Kalas hesitated, and Glendenhook noted a wry smile spread under the metal cage of his great plumed helmet.

"We fly the flag of Honce-the-Bear, the flag of Prince Midalis," the abbot pressed on. "For it is he who was second in the royal line."

"The affairs of state are not your concern, good Abbot," Duke Kalas replied, and there was no angry edge to his voice. "It is up to the throne of Ursal, and not the Abellican Church, to determine the proper pennant of the kingdom."

"Agreed," Abbot Glendenhook replied immediately. "And yet in this the Abellican Church cannot remain silent, for the rise of King Aydrian is not an incident pertinent to the state alone. We know of his allies, Duke Kalas. But enough of this shouting." Glendenhook stepped back from the wall and called down, and the gate of St. Gwendolyn creaked open.

"Under rules of truce," Glendenhook called back out over the wall.

With a look to his knights, the duke led the entourage forward into the small courtyard of the abbey.

"You were wise in opening your door," Kalas said to Glendenhook and Sovereign Sister Treisa when he and one other Allheart met with the pair in Glendenhook's private quarters a few minutes later. "Some chapels were more stubborn in their disregard for King Aydrian. They are being rebuilt."

"A duty that no doubt does swell the heart of Duke Kalas," said Glendenhook.

Kalas shot him a dangerous look.

"Why bother with the pleasantries?" the abbot asked. "We know why you have come, and you understand why we have chosen to fly the flags you see atop our abbey. Your hatred of the Abellican Church is not unknown to us, good Duke. Nor is its source, and for many years has the death of Queen Vivian weighed heavily upon the shoulders of every Abellican."

Glendenhook knew that he had touched a nerve with so straightforward an opening. Little had shaped Duke Targon Bree Kalas' life more than the death of King Danube's first wife, Queen Vivian. Summoned to her side, Je'howith, at that time the abbot of St. Honce, had worked feverishly to save her, but alas, he had arrived at her side too late. That blow had stung King Danube, but had wounded Duke Kalas even more profoundly, leaving a scar in his heart that manifested itself regularly in tirades against the Abel-

lican Church. For more than two decades since Vivian's death, Duke Kalas
had been one of the greatest critics of the Church, a critic who had erupted
many times concerning the leadership in Palmaris, and on any other issue,
even the pilgrimage to Mount Aida. The troublesome duke had been the
subject of many heated discussions at St.-Mere-Abelle during the years when
Glendenhook had served there as a master, under Father Abbots Markwart,
Agronguerre, and Bou-raiy.

"Queen Vivian is not the issue here," Duke Kalas said through gritted
teeth.

"Is she not?" Abbot Glendenhook replied, measuring every wince on the
duke's face as he spoke. He wanted to reason with Kalas, not push the man
into an explosion.

"My march is to spread the word of King Aydrian, and nothing more,"
Kalas replied. "Those who oppose him will be defeated, of course, whether
that opposition comes from village leaders, noblemen, or the Abellican
Church. Your abbeys exist because of the generosity of Honce-the-Bear's
throne. Do not ever forget that."

"The throne has long understood the stabilizing influence of the Church
as its partner in holding the kingdom strong," Sovereign Sister Treisa put
in. "Ours is a partnership of mutual benefit."

"And so, when you fly the flag of King Aydrian and accept him as your
sovereign—"

"Our sovereign is God alone," the feisty Treisa interrupted.

Duke Kalas looked at her hard, then softened his face into a smile and
nodded his deference. "As you believe," he said with a polite bow. "Allow
me to restate my position. When you fly the flag of Aydrian, should any
secular pennant wave above your abbey, and accept him as the rightful king
of Honce-the-Bear, then accept my march here as a cause for celebration
and not fear."

"Your king has made such acceptance difficult," Abbot Glendenhook
replied. "For his decrees apparently extend beyond the accepted domain of
his kingdom."

"Men of your Church came to him, not the other way around," Duke
Kalas answered. "Abbot Olin saw the truth of King Aydrian and embraced
him."

"As did Marcalo De'Unnero," said Treisa.

"Hardly a man of our Church," Glendenhook was quick to add.

Duke Kalas chuckled. "And none of my affair," he said. "Though I will
assure you that Marcalo De'Unnero would kill you if he saw the flags you
fly."

"Then do inform him," Treisa said defiantly.

Duke Kalas and Abbot Glendenhook both widened their eyes at that remark, and the other Allheart in the room gasped aloud.

But Treisa pressed on. "How could one as noble as Duke Targon Bree

Kalas, friend of King Danube, throw in with the mad dog De'Unnero? Have you so forsaken your longtime friend? Is the loyalty of the Allheart Knights such a frail thing as that?"

"Tell your woman to take care her words," Kalas warned Glendenhook.

"Her words are my own," the abbot answered.

Kalas looked as if he was about to strike out physically, but Glendenhook, taking his cue from the determined sovereign sister, continued. "Abbot Olin has made of himself an outcast to St. Abelle and the Church that bears his name. I expect that a replacement for him will be appointed at St. Bondabruce very soon."

"His monks love him and follow him devotedly, and believe that he, and not your friend Bou-raiy, should now lead the Abellican Church."

"Then the replacement will come from St.-Mere-Abelle, or from neighboring St. Rontlemore in Entel," said Glendenhook.

"The replacement," Duke Kalas mused. "A short-lived appointment, no doubt."

"Because the crown does not accept its place in the kingdom," Glendenhook replied. "The affairs of the Church must be left to the Church! You would march with an army to St.-Mere-Abelle and right Abbot Olin's perceived wrong?"

"I will march wherever King Aydrian determines that I must march," Kalas shot back. "To St.-Mere-Abelle—through St.-Mere-Abelle! It hardly matters."

"It is not the concern of the king!"

Duke Kalas snorted and shook his head. "You do not understand," he said quietly. "Aydrian has changed everything. Once, at the end of King Aydrian's own sword, I fell into the hands of death. No, Abbot, not your friend Bou-raiy himself, could have . . ." He stopped and gave a little laugh. "And yet, I live," he finished, looking Glendenhook right in the eye. "I live because now is the time when Honce-the-Bear has brought forth a king with the power over death itself!"

Abbot Glendenhook shook his head in confusion and looked to Treisa, who seemed equally perplexed. "What babble is this?" the sovereign sister asked. "No man has such."

"Certainly no Abellicans," Kalas spat. "When Queen Vivian lay dying, could the fool Je'howith save her? You priests promise eternal life. Well, on my word, Aydrian has shown himself the master of death itself. You condemn him, and me, because you cannot comprehend, because you are so wound within your rituals and false promises that such a king as Aydrian is beyond your comprehension."

"As was the Miracle of Avelyn?" Treisa countered. "Was it not Saint Avelyn who rescued the kingdom—your friend's kingdom—from the ruins of the plague?"

"Saint Avelyn?" Duke Kalas scoffed.

"Soon to be."

"So it has been said for many years," remarked the duke, but then he waved his hands and spun away. "It is of no matter. Avelyn is hero to the people of Honce-the-Bear—even Jilseponie once wore that mantle. They are of no concern anymore. Aydrian is king, and woe to any who oppose him."

"You can so deny Prince Midalis, who was your friend?"

Duke Kalas stiffened at the remark and steeled his gaze. "Prince Midalis would understand and accept if he understood Aydrian as do I."

Glendenhook's jaw dropped open. "What has this young Aydrian done to you? What bewitchery is this?"

"It is the only honest 'bewitchery' that I have ever seen," Kalas spat. "Unlike the falsities of the Abellican Church."

The two men stared long and hard at each other.

"You will open your gates to the soldiers of King Aydrian," the duke demanded. "You will fly the proper flag."

"And if we do not?"

"Then I will open your gates posthaste," Kalas calmly explained, and he walked out of the room, sweeping up his fellow Allheart in his wake.

"What are we to do?" Abbot Glendenhook said to Treisa when they were alone.

The woman looked at him and smiled with true serenity, completely accepting her fate.

Abbot Glendenhook returned that smile a moment later, then moved in and kissed the beautiful sister on the cheek. He swept out of his office, moving to the front wall. They had made their statement here with the flags, and now he intended to make another.

"Duke Kalas!" he shouted down from the wall at the group of men even then turning their To-gai steeds back toward their line. As one, the Allhearts turned back. "Be gone with your army. This is the house of God."

"Open your gates, Abbot Glendenhook," the duke warned.

"We will open our gates here at St. Gwendolyn and even at St.-Mere-Abelle when your King Aydrian assumes his proper place," the abbot yelled at the top of his voice, wanting as many of Kalas' men as possible to hear. "When the criminal Marcalo De'Unnero is imprisoned and Abbot Olin is turned over to Church authority for judgment. Until then, St. Gwendolyn is closed to you."

Duke Kalas again seemed more pleased than concerned.

"Duke Kalas!" Abbot Glendenhook shouted down again as the man turned away once more. As he called, Glendenhook fished into his belt pouch, finding a particularly heavy gemstone.

The duke turned about.

"What is your intention?" Glendenhook demanded.

Duke Kalas turned his mount about to face the abbot squarely. "I spread

the word of King Aydrian across the breadth of Honce-the-Bear," he replied. "For those who accept the word, there is alliance and friendship from
the crown. For those who do not, there is only the sword."

"St. Gwendolyn will not open her gates!"

"Then I declare you enemy," Duke Kalas called.

Abbot Glendenhook lifted his hand toward Kalas and focused his vision
through the images sent to him from the stone. He saw all the fine armor
the man wore more vividly then, as if the rest of the world had dulled to his
senses. He focused on one spot in the duke's armor, the plate covering the
man's heart, and he let the energy of the gemstone build in his heart and soul.

Kalas was shouting out something to him, but he did not hear. Behind
him, Sovereign Sister Treisa cried out, but he didn't register any of it. All
that mattered was the gemstone and its mounting energy; all that mattered
was this one wound he intended to give to young King Aydrian.

Glendenhook gave the lodestone all the power he could muster, tightening and strengthening its magnetic attraction to that one spot on Duke
Kalas's armor. And then, with a cry, the abbot let the bullet fly.

So fast was its flight that the very air crackled about it, and the ring as
the gemstone smashed against Duke Kalas' chest sounded as loudly as an
abbey bell.

Duke Kalas flew backward from his mount, landing hard in the dirt.

"What have you done?" Treisa cried, running up beside the abbot.

"I have sent a loud message to King Aydrian that the Abellican Church
will not buckle to unreasonable demands of the state!"

Below them on the field, some of the Allhearts shielded the fallen duke
while others leaped down from their mounts and lifted him. Other men
rode out from the army ranks to assist in bringing Kalas back.

At once the catapults fired and huge stones pounded against St. Gwendolyn's walls, crumbling the ancient stone. And then came the charge, more
than twenty thousand strong, shaking the ground beneath the abbey, and it
seemed as if the place would simply collapse beneath the thunder.

Abbot Glendenhook ran all about, gathering his brothers to him and ordering them to stand down. "Offer no resistance," he commanded when he
had them all assembled in the nave of the abbey's great chapel. "We have
made our statement."

A brother at the back of the hall, peering out the doors cried, "They have
breached the gate!"

"Close the door, brother," Abbot Glendenhook bade him. "Come and
sit, and pray."

A few moments later, the doors of the chapel burst in, and soldiers swept
into the place.

"Join us in prayer, my friends," Abbot Glendenhook said to them.

He was the first to fall, beaten down under the weight of a shield rush,
then pounded into submission. His frightened brothers and Sovereign Sister Treisa were similarly dragged away.

*   *   *

Two surprises greeted Glendenhook later that afternoon, when he was dragged, half-dead, to the same room where he had met with Duke Kalas that morning.

"And so we meet again," said the first surprise, Duke Kalas himself, sitting in Glendenhook's own chair and still wearing his now-dented, but intact, armor.

Glendenhook was roughly placed in the chair across the desk from the duke.

"Never underestimate the Allheart armorers, good Abbot," Kalas explained. "They designed our fine suits with just you troublesome Abellicans in mind."

"Had I been stronger," Glendenhook remarked under his breath. "Had it been Jilseponie behind the weight of that stone . . ."

"Had it been King Aydrian, then I assure you that my armor would have shattered like glass," Kalas replied. "But no matter. Your cowardice was open for all to see."

"You declared us your enemy, not I."

"And I rode under a flag of truce," Duke Kalas countered. "Yours was the attack of an assassin—not a popular role to play, wouldn't you agree?

"But no matter," the duke said again. "St. Gwendolyn flies the flag of King Aydrian and is thus incorporated once more into the kingdom of Honce-the-Bear. All of her monks, brothers and sisters alike, will be properly interrogated."

"Brothers and sister, you mean," Glendenhook said, wanting to score some point at least, in referring to the escape of the bulk of St. Gwendolyn's monks.

But Duke Kalas merely smiled and motioned to a man at the side of the room, who immediately turned and pulled open a side door. Two soldiers came through, holding a battered Master Belasarus between them.

The monk was shaking his head and crying. "We tried," he pleaded with Glendenhook. "They were waiting for us, just five miles up the coast."

Glendenhook's mouth drooped open, despite his desire to hold strong in the face of Duke Kalas.

Duke Kalas waved his hand and the soldiers dragged Belasarus back out of the room.

"Now, as I was saying," the duke went on casually, "they will be interrogated and those who accept King Aydrian will find that he is a beneficent ruler."

"And those who do not?"

"Will face the court of Abbot Olin, no doubt," Kalas replied. "I care little."

"And what of my fate?"

Duke Kalas looked away. "I sympathize with you. I truly do."

To Glendenhook's surprise, he found that he believed the man. "Then I am to face the wrath of Olin and De'Unnero as well."

"Your unprovoked attack was made on an official of the State, not of the Church," the duke replied, and he looked back at the doomed abbot. "You will be tried, of course, but you know, as do I, that such a trial is but a formality. There can be no doubt of your crime."

Glendenhook's gaze lowered.

"I might be willing to call for a finding of mitigating circumstances, lessening your sentence," the duke offered, and Glendenhook looked back up at him.

"But in return, I would have to proclaim Aydrian as rightful king of Honce-the-Bear," the abbot reasoned.

"That is the first part, yes."

"You would demand of me that I support Abbot Olin and Marcalo De'Unnero?"

"I assure you that in doing so, you would alleviate much suffering that will soon befall your brethren," the duke answered. "And if all of your foolish Church would cooperate, the kingdom would know less confusion and less war."

Abbot Glendenhook thought on that for a few moments. "Perhaps there are some things worth dying for," he said quietly.

"I bid you reconsider," Duke Kalas replied. "For your own sake and for those who will errantly follow your lead to their deaths."

Glendenhook sat back once again and closed his eyes, looking deep into his own heart and soul. He had never been the most pious of Abellican brothers, but rather, more of a pragmatist, as was his mentor, Father Abbot Bou-raiy. On the surface, this predicament seemed the epitome of such a dilemma, principle versus pragmatism, and for the first time in his life, Abbot Toussan Glendenhook felt himself truly tested at every level. This was the ultimate pragmatic moment, obviously, but so too, the ultimate denial of his faith.

He thought of his true inspiration in life, Sovereign Sister Treisa, and answered with a voice strong in conviction.

"Build your gallows."

❖ 30 ❖

The Apology

"You're a long way from home," Pony remarked. The words just fell out of her mouth in her astonishment at seeing Belli'mar Juraviel suddenly appearing at the entrance of the cave where she and Bradwarden had put up for the night. Outside a blizzard raged, wind blowing the snow sidelong and piling it high against the sides of trees and hills.

Pony's remark was true enough, for they were far to the east of Dundalis now, and even that place was far from Juraviel's home.

Juraviel trembled a bit, but did not reply.

Recovering from the shock of seeing Juraviel, Pony went on. "I believe that your Lady Dasslerond and I said all that needed to be said, Belli'mar Juraviel," she said curtly, and she felt Bradwarden's strong hand on her shoulder as she spoke.

"Easy, girl," the centaur advised. "This one's ever been yer friend."

Pony turned on him sharply. "Enough of a friend to tell me of his Lady's—"

Bradwarden stopped her by placing a finger over her pursed lips. "There's something bigger amiss, unless I miss me guess," he said softly, and he turned back to the obviously shaken Juraviel.

"The girl's right, elf," Bradwarden said to him. "Suren that ye're a long way from yer home—farther than I've ever seen any elf wander in a long time, to tell the truth, unless ye're lookin' to find Andacanavar, yer ranger friend, out and about."

Juraviel shook his head slowly.

"You came to see me, then," Pony reasoned. "Well, know that I have nothing left to say to you or to any of the Touel'alfar. Of your people, I hold least enmity to you, but after what you did to me, I doubt that I could ever call you 'friend' again. Please begone." As she spoke, the woman dropped her hand into her pouch of gemstones, preparing to defend herself should Juraviel or any other elf that might be hiding in the area make a move against her.

In response, Juraviel slowly lifted his hand and opened it, revealing the emerald gemstone that was the heart and soul of his people, and of Andur'Blough Inninness.

"Lady Dasslerond is no more," he said softly.

Pony's eyes widened and Bradwarden gasped.

"She gave herself to Andur'Blough Inninness, wrapping the valley in her life's essence to shield it from searching eyes."

"I would not have come back," Pony stammered.

"Not yours."

"Yer son," Bradwarden reasoned. "Aye, but the new king went hunting for the elves that trained him!"

"Many of my people are dead at Aydrian's hand," Juraviel confirmed. "He marched to our valley with hundreds of warriors. We tried to stop him. We tried to defeat him, or turn him aside. But he is powerful. So powerful."

"What are you saying?" Pony demanded. "Aydrian attacked?"

"We tried to turn him aside, to dissuade him from his designs of conquest," Juraviel explained. "But he crushed our resistance through his power with the gemstones."

"And so yer Lady went out to face him?" Bradwarden asked.

"She went out to deny him, in the only way she knew," the elf explained. "She gave herself to this gemstone; and wrapped in her life's essence, Andur'Blough Inninness is lost to the world until the conditions of her enchantment are met."

"And Aydrian cannot break this enchantment?" the centaur asked. "Well, it seems he's not all-powerful then!"

"He cannot," Juraviel replied.

"Then why are you out here?" Pony asked. "Why isn't Juraviel with the rest of his people in their hidden valley?"

"It is hidden from all, human and Touel'alfar alike," he admitted, and that widened the eyes of both Pony and Bradwarden.

"A desperate enchantment indeed," the centaur remarked.

"We are homeless, and hiding."

"Out here?" Pony asked incredulously.

"I have come alone," the elf explained. "The gemstone of the Touel'alfar holds many powers, including one that allows me to travel great distances quickly. Still, it has taken me several days to find you."

"And now you have, and I bid you go away," said Pony, and Bradwarden clasped her shoulder again and gave a squeeze.

The woman turned sharply on the centaur once more. "What do you expect of me?" she asked, then whirled back on Juraviel, her blue eyes clearly reflecting the anger and pain she felt at that moment. "And what do you expect of me?" she asked the elf. "I thought that you, above all your people, were my friend."

"I was always your friend, Jilseponie," Belli'mar Juraviel quietly replied.

"But you were always Touel'alfar first," the woman snapped.

Juraviel lowered his gaze, conceding the point. "I erred," he admitted.

"An apology from an elf ain't no small thing," Bradwarden said softly.

"An apology because he needs me now," the woman reasoned. "Is that not so?" she asked Juraviel.

"Lady Jils—" Juraviel began, but he stopped short and took a deep breath. "Pony," he corrected. "I come to you because it is right that I come to you. I should have come to you with news of Aydrian as soon as Markwart was thrown down and peace was restored to the land."

"Yes, you should have." There was no compromise in Pony's stern tone.

"We all should have, and I spoke with my Lady Dasslerond more than once on that very subject," Juraviel went on. "But we did not. It was her choice that Aydrian was the price of our involvement in aiding you and Elbryan against the errant Markwart."

"Her price!" Pony roared.

"It was her choice to make, not mine. When one is appointed to rule Andur'Blough Inninness, she does so with advisement, perhaps, but not through a poll of her subjects. The rules were Lady Dasslerond's to make, and mine to follow. You have known that about us for many years; never have I misled you on our rule. We are not a people who make our choices independently of Lady Dasslerond's rule—not even my friend Tuntun who died beside you and Elbryan in the bowels of Mount Aida."

The mention of Tuntun did set Pony back on her heels a bit, and stole a bit of her angry edge. Gallant Tuntun had given her life to save Pony and Elbryan, had offered herself up to a most horrible death to serve the greater cause of defeating the demon dactyl. The mere mention of her reminded Pony of all the good the Touel'alfar had done for her and for those she had loved. The elves had saved her and Elbryan on that terrible day three decades before when the goblins had overwhelmed Dundalis. The elves, particularly Belli'mar Juraviel, had been with her throughout her ordeals, and had indeed saved her life that fateful night on the field outside of Palmaris—and had saved Aydrian's life as well.

"My Lady was wrong in her choices regarding your son," Juraviel admitted. "She knew that before she gave her life. I apologize to you for her, as well as for myself. It will forever haunt Belli'mar Juraviel that he failed Pony as her friend."

His words had Pony's legs going weak under her. She knew that he meant them, profoundly, and saw the honest pain that was etched on his fair elven features.

"There is nothing that I can do now to undo that which has happened," Juraviel went on. "But now we face—together, I hope—a trial as great as that brought upon us by the advent of the demon dactyl. Your son, this tyrant Aydrian, desires no less than did Bestesbulzibar."

Pony slumped back against the wall and slid down to a sitting position.

She noted that Bradwarden, hovering over her, silently asked her permission, and so she gave a slight nod.

"Well, ye might come in then outa the cold," the centaur told the Touel'alfar. "I just bringed in some more logs and me friend here's to get the fire blazing again soon enough."

Juraviel moved in tentatively and sat down opposite the low-burning fire pit from Pony. They said nothing as Bradwarden dropped some more kindling on the coals and Pony took out her ruby gemstone and her serpentine. She brought a white-glowing shield up over her hand and forearm, then thrust the hand among the logs and called upon the powers of the ruby. In seconds, she had a fire blazing.

Then she sat back, her blue eyes staring at Juraviel above and through the leaping orange flames. She didn't speak at all, and made no motion for him to do so.

And so they sat quietly for a long time, just getting the feel of one another again—as friends and not as enemies.

"Lady Dasslerond believed that your Aydrian was the only hope of our home," Juraviel finally explained. "He alone could defeat the spreading rot of the demon dactyl, so she believed. And so she kept him as her weapon. In her mind, the Aydrian who was your son died that night on the field, and while you were saved, he was not. Not truly. What was taken from you was not your son, but rather the hope of Andur'Blough Inninness.

"I know that it must sound horrible to you to hear it put so callously," Juraviel continued. "But you must understand that our entire existence is threatened. Even saying all of that, I tell you without condescension and without condition that my Lady was wrong in her assessment, and in trying to use any man in such a manner."

"And we see the result."

"Her price has been ultimate," Juraviel reminded. "But now we must get beyond her grave error and salvage what is left of the world." He gave a helpless little laugh—a curiously human gesture, and nothing Pony had never heard from him or any other elf before.

"The great irony here is that the root of my Lady's error was my own doing, I fear," Juraviel explained. "It was I who pushed Lady Dasslerond and my people too close to the affairs of humans. We became more involved than ever since the time of Terranen Dinoniel—and the world was certainly a different place back then. And now here I am, risen from the ashes of my ruined homeland, once again to interject myself and my people into the affairs of humans."

"Instead of running away and hiding."

"Indeed," the elf agreed. "We could do that. We have found our kin, the Doc'alfar, and they have extended their hand to us. We could allow Andur'Blough Inninness to fade from our memories, and find a new way and a new life far removed from Aydrian and Jilseponie and all other humans."

"Then why are you here?"

"Because he's knowing that yer Aydrian, this thing yer Aydrian has become, was partly the doing o' him and his kin," Bradwarden reasoned.

Pony regarded the centaur, then slowly turned back to regard the diminutive figure sitting across the fire.

"He speaks the truth, my friend," Juraviel answered her unspoken question. "We of the Touel'alfar bear great responsibility for King Aydrian and the monster he has become. And so I come to you, out of mutual need, and offer to you my services."

"The armies of humans are vast," Pony reasoned. "And if Aydrian is as powerful with the gemstones as we believe, he would seem unstoppable." She gave a little shrug. "My people will survive the tempest that is Aydrian. The human lands will go on long after he is dead, long after we are all dead. Your own numbers, though, are diminished, by your own admission. Go and hide, Juraviel—I tell you that as your friend. Go and hide your people away. Your warriors are magnificent, I agree, but you do not number enough to offer any true advantage to our cause. We will win or we will lose, and not a hundred elves could possibly tilt the balance."

"I do not intend to throw my warriors in battle before your Aydrian ever again," the elf agreed. "We cannot afford to lose many more, else we will cease to exist altogether!"

"Then what're ye to offer?" asked Bradwarden.

Juraviel again held aloft the emerald. "You have allies," he explained. "There lives in To-gai, south of the mountains, a ranger trained by me, the warrior woman named Brynn Dharielle, who has risen to lead the To-gai-ru to freedom from their Behrenese oppressors. Even now, Aydrian has reached southward to Behren, and even now, my couriers are advising Brynn to oppose him."

"There's the first glimmer I heared in a bit," Bradwarden said hopefully, and he nudged Pony.

"With this gemstone, I can travel great distances in a short time," Juraviel explained, holding forth the emerald once more. "I can take few others with me, and so I will be of little help in moving armies or the like. But in securing a line of communication between those who would oppose Aydrian, and in scouting the movements of Aydrian's forces, we Touel'alfar are without equal."

Pony stared at him while she digested the information, and while the potential gain to her cause began to blossom in her thoughts. She had understood the desperation of her situation in coming to Vanguard in search of Prince Midalis. She knew that it was likely that Aydrian had already grown too strong to be supplanted by Midalis, even with her support.

But now this. Now the possibility of finding all the loose threads opposing Aydrian and weaving them into a single force . . .

"I accept your apology, Belli'mar Juraviel," the woman remarked quietly. "Help me. Help me make the world as it was."

"And help you to defeat your son?" the elf reasoned.

Those words stung Pony's sensibilities despite her logical agreement, and she knew not from where her response came, "Help me to save my son."

She saw the look of concern shared by Juraviel and Bradwarden at that curious reply, and she understood that look better than she understood her own reasoning.

Still, the woman did not back down from her impetuous statement.

For if she surrendered hope itself, there would remain nothing else.

Lining Up

A ided by Aydrian's use of the gemstones, their journey had been swift, even against the cold winds of winter. Despite that, the returning soldiers and the king who led them were all relieved to see again the walls of Palmaris that cold and wintry day near the end of the second month of God's Year 847.

Riding before the column, the first thing Aydrian noticed was that the wall was manned by Ursal soldiers, his loyal Kingsmen. "Marcalo has held Palmaris strong, it would seem," the young king remarked to Sadye, who rode at his side.

"Could we have expected any less of him?" Sadye asked.

Aydrian slowed his mount and turned a suspicious glance at her.

"What?" Sadye prompted.

"You still love him."

Sadye looked back to Palmaris and gave a halfhearted shrug. "My respect for him has not diminished—should it have?"

Now it was Aydrian's turn to look ahead to the city and shrug.

"You've placed Marcalo in a position of great importance to the security and expansion of your kingdom," the woman went on. "Why?"

When Aydrian didn't immediately answer, she did it for him. "Because you know of his value. You even got Abbot Olin out of the way, because you understand that having Marcalo De'Unnero as the Father Abbot of the Abellican Church will ensure the security of the throne. He is no less ambitious than you—it is just that his ambitions are now more tightly focused."

"You still love him."

"If I do, it is because I still respect him and his ambitions. And so do you."

That last statement brought their gazes back together. "We have no room for jealousy here," Sadye said quietly to him. "Not from you, and not from Marcalo. Though, of course, you will hold so many of his desires as a great sword over his head that he will have no choice but to hide away any jealousy he might hold."

"If he has known Sadye as I have, he would have no greater desire than to hold her," Aydrian said, lowering his gaze to the road ahead.

Sadye's burst of laughter spun him about immediately.

"The words of a boy," the bard explained, and she continued to chuckle. "Tell me, Aydrian Boudabras, who will rule all the world: would you give it all up? Would you forsake your plans and abdicate your kingdom if I asked it of you? I could promise you in exchange all the love you desire and more."

Aydrian just continued to stare at her, not sure how to react.

"Would you?" the woman demanded.

Again, when Aydrian didn't respond, Sadye answered for him. "Of course you would not! There are different layers of desires. So many men become trapped in their immediate needs that they cannot look ahead to a greater future road. Neither you nor Marcalo De'Unnero is among that short-sighted breed. Yes, there will be anger between you two when Marcalo learns that I have moved from his side to yours, but that tension will not threaten the greater goals you both seek. At least, I hope it will not."

Aydrian said nothing, but picked up the pace again, leading his force to the city's western gate, bringing them under the comforting and distracting sound of the cheers of their comrades.

He was not the first of his people to walk among the To-gai-ru, but Lozan Duk felt the many stares upon him as he was escorted across the city of Dharyan-Dharielle to the palace of the Dragon of To-gai.

He walked into the grand structure, along hallways tastefully decorated, but not overdone with fineries, as was the reputed way of most human rulers. Tapestries lined the corridors, with statues and pedestals set before them. Golden bowls placed upon those pedestals were filled with the most precious commodity of this arid region, water, and from the splash marks and footprints, Lozan Duk could tell that visitors were welcomed to move up and refresh themselves. On both sides a long window, filled with multi-colored glass, lined the top of the corridor's walls, and sun rays streaming through splashed the light tiles of the floor with rose and blues and greens.

At the end of one long hall and through great double doors, Lozan Duk looked again on the strange woman who had accompanied the Tylwyn Tou traveler through Tymwyvenne years before. It struck him how greatly Brynn Dharielle had grown in those few years. Physically, she seemed much the same petite and beautiful young woman he had known, but in her light brown eyes, Lozan Duk now saw the depth of wisdom and a simmer of de-termination where before he had seen only the sparkle of youthful inno-cence. He was glad to see that she was not prettily dressed, obscuring her natural grace and beauty beneath outrageous headdresses or voluminous and gaudy robes, as was the case with much of the human hierarchy.

Her smile, one of inviting warmth, would have seemed far less so under the weight of such a disguise.

"Greetings, Brynn Dharielle," the elf said in his native tongue, one that was not far removed from the language Brynn had learned in her years with the Touel'alfar.

"It is good that you have come," Brynn replied, the flow of her words a bit more stilted. "My heart is gladdened to see the face of an old friend."

Lozan Duk waited a moment while Brynn turned to the middle-aged man standing beside her throne and whispered to him, apparently translating.

"I had thought your kingdom secured," the elf said when she turned back to him. "Surprised I am to find an army sitting outside your walls."

"It is a long and complicated story," Brynn replied. "One that may concern you, or may not, depending on why you have journeyed so far."

"To bring you tidings of the lands north of the mountains," the elf explained. "Much has happened."

Brynn translated quickly to Pagonel, then sat quiet and bade Lozan Duk to continue.

"Your friend Aydrian has assumed the throne of the northern kingdom," Lozan Duk told her.

"That is already known to me. He reaches his arms out to our neighboring kingdom of Behren, as well, coming openly as a friend, but in reality, I fear, as a conqueror."

"Know that your fears are justified," the elf explained. "Aydrian marched his army west to the land of the Tylwyn Tou."

Brynn's eyes widened and she gasped.

"He defeated Lady Dasslerond herself; and in her death, she has sealed away her valley from all, even her own people. It was Belli'mar Juraviel who sent me to you to warn you of Aydrian's imperialistic bent. Know beyond doubt, Brynn Dharielle, that your friend of old is now no friend to either Tylwyn Doc or Tylwyn Tou."

"Then your people stand beside your cousins?" Brynn asked after translating the news to Pagonel.

"We are one people again, under the leadership of both King Eltiraaz and Belli'mar Juraviel." He held forth his hand, palm up and showing a large blue sapphire. "The gemstone of my people, sister stone to the emerald that held within it the heart of Andur'Blough Inninness. King Eltiraaz and Lady Dasslerond united the stones once more, as they united our peoples. With this gem, Belli'mar Juraviel, who now wields the emerald, and I can find each other from across the known world."

Brynn, somehow not overly surprised, accepted the words without question and turned to explain them to Pagonel, who did indeed seem more than a little curious and impressed.

"The Tylwyn people are on the run," Lozan Duk told them, changing the subject as he stowed away his precious stone. "We are in hiding from Aydrian's hunters, and while I was sent south to find you, Belli'mar Juraviel has gone north and east in search of Jilseponie, Aydrian's mother. Many have been set about as scouts, for it is our hope that we will serve as the communication between those who must oppose King Aydrian."

"But how long has passed since the fall of Lady Dasslerond?" Brynn asked. "Even if you and your cousins were to stretch your line from Dharyan-Dharielle all the way to the far north, the news will not travel quickly."

"Lady Dasslerond fell just over two weeks ago," Lozan Duk explained.

"Then how . . ."

"The emerald Belli'mar Juraviel holds facilitates his travel—and my own! I was on the southern edge of the Path of Starless Night when he found me from my call, only two days ago. I had come south to meet this dragon, Agradeleous; but alas, the great wurm was not in his lair."

"He is here."

That brought a smile to the pale face of the Doc'alfar. "Belli'mar Juraviel told me of the dire news in the north, and of the danger that is Aydrian, and bade me come here to find you and tell you that we will not forsake you and your people at this dark hour."

"Two days ago?" Brynn asked. "The Path of Starless Night is a week's march."

"Belli'mar Juraviel took me with him through use of his magical gemstone," Lozan Duk explained. "I would have arrived before dusk yesterday, but Belli'mar Juraviel put me down outside your city, neither of us knowing that an army had encircled the place. It took me all the night to weave my way through the human soldiers."

Brynn translated it all to Pagonel, then sat back to digest the information. "It would seem that all of my worst fears of Aydrian are true," she said to Pagonel.

"Abbot Olin seems more the emissary and less the rogue, then," the mystic replied. He put a hand up to stroke Brynn's black hair, prompting her to look directly at him.

"There is a great sadness in you," Pagonel remarked.

"You did not know Andur'Blough Inninness," Brynn explained, "and thus you cannot understand the significance of its passing. And you did not know Lady Dasslerond. In truth, she was more of a mother . . ."

Brynn's voice broke apart, and she sucked in a deep breath and shook her head. She tried to steady herself, knowing that she had to be strong, that she would likely face some serious challenges even beyond the army that now laid siege to her city. But even as she tried to steel herself, Lozan Duk's words began to sink in even deeper. Images of her youthful days beside Dasslerond and the elves came flooding back to her, and she had to bring one hand to her face to find enough focus so that she did not begin sobbing openly.

Finally, she caught enough of her breath to instruct her guards to show Lozan Duk to a comfortable room, then to explain to the Doc'alfar that she would call on him shortly.

"You wish to be alone?" Pagonel asked her quietly as the elf departed.

Brynn started to answer that she did, but she thought it over and realized otherwise. "Come with me," she bade her dearest and most trusted friend and advisor. "Hold me when I need you to, and listen to my tales of Lady Dasslerond and Andur'Blough Inninness."

Pagonel nodded and moved around the arm of the chair, taking Brynn's hand and helping her to her feet.

Before they had even reached her private rooms, the Dragon of To-gai had already begun an animated telling of some of her fondest memories of her years among the elves.

They plodded through the deep snow uncomplaining, with Bradwarden leading the way and piping his songs, and Pony and Symphony following close behind.

Far ahead, Belli'mar Juraviel ran atop the snow with hardly an effort, and every so often he stopped and called back to them, correcting their course. He had already used his emerald to locate Prince Midalis and his entourage, and had meant to take Pony and the centaur to the prince through the same magical means. But to the relief of them all, Juraviel had found that Midalis was not so far away—less than a day's march.

Pony's delight at seeing her old friend was only heightened when she at last entered the small cottage he was using as his temporary quarters to find another old and dear friend standing beside him.

"All the grim tidings diminish against the splendor of your arrival, dear Jilseponie," Prince Midalis said, and he sprang from his chair and swept around the desk, wrapping Pony in the tightest of hugs.

"You've heard of my son, then, and his march across the kingdom that should be your own," Pony replied.

Prince Midalis pulled back from her and turned to the grinning man standing at the side of the room. "Good Captain Al'u'met took upon himself and his crew great risks to sail across the Gulf of Corona even as winter was settling in. A gale could have swamped them, but they pressed on anyway, in the knowledge that it was critical to deliver the tidings from Abbot Braumin of St. Precious."

"Though I fear that good Braumin is no longer in that position," Al'u'met put in. "The army of Aydrian approached Palmaris even as I sailed, and we have reason to believe that the city was overrun in short order."

Pony nodded.

"Because the fleet of Ursal—a portion of it, at least—has sailed past the city and into the gulf," Prince Midalis added. "A flight ship from Pireth Dancard arrived only three weeks ago, after having been pursued nearly halfway across the northern stretches of the gulf. Had not a storm arisen, she would have been caught by the pursuing warships—warships flying a pennant that showed both the bear rampant and the tiger rampant. Apparently, this perversion is the flag of Aydrian Boudabras."

"Boudabras," Pony whispered, the first time she had heard that name.

"An elvish word," Bradwarden explained. "The word of a great storm, maelstrom."

"How fitting," Prince Midalis said dryly.

"We will have a difficult time of discerning exactly how much of the land, and sea, Aydrian has secured," Pony reasoned. She looked all about, settling on a view outside the window, where the snow had begun to fall once more. "I know not this town. How far from Vanguard are we?"

"A week's march," Midalis explained. "The ground is defensible here, and here, we are already well on our way to Palmaris."

"You expect to begin your counterattack there?"

"It seems the logical choice."

"Logical and obvious, to young Aydrian as well, not for doubting," Bradwarden interjected.

"I do not have a fleet that can match that of Ursal," Prince Midalis retorted, and the desperation and frustration was clear in his voice. "The land route to my throne goes through Palmaris, and so through Palmaris I must go."

The centaur gave a polite bow.

Pony glanced at the other three in the room in turn, settling on Bradwarden for a bit, silently asking him for agreement, and when he nodded his understanding, she turned directly to Midalis. "We found you with help from another friend," she explained. "A powerful ally to our cause. You know of the Touel'alfar?"

The prince's expression grew curious indeed, his gray eyes, telltale as a mark of the line of Ursal, widening considerably.

"They will scout the lands for us," Pony explained. "They have ways to determine the movements of all. With the help of the elves, we will discover the vulnerable areas in Aydrian's line, perhaps."

"Even if this is true—and it is welcome news indeed!—our options remain limited," Prince Midalis answered. "If we are to take the war to Aydrian, then we must march south, and it will be of no small consequence to pass by Palmaris. Over the weeks, my scouts and commanders have given me much insight, and I have found but three choices, and three hopes. The first is that Aydrian will choose to divide the kingdom, with him taking the region south and west of the gulf, and leaving Vanguard alone."

"It's not what we're seein' from him," the centaur remarked.

"The second is that he will choose to attack Vanguard, either by land or by sea," Midalis went on. "In either case, he will find the fighting difficult, for I, too, have discovered an ally. I have set my army west of Vanguard, defending against any land invasion, though I do not expect one in the throes of winter. The city of Vanguard is well defended, as well, and we could return there quickly, if needed. But again, it would be of great fortune to us should Aydrian decide to sail the gulf in this season. Likely, more than half his forces would be taken to the bottom."

"He'll not come north until St.-Mere-Abelle is conquered, I would guess, and that will be no easy task," Pony agreed.

"And just north of Vanguard city, and to the east, my ally has encamped, and they will defend my land as fiercely as my own subjects."

"Andacanavar has come to your aid," Pony reasoned.

"And Bruinhelde," Midalis explained. "I do not expect that they will march with me when I go south to dislodge King Aydrian, but if he brings the battle to Vanguard, he will find my army strengthened by my loyal neighbors from the north."

"And what're ye to do if word comes from Aydrian that he's givin' ye yer kingdom north o' the gulf, and that he's takin' all the rest?" Bradwarden asked.

The prince squared his shoulders, seeming every bit the man, the king, that his brother had been before him. "Honce-the-Bear is my kingdom, not Vanguard," he said. "I deny Aydrian's claim, and will fight him to my death or his own." As he finished, he looked at Pony and winced, perhaps only then realizing to whom he was speaking.

But then Pony dismissed that tentative look by saying, "And I will fight beside you, to the bitter end."

"Let us plan our first moves, then," said Midalis.

"Belli'mar Juraviel of the Touel'alfar is already on the move," Pony informed him. "His scouts will scour the land in short order. We will have one advantage in this battle for your kingdom, that of information." She turned to Al'u'met, a wry grin suddenly spreading on her fair face. "Tell me of Pireth Dancard, good Captain. Take me to the sea and point out the direction."

"What're ye thinkin', lass?" Bradwarden asked.

Pony's response came through a wicked smile. "I'm thinking that we should find every loose thread that Aydrian shows around the edges of his blanketing army and tug them hard until the whole of it unravels."

Most of all, the city seemed secure. Soldiers marched along the streets in orderly fashion, and the walls were thick with sentries. Defensive fortifications were under construction at every point along the wall, including many new catapults and ballistae.

Aydrian could hardly contain his smile as he moved through the streets of tamed Palmaris, to the cheers of soldier and townsman alike.

"Marcalo has done a magnificent job in putting the city in line, it would seem," Sadye was happy to say at his side.

Aydrian didn't answer, but just kept looking around at the beehive of activity that was Palmaris. He and his charges made their way to the eastern end of the city, to the great square outside of St. Precious, where Aydrian's commanders put the soldiers in line, rank upon rank.

The doors to the great abbey creaked open and Marcalo De'Unnero came forth, flanked by a dozen Abellican monks. He walked up to stand right before the king, who dismounted.

"Welcome back to your city, King Aydrian," De'Unnero said when the cheering of the multitudes gathering about the square had at last ended. "You will find Palmaris most accommodating, I assure you."

"Accommodating and secure," Aydrian replied.

"More so than ever before," the monk said with great pride and great conviction. "The garrison has spent the entirety of the season at work in preparing the defenses. Should our enemies choose to march south to this city, they will find the place a singular fortress designed to hold them back."

"Any word from Duke Kalas?" Aydrian asked.

"He has pushed across the breadth of the land, and last word had him fast approaching St. Gwendolyn," De'Unnero replied. "And his army has swelled to many times its size, with new recruits rushing in to join in the glory of King Aydrian."

Aydrian beamed and looked to Sadye, who verily glowed at the news. "And what of the Church?" he asked.

"When St. Gwendolyn falls, if it has not already, then there will remain but two opposing abbeys: St.-Mere-Abelle and St. Belfour of Vanguard," the monk replied. He wasn't looking at Aydrian as he spoke, however, but rather at Sadye, who continued to stare at her liege, offering a look that was not hard to read.

Aydrian hesitated a moment to take note of De'Unnero's shifting expression as the monk looked over the woman. "Duke Kalas will turn his march to St.-Mere-Abelle as soon as St. Gwendolyn is secured?" the young king asked, thinking it wise to distract the monk at that moment.

De'Unnero looked at him and blinked a few times, as if coming back to the situation at hand. "He will," the monk stammered. "Of course he will. As we determined."

De'Unnero's gaze went immediately back to the woman.

"Let us continue this in the warmth of your private quarters," Aydrian bade, and he turned to his commanders. "Dismiss the troops. Give them two days to rest and warm their bones, and then join in with the work already at hand here in Palmaris. I will not leave this city to be plucked from my grasp by the eager Midalis, but I expect to be on the road as soon as the weather begins its turn to spring. We will meet up with Duke Kalas in the southland, and then march together to the gates of St.-Mere-Abelle." He turned back to De'Unnero as he again made pointed reference to that most coveted prize. "Father Abbot Bou-raiy will open those gates, or we will knock them down."

The two men sat together in a small room a short while later. Sadye had moved to join in, but Aydrian had dismissed her, telling her to go to Chasewind Manor and find some much-deserved rest. She had tried to argue, but only briefly, before Aydrian had fixed her with a glare that had told her there would be no debate on this matter.

So he sat alone with De'Unnero, and he felt the keen tension within the man, a mixture of eagerness and anger.

"I have begun training on nearly fourscore new monks," De'Unnero explained, pacing back and forth in front of the blazing hearth while Aydrian reclined in a comfortable chair. "This war will no doubt deplete the Abellican ranks by more than half, and I intend to fill those positions quickly and efficiently. And I assure you, all of my monks are being trained in the gemstones from the start of their duties. I will have enough magical power ready to help counter the barrage we will no doubt face at the hands of the brothers of St.-Mere-Abelle."

"Well thought out," Aydrian replied. "As were your decisions to fortify the city. I plan to march with you to St.-Mere-Abelle; indeed, I plan to knock down those gates myself, if need be. But perhaps it will not come to that. Perhaps I can persuade Abbot Braumin to serve as an emissary, even if I have to take his body as my own."

The young king didn't miss the cloud that suddenly crossed De'Unnero's face.

"You've killed him," Aydrian reasoned.

"He escaped," De'Unnero corrected. "A friend rescued him, though at the cost of his own freedom."

"A friend?"

"Roger Lockless, companion of your mother," the monk explained. "I have thrown him in a deep dungeon. He is likely already dead, but if not, then he surely wishes that he was."

Aydrian shook his head and tried hard, but futilely, to hide his mounting anger.

"But it has proven a fair trade, I believe, for Roger Lockless was once the baron of Palmaris, and can be used as easily as was Abbot Braumin to keep the people of the city in proper order. And the man brought information with him of the whereabouts of our most dangerous enemy, the one you allowed to walk out of Ursal."

Aydrian smiled at the monk's unrelenting sarcasm concerning his mother. "If my mother is our most dangerous enemy, then the kingdom is already mine, I would say."

"She moved north from the city before our arrival, to Dundalis, likely," De'Unnero explained. "But she is gone from there, I believe, and on the road to the east. She seeks Midalis."

"Then let her die in his arms."

"Take heed of her, for the people love her," De'Unnero warned. "And she is no minor force, trained in both the blade and the gemstones."

"And I have slain her trainer," Aydrian said.

"Elbryan was her trainer, and I claim that kill," the monk corrected.

"His trainer, then," Aydrian agreed.

"Ah, so you found your Lady Dasslerond and her people."

"The Touel'alfar will be of no consequence to my reign—those Touel'alfar who remain alive, that is."

De'Unnero stared at him for a long time, and Aydrian saw the sincere admiration on the man's face. "Still," the monk said, "we should not take Jilseponie and Midalis lightly."

"And I do not," Aydrian assured him. "It would seem that we have but one more obstacle in our path to claiming all of the southern kingdom, that of St.-Mere-Abelle. She will stand strong against us, I am certain, but at the

least, we will damage and demoralize her, and hole her monks up tight behind their walls. When Midalis comes, if he is so foolish, then St.-Mere-
Abelle will be of little help to him. Your Palmaris must only hold him back
for the week it will take us to swing our army back here across the river and
properly destroy the line of Ursal."

"Easily achieved with but a few thousand warriors," De'Unnero assured
him. "Little magical power will accompany Midalis, other than that of your
mother."

"And if Midalis does not come, then we will play the waiting game, finishing off St.-Mere-Abelle before turning our eyes to the region north of the
gulf," Aydrian replied. "Perhaps we will have to wait until the spring of
next year to begin that final march, but with all the southern kingdom secured, and Behren added to our hold, we will only grow stronger while Midalis hides among his tall trees. The ending, it would seem, is inevitable."

"We always knew that it would be," said De'Unnero.

Aydrian waited for the monk to stop pacing long enough to look at him
directly. "You will soon enough become Father Abbot," he said.

"I already am," De'Unnero countered. "St.-Mere-Abelle is isolated, if
Duke Kalas completed his march, and I cannot believe that he has not. No
abbey of southern Honce-the-Bear is any longer aligned with the mother
abbey and Fio Bou-raiy. He has lost before St.-Mere-Abelle even falls."

"Then I salute you, Father Abbot De'Unnero," Aydrian said. "Perhaps
we should hold a formal ceremony announcing your ascent before we
march upon St.-Mere-Abelle."

De'Unnero paused for a bit, then nodded.

"So tell me of your new Church," Aydrian prompted. "You will not en-
dorse the final canonization of Saint Avelyn, I would guess."

"Of course not."

"And you will return the Abellican Order to its cloistered roots, where
the sacred gemstones are held tight by the brethren alone and their magics
are not so openly offered to the common peasants?"

"Of course, as you already know," De'Unnero said. "Indeed, in your absence, my brothers have collected many of the gemstones from the folk of
Palmaris—reimbursing them, of course, as we discussed. The old order is
already returning to the land, elevating the Church above the ordinary, as it
once was. But you know all of this, so why do you ask?"

Aydrian stared at him long and hard, locking the monk's gaze with his
own. "I sent Sadye to Chasewind Manor," he said bluntly. "There she will
remain. With me."

De'Unnero narrowed his eyes, sucked in his breath, and stood very still,
his hands clenched at his side.

"I offer her back to you," the young king said. "Wholly. But only if you
are willing to forsake that other prize you so crave."

"Take care your words," De'Unnero warned.

Aydrian rose from his chair and calmly walked to the hearth, pointedly putting his back to the monk, showing De'Unnero that he did not fear him in the least. "I am quite beyond you now. You know this. You desired the Abellican Order, and I have delivered it to you." He turned about to face the monk. "To you alone. How convenient, was it not, that I sent Abbot Olin south to the land he most desired?"

"And in exchange, you take my wife?"

"I did not take anything that was not offered," Aydrian replied.

De'Unnero started forward, as if to attack, but stopped himself abruptly. Aydrian did not even make a move to defend himself.

"Allow her to become queen of Honce-the-Bear," Aydrian said. "You know that she desires such. Of course, she does! And why should she not? I have my kingdom, I give to you yours. What life will Sadye know at your side? That of a secret consort, to be whispered about and gossiped over by every other brother of the Abellican Order, and by the peasants, as well. What life is that for the woman who has served us both so brilliantly?"

De'Unnero trembled as he stood there, hardly seeming mollified.

"But it is not your choice, after all," Aydrian went on. "Nor is it mine. It is Sadye's to make, and so she has. Now I ask you to let her go without penalty. Fondly hold those times that you had side by side, my friend, but recognize the truth. Your position has outgrown her. You cannot lead the Church in its former image and glory if you openly hold a wife!

"Be sensible, my friend! You are stepping into a most delicate situation. Obviously so! You would so risk everything to hold Sadye at your side?"

"And if I would?" the monk spat.

"Then I would sooner make peace with Fio Bou-raiy than elevate such a fool to the position as leader of the Church of Honce-the-Bear," Aydrian bluntly replied. "This is no idle threat, Marcalo De'Unnero. You desire the Church, and I hope to give it to you. But if you will not hold fast your responsibility above all else, then I will not deliver St.-Mere-Abelle!" He drifted forward as he spoke, so that he and De'Unnero were face-to-face, barely an inch apart. "Choose wisely."

Aydrian clearly recognized the hatred that De'Unnero masked and the tension in the man's arms that revealed his desire to reach up and throttle Aydrian where he stood.

But Aydrian knew that the monk would not strike out at him, for Aydrian understood the truth of Marcalo De'Unnero's heart.

St.-Mere-Abelle would be his bride.

The First Nibble

W hat struck Pony most about Pireth Vanguard, the city of
Honce-the-Bear's prince for so many years, was how small
the place truly was. It didn't even seem a city by the standards of the woman who had lived the majority of her life in Ursal and Palmaris, but rather, a village surrounding a castle fortress set at the head of a
sheltered bay, overlooking many long docks and wharves. There were out-
lying farms, but they were not huge, unlike those outside of Palmaris. Neither were the roads truly definable structures. They were cart paths and
nothing more, and seemed as if they were often and easily redefinable.

Pony had once served in the Coastpoint Guards and had spent considerable time at Pireth Tulme, the southernmost of the three fortresses—Tulme,
Dancard, and Vanguard—that protected the Gulf of Corona. Vanguard
was surely larger than that guard tower. But still, Pony had always imagined
Pireth Vanguard to be much grander than this, along the lines of Palmaris,
perhaps, with a great seaside castle surrounded by many streets and houses.
How surprised and dismayed she was when Prince Midalis had explained
to her that the population of all of Vanguard, this vast stretch of forested
land, was not equal to that of Palmaris city alone. Given that, she had to
wonder how they could hope to mount any kind of a threat against Aydrian,
who controlled nearly all of the southland?

The other thing that Pony noticed when she, Bradwarden, Prince Midalis,
Captain Al'u'met, and Abbot Haney of St. Belfour entered Pireth Vanguard,
was that the docks were nearly free of vessels. In fact, the only ship of any
note that was in dock was Captain Al'u'met's *Saudi Jacintha*, and she was
fully crewed, with sails untied should she need to put out fast.

"We must be ready to strike camp and march quickly as soon as the
weather breaks," Prince Midalis opened when the group settled into one of
the large tower rooms overlooking the harbor.

"In whichever direction Juraviel's telling us to strike," Bradwarden added.
The talk became more of the same planning that they had gone over be-

fore, and Pony tuned out of the discussion rather quickly, after inquiring of Abbot Haney about the health of Master Dellman, an old friend who had stood with her and Elbryan and Braumin Herde in the last days of Markwart.

"He is well," Abbot Haney had replied. "Though he fears for his old friend, Abbot Braumin."

As did they all, Pony mused, knowing full well the grave implications of having Marcalo De'Unnero returned to Palmaris. She put those dark thoughts out of mind quickly, though, and forced herself to focus on the situation at hand. They had to find a way to strike and strike hard, to win some early decisive victories against Aydrian so that Prince Midalis could gain credibility with the common folk of Honce-the-Bear once more. As long as Aydrian seemed in complete control, Pony knew, it would be impossible to drum up any undercurrent of support for the rightful successor to her late husband.

The meeting was short, as they had little to truly discuss until they had some better idea of their enemy's positioning. But even as Prince Midalis began to call for its end, a trio of other guests arrived, which changed the complexion of the place considerably.

"Greetings to you, fair Queen Jilseponie," said Liam O'Blythe, the close friend of Prince Midalis. He wasn't nearly as imposing a figure as Midalis, with his short red hair and slender frame, and a smile that always seemed about to erupt across his freckled face.

Pony gave him a warm look.

"By the gods of the high mountains, it is good to see you once more, my old friend!" boomed the second of the newcomers, the giant Alpinadoran ranger, Andacanavar. He strode into the room, moving right to Pony, and wrapped her in a great and warm hug. "Even though it seems that trouble's always not far behind you!"

He pushed Pony back to arm's length and the two shared warm smiles, and Pony turned to regard Bruinhelde, the Alpinadoran leader who had done so much good for his people in the time of the rosy plague. These two strong and visionary men had put aside their race's typical mistrust of anyone who was not Alpinadoran, and had led their people in great numbers to Mount Aida in the days of the plague, saving perhaps a devastating secondary outbreak in the cold northern kingdom. The last time Pony had seen the pair was at her wedding to King Danube, when Andacanavar and Bruinhelde had accompanied Prince Midalis to the ceremony, arriving unexpectedly to the delight of both Pony and Danube.

And now here they were once again, with a large number of their warriors camped to the east and north. What a testament to Prince Midalis, Pony thought, that he had so strengthened the bond between Vanguard and Alpinador, two traditional enemies.

"So it's your boy who's bringing all this trouble, I'm hearing," Andacanavar remarked. "A boy trained by the Touel'alfar."

"A boy . . . a young man," Pony corrected, "who has recently exacted his revenge upon the fair folk of Andur'Blough Inninness."

Andacanavar's bright blue eyes narrowed suspiciously.

"Lady Dasslerond is dead," Pony admitted. "And her people are on the run, locked from their valley by the same desperate enchantment that Dasslerond used to keep Aydrian from burning the place down."

The barbarian ranger did a good job of keeping his expression calm and controlled, but Pony sensed the sudden surge of rage within him, an anger clear to her from the man's great hands that were still clamped upon her shoulders. Andacanavar had seen seven full decades of life and more, but there remained within him a strength that was frightening indeed!

"Your friendship with these strange creatures you call Touel'alfar has ever been a curiosity to me," Bruinhelde said to Andacanavar, and his command of the common Honce-the-Bear tongue surprised Pony. "What does this mean to you, my friend?"

"It means that this King Aydrian has stepped beyond the bounds," the ranger grimly replied. He looked from Bruinhelde to Prince Midalis. "I am here as your ally. We came from Alpinador to support our friend. But know now that this has gone beyond that call." The giant man turned back to Pony. "Your son has made of me a mortal enemy. Understand this."

Despite her determination to see Aydrian taken down and Prince Midalis restored to his birthright, the words still stung Pony. For in looking at the determination and outrage simmering behind those bright blue eyes of the giant ranger, she could well envision the death of Aydrian.

But she could not refute Andacanavar's words, for he was a ranger, elven-trained, a student of Dasslerond and her people. Would not her dear dead husband Elbryan similarly do battle on behalf of Andur'Blough Inninness, as fiercely as his father and Pony's own father had defended Dundalis from the goblin hordes those decades before?

Pony offered a nod to Andacanavar, and felt his iron grip relax a bit.

With the arrival of the Alpinadorans, Prince Midalis called the group back to order, wanting to fill in the newest arrivals on all the details thus far. Pony excused herself, though, and allowed one of the prince's guards to escort her to a small private room.

She knew that it was time for her to do a bit of scouting on her own.

Pony went back through that same room, her spirit flying free of her body, a short while later. Only Bradwarden and Andacanavar seemed to sense her presence as she passed by them, crossing through the stone wall as if it were as insubstantial as smoke, and out into the open air.

A storm was brewing, with cold sleet lashing the tower walls and the ground, but it was of no concern to the spirit of Pony, any more than the minor inconvenience that it reduced the visibility to her spirit eyes.

Using Captain Al'u'met's directions, the woman lined herself up on the docks of Vanguard, then rushed away over the open water, flying straight and flying fast across the miles. She moved up high as she flew to widen her perspective, and a short while later, she saw the dark island and tower of Pireth Dancard.

She moved in fast, flying low and circling the island, to see the fifteen warships of Earl DePaunch. Twelve were moored offshore, not far from the dock area. Two others, apparently under repair, were tied up to the docks and heavy with guide ropes and canvas. The last was nearly out of the water altogether, up on great skids to the side of the dock. She had been severely damaged, obviously, and a good deal of her decking was missing, along with one of her masts.

Pony went out to the dozen seaworthy vessels and flew onto one and then another, even searching belowdecks. As she had expected, they were nearly deserted, with all the crews ashore, buttoned up tight against the continuing wintry weather.

Pony went ashore as well, sweeping through the town, then the fortified keep itself. No small force had come to Dancard, she realized, and once more she was reminded of the daunting task that lay before her and Prince Midalis. If the prince took his entire fleet and entire army south to Dancard, he would find himself in a brutal battle indeed—and this was a tiny fraction, no doubt, of the forces Aydrian had mustered. Yet even this small force might hold Prince Midalis at bay.

Pony began to feel the weariness of the gemstone use profoundly then. She hadn't used the stones much in the last years and had almost forgotten how taxing extended spirit-walking could be. She left Pireth Dancard in a rush, sweeping back to the north and her waiting body.

When she was back in her corporeal form, she wanted nothing more than to curl up and go to sleep. But she knew that her information should be passed along at once, and so she dragged herself out of her room and back to the conference room, where the others were still gathered, though now they were eating and drinking more than discussing any strategy.

All eyes turned upon the bedraggled woman when she entered.

"Are ye all right, girl?" Bradwarden asked.

Prince Midalis was the first to Pony's side, sliding his arm under her shoulder to support her.

"She is weary from gemstone use," Abbot Haney remarked.

"I am," the woman agreed. "In the last hours, I have paid a visit to Pireth Dancard. It is as we feared, with fifteen great warships moored or in dock, and a host of Honce-the-Bear warriors manning the tower."

Pony settled back on some cushions that Haney brought over.

"Young Aydrian moved quickly to seal off the gulf," Captain Al'u'met remarked. "Dancard is the most obvious resupply stop for any ship attempting to cross, and certainly a necessary respite for any large flotilla."

"He's making sure that ye come by land, if ye come," Bradwarden reasoned.

"Or he's allowing himself a secure resupply to support his fleet if he chooses to strike straight across the gulf at Pireth Vanguard," Prince Midalis added.

"A strong position, either way," said Captain Al'u'met.

"Then one we must take back," the prince replied.

"Dancard is a considerable fortress," Pony warned. "To say nothing of battling a dozen or more of Honce-the-Bear's finest warships."

"The ships are moored?" Al'u'met asked.

"Tied down for the winter," Pony replied. "And barely crewed."

"Because they know we cannot attack until the turn of the season," Midalis reasoned.

"Or maybe we can," Al'u'met said, and he looked at Pony as he spoke.

The woman returned his smile, understanding full well what the captain was considering, because in truth, she was already thinking the same thing.

"To sail a flotilla across the high seas in this season would be folly," Prince Midalis argued against the obvious sentiment. "A rising storm would wipe out all that I have to offer—and to send any less would weaken greatly any hope that we have of defeating a fortified Pireth Dancard."

"Even if you brought all of your forces," Pony interjected, "you would find Pireth Dancard no easy target. The warriors who came in under Aydrian's banner are well trained and battle-hardened, and have more than a few Allheart Knights among their ranks."

"And likely some gemstone-wielding brothers," Abbot Haney added.

"Then the choices would seem limited," said the prince. "We could march to Palmaris, or dig in here and battle any seaborne forces that King Aydrian sends across the gulf in the spring, or summer if he chooses to wait that long."

"Or we could go and steal the mobility from those forces he has placed in Pireth Dancard," Pony explained. "And strengthen our fleet in the process."

That had more than a few gazes turned the woman's way.

"I will take a group of sailors to Pireth Dancard posthaste," Captain Al'u'met picked up the reasoning. "With Jilseponie's guidance, we might steal some of Aydrian's warships, and perhaps scuttle those we cannot pilfer."

"A winter storm . . ." Midalis began.

"Then we will watch for winter storms," Al'u'met explained, and he looked back to Pony. "They come from the west and northwest, unerringly. If you can fly out to Dancard, then surely you can go out to the western edges of the gulf and beyond, and find us a stretch of fair weather."

"As far as I must," Pony agreed. She moved from her pillowed seat to kneel right before the seated Midalis. "This is our first chance," she explained. "The deep of winter has their guard down. We can go in, strike fast and hard, and be away at once. Even if we can capture only a few of the ships, and scuttle a few others, the attack might well broaden our options when the season turns."

"But how many can Al'u'met's *Saudi Jacintha* carry?" Midalis argued. "It will take fifteen men, at the least, to put one of Honce-the-Bear's great warships out onto the open seas. Even if we loaded *Saudi Jacintha* to sit to her rail in the water, Captain Al'u'met could not carry enough men to capture and sail more than three ships."

"Then we need to send more ships," Pony argued.

"Our fishing vessels could not possibly withstand the winter seas, even if no storm blew through," said the prince.

"But our longboats could," came a voice from across the room, the resonating baritone of Bruinhelde.

Pony, Midalis, and all the others turned to regard the giant Alpinadoran, all of them wearing expressions of complete surprise—all except for Andacanavar, that is, who sat next to his friend Bruinhelde, his great muscular arms crossed over his wolf-fur tunic.

"It seems a fine plan," Bruinhelde went on. "We have agreed that we must strike King Aydrian at his weakest points. This is one."

"Even if Jilseponie scouts all the way to the edges of the gulf, she will guarantee us only enough clear weather to get to Pireth Dancard, if that much," Prince Midalis warned the man. "Through the week and more of the return trip, we will be vulnerable to gales."

"The seas off Alpinador are always rough," Andacanavar replied, "the waters always deathly cold. Yet my people have gone down to the sea in boats for as long as the tales reach back. Accept Bruinhelde's offer as that of a friend, and let us strike a blow at King Aydrian."

Prince Midalis looked all around at the others, and Pony understood that he was searching for some support, some counsel. When his gaze settled last upon her, the woman offered a smile and a determined nod.

Prince Midalis looked over at Bruinhelde. "Lay plans for our transport with Captain Al'u'met," he bade the man. "I pray you fetch enough boats that we may strike hard at Pireth Dancard, perhaps to carry enough men to steal all of Aydrian's ships anchored there."

"Go out this very night," the prince instructed his friend, Liam. "Find our best and most fit sailors, particularly those who might have once served under the duke of the Mirianic and thus have experience in crewing the great warships."

Liam O'Blythe seemed a bit hesitant about all of this. He glanced at Pony one last time, then finally gave a resigned nod.

With that settled, Prince Midalis turned to Abbot Haney. "We will need gemstone-wielding monks to accompany our run," he explained.

"Our run?" the abbot echoed. "Surely you cannot go along, my Prince."

Midalis' responding expression showed his incredulity. "Do you believe that I would send anyone if I would not go myself?"

"You are the cornerstone of the resistance to King Aydrian," Abbot Haney argued. "The only credibility that we have to any resistance at all, outside of the Abellican Church. To risk your life—"

"It is all a risk, good Abbot," Pony interrupted, her words and firm expression cutting the argument short. She looked back at her friend Midalis, the man seeming so much a younger and more trim version of her late husband. "We will ride the bow of *Saudi Jacintha* together, you and I," she said, her eyes glowing with intensity. "We will cripple and strand this force that has conquered Pireth Dancard, and we will let those warriors on the island know that it was Prince Midalis who came against them and soundly defeated them!"

The prince showed true gratitude in his determined nod of response.

The meeting broke up then, with all heading off to make their preparations. Pony spent a few moments whispering assurances to Prince Midalis, then caught up to Bradwarden and Andacanavar in the corridor outside.

"Words wonderfully placed, milady," the ranger said, and he took up Pony's hand and gave it a kiss. "As was your quick thinking in going right out to Pireth Dancard, as you did. It is no puzzle to me that this young Aydrian is as strong as he is, though a bit misguided."

"More than a bit," Bradwarden put in.

"From Jilseponie's womb, with Elbryan as sire . . . has there ever been one in all the world of better breeding?" Andacanavar went on.

"A trio of rangers, that family," Bradwarden agreed, but his words brought a scowl to Pony's face.

"Bah, but you are a ranger, woman, though 'twas never formally proclaimed," Andacanavar said against her frown. "And Lady Dasslerond was all the more a fool to treat you otherwise, and to deny you the knowledge and love of your son."

Pony accepted the compliment gracefully, placing her free hand over Andacanavar's as he still held her other. "We will repair the errors of Dasslerond," she assured the man.

"I know all that you have done already in your young life, good woman," Andacanavar replied. "I've not a doubt."

They sailed and rowed out on the heels of the storm, for Pony had used the gemstones and scouted far to the west and found nothing but clear weather. Al'u'met's *Saudi Jacintha* led the way, carrying many of the leaders, Pony, Bradwarden, and Midalis included. Behind came a line of Alpinadoran longboats, low in the water but with their high, decorated prows standing tall. Fifteen oars lined either side of each sleek vessel and a single mast was set in the center of each. They were not as swift as the *Saudi Jacintha*, except when the strong crews bent their backs over the oars. But they were seaworthy, incredibly so, and they bobbed along the constant wintry swells with ease.

On the second day out from Pireth Vanguard, Pony again fell into her soul stone and spirit-walked out to the west, roving far in search of brewing bad weather. Her report that no storms were in sight assured Al'u'met that they would make the fortress, at least, and begin their turn back to the north.

"We should make secondary plans," Prince Midalis said to Pony later that same day, *Saudi Jacintha*'s sails full of wind, the sleek cutter speeding along. "If we arrive at the fortress and find that a storm will catch us before we can get back to Vanguard's sheltered docks, then we'll do better by taking the island and mooring there."

"You'll have a difficult fight on your hand," Pony replied.

"Better that we lose men to battle than to a storm," said Midalis. "If those who lose friends and family know that their loved ones died battling the scourge Aydrian, then they will hold more patience for the long war that we must endure."

The callousness of the words struck Pony hard, but only for a moment. She understood the truth of war and knew that her friend had to be thinking like a warrior. His words were unsympathetic because he had to be callous, to a degree, if they were going to have any chance of mounting a full-fledged war with Aydrian.

"You have no desire for any of this," she said. "Yet you surely have the belly for it."

Now it was Midalis' turn to look curiously at his friend. "The belly for it?"

"When Elbryan and I had to turn our fight from goblins and the monstrous minions of the demon dactyl to the human minions of Father Abbot Markwart, it nearly broke us," the woman admitted. "There is such a profound difference between battling a creature you know to be evil and one that you understand is without true choice. I have little heart to kill a man, and yet, I know that is precisely what I will likely find myself doing, if I am to ride beside you."

"But you do so, as do I," the prince remarked. "Because we both understand that the end result will be less tragic for the people than avoidance of the battle."

"That is my sustaining hope," Pony said quietly, and she stared out at the rolling dark waters of the wintry Mirianic. "In a strange way, I think Aydrian feels the same."

"By stealing the throne?"

"By claiming what he erroneously believes to be his birthright," the woman explained. "I expect that he sees the world under his control as a world he can influence positively."

"Would any tyrant view it otherwise?"

"No, of course not," the woman said, her voice even quieter. She reached into her pouch and brought forth a handful of various magical gemstones. "How many will I kill when I loose the energies of these?" she asked.

Prince Midalis put his hand on her shoulder and gave a squeeze, then leaned in so that he was very close to her as he whispered his assurance. "As few as possible."

Pony offered him a grateful return look, and the man backed away.

"We have caught a strong tail wind on the heels of the storm," he said. "A couple more days and we will have our first victory."

They came within striking distance of Pireth Vanguard one dark night without incident, and without, as far as Pony could tell, any storms brewing anywhere to the west of them along the gulf. Once again, her spirit-walking proved invaluable, allowing the fleet to regroup just outside the viewing and hearing range of their enemies. While Midalis organized the strike forces, Pony again went to the moored dozen warships, her ghost moving through each of them in turn to make sure that none was heavily crewed.

"Now the question is, how do we get there without alerting those along the docks, and those ships moored closer in?" Midalis asked when the woman returned to her physical body and walked out on deck to join him, Captain Al'u'met, Bruinhelde, and Andacanavar. "And how shall we find all of the proper targets in the dark of night?"

"My boats go in under sail alone," Bruinhelde told them.

"And I will mark the way," Pony added. She fished out a piece of amber and held it up for the others to see. "With this, I can walk across the water, silently and swiftly. I will go from ship to ship and set a candle, unseen by the crew." She looked to Al'u'met, and the captain nodded and moved to a small hold to the side. He reached under the lid of the box, produced a small sack, and handed it to her.

Pony set it down and fished through it, retrieving a hollow half globe carved of wood. "The captain and I thought it might come to this," she explained. "And so he had one of his skilled woodcarvers make these." To demonstrate, she placed the candle into the globe and set it upon the deck. "The only ones who will see the light of the candle will be those at whom the hollow is aimed," she explained. "Those on the docks or in the other ships will remain oblivious."

"The girl thinks o' everything," Bradwarden said with a great snort. "Ah, but I've trained that one well, I have!"

"There is one ship grander than the others," Pony continued, turning to face Midalis directly. "And she is the most heavily crewed, with a score of men, at least, aboard her."

"Then that is my target," the prince replied.

A dozen Alpinadoran longboats set out soon after, gliding quietly toward the distant island, barely a dark blot on the horizon under the light of a quarter moon. Pony stood beside Midalis and Bradwarden, who held his great longbow in hand.

"I fear to let you run off alone in the darkness," Midalis admitted to her.

Pony turned an incredulous look over him.

"Yes, yes," the man said, waving his hands in the air to ward off her retort before she could scream at him.

But Pony merely chuckled. "Then come with me," she offered. "Let us run together to mark the outer ship, then you and I will take the flagship before this boat even arrives."

"You can do that?"

Pony smiled all the wider and offered him her hand. When he took it, she led him to the very edge of the boat as it glided along barely above the dark water. With a glance back and a wink at Bradwarden, the woman casually stepped off, pulling Midalis behind her.

It was an easy enough task for Pony to coordinate the two stones, hematite and amber, so that she could include Midalis within the power of the water-walking. Together the two ran ahead of the slow-moving fleet. Soon enough, they were in sight of the dark warships' silhouettes, skeletal masts rising into the night sky. To the side loomed Pireth Dancard, darkened at this late hour, with only the hint of a glow coming from one window halfway up the main tower.

Pony led Midalis to the far left first, coming to the warship farthest out. They reached her and managed to scramble up over her side without incident. Pony motioned the proper direction to the prince, then reached into another belt pouch and pulled forth a candle and a shielding globe. She set it down low on the rail, between two balustrades, blocking the light with the globe from all directions save one, the one facing out toward the approaching fleet.

Then the two went over the side and on to the next ship in line, repeating the process. They had five marked when they noted the approach of the silent fleet, and knew that they were running short on time.

"They will find the others without our assistance," Pony assured Midalis, and she took his hand and started off toward the vessel moored in the center of the second rank, the closest ship to the wharves.

They went aboard easily, and both knew at once that this ship wasn't nearly as deserted as the others. Pony didn't hesitate, though, but motioned for Midalis to follow as she headed straight for the large deck cabin set at the stern of the large three-master.

"Are you ready?" Pony asked.

The man just grinned, obviously thrilled by his companion's unexpected daring.

Pony walked through the door, guiding Midalis to the side of the outside jamb as she did.

The men inside, nearly a dozen, looked up from the coin-covered table that was set between them.

"What're . . . ?" one started to say.

"Greetings," said Pony.

Several of the men stood up; a couple went for their weapons.

"Earl DePaunch sent us a bit of funning, did he?" one sailor asked lewdly.

"Bah, this one's a bit old for that!" another added.

"Do none of you recognize me?" Pony replied, filling her voice with sad resignation. "And for all those years that I sailed beside you, on *River Palace*."

That widened a few eyes.

"Queen Jilseponie!" one man gasped, and now they seemed even more confused, and more went for their weapons, though those who already held theirs let them slip down toward the floor.

"So quick were you all to forget," Pony scolded. "Me, and your proper royal line!" As she finished, she pulled Prince Midalis from around the corner.

One man screamed, another fell over trying to leap up from his seat, and two lifted weapons, gave a unified battle cry, and leaped forward to attack.

But Pony was the quicker, lifting her hand and jolting the pair with a sudden blast of lightning that lifted them into the air and threw them to the back of the room.

Other men moved as if to ready an attack, but Pony waved her hand about. "Shame on you all!" she scolded. "I bring you your rightful king!"

"Aydrian is king!" one sailor growled back.

"So says Aydrian," Prince Midalis calmly replied. "I intend to tell him differently, and you"—he paused and pointed all around at them—"all of you, would do well to consider the choices that lie before you. I understand that you have been misled, and will pardon you to a man. But only if you choose wisely!"

As he finished, they all heard a commotion on the deck behind.

"Bah, now ye're to get yers, phony prince!" one man cried, and the others growled and bristled, some shaking their weapons.

But then they all dropped back as the giant centaur came in the door between Pony and the prince, Bradwarden's huge bow drawn and readied with an arrow that seemed more a spear.

"I'm thinkin' that any smart ones among ye might be dropping yer weapons to the floor," he said. "One o' yerselfs that don't'll be getting pinned to the back wall, to be sure!"

Pony lifted her gemstone again to add her weight to the threat, and Midalis drew out his fine sword.

"Weigh anchor!" came a cry from the deck. "Four ships taken already, milord! And more to fall soon enough."

"You will pardon me if I borrow your ship, good soldiers of Honce-the-Bear," Prince Midalis said, offering a salute with his sword. "Any who wish to sail with me, may indeed. Any who prefer Pireth Dancard will be placed on a rowboat and shoved away!"

"I must be away," Pony said, and she slipped to the side and kissed Midalis on the cheek for luck. "Don't you be sailing too far from me!" she added. "And keep your beacons bright against the darkness."

She ran out then, pausing to salute the men, Alpinadoran and Bearman alike working hard at pulling up the anchor. Pony went over the side without hesitation, engaging the amber's water-walking powers once more. She rushed for the shore, where a bit of activity was beginning—likely the soldiers reacting to the noises out in the bay.

Pony came up on the wharf a moment later, stepping lightly onto the planks and dropping the amber's power, replacing it almost immediately with the blue-white sheen of the serpentine shield. Her glowing appearance at once drew attention, with confused defenders screaming and pointing.

From there she ran to the deck of the ship to the left of the wharf, the one appearing the most seaworthy. Several sailors opposed her, moving all about and drawing forth their short swords.

Pony lifted her hand, holding a ruby, and brought forth a pillar of flame about herself. "You know me as Queen Jilseponie!" she shouted at them, and the pillar flared outward briefly, warding them away. "You know my power with the magical gemstones. I warn you only once to be gone from this ship, and from the one across the wharf!" As she talked, she headed for the ladder leading belowdecks, and she quickly went down, leaving a trail of smoking footprints behind. She nodded gratefully when she heard the men scrambling above, their footfalls moving toward the wharf. She even heard one go splashing into the water.

Pony reached deep inside the ruby, gathering its power.

And then she let it loose, in a tremendous fireball that roared up through the cracks in the planking, blowing out many planks as it went, igniting all the ship.

Pony ran up the ladder before it was consumed, feeling just a little warmth from the conflagration. She held her serpentine defensive shield strong and ran across the wharf and onto the opposing ship.

An arrow whistled past her head!

The woman didn't waver, but went right to the middle of the open deck. She noted a sailor still aboard—there might have been several.

But she couldn't hesitate, not now. Not with the island coming awake and all the soldiers on their guard.

The second ship went up in flames. A man, engulfed in fire, leaped from the burning decking into the water.

Pony ran out, not onto the wharf, but the other way, calling forth the amber again and dropping the serpentine shield as soon as she was free of the second conflagration. She ran full out for the shore and the third and final ship, the one in dry dock, and she quickly put that one, too, to the ruby's consuming fires.

Then she ran down the beach and waded out into the cold water, moving near the second flaming ship to find the man who had leaped off in flames. She found him bobbing in the surf, near death. Gently she reached under his heaving chest and turned him to his back, then slowly dragged him around the bow of the ship, out of sight from the wharves and land.

Pony pulled forth her hematite; she knew that this was insanity, but simply couldn't bring herself to leave this poor unfortunate soul in so much agony. She held him close and fell into the soul stone, calling up its healing powers and sending them with all her strength into the dying man. She felt his spirit falling away from her, but charged down the dark path after it, reaching for him, calling to him.

The man's eyes opened, and he gasped and spat out some water.

"Know that Prince Midalis' mercy saved you this day," the woman said. "He is the rightful king of Honce-the-Bear and will come again in glory to defeat Aydrian. Tell your friends, in quiet confidence, that Prince Midalis dreads the blood he knows must be shed to restore him to his rightful throne."

She helped the man stand on his own then, and pointed him toward the shore, and only then did she realize that a pair of other soldiers were watching her, with drawn bows.

She looked at them, knowing that they had her dead to rights. She even started to lift her arms in a show of surrender.

But the two soldiers looked at their miraculously healed mate wading toward them, and lowered their bows. One of them went to the wounded man to help him ashore and the other offered Pony a nod.

The woman went out into the darkness, bringing forth the amber to lift herself from the numbingly cold water. She heard much commotion out there on the water, including the sounds of battle from more than one of the warships.

Behind her came the thrum of catapults, and the swish of flaming pitch balls soaring overhead, to fall hissing into the water.

Above all the tumult, the woman heard one voice clearly, that of Prince Midalis ordering all who had secured their ships to put out at once. Accompanying that voice came the piping of Bradwarden, spurring the men on with a rousing tune.

Pony held her position in the dark, off to the side from the three burning ships, and watched. She winced as one of the ships putting out got hit squarely by a flaming missile, and a moment later, she keenly heard the screams echoing across the dark waves. Off to the side, another ship went up in flames, this time from something that happened on the deck itself, likely in the struggle for control of the vessel. Soon after, she heard calls for help and many splashes as men abandoned the burning ship, and heard Alpinadorans calling out directions to retrieve their swimming kin.

Another ship got hit from a shore battery, the flagship Midalis had pilfered, and at that terrible moment, Pony wondered if this expedition had been worth the effort and the cost!

But all the moored ships save three were still moving away from shore, gliding out into the darkness toward a distant beacon—the signal fire burning atop the mainmast of Al'u'met's *Saudi Jacintha*, the assigned rally point. One ship held in the water, burning badly and sure to go under, and another, apparently controlled by her original Honce-the-Bear crew, was gliding in fast for shore.

Pony couldn't let that happen. She ran along the water to intercept, crossing dangerously close to a rowboat that carried several of the men from the ship she and Midalis had taken. If they noticed her, though, they said nothing, and the woman ran on, coming up in front of the warship. She fished her pouch for a malachite, then brought forth its powers of levitations, lifting her over the prow and forecastle. Even as she set down on the deck, soldiers came at her, but Pony drew out her sword and met the charge.

One man thrust straight in. An inner downward circle from Pony's blade brought it over then down beside the thrusting sword and she easily turned it out wide. Pony went right past the man as he stumbled, overbalancing from his unexpectedly clean miss. The warrior woman stopped short and parried the attack of a second man while she kicked out hard at the first, pushing him along farther toward the rail. He hit that rail and caught himself, then turned about.

But there was Pony, charging in, her sword stabbing, stabbing, left and right, forcing him to retreat where there could be no retreat.

He went over the side into the dark water.

Pony swung about, her sword coming across hard to ring against that of her second attacker. A sudden thrust had him in fast retreat, and a second forced him to turn and dive down and roll away. But then Pony had to do likewise as a spear flew past. She came back suddenly, hitting the swordsman with a series of sudden thrusts, some of which got through to stick the man hard.

Up came the blue-white glow. "Off this ship!" Pony cried to her enemies. "Begone, says Queen Jilseponie! For I bring forth the fires of the ruby, and take this ship with flames as I burned those three at the shore!"

She thought her words effective, particularly when the man nearest her threw his sword to the deck and ran to the rail, diving overboard into the dark waters. But then she felt the stabbing pain suddenly as an arrow zipped across the deck to slam her hard in the side, so near to the scar left by her last grievous wound.

Pony lurched and felt her hold on the serpentine diminish suddenly. She tried to reengage it, but had no time to be sure of anything other than the power of the ruby.

She brought forth a fireball—not a large one, but an effective blast that had all the front of the ship burning.

From a distant place, Pony heard the screams and shouts of protest from the sailors still aboard. She stumbled along, feeling the intense heat, nearly collapsing from the pain, her mind straying.

She could smell her hair burning.

She had to hold her focus. She had to find the amber and be gone.

She knew all of that, of course, but it was hard, so hard, to know anything at all beyond the burning agony of the arrow wound and the conflagration closing in all about her . . .

Then she was out on the water, walking somehow, stumbling about toward the distant ships. And then she felt the numbing cold again, and it took her several moments to realize that she had lost her concentration, that she was not atop the water anymore, but *in* the water.

And she was not moving out after Prince Midalis and her friends, but was being pushed back toward the rocky island.

It was all dark and all cold and she had no energy left to offer the gemstones. She felt no more pain in her side, though, and strangely so. She just felt . . . somehow at great peace, as if she had moved beyond all sensation of pain.

Options

"We surprised and wounded them," Pagonel said to Brynn and the other leaders of Dharyan-Dharielle as soon as the courier from Yatol De Hamman had gone. The man had come in under a flag of truce, and had insisted that the battle had all been a terrible mistake, a result of a miscommunication between Jacintha and Dharyan-Dharielle. The courier had expressed apologies from Yatol De Hamman, Yatol Mado Wadon, and, pointedly, from Abbot Olin.

"Too many of De Hamman's soldiers remember the last siege of this city," the mystic reasoned.

"It took them weeks to bury their dead the last time!" Tanalk Grenk added. "And if they press the attack once again, there will be none of them left alive to bury the stinking corpses!" The man's typically fierce words brought nods and cheers from all the others in the room.

Brynn shot Tanalk Grenk a look of sincere admiration. He had grown in stature over the last few months, from the warlord of a single tribe to a spokesman for all the warriors of To-gai. She trusted in him implicitly, and had given him the most important and delicate missions to perform, always with complete confidence that he would accomplish the tasks beyond her wildest expectations—as with his ride to the rescue of Dharyan-Dharielle when De Hamman had attacked. Brynn had sent Grenk and his force out along the plateau divide to make sure that there were no easily exploitable weak spots along the border. As ordered, Grenk had solidified the defenses of every possible route over the plateau divide into central or northern To-gai, he had had the wisdom to go beyond that. When his scouts had informed him of De Hamman's move to the north, Grenk had assembled a crack corps of elite riders and shadowed the Behrenese army's movements, secretly putting his force into position in the shadows of the plateau divide a short ride from the city. When De Hamman had attacked, Grenk's cavalry had come in at exactly the right time, and at exactly the right place.

Even more impressive, Grenk had set up a line of communication, using the sun reflection system that the To-gai-ru had long ago perfected, and was now orchestrating the arrival of yet another secondary force, one ready to strike hard at De Hamman's flank yet again if he persisted in attacking the city. It was a daring move, perhaps even desperate, for in shifting so much of To-gai's forces this far north, the warrior leader had badly exposed their southern flanks.

But Brynn agreed with his reasoning, especially when he had given her all assurances that he had sent many scouts into the desert to the south. As far as he could tell, De Hamman's army was the only organized Behrenese force in all the region.

"Their admission that Abbot Olin was intimately involved in this march does not bode well," Brynn remarked. "Particularly in light of our guest Lozan Duk's information. King Aydrian of Honce-the-Bear looks beyond his borders, it would seem; and all of our suspicions about Abbot Olin's true role in coming south of the mountains seem confirmed."

"Are we to war with Behren *and* the Bearmen north of the mountains?" one of the other leaders asked.

A cloud passed over Brynn's face—and Pagonel's as well—at that dim prospect. To-gai was not a heavily populated country. The To-gai-ru possessed no magic other than Brynn's sword, little in the way of true armor, and few resources with which to build engines of war. Their one advantage, other than fierce riders and fine ponies, would be Agradeleous, and the Behrenese had learned effective countermeasures to the dragon. In all practicality, Brynn understood that she could not raise an army strong enough to defeat a united Behren alone on even ground, and had, in fact, only survived against the forces of Chezru Chieftain Yakim Douan because Pagonel had turned the Chezru court against their leader and thrown the country of Behren into chaos. If Abbot Olin and Mado Wadon were uniting Behren once more with an eye toward To-gai, Brynn would find the defense of the city impossible, and the defense of her entire country improbable—and all of that with only minimal involvement from the northern kingdom. If Honce-the-Bear threw in her weight with Behren in full, To-gai would surely be crushed. Brynn knew that, so did Pagonel, and so did every other warrior in the room, even proud Tanalk Grenk.

"I fear that Abbot Olin is biding his time," Brynn said. "The army has not decamped and begun their march home in any meaningful way."

"He expects that King Aydrian will come and strengthen him," Lozan Duk reasoned when the woman translated her thoughts into elvish.

Brynn nodded and explained the elf's words to the others.

"Or Abbot Olin believes that he must strengthen his hold over Behren more completely before throwing his army at Dharyan-Dharielle," Pagonel said. "No doubt many of Yatol De Hamman's warriors were not pleased at the thought of doing battle with the Dragon of To-gai yet again. But if he holds Behren secure, then the force he can muster against us will be much more impressive and truly overwhelming. Sheer numerical advantage will bring strength to the Behrenese morale, and we will be hard-pressed."

"Then are we to attack?" Brynn asked. "Or to continue to strengthen our defenses in the hopes that we will wound our enemies so greatly that they will reconsider their designs on the city?"

"I will go to Jacintha as your emissary," Pagonel decided. "Let me fathom better the intentions of Abbot Olin and your friend King Aydrian."

"You will be gone a month at least," Brynn argued. "Do we have such time?"

To the side, Lozan Duk put a quizzical look over her, and the woman translated the mystic's intentions.

"I will call to Belli'mar Juraviel," Lozan Duk offered. "We will get your friend to Jacintha and back again in short order."

Later on, the Doc'alfar sat cross-legged on the flat roof of a small tower, the blue sapphire of his people in his lap. He put his thoughts into the gemstone and envisioned the emerald held by Juraviel.

And then he felt the contact, and he called to his golden-haired cousin. For a long while, Lozan Duk held that meditative state, guiding Juraviel with his thoughts.

Less than an hour later, Lozan Duk blinked open his eyes, to see Belli'mar Juraviel standing on the tower top before him, magical emerald in hand.

With the pressing business at hand, the reunion between Brynn and Juraviel was kept short; the two had barely an hour together while Pagonel prepared for the journey to the east. Juraviel offered his promises that they would speak at length about the events in the northern kingdom when he returned, then he led the mystic up to the top of the city's eastern wall and bade Pagonel to take his hand.

Juraviel called to the emerald, and Pagonel watched the ground distort suddenly, folding as if it were a rolling wave. He followed Juraviel's lead in stepping forward off the wall, then the ground unwound suddenly and Pagonel found himself standing far to the east of Dharyan-Dharielle, east even of the line of Behrenese warriors.

"An amazing feat," Pagonel congratulated.

"The emerald's powers are few, but the stone is powerful in that which it does," the elf answered. "The distance distorts for the wielder and those in the immediate area alone, and only those for whom the wielder wishes the distance distorted. Only you and I could have walked from that wall, for only you and I could even see the distortion." Juraviel closed his eyes and called again and the land rolled up. He and Pagonel took their next mile-long step.

They found themselves in the foothills outside of Jacintha with still several hours to go before the dawn. Pagonel bade the elf to wait for him there, and started off toward the city.

"If I have not returned to you by sundown, then return to Brynn," the mystic instructed.

"That would be a tiding of war," Juraviel replied. "For something so important, I will give you two days to return."

Pagonel agreed and walked away, arriving at Jacintha's gate even as the first light of dawn began to peek in over the eastern horizon.

Recognized by the gate guards, Pagonel was not turned away. But they made him sit in the guard tower for several hours, refusing to rouse Yatol Mado Wadon and Abbot Olin so early. Finally, Pagonel was escorted across the city to Chom Deiru, and there, in the palace, he was made to wait once more—while the lords ate their breakfast, it was explained.

If they were trying to rattle the mystic, they did not succeed, for patience was the true mark of any Jhesta Tu. Pagonel would allow them their vanity and superior attitude; it did not matter.

"Ah, so it is Pagonel himself," Yatol Wadon said when at last Pagonel was escorted onto the eastern balcony setting. The place was a garden of great flowers and singing birds, and trees perfectly placed to create equal areas of shade and sun throughout the long daylight hours. A waterfall splashed into a small pond at the side, providing comfortable mist and a cool and welcome dampness to the air. Brightly colored fish, red and orange mostly, swam about in the pond.

Five men were seated about two small tables, including Abbot Olin and Mado Wadon, another Yatol whom Pagonel did not know, another Abellican monk, and a Honce-the-Bear soldier—of high rank, the mystic presumed, given his much-decorated uniform.

"Had we known that the Jhesta Tu who came knocking at our city was the emissary of Brynn Dharielle, we would have set another place for breakfast," Yatol Wadon went on. "Please, sit and join us. I will have more food brought out at once."

Pagonel held his arm out to block the servant even as the man started away. "I have little time. I have come swiftly from Dharyan-Dharielle," the mystic explained. "From a city under siege."

"You left before my—before our—emissaries arrived, then," Abbot Olin put in. "With all apologies to Brynn Dharielle that the attack was a terrible mistake."

"I was there when the emissary relayed your message," said Pagonel, which brought curious looks from both the leaders, since that had occurred only the day before! "I come in response to the claim."

"Brynn Dharielle does not believe our words?" Abbot Olin asked.

Pagonel paid more attention to the subtle notes in the man's voice than to the actual words. He recognized something there, some truth in Abbot Olin's heart, as if the man *were hoping* that his conclusion was correct.

"Following the actions of Yatol De Hamman, we thought it prudent to confirm those words before standing down," Pagonel replied.

"Of course, of course," Abbot Olin said, with unconvincing friendliness.

"And where are our manners, Yatol Wadon? Pagonel of the Jhesta Tu—or are you of the To-gai-ru once more?—I give you Master Mackaront of St. Bondabruce, my trusted second, and Bretherford, the Duke of the Mirianic, commander of the mighty Ursal fleet."

"And I am Yatol Sin-seran," said the other man, when it became apparent that Abbot Olin had no intention of including him in the introductions—a point that Pagonel did not miss.

The mystic, though, kept his eyes on the duke of the Mirianic through it all, seeing something there. Disgust?

"You are a long way from home, good Duke," Pagonel offered with a bow.

Pagonel noted that Duke Bretherford had offered no hint of disagreement to his words.

"The same could be said of a Jhesta Tu mystic," Abbot Olin put in.

"I—and Brynn Dharielle—of course expect that Yatol De Hamman will be recalled with his legions to Jacintha," Pagonel replied.

"I will see to it," Yatol Wadon started to say, but Olin interrupted him with, "Is not Yatol De Hamman properly encamped upon Behrenese soil?"

Pagonel noted Yatol Wadon's slight wince, and noted, too, that Bretherford obviously did not share the enthusiasm of his companions, even less so than did Mado Wadon.

"Their presence on the fields surrounding Dharyan-Dharielle forces the city into a state of war readiness," Pagonel countered.

"Only if you do not trust us," said the smug Abbot Olin.

"And we are in a state of siege, for all practicality," the mystic went on. "Are we to allow our traders to wander down the eastern road through the lines of an army recently scarred by battle against us?"

"You seemed to get out easily enough," Abbot Olin dryly replied.

"I had ways not available to others."

"The mysterious Jhesta Tu," Yatol Sin-seran said, his voice full of mystery and sarcasm.

"Will your army stand down?" Pagonel asked, ignoring the fool.

Yatol Wadon started to answer, but again, Abbot Olin cut him short. "That is the decision of Yatol De Hamman, as he is charged with securing the borders of Behren. He will go where he needs to go to accomplish his task in full, and so long as he remains on Behrenese sovereign soil, then he is well within his rights.

"And we were truly surprised to learn of the events that precipitated the unfortunate battle," Olin went on. "Dharyan-Dharielle was to remain an open city, was it not? And yet, Yatol De Hamman has informed us that his decision to attack was based on the breaking of the treaty by Brynn Dharielle. Perhaps he was a bit rash in his judgment, but you should inform your leader that treaties are more than words on parchment. All parties to them are honor-bound or the treaties are worthless."

"The city is open to scholars and travelers," Pagonel replied. "We could not admit an entire army, one that outnumbers our own garrison by more than five to one. Above all other edicts, Brynn Dharielle is charged with the security of Dharyan-Dharielle and To-gai. Her people live there; she cannot expose them to mortal danger."

"Interpret it as you will," Abbot Olin warned. "But break the treaty at your own peril. Dharyan-Dharielle has not worn that name for long, and the city is, or always was, Behrenese at its roots, and those roots are within the memories of every soldier on the field."

"You believe that Yatol De Hamman had the right to enter Dharyan-Dharielle with his army behind him?" Pagonel asked, pointedly turning to Yatol Wadon as he did.

"That is, perhaps, a point for discussion," Abbot Olin answered anyway. "But certainly by treaty, Brynn Dharielle was given little right to refuse them entrance."

"I agree that the words of a treaty are to be honored," the mystic said, never taking his eyes from Yatol Mado Wadon. "As is the intent behind the treaty."

He did note a slight nod of agreement from the Chezru priest, but Yatol Wadon did not openly reply.

Pagonel turned to survey each of them in turn. Yatol Sin-seran was no ally, he recognized immediately, nor did Master Mackaront seem to him in any way of different heart than Abbot Olin. Once again, though, Duke Bretherford caught his attention. The mystic clearly saw a conflict behind the man's tired eyes.

Pagonel quickly took his leave and wasted no time in the city, returning at once to Belli'mar Juraviel in the foothills to the north.

"Abbot Olin's demeanor would agree with everything you have warned us of concerning young King Aydrian," he reported. "He will find an excuse to retake Dharyan-Dharielle for Behren—his Behren."

"Aydrian was nothing if not ambitious," the elf replied.

"But when a leader reaches so far, he may leave untended business closer to home," Pagonel said. "I did not note equal enthusiasm from one of the other Honce-the-Bear noblemen in attendance."

"Bretherford, Duke of the Mirianic," the surprising elf replied.

Pagonel shot him a curious look.

"I traveled down to the dock area, and recognize the flagship of the Ursal fleet," Juraviel explained. "In the days of Elbryan, and then with Jilseponie, Aydrian's mother, as queen, we of the Touel'alfar learned much of the personalities of those leading the armies of Honce-the-Bear. My Lady Dasslerond feared an attack from Jilseponie's court, as she never truly understood the truth of the goodly woman."

"So you know Duke Bretherford?"

"I know of him," Juraviel explained. "He was a man loyal to King Danube."

"And perhaps not so loyal to Aydrian."

"A man caught in the web Aydrian has spun," said Juraviel. "What choices were put before Duke Bretherford, or any of the others, if Aydrian assumed the throne with overpowering forces?"

Pagonel sat back against a boulder and considered the words for a long while, playing them against the reactions and expressions he had noted from the duke of the Mirianic. "Perhaps we could offer him an option?" the mystic asked more than stated.

"Stepping to his flagship would be no difficult task," said Juraviel. "But what might you tell him in opposition to Aydrian? Would you reveal the conspiracy of Jilseponie and Prince Midalis?"

"Would I be telling him anything that King Aydrian does not already know?"

Now it was Juraviel's turn to sit and consider the reasoning for a moment. "Let us go down to the rocks near to Jacintha's gates," the elf remarked, and he lifted the emerald stone and offered Pagonel his hand. "We can watch for Duke Bretherford's skiff to return him to his flagship, then we can decide."

Twinkling stars blanketed the sky and the quiet sea lapped softly against the planking of the Honce-the-Bear warships. Most of Jacintha slept, as did most of the sailors on the ships, and so no one noticed when Juraviel and Pagonel stepped aboard *Rontlemore's Dream*, the flagship of Duke Bretherford's Mirianic fleet. Juraviel remained aft, easily hiding amidst the rigging and weapons' lockers, while Pagonel calmly and openly strode toward the center of the deck.

So surprised was the poor watchman at the sight of the mystic that he nearly tumbled off the deck and into the dark water!

"Hold!" he cried. "Hold! Attack! Attack! To arms!" He stammered and stuttered, falling all over himself and trying to ready his bow.

Suddenly, Pagonel, moving with the speed and grace that only a Jhesta Tu mystic might know, was flanking him, with one arm up to hold tight to the bowstring.

"Be at ease," the mystic started to say, but the man whirled and tried to stab his long knife into Pagonel's belly.

Pagonel caught the hapless sailor by the wrist and easily halted his progress. "Be at ease," he said again, and he gave a slight and deft twist, turning the man's hand down over his wrist and taking the knife from him so smoothly that it would have seemed to an onlooker to have been willingly given over. "I am no enemy, but a man come to speak with Duke Bretherford."

Other sailors were there, then, circling cautiously.

Pagonel handed the knife back to the stunned and overwhelmed watchman and moved a step to the side, showing his empty hands. "This is no attack, but a conversation long overdue," he explained to them all. "Pray tell your Duke Bretherford that Pagonel, emissary of the Dragon of To-gai, has come to speak with him. He will understand."

The men glanced all around at each other nervously, seeming unsure of how to react. They all held bows ready, and Pagonel was well aware that they could cut him down where he stood.

"If you shoot me, and I am sincere in my words, then your duke will not be pleased," he told them. "If you rouse him, and he sees me as an enemy, you have lost nothing and have cost yourselves no more than the anger of a man awakened in the night. Less anger, I would think, than that of a man who has learned that a valuable friend had been killed by his frightened underlings."

A nod from one of the archers had another of them running off to fetch Duke Bretherford.

A few minutes later, Pagonel stood in the duke's private room, alone with the short, stout man.

Bretherford sipped rum and stared out the window, taken aback, but surely not surprised, by the mystic's reports that Jilseponie and Midalis were in the north, gathering strength to oppose King Aydrian.

"How do you know such things?" Bretherford did question. "Vanguard is a long way from Behren, and a longer way from To-gai."

"The opposition to the recent events of Honce-the-Bear's throne is more widespread and coordinated than you might believe," Pagonel replied. "And surely, being of a kingdom that is rife with gemstone magic, you understand that distance is not always the truest measure of closeness."

Bretherford turned to face him. "And perhaps you do not understand the power of King Aydrian, nor the loyalty of many of those who support him."

"Many of those?" Pagonel echoed. "Would that include Duke Bretherford? You were once a friend to King Danube, I was told. And to his brother, perhaps?"

"You know nothing of what you speak, Jhesta Tu," Bretherford spat back. "Do not presume—"

"I know that I am alive, and was granted a private audience with you," Pagonel interrupted. "I would believe that you know enough of the Jhesta Tu to understand that I could have come in here and killed you quickly, yet you chose to meet with me."

"To gather information for Abbot Olin and King Aydrian, perhaps."

"Perhaps," Pagonel agreed with a bow.

Bretherford swallowed the last of the rum, then tossed his glass aside to clunk on the wooden floor. "What would you have me do?" he asked with helpless frustration.

"I would have you keep hope, wherever that hope might lead you," Pagonel replied. "I would have you pay keen attention to the events that will shape the world. I would have you, in the end, choose with conscience and courage, and not cowardice. No more can ever be asked of any man."

With that, Pagonel bowed again, and walked out the cabin door. He passed the many soldiers who had gathered on deck and walked to the bow, where Juraviel met him with an extended hand. Before the soldiers curiously following Pagonel ever got near enough to see, he and Juraviel took a giant, magical step back to the rocky shoreline north of the city of Jacintha.

"An ally?" Juraviel asked.

"I know not," Pagonel admitted. "But continuing information may well lead him in that direction." He looked at the elf directly. "This stone you carry, combined with the powers of the gemstone of the Doc'alfar, will prove to be our greatest advantage, perhaps. I beseech Belli'mar Juraviel to lead his people and his pale-skinned cousins more deeply into this conflict."

"We are small in number, and no match for Aydrian and his charges."

"But you are our eyes and ears and mouths," Pagonel explained. "When Brynn Dharielle freed To-gai from Behren, she did so because she knew more of her enemy than they could understand of her. Mobility and cunning strikes won the day for To-gai."

"That was a war for freedom," Juraviel countered. "This is a struggle against the homeland of King Aydrian. Eventually, whatever we might, we will have to do battle with him and his great armies directly. No treaty and no minor victories will grant us what we desire. Not in Honce-the-Bear, at least, though there remains more hope for the kingdoms south of the mountains."

"Minor victories might bring hope to potential allies, and lead them to join our cause," the mystic replied. "What role will Belli'mar Juraviel and his people play?"

"It was Lady Dasslerond's step into the affairs of humans that led to the catastrophe that is Aydrian," said the elf.

"Then it is Belli'mar Juraviel's responsibility to help put things aright."

Juraviel mulled those words over for a long while.

Help from Beyond

There was no pain. There was no cold. There was no physical sensation at all. Time and space seemed to have no meaning to her.

It took Pony a long time to recognize that she had entered the spirit realm, the same one in which she walked out of body. No, it was more complete than that, obviously, for she saw no sign of the true physical world about her, and no apparent portal back to that world of substance and color. This was more akin to the place she had gone to battle the spirit of Father Abbot Markwart that long-ago day in Chasewind Manor, the only other time she had ventured so far into the nether realm. That memory of a specific real-world event sparked other thoughts in Pony, but only gradually did the specifics of the fight at Pireth Dancard begin to come back to her. Only after a long while did she remember her desperate flight, and getting shot with the arrow, and then the ocean taking her in its grasp and pulling her back.

Am I dead?

She didn't voice the question, for she had no physical voice at that time. Nor, as she continued to glance around at the seemingly endless plain of gray swirling mists, did she require an answer. She was not a part of her corporeal body, she realized, and to her understanding, that could only mean one thing.

It occurred to her then that she might soon become a shadow in an Oracle mirror—in her son's perhaps. Maybe this was the answer; maybe in death, Pony could reach misguided Aydrian in ways that never manifested to her in life.

Is this it? her thoughts cried out again. *Am I dead? Elbryan!*

Go back, came an answer in the woman's thoughts, and though it was not the sound of physical words, it was a "voice" that Pony recognized.

It was Elbryan! She knew that it had to be Elbryan!

And then she saw him, or rather, felt his presence, and though there was no physicality to any of this, she knew that he was there, not far from her, standing, or hovering, before her.

Elbryan, her thoughts reached out to him. *Oh, my love! I am so weary.* Pony willed her spirit forward, looking to embrace him, soul to soul. But as she approached, he retreated.

Go back! came the plaintive cry in her head. *You cannot be here. Not now! You cannot forsake our son when his hour of need approaches!*

Pony halted her movement, and she knew that if she possessed a physical jaw at that moment, it surely would have been hanging open.

Go back!

Elbryan, do not chase me away!

Go back!

Aydrian is beyond me, beyond all the world. There is nothing—

Go back! Elbryan's call seemed even more insistent to her, and every time she tried to counter, to tell him that she was weary, that she had rightly passed and that she was content, that she was ready, he simply answered, *Go back!*

Pony turned herself about to see that region whence she had apparently come. There was just the mist for a long, long while, but gradually, the woman began to make out a circular, darker area, like the entrance to a tunnel.

Go back! Elbryan implored her. *Quickly! Time is running out!*

The woman moved toward the darkness and saw that it was indeed a tunnel, and as soon as she entered, she saw a distant speck of light, a long, long way from her.

Quickly! Oh, fly, my love! came Elbryan's call, and Pony, despite her feelings and her weariness, flew off as fast as she could, trusting in Elbryan above all else. The light grew and grew until it stung her spiritual eyes, and still she flew on toward it. She heard one last, fleeting call as she burst from the darkness of the tunnel altogether, again Elbryan's voice, saying, *Two shadows live in Aydrian's mirror!*

Bradwarden, Prince Midalis, and Captain Al'u'met watched the listing ship slowly turning in the water and gradually dipping lower. The last of the raiders were off her, as well as all the supplies they had time to scavenge. Of the twelve ships moored in the waters off Dancard, eight were still afloat, not counting the one now spinning down to its death. Even more promising, six of those eight were completely undamaged, and the other two seemed seaworthy and in need of only minor repairs. Midalis and his raiders had lost one to the shore batteries, and a second had been scuttled in the harbor, since there had been too many Ursal soldiers aboard to steal her away easily. During that struggle, several lightning bolts had reached out from shore, lighting fires, dropping combatants to the planking and scorching the deck. A third ship had escaped back toward the shore; but reports said that it, like those in dock, had gone up in flames. Despite the losses, the raiders had gotten away with nine ships, having only thirteen people missing and a few others slightly injured. By any standards, the raid had been a tremendous success.

Except . . .

Where was Pony? She was their greatest ally, the most potent weapon in Midalis' arsenal, and the symbol of hope that bound them all. She had not come out from Pireth Dancard that dark night. Al'u'met had kept the signal fires burning on all the ships throughout the night, but she had not returned to them, amber in hand.

"She might be imprisoned in that tower," Prince Midalis muttered, turning from the spectacle of the sinking ship, its long mast leaning out at nearly a forty-five-degree angle, to the distant speck of Pireth Dancard on the northeastern horizon. "And I'd not trade her for all the Ursal fleet. Not for my kingdom complete!"

Bradwarden patted the prince on the shoulder. "Might be time to sail back to the island and get our girl back, then," he reasoned, and that brought a hopeful smile to Midalis' face.

"And in so doing, destroy the integrity of Jilseponie's death, if dead she is," came a voice from behind, and the trio turned to see huge Andacanavar approaching. "You've got a score of Alpinadoran longboats, this fine boat here, and eight Ursal warships; but every one of them is carrying only a skeleton crew, and few warriors armed to do battle ashore. If we go charging in, we're to lose a few boats to the catapults, and then we'll find a pitched battle on the docks. Are you so willing to risk everything for one heroic woman? Because if you lose here, my friend, you've nothing left with which to oppose Aydrian."

"And if I am willing to take that chance?" Prince Midalis replied. "Will Andacanavar and Bruinhelde and his warriors stand beside me?"

"I'm not for saying," replied the ranger. "But I'd not expect it. Bruinhelde will ask my advice, and that advice will be to sail back to Pireth Vanguard."

Al'u'met seemed quite surprised, and Midalis openly angry, but Bradwarden nodded and tightened his grip on the prince's shoulder. The centaur understood Andacanavar, and his motives and thinking. Andacanavar was a ranger, as Elbryan had been, as they both considered Pony to be. Rangers understood the ultimate sacrifice.

Rangers also understood that it was insulting to one who had so sacrificed himself—or herself, in this case—then to choose a course that minimized the victory brought about by that sacrifice.

"I'll not throw away all the gains made here last night," the ranger explained.

"Or do you fear to lose Alpinadorans for the sake of a Honce-the-Bear woman?" Prince Midalis accused.

Andacanavar's expression was locked somewhere between pity and disillusionment. "I accept your words as the frustrated cries of a man wounded," he said. "But they are not the words of a man who would be king. I advise both Bruinhelde and you to refrain from a foolish attack, for the sake of my kinsmen, yes, but also for the sake of Prince Midalis and his hopes for his kingdom. They have Abellican monks ashore and your best counter to the gemstone magic is missing. Take your fleet beside Bruinhelde's and sail fast back to Vanguard, before a winter storm catches you and scuttles every ship."

"You would just leave her?" Midalis asked.

"I would not, nor, do I suppose, would Bradwarden or good Captain Al'u'met here," the ranger answered. "You go, and if Captain Al'u'met agrees, then let *Saudi Jacintha* patrol the area near to Pireth Dancard to try to find out what happened to our lost friend. With her sails full of wind, Captain Al'u'met's fine ship will outrun anything you have at your disposal. Let us all hope that we beat you back to Pireth Vanguard, and with Pony aboard beside us!"

That had the other three looking at each other, and gradually coming to agreeing nods.

"And if she is a prisoner?" Prince Midalis asked.

"Then me and the ranger here'll go ashore and tear down that tower and everyone in it," Bradwarden proclaimed, and so cold and even was his voice that no one even began to question his proclamation.

Prince Midalis stepped past the others, moving back to the rail, and cast a forlorn glance at the distant island. "It pains me to leave her."

"It's what you must do," Andacanavar said. "For Pony's sake, most of all—especially if she is imprisoned or . . ."

Prince Midalis swung about to stare at him, the look in the man's eyes stealing the barbarian's words.

"We will find her," Andacanavar said.

A bright morning sun forced Pony to open her eyes.

She lay on her back in the cold sand, staring up at the bluest of skies, and only a single grayish cloud began to creep into her field of view.

No, it wasn't a cloud, she suddenly understood, and with great effort, she managed to turn her head a bit to the side. And then she remembered.

She realized then that she was lying on a seaweed-strewn beach on Pireth Dancard, her feet just above the roiling tide line. To her right ran a rocky jetty, far out into the sea, and beyond that rose a light gray smoke—the dying fires from the three burning ships, she assumed.

Startled and suddenly afraid, Pony moved to sit up—or tried to, for a pain more ferocious than anything she had ever known assailed her, sending waves of agony, burning and nauseating, rolling through her prone form. The woman gasped, unable to catch her breath, unable to lift her chest to draw in any air. She started to move her left arm, and hit resistance, and desperately looked down.

Pony saw the tail end of the arrow protruding from her ribs, and in looking at how little was showing, she realized just how much had sunk into her. With sudden panic, she felt the sting across the way, where the arrowhead had ended against the inside of an opposite rib!

She knew at once that she should be dead, and knew at once that she soon enough would be. Instinctively, she started to move her right hand, and only then did she realize that she held a pair of gemstones in it. Without even bringing the hand up to ensure that she held the right stone, Pony fell into the waiting magic. She sensed the amber, and reasoned that even in her semiconscious state, she must have used it to keep herself above the tide. Then she felt the powers of the hematite, and went into it with all of her meager remaining strength.

She gasped in some air, then a second breath, and the moment of panic abated just a bit. But how could she hope actually to defeat this terrible wound? she wondered. She could keep herself functioning only through the gemstone, but her energy here was not limitless.

She told herself that she had to push the arrow through and so she stubbornly angled her right arm, placing her palm against the base of the shaft. She closed her eyes, fell into the soul stone more deeply, and steeled her resolve. She sucked in as deep a breath as she could manage, and started to push.

The wave of agony ended that, stealing all of her strength before she could budge the arrow at all.

Pony fell back in dismay. There was no way she could remove the arrow, no way she could possibly muster the strength needed to break it through.

She fell into the soul stone yet again, and took another deep breath, and, somehow, managed to sit up.

In looking at the beach before her, the woman could hardly believe that she had not been smashed to bits on the multitude of sharp, barnacle-covered rocks. Every incoming wave buffeted them, sending a high spray of white foam into the air.

Elbryan had been with her, she understood, for there was no other explanation. Elbryan's spirit had come to her in her moment of desperation, had helped guide her to this spot, had helped to keep her focused, even in her semiconscious state, on utilizing the soul stone to get through the night. There was no other explanation. Pony had been touched, literally, by a guardian spirit!

She should be dead. For the second time.

That thought alone nearly dropped her back to the sand; but she remembered, too, what Elbryan's spirit had told her in her visit to the nether realm. She was not done here, and could not surrender to her wounds. Somehow, beyond her own understanding, she walked into the ocean, not only keeping the soul stone working enough so that her body did not succumb to the grievous wound, but activating the amber, as well.

She moved out from the beach, out into the open ocean. Soon after she cleared the jetty, she heard cries behind her—from the wharves, she realized.

Pony didn't look back. She just kept walking away from the island, hoping that she would get out of the range of archer and catapult alike before those cries were relayed back to the artillerymen.

The roll of the waves beneath her feet only made her even more nauseous, but the woman stubbornly put one foot ahead of the other and trudged on. A couple of times, she lost her focus on the soul stone, and found herself gasping for breath. A couple of times, she lost her focus on the amber, and went down into the cold sea.

Shivering, her skin blue, her energy fast failing, Pony soon enough lost all sense of where she was, and even of what she was doing. But there was someone else there, with her, guiding her, helping her to keep the gemstones in her hand, as if Elbryan was walking beside her, his hand cupped over hers, holding it closed.

The sun beat down on her, but it offered her no warmth.

Somehow, she continued. Her eyes were closed, she had no idea of where she was going, but she continued.

So lost was Pony, so devastated and disoriented, that she never saw the sails of *Saudi Jacintha*, nor heard the shouts of Bradwarden and the others when they spotted her walking on the swelling azure sea. The swift ship came right beside her in short order, but the wounded woman only kept walking, oblivious to it, and oblivious to the gasps of those who loved her at the rail, all of them shaken to their core by the sight of her devastated form.

Pony felt herself lifted from the surface of the sea, and that physical contact broke her from the trance. Andacanavar laid her down gently on *Saudi Jacintha*'s deck, his strong hands going to the arrow embedded so deeply in her side.

Pony heard him say, "I know not how she is even still alive!"

"Ah, me Pony," she heard Bradwarden say from far, far away. "Oh, ye poor stubborn lass. Don't ye know when time's come to let go?"

Pony opened her eyes to see both the ranger and the centaur hovering over her, with Al'u'met down at her feet, taking a blanket from a crewman and then gently covering her. She wanted to answer the centaur, but she had not the strength to speak aloud.

"What can you do?" Captain Al'u'met asked. "Do something!"

"I can't pull the damned thing out or it'll take half her insides with it!" the ranger cried. "And she'd not survive me pushing it through!"

"How'd she survive this long, is what I'm asking?" remarked Bradwarden. "Suren them wounds're mortal, and should've killed her long ago."

"Gemstones," remarked Al'u'met, who had moved up to Pony's side to tuck her hands under the blanket.

Pony felt him lift her arm and gently loosen her fingers enough to show the amber and gray stones she held.

"Don't ye take that gray one away!" Bradwarden cried. "Ah, but that's the key. She's using the stone's healing powers to keep herself livin', though I've no idea where the woman's findin' the strength in her condition." The centaur clenched her hand tightly, moving it to his breast. Then he bent down very low, and whispered into Pony's ear. "Hey now, me good lass, ye reach inside o' me with yer soul stone. Ye take me strength—I know ye can."

Pony heard the words, and she felt the connection with the amber go away—Bradwarden had interrupted it, she somehow understood. He was making her focus on the one; he was inviting her to leach his great strength.

Hardly aware of anything through the haze of numbing cold and sharp agony, the woman did go deeper into that stone, establishing a connection to the centaur, feeling the solidity of the creature, the unbelievable health and strength.

Bradwarden, her thoughts cried out.

Ye take me strength, me lass, his spirit answered. *Ye take all ye're needing!*

Pony hesitated. Her wound was mortal—and would be so even to one of Bradwarden's great equine constitution.

"Ye take it!" he shouted, and imparted telepathically, as well.

Despite herself, Pony's instincts made her reach out; Elbryan's plea to her, that she could not yet die, made her reach out. She felt a sudden surge of energy injected into her battered form.

She fell into that warmth, that strength, leaching at the mighty centaur.

And then sheets of fire erupted within her, and she heard herself cry out, screaming more loudly than she had ever before, for the pain was more acute than anything the woman had ever imagined.

"Fight on, lass!" Bradwarden shouted at her between her screams. "Find me heart and take it as yer own!"

Pony knew that she should not, knew that to do so would kill her friend! She would take his life energy, all of it, for nothing less would suffice!

But the pain commanded her to grab on more tightly; she could not deny the call of that fiery agony.

She heard a snap from somewhere far away, and then felt a sudden sliding sensation across her inner chest, as if her life force were sliding out of her corporeal form.

She fell back in the fog, hoping that Elbryan would meet her in death once again.

Harvesting the Crop
of Friendship

"It is as we feared, then," Brynn reasoned when Belli'mar Juraviel and Pagonel arrived back in Dharyan-Dharielle with news of Abbot Olin.

"Abbot Olin insists that the strike against us was in error, but there is little mistaking his intent," Pagonel confirmed.

"I'll not stay holed up in the city," Brynn remarked, and she moved to the window of the tower overlooking Dharyan-Dharielle's eastern wall and the encamped Behrenese army beyond. Over the last couple of days, the Behrenese force had shifted to the east, but not far, and while some caravans had moved off down the eastern road, Brynn had suspected that it was all a ruse, and that De Hamman wasn't leaving at all. Pagonel and Juraviel, great-stepping through that region, had confirmed those suspicions, for a second Behrenese camp had been constructed, just to the east of the first.

"They have moved away from the western borders," the woman observed. "They leave that path open to us, that we might flee back to the steppes of To-gai."

Tanalk Grenk entered then, with a sheepish-looking Pechter Dan Turk beside him and Lozan Duk and Belli'mar Juraviel coming in on their heels. There had been talk of expelling the Behrenese emissary from the city, mostly from the fierce Grenk and his followers, but not only had Brynn dissuaded them from that course, she had insisted to Pechter Dan Turk that he remain in Dharyan-Dharielle.

"Is that what your Yatol Wadon desires, Pechter Dan Turk?" the woman asked.

The man looked all about in panic, obviously not understanding the question, for he had not heard Brynn's previous statement.

"Yatol De Hamman moves his force about to the east, inviting us to flee back to the steppes of To-gai," Brynn explained.

"You bade him to leave," the Behrenese man replied. "Perhaps he does so, yes?"

"No," said Pagonel. "He makes us think that he leaves, that he might bide his time and gather more strength from Jacintha."

"What is the image of Behren that Yatol Mado Wadon truly desires?" Brynn asked.

The man stammered and seemed at a loss.

"We are not your enemy," Brynn said to the man. "I beg you to speak freely here, without fear of repercussion."

"Yatol Wadon wishes Behren to remain united," the man explained.

"Does that include Dharyan-Dharielle?" Brynn asked. "Would he so quickly go against the very treaty that allowed him to conquer Jacintha in the first place?"

The question, the accusation, seemed to wound Pechter Dan Turk.

"What is in the heart of Pechter Dan Turk?" Brynn went on. "Do you desire to see Dharyan-Dharielle back in the Behrenese kingdom?"

"I desire peace, good lady," the man replied, and for the first time, it seemed as if he was speaking from the heart, and not from fear. "Behren has been shattered by the deception of Yakim Douan. You cannot understand how profoundly his lies brought rot to the heart and soul of my land and my people."

"Oh, but I can," said Brynn.

"Yatol Mado Wadon sought to reunite the kingdom under Jacintha, for only Jacintha holds enough power to keep the tribes from falling into complete chaos once more," the emissary explained.

"And Abbot Olin helped Jacintha to accomplish that," reasoned Brynn. "So tell me, who is it that presses Jacintha to regain Dharyan-Dharielle? Is this the desire of Yatol Wadon, or Abbot Olin?"

"Good lady, I have no answer for you," the man admitted. "My master has never indicated . . ."

"Then perhaps it is Abbot Olin," Brynn reasoned. "Exacting a level of control over Yatol Wadon. Taking full advantage of your master's desperate struggle."

Pechter Dan Turk started to answer, but then just half shrugged and half nodded, unwilling to agree or deny.

"Mayhap we should send Yatol Wadon this one's head to tell him that we do not accept his proposal," fierce Tanalk Grenk said, and he stared hard at Pechter Dan Turk.

The man seemed very small at that moment.

Brynn walked right over, though, insinuating herself between the two and shooting a fierce scowl right back at Tanalk Grenk. "What does Pechter Dan Turk think of the recent battle?" she asked. "To whom does Dharyan-Dharielle belong? Or do you prefer the name simply as Dharyan?"

The man bit his lip.

"Speak freely," said Brynn. "On my word, there is no consequence here to your honest words."

"The city's rightful name is Dharyan-Dharielle," the man said. "It was fairly given in treaty, and to the gain of both our peoples, so I believed then, when I advised Yatol Mado Wadon. And so I believe now!"

"Then go out from here," Brynn bade him, and Pechter Dan Turk's expression became incredulous. "Go to Yatol De Hamman and discern his intentions. He will likely send you back to us with word that he is breaking camp and returning soon to Jacintha."

"And what am I to tell him from Brynn?"

"Tell him that you are no friend to Brynn," the woman instructed.

The man studied her for a long while. "You would have me spy against my own people," he reasoned.

"Only if you consider Abbot Olin to be of your own people," Brynn replied. "For this is the doing of Abbot Olin, not Yatol Wadon. And perhaps Yatol De Hamman truly intends to leave. If he believes that you are no friend to me, then he will likely speak truthfully to you."

"And you would have me report back," the emissary added.

Brynn shrugged. "That will be a choice for Pechter Dan Turk to make, and I will accept whatever choice that is. If Yatol De Hamman indicates that he means to expel me from the city, then perhaps you will come to understand the truth of my fears, that Abbot Olin—not Yatol Wadon—controls Behren, and in that revelation, perhaps you will believe that I am a better friend to Jacintha than the Abellican abbot."

The man paused and seemed as if he wanted to reply. But he said nothing, except, "I go," and with a bow, he walked from the room.

"He could betray us," Tanalk Grenk remarked as soon as he was gone.

"There is nothing to betray," said Pagonel.

"He could return with a lie from Yatol De Hamman," Grenk reasoned.

"We know the truth of Yatol De Hamman's intentions, whatever Pechter Dan Turk might say," Brynn answered.

"Then what was the point of sending him?"

"To give us a voice in Jacintha later on," said Brynn, "should we survive the onslaught of Yatol De Hamman." She turned to the elves, who were standing quietly off to the side. "You have met with Agradeleous?"

"The dragon is in fine spirits," Juraviel informed her. "And well on the mend. His wing should support him in flight within a few days' time."

"But the danger to him remains, should he take wing at all," Pagonel reminded. "The army of Behren has built weapons to counter Agradeleous, and at the end of the war for To-gai's freedom, those weapons had the dragon in worse condition than he is now. The Behrenese had us beaten, and only their own inner turmoil pulled them from our gates."

Tanalk Grenk gave a bit of a snort at that, but even he did not openly disagree with the reasoning.

"And now those weapons, in the ranks of Yatol De Hamman, do not even constitute the greatest threat to Agradeleous," Pagonel finished.

"The Abellican monks," Brynn remarked.

"They sorely stung the dragon—ever has Agradeleous held great respect for gemstone users, or magic users of any kind."

Brynn nodded throughout the mystic's response. She remembered keenly the time she had flown Agradeleous south about the Mountains of Fire, the land of the Walk of Clouds monastery, which served as home to the Jhesta Tu. Agradeleous had little desire to go anywhere near the magical mystics. Brynn looked back out the window, weighing it all. What she knew beyond doubt was that to try to hole up in the city would eventually prove disastrous, for she and all her forces could not hope to resist the overpowering Behrenese for long. Neither did the prospect of retreating into To-gai appeal to her, particularly given Juraviel's assessment of Aydrian, and the observations of Abbot Olin's entrenchment in Jacintha.

To Brynn, the lack of options all pointed her in the same direction, and that course seemed even more plausible given Pagonel's report of potential unrest within the Honce-the-Bear ranks in Jacintha. She turned back to the group, and the look on her face, so full of determination and sheer grit—an expression that she had worn before most of these same allies for so very long—told them her intentions before she ever spoke them aloud.

"We must shatter this siege before help can arrive," she stated. "We must cut our enemy's ranks apart and send the Behrenese fleeing in terror. We must steal the momentum of their heretofore glorious march and remind them why they once so feared the Dragon of To-gai."

"Our charge will shake the ground beneath their feet!" said an enthusiastic Tanalk Grenk, but the fire seemed to dull quickly, as he added, "But understand, my lady, that such a battle will cost us much in To-gai-ru blood. The Wraps—" He caught himself and stopped, and that, along with his caveat here concerning the battle, showed great progress to Brynn's scrutinizing eyes. Tanalk Grenk was learning to temper his fierce To-gai-ru warrior heritage with the calm understanding of the greater picture that would prove a necessary wisdom within any leader.

"The Behrenese," the man corrected, "are numerous and will not be caught unawares. Without the walls before us, they will sting us with their arrows before battle is ever joined. But we will go, with all of our hearts, if Lady Brynn asks it of us!"

Brynn nodded. "To go out in frontal assault against the encamped army would be folly," she said. "Our greatest weapon here is Agradeleous. The dragon, unchallenged, will strike fear into the hearts of the Behrenese, and his fiery strafes of their ranks will split them asunder and send them running across the open desert sands. But to do that, we must first prepare the battlefield, and our enemies, to our liking."

She turned to Juraviel. "Could you take Agradeleous with you, using your emerald?"

"If the dragon was in his humanoid form, perhaps," the elf replied.

"Then what if you take him out secretly behind Behrenese lines?" Brynn asked. "And Pagonel and me, and some other warriors."

"One at a time," the elf reminded.

"In the dark of night," Brynn agreed. "You set us down, and in position to strike at those positions that would most threaten Agradeleous, and then I shall unbridle the beast, to our enemy's doom."

"You would play the role of assassin before that of warrior?" Pagonel asked.

"I would secure Dharyan-Dharielle and To-gai, by whatever means," Brynn replied without missing a beat, and the nod of the Jhesta Tu told her that he agreed with her reasoning. "If we, if Agradeleous, can enact a devastating first strike against the Abellicans and Yatol De Hamman's war engines, then we shall gain the upper hand and shatter this siege."

"To what end?" asked Juraviel, and all looked at him curiously.

"Will you then return to hide behind your walls, and await the march of Abbot Olin?" the elf asked.

"I will take the fight all the way to Jacintha, all the way to Abbot Olin," Brynn answered.

"Then let me go out to the north at once and see if I might find us an ally," Juraviel asked. "The winter nears its end up there, offering more mobility to those who would oppose Aydrian."

"And more mobility to Aydrian, should he decide to reinforce Jacintha," Pagonel warned.

"But do go, and return as soon as you may," Brynn said to the elf. "We must gather all the information possible before we can execute this plan." She turned her look upon Lozan Duk. "When you arrived here, you told me that moving through the lines of Yatol De Hamman had been of little difficulty."

The Doc'alfar grinned from pointed ear to pointed ear. "Give me two nights," he said, "and I will have every area of Yatol De Hamman's encampment mapped out for you in great detail. If Juraviel can delay for just a few hours, he and I can bring in many of my kinfolk, who are now stretched from the To-gai plateau to the southern entrance of the Path of Starless Night."

All of them looked about to each other then, everyone offering a grim and determined nod. The meeting broke up, with all heading to their respective duties, but Pagonel lingered to speak with Brynn alone.

"You will need assurance that our suspicions of Abbot Olin's intent is correct, that he means to attack and overrun Dharyan-Dharielle," the mystic reasoned.

"I expect Pechter Dan Turk to return and erase any hopes that I might otherwise have," said Brynn.

Pagonel nodded, and Brynn could see the sincere admiration in his brown almond-shaped eyes, the mark of his To-gai-ru heritage. She knew then, in that look from her greatest mentor, that she had played the situation perfectly on all counts.

Still, in looking again out the window at the overwhelming enemy force, Brynn realized that it would take more than that for her to truly win through.

For the second time, she blinked open her eyes to see the sun. The sun in the land of the living, from whence Pony believed she had departed forevermore. She was in a cabin in a ship—on *Saudi Jacintha*, she remembered— wrapped tightly in warm blankets and near to the cabin's one window.

"Welcome back, lass," said Andacanavar, kneeling by the side of her bed, which still made him tower over the prone woman. "We thought you'd left us. Praise to Bradwarden for understanding the gemstones and leaping in to your rescue."

The words rattled around in Pony's head for a bit, conjuring images of those terrible and desperate moments out on the deck. Bradwarden! She had tapped his life force with the soul stone! She had reached out and taken his energy as her own!

Panicked, Pony tried to sit up, but the pain, and Andacanavar's strong arm held her down. "Rest easy, my friend," the ranger said softly. "We've two more days to Vanguard, and you will need all of that time and more to stand strong once again."

"Bradwarden?" Pony gasped breathlessly. "Where is Bradwarden?"

"Out on the deck, resting comfortably," Andacanavar replied. "He is exhausted from his ordeal in battling your wounds with you—exhausted but well on the mend."

"I took too much!" Pony insisted. "Speak truly to me, for I know that he could not have survived the leaching of the soul stone!"

Andacanavar gave a small laugh. "You took much indeed," he agreed. "And we all thought we had lost the centaur—and nearly lost Captain Al'u'met when Bradwarden toppled over toward him! But the hardy Bradwarden rebounded well, I tell you in all honesty."

Pony shook her head; it didn't make sense. "Too much," she argued.

"He mentioned something about an armband," Andacanavar explained. "A red armband."

That settled Pony back, her thoughts whirling and all of the questions popping into them leading her in a positive direction. She had forgotten the enchantment of that armband! The elves had given it to Elbryan, and on a human, its healing magic had worked well. But on the centaur, the powers had somehow extended beyond anything Pony had ever known. When Mount Aida had collapsed during the defeat of the demon dactyl, a large section of the mountain had crushed Bradwarden and should have killed him. But that enchanted armband had not allowed the centaur's life force to flee his corporeal form: it had kept him alive, on the very precipice of death, for weeks and months.

And now it had saved him again, and had saved Pony, as well.

"Tell me of the raid," said Pony. "How great the gain, and how great the losses?"

"A success by any measure," Andacanavar told her. "Eight great warships accompany our fleet now, and King Aydrian's expeditionary force is stranded on Pireth Dancard. The mainland is a long swim."

Pony shared in his laughter, as much as her aching side allowed. "We must not rest on this one victory," she said in all seriousness. "Aydrian will move quickly to even the score, and to the support of Pireth Dancard."

"With the additional ships, Prince Midalis can load a significant force aboard and invade that island fortress."

"Better not to fight them in defended holes, I think."

The ranger gave a shrug. "Planning for another day. We will make Vanguard soon enough, and there decide our next course of action."

"Our?"

Another shrug. "Bruinhelde holds great respect and admiration for Prince Midalis," the ranger explained. "They are brothers by deed, if not by blood, and have shared much. If Bruinhelde believes that Honce-the-Bear is better served by Midalis than by Aydrian, if he comes to believe that Alpinador will be threatened should Aydrian defeat the rightful king, then he will likely march with Prince Midalis."

"And will that be your advisement to him?"

"We will see," the ranger replied, lowering his voice and putting a finger over Pony's mouth to prevent her from continuing. "Rest, my friend. We've a long road ahead."

Saudi Jacintha caught up to the rest of the fleet and led the way into Pireth Vanguard on the front winds of a budding winter storm. Barely had the ships been safely sheltered and moored, with the Alpinadorans pulling their longboats right out of the water, before terrific winds and great swells battered the coastline of Vanguard, sweeping through the Gulf of Corona and out into the deeper Mirianic.

Still, the season was getting late, with spring fast approaching, and the prince's charges believed that it would not be long before the trails to Caer Tinella were clear of snow and the gulf became reliably navigable once more. And so the planning began in full, as both Pony and Bradwarden recovered from their wounds. They planned for the defense of Vanguard, should it come to that, and for the offensive they hoped to launch against King Aydrian.

The mood of Pireth Vanguard was not hopeful, however, despite their determination and the great victory they had won at Pireth Dancard. For they knew, from reports and from common sense, that Aydrian was making great gains in the southland. He had even scattered the Touel'alfar, and that was no small feat! Prince Midalis knew that he must fight, but he and all of those around him understood the desperation of that prospect.

Five days after their return to Pireth Vanguard, the darkness of the mood only deepened, for Belli'mar Juraviel arrived with news gathered by his many scouts of the happenings in the southland of Honce-the-Bear, of Duke Kalas' march and swelling ranks, of Aydrian's departure from Palmaris at the head of a second army, of the fall of St. Gwendolyn and the execution of Abbot Glendenhook.

But Juraviel also brought with him other news, from the lands south of the Belt-and-Buckle, of the second resistance building against King Aydrian's encroachment into Behren. And, more hopeful still, of potential erosion within Aydrian's own ranks.

Namely, Duke Bretherford. Pony knew Bretherford; he had accompanied King Danube to Palmaris during his courting of Pony for those years, and had been the one to sail her back to Ursal upon *River Palace* when she had returned to Danube's side after their short separation. Bretherford had not been a supporter of her marriage to Danube, but he had been truthful with Pony throughout their relationship, and had never personally attacked her. More than anything else, Pony had understood Duke Bretherford to be a loyal friend of her husband the king.

"What do you think Duke Bretherford will do if Brynn breaks out of Dharyan-Dharielle and takes her army against Abbot Olin in Jacintha?" Pony asked at the meeting, after Juraviel had told her and the gathered leaders of Yatol De Hamman's siege of Dharyan-Dharielle and Brynn's plans to break it.

"He'll fight for Abbot Olin," Prince Midalis answered before Juraviel could, and the elf seemed in complete agreement. "Duke Bretherford will side with Honce-the-Bear against either Behren or To-gai, whatever his feelings for the present king."

Pony looked at all of those gathered, her expression turning sly. "Unless we give him a reason not to," she remarked.

"What're ye thinking, lass?" Bradwarden asked.

"Would Duke Bretherford be so willing to support Abbot Olin if Prince Midalis joined Brynn in that fight against Abbot Olin?" Pony replied.

"Are you suggesting that we load up our newly acquired warships and sail all the way to Jacintha?" asked an obviously surprised Prince Midalis.

"It is a risk," she admitted. "But what do you think the effect upon Aydrian would be if we arrived in Jacintha at the same time as Brynn Dharielle, squeezing Abbot Olin and all of his warriors in a great vise? And what might Aydrian think—and more importantly, what might the other nobles of Honce-the-Bear think—if Duke Bretherford came to side with Prince Midalis?"

"It would be a great victory," Midalis admitted. "Greater than Pireth Dancard by far."

"But is it worth the risk of sailing so far and so fast?" Liam put in. "We've hardly put the winter behind us, after all."

Everyone turned to Prince Midalis for a verdict on that remark, and the man sat back in his chair and closed his eyes for a long, long time.

"If we stay here and wait for Aydrian, we might give him a difficult fight, especially if Bruinhelde and his warriors support us, as I know they shall," the prince began. "But in the end, though we might beat Aydrian back, or stay hidden away enough so that he comes to believe that Vanguard is not worth his trouble, we will hardly be able to counterstrike forcibly.

"If we sail out or march out to take the battle to southern Honce-the-Bear, as I know I must, the odds are far from favorable," Midalis went on. "We would need to have people, including many soldiers and even Allheart Knights, come over to our side in great numbers to have any chance of standing against the army Duke Kalas has apparently assembled. With those realities put before us, and given our friend Juraviel's information, is an attempt to enlist the support of Duke Bretherford such a far-fetched and risky proposition?"

"We have to pull at the loose ends of this tapestry Aydrian is weaving to blanket the land," Pony reminded, and she gave a little shrug and a wink as she finished, "Besides, I have always wanted to see Jacintha."

"If we find negotiation with Duke Bretherford and turn him to our side, or even if we just join in the battle and assure that Abbot Olin and Duke Bretherford are defeated in Jacintha, our gain will be great," Juraviel insisted. "If Duke Bretherford comes over or his fleet is sunk, then you will control the seas, Prince Midalis, and it will be much harder for Aydrian to know your location."

"In that case, he could just march for Vanguard," the prince warned.

"And you could debark your seaborne forces behind him, anywhere along Honce-the-Bear's long coastline, and begin eroding his base of support and supply," the elf countered.

"We become more elusive if we gain uncontested control of the seas," Pony agreed.

Prince Midalis looked at her, silently pleading with her, she knew. She had gained his trust long ago, on Mount Aida, and he needed to trust in her again. She offered him a warm smile and a determined nod.

"To the Mirianic we go," Prince Midalis announced. "Tell Captain Al'u'met to organize the sail."

Soon after, Pony accompanied Midalis to the tent of Bruinhelde in the Alpinadoran encampment northeast of Pireth Vanguard. The two were surprised indeed—and so was Andacanavar, who was also in attendance—when the Alpinadoran chieftain announced that he would accompany the prince on his southern sail, with many warships and the hopes of a great victory.

"You have sown the seeds of trust and friendship," Pony said to the prince, as they rode back toward Pireth Vanguard later that day.

"A crop more fruitful than I ever imagined," said Midalis.

"Because you sowed them honestly, and without any ulterior design," said Pony. "Bruinhelde knows that you came to him in sincere friendship for the benefit of both your peoples. When he followed you to Mount Aida, he found that his acceptance of your offers of friendship in the time of the dactyl were well-founded. And so he is willing to stand beside you."

"All the way to Behren," Midalis said with a helpless laugh.

"All the way to Behren," Pony echoed.

CHAPTER

❖ 36 ❖

Counter Winds Blowing

"Little did we realize how fast and great our rise would be when last we passed this city's gates," Aydrian said triumphantly to De'Unnero and Sadye as they and Duke Kalas rode beside him into the city of Entel. The ride across Honce-the-Bear had been easy and most gratifying, with crowds lining every way to cheer for the new king. What a testament to Duke Kalas' influence and strength, Aydrian had realized, for the man had securely locked up the entirety of the southern kingdom in Aydrian's name, with but two notable exceptions: Pireth Tulme to the north, upon which Duke Kalas' armies were even then descending, and St.-Mere-Abelle, to the north and west.

The side trip to Entel had been Kalas' idea, mostly to check on Abbot Olin's progress in the south and to ensure that this great city, more populated than Palmaris, even, remained firmly under control during Abbot Olin's absence. The Abellican Church had always been strong here, but strong in two separate factions. St. Bondabruce, the great abbey, had long held firm under Abbot Olin and his preoccupation with Behren, while the smaller and older abbey, St. Rontlemore, had stayed more a friend to the line of Ursal and the Abellican Church proper, more closely tied to St.-Mere-Abelle.

Duke Kalas had feared that St. Rontlemore might be using Olin's absence to gain a stronger foothold in Entel, but if that was in any way the case, then the welcome for King Aydrian did not show it! Thousands turned out, the whole city it seemed, waving red kerchiefs, as had become the custom for greeting the young king, and all the state flags flying over the main houses of power, the lords' mansions, St. Bondabruce, and St. Rontlemore, were the newer version, the bear and tiger rampant, facing off over the evergreen symbol of the Church.

"St. Rontlemore has shown great wisdom in this," De'Unnero remarked when he noted that banner over the ancient abbey.

"Because Duke Kalas has so completely cut them off from St.-Mere-Abelle," Aydrian replied. "Their mother abbey has deserted them, as far as they can tell."

"I do not trust in their loyalty," Duke Kalas admitted. "The brothers of St. Rontlemore might be pragmatic more than wise, and if that is so, they likely hold the old flag of the Ursal line ready to hoist should the situation change."

"We need not worry over that once St.-Mere-Abelle has fallen," Aydrian remarked, and he looked to De'Unnero, who nodded his agreement and couldn't hide just a bit of a grin.

"I have long sent word to Duke Bretherford in the south," Duke Kalas said. "I expect that Abbot Olin will be here to greet us, or that he will soon arrive."

"Not soon enough, if he is not already here," said De'Unnero. "We have left a dangerous foe behind us in St.-Mere-Abelle, and with spring fast warming the winter trails, Prince Midalis might not be far behind."

"Palmaris is well defended, as is Ursal," Duke Kalas strongly replied, as if he had taken the words as an affront.

"Nothing would please me more than to hear that Midalis and St.-Mere-Abelle were both now attacking Palmaris," said Aydrian. "Let them play their hands."

"Midalis will not be without support, wherever he arrives," warned De'Unnero.

"Wherever that may be, I will crush him," Aydrian assured the man. Aydrian didn't miss Duke Kalas' slight grimace at that remark; he understood the duke's reluctance. Prince Midalis had been his friend for a long time, after all, and the brother of the man who had been Kalas' dearest companion for many years. But it did not matter, Aydrian knew. Duke Kalas would not flee his side when Midalis arrived.

"And the sooner we are rid of him, the sooner I can secure the kingdom in total and turn my attention toward helping Abbot Olin finish off the Behrenese," Aydrian went on. "Then where, I wonder? To To-gai in the far southwest? To the cold lands of Alpinador?"

He stopped as they pulled their horses up in front of the great iron gates of the fence surrounding St. Bondabruce. They were warmly welcomed by a host of eager brothers and led into the main audience chamber of Abbot Olin. It was a vast and airy space, not as cavernous as the audience halls of Castle Ursal perhaps, but actually more so than the tighter quarters of St.-Mere-Abelle, with its huddled architecture keeping it warm from the cold Mirianic winds. St.-Mere-Abelle was many times the size of St. Bondabruce, and held more than ten times the number of brothers. The treasures of the mother abbey were priceless, with gold-trimmed tapestries and ornamental chalices and artifacts from every age of the Abellican Church, and many more that even predated the old religion! In terms of wealth, gemstone cache, library, and artworks, St. Bondabruce did not come close to comparing to St.-Mere-Abelle, nor did the Entel abbey have any of the more spectacular architectural items, like the ornate stained-glass window that looked out on All Saints Bay from the main keep in great St.-Mere-

Abelle. But with the more hospitable southern climate, St. Bondabruce did not need the low ceilings of its northern sister abbey, so the place was anchored by soaring minarets. The ceiling in this audience chamber was no less than fifty feet high, all painted in the bright colors and designs more typical of Behren than Honce-the-Bear.

The furnishings also showed great Behrenese influence, with rich, brightly colored fabrics and airy net weaves across the wide backs of chairs. Abbot Olin had done much to influence that, they all understood, and seeing the place again only reminded Aydrian of how fully he had put Olin out of the way by sending him to his favored haunts in the south.

"King Aydrian," greeted an older, neatly trimmed man, moving out quickly from a side door in the audience hall. He rushed up before Aydrian, dipped a deep and polite bow, and motioned for the young king to take the abbot's throne seat as his own.

"Greetings, Master Mackaront," Aydrian replied, recognizing the man from their journeys to the southern waters, when De'Unnero and Aydrian had secured the services of the pirate, Maisha Darou, and his fleet. "Pray you go tell your Abbot Olin that we have arrived, and that time is of the essence."

Mackaront shifted somewhat nervously, a movement that none of the four visitors missed. "Abbot Olin remains in Jacintha," the man explained. "The situation there is quite fluid, and he feared that leaving now could be detrimental to our purposes."

Aydrian studied the man carefully, then nodded and did sit down upon Olin's own chair. "Quite fluid?"

Mackaront glanced around and cleared his throat. "I assure you, King Aydrian, that Behren is secured," he began, trying to appear more confident than he sounded. "At least, the newer kingdom of Behren is now secure under the control of Yatol Mado Wadon, who is no more than the public voice of Abbot Olin. The tumult within Behren is as you believed, and Abbot Olin found his services required—at any price."

"But . . ." Aydrian prompted, for the words of victory hardly matched the man's nervous demeanor.

"In Behren's war with To-gai, concessions were made," Master Mackaront explained. "The city of Dharyan was given over to Brynn Dharielle and the To-gai-ru, and we have found a difficult time in . . . in getting it back."

Aydrian paused for a moment, then laughed aloud. "Abbot Olin has done battle with Brynn?"

"Through his emissary, Yatol De Hamman, yes."

Aydrian laughed again.

"Yatol De Hamman's march through the kingdom was a complete success," the stammering Mackaront added, obviously confused by the laughter. "Every city fell to Jacintha. Concerning the new incarnation of Behren, your dreams have been all but realized, and will be soon, I do not doubt, as

Abbot Olin increases his hold over the populace. But the army is weary of battle, and has great fear of Brynn Dharielle, the Dragon of To-gai. Thus, I was sent back to Entel, to find audience with you and bid you to spare more soldiers for Abbot Olin."

"The force I have already given to him is considerable," Aydrian countered.

"But much of it involves the fleet, and that will be of little use inland against Dharyan-Dharielle," Master Mackaront explained. "Abbot Olin believes that with another five thousand Kingsmen, he can seize Dharyan-Dharielle within three weeks and complete the reunification of Behren."

"And then press on?" Aydrian asked.

"If Dharyan is recovered, the To-gai-ru will have little resistance to offer," Master Mackaront said hopefully. "If you were to send ten thousand instead of five, Abbot Olin could sweep all resistance from the steppes before the turn of the year! Such a victory, led by men of Honce-the-Bear, would also strengthen Abbot Olin's position in Jacintha. He could quickly make Yatol Mado Wadon fully irrelevant, and all the lands south of the Belt-and-Buckle would be yours."

"Hmm," the young king mused, dropping his chin into his hand. "There remains only one problem then."

"My King?"

"The fact that I specifically instructed Abbot Olin not to go against Brynn Dharielle," said Aydrian, his voice suddenly turning angry.

"The battle was inadvertent," Master Mackaront backpedaled. "An error in judgment by Yatol De Hamman, whose head was doubtlessly filled with images of greater glory. But now that the fight has begun . . ."

"Abbot Olin will stop it, and with his sincere apologies," Aydrian told him.

"We can defeat her, my King," Master Mackaront assured.

"Is there something deficient in your hearing, master?" De'Unnero sternly interjected.

Aydrian waved the fiery monk off. "Please speak openly, master," he bade.

Master Mackaront cleared his throat again. "The city nearly fell to De Hamman, and that despite the surprise return of the dragon and a second horde of To-gai-ru warriors," he explained. "They are besieged within the city now, with nowhere to run. Never will we see so great an opportunity as this one at hand. On the open desert or open steppes, the Dragon of To-gai is a far more formidable foe."

"Is this Dragon of To-gai a woman, or is it a beast?" De'Unnero asked.

"It is both," Mackaront explained. "The woman, Brynn Dharielle, is called the Dragon of To-gai because of the great beast she controls."

"A dragon?" Sadye put in. "A *real* dragon?"

"Had I not seen it with my own eyes, I would not disagree with your obvious doubt," Master Mackaront replied. "A real dragon indeed, huge and terrible. But the warriors of Behren have done battle with it for years now, and they know how to beat it. Aided by the magic of the Abellican brothers, they will bring the beast down."

"There remains only one problem then," Aydrian reiterated, his voice thick with sarcasm.

"Yes, my King," the master of St. Bondabruce agreed, and he lowered his eyes.

"Abbot Olin is not to battle Brynn," Aydrian declared. "Not now. Not if all the southland was handed to me in a victory chalice. I do not wish to war with Brynn. I have other plans for her."

That brought curious stares from the others in the room, Aydrian noted, particularly from Sadye, who seemed less than pleased. She was particularly irked by his familiar tone regarding Brynn, he realized, and he had to fight hard to keep his grin hidden.

"Abbot Olin has all the forces that can be spared at this time," Aydrian said flatly to Master Mackaront. "The season grows warmer and our dangerous foe to the north will likely march. And there remains the issue of St.-Mere-Abelle—you and your abbot do remember that place, do you not?" Aydrian looked at De'Unnero as he finished, though, and not at Mackaront, and he was pleased to see the eager glow in the monk's eyes—and in those of Duke Kalas, as well.

"Yes, my King."

"Would you have me lessen my pressure upon the perverted Abellican Order and delay my conquest of the mother abbey so that your abbot can collect miles of windblown sand for my coffers?"

"No, of course not, my King."

"Then go quickly and tell Abbot Olin to surrender his visions of To-gai and use the forces I have given to him to strengthen his hold on Behren. When I am finished here, I will join him in Jacintha, with all the strength of Honce-the-Bear behind me. Brynn Dharielle will be brought into my fold, one way or another. Now be gone."

"Yes, my King." With that, Mackaront bowed and exited the room, and headed straight out the front door of St. Bondabruce.

"I am surprised that Abbot Olin did not come to meet with you personally," Marcalo De'Unnero observed.

"Nor Duke Bretherford," added Kalas. "Perhaps the abbot's hold on the southland is not as strong as he believes."

"Let us hope that it is," Aydrian replied. "Because he must hold with those forces I have entrusted to him. I'll not turn my eyes from the north now, not with St.-Mere-Abelle unconquered and Prince Midalis not yet discovered. Have we word from Earl DePaunch?"

"None since the runner ship arrived in Palmaris from Pireth Dancard announcing that the fortress had been taken," Duke Kalas admitted.

"The weather has turned fair enough for DePaunch to risk a journey southward by a courier ship, surely," said De'Unnero.

"Perhaps one has landed in Palmaris during our march," the duke replied. "We cannot know."

De'Unnero started to respond, his voice rising with agitation.

"It is not a matter of concern to us at this time," Aydrian interrupted. "Set your sights on Pireth Tulme—I wish to have it secured in short order. And set your sights upon St.-Mere-Abelle. If Prince Midalis makes an appearance, we will destroy him. If not, then let us secure the whole of the southland, the mother abbey included. Our position will only be greater in that event should the prince come south."

"And what of the eager DePaunch?" De'Unnero asked, doing nothing at all to hide his continuing contempt for the young upstart.

"I will see to him," said Aydrian. "Along with his victory in the gulf, when Pireth Tulme is ours, St.-Mere-Abelle will be completely isolated. As will Prince Midalis. Time works against the prince, not for him. Even those peasants who might have supported him have warmed to the thought of King Aydrian, no doubt."

"They are a fickle lot," Duke Kalas agreed with a derisive chortle, a sentiment that was shared by everyone in the room.

The now-formidable armada of Prince Midalis swept out of Vanguard harbor, sails full of wind. Sleek *Saudi Jacintha* centered the fleet, her prow smoothly cutting the dark waters while the heavier, stolen Honce-the-Bear warships bounced and splashed along beside her.

The spirit of Aydrian, hovering over the gulf waters, wasn't nearly as surprised that the efficient prince had so quickly turned the ships back out as he was to discover the trailing fleet of Alpinadoran longboats.

So, Midalis had made some allies in Vanguard.

Any thoughts that Aydrian had harbored of sending the rest of his fleet out from Palmaris to confront the prince flew away now, in light of the size and strength of this armada. When the young king's spirit had flown past Pireth Dancard, to see the charred skeletons of three warships and the tip of the mast of a fourth one, sunken in the bay, he had easily deduced the source of that disaster. His subsequent scouting of the island, to see that Earl DePaunch and the rest of his soldiers were still ashore, had made it fairly clear to Aydrian that the rest of the missing fleet had likely been stolen.

And here they were, sailing south from Vanguard, stacked with enemies of his crown.

In a way, Aydrian was glad to see the force moving against him—finally he knew the intentions of Prince Midalis. And given the size of the fleet, he knew, too, the general size of Midalis' force. Fifty boats, most of them longboats and only nine heavier warships.

Not more than five thousand warriors.

The young king wished that he could become a more substantial physical force at that moment, a great gale to circle behind the armada and fill their sails even more. Not to sink them, but to urge them on, to push Midalis more swiftly to the coast of southern Honce-the-Bear.

Then it would be over and he would be unopposed.

His pleasant musing was sharply interrupted, though, as a wave of energy overcame him. Suddenly, Aydrian's corporeal form seemed so much farther away, almost unattainably so! Panic welling, the young man soared back to his body in Entel, and rushed into it, coming awake and gasping repeatedly.

Gradually, he calmed and realized what had happened, and he forgave himself his moment of panic and misunderstanding.

He wasn't used to losing.

He recognized that sunstone antimagic had defeated him. Certainly it was easier to put up a sunstone antimagic wave than to utilize the spirit-walking ability of the soul stone. Even a much weaker gemstone-wielder could defeat the latter with the former.

Still, someone had noted his intrusion, it seemed, and he had been nowhere near to the fleet of Prince Midalis. Someone on the decks of one of those ships was apparently quite familiar, and proficient, with gemstone magic.

"Mother?" Aydrian asked slyly into his empty room.

At the front rail on the prow of *Saudi Jacintha*, Pony looked out at the dark waters and let the salty breeze blow through her hair. She had come up here alone to meditate on all the circumstances surrounding her, to consider the course of Dasslerond more completely, and now the attempts by Juraviel to help her put things aright.

To consider the man standing on the deck behind her, Prince Midalis, and the desperate gamble they were all now taking to try to find some weakness in the growing strength of Aydrian.

To consider Aydrian, her son, so lost and wayward, so wrongly guided.

And to consider Elbryan. Had it been a dream, a delusion wrought by weakness and agony? Had she really descended into the realm of death when she had been shot by that arrow along the waters offshore of Pireth Dancard? By all common sense, she knew it had to be a delusion; but if so how had she maintained enough of a connection to her soul stone to prevent that surely mortal wound from finishing her off?

Had it really been the spirit of Elbryan guiding her, holding her hand and holding her heart through the gemstone?

Pony didn't know, and that only made the spirit's last words to her even more confusing.

"We make fine progress, but Captain Al'u'met fears that the strong tail wind portends a brewing late-season storm," said Midalis, coming up beside her.

"No storm," Pony assured him, for she had scouted far out to the west the previous night. She knew that they would be well beyond Pireth Dancard, at least, before any storm could catch up to them, and knew, too, that if they got around the northeastern tip of the mainland, beyond Pireth Tulme, then the sailing should be smoother and much safer.

"Captain Al'u'met explained that running the eastern coast in the spring and summer is quite safe," Midalis remarked, echoing her thoughts exactly.

"The farther south we sail, the safer the waters in this season," she replied.

The two stood in silence for some time, then, just looking out at the shining dark waters and the occasional white-tipped breaks. Directly below them, the water splashed and flew as *Saudi Jacintha* swept on.

"I never would have found the courage for so bold a move without you," Prince Midalis said quietly a short time later.

Pony turned and regarded him curiously.

"The strike against Dancard, and now this," Midalis explained. "You have brought more with you than you understand in your journey to join me."

"More a flight from Aydrian than that," Pony admitted.

Prince Midalis offered a smile and a nod. "Do you really believe that Duke Bretherford will be swayed?"

"The Duke Bretherford that I knew was loyal to your brother."

"As was Duke Kalas," Midalis reminded.

"But unlike Kalas, Bretherford was never blinded by ambition," Pony explained. "It is surprising that Duke Kalas threw in so readily with Aydrian— unless you consider how profoundly the man despises me."

"Then he is a fool," Midalis said to her, and he reached over and dared to stroke her blond hair.

Pony just kept looking back out at the water, accepting the comforting pat.

"Then Duke Bretherford never despised Queen Jilseponie," Midalis reasoned.

"I would not have called us friends, but neither were we enemies. I have always been fond of Duke Bretherford, and he was quite blunt and honest with me—perhaps the only one in your brother's court to act so."

Midalis came to the rail beside her and leaned out on crossed arms. "It is such a desperate plan, isn't it?"

"Less so than our strike at Pireth Dancard a few weeks ago when the seas were far more dangerous, I would guess," Pony replied. "Duke Bretherford's fleet outside of Jacintha is not so formidable, from what I have gathered from Belli'mar Juraviel. If the duke turns on us, we should defeat him."

"I mean all of it," Prince Midalis clarified. "This whole attempt to unseat your son, whose army, by all accounts, is . . ." He stopped and looked hard at Pony, who had suddenly turned away, glancing all about and wearing an expression of suspicion.

"What is it?"

Pony held up her hand to cut short the inquisition and just went on glancing about. "How could I have been so foolish?" she asked, and her hand went to the pouch on her hip.

"What is it?" Midalis demanded.

"It is Aydrian, I believe," the woman answered, and she drew forth her hand and sorted through the stones until she held a sunstone alone. Pony fell into that stone and called forth its antimagic energies, then threw them out wide to the waves. Sometime later, the woman gave a sigh and considered her friend.

"Aydrian sought us out spiritually," she explained. "I think it was he, or one of his lackeys."

"Perhaps it was one of the brothers within St.-Mere-Abelle."

"Let us hope," said Pony.

"You dismissed the magic with the sunstone?"

"It is not so difficult a feat," she explained. "The sunstone is an easy defense against such intrusions, for the first hint of its power forces a spirit to flee back to its dispossessed body."

"Could you not have gone out with the soul stone instead?" the prince asked. "To determine the source of that . . . feeling?"

Pony thought on it, then just shook her head. The prince had a point, she knew, but she knew, too, without a doubt, that she simply did not wish to meet Aydrian in any form at that time.

"I will be more vigilant," she promised.

"If he knows . . ."

"Then he knows only that we have sailed out of Vanguard, nothing more. Our destination could be Palmaris. Or St.-Mere-Abelle. Or Pireth Tulme. He cannot know. And we have a significant part of his fleet, even should he guess our course. What might he throw against us that we cannot defeat out here on the seas?"

It was true enough, she knew, and she joined Prince Midalis in looking around at that time, at the great warships sailing off to either side of *Saudi Jacintha*'s wake and the multitude of Alpinadoran vessels keeping pace all about them. It was a comforting sight indeed, for there was truth in Pony's statement, and it seemed possible at that time that Prince Midalis might seize complete control of the seas in short order. Taking the land might not prove so easy.

Playing on that thought, Pony turned to the man. "Pireth Dancard," she said.

Midalis looked at her curiously.

"Perhaps we should visit the island fortress once more, on our way through the gulf," Pony explained. "They, resident and invader alike, have been trapped there for weeks now. Perhaps the sight of Prince Midalis will offer hope to your loyalists and make Aydrian's supporters reconsider their course."

"You would have us slow our run to the south?"

"Nay," the woman answered, a grin growing on her face. "Let the fleet sail on, with only *Saudi Jacintha* lagging behind. Or better still, let us bid Captain Al'u'met to open wide his sails and outdistance the fleet to Dancard, where we can wait. You and I can go out from her—I will get you to Dancard with the gemstones."

"And then what?" the prince asked incredulously. "We, two, do battle with an Ursal legion?"

"We two learn what we might learn, and strike wherever we might," Pony said, and now her grin spread wide across her face.

Prince Midalis looked at her for a long while before a similar grin began to widen on his handsome face. "You are a gambler, aren't you?"

"Not when I see a more reasonable course," Pony admitted. "You know of one?"

The prince only laughed.

They came ashore in the dark of night, stepping from the lapping waves onto the surf-rounded rocks not far from the spot where Pony once lay wounded. Behind them, a mile out to sea, *Saudi Jacintha* sat at anchor, while the rest of the fleet sailed on from the north, trying to catch up to the swift ship.

As they moved up the beach to higher ground, they saw the lights of the tower fortress off to the left and the darkened shapes of the buildings of Dancard town along the rocky slopes to the right. One place within that quiet community seemed to be bustling, though, and the pair let it be their beacon as they made their way.

"A common room," Pony observed quietly from the shadows beyond the windows.

"Filled mostly with townsfolk, it seems," said Midalis, bending a bit for a better angle as he peered into the glow. "But soldiers, too, no doubt."

"I want to run in there and proclaim your presence," Pony admitted. "I want to lead you to the tower and take it back for the rightful crown, here and now."

"You promised Bradwarden and Andacanavar that this was merely an exploratory journey," the prince reminded her.

It was true enough, Pony had to admit. When she and Midalis had announced their plans for this diversion to Pireth Dancard, the centaur, in particular, had howled in outrage, and had kept on howling until he got concessions from the pair that they would use all precautions here.

The sound of talking from farther down the road behind the pair had them ducking deeper into the shadows, and they watched as a group of five men—fishermen of Dancard, obviously, and not professional soldiers—ambled into sight.

Pony and Midalis exchanged a glance, and then the woman stepped out to block the road before the group, while the prince sank deeper into the shadows.

"Greetings," she said.

The men stopped, nearly falling all over each other. "Eh, Connie girl, is that you?" one asked.

"Nah, that's not Connie," another was quick to add. "Who are ye, girl?"

"Hardly a girl anymore," Pony said and she moved a bit more into the light and pulled back the hood of her cloak, shaking her blond hair free.

"Who are ye then?" the second man asked. "Ye're not one from Dancard that I'm knowin', and I'm knowin' all from Dancard town. Did ye come in with them soldiers, then? A trollop for the morale o' the men?"

That brought a few hopeful smiles from the others, and Pony merely laughed. "Hardly," she replied. "I am a herald, come to Dancard isle this night."

"This night?" one man balked, and he and the others glanced down toward the dark ocean as if expecting an invasion fleet to even then be gliding in. "I heard o' no ships putting in to Dancard this night!"

"Because I was on no ship," Pony replied calmly. "And I am no trollop. I am a herald, as I said, bearing news of Prince Midalis of Vanguard, the rightful king of Honce-the-Bear."

The men all stammered, but really said nothing intelligible for a long while.

"Are ye now?" one of them finally managed to ask.

"The same Prince Midalis who led the attack against the fleet of Ursal that came to Pireth Dancard," Pony went on. "The same Prince Midalis who stranded the soldiers here by sailing off with their ships."

"Bah, she's one of Earl DePaunch's spies!" another man cried. "He's testing our wits here, wanting to see if we're thinkin' in favor o' Midalis. Scoot her on her way and let us get to the bottles!"

"Aye, she's no herald," another agreed.

"Then why did she bring me along with her?" asked Midalis, stepping from the shadows to stand openly before them, his hands on his hips, holding wide his cloak to reveal the crest of the bear rampant, the crest of his family, emblazoned upon the one piece of armor he wore this night, a half breastplate that covered the left side of his chest.

Indeed, the men did recognize Midalis, for he had been through Dancard on several occasions, including his return trip from the marriage of Pony and his brother only a couple of years before.

The men gave a communal gasp.

"Are ye to kill DePaunch then and get his bullies off our island?" one dared to ask a moment later.

"Aye, the dog that he is," another said, and he spat upon the ground.

"He put Warder Presso to the noose, he did," said another.

"Warder Presso?" Pony asked suddenly, the name sparking recognition.

"Aye, our leader here before DePaunch," the man answered. "A good man. Coastpoint Guard for years and years."

"You knew him?" Prince Midalis asked Pony.

"I knew a man by that name in Pireth Tulme, many years ago," the woman answered, and her tone turned very cold as she asked the townsman, "Where is this Earl DePaunch?"

As one, the group turned up toward the tower.

"What are you thinking, Jilseponie?" Prince Midalis quietly asked.

She didn't answer. She didn't have to answer to convey her intentions. "Stand strong in your faith in the line of Ursal," she said to the townsfolk, and she turned and started off into the darkness, heading for the distant tower.

"My prince?" one man asked, obviously not knowing what he should do and obviously expecting some trouble!

"Go to your revelry," Prince Midalis explained. "You are not forgotten here, though it may be some time before I can return to you. But I will return to you, on my word, should I reclaim the crown of Honce-the-Bear." And then, knowing well that Pony wasn't waiting for him, the man sprinted off into the night.

He caught up to her along the road out of Dancard town, moving determinedly toward the tower. "Jilseponie," he warned, grabbing her by the arm. "We promised Andacanavar and Bradwarden that we would avoid trouble."

"No trouble," the woman returned. "But I've a few words for this Earl DePaunch." She looked Midalis in the eye, and even in the dark of night, he could see the intense sparkle in her blue eyes. "For the man who murdered Warder Constantine Presso."

The woman stormed on, sweeping Midalis along in her wake. As they approached the tower of Pireth Dancard, they saw a pair of guards standing before the closed doors, long spears held ready beside them.

"Stand and be counted!" came the demand.

"Open the door!" Pony shouted back.

"What is the meaning of this?" one of the guards roared at her. "Back to your homes, peasants!"

"Is that how you name your former queen, and the prince of Honce-the-Bear?" Pony yelled right back at him, pulling back the hood of her cloak. "Stand aside for Prince Midalis, or risk being hanged as a traitor to the crown!"

How wide those two sets of eyes looked, reflected in the torchlight! The men gawked for a moment, then looked to each other, then back at the surprising pair. One stammered, "What? What?" over and over again, while the other slunk back and seemed on the verge of a fast retreat.

"Open the door!" Pony demanded.

"I cannot, milady," the flustered soldier cried, and he halfheartedly lifted his spear before him, while his partner moved more forcibly to intercept the still-approaching pair.

Or at least, the man tried to intercept, for in the flash of a sizzling, bluish silver bolt, he was flying away, to crash against the tower side and crumple to the hard ground.

The other man fell back, and then screamed out as another bolt blasted forth from Pony's hand, aimed not at him, but at the door he partially blocked.

The door fell in, the guard stumbling down atop it, and Pony and Midalis simply walked right by.

"Where is Earl DePaunch?" Pony asked the shaking and prone guard.

The man pointed to the stairway set in the back of the circular tower's base.

Up went Pony, with Midalis following close behind. They moved quickly right through the second floor, the barracks, taking little heed of the men, some sleeping, some groggily asking what the commotion was all about.

By the time they got to the third-floor door, some of those soldiers were crying out for them to stop, but they merely pushed on, then closed and barred the door behind them.

A hallway loomed before them, a door on either side and one at its end.

"Which one, I wonder?" Pony asked, and Midalis just shrugged.

"If this is another squabble over some peasant's livestock, I will..." came a complaint for the end of the hall, as the door opened and a man stepped to its threshold. He wore a nightshirt, but it was of fine silk, obviously imported from Behren, and he had a distinct look of nobility about him, with his perfectly groomed hair and beard.

"Earl DePaunch, I presume," Pony said to him.

The man looked at her curiously for just a moment, and then his eyes widened so much that it seemed as if the balls would just fall from their sockets and roll about on the floor!

"Queen . . . queen," he stammered.

"And prince prince, too," Pony dryly replied.

The man disappeared, slamming the door and giving a shriek, and Pony methodically moved to it, and through it, just in time to see the tower top's trapdoor slam shut above her.

"Block it! Block it!" she heard the muffled cry of the earl. "Put your bodies atop it, you fools!"

Pony looked to Midalis and smiled wryly. "See? No trouble." She lifted her hand and found her way into the graphite.

The trapdoor blasted apart, launching the two unfortunate soldiers lying atop it into the air.

One was still down, barely conscious, the other up on one knee, shaking his head so forcefully that his lips made a flapping sound, when Pony climbed through onto the rooftop.

A sword met her ascent, coming in hard from the left, but the woman had anticipated the attack, of course, and so she had her own sword in hand, meeting the attack with a deft parry, a subtle turn, and a sudden sweep that sent the other blade flying away into the night.

The Kingsman started to come at her again, but she eyed him dangerously. "Be reasonable, friend," she said. "Do not make me kill you."

The man, as if only then realizing that he had no weapon in hand, backed away and held his hands up before him.

"To arms!" the terrified DePaunch cried, leaning over the tower's edge across the way from Pony. "To arms! Giulio Jannet, where are you?"

"Nowhere that will do you any good, traitor," Pony said, and Earl DePaunch gave a little shriek and rushed to the side as Pony steadily approached.

"Tell me of Warder Presso's hanging," Pony bade him. "Tell me in detail how you murdered my old friend."

"I represent King Aydrian," the stammering earl replied. "I am a soldier in the army of Honce-the-Bear."

"You are an Allheart Knight, sworn to protect the line of Ursal!" Pony corrected. "The line that names this man as king!" She swept her hand out toward the somewhat amused, somewhat nervous, Prince Midalis.

He stood by the shattered trapdoor looking down, and remarked, "I do believe that we will soon be joined by interested others."

That seemed to give Earl DePaunch some backbone—he stood straighter, at least, and motioned for his soldiers to act.

One started to, but Pony was quicker. She rushed the nobleman and put her sword tip to his throat, her other hand reaching into her gemstone pouch. "Do tell your soldiers to leave."

"Help me!" the man cried. "Help me! Kill them!"

Pony snapped her hand up to the earl's chest and engaged her new gemstone, forcing its powers to encompass the man instead of herself. His body weight stolen by the malachite's levitational magic, the man went up on his toes, then right off the ground, lifted by Pony. With a shrug, she sent him flying out over the tower's edge.

"Yes, do kill me," she said, turning to face the others.

The three Kingsmen, and a fourth coming up through the trapdoor, hesitated.

"Leave her!" Earl DePaunch screamed frantically, flailing his arms and legs. "Do not harm her! Do not break her concentration!"

With that settled, Pony motioned for the men to throw aside their weapons and move back over to the trapdoor.

"I demand the surrender of Pireth Dancard to the rightful king of Honce-the-Bear, Prince Midalis Dan Ursal!" she called to DePaunch.

DePaunch stammered and stuttered, but was too afraid to argue with her.

"If you so believe in your young King Aydrian, then you should deny my claim here and now," Pony chided. "Tell your men to slay me, Earl De-Paunch. Tell them to attack with all their hearts, in faith that you served your king well as you fell to your death."

The sound that came from Earl DePaunch's lips sounded distinctly like a whine.

"I deny your claim!" came a cry from below, and Pony and Midalis looked over the tower's lip to see an Abellican monk standing before the tower, soldiers all about him. "The kingdom is Aydrian's, and the church is claimed for Father Abbot Marcalo De'Unnero." The monk looked about, ordering the soldiers into the tower, and he seemed to have many allies down there with him, all willing to sacrifice DePaunch, if it had to be.

"If I angle it correctly, I might be able to drop DePaunch atop the fool," Pony remarked to Midalis.

But Prince Midalis cupped her hand with his own. "Remember who we are," he said. "Set the man down."

Pony stared at him incredulously, but Midalis jumped aside and gathered up a rope that was lying beside the ballista. He tossed one end out to the earl, and when the man caught it, he gave a sudden tug that brought the weightless DePaunch flying back over the tower top, where Pony released him from the magic. He fell hard, skidding down, but scrambled right back to his feet.

"A wise choice, Prince Midalis," DePaunch said, trying to regain some of his lost dignity. "Perhaps I might speak on your behalf to King Aydrian."

He didn't quite get Aydrian's name out before Midalis' left hook smashed him in the face, dropping him like a stone.

"Think well on your position here, Earl DePaunch," the prince warned. "You are isolated; the seas are mine, as the kingdom soon will be. I'll not forget your treason, sir, nor your murder of Warder Presso."

"Who was my friend," Pony added, moving by and glaring at the squirming man. "We will speak again."

They had to leave then, for the tower below was filling with soldiers, and even the three guards on the top with them seemed to be gaining some confidence.

"You should all consider your positions well," Pony said to them, and she sheathed her sword and took out a second gemstone—which made the soldiers shrink back even more! "King Danube is dead, but his line lives on. Aydrian is not of that line, and is not the rightful king of Honce-the-Bear."

She took Midalis' hand then, and engaged her malachite gemstone, running to the tower's lip and leaping away. As soon as they were airborne, Pony reached into the second stone, a lodestone, and used its energies to find a metallic source across the way in Dancard town. She strengthened the lodestone's focus on that metal, using the magnetic energies to propel her and Midalis along through the dark Dancard night.

She brought them down easily, releasing the malachite. On they ran down to the surf, the sound of a dozen horns blowing furiously behind them. Now with amber in hand, the clever woman and the prince sprinted out across the dark waters toward the waiting *Saudi Jacintha*. "I should have dropped him to his death," Pony lamented, when they were safely away.

"His terror weakened him in the eyes of his juniors," Midalis remarked. "Your action, had you killed him, might have brought an attempted revolt, but that would have done little but get the townsfolk slaughtered. We cannot support them now, because we've not the time nor the resources to do battle with Pireth Dancard at present. Our business is in the south, remember?"

Pony had to agree. "You have support in Dancard—Earl DePaunch's stay there will not be without incident."

"And there he will remain, until we decide otherwise. You shamed him to his soldiers and now they know the truth of my intent. We have won a significant victory here."

Pony wasn't quite so convinced, but she understood that it had to be good enough. Still, within Pony there loomed a desire to slip ashore and cripple the batteries, and to finish with DePaunch and all the other leaders. Then let Midalis' warships sail in, and see how much resistance the island offered! But Midalis was right, she knew. What would they do with the crown's soldiers even if they came over to the prince's cause? They had no more room on their ships.

Her friend was right, she knew. Let Aydrian's men sit there on that rocky island and fester.

And let DePaunch suffer with his fears.

For now.

CHAPTER

❖ 37 ❖

The Value of Knowing

"I was told to come here and convince you that the withdrawal is well under way," Pechter Dan Turk said to Brynn, Pagonel, and the other leaders of Dharyan-Dharielle. "You are to be mollified, to purchase the weeks that Yatol De Hamman needs to strengthen his force."

Brynn looked past the words, to the torn feelings she read clearly in Pechter Dan Turk's eyes. It was killing the man to so betray his own people, she knew, and he was doing so only because he had honestly come to believe that it was Abbot Olin and Honce-the-Bear, and not Yatol Wadon and Behren, that were truly in command here, and truly set to benefit. Olin was using Behrenese blood to expand the empire of King Aydrian and the Abellican Church.

Brynn looked around to the others in the room, to see the gamut of emotions, from the doubting expression on the stern face of ever-skeptical Tanalk Grenk to the sudden exuberance displayed by some of the younger leaders.

"Those hundreds who have apparently left De Hamman's force," Brynn began, "how far have they retreated?"

"Within an hour's march," Pechter Dan Turk replied. "A few miles along the road and no more. Yatol De Hamman will not allow himself to become truly weakened when there is any possibility that you might come forth from Dharyan-Dharielle."

"Then why march at all?" Tanalk Grenk put in.

"Because if we believe that he is coordinating the retreat of his army, we will not come forth," Pagonel explained. "Yatol De Hamman does not wish a battle against us at this time."

"His force is greater than anything To-gai could muster," Tanalk Grenk argued. "Our walls keep him at bay, but would we win if we charged out from those walls?"

"It would be a difficult battle," Brynn admitted. "But we would prevail." She wasn't sure she really believed that last statement, for she understood

379

that De Hamman's force was not only mighty in a conventional sense, but that they had added several elements—quick-aiming and versatile ballistae and the Abellican gemstone-wielding monks—to counteract Brynn's greatest advantage: Agradeleous. For the To-gai-ru to ride out, for all their ferocity, would be to throw themselves into a maelstrom. They might win anyway, Brynn believed, for she thought a To-gai-ru warrior to be worth two Behrenese, but it would be a bloody and difficult battle, one that would leave her army depleted and battered. It would be very hard to accomplish a rout with that second Behrenese force returning fast to join in, for the initial defense would not break and run in their faith and understanding that help was coming fast.

The woman felt a slight pang of guilt in so deceiving Pechter Dan Turk, though, but she could not put her trust completely in the man who was already working as a double agent. He had gone to De Hamman ostensibly to report on her and the defenses of the city, but had instead returned in a polar opposite manner.

Her words stirred several private whispered conversations, mostly among the ferocious To-gai-ru leaders who believed in their hearts that they could overrun the Behrenese all the way to Jacintha and the coast.

"Yatol De Hamman's retreat will not suffice," Brynn said, her tone and volume silencing all other conversations in the audience room. "If you would have us break out of Dharyan-Dharielle and ride to the support of Yatol Mado Wadon, then you must convince Yatol De Hamman that we are weaker than we appear, and that he must send more of his forces away, and farther away. Only then will we come forth."

Pechter Dan Turk stiffened and bristled at the blunt request, but it was not an unexpected reaction. Brynn had just asked him to place his country's main army into near helplessness, after all!

"If you can do that, then I will rout De Hamman and scatter the army of Behren," Brynn went on, honestly and bluntly. "You will precede our ride to Jacintha, where you will place all of the blame for this disaster squarely on the shoulders of imperialistic Abbot Olin. You will assure Yatol Wadon that if Abbot Olin is expelled in full, To-gai will not work against Yatol Wadon's efforts to hold his kingdom united."

"Unless I am hanged by the neck for deceiving Yatol De Hamman," the man said.

Brynn had no answer for that. If Abbot Olin was firmly in control, which they all prayed was not the case, then Pechter Dan Turk's fears were indeed justified and his execution would be a likely consequence.

"Great men are made through great risk," Pagonel said at her side.

"You must do that which is in your heart, Pechter Dan Turk," Brynn added. "We have agreed that Behren is not in Behrenese hands at this time, and that Aydrian, and not Brynn, is the threat to your homeland. I offer you a partnership in fixing that problem, but I do not diminish the pain that I know you are feeling in your heart. I say to you that Abbot Olin must be disgraced, and that such an event can only be brought about with Behrenese blood."

"You ask me to lay open the defenses of my country," Pechter Dan Turk replied. "You ask me to sacrifice Behrenese warriors."

Brynn's answer straightened the man again, mostly, she knew, because Pechter Dan Turk understood that she was correct.

"I do."

Long streaks of blue-white lightning split the nighttime sky, outlining the roiling and rising tower of dark clouds. Waves lashed the sandy beach to the west of Pireth Tulme, tossing about the Alpinadoran longboats and tilting the Honce-the-Bear warships so violently back and forth that their mast tips drew semicircles against the backdrop of the sheet of rain.

Pony and Prince Midalis pulled their cloaks tight against that rain, though Andacanavar seemed perfectly unbothered by it and Bradwarden merely paused in his piping every so often and shook his bushy head vigorously.

"It feels strange to me to come ashore here," Prince Midalis remarked. "Do I arrive as a conquering foreigner to this land that should be my own to rule?"

"With the help of the Touel'alfar, we will put things aright," Pony promised.

"If the storm doesn't sink the lot o' our ships," Bradwarden said with a great belly laugh—one that was not shared as three other sets of eyes glanced back at the rain, the wave-lashed beach, and the rocking ships. They had come in before the start of the storm and were relatively confident that their anchors would hold, but still, any losses incurred by this armada could prove devastating to the cause of the already outnumbered minions of Prince Midalis.

The good sign, though, was that the storm had come in around the tip of the mainland, out from the wider Mirianic beyond Pireth Tulme. While the winds were blowing from the northeast, wrapping around the great vortex of the storm, those winds had carried up warmer southern air. For those who understood the seasons of Honce-the-Bear along the Gulf of Corona, as did Captain Al'u'met and Prince Midalis, the storm seemed a herald for the onset of spring, and a promise for better sailing weather beyond its windy borders.

Pony squinted against the rain and wind and made out the firelight of a farmhouse in the distance. She pointed it out to her companions and started off toward it, and soon after, the friends moved into the dry and dark comfort of the farm's barn. Bradwarden stayed by the door and continued his piping, the call to Belli'mar Juraviel. For Pony had seen Juraviel in one of her soul stone scouting journeys, and the elf had sensed her spiritual presence and had bidden her to come ashore, in this region. Now they could only hope that Juraviel would hear the song of Bradwarden.

"We should set off before the dawn," Prince Midalis remarked, and he shrugged off his soaked cloak. "And use this opportunity, since we are ashore anyway, to retake Pireth Tulme."

"You'll not hold it," Andacanavar reminded. "Those armies that took it for King Aydrian are not far."

"Let us take it and leave it deserted," the prince explained.

"A signal to Aydrian that you have not forsaken the kingdom," Pony reasoned. She similarly pulled off her cloak and shook out her dripping hair, running her fingers through it to push it back from her face.

"Aye, and a signal to the folk of the kingdom that they may find an alternative to this usurper," Prince Midalis explained. "We will attack and overwhelm Pireth Tulme, putting King Aydrian's puppets onto the open road with news of the defeat. Let Aydrian retake it without a fight—the embarrassment of the defeat will sting at this proud young man."

Pony smiled, finding herself in complete agreement. This was just the sort of opportunity that they had to seize at every opening, just the sort of necessary unraveling of the tapestry that Aydrian was laying across the land. What effect might the loss of Pireth Tulme have on those men serving the usurper king? Pony knew from her own scouting that the fortress had been taken by force, that the Coastpoint Guards who had held Pireth Tulme had resisted Aydrian, much as those people out on Pireth Dancard had opposed the assault of Earl DePaunch.

Before they could continue the conversation, Bradwarden stopped his piping and gave a great bellow of greeting to a diminutive figure that moved into the open doorway of the barn. Belli'mar Juraviel seemed as if the rain hadn't even touched him, as if he had somehow wandered through the gale without getting wet.

Pony wasn't surprised.

The elf came forward, smiling warmly, and Bradwarden pulled the door closed. Immediately, Pony used her ruby to ignite the small pile of wood they had gathered.

"It is good to be back, my friends," Juraviel said, squeezing the hands of Andacanavar, Bradwarden, and Midalis, then exchanging a warm hug with Pony. "I bring you tidings from the land south of the mountains, as well as from your own kingdom."

"Brynn Dharielle met our hopes for a distant alliance with acceptance?" Prince Midalis asked.

"Brynn fears Aydrian and the Abellicans," Juraviel replied. "They overstepped themselves, I believe, for she was attacked in her city. Even now, she is preparing to break out and march to Jacintha. Her goal is to expel Abbot Olin from Behren, and nothing less."

The elf paused, but they all held silent, their unasked question evident enough.

"Brynn will welcome the support of Prince Midalis," Juraviel confirmed.

"Her role beyond Jacintha and Behren will no doubt be limited, but if she can aid in expelling Abbot Olin and handing Aydrian a sound defeat down there, that will be no small thing."

Pony sighed, for she had been hoping for more, had been hoping that Juraviel would offer news of To-gai's willingness to sail north to Entel and fight for the cause of Prince Midalis. But in truth, she realized the improbability of that.

"No small thing indeed!" Prince Midalis echoed, apparently more than satisfied.

"My path here was not direct," Juraviel went on, "for my people are scattered about Honce-the-Bear, gathering information as they go." He reached under his traveling cloak and brought forth a rough map of Honce-the-Bear, spreading it carefully on the ground before the fire. "King Aydrian marches east from Entel to Ursal and is even now crossing Yorkey County," the elf explained, pointing it out on the map. "He has sent the bulk of his force north to sweep opposition from the lands between Pireth Tulme and Palmaris, and the various bands of soldiers seem to be congregating just south of St.-Mere-Abelle Abbey."

"The grandest prize of all," Prince Midalis remarked.

"They have done well in keeping their line strong at most points, particularly those that might be struck by sea," Juraviel explained. "But there are some notable weaknesses."

The others looked about and smiled. "What gains we shall find with the help of the Touel'alfar," declared Pony.

"We can strike where he is most weak," Prince Midalis agreed. "And be gone before he can retaliate."

"Thus was how Brynn Dharielle defeated Behren," said the elf. "And then, after years of teasing victories, she held them off from behind the walls of a city, making the war too costly for the Behrenese to continue."

"But we will not defeat Aydrian in such a manner," said Midalis. "He will not relent. Eventually, we will have to face him and defeat him."

"True enough," Bradwarden agreed, "but I'm thinking that ye should be taking what ye can find until the time's come to fight Aydrian directly."

"Of course," said the prince, and he and the others turned to Juraviel.

"St. Gwendolyn is undefended," Juraviel explained. "It is practically deserted, for though Marcalo De'Unnero is working hard to fill the void of Abellican monks, most of whom will not go over to Aydrian's side, he has few at his disposal, and most of those travel with the armies, training in the gemstone magic as they go."

"Why would any go over with the dog De'Unnero?" Pony asked, her voice gravelly and angry at the mere mention of the man.

"Aydrian's soldiers have set the appearance of defense along the coastal regions about St. Gwendolyn," Juraviel went on. "But the appearance only, for the fortifications are truly undefended. Also, they have altered the two guiding light towers along the rocks near to the abbey, hoping to scuttle any approaching ships on the rocks, no doubt. But some of my people will be there with torches, to guide your landing correctly."

"Your value to my cause cannot be overestimated, good Juraviel," Prince Midalis remarked. "This information and guidance gives me hope."

"Retake St. Gwendolyn in five days' time, and we will meet again there," the elf finished. "I hope then to have news of Brynn's breakout from Dharyan-Dharielle and her march to Jacintha, and we can coordinate the next movement."

"First Pireth Tulme will fall," said Prince Midalis. "But St. Gwendolyn it will be, in five days."

Juraviel rose immediately and bowed. "I am off, then, back to Brynn Dharielle," he explained. "Go with speed and go with strength, Prince Midalis. The hopes of more than your people rest upon your able shoulders." With another bow, the elf lifted his hand, the shining emerald in his palm, and in the blink of an eye, he disappeared.

Pony felt the sudden tension within Prince Midalis, an eagerness to be done with all of this. She put her hand on the man's shoulder. "Patience," she counseled. "Patience."

"Your agent is quite effective," Lozan Duk told Brynn. "Whatever Pechter Dan Turk has said to Yatol De Hamman has had an immediate effect. Those who already departed the Behrenese force have moved farther back—beyond half a day's march already. And more have left the Behrenese line, moving to the original position taken by those first departed."

"What of the Abellicans?" Brynn asked. "And the dragon-hunter ballistae?"

"Still in position, except that the leader of the Abellican contingent has long flown—for Jacintha, I would guess."

Brynn mulled over the report. She knew exactly what Pechter Dan Turk had done, for she had coached him in full before sending him out of Dharyan-Dharielle. The agent had told De Hamman that the To-gai-ru would not relax their guard with those supposedly departed warriors close enough to return quickly. He had told De Hamman that if the defenders of Dharyan-Dharielle came to fear that the Behrenese were merely buying time to reinforce their lines, they would come forth with all their strength. In effect, Pechter Dan Turk had merely told Yatol De Hamman the truth, but he had done so with the misleading representation that the To-gai-ru fears could be minimized to the point of inaction.

So Yatol De Hamman had stretched his line, but he had erred, Brynn believed, for he had moved a significant part of his force beyond the range of immediate reinforcement. Whereas before, the Behrenese could have held strong against the attempted breakout from Dharyan-Dharielle with the comfort of knowing that support was well on the way, now those still encircling the city would understand that they would have to win out against the fury of Brynn unleashed.

But she would have to strike fast, Brynn knew, to take advantage fully of the situation, and so she was quite relieved later that same day when Belli'mar Juraviel returned from Honce-the-Bear, bearing with him the good news that her allies opposing Aydrian in the north were making some gains and bearing, too, the emerald that would allow her attack to become more swift and more deadly.

That same night, the sun barely gone behind the plateau divide, the first stars coming to life above, Belli'mar Juraviel began the magical transport. He took Pagonel out first, depositing the mystic alongside a group of Doc'alfar behind the lines of De Hamman's main force and near to the tents that housed the Abellican monks. Next came Agradeleous, to join Pagonel and the Doc'alfar infiltrators.

Juraviel made three dozen trips, before sheer exhaustion from magic use forced him to relent. He did manage to join up with Pagonel, the dragon, and his Doc'alfar kin, though, wanting to be in on the most important assault of the night. He remained with the mystic and the dragon while the Doc'alfar set off, quieting the various sentries scattered about the encampment.

Just before dawn, the southern and eastern gate of Dharyan-Dharielle flew wide, and out came the charge of the To-gai-ru, led by Brynn on the east and Tanalk Grenk on the south. At that same moment, Pagonel, Juraviel, and several of Cazzira's kin burst into a tent of Abellicans, cutting them down even as they tried to scramble out of their beds. It pained Pagonel to be a part of that type of assault, for they were in no position to take prisoners. He tried to hold back his strikes so that they would incapacitate rather than kill, but still, before the group rushed back out, four of the five monks were dead, and the other's hold on life was tenuous at best.

In the tent to the side, Agradeleous was even less discriminating. The dragon tossed aside the lone guard at the tent flap, hurling the poor man a full thirty feet. Then the dragon tore through and leaped upon the startled, and still half-asleep, Abellicans. Agradeleous wasn't in his great dragon form, but even in his humanoid, lizardman form, his power proved overwhelming. A single swipe of his arm across one monk shattered half the bones in the man's chest, a kick with one scaly leg disemboweled a second.

The dragon emerged even as Pagonel, Juraviel, and the others were coming forth, to the sound of blowing horns and the mad scramble of the encampment coming to life and running to defensive positions.

Pagonel surveyed the scene and noted the efficiency of the more professional soldiers, particularly the men of Honce-the-Bear. But this force was as much comprised of impressed peasants as trained soldiers, and those frightened peasants surely got in the way of the preparations.

And the two fierce regiments of To-gai-ru came on straight and fast.

"I take to the air!" Agradeleous declared, and there came the popping of bone and the ripping of scaly skin as the dragon reshaped into its natural, beastly form.

Only then, with the spectacle of the dragon rising behind them, did the Behrenese seem to realize that they had been infiltrated from behind. Screams and shouts went all through the ranks, many calling for the turning of the ballistae. Desperate pleas to destroy the dragon echoed through the still-dim morning.

But those ballistae crews did not respond, for the Doc'alfar had slipped in among them, working with deadly precision. Wooden staves and spears made whistling sounds as they whipped through the air, before landing hard upon defenseless artillerymen, laying them low.

The To-gai riders crashed through the forward lines with little resistance, cutting down with impunity the Behrenese, most of whom seemed more concerned with fleeing than with fighting. Brynn's group did come to a stall, though, as they were met by two squares of Bearmen, shields locked and spears leveled.

But then Agradeleous flew past, fiery breath strafing the confused Bearmen, immolating the central ranks and defeating the integrity of the formation.

Still the ballistae didn't let fly at the great wurm, despite the cries and despite the attempts at reinforcing the crews.

For the Doc'alfar were still there, hiding, slipping out and killing any who neared the devastating war engines.

Agradeleous flew without fear, brushing aside the few arrows that reached up for him and returning every shot with a gout of flame or a slashing claw as he flew past.

Astride Runtly, Brynn moved to a high vantage point as the sun crested the eastern horizon. Pechter Dan Turk had done his job very well, she realized, for the Behrenese had been caught completely by surprise. Without any answer to the dragon, or this force of assassins that had somehow landed strategically behind them, and with their Bearman allies torn apart, all semblance of a defensive stance had flown. The Behrenese were scattering to the desert sands.

Down the eastern road, a second force approached swiftly, but those too soon turned and scattered, for they found themselves unexpectedly outnumbered, and by To-gai-ru warriors, as fierce and mighty as any in the world. And worse, the approaching Behrenese saw the dragon, the mighty beast of To-gai, flying free with no countermeasures leaping up to stop him.

Pagonel joined Brynn on that higher ground soon after, escorting a tearful Pechter Dan Turk and an outraged and bound Yatol De Hamman.

"Treachery!" the Yatol screamed at Brynn. "We declared a truce!"

"You assumed the posture of a truce, but only so that you could purchase the time to strengthen your line for the assault on Dharyan-Dharielle," Brynn calmly corrected.

"You have no evidence of this!"

"I need none, beyond what my scouts and my sensibilities have shown to me."

"Prepare for war, Brynn Dharielle," the outraged Yatol fumed. "For you have brought this on!"

Brynn slid down from Runtly and moved to stand right before the man, locking stares with him and not blinking at all. "You brought this on, as the lackey of Abbot Olin of Honce-the-Bear," she said evenly. "Feign innocence as you will, but I know the truth of it." She moved even closer, so that there could be no misunderstanding, so that Yatol De Hamman could feel her hot breath on his face. "Know that To-gai is free, and that Dharyan-Dharielle is mine. I will defend my people, even if I have to kill every Behrenese man, woman, and child. Even if I have to loose the power of Agradeleous upon a defenseless Behrenese village. You should have learned the lessons of the last war, Yatol De Hamman." She looked out over the field as the sunlight grew, drawing the man's gaze with her own.

To row after row of Behrenese dead and wounded. To the buzzards, already landing on the hard sands, awaiting their morning feast.

She turned back to regard De Hamman, and saw that the man seemed suddenly broken, the fight torn from him by the realization of his horrific defeat. "Abbot Olin sends you to conquer To-gai even as he strengthens his hold over Behren," she explained.

"You fought beside him against Yatol Bardoh!" the man protested.

"I fought against the dog Bardoh, in support of Yatol Mado Wadon," Brynn corrected. "Had I been offered the honest choice of Bardoh or Abbot Olin, I would have turned my power against Honce-the-Bear that day in Jacintha, do not doubt."

"Abbot Olin is friend to . . ."

"To King Aydrian, and not to Behren, and you know the truth of it," Brynn argued.

Yatol De Hamman gazed out to the east, to the flight of his remaining force. There was neither organization nor defensive posture driving them, just sheer terror, and that seemed quite fitting to him at that terrible moment.

"Behren will fall to chaos," he lamented. "Without strength from Jacintha, the tribes will revert to rivalry and warfare."

"Better to that than to the Abellicans and their imperialistic king," Brynn added.

She motioned to Pagonel, who pulled the defeated Yatol away, leading him to the other prisoners being assembled on the field. As soon as they were gone, Brynn offered a sympathetic look to poor, torn Pechter Dan Turk.

"You have chosen wisely," she assured the man. "For the good of your people, ultimately. I know that you do not see that at present, not with so many of your countrymen lying dead—"

She stopped as the man leaped aside suddenly, his hand coming out from under his cloak, revealing a long and slender dagger.

"Free them!" Pechter Dan Turk yelled at her.

Brynn went into a defensive stance immediately, shaking her head, pleading with the man not to force her to use her sword.

Pechter Dan Turk did not advance, however. "Free them," he said again, quietly this time. "On your word."

Brynn stood straighter, lowering her blade, fully confused.

Pechter Dan Turk gave a resigned little shrug. Then he plunged the dagger into his own chest and stumbled backward.

Brynn ran to him and grabbed him by the arm, trying to ease his fall to the sand. She started to cry out for some assistance, but recognized at once the futility of that course. She hugged the man's head close to her own, and whispered her promise that Behren would be free. She wasn't sure if Pechter Dan Turk heard her, though, for when she moved back, the life had flown from his vacant eyes.

Brynn put aside her own tears with a deep breath. She laid the man down gently, then moved to Runtly and leaped astride.

The day was young; the march to Jacintha had only just begun.

As soon as the morning light revealed the size of the force arrayed against them, the unfortunate soldiers stationed at Pireth Tulme threw down their arms and surrendered the fortress.

Exacting only the promise that they would not take up arms against him, Prince Midalis put them on the road and set them free. Then the great fleet pillaged Pireth Tulme fully, filling their holds with foodstuffs, weapons, and armor. They were gone before the sun had reached its midpoint, sailing fast on the tailing winds of the departing storm, around the tip and down the eastern coast of Honce-the-Bear.

The weather held favorably, and three days later, the fifth day after Belli'mar Juraviel's departure for the southland, they approached the coast just to the north of St. Gwendolyn Abbey. As Juraviel had promised, torches waving on the bank guided them in under the cover of night, and soon enough, the army of Vanguard and Alpinador was ashore once more, forming up and marching at once to the west, off the beach, then to the south.

Unlike at Pireth Tulme, the soldiers and monks who had been left in control of St. Gwendolyn tried to resist the approach of the prince and his army. They had little to offer in the way of defense, though, especially since repairs on much of the destruction Duke Kalas had wrought upon the battered old abbey had not yet even begun.

Some of those defenders, Abellican monks, tried to respond to the charge with gemstone magic, but anticipating as much, Pony was more than up to the task of countering. With sunstone in hand, she quieted the lightning blasts, then she responded with her own stunning bursts from a graphite, shattering stone and throwing down the defenders.

Andacanavar and Bruinhelde led the main charge to the gates of the abbey proper, and the sheer weight of the Alpinadoran press sundered those gates and sent the few defenders behind them fleeing in terror for the deeper holes in the abbey's substructure. Yet even there, they found no place to hide.

When Belli'mar Juraviel returned to Prince Midalis as promised later that same night, St. Gwendolyn had been taken.

"The news from the south is promising, as well," the elf told them. "Brynn has routed the army surrounding Dharyan-Dharielle."

"She does seem to do that quite a bit, from the tales you tell," Pony remarked.

"There is little unity among her enemies," Juraviel replied. "And Brynn has learned to exploit that well. She is well-advised, and wise in her understanding of the motivations of men."

"What then will she make of young Aydrian?" Prince Midalis asked.

Juraviel had no answer to that.

"We have sent out runners to the nearby towns, to tell them of the return of Prince Midalis," Pony explained. "To let the people know that there is indeed opposition to Aydrian and to give them hope that the kingdom will be restored."

Juraviel watched Pony closely as she made her remarks, recognizing that there was an undercurrent of turmoil behind the stated determination. "Or to warn them, perhaps, that there will be warfare raging all about them?" the elf asked.

"That, too," Pony admitted, after a pause and long sigh.

To her side, Prince Midalis put on a curious expression, the man obviously a bit taken aback.

"I fear that you place too much hope in the common people of Honce-the-Bear," Juraviel said bluntly to the prince. "Most of this is far beyond them, I would guess. Above all else, they desire peace and stability."

"Your own reports to me show that many have flocked to the side of Duke Kalas," Midalis replied.

"True enough," said Juraviel. "And yes, you must offer them an alternative to King Aydrian. The folk of this kingdom are unlike our friends from Alpinador." He gave a deferential nod to Bruinhelde and Andacanavar. "Unlike the To-gai-ru now led by Brynn, and unlike the folk of Behren, even. Honce-the-Bear has been a singular kingdom for many centuries— that unity and stability is all that the folk know. They look to Ursal and St.-Mere-Abelle for protection and guidance. With the emergence of Brynn, the To-gai-ru are beginning to experience this for the first time. With the fall of the Chezru chieftain in Behren, the folk there are in disarray, but not as much so as would be the folk of Honce-the-Bear should the crown diminish. Despite centuries of central guidance from the Chezru chieftain, Behren's ties remain strong to individual tribes. Only in Honce-the-Bear have the common folk so blended as to become truly one people.

"And so they are unsettled, and so they are scared," Juraviel went on. "And you do well in assuring them that the line of Ursal remains vital. But I warn you now, from all that I have learned, from all that my many scouts have shown to me and told to me, do not expect the common man of Honce-the-Bear to rise up against King Aydrian when he, flanked by All-heart Knights and legions of Kingsmen, seems so unbeatable."

Prince Midalis nodded his agreement. "That is why we strike wherever the opportunity allows," he said. "We will build support slowly, and wear away at the edges of Aydrian's seemingly impregnable hold."

"And that is why you must return to your boats at once," said Juraviel. "That is why you must sail to the south, to Jacintha, and help Brynn deal Aydrian his greatest defeat yet."

All eyes turned to Prince Midalis and his skeptical expression. "You ask me to go to war with the Behrenese and To-gai-ru against my own people," he said.

"Against King Aydrian," Juraviel replied. "Is that not what you do even now? Is that not what you did in taking Pireth Dancard? Pireth Tulme? St. Gwendolyn?"

"You ask me to join a foreign country against Honce-the-Bear," Midalis clarified, and it seemed as if he was gaining some confidence here. "There is a difference, and one that the people of Honce-the-Bear will understand distinctly, even if you do not."

The group grew silent then, for a long while, and Juraviel looked to Pony directly.

"Perhaps you should look beyond the sensibilities of Honce-the-Bear to find your answers here," she said to Midalis, and she took the man's hand and moved in front of him.

"Those sensibilities will be poignant when news of the war in the south drifts over the mountains," Midalis countered. "What will the mothers and children think when they are told that their husbands and fathers, their brothers and sons, are dead, and at my hands?"

Pony squared her shoulders and didn't blink. "What leader of Honce-the-Bear do you presume yourself to be if you would allow our kingdom to unlawfully invade another?" she said bluntly. "What leader of Honce-the-Bear do you presume yourself to be if you would allow Aydrian, through Abbot Olin, to prosecute a war that will leave hundreds, if not thousands, of your own people dead? To say nothing of the innocents of Behren and the brave warriors of To-gai who rise to their cause."

Prince Midalis seemed to shrink back then. He shook his head and looked all around at the surprised expressions worn by those around him.

"Go and turn Duke Bretherford back to that which he, too, knows is right," Pony begged the man. "Go and stop Abbot Olin."

Prince Midalis mulled over the words for a while, then gave a helpless chuckle. "To the boats, then," he said, still shaking his head.

Hopes and Dashed Hopes

Braumin Herde felt better, physically, but hardly so emotionally, given all the news filtering in from the surrounding countryside, of the securing of Palmaris in the name of King Aydrian and the triumphant march of Duke Kalas. The former bishop stood in the great audience hall of St.-Mere-Abelle, to the side of the wide staircase, staring up at the huge stained-glass window that bore the image of the upraised arm of Avelyn.

In that miraculous arm lay the promise of eternal life, and it was one that Braumin Herde needed to hear in his mind clearly now, with his own mortality looming so close. For the armies were coming, there could be no doubt, and resistance to King Aydrian seemed practically nonexistent. Staring up at the image brought Braumin back across the years, the long years, to his days huddled in the catacombs of this very abbey, listening to kind old Master Jojonah recount the tales of Avelyn and Elbryan and the coming of the demon dactyl. He remembered his flight from St.-Mere-Abelle and the deranged Father Abbot Markwart, alongside Brothers Viscenti and Castinagis, and Dellman. Yes, Brother Dellman! Braumin Herde hoped that the man fared well up in cold St. Belfour of Vanguard. Loyal Brother Dellman would stand with Prince Midalis, Braumin knew, all the way to his death beside the nobleman, if need be.

The distinct clicking of heels on the hard floor caught Braumin's attention. He knew from the cadence and steadiness of the footfalls that it was Father Abbot Bou-raiy crossing the floor before the man even sidled up to him.

"You approve?" Bou-raiy asked, and like Braumin, he was staring up at the great window.

Braumin Herde considered the question and the man's distinctly defensive tone. For up in that depiction of the Miracle of Avelyn loomed another figure, a one-armed Abellican. "No tribute might we offer to Brother Avelyn to fully appreciate his worth," Braumin replied. He noted that Fio Bou-raiy shuffled a bit, seeming uncomfortable.

"I came to see the truth of that, you know," the Father Abbot said after a long pause.

"I know." Braumin turned to the man and stared at him until that gaze brought Fio Bou-raiy's attention from the window. "The piece is beautiful," Braumin stated. "The artisans have outdone themselves, which is only fitting since they depicted perhaps the greatest miracle in the history of mankind. And fitting, too," he added, because he knew that Bou-raiy needed to hear it in this desperate time, "that the image of the Father Abbot possessed of the foresight to so magnificently illustrate the beauty of St. Avelyn is depicted, as well. I can see the doubt on your face in that depiction, Father Abbot, and your reluctance to travel to the Barbacan to partake of the miracle only makes the image all the more powerful."

"You are too kind," the Father Abbot replied.

Braumin Herde looked back at the window. "We all live with our doubts, every day," he said quietly. "We all question our faith, and when our lives are imperiled, we question the worth of our principles, as well. Certainly that was true of St. Avelyn. Did you know that he was a drunkard when Jilseponie found him?"

Fio Bou-raiy gave a little laugh—something so uncharacteristic from the always-serious man.

"The true miracle of Avelyn is his gift to us of insight," Braumin Herde went on. "He understood that the Abellican Church must be for all people, or it is for none. He understood that the powers of the sacred gemstones must not be hoarded for personal or institutional gain, but must be wisely and discreetly used to better the lives of all the people."

"He was terrified when he faced the demon dactyl," Braumin reasoned. "I know that he was. For a moment, at least. He knew that he was facing his own death. He was terrified."

"But he persevered, to the benefit of all the world," said Father Abbot Bou-raiy.

"As shall we, brother," Braumin Herde assured him.

"One of our couriers returned this morning," the Father Abbot said. "Bearing, intact and still with seal, the declaration of Avelyn as saint. I was too late. I should have completed the process long ago—or certainly with greater haste once I learned of the rise of King Aydrian and the return of Marcalo De'Unnero. Many of my couriers have been captured, I fear, or have fled back in terror before the darkness that is Aydrian. The people will not know."

"The people will know," Braumin replied, and he looked again at the older man. "The truth cannot be buried, not for long. Do you not remember Master Jojonah and his fellow conspirators, myself among them?"

"I remember," Fio Bou-raiy replied, his voice growing gravelly, his tone husky.

Braumin watched the man wince, more than once, and suspected that he was remembering the execution of Master Jojonah, a sentence that Bou-raiy had approved of, like so many of the other followers of Father Abbot Markwart.

"Perhaps that is the second true miracle of Avelyn," Braumin offered. "That we all err—terribly so. Avelyn was a sinner and surely played a role in the death of Master Siherton. Yet he was forgiven, obviously, for how else might one explain the Covenant? We are the children of a merciful God."

"De'Unnero does not understand that," said Bou-raiy. "His is the God of fire and vengeance."

"Then let us hope that our merciful God is also a God of justice."

That brought a smile back to the tortured face of Father Abbot Bou-raiy.

"The defensive preparations continue?" Braumin asked.

"Night and day. More than a thousand able commoners have flocked in to St.-Mere-Abelle since the onset of the march of Duke Kalas, and all are being trained to fight, or to man the engines of war, thus freeing up more brothers to do battle with the sacred stones."

"I remind you that St.-Mere-Abelle has never fallen," said Braumin. "Not to any enemy. Not to the great powrie fleet that attacked us in the time of the demon. Not to the goblin hordes that descended upon the civilized lands in the time of Father Abbot Des'Coute. Not to the errant judgments of Father Abbot Dalebert Markwart. Not to the plague, in all its incarnations. Our walls are strong, though not nearly as strong as the faith that truly holds us firm."

"Fine words, brother," said Bou-raiy. "We will speak them together, and loudly, for all to hear, when King Aydrian comes knocking."

Bou-raiy offered a slight bow to Braumin and left the room.

Braumin remained there for a long while, staring up at the grand depiction of the arm of Avelyn, considering the implications of the many pivotal decisions of his life.

He believed that St.-Mere-Abelle and the entire Abellican Order was now facing its greatest challenge in the history of the Church. He doubted that the abbey walls would hold back the tempest that was Aydrian and fully expected that he would be dead before the turn of the autumn season.

But he was at peace.

"Pireth Tulme and now St. Gwendolyn," Duke Kalas fumed, crumpling the parchment. He took a step forward and the runner who had arrived with the disturbing news of Prince Midalis' victory blanched and seemed ready to faint dead away. "I knew that we should have left greater forces to defend each."

"Prince Midalis' army was not that powerful, by all reports," said Sir Blaxson Tre'felois, one of Kalas' finest commanders, the field general of the Allheart Brigade's most dependable company. "We could arrive at St. Gwendolyn within three days."

Kalas was shaking his head before the man ever finished the thought. "Prince Midalis has already deserted the place, as he deserted Pireth Tulme," he explained.

"Because he knows that he cannot stand against us."

"And so he wears at our edges," said Kalas. "Hoping to erode support for King Aydrian among the populace. I would do the same if I were in his unenviable position."

"Unenviable because we know that he will achieve minor victories alone," Sir Blaxson remarked. "In the end, he must face us and must face King Aydrian."

"Where is King Aydrian?" Duke Kalas asked.

"Last reports placed him in Ursal with Father Abbot De'Unnero," Sir Blaxson replied. "Though by now, I suspect that he is back on the road, perhaps heading to join us as we complete the encirclement of St.-Mere-Abelle."

Duke Kalas shook his head. "We will reach the gates of St.-Mere-Abelle before his arrival. And I wish to construct batteries along the shore to either side of the abbey. If Prince Midalis' fleet has any intention of sailing into St.-Mere-Abelle's minor docks, we will defeat that notion."

"You believe that Midalis has turned back to the north from St. Gwendolyn?"

Kalas nodded. "I would. Summer draws near and the sailing through the gulf is clear. Prince Midalis' retreat from both Pireth Tulme and St. Gwendolyn show that he understands his weakness. He must seek more aid, and with Pireth Dancard closed to him, that can only mean St.-Mere-Abelle." Kalas nodded as he considered his own planning. "Send word to Palmaris," he instructed. "The rest of the Masur Delaval's fleet is to set sail at once for St.-Mere-Abelle."

"Prince Midalis' armada is formidable, by the words of King Aydrian himself," Sir Blaxson warned.

"We will not engage Prince Midalis at sea," Duke Kalas assured him. "Let us beat the prince to St.-Mere-Abelle. Our fleet need only to destroy the abbey's docks, and that should prove no difficult task with our soldiers pressing the monks hard at their wall. After that, let our warships settle under the protective range of our coastal artillery."

"Then St.-Mere-Abelle must stand alone, as Prince Midalis must stand alone," reasoned Sir Blaxson.

Duke Kalas squared his shoulders. "We must keep our two great enemies separate."

Braumin Herde was quite surprised later on when Master Viscenti entered his private chambers to announce a guest—a female. He was even more surprised when that guest, To'el Dallia of the Touel'alfar, walked in behind the nervous master!

"Juraviel's kin?" he stammered. "How . . . what are you doing here?"

"The Touel'alfar have aligned themselves with our cause," Master Viscenti answered. "They serve as scouts and liaison between St.-Mere-Abelle, the forces of Prince Midalis, and another potential ally doing battle with Abbot Olin in Behren."

"In Behren?"

"Aydrian reaches far and wide," To'el Dallia replied. "Too wide, let us hope."

"The news is both good and bad," Master Viscenti explained. "Prince Midalis has won three minor victories and seeks his fourth, which will be the greatest yet. But he is in the far south, while Duke Kalas and his forces even now march to St.-Mere-Abelle. Prince Midalis will offer us no support for the early stages of defense."

"And if Prince Midalis wins in the south, Aydrian will likely attack St.-Mere-Abelle even more forcefully," the elf added.

"You sound as if you know him," said Braumin.

"I do indeed. I was his trainer in Andur'Blough Inninness. I taught him the ways of the ranger, though his temperament unfortunately did not match that calling. He has become the catastrophe of my home and my people, and will be the darkness of all the world if we cannot stop him." The diminutive creature paused and nodded grimly at Braumin Herde. "And you must stop him here."

"You have spoken with Father Abbot Fio Bou-raiy?"

"She has," Master Viscenti answered. "Though she was nearly attacked by the gate guards when she so boldly arrived before them!"

"To see such a legend come to life," Braumin reasoned. "I can understand their trepidation!"

"We will meet with Father Abbot Bou-raiy in a short while better to coordinate our plans," To'el Dallia explained. "But I wished for you to be there, as you are less a stranger to my race than your peers. Jilseponie speaks highly of Bishop Braumin."

"Not as highly as Bishop Braumin speaks of Jilseponie," the man replied.

"This is all too surprising," Braumin went on, shaking his head and running his hand through his thinning hair. "And most welcome. If Aydrian easily claims St.-Mere-Abelle, then it will only be a matter of time before he catches up with Prince Midalis. Who will be left to oppose him?"

"We will hold," Master Viscenti said, his teeth gritted and chattering as he continued his typical trembling. "We will make Aydrian regret ever coming against the walls of St.-Mere-Abelle!"

"Let us hope, brother," said Braumin, rising and walking past the man into the hall. "Let us hope."

They came in sight of the great abbey's mile-long wall late one afternoon, and there set camp, their own lines so long that they were easily able to form a semicircle about the place, with men both north and south of the abbey looking out over the dark waters of All Saints Bay. Assembly of great catapults and spear-throwing devices began immediately at both of those points, while all along the line other soldiers went about the task of setting up the tents.

From somewhere near the middle of that line, directly across the beaten field leading to the abbey's great gates, Duke Kalas sat and watched, and waited for word of the ships approaching from Palmaris. He could not attack St.-Mere-Abelle's docks by land, for they were located far below the abbey's eastern wall, which was built upon a cliff face. He needed the ships to take out the long wharf, and to patrol the waters under the watchful eye of his artillery crews.

Early the next morning, sails appeared along the coast to the west.

Duke Kalas went into action immediately, forming up the ranks about the center of his line. He used his Allhearts and Kingsmen more as prods against the peasant army than as a leading strike force, forcing the all-out assault upon the abbey's front wall. In short order, the ground was shaking under the charge of more than twenty thousand men. Behind them, the duke's batteries of catapults launched huge rocks high and far into the air to smash down among the structures of the abbey.

The response reaching out from St.-Mere-Abelle's walls was no less spectacular, with lightning bolts, lines of magical fire, and responding catapult fire slicing through the duke's ranks. Men died by the score, but they kept up the cry for King Aydrian and charged on.

The monks slaughtered them.

Duke Kalas, still sitting astride his pony across the field, grimaced with every magical discharge, with every scream. He glanced continually over to his left, awaiting the signal.

"You fool!" came an unexpected roar beside him, and he turned to see a fuming Marcalo De'Unnero. "Who gave you orders to attack the abbey? You were to encircle and besiege, nothing more!"

Even as the monk ranted along, Kalas noted the signalman to the north of the abbey waving his flags, red and blue. Red indicating that the docks had been destroyed; blue showing that the fleet had slipped away.

The diversion had worked.

Kalas called to the trumpeters beside him, ordering them to blow a retreat.

"You have lost hundreds!" De'Unnero yelled at him. "And what have you gained?"

"I—we—have gained the sea access to the abbey," Kalas calmly explained. "St.-Mere-Abelle's docks are destroyed and the waters about the abbey are now secured—and will grow more unfriendly to Prince Midalis and his raiding fleet with every passing hour." The Allheart commander, his face a mask of complete confidence, looked back at St.-Mere-Abelle, seeming quite pleased with himself.

"Now they are isolated and properly besieged," he explained.

De'Unnero looked all around at the retreat, and at the many dead lying on the field near to the abbey's gates. "If Aydrian and his secondary force were here, we could have overrun them," he insisted.

"But Aydrian is not here, nor will he arrive anytime soon, from what my scouts have told me. Now the monks of St.-Mere-Abelle cannot flee, nor can Prince Midalis slip in to reinforce their ranks upon those strong walls."

Duke Kalas knew that it was tearing Marcalo De'Unnero apart to admit that he was wrong, and so he took the man's silence, even with the dismissive wave of his hand as he walked off, as compliment enough.

CHAPTER

❖ 39 ❖

Playing the Fears

"You could have slaughtered them," Yatol De Hamman said to Brynn as they looked down into the windswept and sandy valley where a splinter of De Hamman's army was in full flight from the To-gai-ru forces who had circled about them and turned them back to the southwest. All around this northeastern side of the circular valley loomed the silhouettes of To-gai-ru horsemen, awaiting a signal from Brynn to sweep down upon the helpless Behrenese.

But that signal would not come.

"I have no desire to slaughter Behrenese, or Bearman, or any people," Brynn replied.

"Your attack upon my forces outside of Dharyan-Dharielle would indicate otherwise."

Brynn walked Runtly around to put her directly in front of the Yatol, who sat upon a yellow nag, a horse too old to run away even if De Hamman had had the courage to try such an escape.

"You and I both understand the truth of that situation," the woman said with unnerving calm. "My information about your intentions—to reinforce and overrun the city—was correct. Your inability to admit as much is your failing, Yatol De Hamman, and not mine."

Yatol De Hamman chewed his bottom lip and pointedly looked away—but he could not maintain that distant stare for long and kept glancing back at the imposing woman.

Brynn never took her eyes off him, and neither did she even blink.

Behind the Yatol and to the side, Pagonel cleared his throat. "I will take Agradeleous back to the skies to seek out any other groups intent on retreating to Jacintha," he said.

"Turn them," Brynn agreed. "None are to reinforce Abbot Olin's garrison."

Such had been the plan all during the week-long march out of Dharyan-Dharielle. Brynn and Pagonel had taken Agradeleous up scouting, and with the great dragon flying about with impunity, their advantage had proven tremendous. One by one, they had encountered the pockets of fleeing Behrenese, and one by one, they had turned the men from the eastern road, often scattering them to the desert sands, or driving them like cattle toward the nearest city or oasis. There had been only a trio of minor battles, routs for the To-gai-ru, and even in those, Brynn had quickly stayed her hand, minimizing the enemy losses. In fact, since the Behrenese retreat from Dharyan-Dharielle, the largest number of casualties among the defeated force's ranks had been in the accompanying force of Bearmen, many of whom had been turned upon by the outraged Behrenese and slaughtered in the sands.

"Do you believe that you can defeat Jacintha?" Yatol De Hamman dared to say.

"I believe that Jacintha will defeat herself—if she has not already done so."

Yatol De Hamman put on a quizzical look.

"You would surrender your country to King Aydrian?" Brynn continued. "You would surrender your heritage and your ways to the imperialist northmen?" She could see from the man's expression that she had touched a nerve here. Yatol De Hamman understood the truth of Abbot Olin, Brynn believed.

"What gain, Yatol De Hamman?" she asked. "Or more to the point, what sustained gain?"

"What do you mean?"

"Yatol Mado Wadon's position becomes secured," Brynn reasoned. "He assumes the mantle of Chezru chieftain. That is what we all desired when Yakim Douan fell and our war ended at the gates of Dharyan-Dharielle."

"A goal that was realized!" the Yatol argued.

"Not so, because the title of Chezru chieftain became subordinated to the desires of Abbot Olin," said Brynn. "I know that you understand the truth of this, as surely as I know your true intent in overrunning Dharyan-Dharielle. So tell me, was the attack upon my city the order of Yatol Wadon, or of Abbot Olin?"

"It was an error."

Brynn gave a helpless laugh. "You are a fool. Hold fast to your pride and your lies, if you so choose. I will rescue the identity of Behren from the designs of King Aydrian of Honce-the-Bear with or without your help."

"You believe that you can defeat Jacintha," the Yatol said derisively.

Brynn looked around at her considerable force, some thousand To-gai-ru warriors. In the open desert, she could take on an army twice, perhaps even thrice, her size, but against a fortified city, she knew that many of her greatest advantages, primarily the mobility and skill of her forces, would be for naught. "I could not hope to defeat Jacintha," she admitted. As she watched Yatol De Hamman's shoulders square, she added teasingly, "Alone."

That put a fearful expression on the man's smug face.

"Not even with my dragon friend," Brynn admitted.

"Have you resurrected the spirit of Yatol Bardoh, then?" the Yatol spat. "Do you think to pit Behrenese against Behrenese."

"An imperialistic king makes many enemies," was all that Brynn would say. She held her expression sly and walked Runtly away.

Leaving a flustered De Hamman sputtering on his ugly yellow nag.

"Those few who managed to return . . ." Yatol Wadon stammered, hardly able to get the words out. Not that he needed to say them, in any case, for his audience—Abbot Olin, new Yatol Paroud, and Master Mackaront just returned from Entel—understood the message quite clearly. De Hamman had been routed outside of Dharyan-Dharielle. Brynn had pulled yet another trick on them, and the Behrenese force, already so tentative about doing battle with the infamous Dragon of To-gai, had broken ranks and fled, and were still fleeing, by all accounts, in ever-shrinking numbers.

Yatol Wadon's inability to express his outrage was certainly understandable.

"Your losses were not so great, by every report," Abbot Olin replied, seeming unperturbed by it all.

"Not so great?" Wadon yelled at him. "Hundreds, perhaps thousands, have been slaughtered, and worse, the remaining thousands are scattering to the four winds. You cannot begin to understand the depth of this; Behren is not like Honce-the-Bear."

"The victory has lured Brynn Dharielle out of her hole," Abbot Olin calmly replied.

"The To-gai-ru are more dangerous on the open sands," Yatol Paroud dared to interject.

"Not against Abellicans," said Abbot Olin.

"A shrinking number," Paroud dryly reminded, and Olin shot him a hateful look.

"Enough!" demanded Yatol Wadon.

"Where will Brynn carry the fight?" Abbot Olin said. "Will she run across the desert, striking haphazardly against the smaller towns? Will she attack Jacintha? Surely that would be the purest folly."

"In the open desert, then," reasoned Yatol Wadon.

"To what gain?" Abbot Olin asked, and he rose from his seat and moved about the room, more animated than any had seen him in a long while. "Time does not work in favor of Brynn Dharielle. She has few resources, and the toll on her army will be great. She cannot defeat us, so likely she will sate her warriors' hunger for revenge and then retreat into her hole. All we need do is regroup our forces and wait her out."

Yatol Wadon glared at the man.

"So we do not reunite Behren at this time," the abbot went on. "Dharyan will have to wait until King Aydrian can fully turn his attention to Behren. It will not be long."

"Even when reinforcements from Honce-the-Bear arrive, Brynn will be within her secure walls, and with her dragon beside her," Yatol Wadon argued. "That is no minor thing!"

"In the face of King Aydrian, it is indeed," said Abbot Olin. "If the dragon arrives on the field before the king of Honce-the-Bear, he will destroy it, and with ease. You see the fight at Dharyan as a disaster, my friend, but you are not scrutinizing the details well enough, I fear."

Yatol Wadon's glare softened just a bit, showing some intrigue.

"My monks stung the dragon profoundly," Abbot Olin explained. "Their lightning knocked it from the sky, and yet all of their bolts combined are minuscule compared to the power of Aydrian."

"All of your monks are dead," Yatol Wadon reminded.

"They were minor brothers, I assure you, and easily replaced. We must hold strong and pick our fights with this impudent wench of To-gai carefully until King Aydrian can come more fully to our side. Brynn may gain victories over small towns, but she will lose warriors with each win, and those will not easily be replaced. The strain on To-gai will prove too much, and she will turn for home, then we will send out a second army to ensure that Behren is secured, and then, when King Aydrian arrives, we will destroy the woman and her pitiful forces."

Yatol Paroud was nodding, his eyes verily glowing as he listened to the promises of ultimate victory. But Mado Wadon was a long way from sharing that enthusiasm. Did Abbot Olin not even care that thousands of Behrenese citizens were surely to be slaughtered? Did he not appreciate the divisive power of the various Behrenese factions, ancient tribes, and bloodlines, that demanded allegiance to traditions that went beyond the kingdom or even beyond Chezru itself? For hundreds of years, Behren had been united as a kingdom in theory, but even in the last days of Yakim Douan, the political structure had often been more tribal in nature.

"The last reports put Brynn Dharielle near to Dahdah Oasis," Yatol Wadon offered. "And moving eastward, toward Jacintha."

"With how many warriors?"

"Perhaps a thousand," Yatol Wadon answered honestly, and in truth, when he spoke the words aloud, they seemed almost laughable. It would take an army many times that size to have any chance at all of overpowering present Jacintha, with nearly ten thousand Honce-the-Bear warriors supporting their ranks. "And she has her dragon."

"Then let her come on," said Abbot Olin. "Let her grow too confident with that beast of hers and charge our walls. Master Mackaront brought a score more brothers on his return, all of them armed with graphite and serpentine, the stone of lightning and a shield that will defeat even dragon fire. Her confidence, if she approaches as you believe, will be her undoing, and horribly so. How tall will Yatol Wadon stand in the eyes of his countrymen when he emerges from Jacintha victorious over the Dragon of To-gai?"

Yatol Wadon considered the words, then nodded slowly.

"Our only vulnerability here is my fleet, and thus I have ordered Duke Bretherford to put out farther from shore and to the north, out of sight of

Jacintha harbor. If Brynn and her beast pursue him into Honce-the-Bear waters, she will invoke the immediate wrath of King Aydrian, and not a flight of a hundred dragons could save her then.

"Fear not," Abbot Olin finished as he headed for the room's door, Master Mackaront in tow, "for Brynn Dharielle's moment of opportunity is fast slipping away, and she knows it. She will run for home if she is wise, but she knows, as do we, that she cannot win in the end."

"Whatever the cost?"

Abbot Olin turned as he reached the exit, showing Yatol Wadon his smirk. "Of course."

"She cannot take Jacintha, master," Yatol Paroud remarked.

"She can create great dissension," Yatol Wadon warned. "She already has. It may take us months to regroup the remnants of Yatol De Hamman's force, and without them . . ."

"We are even more dependent on Abbot Olin," Yatol Paroud finished, and the words seemed to surprise the man even as he spoke them, as if a great revelation just then came over him. "My Yatol, you do not believe—" he stammered.

"That this is proceeding exactly as Abbot Olin had hoped?" Yatol Wadon interrupted. "No, I do not think this to be his design. I believe that he laments the defeat at Dharyan-Dharielle—he would have liked nothing more than to report to his king that the city had been taken."

"Our spies were set in place behind the bookcase when returned Master Mackaront met with Abbot Olin," Yatol Paroud reasoned. "They heard the edict of King Aydrian that the Bearmen were not to do battle against Brynn. Their inference from the tone and wording was that King Aydrian meant to strike an alliance with Brynn."

Yatol Wado Madon turned to the window overlooking Jacintha harbor, his lips growing very tight. He tried hard not to believe Paroud's suspicions, but he found it hard to make a logical argument.

"My master, is it possible that Abbot Olin came here to oversee the destruction of Behren?" Paroud asked, and Yatol Wadon winced. "Is it possible that he helped us in our fight with Yatol Bardoh only because he perceived Yatol Bardoh to be more of an obstacle standing before his King Aydrian?"

Again Yatol Wadon had no answer for the man. He knew that Behren was in serious trouble—more so than Abbot Olin seemed to believe. Yatol De Hamman's army had very likely split apart into its tribal factions, and those bands of warriors were running free across the countryside, afraid and angry. It was possible that while he sat here in secure Jacintha, Behren was already beginning to tear itself apart across the desert sands.

And if the country fell into complete turmoil, particularly with Brynn Dharielle and her dragon running free about the land, Yatol Wadon would be powerless to put it back together—without the dominating assistance of Abbot Olin and his eager young King Aydrian.

Yatol Wadon continued to stare out at the harbor, where the Honce-the-Bear warships were still anchored. He almost hoped that Brynn and her dragon would swoop across his field of vision then, and lay waste to that fleet.

That foreign fleet.

Within the hour, Duke Bretherford's warships unfurled their sails and pulled up their anchors. The half dozen Honce-the-Bear ships sailed north-east, going out from the coast and back toward the safety of Honce-the-Bear waters, while Maisha Darou's pirate fleet headed out along the coast to the south, cut free of their duties for the time being. With bags of precious gems in hand, Darou set his course, as instructed, for the safety of the pirate shoals, and the promise of a well-deserved rest.

For Duke Bretherford, departing Jacintha was no hardship. The man had heard the reports of the disaster at Dharyan-Dharielle, and while the vast majority of that routed force had been Behrenese and not Bearman, some of the reports filtering in from the retreating forces spoke of retribution against the northerners by the fleeing Behrenese.

Duke Bretherford couldn't care less for Behren; he was more concerned with the turmoil in his own land. He planned to stop at the island of Freeport to resupply, then to put into Entel for news of King Aydrian and Prince Midalis.

Early the next morning, just east of the easternmost peaks of the Belt-and-Buckle, word came to the duke in his cabin that a second fleet was sailing south to intercept. With news that these were caravels, Bretherford wondered if Aydrian was sailing to Abbot Olin's aid. As soon as he arrived at the prow of *Rontlemore's Dream*, though, the duke understood differently.

For this approaching armada sailed under the bear rampant of the Ursals.

"Battle sails!" Duke Bretherford called, and the message was relayed across the decks to the other warships.

The duke continued to stare out as more and more ships came visible.

"What are those?" asked the sailor at Duke Bretherford's side.

"Alpinadoran longboats," the old seaman replied. "The prince has brought some friends."

The approaching warships similarly dropped to battle sail, except for one, a sleek schooner that Duke Bretherford recognized as *Saudi Jacintha*, the pride of Palmaris' merchant fleet. "Captain Al'u'met," he muttered, for he knew of the man, and knew him to be an old and dear friend to Queen Jilseponie.

Saudi Jacintha ran a white flag of truce up her guide line and continued her approach until she was within a hundred yards of *Rontlemore's Dream*. There, she banked low in a sharp turn and tacked against the sea breeze, holding her position.

"Signal for them to approach under agreed truce," Duke Bretherford told his signalman.

"We would expect nothing less from honorable Duke Bretherford," came a voice from behind them, and the duke nearly leaped out of his boots and overboard. He swung about, as did everyone else in the area, to see three people—a diminutive Touel'alfar, Queen Jilseponie, and Prince Midalis—simply step as if out of nowhere onto the deck. All three held hands, and all were covered with a bluish white glow.

The crew stumbled all over themselves, going for their weapons; from the back of the deck, several archers leveled their bows.

Pony held a ruby for Bretherford to see. "I could put your ship to the flame," she said quietly. "Do not make me do that, I beg."

"The flag of truce holds," Prince Midalis added. "We are here to parley."

Staring at the ruby, Duke Bretherford hardly heard the prince. He was not ignorant of Jilseponie's prowess with the magical gemstones, and he well understood that devastation her fireball would wreak. He motioned for his archers to put up their bows, and for the rest of the crew to stand down.

"My cabin," he said, motioning to the door across the deck.

"Right here," Prince Midalis corrected. The prince looked at Pony, then stepped away from her, releasing her hand, and immediately emerged from the serpentine fire shield.

"I am Prince Midalis, brother of King Danube Brock Ursal," he began powerfully, and he paced about so that he could look into the eyes of each man on deck. "You know me. You served my brother well. And you know, too, that this young man who has seized the throne of Honce-the-Bear is not your rightful king. I claim the throne as my own, and demand fealty!" Astonished looks came back at him, and more than a few doubtful whispers. From the front, Duke Bretherford heard the name of King Aydrian whispered more than once.

"Aydrian is king, by your brother's own words," the duke argued.

"Those words were twisted, and errantly spoken, and you know the truth of it," Pony retorted.

The duke merely shrugged. To him, the point was moot.

"I will have your fealty, or I will have your surrender, Duke Bretherford," Prince Midalis remarked, and when Bretherford squared his shoulders defiantly, he added, "I have fifty warships at my disposal, as well as Queen Jilseponie and her gemstones, Andacanavar, the ranger of Alpinador and his mighty warriors, and . . ." He paused and pointed to Juraviel. "And other allies whose powers you cannot begin to understand. Do not make me kill my misled countrymen, I beg of you."

"Aydrian has claimed the throne," Duke Bretherford replied. "The entire southland of Honce-the-Bear is his, and you cannot hope—"

"What I hope and do not hope is of no consequence to you, Duke Bretherford," Prince Midalis cut him short. "As you were friend to Jilseponie and Danube, I offer you this opportunity to put aright your ill-chosen course."

"He has Kalas and all the Allhearts, and all the Kingsmen, and a mercenary army that at least equals their size," Duke Bretherford replied. "Do you believe that you have any chance at all of defeating him?"

"Was I given a choice in the matter?" Prince Midalis asked him. "Would you have me surrender my courage and virtue and all that I hold dear to acquiesce to this upstart usurper who has stolen my throne?"

"You cannot defeat him," Bretherford said again.

"And you cannot defeat me, not here and now," said Midalis. "Nor can you hope to outrun me. I will have your ships, or I will sink . . ."

Pony walked beside him and touched his shoulder, silencing him, then walked past to stand right before Duke Bretherford. "I know you," she said. "I understand your sense of honor."

"And you know your son Aydrian," Bretherford argued. "You know his power!"

"I do, and perhaps all of this resistance is folly."

"Then find another way."

"No, and I beg of you to join with us! Aydrian has Honce-the-Bear, from Palmaris to Ursal to Entel to Pireth Tulme, but we own the sea."

The duke began to shake his head slowly.

"Join us!" Pony said again.

"Am I to switch allegiance whenever a force mightier than my own comes against me?" Duke Bretherford roared at her. "I am a duke serving the king of Honce-the-Bear!"

"And that king is rightfully Midalis Dan Ursal!"

"What would you have me do, woman?" the flustered Bretherford cried. "Would you so demand dishonor from me?"

"I would ask of you only what I have asked of myself," Pony quietly replied. "I would ask that you follow that which is in your heart."

Bretherford leaned back against the rail and rubbed his ruddy face.

"If you fight me, I will show no mercy," Prince Midalis warned. "We have not the time."

"We sail to Jacintha to help Brynn Dharielle defeat Abbot Olin," Pony explained, and the duke's jaw dropped open with astonishment.

"How could you know?"

"The movements are not independent of each other," Prince Midalis assured the man. Again, Bretherford could only rub his face and ponder.

Pony moved next to Prince Midalis and whispered into his ear. After a moment, the prince nodded his agreement.

"I grant you this alone, out of friendship and faith," he told the duke. "Poll all of your men. Offer them the choice of King Midalis or King Aydrian. Those who hold allegiance to the line of Ursal will sail with me in glory. Those who side with the usurper, Aydrian, will be put ashore in Entel. All of your warships are mine in any case."

"Follow that which is in your heart," Pony said again.

"We cannot win," Bretherford lamented, and he noted the smiles widening as his mention of "we."

"Then we will die in a righteous cause," said Prince Midalis, and he pulled a flag from a sack hung on his belt, the pennant of Ursal, and tossed it to the duke. "And five others inside," he explained, and he took the sack from his belt and tossed it to the deck at Bretherford's feet. "We await your decision."

As he spoke, he stepped back between Pony and the diminutive elf, who held up his hand to reveal a shining emerald gemstone.

And then they were gone.

The startled Duke Bretherford spun about to regard *Saudi Jacintha*, which was even then finishing her turn in the water, swinging her sails to fill them full of wind, and moving away, while the rest of Midalis' considerable fleet closed fast, with a line of Alpinadoran longboats swinging wide to the east.

"We will sink them all, my Duke!" one sailor cried, and others cheered and ran for their weapons.

Duke Bretherford looked at the flag in his hands, then up at the pennant of King Aydrian waving in the wind overhead. He ordered his sailors to stand ready and quickly moved to his private cabin, pouring himself a jigger of rum. He held the small glass up before him, swirling its contents about, losing his thoughts.

And then he swallowed the contents in one great gulp, and in frustration and rage, threw the glass across the room. It hit the wall hard, but at an angle that offered the strength of the thick glass, and so it did not shatter, but tumbled down to bounce across the floor. Then it went into a roll, and it seemed to Duke Bretherford like the roll of the uncertain sea below him, and like the uncertain emotions rolling within him.

Most of all, Jilseponie's parting words echoed within his thoughts. *Follow that which is in your heart.*

For that was the truth of it, was it not? In the end measure, that was all that any man could do.

Duke Bretherford had never been taken in by the grandeur that was Aydrian, or by the resounding accolades of the young usurper offered by Duke Kalas. Duke Bretherford had known King Danube well, and had loved the man dearly. And Bretherford, above all the other of Ursal's nobles, knew well that the temperament of Prince Midalis was akin to that of the dead king.

Bretherford looked down at the small glass, settled now and rolling no more, save the occasional shift as the boat rolled in the sea.

Settled, too, were the duke's emotions. At long last settled, though he believed his epiphany now, his decision to follow Prince Midalis would likely deliver him soon enough to the netherworld.

So be it. He would die knowing that he held intact his honor and his loyalty to the line of Ursal.

He would die knowing that he had indeed followed that which was in his heart.

*   *   *

"They will arrive soon after midday, by Duke Bretherford's estimation," Belli'mar Juraviel informed Brynn.

The warrior woman stood up and walked to the edge of the rocky outcropping. Below her to the southeast, Jacintha spread out wide. "This Duke Bretherford, he will prove a valuable ally?" she asked.

"Better that he fight with us than against us," Juraviel replied. "The number of forces he brings with him is small—more than half of those who sailed with his small fleet opted to be put ashore in Entel, as per Jilseponie's offer in the terms of surrender, to continue their service to King Aydrian. But he is a nobleman of Honce-the-Bear, and well regarded among his peers. Perhaps his decision will cause others to recognize their folly, or to find their courage."

"You do not believe that," Brynn remarked.

"No, I do not," the elf admitted after a short pause. "My scouts place King Aydrian in firm control of the vast majority of Honce-the-Bear's population and military. But with Duke Bretherford's conversion, our allies in the north command the seas, and that is no small thing."

Brynn nodded, not wanting to further a pointless argument. She and Pagonel had discussed this at length and had come to the conclusion that the cause in Honce-the-Bear was not promising. The numbers of the prince's army could not carry him across the land, nor even very far inland. He seemed in danger of becoming to Honce-the-Bear what Maisha Darou was to Behren: a thorn and elusive irritation, and little more.

To their cause in Behren, though, and in To-gai by extension, Prince Midalis and Duke Bretherford might prove invaluable.

"Your journey through Jacintha last night was fruitful?" the woman asked.

Juraviel motioned for Brynn and Pagonel to follow around the side of a boulder, where the burning torch had been set, sheltered from any eyes looking out from the city. He produced the map of the city that Brynn had provided and carefully spread it out on a rock. "The stable and supplies," he said, pointing to an area in the northeastern corner. "The soldiers of Honce-the-Bear brought tons of hay with them and the bales are piled floor to ceiling in several buildings."

Brynn's expression tightened; it went against all of her To-gai-ru instincts to attack a stable. The nomadic people loved and appreciated their horses above all else.

"Not far from there lies a warehouse of pitch," Juraviel went on, sliding his finger more toward the center of the city.

"You can identify these structures from the air, in the dark of night?" Pagonel asked, and the elf nodded.

Both went quiet then, and stepped back from Brynn. She felt their eyes upon her, and knew that her tearing emotions were playing out clearly on her face.

"I hate this," she remarked.

"But you hate the alternative even more," Pagonel reminded.

Brynn looked up from the map to regard her trusted advisor. In her mind, she could hear the screams of men and woman, and the shrieks of terrified horses. In her mind, she could see the flames leaping high above Jacintha. The orange flames, the purest of destructive forces.

"Aydrian plans to conquer the whole of the world," she heard Juraviel remark.

"Aydrian destroyed Lady Dasslerond, and meant to bring complete ruin to Andur'Blough Inninness," the elf added a moment later.

Brynn didn't disagree with the reasoning, nor with the point that her former companion had to be stopped. But it wounded her to her soul to know that she would have to go through the bodies of innocents to get near to him.

"Let us light the way for our allies," the woman said.

Two hours before the dawn, Brynn, Pagonel, and Juraviel climbed onto the shoulders of mighty Agradeleous. From on high at the southeastern peaks of the mountain range, the dragon leaped out and spread his wings wide, catching the updrafts rising up the cliff facings from the warm ocean water. Agradeleous went very low, under the fog that clung to the sea, and soared out across the dark waters, gradually turning to the south, then all the way back around to the northeast. He came over Jacintha's docks in a sudden rush, eliciting cries of terror from those few people awake and about. That call did not rally the soldiers along the city wall facing the docks nearly quickly enough, though, and so barely a bow was lifted against the passing dragon as he rushed overhead.

Juraviel pointed out the pitch warehouse first, and though the building was constructed mostly of stone, Agradeleous' fiery breath found its way in through the cracks and ignited many of the piled kegs.

The next target loomed before them as they continued their flight back toward the black silhouettes of the mountains in the north, and this time the strafing run showed more dramatic and immediate effects. Mounds of dry hay exploded to fiery life in Agradeleous' wake.

Brynn didn't, couldn't, look back, but the screams caught up to her almost immediately.

The dragon, obviously enjoying the destructive spectacle, banked as if to turn back, but Pagonel yelled to him to hold fast his course, reminding him that the weapons and the Abellicans were no doubt already being raised against him.

Among the rocks of the mountains a short while later, Brynn Dharielle did step forward and look down upon the spectacle of Jacintha and the huge fire leaping into the predawn air along the city's northern wall. All the horizon glowed orange from the flames and a cloud of the blackest smoke lifted into the air and spread wide, blocking out the stars.

Brynn put the implications firmly out of her mind. "We approach at first light," she informed her companions. "We must keep their attention to the west."

The soldiers on Jacintha's western wall, their ranks thinned by the many pulled to fight the raging fires, were greeted at the dawn's light by the horsed ranks of the Dragon of To-gai. Astride their pinto ponies, short bows in hand, the To-gai-ru warriors stretched that line long and thin, just out of reach of the Jacintha archers.

Not so the catapults, though, and one by one, they sent great missiles arcing toward the To-gai-ru.

But the riders were too mobile to fall victim to such an attack and they dodged the missiles with impunity, all the while hurling taunts and insults back at the city.

"It is a common Ru ruse," Yatol Wadon said to Abbot Olin. "They try to goad us out from behind our walls that they can slaughter us on the sands."

"Horsed demons," Abbot Olin growled. "They strike in the dark of night and flee. Cowards one and all!"

"Cowards who win when they should not, time and time again," Yatol Wadon warned.

"Against the Behrenese," Abbot Olin snapped back contemptuously. "They do not appreciate the might of the Bearmen."

"With their bows and astride their fine ponies, they are unmatched."

"And how will their feeble bows fare against Bearman armor?" the abbot fumed. "Or against Abellican magic?"

The Yatol merely shrugged.

"I will be done with this troublesome wench here and now," Abbot Olin declared. "And she is all the more troublesome because your people fear her! It was fear alone that shattered the ranks on the field outside of Dharyan. Had Yatol De Hamman re-formed his forces, he could have won a great victory."

"We have been given good reason to fear her," the Yatol put in.

"Then let us reverse that, here and now. If Brynn Dharielle will stand against the might of Honce-the-Bear, then I will slaughter her people wholesale. If she turns and flees, as she must, then let your soldiers witness the rout and know that the reality of the Dragon of To-gai does not match the legend!"

"I fear such a course."

"You fear everything," Abbot Olin retorted. He stormed out of the room, calling to his commanders to organize a charge.

"You have securely removed the dragon?" Pagonel asked Brynn, as he stood with Belli'mar Juraviel near the center of the To-gai-ru line beside Runtly and the woman.

"I sent him to Dharyan-Dharielle to deliver news of the battle," Brynn explained. "He will return along a course south of the city and will seek us out, wherever we are."

Pagonel patted her leg and nodded his agreement. It was vital to keep the bloodthirsty dragon out of the battle at this time.

"This will work," Brynn said determinedly.

"And if it does not?"

"Then I will ride across the desert sands to Alzuth and sack the city," the woman answered. "And to every town between Alzuth and Dharyan-Dharielle. And the mercy I have extended to those fleeing Behrenese soldiers will be no more."

Again the mystic nodded.

"But this will work," Brynn added.

Pagonel recognized it to be a question and a desperate plea, more than a statement. "Even Yatol De Hamman has come to agree," he assured her.

Only a few moments later, the great gates of Jacintha burst open and the Bearman army flowed forth.

"Shoot well and shoot high," Pagonel said to Brynn, and he offered his hand to Juraviel.

In an instant and with the green flash of an emerald, the two were gone.

The soldiers of Honce-the-Bear formed their ranks and began their charge, centered by a line of heavy cavalry that shook the ground.

With precision unmatched in all the world, the To-gai-ru waited until the last possible moment, until lightning bolts began to reach out and even take some down, then turned and rode off. As one, it seemed, they lifted legs over saddles and turned about, standing straight in one stirrup and facing backward, bows coming to the ready.

Their first volleys flew away, perfectly aimed.

Not a Honce-the-Bear soldier, nor a Honce-the-Bear mount, was struck.

Having Pagonel, Brynn Dharielle's closest advisor, stride from the shadows at the side of his audience chamber, was not something that Yatol Wadon could have expected at that moment.

The Yatols at Wadon's side gave a communal shriek and the guards charged forward to their leader's defense.

But Pagonel stopped far short of the throne and held up his hands in a sign of unthreatening greeting.

Old Yatol Wadon leaped up from his chair and ordered his guards to stop, but then turned an angry eye upon the mystic.

"The fires rage in Jacintha," Yatol Wadon stated. "This is hardly the time for parley."

"If I were still allied with Brynn Dharielle, I would agree with you," the mystic replied. "But I have abandoned her cause, as I scorn the cause of Jacintha."

That curious statement had Yatol Wadon squinting and shaking his head.

"Those causes are one and the same," Pagonel insisted.

"Brynn attacked Jacintha last night," Yatol Wadon argued.

"And brilliantly so," the mystic replied, "following the specific instructions of Abbot Olin."

Yatol Wadon fell back in his seat and those around him gasped and looked to each other in confusion. "You lie," the old man said.

Pagonel dipped a low bow. "Only of late has Brynn Dharielle discovered that this was all a ruse," the mystic explained. "And by that point, her land was too threatened for her to deny the call of Abbot Olin and King Aydrian, who was once her friend.

"Honce-the-Bear will have Behren, without opposition, when this is ended," the mystic went on. "The reign of the Yatols and Chezru will be ended, buried beneath a version of the Abellican Church that will satisfy the needs of the desperate people. Abbot Olin of Behren will sign a treaty with To-gai, granting the To-gai-ru their sovereignty—though in truth, they will be subjugated under the will of King Aydrian."

"This is impossible!" one of the other Yatols cried out.

"The Bearman army are being welcomed back into the city?" Pagonel asked.

"Yes, triumphantly so, after chasing the devil Rus away!" the Yatol answered.

"And in their charge out from Jacintha, how many were slain?"

That brought a curious look upon the face of the man, and several others. "Their fine armor . . ." the man began tentatively.

"Then how many horses were shot out from under them?" Pagonel asked, and the man went silent. The mystic turned to Yatol Wadon. "Have you ever known the To-gai-ru to shoot so poorly?"

Yatol Wadon considered it all for a moment, then stubbornly shook his head. "This is impossible!" he roared. "What you speak of is—"

"Even now a great fleet of Honce-the-Bear approaches your docks," the mystic interrupted, and he motioned toward the room's eastern-facing window.

Men bristled and turned about, several running over to view the harbor. Their cries of dismay were all the confirmation Yatol Wadon needed.

As luck would have it, Abbot Olin and Master Mackaront stormed into the room at that moment, followed by one of the guards who had slipped out at the appearance of Pagonel.

"What is the meaning of this?" the old abbot demanded.

Yatol Wadon, his eyes burning with fires of outrage, looked at Pagonel, then back to Olin. He motioned to his guards. "Arrest him!" he commanded.

Abbot Olin's face twisted in confusion. "Are you mad?"

"If you mean angry, then know that I have never been so mad in all my life," the Yatol replied, and his soldiers surrounded the pair and roughly grabbed them.

Abbot Olin cried out and his own soldiers charged into the room then, and Yatol Wadon's remaining guards leaped upon them. As did Pagonel, the mystic flowing through the ranks, taking down soldier after soldier with devastating blows.

Soon enough, the room was secured for Yatol Wadon.

"Take that lying fool away," Yatol Wadon instructed the men holding Olin. He turned to Master Mackaront. "Release him," he instructed, and he walked forward to look the man in the eye even as the screaming and protesting Olin was dragged from the room.

"I will have your head on a stake!" the abbot shouted, the last words he said before the butt of a spear smashed him in the face, silencing him.

"Your plans are known to me," Yatol Wadon said to Mackaront. "And they have failed."

The man started to respond, but Wadon slapped him across the face.

"You would sacrifice all of Behren in the name of your King Aydrian," Yatol Wadon spat.

Mackaront glared at him.

"Go back to your foul king," Yatol Wadon told him. "Turn your fleet aside."

"My fleet?" Mackaront asked, and Yatol Wadon slapped him across the face again.

"Begone from Jacintha with all of those who would follow you!" Yatol Wadon yelled at him. "There is no room in Behren for your King Aydrian!"

Master Mackaront stiffened and continued to glare, but he said nothing. He gave the slightest of bows and turned away.

Word spread quickly from Chom Deiru, and fighting erupted throughout the city, Bearman against Behrenese and Behrenese against Behrenese. From the audience chamber, Pagonel and several of the Behrenese leaders watched it all. Yatol Wadon was there, as well, and in great distress.

At one point, as the great fleet neared the docks, Yatol Wadon turned to his advisors and ordered them to secure against the invasion.

But Pagonel stopped him, pointing excitedly out the window. "They fly the flag of Ursal!" he cried, pointing out toward the armada. "And the Alpinadorans are beside them!"

Yatol Wadon stared at him incredulously.

"Prince Midalis has won out at sea!" the mystic cried, and he clapped the old Yatol on the shoulders—a movement that nearly incited the nearby guards to violence. "That was my one fleeting hope!"

Wadon's expression became even more incredulous, like a man caught in a whirlpool that was beyond his comprehension.

"Do you not understand?" the mystic asked, becoming far more animated than usual—and in that arm-waving, he flashed a subtle and predetermined signal to Belli'mar Juraviel, who was still hiding in the shadows at the far end of the hall, to go out to Prince Midalis with news of the turn of events. "These are not enemies who sail into Jacintha, but allies!"

"How much of a fool do you take me to be?" Yatol Wadon demanded.

"Prince Midalis himself, the rightful king of Honce-the-Bear and the sworn enemy of Aydrian and Abbot Olin is on those ships, I do not doubt. The rescue of your city is at hand, Yatol Wadon, and by an outside force that will not remain to question your rule."

So flabbergasted was Yatol Wadon that his knees buckled beneath him and he would have fallen to the floor had not Pagonel caught him by the arm. So many thoughts rushed through his mind. He knew that he had been badly deceived, but he wasn't sure whether that deception had come from Abbot Olin or Pagonel!

He thought of retrieving Olin at that time, but he knew that it had already gone past that point. When the vicious man had claimed that he would see Yatol Wadon's head on a stake, he had meant it.

"Chezru, what are we to do?" asked one of the confused Yatols at Wadon's side.

Yatol Wadon looked down at the tumult that was sweeping across Jacintha. He had no idea.

❖ 40 ❖

The Unselfish Choice

Brynn walked Runtly through the battered Jacintha streets. Fires burned in many places throughout the city, though the main conflagration at the stables and stockpiles was out now, burned down to a blackened and smoldering field of debris. There was still fighting in the city, though the sun was setting and every street was littered with dead. No one really knew who was fighting whom anymore, and even in flying over the breadth of the place on Agradeleous, Brynn had discovered no pattern to the small and vicious battles. All that she knew was that Jacintha was shocked and shattered, a place of complete chaos. Prince Midalis and his fleet had landed at the docks with little opposition, and now held that region secure. The formal Jacintha guard had set up a perimeter around Chom Deiru. And a contingent of the Bearman force had broken out of the city soon after returning from their futile chase of Brynn. They had marched into the foothills of the Belt-and-Buckle and showed no signs of planning to return.

Belli'mar Juraviel had assured Brynn that Lozan Duk and the other alfar would watch them all the way back to Entel.

The Bearman force that had escaped was not nearly as large as the one that had first marched to Jacintha, though. Perhaps a third of the warriors were running home, but that left somewhere around seven thousand remaining in the city.

In moving through now, winding Runtly around lines of heavily armored corpses, Brynn understood that most of them were dead. At one point, Brynn's troupe passed a spot where five men hung by the neck from high windows, and four of them wore the brown robes of Abellican monks.

"You played on the city's every fear," Brynn remarked to Pagonel, who rode beside her.

"Yatol Wadon still has no idea of what to believe," the mystic agreed. "He suspects that I lied to him, I think, but his hatred of Abbot Olin made him an easy target for my words."

"Did it not pain you to so deceive the man?" demanded Yatol De Hamman, who rode behind the pair, sandwiched by To-gai-ru guards, including Tanalk Grenk.

"All of this pains me," Pagonel replied. "As your force pained me when you attacked Dharyan-Dharielle without provocation."

That shrank the imperious Yatol back in his saddle. "What good can come from this?" he did manage to ask. "Jacintha is laid to waste. Without the calming strength of the city, rogue warlords of like mind to my old nemesis Peridan will tear Behren apart!"

"Two things will result," Brynn answered, and she looked to Pagonel.

"Behren, whatever form the country takes, will again be for and of the Behrenese," the mystic said.

"And Behren will threaten To-gai no longer," Brynn added. "Whatever happens within your country, Yatol, you and your peers will never convince your people to ride against me again—especially after I sign a treaty with Prince Midalis of Honce-the-Bear and the leaders of the Alpinadorans who have so unexpectedly come to Jacintha."

"Honce-the-Bear is ruled by another," Yatol De Hamman reminded.

"And if he returns with designs of conquest upon Behren, then know that To-gai will stand beside you to expel him."

The Yatol started to answer, but just shook his head and spat upon the ground.

Brynn couldn't really fault him for his attitude; his capital city was in shambles. This catastrophe seemed to her the physical equivalent of the emotional destruction wrought by the deception of Yakim Douan. Brynn wasn't proud of the role she had played in this—every body lying along the street brought her great pain. But neither did she regret her decision to strike and strike hard in response to Abbot Olin's advances against Dharyan-Dharielle and against Behren itself.

The many soldiers around Chom Deiru eyed Brynn's group dangerously, but none made a move against her—since Agradeleous, in his still-imposing lizardman form, was walking beside the To-gai contingent.

Chom Deiru had not escaped the warring unscathed, obviously. Though cleared of bodies, the great steps leading up between the pillars that flanked the front entrance had been stained a deep crimson, the great doors of the palace had been sundered; one was somewhat back in place, but tilting badly. The polished stone walls showed the scorch marks of Abellican magic, and an entire area to the left of the doors had been crumbled and broken. Many ballista bolts lay about the corners of the square before Chom Deiru, and the remnants of pitch missiles marred the blasted ground, as the Behrenese had obviously turned their city artillery upon the palace attackers. Brynn had heard the reports of the vicious fighting here, as many of the warriors from Honce-the-Bear had gone in to try to rescue Abbot Olin. Brynn could only imagine the fighting that had occurred right on these steps, Chezhou-Lei against Allheart Knight.

Without slowing, the woman walked Runtly right up the steps and through the broken doorway into the palace's grand foyer.

"Direct me to Yatol Wadon," she instructed one of the startled guards inside.

"You cannot bring your horses in here!" the soldier cried, waving at all of them to turn about.

Brynn walked past him, brushing him hard enough with Runtly to send him stumbling aside. There would be no sign of weakness, the victorious woman decided. She looked at another guard, a younger man, who was trembling so hard that he seemed in danger of knocking himself unconscious with the long handle of his halberd.

"Yatol Wadon?" she asked.

The man started down the hallway.

Brynn did dismount before the threshold to Yatol Wadon's audience chamber, and the guide moved to take Runtly's reins.

Brynn held him back at arm's length. "If you touch my horse, my dragon back there is under explicit instructions to eat you," she calmly explained.

The man stuttered, blanched, wobbled as if he would simply faint away, and stumbled back with a shriek.

"Brynn," Pagonel said softly.

"Now none of them will touch our horses," she replied.

"True enough," the mystic admitted.

It wasn't hard for Brynn to sort out the gathering inside the audience hall. She knew Wadon and his advisors, of course, and Duke Bretherford. Several other men and women of Honce-the-Bear stood to the side with Bretherford, and one in particular seemed to stand above the others. Prince Midalis, Brynn guessed.

As for the woman standing beside him, Brynn didn't even have to guess. She knew Aydrian's features, the eyes and those full lips, and so she knew at once that this was the famous Jilseponie, his mother, the wife of Nightbird, the wife of King Danube.

Just behind Prince Midalis and Jilseponie stood a pair of huge men—Alpinadorans, obviously.

Brynn stopped just inside the door and handed Runtly to one of her attendants, and then she, Pagonel, and Tanalk Grenk came forward. She started for Yatol Wadon, as protocol demanded, since he was host, but changed her mind and veered to the side, moving right up to Jilseponie, where she dipped a low and polite bow.

"So much I have heard of you, Lady Jilseponie," she said, and Pagonel moved right to her side and translated. And then he turned to the Alpinadorans and started to translate, as well, but they stopped him, assuring him that they understood the language of Honce-the-Bear.

"Is there any language you do not speak?" Brynn asked the mystic.

"Working on my elf," Pagonel replied. "And my powrie is nowhere near as good as it should be."

That elicited a smirk.

"Your own deeds are fast becoming legend throughout all the lands," Pony replied, and Pagonel translated. Pony turned, then, and stepped aside, ushering one of the large Alpinadorans, a much older man, to move up and stand before Brynn.

"With all my heart and all my soul, I offer you my sword, ranger of To-gai," Andacanavar said in perfect elvish, and Brynn's light brown eyes widened indeed!

"Andacanavar of Alpinador?" the woman stammered.

"I am indeed," he answered. "And honored to be in your presence." He bowed very low, taking her hand up and kissing the back of it before rising to his nearly seven-foot height once again.

Brynn found that she could hardly catch her breath—and for the woman who had seen so much of the world, who had met a dragon and conquered a great enemy, it took a lot to shake her.

Andacanavar was a lot.

An obviously impatient Yatol Wadon cleared his throat then, turning them all to regard him. "May we dispense with the pleasantries?" he asked sharply, and the various translators went to work.

"Unpleasantries?" Brynn asked. "Are we not among friends?"

"I would have thought as much," Wadon sharply retorted, "before your Jhesta Tu spy so deceived me!"

Brynn looked to Pagonel, who merely bowed, seeing no need to cover his complicity.

"I should have him killed here and now!" Wadon shouted, coming forward in his throne, and the soldiers lining the room stiffened and clutched their weapons more tightly.

"I would get to you before your guards got near to us," Brynn warned. "Though I believe that Pagonel would beat me to your throat."

Over by the door, Agradeleous snorted, sending forth a gout of flame that licked the tiles of the grand floor, and all the soldiers seemed to shrink quite a bit, from Brynn's perspective.

Yatol Wadon settled back in his chair.

Brynn turned to the door and nodded, and one of her soldiers stepped back and pulled Yatol De Hamman into the room, shoving him forward. The Yatol straightened and brushed himself off in an attempt to regain some of his dignity, then moved forward to bow before Wadon.

"If I believed for a moment that Yatol De Hamman had acted under orders of Yatol Wadon and not Abbot Olin when he attacked my city, the carnage in Jacintha would have only just begun," Brynn assured Wadon. "I offer you the benefit of my suspicions here—take care how you abuse them."

Wadon seemed to retreat back even farther into his great throne. He trembled visibly, and seemed as if he was about to burst into a fit of wailing, but to his credit, he managed to get past it.

"Abbot Olin is in chains," he explained.

Brynn nodded.

"The Bearmen are of no consequence to Jacintha and Behren at this time," Yatol Wadon went on, and he turned to Prince Midalis, who offered an assenting nod as his words were translated. "They will sail, posthaste."

"We have much to accomplish in our own land," Midalis explained, turning to the Dragon of To-gai. "Your alliance would be most appreciated."

The words stung Brynn, and she turned to Pagonel, needing his support. In her heart, she recognized the danger that was Aydrian and knew that he had to be stopped. But what assistance might To-gai offer in a struggle north of the great mountains? She could ill afford to send her warriors away on such a crusade with Behren in such turmoil right below the plateau divide!

"You will have my offer of friendship, Prince Midalis," she stated. "And when you have recovered your throne, our people may know a time of great alliance and trade. But your war is not the concern of To-gai, though I will tell you that if your enemy, Aydrian, who is known to me, returns to Behren with hopes of conquest, my people will battle him to the last."

Prince Midalis seemed more than a little disappointed as those words were relayed to him, but to his credit, he nodded and bowed in acceptance.

"And I intend to travel with Yatol Wadon to Entel to meet with King Aydrian," Brynn startled them all—particularly Mado Wadon!—by announcing. "I wish to see my old companion and let him know that I do not approve of his movements. Fear not, Prince Midalis, for there will be no alliances between us beyond an agreement that our kingdoms will not war."

"I have agreed to no such meeting!" Yatol Wadon protested. "You would ask me to leave Jacintha at this time?"

"Send an emissary—Yatol De Hamman perhaps—if you must," Brynn said to him. "We need to speak with this opportunistic young man. Pagonel will accompany me—I have room on Agradeleous' neck for one more."

The mention of riding on the dragon had Mado Wadon sinking even deeper into his throne. "Yatol De Hamman, then," he squeaked, and De Hamman swallowed hard.

Brynn turned back to Midalis. "You will put back out to sea?"

"As soon as we come to believe that Jacintha is secured, and free of Aydrian's soldiers," the prince confirmed. "Yatol Wadon has graciously allowed us to resupply in full. We arrived to right the wrongs of Aydrian in Behren, and nothing more."

Brynn knew that the man was speaking merely for diplomatic gain. Prince Midalis had wisely seized the opportunity of joining in the fight against his adversary's weak point. She gave no outward indication, though, no grin or smirk. "Fare well, then, in all your endeavors," she said, and she moved over and offered Midalis her hand, then shook Pony's as well.

She started to offer Andacanavar her hand as well, but the big man wrapped her in a sudden hug.

"You know what Aydrian did to Lady Dasslerond and her people?" the barbarian ranger whispered as he held Brynn close.

"I do."

"Take care how you deal with young Aydrian," Andacanavar warned. "He is the most dangerous man in all the world."

Brynn didn't doubt that for a minute.

"I will return for you soon, within a week or two," Brynn said to Yatol De Hamman. "After I have arranged our meeting with Aydrian."

She left with her entourage then, moving back out of Chom Deiru, then across the torn city. Not far outside of Jacintha's gate, back near the foothills of the Belt-and-Buckle, they met up with Belli'mar Juraviel.

"You will sail with Prince Midalis and Jilseponie?" the elf asked hopefully.

"Our war with Aydrian has ended," Brynn explained. "Unless he turns his eye to the south once more."

It was fairly obvious to all around that the surprising proclamation did not settle well on Juraviel's delicate shoulders. The elf moved forward suddenly, hopping right before Brynn. "He will come south once more!" Juraviel cried. "If Aydrian wins out against Prince Midalis, he will march south with several times the forces he sent behind Abbot Olin. He means to conquer the world—can you not see that?"

"His people will be a long way from home indeed if they mean to strike at To-gai," Brynn answered. "Too long, I would guess, for even Aydrian properly to wage war."

"That is a dangerous gamble."

"No more dangerous than emptying my country of her warriors to chase Aydrian across his homeland," Brynn replied. She started to look to Pagonel for support, but changed her mind and remained focused on Juraviel instead. She had already worked through her feelings in debate with the mystic; there was no reason for her to answer to anyone but herself now.

"The Behrenese will likely splinter into their ancient tribes now, and many of those stalk about the desert below the To-gai plateau," Brynn explained. "If they see the opportunity to raid into To-gai, they certainly shall. I'll not give them that opportunity, nor will I offer Yatol Wadon the hope that he can reunite Behren yet again and successfully march against a scantily defended Dharyan-Dharielle!"

"Without your help, it is unlikely that Prince Midalis will prevail," Juraviel argued.

Brynn didn't answer.

"Do you not care?" the elf accused, his voice as angry as Brynn had ever heard it. "Do you not care that Lady Dasslerond is dead by Aydrian's deed? Do you not care that Andur'Blough Inninness is lost to the world?"

The words stung Brynn to her heart. Never had she been so torn in her loyalties. Of course she cared, and deeply so! But this wasn't about her, she knew, as Pagonel and her experiences here had taught her. Her decisions were not her own to make, based on her own desires, for if she did that, then she would be no better than Aydrian! She was the leader of the To-gai-ru; an entire nation of proud people depended upon her and trusted in her to make the best decisions for their benefit.

She would not betray that trust. Brynn knew that to load her warriors on the boats and land them in Entel so that she could do battle with Aydrian would leave her country badly exposed to the immediate threats, and that, she could not do.

"I want you to get word to Aydrian," she said to the elf, "that I and an emissary from Yatol Mado Wadon, who leads Behren, wish to meet with him under a flag of truce in the city of Entel in three weeks' time. Inform Aydrian that Abbot Olin has been repelled."

Belli'mar Juraviel stood very still, staring at her.

"You can do this?" Brynn asked.

The elf looked to Pagonel, then past him, to Tanalk Grenk, who stood scowling, his strong arms crossed over his chest.

It was Brynn who answered his silent plea, though. "I cannot do what you wish of me, my friend," she said calmly. "All the world will mourn the loss of Andur'Blough Inninness, but To-gai is not the answer. My people are not the retributive arm of Belli'mar Juraviel's army."

Juraviel snapped his head about to stare at Brynn again, his face showing both anger and remorse. He started to remark that he never asked that of her, but Brynn cut him short when she asked, "Will you get word to Aydrian for me?"

Juraviel visibly relaxed and even managed a friendly smile. He brought forth his emerald, offered a helpless shrug to Brynn, then stepped far, far away.

"I know how difficult that was for you," Pagonel said quietly, moving up right beside the To-gai leader. "You chose wisely, and generously for your people."

Brynn was glad to hear that affirmation, though Pagonel had counseled as much to her in their meetings before they ever had ridden against Abbot Olin. She wondered what her meeting with Aydrian might be like. She hadn't seen him in over five years; he would be a man now, a king among men.

And they would no longer be friends. Whatever Aydrian might say to her, whatever justification he might offer, to Brynn Dharielle, the ranger of To-gai, there could be no excuse for his actions.

"We have placed the notices all about the city of Entel," one of the Touel'alfar scouts informed Juraviel only a couple of days after Juraviel had arrived back in Honce-the-Bear to secretly spread the word that the leaders of both To-gai and Behren wished to parley with King Aydrian in the city.

Soon after, Juraviel conferred with scouts outside of Ursal, where similar notices had been placed, and then outside of Palmaris. His contact in Palmaris added some other information, though, that had Juraviel more than a little unsettled.

"We must go to him," Juraviel replied to the disquieting news.

The elven scout shook his head. "There is no way to get near to him. Even with the emerald of Andur'Blough Inninness, we would need to fight our way in to his side."

Juraviel closed his eyes and forced himself to calm down. He wanted to go anyway, but understood that this wasn't about his desires. He couldn't risk everything for the sake of this one man, friend though he might be. "Keep your eyes ever turned his way, then," he bade his scout. "If an opening is to be found, let us find it."

The scout nodded, and Juraviel went on his way.

His pass back through Yorkey County brought him the welcome news that King Aydrian had posted a response indicating that he would agree to the meeting.

The elf hurried back across the mountains to Jacintha, determined to catch up with Pony before Prince Midalis sailed. She would need to know.

She walked her borrowed horse along the destroyed streets, past the crumbled houses, the barricaded doorways, and the bodies. So many bodies. Jacintha would be a long time in recovering from the battle and the rioting. Even now, more than a week after the expulsion of Abbot Olin, Pony could hear the cries of outrage and pain, as opportunistic gangs made their way across the chaotic city.

Pony tried hard to ignore it all. The fate of Jacintha was beyond her control. Still, she winced whenever a scream echoed through the air.

There were no stars out this night, as a blanket of heavy clouds had rolled in off the ocean. Pony hoped that it would rain, that God would wash away the pools of blood and gore.

She was relieved when she passed out the city's western gate a short while later. She could see the campfires of the To-gai-ru force up in the north, so she turned her horse and walked along.

Within the hour, the cries of To-gai-ru sentries halted her. She offered no argument as they came out, surrounding her horse. She couldn't understand their commands to her, but she did dismount, and even surrendered her sword, though she kept her pouch of magical gemstones and even managed to slip a graphite unnoticed into her palm. If she had to, she would send forth a burst of stunning energy.

She was not mistreated, however, and was led straightaway to a centrally located grouping of tents, nestled on a sheltered plateau. There, Pony found Brynn and Pagonel, and they welcomed her warmly.

"May we go off alone and talk?" Pony asked after some formal greetings.

Brynn waved her guards away and led the pair to the southern lip of the plateau, away from the lights and bustle of the encampment. From that high vantage point, they could see the dark shapes of Jacintha far below, and beyond that, the campfires of a large group of soldiers and refugees who were returning to their homeland of Cosinnida with Yatol Paroud.

"Hundreds are dead," Pony lamented.

"My reports put the number into the thousands," Brynn corrected after Pagonel had interpreted the words. "Perhaps into the tens of thousands."

Pony didn't disagree with the estimate; never had she witnessed such brutality, man against man, as had occurred in the turmoil of Jacintha. Groups seemed to be operating independently, fighting anyone who came against them, or even near them, without bothering to determine if they were friend or foe.

"And there is fighting beginning anew in other regions of Behren," Brynn went on. "Yatol Wadon will find his task of reuniting the kingdom daunting, perhaps impossible."

"Is that a bad thing?" Pony asked.

"Only if the imperialistic Bearmen return," said Brynn. "In that case, opposition to Aydrian and Honce-the-Bear will be minimal, I fear. He will find allies among the various tribes."

"Aydrian will not return here," Pony vowed.

"They are a tribal people, in their core," Pagonel added, speaking it consecutively in both languages. "They will cluster together in their respective cities and regions, and defend their borders from any who would try to dominate them."

They stood in silence for a short while after that, just looking down at the devastated city.

Pony appreciated Brynn's patience here. The Dragon of To-gai didn't press her at all to reveal the meaning of this unexpected visit.

"Have you considered what you will say to my son . . . to Aydrian?" Pony finally asked.

"Brynn travels to Entel to deliver the news of Abbot Olin's defeat," Pagonel answered, before he even translated the words to the To-gai warrior woman. "And to warn Aydrian against his apparent designs on the kingdoms south of the mountains. She will offer truce, but not alliance."

Pony waited for Pagonel to explain the exchange to Brynn, then bade the mystic, "Ask her if she will deliver for me a message to Aydrian. Tell him that Yatol Wadon has generously turned the prisoner Abbot Olin over to my care and that I wish an exchange."

Pagonel interpreted the request for Brynn, then assured Pony that they would arrange it.

Pony explained the situation at length to Pagonel, who in turn spelled it out for Brynn.

"Your message will be delivered," Brynn promised. "And with my insistence that King Aydrian agree to your terms."

Pony nodded her gratitude, and the three turned back to the distant sights of Jacintha and the encampment. Eventually, the woman who had been queen turned as if to ask something else.

But Pony hesitated and seemed uncomfortable.

"What else do you wish of me?" the perceptive Brynn asked.

"You knew Aydrian," Pony began haltingly. "When he was young. I wish to know . . ." Her voice trailed off into a sigh.

Brynn's smile widened as Pagonel translated the words. "There is much I wish to tell you about him," the ranger answered. "I did not see him daily in Andur'Blough Inninness, but enough to share with you many memories."

"I would enjoy that," said Pony.

The trio spent the remainder of the evening out there in the dark, with Brynn telling Pony so many things about the life her son had lived in the valley of the elves. She didn't hide the truth of the headstrong young Aydrian behind empty compliments, but she spoke of many of his arguments with Lady Dasslerond with a wide grin upon her face.

For Pony, it was all bittersweet. She loved hearing that Aydrian had found some bit of joy and innocence in his youth, at least.

But that only made her realize even more poignantly how much she regretted all that she had missed.

❖ 41 ❖

Necessary Disengagement

"Olin has failed," Aydrian informed Sadye. He was still holding the notice that had been posted anonymously in Ursal, requesting that he meet with the leaders of To-gai and Behren to discuss an end to the hostilities.

"Failed?"

"He invoked the wrath of Brynn Dharielle, and she joined with the Behrenese to defeat him," Aydrian explained. "Even as Master Mackaront was requesting that I send more soldiers to Jacintha, To-gai was rising against Abbot Olin."

"Do you question your decision not to send the soldiers?"

"No," Aydrian said without the slightest hesitation. "Our fight is here. St.-Mere-Abelle remains strong and Prince Midalis is running free about the coast, with support from Alpinador. I cannot send ten thousand more warriors so that Abbot Olin can realize his dreams beyond the borders of Honce-the-Bear!"

Sadye moved right beside her lover and gently slid her arm about his waist. "How big a loss have we suffered?" she asked quietly. "How many were killed?"

"I know not," Aydrian admitted. "There have been reports of a large force crossing the mountains to return to Entel. Olin took ten thousand with him; it will be a simple matter of subtraction to determine our casualties. There is one great concern to me, though: where is Duke Bretherford? Surely he could have sailed from Jacintha to Entel by now."

"The reports from Entel," Sadye remarked under her breath, for they had heard whispers that a large force had been deposited along the beaches outside of Entel, and that many were claiming to be the remnants of Duke Bretherford's fleet after it had been conquered by Prince Midalis. Aydrian hadn't put much stock in those scattered and confused reports, nor had anyone else outside of Entel; but now they suddenly took on a deeper resonance.

"Is it possible that Prince Midalis sailed all the way to Jacintha to wage war with Abbot Olin?" the young king remarked.

"You sound as if you almost hope that to be the case," said Sadye.

"Oh, but I do," Aydrian replied, and he went on with a leading voice, "If Midalis is so far to the south . . ."

Sadye looked at him curiously, studying his widening smile and considering the way he spoke the words. "Then Vanguard is less guarded," she reasoned at last.

"And our force at Dancard can be retrieved and sent at once across the gulf."

"Prince Midalis seems to be well informed of our every move," Sadye cautioned. "If he sails fast and chases that force to Vanguard, they will be trapped."

That was the rub, Aydrian knew. Prince Midalis seemed to know their every move. He had retaken the nearly deserted Pireth Tulme in short order, and had avoided all the traps they had set about the coastline below St. Gwendolyn. And now, apparently, he had discovered Abbot Olin's troubles in Jacintha. Something wasn't right, but Aydrian couldn't quite yet put his finger on it.

"Let us travel to Entel and meet with Brynn Dharielle and the victorious Yatol," he suggested. "They will tell us more, whether they wish to do so or not."

By the time Aydrian and Brynn rode back into Entel that early-summer morning, the young king had gotten confirmation that Prince Midalis had indeed joined in the fighting against Abbot Olin. Hearing the reports from some merchants on the road in eastern Yorkey County, Aydrian had retreated to his wagon and to his soul stone, and had personally gone out, his spirit flying across the winds to the Entel coast, and then down and around the Belt-and-Buckle until Jacintha came into sight. He wasn't able to maintain his vision of the place for long, for that pesky sunstone shield held strong against him.

Of course, that alone told him that he had come near to his mother. He had seen enough to realize the truth anyway. Many Honce-the-Bear warships were anchored in the Jacintha harbor, alongside oared craft of an unusual design, which Aydrian figured correctly to be Midalis' Alpinadoran allies.

A second bit of news greeted Aydrian in Entel, as well: that Duke Kalas and Marcalo De'Unnero had surrounded and besieged St.-Mere-Abelle, and had sealed the docks.

That was something positive, at least.

The Entel meeting was arranged in a small farmhouse west of the city, a secluded location where the interested parties might find the privacy needed to conduct such business. Aydrian was there first, along with his entourage. He waited before the hearth, staring into the flames. It wasn't really cold enough to warrant a fire this night, but the young man desired one so that he could lose his thoughts in the swirl of orange.

Sadye sat right beside him, wrapping his arm with both of hers and resting her head upon his strong shoulder.

A knock on the door startled them both. Aydrian stood up and helped Sadye to her feet, then brushed himself off and straightened his shirt.

"Allheart Mallon Yank, my King!" came the proclamation, and then another knock.

"Do enter, Allheart," Aydrian formally replied.

The door creaked open and an old and very dignified-looking nobleman strode in, his posture perfect, his Allheart armor impeccable, and his helm tightly tucked under his arm. "I give you Brynn Dharielle of To-gai and Yatol De Hamman, who speaks for the Behrenese," the man explained, and he turned about and swept his arm toward the door.

Brynn led the procession into the room, and Aydrian had to catch his breath at the sight of her. He hadn't seen her in more than five years, but he recognized her from the instant she appeared in the door. Those eyes! Aydrian would never forget those light brown eyes, contrasting so starkly with the woman's raven hair. He couldn't contain his smile, and forgot his protocol altogether, sweeping forward as if to embrace her.

Brynn's icy stare stopped him cold, even forced him back a step.

Two men walked in behind, one wearing the robes that Aydrian recognized as those of a Yatol priest—De Hamman, he figured—and the other plainly dressed. This second man drew Aydrian's attention more than the Yatol. He appeared in his midforties, but walked in such a way, with soft steps and certain balance, as to make Aydrian believe him to be a warrior.

"Greetings, King Aydrian," Yatol De Hamman began, his command of the Bearman tongue fairly solid. "I am an emissary from Chezru Chieftain Mado Wadon, and speak for Jacintha."

"Chezru Wadon could not be bothered to make the journey himself?"

That took the stupid grin from Yatol De Hamman's face. "The treachery of Abbot Olin has brought great distress to Behren," he retorted, and he didn't even note the scowl that Brynn shot his way for so easily offering such information. "The city is in flames because of the abbot, and war rages across the land!"

"Enough, good Yatol," Brynn said in a language that Aydrian didn't understand. She turned immediately and spoke to him directly, using the language of the Touel'alfar. "Great devastation has been inflicted upon Behren. Abbot Olin has brought shame to the Abellican Church and to Honce-the-Bear, and has represented you as an imperialistic conqueror." She stared hard at Aydrian then, and added, "Would Lady Dasslerond agree?"

Aydrian couldn't help but offer a smirk at the mere mention of the elf's name. "Have you come to declare war?" he asked bluntly.

"I have come to demand peace," said Brynn. "And to warn you to honor the border between your lands and mine—and ours," she finished, turning to include Yatol De Hamman in the mix.

"Abbot Olin went beyond his edict," Aydrian told her.

"And that was?"

"To help Behren to find stability, and nothing more," said Aydrian, rather unconvincingly. "To determine whose cause was just and use the forces at his command to solidify that man's hold on the shattered kingdom."

"A gesture from the beneficent ruler from the north?" Brynn asked, not hiding her skepticism in the least.

"Exactly."

Brynn glanced back at the other two men, then turned back on Aydrian, her expression sour. She came forward a step, so that she was very near to the young king. "Aydrian, what are you doing?" she whispered, though if she had shouted the elvish words, no one else would have understood them anyway. "What did you do to Lady Dasslerond?"

Aydrian's face went very tight.

"You came to Behren with intent of conquest," said Brynn. "And you stole this kingdom you now command. What are you—"

"Stole?" Aydrian retorted. "My mother was the queen, do you not know?"

"Your mother bitterly opposes your rule," Brynn replied.

"And how might you know this?"

Brynn stared at him for a long while, then stepped back. "I have come to form an agreement of nonaggression," she said in the language of the To-gai-ru, and Pagonel translated it into Bearman. "Your place is not south of the mountains, except on invitation from Chezru Wadon or myself. If you accept that place, then understand that the events in Honce-the-Bear are not the concern of To-gai, or of Behren."

As Pagonel translated, Yatol De Hamman echoed his agreement.

"Very well then," Aydrian said, turning and motioning to the long table that had been set up deeper within the room, complete with piles of parchment, writing quills, and inkwells. On a motion from Aydrian, a pair of scribes walked out from the corners of the room and took their places opposite each other.

Aydrian and Sadye sat on one side, with Brynn and Yatol De Hamman taking the two vacant seats across from them, and Pagonel standing directly behind Brynn.

The terms were simple enough, with Brynn and Yatol De Hamman promising not to attack Honce-the-Bear, and Aydrian agreeing to keep his armies north of the mountains. Agreed upon without delay, they set the scribes to work, and soon enough, the three leaders signed.

"Is there anything more?" Aydrian asked, eyeing Brynn with every word, and just to make sure that she understood his meaning, he repeated the question in the language of the Touel'alfar.

"There is so much more that I need to say to you," Brynn answered, again in the elvish tongue. "Who are you, Aydrian? What have you become?"

"Everything that Lady Dasslerond hoped I would become, and more," he answered flippantly.

Brynn narrowed her brown eyes. "I know what you did to her, and to Andur'Blough Inninness."

"And how might you know that, pray tell?"

Brynn didn't reply to the question, instead changing back to the language of her people and offering, "There is one other matter, concerning the disposition of a prisoner."

Pagonel translated.

"Do tell," Aydrian prompted.

"We have Abbot Olin, and will return him to you," said Brynn.

"How generous. Can you not afford enough rope?"

"But in exchange for one you hold," the woman went on. "His name is Roger Lockless, and he is kept in the dungeons of Palmaris. Abbot Olin will be traded for him, if you so agree, at a time and place of your choosing."

Aydrian laughed aloud as Pagonel translated it all. "Ah, my mother," he said. "Ever the sentimental and loyal fool."

"You know nothing of your mother," Pagonel dared to reply.

Aydrian stared at him hard. "Who are you?" he demanded.

Pagonel offered a slight bow and deferentially receded a step.

"Abbot Olin for Roger Lockless?" Aydrian said to Brynn directly, reverting to the elvish tongue.

"It seems more than fair from your perspective."

"Then why?"

"Because he was a friend to your mother, and she would see him free."

"That alone tells me that I should refuse you," Aydrian said coldly. "Anything that brings comfort to my mother is of no interest to me."

Again came that judgmental, disapproving look from Brynn, but Aydrian held strong. He shoved his chair out from the table and crossed his powerful arms over his chest. "Your request is denied. Hang Olin from the tallest tower in Jacintha, or from the mast of Prince Midalis' own ship. I have no interest in him. He failed me and disobeyed me, and the result, by your own admission, is that Behren has been reduced to utter chaos."

"Behren has its trouble, indeed," Brynn agreed. She came forward in her chair, leaning right over the table to stare hard at Aydrian. "But I warn you, if you come south to take advantage of that chaos, you will find a unified Behren standing against you, and beside a To-gai ally." The woman backed off just a bit, and reached out one last time. "Aydrian. Aydrian! You know me as your friend. We were nurtured together—"

"You were nurtured while I was tortured!" the young king roared back, and he leaped from his chair and leaned over the table, so that his face was but an inch from Brynn's. "Who am I? I am the nightmare of Lady Dasslerond! I am the maelstrom."

"You killed her!"

"I wish I had!" Aydrian snapped back. "But no, I was robbed of that pleasure by the witch herself!"

Brynn slammed the table, and Sir Mallon Yank rushed forward, as if to cut in front of Brynn.

Of course, Pagonel was far the quicker, spinning past the yelping Yatol De Hamman to easily intercept the Allheart. Mallon Yank went for his sword, but Pagonel caught him by the wrist as he closed his hand over the hilt, and with a proper press on the sensitive areas, locked the man's hand in place.

Yank responded by swinging his left for the mystic, but Pagonel easily avoided the lumbering blow, stepped back, and pushed the man along in his swing, knocking him off-balance and turning him right about. The mystic's foot planted against the stumbling Allheart's rump and shoved him hard across the room, to crash into the far wall, where he stumbled down in his heavy armor and floundered about.

Yatol De Hamman yelped again and ducked for cover; Aydrian's hand went to his sword, as did Brynn's.

Outside, the guards cried out, and then they screamed out, and a great roar shook the house. The door burst open and the lizardman Agradeleous stepped to the threshold, smoke wafting eagerly from his nostrils.

Brynn threw up her hands and stepped back, shouting, "Enough!"

But then something strange happened, something unexpected and frightening beyond anything the onlookers could have anticipated.

For Aydrian looked at the dragon, and Agradeleous at he, and both roared out in revulsion! Agradeleous bared his great fangs and seemed as if he meant to immolate the entire room, but Aydrian was the quicker, lifting his hand from his pouch and covering himself in a blue-white serpentine shield, and then blasting a bolt of lightning at the dragon that knocked Agradeleous back out of the room.

"Enough!" Brynn cried again, and she leaped forward at Aydrian, who turned on her angrily.

"You would consort with such a beast, and yet you question my actions?" the young king yelled at her. "Begone from here! At once!"

Brynn saw that there was something deeper here, something almost feral within Aydrian. How could he know anything of dragons? Why had he acted so violently, without the slightest hesitation?

And why had Agradeleous?

Brynn stared at him for just a moment longer, then rushed out the door, fearing that her dragon would assume its greater form and simply stamp the house flat.

She found Agradeleous hardly in a position to do so, for Aydrian's bolt had stung him and stunned him. He was many feet back from the doorway, sitting in the yard, and seemed more shaken than Brynn had ever before seen him.

"Quickly, let us be out of here," Pagonel said to her, moving by and taking her by the arm. He pulled her past the dragon, with Yatol De Hamman moving even faster and farther.

But Agradeleous did not stand to follow.

"Agradeleous?" the mystic asked. He let go of Brynn and rushed back around to regard the dragon directly, to see the curious expression. Was it rage? Fear?

"Come along," the mystic prompted.

The dragon stood up, still staring with obvious murderous intent at the house.

"The treaty is signed," Pagonel went on. "Our business here is done. Let us be gone from this place."

"Long gone," the dragon finally agreed. "Long, long gone."

"Aydrian!" Sadye yelled, grabbing the young king as he broke from his pacing and stalked determinedly toward the door.

Aydrian turned on her, his eyes glowing with outrage, his expression more ferocious than Sadye had ever seen. But she, who had tamed the weretiger within Marcalo De'Unnero, did not back away.

"What are you doing?" the woman asked, and as Aydrian's muscles tightened with tension, she tightened her grip upon him.

"What was that?" the woman calmly asked.

"A dragon," Aydrian explained, though his teeth were so tightly gritted that he could hardly push the words through. "The second oldest of the races and the most vile by far!"

Sadye shook her head with every word. "You knew that Brynn Dharielle was rumored to possess such a beast," the bard reasoned.

"So?"

"So explain your reaction," Sadye replied.

That simple question did ease the tension from the young king and put him back on his heels. He had indeed heard the stories, and had eagerly anticipated the prospects of seeing the creature—had even fancied himself taking the dragon as a fitting mount to the man who would rule the world. Sadye's confusion was justified, he realized. What indeed had just happened?

"I cannot explain," he admitted. "The revulsion within me—I had not anticipated . . ."

"Were you not joking earlier that you would desire such a beast as a mount?"

"I would desire its vile head as a trophy, and nothing more!" Aydrian roared.

"Aydrian?"

Again, the surprising outburst had Aydrian shaking his head with more surprise than anyone in his audience.

"My liege, I will rouse the troops at once," Sir Mallon Yank declared. "We will bring down the beast and deliver its head!"

"You will stand down," Aydrian replied immediately. "The southerners arrived under a flag of truce, and we will honor that."

"Yes, my King."

"The unfortunate outburst is to be forgotten," Aydrian told them all. "We have signed a treaty and will hold to it, as will Brynn and her people, and the Behrenese. The issue of the southland is settled for now, to my relief. Let us turn our attention fully to our own lands now, and be done with Prince Midalis and the rebellion."

It was news that they were all glad to hear.

"Perhaps the next time you request a gathering with Brynn, you would be wise to advise her to leave her beast in To-gai," Sadye said quietly to Aydrian, while the others went about straightening the room and ensuring that their guests were long away.

Aydrian wrapped his arm about the woman's shoulder and laughed. "Wise indeed," he agreed. "Wise indeed."

42

Pecking Away

Upon returning to Jacintha, Yatol De Hamman was not pleased to learn that fighting had broken out anew along the southern sections of the city. "There is no order! All of Behren is in chaos because of you," he accused Brynn. "Fool woman!"

Brynn didn't shrink back an inch from the blabbering man. "Push my patience at your peril, Yatol," she calmly replied. "Had you not attacked my city, I would not have marched forth in response." He started to protest, but Brynn raised her hand into his face and spoke over him. "Spare me your talk of a mistake. There is no time for that anymore. Your country is in ruin, and you have no one to blame but Abbot Olin—and yourself.

"So go back to your home, Yatol," the woman went on. "Secure your province and release this anger you hold toward me and toward To-gai. It is an unhealthy practice, I assure you." That last threat had been not the least bit disguised, and Yatol De Hamman blanched and swayed back from the imposing warrior woman.

"Let us return to your people," Pagonel offered from behind Brynn.

"Indeed," Brynn replied. "I have had more than enough of the Behrenese."

They found the To-gai encampment up in the foothills easily enough. Many of the warriors had gone home by then, leaving only fourscore patrolling the region. Tanalk Grenk was there, however, patiently awaiting Brynn's return.

"To-gai's conflict with Honce-the-Bear is at its end," Brynn explained to the man. "King Aydrian has been warned to stay north of the mountains, and given his loss here, it will be a long time before he can turn his eyes south to us once more. When the issue of his struggle with Prince Midalis is settled, To-gai will go to the victor in parley again, to reaffirm the treaty we have signed."

"You have done well for our people," Grenk congratulated, and he offered a respectful bow. "Yet again."

"My efforts have been no less fruitful than your own," Brynn replied. "Your actions and leadership saved Dharyan-Dharielle, and allowed us to break out from the besieged city." The woman paused and looked to Pagonel, taking strength in his serenity.

"And that is why it is with complete confidence that I hand the leadership of To-gai into your able hands, Chief Tanalk Grenk," Brynn explained, and for perhaps the first time in his entire life, the powerful To-gai-ru warrior seemed as if his legs would not support him!

"My lady?" he stuttered.

"My road takes me north," Brynn explained. "By his deeds has Aydrian named himself my enemy, and I cannot go quietly home while he continues his errant course."

"An enemy of Brynn Dharielle is an enemy of To-gai!" Tanalk Grenk said determinedly.

Brynn offered him a grateful smile and patted his shoulder. "Aydrian's misdeeds against the Touel'alfar are no business of any To-gai-ru except for me. I am a ranger, as surely as I am To-gai-ru. I could not ask my warriors to follow me across the mountains. I could not risk the welfare of To-gai in my defense of Lady Dasslerond, who was as my mother. I am going north to do battle with Aydrian because I must. To you I entrust the leadership of our people, and I have no doubt that you will perform magnificently. To you, I entrust the care of Runtly, who is precious to me."

"And when you return?" Grenk asked.

"I will take back my pony, but that is all," Brynn replied. "My abdication is complete. If ever I am needed by To-gai, I will be there, by your side, but if I return from Honce-the-Bear, my road will be . . ." She stopped and glanced over at Pagonel, who smiled and nodded.

"You are going to study with the Jhesta Tu," Tanalk Grenk reasoned.

Brynn smiled and continued to look to the mystic. "If I am fortunate enough to live through the trials with Aydrian," she admitted.

When she turned back to Tanalk Grenk, she was surprised to see that he didn't appear ready to argue, nor was he puffing his chest with pride. "If I serve To-gai half as well as did Brynn Dharielle, then my name will be legend among our people," he offered, and he bowed so low that it seemed as if his face would touch the ground, and when he came up, Brynn saw the hint of tears in his dark eyes.

"I would ride with you anywhere in all the world, against any enemy," he said. "I would battle the dragon itself if you but asked. You cannot know . . ."

Brynn interrupted him by moving forward and wrapping him in a great hug.

"I could not go and do what I must, were it not for you," she whispered to the man. "I leave To-gai in all confidence that she will be safe and well led."

Tanalk Grenk nodded, and Brynn hugged him again. Then she gathered up Pagonel and walked off the plateau encampment, down to where Agradeleous waited.

The eagerness of the dragon had the woman more than a little concerned.

"He is worth killing," Agradeleous explained to her.

"And you mean to do that?"

The dragon fell back and the eager sparkle in his reptilian eyes dimmed considerably. "Better for another, that task," he said. "For me, I will fly about the beast's kingdom, putting towns to the flame!"

"No," Brynn replied, and she closed her eyes against the memories evoked by Agradeleous' obvious hunger. She remembered well the carnage she had allowed the dragon to inflict upon the Behrenese settlers in To-gai, and knew that forevermore she would hear their terrified screams in her mind. Her fight in the north was not with Honce-the-Bear, however, but with Aydrian—specifically Aydrian.

She would not turn Agradeleous loose in such a manner ever again.

They spent the night in preparation, Pagonel and Brynn determining how they might best serve Prince Midalis, and then they were off with the dawn's light, flying east to find the prince and his navy.

Three more catapults came on-line that day on the field outside of St.-Mere-Abelle, and Duke Kalas wasted no time in adding them to the bombardment. At any given moment throughout that morning, a trio of boulders were in the air, soaring out far and wide to smash down among the structures of the great abbey, or mostly, along the front wall near to the great gates.

Responding fire from the abbey's artillery proved sporadic at best, and wholly ineffective. Nor could the monks reach out this far with their gemstones.

Every so often, Kalas' artillerymen changed their tactics and loaded up with smoldering pitch and elevated the firing angle, and then with a great whoosh, they launched all fifteen of the massive catapults together, sending a wave of fire soaring over the abbey wall.

"Are you enjoying this as much as I?" Kalas asked De'Unnero as the two stood and watched the continuing bombardment.

"You would knock it all down if you could," the monk replied.

Kalas didn't even bother to reply, just stood there watching, a superior grin upon his face.

"Are you not just giving them more ammunition to throw back at us?" De'Unnero asked.

"That is why we throw the pitch over the wall, but launch the stones in short, so that most smash against the front wall and bounce down beyond their reach. Not that it would matter. When King Aydrian arrives and tells us to charge in, the monks will run out of time long before they will run out of stones to throw."

"He will arrive soon?"

"Tomorrow, from what I have heard."

"And what of the rumors from the southland?"

"By all reports, Abbot Olin was defeated and captured," Duke Kalas answered. "By all reports, Prince Midalis played a hand in that defeat. I fear that King Aydrian perhaps reached too far and too fast."

"No," the monk argued. "It was not Aydrian's error, but Abbot Olin's. He should have stepped more carefully—he had enough warriors at his disposal to hold strong against any opposition, had he kept his focus upon Jacintha and Behren alone."

"Do you think they are afraid?" Duke Kalas asked, indicating the great abbey once more.

De'Unnero turned back to regard the ancient structure. "They are concerned, of course," he replied. "But they know that you'll not knock down their solid walls from out here. And they know that they can withstand a siege forever and ever—the abbey is fully self-supporting. The brothers understand that to take St.-Mere-Abelle, you, or Aydrian, will have to charge those walls. The monastery has been attacked many times, good Duke. Never has it fallen."

"Never has it faced the wrath of Aydrian, or the combined armies of Honce-the-Bear," Kalas was quick to answer. He put on a sly look, and offered, "Nor, perhaps, the wrath of Marcalo De'Unnero."

"St.-Mere-Abelle will fall," De'Unnero agreed, but far from jubilant, his tone was somber. De'Unnero wanted the abbey taken, of course—this was the moment of his ascension. But it pained him nonetheless to know that to put things in the Church aright, he would have to bring down the formerly unconquerable fortress. There was some mystique about St.-Mere-Abelle that appealed to the warrior monk: unconquerable, indomitable, ageless.

"Do you think they have had enough shaking for the morning?" Kalas asked.

"Take care you do not pile your missiles too high before the walls," the monk warned. "Else we'll have to move them aside before we batter at the gates."

Duke Kalas snorted and turned to look over his shoulder. "The artillery is to stand down!" he called to one of his nearby undercommanders, and the man saluted and ran off to relay the command.

"We will resume tomorrow morning," Kalas explained to De'Unnero. "And every morning thereafter."

He chuckled as he considered a black line of smoke rising from behind the abbey's wall, the result, no doubt, of the last pitch barrage. "We will wear away their resolve," he promised. "And then St.-Mere-Abelle will fall to Aydrian's control."

Marcalo De'Unnero eyed the man for a long time, but resisted the urge to correct him on that last part. St.-Mere-Abelle would fall, true, but control would cede to him, and not to Aydrian.

Later that day, a runner arrived with word that Prince Midalis had come ashore in the east yet again.

"St. Gwendolyn?" Duke Kalas asked hopefully, for he had left a sizable force in place, hidden within the abbey. "Then at last, the renegade found a fight."

"Pireth Tulme," the runner corrected. "And then Macomber Village."

Duke Kalas looked at De'Unnero, and the monk merely shrugged. Once again, the prince had known exactly where to strike.

"Gather a force and retake the place," said a disgusted Duke Kalas.

"Yes, my lord," the runner replied, and Kalas waved him away.

"Pray that Aydrian arrives soon," Kalas muttered to De'Unnero. "We are in sore need of a victory here, to ensure that the peasants do not start believing in the superiority of Prince Midalis. Though he wins no major victories!"

"He is gambling that he will need none," the monk replied.

Trumpets heralded the arrival of King Aydrian and his force of five thousand the next day. He wasted no time with formalities, or even in surveying the damage done so far to St.-Mere-Abelle, but went straight to the tent offered him as his audience hall, to meet with Father Abbot De'Unnero and Duke Kalas.

"You have heard of Olin's failure?" Aydrian snapped as soon as the pair walked in. He noted, too, that De'Unnero's eyes were not on him, but were on Sadye, and the monk seemed less than pleased to be looking upon her once more.

"Rumors have reached us, yes," Duke Kalas replied.

"They are all true, I assure you," said Aydrian. "Olin attacked my old companion, Brynn Dharielle, and her To-gai-ru kinfolk, and he was soundly thrashed. Of course, it helped Brynn's cause that Prince Midalis happened to sail into Jacintha harbor in support of her war with Olin."

"The prince has proven to be a thorn up and down the coast," Duke Kalas agreed. "Always does he seem to be striking wherever we are not."

"It's the witch with her gemstones," De'Unnero offered. "The witch you let walk out of Ursal."

The two men stared hard at each other, and Aydrian was the first to blink. Perhaps De'Unnero was right here, he knew. Perhaps, in his supreme confidence, he had erred in allowing his mother to walk free. Was she now using her soul stone to scout out the regions along the coast where Midalis could safely strike? Had she gone so far to the south as to recognize the situation in Jacintha, and then guide Prince Midalis to the side of Brynn?

It seemed a bit of a stretch to Aydrian; there were great limitations to spirit-walking, after all. But still, something was obviously going on here.

"Behren and To-gai are no longer involved in our struggles," Aydrian explained to the two men. "I have signed a treaty with both Brynn Dharielle and the representative of Jacintha."

"If they hold to it," Duke Kalas murmured.

"Brynn Dharielle's word cannot be questioned," Aydrian countered. "She has agreed that To-gai will not go to war with Honce-the-Bear, and so they shall not. As for Behren, by all reports, the people there are too busy battling with each other to turn their eyes to the north."

"Then we need not fortify Entel, beyond a force that could repel Prince Midalis," Kalas reasoned.

"Entel is secure," Aydrian assured him. "Prince Midalis will not engage us fully at this time. His strategy is to strike where we are weakest and then to run away."

"He is trying to erode support for you among the people," De'Unnero reasoned. "He is trying to make sure that they understand his viability as their king."

"And to counter that, we need a more substantial victory than the prince could ever hope to gain," said Aydrian. He pointed straight out the door, across the fields to the distant gray-brown structure of St.-Mere-Abelle. "We need to overrun St.-Mere-Abelle, and soon," he explained. "Once the abbey is ours, my armies will be free to fortify the coastline more completely. Where then will Prince Midalis strike?"

"The monastery is already isolated from him, my King," Duke Kalas said, his shoulders going back, chest puffing out as he reported the good news. "St.-Mere-Abelle's docks are in ruin and any ships coming in will be under constant barrage from the cliffs, north and south. Our Palmaris warships huddle beneath the shadows of those batteries. Any attempt by Prince Midalis to come in will prove costly to him, I promise you."

"We have softened the defenses of the abbey, as well," De'Unnero added, and from the look Kalas shot him, Aydrian understood that the monk was speaking up to make sure that he was included in the dispensing of glory. "The brothers within have been awakened every morning by the thunder of boulders and the smell of burning pitch."

Aydrian nodded, pleased by it all. He had little doubt that his army could overrun the abbey, especially with him there, neutralizing the magical response from the Abellicans and mounting more devastating attacks, as well. But he understood, too, that the defenses of St.-Mere-Abelle were as much underground as above, a network of tunnels and fortified subchambers. Aydrian believed that he could get through the gates easily enough—hadn't he done just that against Palmaris? But he understood that the struggle to secure control of the monastery could be long and troublesome.

The young king had been stung quite a bit of late and wanted to proceed with all caution in this most important of all battles. Abbot Olin had failed him and Prince Midalis had surprised him repeatedly.

He could not let that happen again.

Late that day, while De'Unnero, Kalas, and the other commanders began their planning and preparation for the assault on the monastery, Aydrian retired to a darkened tent. He set up his Oracle mirror and sat across from it, staring into its depths, asking himself the many questions concerning the prince's uncanny ability to strike just beyond his reach and to join in wherever he was most needed.

For a long time, nothing really sparked in Aydrian's mind. He kept imagining his mother's spirit, flying across the lands, gathering information for
the prince. But how had she known to go to Brynn? And how had she con-
tacted Brynn completely enough to coordinate any action, as surely seemed
the case, since all reports had the To-gai-ru and the prince's fleet arriving at
precisely the right times to unhinge Jacintha.

A memory flashed in Aydrian's mind, a recollection of his first real battle
with Lady Dasslerond. She had used her magical emerald that day to distort
the ground beneath them, to pull him back to the edge of Andur'Blough
Inninness.

The emerald.

It all made sense, then. The scattered Touel'alfar were not in hiding, but
had joined in the cause against him!

Aydrian's eyes popped open. Could it be true?

The young king fished about immediately for his soul stone and soared
out from his tent in spirit form. If he was correct, then surely he could find
some evidence near the primary points of importance, St. Gwendolyn and
Pireth Tulme.

Near St.-Mere-Abelle.

It took Aydrian a long time that night to locate the spy. He followed the
sensations of life offered by the stone, those same sensations that invited an
out-of-body spirit to attempt possession of any living, reasoning being it
passed near.

And then he found her, To'el Dallia, not far from St.-Mere-Abelle's
northern wall, studying the artillery Duke Kalas had put in place to cover
the coastal approach.

Without going near to the elf, Aydrian soared back to his body and again
popped open his eyes wide.

The Touel'alfar were spying for Prince Midalis. Those wretched little
elves were working toward Aydrian's demise!

But now he recognized that, and now, perhaps, there might be a way
when he could use those spies against the prince. A swirl of possibilities filtered through his thoughts, and he knew that he would have to spend some
time in planning this carefully.

How could he end this war, here and now?

Aydrian wasn't quite sure of the particulars, of course, but he was determined to see it through. He wanted to be done with St.-Mere-Abelle and
put De'Unnero firmly in place. He wanted to be done with Prince Midalis
and get on with solidifying his kingdom so that he could again turn his attention to the southland. He wanted most of all to be done with his troublesome mother. He had sent her away and had wanted her to just go find a
place to hide, that she might wither in misery. Her resilience had surprised
him, but more than that, it had angered him.

He wanted to make her pay.

He went back out in spirit form almost immediately, flying fast to the northwest, back to a place he knew in the region of the small town of Dundalis.

Soon, he was looking down upon a pair of rock-piled cairns, one for his great-uncle Mather and one for his dead father.

The spirit of Aydrian called out to the nether realm.

Even as Aydrian's spirit reentered his corporeal body, a rock on that Timberland grave shifted and rolled away, and then another.

Positioning

ydrian didn't explain his plan to Duke Kalas, figuring the man, who knew little outside the domain of Ursal's noble court, simply would not understand the nuances of it. He did tell De'Unnero, though, and the monk smiled wickedly.

"It is no wonder then that Prince Midalis knows exactly where to strike," De'Unnero said. "I have never been fond of those troublesome winged creatures!"

"Believe me when I tell you that your animus toward them is far less than my own," Aydrian dryly replied.

"You will possess them?"

"I . . . we, will deceive them," Aydrian explained. "And I will ensure that the deception is not discovered until it is too late for Midalis."

"You bring all of your enemies together," the monk mused. "Is that wise?"

"Do you believe that St.-Mere-Abelle can stand against us?"

"Of course not."

"And do you believe that Prince Midalis and his pitiful few thousand will truly trouble Duke Kalas and his skilled warriors?"

The monk pondered that one a bit longer. "Do not underestimate the Alpinadorans," he warned. "And there is the not-so-little matter of . . ."

"My mother," Aydrian finished. "Yes, I know. And have faith that I understand how to take that one from the battlefield—heart, soul, and body."

"You have underestimated her before."

"True enough," Aydrian admitted. "I should have followed your advice and done away with her back in Ursal. She is more resilient than I believed."

"Perhaps that is where her son inherited such admirable traits," De'Unnero replied, and Aydrian rocked back on his heels at that. Had the monk just complimented him? Truly? Things had been so icy between them since Aydrian had announced his intentions toward Sadye that Aydrian had wondered if the rift ever would mend.

But now he saw the truth of it, and upon reflection, he found that he was not surprised. De'Unnero had loved Sadye—likely he still did—but he loved power more. Aydrian, and not Sadye, was the promise of that power.

"Abbot Olin is held prisoner by the Yatols of Jacintha, or by Brynn Dharielle of To-gai," he said. "I expect that he will be returned to us as soon as our business with Prince Midalis is completed."

"Do you ask what I wish done with him?"

"You are the Father Abbot of the Church of Honce-the-Bear," Aydrian stated flatly. "Once St.-Mere-Abelle is ours—within the week, I would expect—there will be no opposition to your rule. I will defer to your judgment concerning old Abbot Olin, though I am far from pleased with him at this time."

"What would you advise?"

"Give him Behren once it is taken and secured," Aydrian replied. "He loves the southland and, as you taught me, it is always best to place your resources in those areas of their greatest desire."

The double meaning of that turned phrase was not lost on De'Unnero, obviously. He quieted and settled back, staring hard at Aydrian.

Aydrian thought to push the point, but changed his mind. There would be no resolution here, the young king understood. Marcalo De'Unnero had gotten past the outrage concerning Aydrian's affair with Sadye, but the simmering anger remained.

Obviously so. Aydrian knew then to keep the monk's focus on the goal at hand, St.-Mere-Abelle, and to keep Sadye and De'Unnero as far apart as possible. In that light alone, the two could continue to work together effectively.

"Construct the house on the northwestern end of the encampment," Aydrian explained. "Tell the workers the importance of the structure they build, that it will be the command post for all of our operations in the region."

"Place the bait," De'Unnero agreed, and he went out and started the work immediately.

Aydrian went back to his own tent, then, where Sadye waited. She started to ask him about his conversation with Marcalo, but he didn't really want to talk about that at that time. He didn't want to talk about anything; he just wanted to enjoy the woman, whom he considered among the greatest gains he had made.

Later on, with construction on the house under way, Aydrian went out with his soul stone and scoured the area, locating To'el Dallia once again and taking heart that she was already looking toward the work area.

Aydrian went out in a wider arc, then, ensuring that no other Touel'alfar were about. Then he flew far out to the west, halfway back to Palmaris, and scoured that area, as well. For this would be the march and turn of Duke Kalas, the ruse, and prying eyes might ruin everything. He did indeed find an elf, resting in the low boughs of an evergreen tree.

One more stooge.

*   *   *

The fleet sat quiet, bobbing slightly on the tiny swells of the Mirianic, the tall trees of the coastline just west of the tip of the Broken Coast barely visible in the south. Fresh from their victory over Pireth Tulme, Midalis' men were itching to go ashore once more. But no new reports had come in from Belli'mar Juraviel, and Midalis would not go in blindly.

He stood on *Saudi Jacintha's* deck that summer morning, leaning on the rail. Liam O'Blythe, his dear old friend, was there with him, offering silent support.

Midalis greatly appreciated the man, and all the others who were so willingly following him along this desperate course. And it was indeed desperate, he knew. Even with the allies he had found, even with the victories he had stolen, the specter of Aydrian seemed far beyond him. Juraviel's assessment of Aydrian's armies named them as perhaps the greatest the world had ever known. How could Midalis hope to counter that?

The song of Bradwarden filtered past him then, calming his nerves and reminding him even more vividly of the extraordinary friends he had found. The centaur stood on deck amidships, Pony and the captain beside him, taking in the warm air and the brief respite; and his song only added to that sense of calm, and seemed as if it softened the waters below, as well.

So much starker then came the call of the lookouts, one ship after another, sighting a great winged form gliding in over the water.

"Brynn and the dragon," Pony said, rushing up beside the prince and Liam.

"And Roger, too, let us hope," Midalis replied.

The great wurm soared past the ships, banking and running the line of them—and more than a few lifted bows or spears its way!

Sighting Midalis and the others, Brynn and Pagonel brought Agradeleous down low beside *Saudi Jacintha*. The dragon hooked the rail with his great claws and held aloft there, beating his wings, as his two riders leaped down upon the deck.

"Where is Roger?" Pony asked before they could even exchange formal greetings.

Brynn looked to Pagonel.

"Your son would not deal for Abbot Olin," the mystic explained. "Roger remains his captive in the city of Palmaris."

"I must go there," Pony said, and she turned to Bradwarden and Prince Midalis, pleading with them. "As soon as Juraviel returns to us, I will have him usher me away to Roger's side."

"Roger won't be liking that," Bradwarden dared to reply. "If ye bring the elf and yerself into danger, ye might be costing us more than ye know. He got caught freeing Braumin, yes? And I'm thinking that yerself and Juraviel are more important to the cause than our friend the bishop."

Pony had no answer, other than to glare at the centaur.

"To-gai and Behren are at peace with Honce-the-Bear?" Prince Midalis inquired of Pagonel.

"The treaty has been signed by all parties," the mystic replied. "Though we fear that if Aydrian proves victorious up here, he will again turn his eyes our way."

"No doubt."

"Brynn has ceded the throne of To-gai," the mystic went on, and that brought surprised expressions from all the onlookers. "Her calling is to avenge Lady Dasslerond and Andur'Blough Inninness, and she cannot involve her people in such a desperate struggle. To-gai is at peace with Honce-the-Bear, but the former leader of To-gai most certainly is not at peace with King Aydrian."

"You have come to join in our cause?" Midalis asked, and there was no hiding the hopefulness in his tone.

"If you will have us," the mystic answered.

Prince Midalis looked all around at the nodding heads and the widening smiles. Fine allies, indeed! "Brynn will fight against Aydrian, to punish him for his actions," the prince reasoned. "Why will Pagonel fight?"

"I fight for my friend, Brynn Dharielle."

"And why him?" the prince asked, motioning with his chin toward Agra-deleous, who had dropped off the ship and was sitting in the water, seeming like some great lizard-headed gull.

Pagonel gave a little laugh as he regarded the wurm. "Agradeleous just likes to fight," he admitted.

Prince Midalis thought on that for just a moment, then realized that if such was the case, better that the formidable dragon was fighting for him!

The direct line took the undead creature right through Dundalis, and so through Dundalis it walked, that dark night. A handful of men out enjoying some drink and the comfortable summer air saw it coming down the road from the north, and hailed it, thinking it a traveler.

It didn't answer—it couldn't, of course—but just kept walking, north-west to southeast, along the road when the road happened to be under its stiff-legged stride, across undergrowth and farms when it was not.

The men hailed it again and moved to intercept.

"Hey there, ye can'no just be walking into town unannounced and all!" one warned.

The undead creature's pace was not swift, and so the men easily moved before it.

It didn't slow, didn't even seem to notice them.

One held out his arm to block, ordering the intruder to stop again.

He got slapped aside, knocked fully ten feet through the air by a single swipe of the powerful creature's arm.

The others moved to attack, but then the creature moved before the light coming from the hearth of one house, and they got a better look at it.

As one, they fell back in terror, crying out in shock and surprise. There wasn't a religious man among the group, but more than half made the sign of the Abellican evergreen in that moment of horrible revelation, and every one called out for help from God.

But the zombie wasn't interested in them. It just kept walking, northwest to southeast, the direct line to the call of its master.

"This is outrageous!" Duke Kalas roared, and he slammed his fist on the table. "Our greatest enemy stands before us, and you would send me and my legions away? What foolishness is this?"

Aydrian stood across the table from Kalas, his chin in one hand. He fought hard to keep the grin off his face, for Kalas was unwittingly playing his part perfectly for the elven audience Aydrian knew lurked just outside the house. He had watched To'el Dallia, his former instructor in Andur'Blough Inninness, very carefully over the last few days, waiting for her to drift toward the new structure near the Kingsmen line, the house that he had obviously constructed as his field throne room, his command center.

Aydrian had also tried his best to monitor the movements of Prince Midalis after the second fall of Pireth Tulme, and he was reasonably certain now that the prince and his fleet were sailing the waters much closer to St.-Mere-Abelle.

In perfect position for the timing of this deception.

"I will not need your thirty thousand to sack St.-Mere-Abelle," Aydrian replied to the duke. "With my five thousand and the war engines, the abbey will quickly fall. That frees you up to begin the great march, to Palmaris and then to the north and east, to Vanguard itself. Prince Midalis cannot hope to oppose you, wherever he might land."

"You take too great a risk," Duke Kalas warned. "St.-Mere-Abelle is formidable beyond your expectations! Never has the abbey fallen in all its long history, and greater forces than yours have arrayed against it."

"But never a force led by one as potent as I in the use of the gemstones," Aydrian explained. "Nor as proficient in defeating the monks' use of the stones. There are no more than seven hundred monks inside of St.-Mere-Abelle at this time."

"And a like number of peasants, if not more," Duke Kalas added, and Aydrian shrugged as if that hardly mattered.

"If I can minimize the monks' gemstone use, we will get through the door, and once that has happened, the monastery will quickly fall," Aydrian reasoned.

"The monks are well trained in conventional battle," Kalas warned.

"Some are fine fighters," De'Unnero agreed. "But most are nominal, at best. King Aydrian and I will find the leadership of St.-Mere-Abelle and decapitate the abbey. Many of the lesser monks will then likely come to see the truth of the new king and the new Church. To do otherwise would be disastrous for them, would it not?"

Duke Kalas continued to shake his head. "Let us overrun the monastery together, in the morning," he offered. "Once that is done, we can better plan the downfall of Prince Midalis."

"That has been our error all along," Aydrian replied. "We have kept our forces too bunched. That is why Midalis has been able to find places at which to strike around our edges. No, it is time to sort our armies into mighty parts. And I am not ready to go against St.-Mere-Abelle quite yet. Even now, I am quietly spying on the brothers within, to learn how best I can exploit their weaknesses. I will destroy the remnants of Fio Bou-raiy's Abellican Church in one week, I expect, but by then, I would have you storming north of Palmaris with twenty thousand warriors. Your other ten thousand are to be dispatched south and east, with three thousand strengthening the garrison of Entel and the other force to patrol the Mantis Arm and the Broken Coast. I doubt that Midalis will land again in the southland when he learns of your march to crush his home, but if he does, we will be ready to meet him quickly and decisively."

"My King . . ." Duke Kalas began to argue, but Aydrian was hearing none of it.

"That is my decision," he said, ending the debate. "I and my five thousand will be rid of the brothers within St.-Mere-Abelle. Then I will instate Marcalo De'Unnero as the Father Abbot of all the Abellican Church and reposition my warriors as I see fit. I hope to join you in Vanguard, my friend, that I can share in our most glorious victory, but I bid you not to wait for me. Let us be done with this, all of it."

"Yes, my King," Duke Kalas replied.

Aydrian nodded and offered a smile, but mostly, he was smiling because he knew that To'el Dallia was likely already on her way to report the momentous happenings.

And the apparent hole in his defenses.

"Your son has erred, and greatly, it would seem," Prince Midalis said to Pony and the others when Juraviel delivered the startling news of Aydrian's redeployment the very next day.

"I have heard the details of the way he overran Palmaris," Captain Al'u'met offered. "I doubt St.-Mere-Abelle will stand against him for long, even with his reduced force."

"But he has exposed himself, and he alone is the source of opposition to my rule," Prince Midalis explained.

"Five thousand," Andacanavar said. "His force is still more than equal to that which you hold at your disposal, and it is headed by the powerful young king."

"True enough," said Midalis. "But we have a pair of rangers of our own." He looked from Andacanavar to Brynn Dharielle. "To say nothing of Jilseponie and the dragon!"

"Forget not the Jhesta Tu who walks beside you, good Prince Midalis," Brynn added after the mystic had translated the prince's words to her.

Pagonel bowed to her before relaying her words to Prince Midalis.

"If we sail quickly and land ashore directly opposite the peninsula from St.-Mere-Abelle, we will arrive on the field before Aydrian's attack," Prince Midalis reasoned. "How much will our arrival bolster the confidence and effectiveness of Father Abbot Bou-raiy and his minions as they ward the assaults of the warrior king?"

"And if we fail, then all is lost," Pony pointed out.

"And if we do not take this opportunity, will we ever again be presented with a chance as great?" Prince Midalis replied. "Duke Kalas marches with an army that is far beyond us. If we retreat now and continue to strike at lesser targets, then St.-Mere-Abelle will fall, as will Vanguard. What is then left to us? Are we to sail forever about the coastline, stinging the king? Certainly, he will build another fleet in time, and likely a stronger one; then even the waters of the Mirianic will no longer be a haven."

The man paused and took a deep breath, then moved right before Pony, placing his hands on her shoulders and locking her gaze with his own. "He has erred," the prince explained. "He underestimates us and our information gathering. He has left himself vulnerable before the gates of St.-Mere-Abelle. Let us strike at him even as he tries to topple the Abellican Church. If we can defeat him and ki . . ." He paused again and sighed.

"And kill him," Pony finished.

"Or capture him," Prince Midalis added. "Then will Duke Kalas continue to support him? Will any of the nobles? And more importantly, will the people of Honce-the-Bear be so eager to rush to his cause? We have already discussed at length that Aydrian's greatest advantage in this has been his proximity to Ursal, while I was far away in distant Vanguard. The people didn't oppose him because they saw no alternative to King Aydrian, and had no way to believe that they could do battle against Duke Kalas and his Allheart Knights. Without Aydrian, his entire false 'kingdom' crumbles. I will be accepted as the rightful king of Honce-the-Bear—even Duke Kalas will have no choice but to admit the truth of it."

"With that many soldiers in his ranks, he might be thinking to make a try for the throne himself," Bradwarden remarked.

Midalis turned to the centaur, shaking his head. "That is not in the character of Duke Kalas," he explained. "He is an Allheart Knight, first and foremost. If we defeat Aydrian here and now, the war will be over and the kingdom will be returned to the line of Ursal."

He stopped and looked around, his expression asking them all for opinions.

"We'll not find a better chance, then," Andacanavar said.

"Let us be done with this," Pony added, eerily echoing the words her son had spoken only the day before.

With Pony's support, not a word of argument came from any of those present.

Within the hour, the fleet of Prince Midalis was on the move once more, sailing west around the tip of the peninsula that held St.-Mere-Abelle along its eastern arm.

At that same time, Duke Kalas and his army of twenty thousand were fast-marching toward Palmaris. By then, however, Aydrian had let Kalas in on his little secret concerning the Touel'alfar spying.

The duke would move west for three days, then pivot back to the northwest.

For by then, Aydrian would know Prince Midalis' intent and landing point.

Duke Kalas would close the vise.

Aydrian spent the next days preparing his force for the attack on the abbey. In the nights, however, the young king went out spiritually to check on the movements.

He didn't bother scouting to the east and south, for the redeployment of the ten thousand to those locations was an honest one, and any spies reporting in would only confirm what To'el Dallia had no doubt relayed to Prince Midalis.

Mostly, the young king scouted about the coast near to St.-Mere-Abelle, and when he found sunstone resistance to his spirit-walking presence in some areas, he had a fair idea of where the prince was heading.

The young king wasted no time in relaying the information to Marcalo De'Unnero, who, in weretiger form, had little trouble in catching up to Duke Kalas' army with the news.

De'Unnero walked into Kalas' tent the evening of the second day after Kalas' departure from Aydrian's ranks.

Before the break of the next dawn, the duke split his ranks and sent a group to the north, marching them fast for the coast, toward the region where Aydrian was now certain Midalis would land.

Midalis would beat Kalas' expeditionary force to that spot, but that was the plan. Let the prince and his forces charge across the peninsula to do battle with Aydrian, while Duke Kalas quietly pursued him from behind.

Aydrian knew it, De'Unnero knew it, and Duke Kalas knew it. Once Prince Midalis came ashore and marched away from his boats, he had nowhere left to run and nowhere left to hide.

The great river hardly slowed the progress of the undead creature. Moving unerringly to Aydrian's call, the zombie walked right into the Masur Delaval. It drew no breath, and so had no air within its form and was not lifted by the water. The currents did drag on it, but they were no match for the strength of the zombie.

Straight was its march.

Straight to Aydrian, its master, who ruled Honce-the-Bear and who ruled the netherworld.

❖ 44 ❖

Maelstrom

Something felt wrong to Pony as she came ashore that midsummer day. All of this desperate plan didn't seem to fit well in her designs for the kingdom of Honce-the-Bear. She had gone out spiritually with the soul stone even as *Saudi Jacintha* had rounded the peninsula's tip, and everything she had been able to discern had seemed confirmation of the conclusions of Juraviel's scouts.

And yet, something just didn't *feel* right to her. It was more than her remorse at not being able to run right off to free Roger Lockless, she knew, and she was not the only one feeling this unease. Even Symphony, freed at last from his confinement aboard *Saudi Jacintha*, snorted and shook his head nervously, and seemed to jump at every touch.

"The great stallion fears this move," Pony remarked to Bradwarden. "I feel it as well, a sense of dread."

"I'm not for arguin' with ye, girl," the centaur replied. "But I'd be thinkin' ye were daft if ye weren't feeling that way. We're taking a mighty gamble here and puttin' all our money on the table."

Pony listened and absorbed the truth of his words. This sortie was different, and more dangerous than anything they had previously attempted. When they had struck at Pireth Tulme and at St. Gwendolyn, even when they had gone to Jacintha to oppose Abbot Olin, they had never moved inland more than a couple of hours' march from their ships and the safety of the Mirianic. Now, though, they were soon to be hard-marching away from the coast for three long days, opening more than fifty miles of ground between themselves and their boats.

"And now we're to face him," Bradwarden remarked a moment later, drawing the woman from her thoughts. "Yer son. Ye're to go against him directly for the first time since he chased ye from Ursal. That's got ye afraid, and rightly so."

"So you believe that we must simply trust in Juraviel's scouts?" Pony asked.

"I'm thinking that if they're right, we've got ourselfs a better chance now than we might ever be seein' again. If yer son's grown too confident and has made a mistake, then we'd be fools not to charge in now." The centaur gave a little chuckle, looking down at her from his full height, and finished, "How dark's the world to be if St.-Mere-Abelle falls to him and to De'Unnero?"

His words were true enough, Pony knew, so she simply nodded and swallowed her uneasiness.

Soon after, she was right beside Prince Midalis, Bruinhelde, and Andacanavar, leading the march across the peninsula.

They charged up the coast with a single purpose: to find the place where Prince Midalis had come ashore. Led by Sir Blaxson of the Allhearts, this splinter group of three thousand warriors knew that they would not be a part of the glorious battle that would soon occur at St.-Mere-Abelle. But they knew, too, and to a man, that their mission here was vital to their king's success.

There must be no escape!

Sir Blaxson understood the great risks involved—his force was in many ways in more peril than Aydrian's own army. Duke Kalas has explained the plans to him, and Sir Blaxson was a seasoned enough warrior to understand that in good part the strategy pivoted on timing and a guess.

Would Prince Midalis really take the bait King Aydrian had offered?

Would the prince come ashore as predicted, and in the time period predicted? For if that was not the case, Sir Blaxson and his soldiers might find themselves face-to-face with Midalis himself, along with an army larger than Blaxson's own, and one that included Jilseponie Wyndon!

Sir Blaxson had warned his men of the potential battle they faced, and his pride had only multiplied ten times over and more when the warriors under his command had taken up the call of King Aydrian and had pressed on more urgently, double-timing their march throughout the day, from long before the dawn until long after the sunset.

They found their reward on the second day after they had splintered from Duke Kalas, their fifth day away from St.-Mere-Abelle. In a sheltered cove only a short distance up the western shore of the All Saints Peninsula, they found the fleet of Prince Midalis.

Alpinadoran longboats had been drawn up onto the shore, while the greater sailing vessels sat at anchor in the distance.

Nearly three hundred men, hardy Alpinadoran warriors all, guarded the beached boats.

When his scouts returned to report the sighting, Sir Blaxson didn't hesitate, forming his line.

"Our duty is here and now before us," he told his men, riding his To-gai pony up and down the length of that line. "The former prince has brought an invader to our fair shores: an Alpinadoran foreigner. A barbaric invader!

These northmen know no quarter, no mercy, and no decency. They will kill our people indiscriminately; they will take our women back to their cold wasteland to serve as bed warmers!

"We must turn them now!" Sir Blaxson cried. "We must kill the barbarians and destroy their vessels. Damnation awaits Prince Midalis for bringing these murderers to the fair shores of Honce-the-Bear! And King Aydrian will deliver him to that damnation, alongside all the traitorous rabble who have joined him!"

The warriors cheered his every word, their excitement building, the sense of righteousness overflowing.

"Death to the barbarians who dare come south to spoil our lands, our women, our children!" Sir Blaxson cried, and he turned his pony to the north, drew forth his sword, and pointed the way.

The charge of three thousand warriors flowed over the high bluffs just south of the sheltered cove, descending fast upon the surprised Alpinadoran guards. Kingsmen archers filled the air with deadly missiles. Sir Blaxson sent his infantry down first, the soldiers breaking left and right as they neared the barbarian line, for through the center came the cavalry charge.

To their credit, the Alpinadorans did not break ranks and flee. In concert with their proud heritage, in agreement with the tenets that guided their warrior existence, they took up their weapons and joined in a song to Dane Thorrson, their god of battle. Side by side, they met the attack with a wave of thrown hammers, then with their own muscle.

Against the infantry, the great warriors of the northern lands killed two Bearmen for their every loss, but strong as they were, the Alpinadorans had no answer for the heavy Kingsman and Allheart cavalry. Even to the sides of the devastating cavalry charge, the Alpinadorans were swarmed and brought down, for the army of Sir Blaxson outnumbered them ten to one.

Few of the Alpinadorans fell wounded, for they fought until all life had left their tall, muscular frames. Those wounded few were shown no mercy by Sir Blaxson, nor did a single Alpinadoran ask for such.

They were put to the sword, joining the dead on the blood-soaked beach.

The task was not finished, however, and Sir Blaxson ordered his men to destroy half of the forty longboats. The other half were dragged back into the surf, manned by Bearmen warriors.

Out they went for the anchored, and barely crewed, warships.

A couple, including *Saudi Jacintha*, raised their sails and headed out. One even managed to begin firing its catapult at the approaching armada, though to no effect.

One by one, the great ships of Honce-the-Bear were reclaimed in the name of King Aydrian.

Watching from the beach, Sir Blaxson puffed his old chest out in pride every time the flag of Ursal was brought down and the bear and tiger of King Aydrian was run up. Those two or three that managed to get away would be of no consequence, he understood. He had served his king and his duke to perfection.

Now Prince Midalis had no retreat.

"Just as Juraviel informed us," Prince Midalis remarked to the others when they came in sight of the high ground north of St.-Mere-Abelle. There in the distance loomed the unmistakable forms of catapults, and even as they watched, the massive war engines were being turned about.

"It would seem that they have noted our approach," Pony said.

"They'll not turn them in time," Prince Midalis assured her, and he lifted his arm into the air. "Ride on and run on, my warriors!" he cried. "Now is the hour of my ascent!"

Beside him, Bradwarden took up a rousing tune on his pipes. Behind him, Bruinhelde and Andacanavar led the Alpinadorans in a song to Dane Thorrson.

But then they all paused in awe, for before them, a great winged shape loomed up over the distant cliffs and rushed at the artillery emplacement. Bearing Brynn and Pagonel, the dragon soared past the terrified Bearmen, his fiery breath igniting one catapult, his great claws overturning a second.

Bradwarden resumed his song; Bruinhelde began to sing.

On came the prince's charge.

Few of Aydrian's men remained to oppose them, with most fleeing to the south and west. A second pass by Agradeleous set yet another catapult ablaze, and this time, with the prince's army closing fast, Brynn and Pagonel leaped down amidst the terrified and scattering soldiers.

Symphony and Pony were the first to join them, the erstwhile queen wasting no time in flashing off a devastating lightning stroke that splintered the wood of the one remaining catapult. The concussion of the blast dropped a dozen men to the ground; and as one, as they recovered their wits, they threw aside their weapons and begged for mercy.

Pony linked with Brynn and Pagonel, and Agradeleous set down beside them. The devastating group overwhelmed another pocket of defense.

And then Midalis and the hordes were there, tearing through the meager force. The high ground was theirs!

From that vantage point, they could clearly see the northern walls of St.-Mere-Abelle. From that vantage point, they could see the dark swarm of Aydrian's army, west of the main, western gate. The path to Aydrian was at hand.

But then a very shaken Belli'mar Juraviel stepped as if from nowhere into the midst of the leaders, wagging his head in distress. "We have been deceived," the elf wailed. "Duke Kalas has turned!"

All heads swung farther to the west, and soon enough they saw the cloud of dust rising into the air, the approach of a great army.

"How is this possible?" Prince Midalis asked the elf. "Why did your scouts not detect . . ."

"Aydrian," came the elf's simple answer. "Aydrian and his gemstones. We have been deceived."

"We cannot fight them all," Pony remarked.

"If we turn now, St.-Mere-Abelle is doomed," the prince replied.

"St.-Mere-Abelle is doomed in any case," Juraviel noted. "Duke Kalas' army is huge."

Prince Midalis looked all around, searching for answers. He seemed to grow more desperate by the moment, but then Pony put her hand on his arm, forcing him to calm himself and to look at her.

"We have nowhere to run," the woman told him.

Prince Midalis nodded his agreement. "Then let us fight," he replied, his voice full of determination.

"So it begins," Aydrian announced, sitting astride his horse before the gates of St.-Mere-Abelle. He turned to a young monk standing beside him. "You have brought the items as I instructed?"

"Yes, my lord," the man sheepishly replied, and he handed Aydrian a quiver of arrows.

Smiling widely, Aydrian calmly told Marcalo De'Unnero to order the catapults to pound at the door, and to begin the charge for the main gates. Then the young king drew one of the arrows from the quiver and held it up before his eyes, marveling at the small ruby that had been secured to its shaft, just below the arrowhead.

He was still staring at it when De'Unnero returned to his side. "You cannot think to . . ." the monk began, but Aydrian merely laughed, stopping him.

The young king took out a soul stone and pulled his great bow, the bow of his father, from the side of his saddle, and, with a fluid movement, strung Hawkwing.

"I have not practiced my archery as much as I should have," he lamented, as the catapults fired and his warriors took up the charge. With a shrug, Aydrian set the ruby-imbued arrow to the bowstring. "Still, I expect that I can place the arrow close enough to the gate towers to cause a bit of discomfort."

Inside the uppermost open rooms in the gate towers flanking the main door of the great monastery, the brothers of St.-Mere-Abelle responded to the assault with blasts of magical lightning, like blue-white arms reaching down to sting and slam the front ranks of the charging warriors.

In the left-hand tower room, flanking Father Abbot Fio Bou-raiy, Bishop Braumin cheered his brothers on, imploring them to throw every ounce of energy they could muster into their initial blasts. Braumin had seen Aydrian quiet the magical response in Palmaris, after all, and he could only assume that the young king would similarly cover his attackers here.

Father Abbot Bou-raiy also implored the brothers, yelling out to them, reminding them that St.-Mere-Abelle had never fallen and telling them that it would not do so now! From both towers and all along the walls at the front of the monastery came a thunderous response. With gemstones and crossbows, with boiling oil and heavy stones, the brothers and the peasant army fought hard against the crush.

Bishop Braumin did notice the group of figures across the field, watching it all, and he knew that Aydrian and De'Unnero were among them. He took little interest in them, however, for they seemed far out of his magical reach; and so he didn't even see the young king, still sitting astride his horse, lift his great feather-tipped elven bow and let fly a solitary arrow.

The missile, to any who noticed, seemed like nothing at all, a minor bolt amidst a swarm of carnage. It arced perfectly through the morning sky, descending to the open tower top room on the right-hand side of the battered gate. Nor did any of the monks notice the presence that accompanied that missile, the spirit of Aydrian, moving out of body, retaining his connection with the ruby set in the arrow's shaft.

The arrow clicked down against the stone, shattering as it hit the ledge of the great open window in the tower.

And then it exploded, a tremendous fireball blasting through the tower room, silencing the magical defenses of the monks in a burst of sudden and terrifying flame.

"By God," Braumin Herde muttered, stunned by the magical display. The man's knees went weak beneath him as he heard the screams from across the way, as he saw one man and then another leap out of the tower, flames clinging to every part of their bodies. "By God."

"Sunstone shields!" Fio Bou-raiy cried desperately, for when he looked across the field, he could see Aydrian lifting his bow yet again. The monks scrambled to produce the proper stones, but they were not in time.

A second arrow came down from on high, arcing into the courtyard behind the gate itself. The ensuing fireball had the peasant force gathered there in defense of the gate screaming and running, many of them with flames leaping from their clothing, their hair, their skin. Even worse for the integrity of the defense, the flames caught on the great beams holding the door, as well.

"Get some serpentine down there!" Fio Bou-raiy cried. "Get some water down there!"

Braumin Herde, his body glowing blue-white now from a serpentine shield he had enacted, fell over Fio Bou-raiy, and worked feverishly to include the man within the shield, even as the third magical fireball went off, this one blasting through the room that contained the leader.

Braumin flew back from the force of the blow, but held stubbornly on to Bou-raiy, even when they crashed against the back wall. Still holding tight, the bishop climbed to his feet and pulled the Father Abbot up with him, then ushered the man from the burning room, down the tower's spiral staircase, and out of the structure altogether.

"Hold as long as you can, then organize a retreat to the cellars," he instructed Master Machuso out in the courtyard. "We must make them fight for every inch of ground. We must make them climb over the bodies of their dead comrades every step of the way!"

The old master nodded his agreement and ran off, rallying the brothers and the peasants against the unexpected devastation, making sure that the sunstone shields were being emblazed all across the battle zone. And indeed, the next ruby-set arrow that soared in from across the way crossed into an area of antimagic, where Aydrian's spirit was repulsed. The fireball did not explode.

"A conventional battle, then," Master Machuso remarked, and he nodded grimly, certain that he and his brethren could give this enemy all that they could handle with or without magic.

His determination turned to great hope soon after, when cries echoed down from the northern stretches of the monastery wall, heralding the arrival of a second force, led by Prince Midalis.

Aydrian and De'Unnero soon heard the rumors, as well, and soon after that, saw the force of Prince Midalis, charging hard from the north.

"We'll pivot and move them out from the wall," De'Unnero reasoned.

"Then Midalis will flee inside the monastery," Aydrian reasoned. "And that, we do not want."

De'Unnero started away, but Aydrian reached down and stopped him, grabbing him by the shoulder. "Look there," the young king explained, motioning toward the west. "Duke Kalas will see to the army of Prince Midalis."

De'Unnero settled immediately as yet another army made its appearance on the field, charging in hard from the west. Duke Kalas had returned, with a force three times the size of the one Midalis had brought. A quick glance to the north and then back to the west showed the young king and the fierce monk the truth of it. Prince Midalis would not make the gate before Duke Kalas.

"Duke Kalas will have the fight without well in hand," Aydrian assured the monk. "Come, let us go to the gate and see to the fight within."

Aydrian had to walk his horse in a zigzag course to avoid the carnage before the gate and walls of St.-Mere-Abelle. He figured that more than a third of his force of five thousand were down, but he didn't care—for the gate had been weakened, and the defenses were tiring. Connected through his hematite, he could tell that there was some sunstone antimagic about, but it was nothing substantial out here, beyond the gate, and certainly nothing that would inhibit the power of King Aydrian.

Like a wave, his men parted before him, opening a line to the great portal.

Aydrian drew out Tempest and leveled the blade, then sent every bit of his strength into the graphite set within the sword, and a tremendous white bolt of lightning shot forth.

The doors shuddered inward; the great locking beams—weakened by the fires and the press—snapped apart.

The swarm flowed into the courtyard of St.-Mere-Abelle.

"Kill all who will not yield," Aydrian told his men and, flanked by Sadye and Marcalo De'Unnero, the young king walked his horse into the monastery's courtyard.

"We're too late," Prince Midalis lamented when he saw the approach of the huge army, angling to intercept him.

"Flee or fight?" Bradwarden asked.

Prince Midalis turned a steely eyed gaze the centaur's way.

"Fight well and die well!" Bradwarden roared, and he took up his pipes.

The men from Vanguard and Alpinador formed into a defensive square about Midalis and Bruinhelde and the other leaders, setting themselves against Kalas' charge.

An arm of the duke's army swung around to the north to seal off any retreat, but the prince's warriors had no intention of fleeing.

As one, the prince and his forces ducked low, as Agradeleous soared above him, Brynn and Pagonel taking the dragon out in a sudden charge. They got near to the opposing army, with Agradeleous even managing to spew forth his breath at one leading group of soldiers, but then such a hail of arrows reached up at them that Brynn was forced to turned her beast about and fly fast away.

"Well disciplined," Pony remarked to Midalis. "Let us see how they deal with me." She reached forth her arm and jolted the nearest group of infantry with a blast of lightning, all of the men falling to the ground and jerking about wildly.

"Ride with us!"

Pagonel shouted to Prince Midalis as Brynn brought the dragon down beside him. "We cannot fight our way through the whole of King Aydrian's army with any hope of stopping him!"

Prince Midalis looked around at the other leaders.

"Go!" Andacanavar shouted at him.

"Be quick!" Bruinhelde agreed. "We'll give these attackers second thoughts!" The barbarian leader turned to his men, then, and shouted, "Fight well and die well!" And that cry was echoed enthusiastically all along the Alpinadoran line.

Prince Midalis scrambled up behind Pagonel. "Find Aydrian," he bade the mystic and Brynn.

"I can smell him," came the growling response from Agradeleous, and the dragon leaped away.

"Neither is our place here," Belli'mar Juraviel said to Pony and Bradwarden. Even as he spoke, they heard Aydrian's thunder, and the cries from inside the monastery's walls. "He has found his way in!" Juraviel shouted. "We must stop him!"

Pony on Symphony and Bradwarden moved close to the elf, who lifted his open hand, showing the emerald of Andur'Blough Inninness. "You are ranger first," he said to Andacanavar.

The big man hesitated and looked nervously to Bruinhelde.

"Go and kill him in battle!" Bruinhelde said without the slightest hesitation. "I'll die singing your name, mighty Andacanavar!"

A moment later, Belli'mar Juraviel and his four companions took a gigantic step, right past the southern edge of Duke Kalas' approaching forces, to appear near the broken gate of St.-Mere-Abelle.

They charged immediately for that gate, striking hard at the stragglers of Aydrian's force. Behind them, they heard the concussion as Duke Kalas' force collided with the warriors of Vanguard and Alpinador.

Pony tried hard not to hear those cries.

Braumin Herde left Father Abbot Bou-raiy and the others in the great hall of the main keep. The former bishop of Palmaris rushed up the wide stairway and ran along the balcony, then went up again, using a circular stair that would take him to the keep's highest level, and up again along the same stairs to the flat and defended roof of the structure.

From there, he could see the sweep of Duke Kalas' forces, locked in ferocious battle with Prince Midalis' men outside the monastery's walls. From there, he could see the great dragon, three figures atop it, soaring about the battlefield, apparently battling on Prince Midalis' side. Braumin Herde had no idea what the fire-breathing beast was all about, or where it had come from, or why it might be allied with the prince, but he was surely thrilled to discern that it was an ally and not an enemy!

Any hope the dragon inspired could not hold for long, though, for Braumin's gaze was inevitably drawn back within the abbey, where pockets of fighting had erupted in every building and all along the wall. Men were dying by the score, Braumin knew, and there was nothing he could do.

He continued his scan, then froze in place, his gaze settling on a group making its way across the courtyard from the broken gate.

"Who is that?" one younger brother asked of him, following his lead.

Braumin Herde couldn't get the names of King Aydrian and Marcalo De'Unnero out of his mouth. "Our worst nightmare," he did manage to whisper.

"What are we to do, master?" the young monk asked, and Braumin glanced over at him, to see several others staring at him for some guidance here.

"Pray, brothers," he said. "Shoot straight and pray loudly."

With a deep breath, Braumin steadied his feet under him and headed back for the stairway and back into the keep.

"The rat has retreated to his hole, it would seem," Aydrian remarked, motioning toward the solid keep across the courtyard and overlooking All Saints Bay.

"Then let us go and kill the creature," De'Unnero agreed.

Aydrian and Sadye paused then, hearing the pop of bone from their companion. De'Unnero was wearing his monk robe, and so they couldn't see the details of the transformation. Under the folds of that robe, they did see the movement of his limbs, though, as his legs transformed into those of a mighty tiger.

"I will join with you inside," De'Unnero explained, and he leaped gracefully away, sprinting across the rest of the courtyard to the base of the keep's solid wall. With hardly an effort, it seemed, the weretiger leaped straight up, landing lightly on the sill of a second-story window.

With a glance back at Aydrian, De'Unnero slipped inside onto the balcony in the great hall. He moved across to the solid railing and peeked over, looking down upon Fio Bou-raiy, who was seated on the single throne and flanked by several of St.-Mere-Abelle's masters.

De'Unnero glanced about, noting the statues set in alcoves at the back of the balcony. The railing was high and solid, providing good cover, and the monk figured that he could get to the stairs easily enough without being seen.

Looking at the stairs, or more particularly, at the huge circular window set in the wall above them, did give him pause, though. The morning light streamed through that window, that image of Avelyn's upraised arm.

Before De'Unnero moved again, he heard the door in the room below crash open, and he knew that King Aydrian had arrived.

It pained Prince Midalis to leave his men. He wanted to stay, with the dragon and the mystic, and the woman with her devastating bow.

And Brynn was nothing short of amazing, up there on Agradeleous, flying cover for the soldiers battling below.

"I smell him!" Agradeleous cried over and over again.

"Then find him!" Pagonel demanded.

With a flap of his leathery wings, Agradeleous lifted higher into the air, then slowly turned about and fell into a dive past the northern edge of the monastery and down over the cliff facing, gathering speed as he went.

Prince Midalis watched the battle until the dragon dove low, the cliffs shutting him off from his warriors, from Liam O'Blythe and Bruinhelde and all the others.

He could still hear their battle cries, however.

He knew that he had to trust.

They plowed through the confusion at the broken gate. If two warriors trained in *bi'nelle dasada* weren't enough to scatter Aydrian's forces clustered there, the sheer strength of Bradwarden and the well-placed arrows of Belli'mar Juraviel surely were.

Pony rolled down from Symphony, falling into place beside the Alpinadoran ranger. As soon as they engaged a group of opponents together, it became apparent that she and Andacanavar couldn't quite find the level of harmony that the woman had once enjoyed with Elbryan. For the barbarian's sword dance had been adapted to fit his physical size and strength. When a soldier charged at him, he parried with a horizontal blade and quick-stepped back, typical of the dance. But then Andacanavar slid his back foot to the side and stepped out wide. Halting his progress, he reversed momentum, coming across with a devastating slash of his elven greatsword that laid low his foolishly pursuing opponent.

Andacanavar's sidelong step left Pony out alone for a moment against two other warriors, but the woman worked her sword quickly and accurately, turning thrust after thrust with apparent ease.

Then Bradwarden stepped up to fill the void left by the Alpinadoran ranger. The centaur stabbed his huge bow out as if it were a spear, just as one of Pony's opponents broke from her and charged at him. The tip of the bow caught the man just below his breastplate and the centaur drove ahead and up, lifting him right from the ground. Arms and legs flailing, he went tumbling back, and when he finally caught himself and tried to come back in, the centaur had that bow leveled his way, an arrow that seemed more like a heavy spear set on its bowstring!

The man screamed and turned and scrambled past a comrade who was charging in to join the fight.

A slight shift put the arrow in line with this newcomer, and the centaur's arrow blasted through his metal breastplate, lifting him from his feet and throwing him back and to the ground.

Off to the side, Pony parried and retreated, then came back suddenly as her opponent lifted his sword above his shoulder. Her reversed movement, a brilliant execution of the sword dance, was too quick for her opponent even to register it. His eyes wide with sudden horror, the man could not hope to bring his sword down to deflect the thrust.

Pony struck true, her sword sliding into the Kingsman's belly, and he fell away, howling and clutching at the wound.

Another man came in fast for Pony's side, but she turned in time to parry.

He never got that close, though, stopping suddenly and grasping at the small arrow that found his throat.

Pony glanced back over her shoulder and then up, to see Juraviel perched atop one of the huge open doors, bow in hand. The elf offered a wink and a nod.

Even as Pony lowered her gaze somewhat, she saw another man fall away, creased by Andacanavar's slashing sword; then another fell to the great ranger as he came out of the slash and right into a devastating long thrust.

The four could stand there and defeat any who came against them, Pony understood. But that was hardly the point, and killing soldiers unwittingly serving Aydrian brought her no joy, and no hope.

Glancing across the courtyard, she saw a robed figure rise up in a great leap, as if magically, along the wall of the great keep, and she knew beyond any doubt that it could be only one man.

"Get me there!" the woman cried to Bradwarden and Andacanavar, and when they looked her way, she indicated the base of the wall across the way.

"Elf!" Bradwarden called, but when he looked at the open door, Juraviel was not to be found. "The hard way then!" the centaur roared, and he and Andacanavar flanked Pony and started across. Few of the soldiers wanted to face them, obviously, but in the chaos that was the courtyard of St.-Mere-Abelle, some did indeed find themselves caught before the charge of the trio.

Bradwarden simply ran one down, trampling him to the ground.

Andacanavar leaped past the centaur and felled two others with a great sidelong slash.

And Pony fell in behind the centaur, intercepted the thrusting sword of a man thinking to stab at the creature's exposed flank. The woman rolled her sword over the attacker's, then drove it down. Sensing a second attacker coming in at her back, she turned and stepped forward, releasing the sword and snapping her pommel up into the first man's face, staggering him. Then she called for Bradwarden, and the centaur glanced back, shifted his weight to his front hooves, and double-kicked with his rear legs just as the second man went rushing by.

By the time the centaur's back legs touched down, Pony had finished the stunned man off and was already moving past him.

Their swath of devastation got them to the wall in short order.

"Help me," the woman bade them, motioning to the second-story window—the same window through which she had seen Marcalo De'Unnero disappear.

Andacanavar hoisted her atop Bradwarden's back, then spun about to join battle with stubborn pursuers.

"Ye ready?" the centaur asked.

"Go!" came the reply, Pony fishing in her pouch for her gemstones. Bradwarden's buck lifted her into the air, and she caught herself with the magic of the malachite, activating its levitation so that she continued up, up until she had gained the ledge.

She went inside as Juraviel reappeared, fluttering to the ledge to replace her. The elf started to follow her in, but then stopped and turned his attention back to the scene below, where a host of enemies had come suddenly against Bradwarden and Andacanavar.

"Good to have ye back, elf!" the centaur cried as one man, against whom the already-engaged Bradwarden could offer no defense, staggered backward instead of charging in, an arrow sticking out from his forehead.

"Someone has to keep you out of trouble, fool centaur!" Juraviel called back.

*   *   *

"How dare you desecrate this holy place!" Fio Bou-raiy screamed at Aydrian, and the Father Abbot came out of his throne to boldly face the approaching young king even as his fellow Abellicans fell back before the spectacle of the magnificent man.

"Desecrate?" Aydrian echoed. "I am returning St.-Mere-Abelle to its former glory!" He hadn't even drawn Tempest from its sheath, but had slipped a lodestone into one hand. Rather than targeting any metal on Bou-raiy directly, Aydrian focused instead on a plate set at the top of the throne behind the man.

"How dare you?" Bou-raiy yelled again, and he lifted his hand toward Aydrian, revealing his own lodestone.

Sadye cried out, but she needn't have worried, for both men let fly their magical stones at the same time.

Despite his anger, which led him to throw more energy into the stone than he had ever before managed, Bou-raiy's missile clanged against Aydrian's brilliant breastplate, making little more than a loud ring.

Aydrian's stone, though, smashed through Bou-raiy's extended hand, shattering bones and even removing two of his fingers. Then it, too, rang loudly as it smacked against the metal plate on the chair—after blowing a hole through the Father Abbot's head.

"You cannot defeat me, you cannot deny me," Aydrian told the stunned masters as Fio Bou-raiy's lifeless body dropped to the floor.

"Then we shall die, but die in the hopes of salvation!" one of the men cried, and he lifted a stone Aydrian's way.

"And damnation to you and to the cursed De'Unnero!" another yelled.

"Indeed!" came a shout from the balcony overlooking the room, and all turned to see Marcalo De'Unnero, standing at the rail and smiling widely.

Sadye took up a song to the glory of King Aydrian. De'Unnero started along the rail for the stairs.

And Aydrian snapped Tempest from its sheath, and melted one of the masters with a lightning bolt that shook the ground and stunned them all.

Crouched in the shadows behind one of the statues along the backside of the balcony, Braumin Herde, dagger in hand, came out fast right behind the distracted De'Unnero.

Even as he went to strike, even as Aydrian moved to destroy another of the masters and even as that man and his fellows moved to return the attack upon Aydrian, the great circular window, the image of St. Avelyn's arm, exploded inward. Black metal twisted and folded, and shards of multicolored glass showered the room, and the image of the upraised arm was replaced by that of a great dragon, wings outstretched!

Despite the explosion and the appearance of the beast, Braumin held his concentration and followed through with his attack, for to him there was no greater monster in all the world than Marcalo De'Unnero. He thought he had his opening, thought he had his kill, the blade stabbing fast for the fierce monk's kidney, but then De'Unnero's hand snapped around so suddenly! The superb warrior caught Braumin's thrusting arm by the wrist and stopped the attack as surely as would a stone wall.

Braumin Herde cried out but pressed on, diving above that block and aiming his free hand for De'Unnero's head.

But De'Unnero's free hand came about as the fierce monk pivoted to face Braumin squarely, and he easily turned the punch aside.

Braumin's thoughts were whirling, for he knew that he was badly overmatched here. Before he could even recognize what was happening, he found himself free of the clench and the press, as De'Unnero fell back.

His first instincts told him to pursue, but Braumin caught himself and tried to retreat instead.

But too late, for De'Unnero had pulled back only that he could set and leap into a spinning circle kick. His tiger's foot came around behind Braumin's upraised, blocking arms, and caught the bishop across the face, knocking out more than a few teeth and sending Braumin flying to the side, to crash hard against the wall.

Dazed and stumbling, Braumin would have fallen to the floor, but De'Unnero caught him and held him there with a series of vicious and devastating blows that shattered his ribs and cracked his cheekbone.

All the world rushed away from the bishop as blackness leaped up to swallow him.

A scream from a voice that he knew so well tore De'Unnero from his murderous frenzy. There ran Sadye, up the stairs, bleeding from many cuts, her face locked in an expression of terror.

She cried out for help.

She cried out for Aydrian to save her.

She did not call out for De'Unnero, and that realization froze the monk in place. He watched as a lithe, black-haired woman dropped down from the dragon, followed by a man whom De'Unnero recognized as Prince Midalis himself! Neither paid much heed to Sadye, though, as they charged down the debris-covered stairs.

A third figure remained on the great wurm, holding the beast steady—until there came an explosion that eclipsed even the thunder of the dragon's unexpected arrival. A bolt of the purest white light reached up at the beast, blinding everyone in the room. Arcs of energy crackled all about the dragon, and the force of the blast blew dragon and rider right back out the shattered window.

De'Unnero recovered his sensibilities and glanced back to ensure that Braumin wasn't going to be getting up anytime soon. He understood that Aydrian was facing formidable enemies, but still, he would have gone to Sadye and not Aydrian.

If only she had been calling *his* name!

The monk growled and ran to the railing, taking in the scene. He moved to leap right over, to drop the thirty feet to the floor and rush to Aydrian's side, but again he was stopped, by yet another familiar voice.

"Brighter would all the world be if Marcalo De'Unnero had died that day in Palmaris," said Pony.

De'Unnero fell back behind the railing and slowly turned to face his most-hated adversary.

Agradeleous fell from the monastery, twirling weirdly as one wing or another unfolded and caught the updrafts rising along the steep cliff face.

"Agradeleous!" Pagonel screamed in the dragon's ear. "I need you!"

The dark stones of the cliff rushed past; the dark waters of All Saints Bay reached up at them.

"Awaken!" the mystic ordered. "I need you! The whole world needs you!"

Too many rocks loomed below them, Pagonel knew, and he had no hope that either he or Agradeleous would survive the fall. That was to say if the dragon wasn't already dead. For the blast of lightning from young Aydrian had been the greatest show of magic, the greatest show of sheer power, Pagonel had ever witnessed.

"Agradeleous!" he cried one last time before they both would have smashed into the surf and the rocks.

The dragon's leathery wings extended suddenly and the beast arched its back, changing the angle. Pagonel nearly fell as the creature's plummet became a sudden swoop, Agradeleous soaring out fast across the waters.

"I need you!" Pagonel cried into the wind, but Agradeleous seemed not to hear him.

"My mortal enemy!" the dragon roared. "From time uncounted! The demon awakens!"

Those words surely put the mystic back in his seat. "What do you mean?" he shouted.

"As it was eons ago, when dragon and demon shared the world!" the dragon roared on, still seeming not to hear him.

Pagonel continued to scream at him, and finally, the dragon took note and stopped his bellowing long enough to listen.

"What do you mean?" the mystic demanded. "This young King Aydrian, trained by the Touel'alfar, the human son of Elbryan and Jilseponie—"

"Is more than that!" the dragon interrupted. "He is not man, this young King Aydrian! Not wholly so. It is the beast, the mortal bane of dragonkind!"

Pagonel nearly swooned. He remembered the encounter at the Entel house, when Aydrian and Agradeleous had first seen each other, when both had launched into a primal fury at the mere sight of the other! Could it be true?

"Then back to wage battle!" Pagonel cried.

The dragon roared in protest and replied, "Not I!"

"This beast must be defeated!" the mystic argued.

"I cannot help you," the dragon admitted. "He is beyond me. He will dominate my thoughts and turn me against you! I cannot resist him!"

Pagonel absorbed the words and tried to find some answer. He heard the continuing battle up and behind him, within the monastery's wall and without. Men were dying by the dozen, by the score. "Then we must trust in our friends, great Agradeleous," he finally decided. "Then we find our place in saving the lives of men! Take me now, I beg you, to the north and the battle joined! I need your voice, great wurm!"

The dragon banked hard to the left, soaring around back toward shore, aiming for the sounds of battle echoing along the northern stretches of the great and ancient abbey.

The glass seemed not to have touched Aydrian, as if he were somehow proof against it. Brynn and Prince Midalis sprinted down the stairs to stand before their nemesis, while those few remaining masters cowered and crawled away, bleeding and terrified.

"So much for the word of Brynn Dharielle," Aydrian said dryly in the elven tongue. "To-gai will not go to war against me?"

"To-gai does not, and will not," Brynn stated.

"Says their leader as she stands before me, sword drawn!"

"I do not lead To-gai any longer. I have come here in response to your attacks on my other homeland, Aydrian."

The young king laughed at her. "Do not be a fool," he said. "Dasslerond is gone, and good riddance to the witch! The world is ours, yours and mine, to rule as we see fit. You would surrender all of that?"

Brynn leveled Flamedancer his way, and, seeing the motion, Prince Midalis drew out his sword as well. "I will stop you," Brynn promised.

"Yield now and be spared!" Prince Midalis demanded, and Aydrian laughed at him.

Brynn started it with a sudden thrust, stepping forward with all the speed and balance of *bi'nelle dasada*, her sword going for Aydrian's armored belly. His parry was easy enough, but Brynn had expected that, and so she retracted and came ahead aggressively yet again, this time stabbing for his face, and this time setting her magical blade aflame.

But Aydrian was thinking far ahead as well, and he ducked and backstepped, slapping her blade out to the side. He left an apparent opening on his left, one that he knew Midalis would waste no time in exploiting.

But the prince did not understand the enchantment of the lodestones set in Aydrian's shining breastplate. His sword slashed in for Aydrian's shoulder, but a wave of magnetism turned it and Midalis hit nothing but air.

Aydrian's sword arm snapped across, cutting at the prince's forearm, and only Midalis' fine training allowed him to keep his moving arm far enough ahead of that blade to prevent a deep and debilitating cut.

Aydrian didn't follow through anyway, for Brynn remained on the offensive. The young king started bringing his sword back to face her, but turned it tip down and fired off a lightning bolt into the floor that staggered them all for a second and allowed him a breather.

Only then did Aydrian realize how greatly his attack on the dragon had taxed him. He had thrown every bit of himself into that lightning bolt, even beyond a rational level. His hatred of the beast had come from somewhere deeper, somewhere more primal.

He was not too concerned, though, for he knew that his magical energy would soon return, and he held all confidence that he could defeat these two even without the aid of the gemstones.

He parried Brynn's next attack, rolling his blade over hers expertly, and was about to counter when he sensed that stubborn Midalis coming in again at his side.

A quick turn and a riposte had the prince staggering backward.

Aydrian couldn't suppress a smile, for he could already feel his magical energies replenishing, could already feel the tug of the graphite and the ruby set in Tempest's hilt.

Time worked on his side.

Men screamed and died all about it, but the creature didn't notice. Singular in purpose, it walked across the field outside of St.-Mere-Abelle, oblivious to the vicious battle raging, oblivious to the war cries and charge of the Alpinadorans, stubbornly pushing back Duke Kalas' flank. Oblivious to the charge of the Allheart Brigade, which cut prince Midalis' force into two separate groups.

The zombie moved to the gates, to the call of its master.

Nothing else mattered.

Not the arguing below, nor the first sounds of battle, not even the arrival and ejection of the great dragon, could turn Pony's attention from this man standing before her, this man who had killed her beloved Elbryan, this man who had ever been her most hated enemy. She could see De'Unnero's arm transforming into a tiger's paw as he calmly stalked toward her, seeming as focused as she in their mutual hatred.

She lifted her left hand. "Go sleep with the demons," she said.

De'Unnero didn't leap aside, didn't turn away, didn't move to respond.

Pony hit him with a blast of magical lightning, one that burned a hole in his robe and staggered him back several steps. But on he came again, stubbornly, too full of hatred even to care.

She hit him with another blast, but a lesser one, and then they were into it, claw against sword, *bi'nelle dasada* against the man's years of training in the Abellican fighting arts. He was quicker than she, and stronger than she, but the woman managed to keep him at bay with her longer weapon.

She saw an opening and stabbed ahead, but De'Unnero was gone. Simply gone, propelled away by a twitch of his powerful feline legs.

Pony spun and slashed, and when her sword again hit nothing, she sent out a stunning wave of lightning magic, emanating in all directions from her form. She heard a gasp and whirled about, meeting De'Unnero's charge with a slash of her sword that scored a hit on his forearm even as his claw painfully tore at her wrist above the pommel.

The monk retreated, as did Pony, and then De'Unnero leaped ahead suddenly.

Pony fended with a series of sudden and vicious cuts, but again she was forced to retreat, and then again as De'Unnero stubbornly rushed right back at her.

He wasn't trying to score a hit on that next attack, she understood, but rather, was backing her up dangerously close to the wide stairway. Mobility was her advantage against the ferocity of the monk, and he was trying to take that away.

Pony hit him with another lightning bolt, and this one seemed to catch him off guard and stagger him just a bit.

But as much as she wanted to, Pony couldn't exploit that moment of opportunity, for another form appeared at her side, rushing up the stairs and brandishing a sword that she knew all too well.

"Good fortune is mine," the woman muttered under her breath and she swung about to deflect Sadye's awkward attack. She stepped right past the turned blades, right up before the bard, and backhandedly slapped her across the face, and then hit her again. She grabbed the woman's extended arm and turned under it, spinning about and dragging Sadye before her as a shield.

That movement stopped the stubborn De'Unnero in his tracks, and put an expression on his face that Pony hardly recognized. Sadness? Confusion? Surely it was nothing she had ever before seen on the face of the fierce and unrepentant monk.

Pony pushed aside her own surprise and tugged down hard on Sadye's pinned sword arm, twisting it so that she could pull Defender free of the woman's weakened grasp. Even as she executed the transfer, Pony raised one foot to the small of the woman's back and kicked ahead, sending her flying for the floor at De'Unnero's feet. Sadye gave a cry as De'Unnero caught her, and started to reach out as if to embrace him. But with a half twist, the monk callously sent the bard sliding away behind him.

On came De'Unnero again, but now Pony possessed a much finer blade. Her riposte came quicker, and she even scored a slight hit as she backed the monk away several steps.

"By God, what hellish enemies have come against us?" one of the brothers of St.-Mere-Abelle cried when he ran along the courtyard beside some of his brethren, a group led by Master Viscenti.

They all paused and looked to the base of the keep, where Bradwarden and Andacanavar were battling mightily against a host of attackers.

"No enemies!" a jubilant Viscenti cried. "Get to them, my friends! Behold, hope has arrived within our walls!" He looked up from the battling duo and saw another familiar form, crouched in the window, his small bow raining arrows on those who opposed Bradwarden and the great Alpinadoran.

And as they made their way to join the warrior, Viscenti saw yet another familiar figure, a magnificent horse trotting about the grounds, riderless. The last time he had seen Symphony, King Aydrian had been riding the steed. Was it possible that Aydrian had been taken down?

"Well met, little one!" Bradwarden cried when the monks finally got there, adding crossbows and a bit of magic to the effectiveness of the already-devastating duo. "We'll chase them all back, we will!"

"Good Bradwarden . . ." Viscenti started to reply, but the words were lost in the din of a tremendous cry, a voice greater than anything any of them had ever before heard.

"STAY YOUR WEAPON HANDS!" Agradeleous roared as Pagonel took him soaring across the breadth of the courtyard. "WHAT WORTH DYING FOR AYDRIAN OR FOR MIDALIS, WHEN THEY ALONE WILL DETERMINE WHICH LEAVES AS KING? THEY ARE JOINED NOW IN MORTAL COMBAT, AND ONLY ONE WILL EMERGE. STAY YOUR WEAPON HANDS, GOOD PEOPLE. ALLOW THOSE TWO TO DETERMINE WHICH IS KING!"

The beast flew overhead and continued its cry, but pointedly banked away from the tower and flew out to the north, where the fighting raged.

The fighting did calm somewhat, though whether that had anything to do with the actual words of Agradeleous, or simply because so many had dived aside and cowered at the mere sight of the great beast, none could tell.

Aydrian continued the rhythm of the battle quite easily, and felt his magical energies rejuvenating. He parried Brynn's next thrust and brought his sword flashing across to intercept Midalis' slash, and even managed to stab back the other way, piercing the side of an Abellican master who was trying to slip away. The man fell with a groan, and Aydrian spun right back, to parry once and then again, as Brynn pressed the attack.

Aydrian wondered which of his opponents he should destroy with his lightning. Midalis, he supposed, for he held hope that Brynn could be brought over to his side. He started to reach into the graphite set in Tempest's pommel.

But a distraction came to him, a sensation, a call from the netherworld that he could not ignore. Initial surprise and even fear fast gave way to an almost giddy sense of superiority as he recognized the source of that call, as he turned toward the door to see his latest creation of magic walk into the room.

"You have come in with rangers at your side, Prince Midalis," he said. "I salute you in your wisdom of acquiring both my mother and Brynn Dharielle!"

"And Andacanavar, fool Aydrian," Midalis retorted. "Surely you have heard the name!"

"Then all the rangers of all the world are gathered here!" Aydrian replied excitely. "What a wondrous sight! Three for Midalis, for I offer my mother that title, and two for Aydrian!"

"Two?" Brynn asked, and she paused in her attacks and skittered back.

Aydrian spun aside, moving around the back of the blood- and brain-spattered throne, thus changing the angle of battle so that all three turned sidelong to the door, so positioned that all could witness the entrance of the zombie Elbryan.

"What have you done?" Brynn gasped.

Aydrian held up a soul stone and fell into it, bringing forth the energies of the netherworld, and all the room was bathed in shadow, a blackish blue glow that emanated from his hand. That nether energy reached out from Aydrian to the ragged zombie, and the creature stood straighter suddenly, and moved less stiffly, and its wounds seemed to heal, as if the body had begun recomposing itself.

A moment later, the creature seemed not a rotting zombie, but Elbryan again, except that his features were all gray and dark.

"Behold Elbryan, the Nightbird!" Aydrian cried. "Welcome, my father," he said to the specter, and he casually tossed Tempest to his ally and motioned at Brynn, as he ordered, "Destroy her."

Before Brynn or Midalis could begin to ask, the specter of Elbryan launched himself in perfect balance across the way, attacking Brynn with such ferocity and cunning strikes that she had to fall back in full defense.

Aydrian turned on Midalis. "King to king, then," he said, and he pulled Hawkwing from off his back and held the unstrung bow before him as a staff. "Honce-the-Bear is mine, fool Ursal. The time of your line is at its end."

Prince Midalis gave a desperate cry and came on hard.

Those bluish black shadows reached up to the balcony as well, bathing Pony and De'Unnero in their strange and unearthly haze.

Then came the declaration of Aydrian, and both combatants worked toward the balcony, then broke off from combat long enough to view the specter of Elbryan.

"Aydrian," De'Unnero muttered beneath his breath, hardly believing the recklessness of the young king.

But when the worried monk turned back to regard Pony, he understood. All along, Aydrian had insisted that Jilseponie was no real threat to him, and that he knew how to take the strength from her. Now, looking at her bloodless face, her mouth hanging open as if she had forcibly to gasp simply to draw breath, the monk surely understood.

De'Unnero laughed at the woman. "He has the power over death itself," he said, and he began a cautious stalk at the horrified and paralyzed Pony. She seemed so old to De'Unnero suddenly, so weak and even pitiful. "Perhaps one day your magnificent son will retrieve your rotting corpse from the cold ground to do his bidding."

De'Unnero stalked in, and Pony just fell back against the wall—Defender's tip pointing down—not even assuming any semblance of defense.

To De'Unnero, it was almost disappointingly easy.

Agradeleous' cry for a halt in the fighting had less obvious effect on the battle raging outside of St.-Mere-Abelle's wall. Outnumbered, but full of their battle lust, the Alpinadorans brought fire into the hearts of Prince Midalis' forces. And Duke Kalas and his Allhearts were not to be outdone!

The skilled Kingsmen archers did not run and cower, but turned their great bows skyward and sent stinging volleys at the dragon and its rider.

Pagonel, an arrow in his shoulder and another in his thigh, knew that he had to take a different tack. He guided Agradeleous down fast for the center of the fighting, where Duke Kalas and the Allhearts had joined in battle with Bruinhelde and the Alpinadorans. Roaring all the way, Agradeleous skidded down, tearing up the field.

Pagonel jumped from the dragon's shoulder, falling into a roll and then coming out of it in a great leap at Duke Kalas himself. The Allheart couldn't begin to get his sword in line to intercept the unexpected human missile, and could only grab on as Pagonel impacted, the momentum taking them both off the back of the horse to crash to the ground.

"Dragon!" the mystic yelled, and Agradeleous roared out the call for a cessation of battle yet again.

Pagonel had Kalas dead, and Kalas knew it, but the mystic leaped back up, and pulled the stunned nobleman up beside him. "There is no need to continue," he explained. "One will emerge, and he will rule the land!"

"They come to our shore unbidden!" the duke protested, pointing across at Bruinhelde and his companions, but even as he spoke the words, it was obvious that Duke Kalas did not really believe them.

"There is no need!" Pagonel shouted, spinning about to face Bruinhelde, and then Liam O'Blythe, who led the Vanguardsmen. "Put up your weapons, I beg. Let no more blood be spilled this day."

Beyond the immediate area, the fighting continued, of course, and even about the dragon and the mystic, the truce, if it was one, seemed a tenuous thing at best. But the battle had indeed diminished somewhat—both without and within the monastery's walls—and that brought a sense of gratitude and calm to Pagonel, that he had done some good, at least.

She had heard many stories of the great Nightbird in her time with the Touel'alfar, of course, but Brynn could hardly believe the creature's proficiency with the blade. He countered her every attempted thrust easily and efficiently, either gliding back just barely out of reach or shifting Tempest ever so slightly to slide Flamedancer harmlessly wide. Similarly, his own attacks came fast and precise, forcing from Brynn every bit of her energy and expertise. Even then, even fighting as well as she knew that she possibly could, she understood at once that she was no match for this legendary ranger. He was too fast and too skilled—as good with the blade as Aydrian, if not better.

But she fought on anyway, with all her heart and all her skill, and tried not to consider the possibility that even if she somehow managed to get her blade past the seemingly impregnable defenses, it might not harm the otherworldly being!

Across the one-step dais that held the throne, Aydrian was similarly overmatching Prince Midalis. He changed his fighting style now to accommodate a staff instead of a sword: feet wide and balanced and hands set wide on the hard silverel-enhanced wood of Hawkwing, Aydrian's movements became more animated, with broader sweeps and sudden turns that sent the staff into an over-and-under spin, side to side and back and forth.

In light of that continual dizzying display, Midalis was backing before he began any offensive move, and found himself ducking in anticipation of strikes that never came forth.

He thought he saw an opening at last, and gave a cry and charged ahead, but Aydrian laughed at him, easily sidestepped him, and cracked Hawkwing hard across his back as he lumbered past.

Two against two, Midalis and Brynn had no chance.

But then, suddenly, it became four against two, as a roaring Andacanavar and a charging Bradwarden entered the fray!

It was the moment of his greatest satisfaction, the moment in which he would at last be rid of the witch, Jilseponie.

De'Unnero hardly felt the first sting in the back of his neck, but as he reached up instinctively with the hand that was still human, a second arrow stabbed him hard. Furious, the monk whirled, to see a diminutive figure perched on the window ledge, launching yet another stinging bolt his way.

Tiger legs vaulted De'Unnero forward in a sudden rush, and Juraviel simply threw his bow at the wild creature. The elf knew that he couldn't get back outside quickly enough, knew that De'Unnero had him caught side to side, as well. So he took the only possible route open to him by leaping straight ahead and to the floor instead, even as De'Unnero's tiger paw swept furiously at the ledge.

Through the monk's legs went the elf, scrambling and crawling furiously for the frozen Jilseponie.

"Pony!" he cried. "Pony! Now is not the time for weakness! Now is not the time for frailty! Pony!"

His last call came out as a gasp as the tiger's paw swept across, smashing him on the side of the head, sending him spinning across the floor to slam hard into the base of the balcony, where he lay very still.

If the words had not gotten through to the horrified Pony, the sight of her friend being knocked away surely did. Even as De'Unnero rose over her once more, she struck hard with her graphite, lifting him backward with a lightning bolt.

She hit him with another one as she stood straight. Growling ferally, the woman hit him yet again, staggering him.

Defender came up in a flash and Pony threw off all the bonds of fear and uncertainty. She led her charge with yet another lightning bolt, though its intensity was somewhat diminished.

And then she was in close to De'Unnero, stabbing, stabbing and slashing furiously, driving him back, anticipating his every move and beating him to the point.

For De'Unnero, the stunning reversal had him back on his paws. This was not Queen Jilseponie, the aging and weakening widow of dead King Danube. This was not the broken woman who had crawled out of Ursal.

No, this was Pony, the wife of Elbryan, the same Pony who had defeated De'Unnero in Palmaris' square those many years ago, the same young and strong Pony trained and adept in the gemstones and in the elven sword dance.

The appearance of Elbryan had done this to her, had transformed her into a creature of pure outrage.

De'Unnero understood at once how badly young Aydrian had miscalculated.

Even when Andacanavar joined in beside Midalis, the two of them coordinating their attacks brilliantly and in perfect harmony, Aydrian found that he could more than hold his own. Something inside of him surfaced, some primordial, instinctual response that had him flashing Hawkwing all about magnificently, that had him turning and dodging, ducking a great slash of Andacanavar's huge sword and skipping back deftly from Midalis' sudden thrust.

And all the while, he countered with Hawkwing, sliding his hands down low on one end to swing it like a club, or moving the lead hand up suddenly and thrusting forward.

On one such thrust, Aydrian stopped suddenly, slid his hand back, and pivoted about, launching a wide and strong swing that had Midalis caught flat-footed. The prince gave a cry and fell away, but got clipped on the shoulder and had to tumble down, his sword skidding from his grasp.

Aydrian didn't pursue, but turned fast on Andacanavar.

"Your time is past, old man," he said, and he went in hard.

The barbarian started a sidelong slash, but stopped cunningly and reversed his strength, stabbing straight ahead instead.

But Aydrian was already gone, spinning to the side around the blade. He brought Hawkwing across hard, smashing the man's elbows, then retracted and slid his hands apart, stabbing the man hard in the side.

The barbarian ranger's backhand slash almost had Aydrian then, but he went down low and moved across under the slashing blade. Hawkwing took Andacanavar on the inside of the knee, driving his leg out wide and stealing his balance.

Aydrian reversed and stabbed up with the staff, catching the ranger in the groin and lifting him up on his toes. Andacanavar roared and punched down hard, but Aydrian was already moving, diving forward between his legs.

As soon as the young king got his feet under him, he cut back the other way, rushing back behind Andacanavar as the barbarian turned about, his great sword leading.

Now one clean step ahead of his opponent, Aydrian brought Hawkwing across with all his strength, and heard the crunch of bone as the hard wood connected on Andacanavar's skull.

The barbarian spun, and continued spinning, all the way to the floor, blood spilling from his ears.

Figuring the man already dead, Aydrian went in anyway, but had to pull up short and spin back at the attacking Midalis. The prince, off-balance, his sword not even securely back in his grasp, stumbled by and took a solid hit.

Midalis tried to turn as he hit the floor, but Aydrian was there, his leg solidly placed to hold the prince awkwardly, and helpless.

Prince Midalis looked up to realize his doom, the specter of Aydrian, Hawkwing high before him.

And so it ends, Midalis thought.

Across the way, Elbryan's swordplay with Brynn took on a new dimension as Bradwarden joined the fray, the ferocious and powerful centaur sweeping his heavy club to and fro with wild abandon.

"We'll get this one, lassie!" the centaur promised. His club went past the retreating specter, who then reversed his footing and charged in through the opening.

But then Brynn was there, intercepting Elbryan's sword and forcing him to back away quickly as Bradwarden's backhand nearly caught up to him.

"Ah, but we're a fine team!" the centaur roared, although Brynn, of course, couldn't understand a word of what he was saying.

With his typical lack of finesse, Bradwarden leaped ahead and gave a roar, and Elbryan came forward as well, spinning to the side.

Bradwarden tried to turn to keep up with the quick ranger, but his hooves skidded on the blood-slicked floor. He tried to scramble to hold his balance, but futilely, and his back legs went out from under him and down he went.

"I breaked me leg!" he howled soon after the snap of bone echoed through the room, and then another equine form came charging through, inadvertently clipping the centaur and sending him skidding and spinning away.

That charging horse staggered Elbryan and Brynn back, as well, cutting directly between them. The reprieve didn't last for long for the Dragon of To-gai, though, for the specter of Nightbird was right back at her, pressing his attack even more furiously.

Determined to face death boldly, Prince Midalis glared up at young Aydrian. "Never will you be king," he said.

Aydrian brought Hawkwing down.

Or started to, until Symphony charged into him, knocking him to the floor.

Prince Midalis recovered his wits quickly and went for his sword. Aydrian, too, rolled right back to his feet. He held his hematite out toward the great stallion even as Symphony started to turn to charge again, and sent a wave of dominating willpower at the horse, filtering it through the magical turquoise set in Symphony's breast.

Aydrian found that he couldn't so easily dominate Symphony as he once had, but he had the beast stalled, at least, kicking and bucking and throwing its head in protest.

Aydrian was ready for Midalis as the man stubbornly came at him again. He blocked a pair of weak attacks, and thrust his staff hard into the prince's belly, taking his breath and sending him stumbling backward, clutching at his midsection.

"It would have been so much easier and cleaner if the horse hadn't come in," Aydrian remarked, and he stalked in for the kill.

In her rage, it was as if the energy of her youth had returned in full. Pony fought with fury, stabbing Defender all about De'Unnero to keep him off-balance and constantly backing. Every time the monk tried to counter, Defender was there, stabbing hard and forcing him aside, and, every so often, Pony hit him with a lightning bolt, a minor sting to be sure. But these nicks and stings were starting to take their toll on the battered De'Unnero.

And so he gathered up his strength and came at her hard and desperately, knowing that time was not on his side.

But Pony knew that, too, so she was not taken by surprise as De'Unnero leaped forward over her extended sword, pouncing for her head.

She smashed him with a lightning bolt, the force of it catching him in his descent and holding him aloft for just a moment—long enough for the woman to bring her sword above her!

Defender slid in under the descending monk's ribs, up into a lung.

Pony spun out from under him, guiding him to the side with her blade. She pulled the sword free as De'Unnero tumbled down, and stabbed him again and again, gashing his arms, human hand and tiger paw, as he tried to fend her, stabbing his leg hard as he tried to scramble away.

He tried to come up, suddenly, reversing direction, but the infuriated woman was ready for him again, bringing Defender down in a hard slash that tore through skin and smashed the monk's collarbone. As his arm went weak under him, De'Unnero lost his balance and fell down flat on his back.

Gasping for breath, he stared up at the victorious Pony.

"And you think those wounds will heal," she said, and she batted his one blocking arm aside and fell over him, thrusting her hand right into the monk's deepest wound.

De'Unnero gasped again, his mouth twisting in a silent question.

"Do you feel it?" Pony asked him, and she drove her hand in harder. "Do you feel that stone, Marcalo De'Unnero?"

She sent her energy into the stone she held inside the monk's body.

A sunstone.

Pony felt the resistance of the healing magic that had sustained De'Unnero in health and youth for so many years, the magic that had allowed him to recover from the mortal wounds she had inflicted upon him in their fight in Palmaris those years before.

De'Unnero's one working arm, his human arm, snapped up and grabbed her by the wrist.

"This time you are dead, Marcalo De'Unnero," the woman promised, and she growled and drove on, the sunstone antimagic pushing through the monk's healing magical shield.

As if resigned to the truth of her words, De'Unnero let go of her and settled back.

As if somehow pleased by this final ending, the monk looked up at her, his face showing acceptance. He looked her in the eye, nodded, and slumped back.

Pony knew that she couldn't stop there. She spun about, to see Juraviel crumpled against the wall, and Braumin lying on the floor, weeping and curled, and clutching at his many wounds.

She heard the fighting down below, and knew that she had to press on. She moved to the stairs, past the sobbing Sadye, and looked down upon the spectacle—down upon her lost husband, Elbryan, brought forth by the abomination that was her son.

There were still pockets of fighting on the field, and some of it was ferocious, but at the center of the lines, where Bruinhelde and Liam faced off against Duke Kalas himself, all had gone quiet. The dragon stood between the forces, eyeing the Alpinadoran warriors and Vanguardsmen almost as hungrily as he regarded Duke Kalas and his Allhearts.

"There is no need of this," Pagonel continued to insist. "Prince Midalis has joined in battle with Aydrian even now. How many must die?"

"And of what intent are you, should Aydrian emerge from that conflict?" Duke Kalas shouted at the opposing leaders, particularly at great Bruinhelde.

"My warriors have come as Prince Midalis' allies," the proud northman replied. "But if the battle is settled within, then our time here is ended."

"Tell them all to stop," Pagonel shouted to the leaders. "I beg of you to save as many brave men as you can this terrible day!"

Duke Kalas stared at him hard for a few moments, then turned to his leaders. "Tell them to stand down!"

"My lord!" came a protest, but Kalas cut the man short by turning away and holding up a hand.

"If you have deceived me, then know that none of Prince Midalis' followers will leave this field alive," he warned the mystic.

Pagonel more than matched that stare.

Right beside him, Agradeleous lowered his head and gave a low growl, smoke issuing forth from his nostrils.

She started down the staircase, but Pony knew that she could not get to Brynn in time. With Bradwarden out of the fighting, Elbryan was dominating the ranger of To-gai. Tempest slapped once, twice, thrice against Flamedancer, pushing it out to the side, and when Brynn tried to bring it to bear, thinking the specter would take the opening and charge, Elbryan fooled her completely by stepping back instead.

As Flamedancer came across, Elbryan worked Tempest over, down, and then under and up, wrapping the blade and powerfully throwing it out to the side, right from Brynn's grasp.

The woman cried out and charged ahead, knowing that she had to get inside the specter's deadly blade. But Elbryan hardly hesitated, hitting her with a left hook that shattered her nose and sent her staggering to the side and to the floor.

"Elbryan!" Pony yelled, coming down more quickly.

The specter turned to regard her, and a light flared in its eyes as it came to recognize the woman. Abandoning the fallen Brynn, Elbryan stalked ahead for Pony, brandishing Tempest.

Pony knew that she couldn't possibly match this man, Nightbird, blade against blade. Even in life, those years ago, she was not his equal, but now . . .

She went at him in a different manner, falling into her soul stone and sending her magical energy at his spirit with all her strength.

She closed her physical eyes, but watched the approach of his shadowy form, and she knew that she was slowing him, at least.

The woman plowed on, throwing all of her strength at the specter, denying his existence, damning him back to the netherworld. But on he came, and she knew that Aydrian had brought him forth too fully for any hope of dismissing him! She could not deny the strength of the creature, nor could she match it, physically or spiritually!

On impulse, the desperate woman changed her tactics. Instead of fighting against Elbryan, she accepted him, with all of her heart. She searched that shadowy spirit, seeking a spark of light in the darkness.

She felt cold as he came over her, felt the hard stairs against her back, though she didn't even know that she had fallen.

Pony opened her eyes and looked up at the man, his face twisted in rage, Tempest's tip in close to her exposed throat.

"Elbryan," she said softly. "My love."

Tempest began to tremble; Pony sensed a struggle within the creature.

"Fight it," she implored him, and she fell deeper into the hematite and stepped from her body, as if to hug her lover spiritually. *You must resist the call of Aydrian!* she telepathically imparted. *Elbryan, my love! Remember all that you were, all that we were. You know me.*

Tempest began to edge away, and when Pony opened her physical eyes once more, she nearly swooned. For the specter's dark features lightened; its skin shed the gray hue and seemed to come alive! The light of life was coming back to him, undeniably so! Pony looked into Elbryan's eyes, those dazzling green eyes that had so enthralled her from the time she was old enough to appreciate the differences between men and women.

Elbryan pulled back his sword suddenly, instead extending his hand, and Pony took it gladly.

"We have to stop our son," she explained as Elbryan reached up and tenderly stroked her cheek.

"What have you done?" came a shout from below, and the pair turned to see Aydrian standing by the throne. Prince Midalis, battered and bloody, crawled on the floor behind him, seeming senseless.

"What have *you* done?" Pony shouted back.

Aydrian closed his eyes and reached out to Elbryan's hand through the lodestones set in his breastplate, and the ranger, still unsettled and confused, had Tempest torn from his grasp, the sword flying across the way, where Aydrian neatly caught it. "You see?" he boasted. "Nothing is beyond me!" He leveled the deadly sword their way.

Pony desperately reached for her pouch, for her sunstone, but realized that she had left it above, with De'Unnero.

"Now you die!" Aydrian promised, and he sent his great strength into the graphite.

But a flaming sword flashed before him, smacking against his blade, turning it aside, and the tremendous lightning bolt split the marble of the floor and ricocheted about the room.

"The second shadow in the mirror!" Elbryan cried to Pony. "He is as Markwart once was!" He grabbed her hand, then, clutching the hematite with her, and together they went through the gemstone portal, throwing themselves at Aydrian in the realm of the spirit even as Brynn battled him physically.

But the duality that was Aydrian was more than up to the challenge, his sword parrying and countering Brynn's attacks even as the darkness within him fended the spiritual assault of both his parents. Pony went at him physically, then, as well, and the three blades rang so quickly and loudly that it seemed like one long toll of a bell.

Pony tried to stay with Elbryan as well, in that darker realm, but there was no break in the darkness that surrounded Aydrian, no opening for them to reach out to their lost son. Indeed, it was as Elbryan had said, so much like their battle with Markwart, but this time, the darkness seemed even more complete.

They made no headway, with sword or with spirit, and gradually, it was the trio who began to tire, and not Aydrian. Tempest rang out with fury—Aydrian even managed a lightning blast that sent Brynn flying backward and to the floor, though she recovered quickly and rushed back in before the young king could gain an edge on Pony.

Brynn pressed on with Flamedancer, Pony wielded Defender magnificently, and Elbryan, so familiar with that other shadow in the mirror, attacked the young king with all his spiritual sensibilities.

But they were battling a fortress that had no weaknesses, a foe who remained ahead of them every step of the way. A foe who did not tire.

They could not win.

Up on the balcony, the battered Sadye, sobbing and limping badly, slid past De'Unnero and Juraviel, struggling for the stairs. She looked down on the titanic battle and cried out to Aydrian.

"Win, my love!" she called. "Kill them all! Aydrian! Oh, my love!"

Behind her, Marcalo De'Unnero heard her words. Aydrian. Her love.

The monk's eyes snapped open.

Defender and Flamedancer came in side by side, angled so that Aydrian couldn't possibly parry both.

But he did, with a sudden snap and twist of Tempest, and he even managed a slight thrust that backed Pony a step. The young king spun out of the clench and went at Brynn, driving her sword up and to the side.

She turned a complete circuit in response, bringing Flamedancer back around, but Tempest was already there, ringing so hard against her blade that her arm went numb.

Pony came back in hard, just in time to save her, but again Aydrian had little trouble in pushing Defender aside and countering the woman's strikes.

And behind Pony, Elbryan's continuing efforts did little against the wall of darkness that encompassed Aydrian.

Then they all heard Sadye's call, and all but Elbryan glanced back at the stairs to see the battered woman stumbling down, to see a form rush up behind her.

To see Sadye stiffen and arch her back as a sword plunged through her body.

Sadye looked down, confused, her eyes wide with shock. And then she fell, facefirst, tumbling down the stairs, the sword, Pony's discarded sword, still stuck through her.

Standing behind her, his life finally fleeing his corporeal coil, Marcalo De'Unnero tumbled after.

Despite himself, Aydrian could not suppress a cry. And in that moment of pain and shock, in that moment of very human loss, there shone a bright seam in the dark shroud that engulfed his spirit.

Elbryan rushed for the light; Pony felt her lover's spiritual tug and joined him, embracing the light, embracing their son. They called to him and pleaded with him. They offered him the love that only parents might know for their child.

They heard the sneer from within the monster, heard the denial all too clearly.

But they felt, too, the warmth that was within Aydrian, buried so far away by this demonic creature that had somehow found its way into his very being.

And so they grabbed at the light that was not the demon, the light that was the humanity of Aydrian.

Outside that spiritual realm, Brynn saw the young king freeze suddenly, his eyes wide in confusion.

She didn't hesitate, charging right up to him and plunging Flamedancer deep into his chest.

Denial

Pony and Elbryan held on to that spark of light as the dark shroud dissipated. But their joy at seeing their son freed of the demon's grasp was short-lived, for almost immediately, Aydrian's life force began to dissipate as well, sliding down, down to the realm of death.

Pony had felt this loss before, when Elbryan had fallen before the demon within Markwart. She recognized it for what it was, and when she popped open her eyes in horror, she saw Aydrian lying on the floor, his chest gashed with a wound that was surely mortal.

"No!" the woman cried and she fell back into her hematite even as she physically collapsed over her dying son. "No!"

Pony cried for Elbryan to join her, and charged along the swirling gray corridor that descended to the realm of death. She saw Aydrian's spirit drifting ahead of her, falling into death. *Not again,* the woman wailed. She had not saved Aydrian just to lose him now!

But this was not a place of bargaining. This was the realm of death, the realm of finality.

Pony didn't slow, throwing herself down that corridor with abandon, crying out for Aydrian, yelling out in denial at death itself, telling the dark realm that it could not have her Aydrian! Not here and not now!

She was more into the spirit realm than she had ever been, completely detached from her body and unsure that she could even find her way back to it! Might she have doomed herself by chasing Aydrian to this dark place?

Pony didn't care at all, didn't give it a second thought. She chased Aydrian, she caught Aydrian, and she hugged her son close, imploring him to return with her to the realm of the living, and denying the shadowy fingers that grabbed for his spirit.

And then Elbryan was there beside her, beside their son, pulling them both back along the winding gray trail, back to the light of life.

As Aydrian had done with Duke Kalas that day on the field after the tournament, Pony now won out against the nether realm. She pulled Aydrian back to his body; she breathed life into him once more, and even as he opened his eyes, she was there, attacking his wound with her soul stone, finding energy where she had none.

Gasping, Pony again fell over the young man as he curled up, sobbing. His mother lifted her head and looked around the room, to Bradwarden, leaning against the wall for support, with Symphony standing before him, pawing the ground defiantly. To Brynn and Prince Midalis, battered and beaten, watching her with mouths agape. To the dead monks and the large and still form of Andacanavar. To dead Sadye and De'Unnero on the stairs.

To Elbryan, standing passively, seeming so very much alive!

A movement by the door turned them all, to see Pagonel, Bruinhelde, and Duke Kalas stride in.

"Move away from him," Prince Midalis said to Pony, his tone unmistakably grim. "This must be finished."

"It is finished!" the woman yelled back, and she held Aydrian all the tighter and shot the prince a warning glare. "You leave him alone! All of you!"

"He has brought great misery to the world," Prince Midalis went on. "You would have us forget?"

"It wasn't he!" Pony shouted. "It wasn't Aydrian."

"The demon possessed him," Elbryan said, and Pony noted that his voice seemed strained and weakened. "That day on the field when he was born, the demon found its way from Father Abbot Markwart into the boy. That demon is gone now."

"You cannot be certain!" Prince Midalis argued.

"Agradeleous can tell us," Pagonel offered. "The dragon will know at the sight of him."

"And when that dragon confirms what I have said, then you will leave him alone," Pony demanded of the prince. "You will pardon him and you will forget him, and you will allow me to leave with him, to our home."

Prince Midalis started to respond, but merely sighed and stepped forward, offering Pony his hand and helping her to her feet.

"The battle is ended?" he asked Duke Kalas.

"Mostly," the man replied. He stepped forward then, taking his helmet from his head and tucking it under one arm. Lowering his gaze to the floor, the proud duke dropped his sword to the ground at Midalis' feet.

"I would be a liar if I said that your actions on behalf of King Aydrian did not wound me to my heart," Midalis offered.

"I accept your judgment," Duke Kalas said softly.

Off to the side, Pony wasn't even paying attention. She was with Elbryan again, and she could sense the truth. He was diminishing.

"None who have known the other side can return to the land of the living," he quietly explained to her, lifting his hand to brush a tear from her eye.

How wonderful that touch felt to poor Pony! For it was the same as it had once been, the gentleness and love she had once known with this man. He was no illusion, but was Elbryan, her Elbryan!

"Do not leave me," she whispered, but Elbryan brought a finger up to her lips to silence her, then followed it with a gentle kiss.

"Never would I, and never have I," he said. "I am there, my love. Always there."

"Elbryan, I cannot live . . ."

"You must," the ghost answered. "Our son needs you now, more than ever. You must see to him and teach him. His path is not ended, as is mine."

Pony shook her head in denial of every word, her tears flowing freely. How could she part with Elbryan again? Suddenly conscious of herself and her appearance, the woman gave a little laugh, an admission that she had to accept this, for all the pain. "You are so young and beautiful," she said to the ghost. "As I remember you." She reached up to stroke Elbryan's face. "And I am grown old and ugly."

He crushed her in a hug and kissed her deeply and passionately. "You are to me exactly as I remember you," he told her. "You are my Jilseponie, my Pony, my friend and my lover."

He felt lighter to her suddenly, and less substantial, and Pony clutched him all the tighter, holding on desperately.

"I will never leave you," Elbryan's voice said, and it diminished as he diminished, returning to the netherworld.

Pony nearly swooned, but caught herself with the same determination that had seen her through all of this. She almost dove back into her hematite, to chase her lost lover, but she understood the truth of it.

He could not come back, could never come back, to the physical world—not fully.

Pony growled and took a deep, deep breath, throwing aside all her tears and all the weakness in her legs. She opened her blue eyes and looked around, and saw that all were staring at her, and that all eyes were moist.

"You will pardon my son, wholly," she said to Prince Midalis. "I demand this of you, and I daresay that I have earned as much. This is all that I ask, that Aydrian and I can leave in peace. For Dundalis, where we will bother you no more."

"I had hoped that you would join me in Ursal," the prince said.

"No more," Pony admitted. "I have nothing left to offer to any, save Aydrian, who needs me most of all."

A call from above reminded them that they had much more to do here, and that such decisions could surely wait. They all turned to see Bishop Braumin sitting at the top of the stairs, covered in blood and reaching out to them for help.

"Midalis is King!" Liam O'Blythe yelled suddenly, charging in the door. "Long live the king!"

*   *   *

"I have so much to do, so much to repair," King Midalis admitted to Pony a short while later. All around them, the monks went about healing the wounded and the soldiers went about piling the dead.

So many dead.

"You have pardoned Duke Kalas?" Pony asked him.

"It will be done," the king replied. "In time. I want him to consider long and hard all that he has done. But yes, I will pardon him. I will invite him into my court, to serve me as he served my brother. He was deceived by Aydrian . . ." He caught himself and smiled warmly at the woman. "He was deceived by the same demon that stole your son from you," he corrected.

"A wise choice," Pony replied. "Vengeance breeds resentment. Remember the story of Constance Pemblebury and take that to heart, my friend. Compassion will serve you well."

"Jilseponie would serve me well."

Pony smiled and managed a little laugh. "Jilseponie is dead," she said, and though it was a joke, obviously, her expression became more serious suddenly, as if she noted some definite truth in her words. "Twice I have personally cheated death," she explained. "In the Moorlands and on the beach of Pireth Dancard. I should have died, but Elbryan would not let me."

"Then credit Elbryan with saving the kingdom."

"But that was not his purpose," Pony explained, and she glanced over to where Aydrian, Bradwarden, and Belli'mar Juraviel sat in the shade of the monastery wall. "He saved me to save my son, and so I shall." She turned and looked Midalis in the eye. "And then I will join him, my husband," she said calmly. "As I rightfully should have already joined him."

King Midalis tried to respond, but it was obvious that he couldn't get any words past the lump in his throat.

"Though I still have much to do," Pony admitted, looking back at Aydrian.

"You will leave us now?"

"My time here is ended," Pony replied, and she moved forward and offered the king a warm hug. "Rule well—I know you shall! For me, I will spend my time in Dundalis, back home again. How long ago it seems, when Elbryan and I would run carelessly about the caribou moss, awaiting the hunters' return or hoping for a glimpse of the Halo."

She stepped back and motioned to her friends. Bradwarden gave a whistle for Symphony and came forward, limping still a bit, though Pony and her soul stone had done wonders with his broken leg.

Another form came running over, as well, calling out for her to wait.

Pony met Braumin Herde with a great hug.

"I cannot believe you are leaving us," the monk said, and he wouldn't let her go.

"You have your Church to restore, and I have my son to save," Pony replied.

Braumin Herde gave a great sigh. A sniffle behind them turned them to see Master Viscenti, standing forlornly, head down.

"What better place to save him than St.-Mere-Abelle?" Braumin slyly remarked.

But Pony had an answer. "Dundalis."

After a long while, they started off, Pony and Aydrian on Symphony, Juraviel on Bradwarden. The elf used his emerald to facilitate their journey, and so within the day, they stepped onto the ferry in Amvoy, crossing the Masur Delaval into the confused city of Palmaris.

Within a short time, they were in the cellars of Chasewind Manor, Pony pushing aside the baffled guard as he fumbled with his keys. She found the correct key on the second try, and if it had taken much longer than that, she would have just pulled forth her graphite and blown the door down.

The wretched form inside stared up at her, but surely didn't recognize her. She fell over him at once, soul stone in hand, but in truth, the warmth of her hug was more healing to the battered man than any magic she might offer.

The very next day, as Palmaris stood down from its defensive posture and prepared to welcome the march of King Midalis Dan Ursal, the friends moved out of Palmaris' northern gate, a weary, but very much alive, Roger Lockless beside them.

EPILOGUE

GOD'S YEAR 857

T he chilly autumn wind rustled through the carpet of brown leaves, and sent those that were even then dropping from the trees into whirlwind dances all about the two friends. White clouds rushed by overhead, more often than not hiding the sun and casting long shadows that seemed fitting this day.

For Aydrian and Bradwarden stood before a third cairn in the grove outside of Dundalis, one they had just piled. A secret arrangement with Belli'mar Juraviel had afforded Pony the title of ranger, and so this ground had been sanctified by Belli'mar Juraviel himself, Pony's cairn given the same blessings and magical protections as those of Elbryan and Mather beside her.

Aydrian leaned on a long-handled shovel and watched the dance of the leaves, and listened to the sad wind. "She just gave up," he remarked.

"Nay, lad, ye're reading it wrong," the centaur replied. "Yer ma died years ago, she did, not once but twice. She told me so, and I'm remembering it well enough to know that she was speaking truly. She was kept alive by the strength of yer dead father against wounds that should've killed her, and for one reason only."

"For me," Aydrian whispered.

"She didn't give up, ye fool boy." the centaur went on. "She knew her job was done." Bradwarden managed a bittersweet smile as he looked to the cairn. "Now she's found her reward."

Aydrian leaned even more heavily on the shovel and stared down at the piled stones. For a long while, neither he nor Bradwarden said anything, but the centaur did lift his pipes and begin a tune that seemed both mournful and joyous, a celebration of Pony's life and the remorse at her passing. How much diminished the world suddenly seemed to them both.

Aydrian replayed the last ten years—years of freedom, they seemed. Under his mother's guidance, he had learned so much more than the elves had ever taught him. Not about what it was to be a warrior, or even a ranger, but about what it truly was to be a human being. He learned to love; he learned to see the world as something beyond his solitary existence. Instead of being the center of his every thought, he came to view himself as part of something much grander and more wonderful. Because of his mother's teaching, he had made many friends in Dundalis, and had earned their respect rather than demanding it.

Darker clouds rushed overhead on the strong winds; a few dead leaves crackled as they swept past.

And then a melodic voice brought the young man from his contemplations.

Aydrian looked up to see Belli'mar Juraviel staring down at him from a low bough. "It is time," the elf said.

Panic flashed over Aydrian, and he looked at the centaur, who stopped his playing and regarded the man. That terror proved a fleeting emotion, though, for Aydrian knew that Juraviel was right, and knew, too, that it was time for him to begin to pay back the world for all the agony he had caused.

"Are you ready, Aydrian Wyndon?" the elf asked directly.

"Have ye no shame then, ye fool elf?" Bradwarden interjected. "The boy's just lost his mother—ye think ye might be givin' him a bit o' time to sort out his own road?"

"His road was determined a decade ago," Juraviel replied.

"His road was forced upon him by yer Lady Dasslerond before he was old enough to even know he was to walk it!" Bradwarden retorted.

"Enough, Bradwarden!" came Aydrian's sudden demand, and both the elf and the centaur turned to regard him.

"Juraviel is right, and it is long past time that I try to atone for all that I have done."

"Then do it, in every action of every day," the centaur argued. "Live a good life now and take yer small steps to atone."

Aydrian was shaking his head with every word, and that made the centaur press on more fervently.

"Ye might be doing good before ye give it all up!" he argued.

"You and I both know the truth of it," Aydrian calmly replied, and the smile on his face was a genuine one.

"Ye're to throw away all that yer mother taught ye?"

"Come, Bradwarden, we both know that my mother did more than teach me," Aydrian answered. "She saved me, and through all that I now have come to understand and appreciate about the world, I know that I must do this, that I must repair that which I have ruined, to the best of my abilities." He looked to Juraviel. "I know that I can never undo all that Aydrian Boudabras did. I cannot give back the lives of those who died in my name, or before my selfish march. But I try, as I must."

Aydrian tossed his shovel to the ground and stepped toward Juraviel, holding his arms out before him in a gesture of complete submission.

They didn't return to Dundalis that cold day, but headed west, Juraviel and the enchanted emerald of the Touel'alfar carting them away with great speed. In the mountains, they found Juraviel's kin, the whole of the Touel'alfar and a good number of the Doc'alfar as well. Cold as the winter's day, Juraviel motioned for Aydrian to step out alone into a clearing. The elf followed him out a few moments later and motioned for his wrist. Aydrian looked back at the others, at Bradwarden, who stood stoically. He hiked up the sleeve of his jacket and held his exposed wrist out to Juraviel.

The elf brought forth his sword and gashed that wrist.

Aydrian felt the sting and the warmth as his lifeblood flowed forth. He held his arm up high, as Juraviel had instructed. A crimson mist filled the air before him, leading him on, and Aydrian began what he understood was to be the last walk of his mortal life.

For three days, he followed the lead of his spewing blood, along the mountain passes. Delirious, hardly seeing the ground before him, he trudged on. He fell often, but picked himself up without complaint, and staggered ahead, compelled by magic and by remorse. In the dark of night, Aydrian led the troupe over the crest of one mountain ridge, and for the first time in more than a decade, the Touel'alfar looked again on their ancient homeland.

Aydrian had led them home.

But the young man's work was not done, for in the absence of the elves, the rot of the demon dactyl had spread. They found the primary source of that stain, a dead tree in a field of blackened grass.

Aydrian, barely conscious, looked to Juraviel for guidance, and the elf, without a trace of mercy showing in his golden eyes, motioned for the man to go and fulfill his destiny. Aydrian walked to the base of the rotting tree. He sat down and he hugged the trunk, and then he gave himself to the earth about him, and to the tree.

Moonlight and starlight bathed him as he sat there. Around the edges of that field of stain, the Touel'alfar took up their evening song, accompanied by the haunting piping of Bradwarden the centaur.

Aydrian fell into a dark, dark place, accepting the realm of death as it rose up to engulf him.

But he found that he was not alone.

His mother was there beside him, coaxing him. His father was there, standing beside Pony. And Andacanavar was there, and another spirit that Aydrian somehow recognized to be Mather Wyndon, his great-uncle.

All the rangers who had passed before him were there, supporting him, bidding him to press on, to offer his life that Andur'Blough Inninness might live.

And the young man, accepting his penance, didn't hesitate, throwing all that he had left to give into the tree, giving of himself so that it might live, so that the rot of the demon dactyl might be at last defeated.

A long, long time later, Aydrian Wyndon opened his eyes.

The elves were all about him, dancing and singing, and reaching up to touch the lowest boughs of the tree, which had blossomed to life.

Weary beyond anything he had ever known, Aydrian fell back and closed his eyes once more.

When he awoke, he was still by the tree, with Belli'mar Juraviel standing beside him, along with a Doc'alfar female and a child elf of about ten years. The young sprite, a boy, had the coloration of the Doc'alfar, with beautifully porcelain skin, bright blue eyes, and raven hair. But Aydrian understood the truth of him so clearly, for unlike the Doc'alfar, this child sported wings.

"Juraviel," Aydrian whispered to the elf.

"Meet my son," the elf replied. "Wyndon Juraviel."

The name startled Aydrian, until he considered all that name had come to mean to the Touel'alfar over the last few decades.

"You said I would not live through the ordeal," Aydrian remarked a moment later.

"I believed you would not, and could not," Juraviel replied. "Little did I know that you would find so many allies in your struggle."

"The rangers."

"Indeed. They lent their strength to you, and in saving you, they bound you, Aydrian Wyndon. I had thought this cleansing of the demon stain to be your last task in life, but I was wrong." He stepped back, revealing Bradwarden, who stood with Tempest in one hand, Hawkwing in the other.

"They are yours now, Tai'Maqwilloq," Belli'mar Juraviel told him. "You cannot repay the world for the misery you have caused, perhaps, but for your own sake, you must try." Aydrian rose and solemnly took the bow and sword.

"And this," the centaur added, tossing him Pony's pouch of gemstones. After a moment, and with a crooked smile, Bradwarden repeated, "And this," and handed him the turquoise Symphony had once carried embedded in his breast. "Symphony had a son, ye know," the centaur explained with a wink.

With all of the elves watching and singing, Bradwarden and the ranger Aydrian walked out of Andur'Blough Inninness the next morning.

"The world's wide before ye, boy," the centaur remarked soon after they were away from the elf-song. "Yer own for the takin'."

"Take care your words, good centaur," Aydrian replied with a grin. "For at one time, I would have taken you literally."

Bradwarden roared with laughter. "Come along then. Let us find ye a proper horse."

"And then where will I go?" Aydrian wondered.

"To Ursal?" Bradwarden asked him. "If ye go in with care, King Midalis might be welcoming ye. He'll be wanting to hear o' yer mother's last years."

"Ursal maybe," Aydrian replied.

"Or farther still?" Bradwarden pressed. "Ye got a kin o' sorts south o' the mountains, ye know. If ye can forgive the lass for puttin' her sword through yer chest, I mean."

Aydrian could only snicker in response to the irreverent centaur. He recognized that Bradwarden was right in his assessment, though. All the world was there before Aydrian.

For the enjoying, and not for the taking.

Behind them, Andur'Blough Inninness was alive once more; before them, the kingdom of Honce-the-Bear was at peace.

So was defeated the rot of the dactyl.

So ended the DemonWar.

IMMORTALIS:

Misery's curse to those who let pride
Propel their journey as spiritual guide,
To count their hopes in fingers' toil
And measure worth in corporeal coil.

What wretched fools these mortals be
Ignoring promise of eternity,
Denying reason's just reward,
Defending riches with the sword.
Averting eyes from higher light,
Existing in fear of eternal night.
How pitiful are those lacking the sense
To accept the call of divine recompense!

What joke it would be to beings of reason
If flesh and blood proves the only season,
If divinity's call is an outrageous lie,
And heaven sits not above earthly sky.
If consciousness falls to black emptiness
And maggots claim souls as part of their mess,
If all of our reason to brightest lights shine,
In false perception of all that's divine.

So tell me not of mere mortal coil
Denying the hopes in worm-holed soil.
I'll fly my way on angels borne
While faithless wallow in mud, forlorn.

On this day and from my pen the answer to dead Calvin of Bri-
Onnaire, whose reason clouded his soul. This answer is for the living. Calvin found his answers long ago.
                        —Brother Niklos Santella, St. Precious Abbey, Palmaris